THE GUARDIANS OF LIGHT SERIES

BOOKS ONE THROUGH FOUR
VOLUME 1
BONUS INCLUSION OF BOOK FIVE

I0660528

KASEY HILL

Azoth Khem Publishing
Huntsville, AL
February 2025

AZOTH KHEM

© Azoth Khem Publishing, 2025

ISBN: 978-1-952880-27-8
First Edition 2020
Second Edition 2025

Azoth Khem Publishing
29931 Copperpenny Drive NW
Harvest, AL 35749
www.azothkhem.com

Ordering Information:
Quantity sales and exclusive discounts are available on quantity purchases by corporations, associations, and others. For details, contact the publisher at the address above. For orders by U.S. trade bookstores and wholesalers, please contact
Azoth Khem Publishing: Tel: (256) 221-5498 or visit www.azothkhem.com

Printed in the United States of America

Kasey Hill Presents

The Guardians of Light Series

CHECK OUT THESE OTHER SERIES BY KASEY HILL

The Guardians of Light Series

Firefly of Immortality
The Shining Ones
Firefly: The Half-Blood Angel
The Valley of the Shadow of Death: Nephilim Rising
Firefly of Immortality II

The Whispering Spirits Series

The Haunting at Foxwood Village
Dark Coven

Short Story Collections

Tales from the Crib: A Collection of Limericks and Short Horror Stories Vol. 1

Dark Woods Series

Devil's Claw

Coming Soon to The Guardians of Light Series

Ashes of Immortality: Black Wings of Death
Ashes of Immortality: Crowned by Ash and Flame
Ashes of Immortality: Crowned by Infernal Flame
Ashes of Immortality: The Shadowed Verse
Ashes of Immortality: Anniel Unveiled
Alpha and Omega
Firefly of the Apocalypse

For my Luxina, the starchild

Note from the Author

Greetings readers! Welcome to the world of The Guardians of Light! In this series, you will find a retelling of the creation story with varying mythologies interweaved into the stories. This book has the first four published books in the series, with five more in the works, as well as an entire world built around the original series. The first book starts off with the backstory of the entire series, following Sophie and Incaendiel as they battle to restore the harmony of light and dark as they wage war against the malevolent God Alpha. As you turn the page into book two, The Shining Ones, their children come into play. There is a prophecy about these children and how they are the key to the New World Order within the Celestial Hierarchy.

As you read through these books, it is imperative for you to read the Prologues and Epilogues, for they have information not available in the book itself. These books were written from years of research into the occult and the studies of many world religions as well as dead religions. I really hope you enjoy the series and the sneak preview into the next release for Volume 2 of the series. Open your minds and let this fantasy world take over, and remember, it's just fiction. Please put aside your religious purviews and have fun reading this alternate version of classical Abrahamic lore. As always, I am grateful for reviews received as they give me the spark to move forward in writing, and sincerely thank you for your feedback!

XOXO

Kasey Hill

Firefly of Immortality

THE GUARDIANS OF LIGHT SERIES

BOOK ONE

Kasey Hill

Azoth Khem Publishing
Huntsville, AL
April 2025

CHAPTER 1

*I*n the beginning

"THE SEAS WILL RISE and crash anew, spreading the waters of the vast deep blue. My arms in yours and your lips to mine, forever our souls to be intertwined. My light is yours as your grace is mine, together our powers are combined. But come morning as the dawn will approach, your hand will falter and let go. You take the dive, selfless and out of control. Just so in the end you may save their souls."

THERE HAS ALWAYS BEEN a war between the angels. It was not over who was heavenly and who was hellish, but rather over existing in heaven, to begin with. That war continues in an eternal battle of bloodshed while the brotherhood shared between them collapses. The Holy War was declared to the countless people of the earth throughout time, leaving them starved of knowledge, and empty of understanding, as to what exactly this war was about. Humanity was deceived into believing that the ultimate power named "God" was a creator of good, and his Adversary, Satan, was evil. The age-long battle of "good" versus "evil" at the tip of everyone's consciousness, yet it was never elaborated upon.

A space unoccupied in the vast array of the cosmos was claimed by a youthful god who called himself Alpha. When he leapt into being, he knew naught of the laws of the universe. He contemplated long and hard about what he would create from this void of space. It was full of darkness and hopelessness.

He had existed in solitude for eons before deciding that he no longer wished to be alone. Therefore, gathering the energy that surrounded him and existed within himself, he created another power to share in his experience; he called her Omega. Never had he imagined that he would create such a gem that enraptured his heart. Pure love streamed between the two of them, and together, they emanated so much love that they shared their plentiful love with the cosmos, causing galaxies to spring forth in the vast spaces of the universe. Their love produced so much power; inadvertently, they generated celestial creatures most like themselves. These beings were called angels and would be forever immortalized as the Elohim, both a cosmic and celestial hierarchy.

When they created this race of angels, their purpose was to be watchers and guardians of the universe. The cosmos was still empty of mortal men, but they wanted everyone to know their duties, and they wanted them to know that humanity, when created, was to be loved as much as their mother and father, if not more.

"You do understand the power and obedience you grant and receive by agreeing to this, do you not?" Omega asked. The angels nodded their heads in approval of their tasks. Disobedience to their mother and father was not a thing they wished to accomplish.

Once all the Elohim had agreed to love and trust the mortals, Omega, the goddess, waved her hand, and a desolate planet that had been molten lava had water crash through it. The raging fire and lava became landmasses, and the water filled in the rest, creating lakes, rivers, and oceans. They placed all sorts of creatures upon the land to roam and create life from the life they were granted. They knew it would take quite some time for these creatures to go through their evolutionary trials, but Alpha and Omega could not wait for these creatures to evolve, so, they created a place outside of space and time that they called the Garden of Eden. They created morning and night for their precious treasures, and every angel gathered around so they could watch these creatures live.

They had yet to put any humans in the Garden, so they spent their time adding animals that they felt deserved to exist forever. Likewise, they placed many species of plant life that would never take root in Earth's soil. It was many years before Alpha and Omega decided it was time to create any humans for the Garden. When the time came, they created one human to exist in the Garden, and they called him Adam. Showering Adam with love and affection, he had everything he would ever need to survive in this Garden. Alpha and Omega were pleased with what their shared power had created. It was beautiful.

However, what brightens the heart and soul does not always last forever. Alpha noticed that there was an unequal balance in the cosmos. There was too much light and not enough darkness to keep the energies in balance. It was a perfect balance of yin and yang energies with just Omega and Himself, but with the addition of their celestial children, the universe was becoming more complicated.

Without Omega's knowledge or the Elohim's, Alpha sought council from beings that had secretly brought him into existence. Alpha was a jealous god at heart, and he knew that if they were to find out about others like him in power, they would turn their backs on him and leave. He traveled across galaxies and into different universes to pull council with the Elder Gods.

"I stand before you as a young god, but no less powerful than any of you. However, my universe is beginning to fold in upon itself, and I haven't the slightest idea as to why. I created for myself a consort, and we then created our own band of cosmic power through our children. Is this addition of power to the light the cause of my troubles? Tell me, what must I do to rectify this flaw in our universe?" Alpha looked into the eyes of the wisest of gods, hoping for rectification.

"You stand before me claiming yourself as powerful as I and yet have no clue as to how to fix your problem. Arrogance will get you nowhere, Alpha," the mighty god Drac thundered.

"Have I not created a universe full of spectrum as you have? Have I not gathered the energy within me to create for myself a mate as godly as yours?" Alpha replied bitterly.

"Even with these accomplishments, you still have no clue as to how to truly rule your universe — you fool. Instead of creating life, you created power. Instead of creating your world, you created an army to bow to you, and then ask why your universe caves in on itself. Such naivety from a boastful young god," Drac sneered.

"Please, I implore you. How do I rectify this situation?" Alpha pleaded, looking between the council faces.

"What was the first thing you did to this universe you created?" A voice called out; Alpha turned his gaze to a stunning goddess that held placement in the council.

"I created light where there was no light," Alpha replied indignantly. The goddess snickered. "Why do you mock me with my decisions of how my universe was brought about? Who do you think you are to condescend me in this tumultuous gift I gave this universe."

"I am the one who created the darkness. I am, in fact, darkness itself. Have you not heard of your Elder God, Tiamat?" she replied sarcastically.

Alpha became nervous as he glanced around to all the benevolent faces. "Apologies, Dark One," he said, taking to his knee in respect. He glanced up at her nervously for fear she may strike him down with her wrath. "How do I fix this chaos I have implemented upon myself?"

The insidious smile she gave him chilled him to his core. "There is but one solution to the universe you have created for yourself. Since so much power exists in the light and is throwing the cosmos into discord, you must choose an adversary to oppose you."

"What do you mean, an adversary?" Alpha, confused by her instructions, rose to his feet and approached the council.

"The natural order and balance of the cosmos are out of sorts. An adversary would balance the energies of your universe, your energies being that of light, and your Adversary being that of darkness. Do not confuse the two as negative oppositions but as positives. The dark and light are drawn to one another and complete a cycle of energy. Right now, the energy of the universe is one-sided and is the root cause for the disruption of your universe." The council all nodded in agreement with Tiamat.

"I still do not quite understand what you mean for me to do," Alpha replied.

"One of your creations must adhere to the darkness and be your counter energy," Tiamat replied. "And you call yourself all-knowing." She chuckled while she toyed with him.

"I must sacrifice one of my own to bring about the balance of the energies," Alpha stated, letting the information sink in. Tiamat nodded. "Does it matter who?" he asked.

"It must be one whose power is in close proximity to your own," she replied.

Alpha sighed heavily as he drank in everything she had told him. "I thank you all for joining council with me. I now know my answer and must implement it immediately." The council nodded their approval of his disclosing statement and faded back to the universes they held power over. Alpha returned to the summit and was greeted by Omega at the gates.

"I was wondering where you were." She smiled at him and wrapped her arms around his neck, kissing him softly on the lips.

"I wasn't far," he replied. "Gather the children, darling. We need to sit down and have a talk with them." Omega wrinkled her forehead in confusion but nodded, acknowledging she would. She assembled the court with a mandatory proclamation that all angels must be present.

CHAPTER 2

To Have Loved and Lost

"YOU LEFT me without letting me know why? Why!!? I demand to know why! But your answer still falls on my deaf ears. I walk from your feet to the reflecting light bouncing in my eyes I walk closer to your heart. And I lay down your flowers right there on the mound of dirt."

I WALKED to the center of the graveyard, maneuvering the way I had remembered it. It had been four years since the day Gramms had died. It still stings as if it were only yesterday. I swear, if I didn't know any better, someone took my emotions after my breakdown, and they were slowly giving them back to me. *Ridiculous right?* I decided to go to her grave for the first time since we had buried her. Everyone thought it would have been best not to visit until the wound had scabbed over. *Could it ever really scab over?*

I sat down at her feet and laid the peonies I bought for her at her headstone. Peonies were always her favorite. I slipped the Bible she had read to me every night that she was over at my house out of my bag. I flipped the pages open and ran my fingers over them. The night Gramms died, she had come over like she had done weekly ever since my young mind could remember. That night seemed no different from any other night. Gramms would come over to cook me dinner while my parents locked themselves away in their room, arguing. We had already sat down and had the big "D" discussion, but they promised to work it out beforehand. Their arguments had started to become rapid in frequency, so I knew the time would be soon.

"What are you cooking tonight, Gramms," I asked, walking into the kitchen.

"Well, do you still like spaghetti?" she asked, winking at me.

"Oh, how did you know it is my favorite?" I asked, chuckling.

I walked over to the stove and lifted the lid off the pot, bubbling with pasta sauce. The aroma filled my nostrils, and my stomach growled in response. Gramms chuckled back at me and cooed, "Tell it not to worry. Dinner's nearly ready." I smiled at her humor and sat down at the table.

Gramms' Bible was laid out and opened midways through to some strange writing. She had to have taken foreign language classes in ancient writings. You could hardly call the scribbles words. "Are you going to read to me again tonight?" I asked, looking up from her book.

"Don't I always?" she replied.

"Mom doesn't like it when you read to me from it. She said you're filtering into my mind nothing but pure nonsense," I said. "Well, that wasn't the exact word she used, but I'd rather not pick up her bad habit of cursing," I added.

Gramms busied herself, making our plates of spaghetti and removed the French bread from the oven. She cut us slices from the loaf of baked bread, served me my plate, and took a seat across from me. We ate in silence for a few moments. Mom's comments always made her upset whenever she spoke out against the family bible.

"Sophie, do you go to church with your mother still?" she asked.

"Yup, Mom said I have to, so I wouldn't be sucked into the evilness of the world," I replied.

"The evil of the world indeed," Gramms said angrily. "Do you know what church really promotes?" she asked coolly. I shook my head. "Throughout time, the church has used this propaganda to fund their war on 'Satan.' Donations and 'offerings' have poured in from billions of churchgoers to pay for new churches to be built to pay the salary of preachers, priests, and even the Pope. Fear and torment have spread worldwide, accusing those who do not bow to the church and its teachings of being a follower of Satan. Hell was the destination of those who did not convert, and death was implemented in the early start of Christianity. The brush upon the blade and cross spread throughout the Middle East and into the European nations. Blood was shed in this "holy" war, and it wasn't the blood of soldiers, but rather the blood of innocence. Your mother is just sucking you into THAT nonsense." She was building in anger.

"What else has the church lied about, Gramms?" I asked, taking slow bites from my food.

"Satan became a front for the church, a way to convert those who were already afraid of dying for not wanting to convert. The image of the goat-like beast papered the painted glass of the Roman Catholic Church and was a warning to those who did not follow word by word the holy text taught that they would end up a slave to him. Demons came next, the minions of Satan. They were angels who chose to fall with him instead of staying with their father in heaven. Thus began the holy war not only on Earth but also in between Heaven and Purgatory. What the church left out, not by choice, but by the influence of 'God' himself, was that the war was instigated by God, not by those who had fallen." She was waving her hands around in the air as she made her points.

I grew quiet and finished eating my food. Overhead, I heard the thuds and thumps coming from my parent's room. I excused myself from the table, muttering that I needed to use the restroom, and inched closer to their door to hear what they were arguing about this time.

"She's fourteen, Lorraine. Your mother needs to stop telling her about her Satanic beliefs before she converts our daughter into a Satanist!" Dad shouted.

"My mother is not a Satanist! She just has a separate set of beliefs than what mainstream religion has," my mother retorted bitterly.

"Well, tonight is the last night. If you want this marriage to work, you're going to have to put your foot down and tell her enough is enough!" I heard their master bathroom door slam shut, and it startled me.

I couldn't believe Dad would say that about Gramms. I slipped back downstairs, and Gramms had already washed the plates we ate from and slipped into the living room. I tried to hold back the tears wanting to roll down my face. Gramms patted the seat beside her, so I walked over to her and curled up beside her.

"I'm sorry you had to hear that, Sophie. Your parents are lashing out at anything they can to fuel their arguments." She smoothed my hair out while she talked to me. "Your hair has always been my envy, your red, bouncy curls. Let me braid it," she said.

I climbed to the floor in front of me, and she ran a brush through my hair. "Did you know that left unknown throughout time, there was a family lineage that started in the early days after the banishment from the Garden?" she asked.

"You mean like the stories you told me as a kid?" I asked.

"Exactly like those stories," she said. "Guardians were created, as an opposition of God, to thwart the war. The lineage held a secret and passed the secret on through a family bible. This Bible told the true story of what happened, and every so often, one was born into the family to help diminish the ideologies that the Father God implemented. It was up to this person to determine what was truth and what was false. This lineage had made it through all the millenniums of war and anguish both sides fought for."

"Well, where is the lineage at now?" I asked.

"We're that lineage, Sophie," she replied.

"You mean your bible is the same bible?"

"Yes, it is," she replied. "Sweetie, it is particularly important that you understand the story of creation. As Guardians, it is vital to our nature that we understand our responsibility from this story. No one knew exactly where the lineage started or when it would end, but it was always up to the chosen person in the family to uphold the beliefs."

Her stories and beliefs came from legends of a fall, not that of Satan, but of the Dark Mother. I knew everyone had heard some form of the creation story. God created Adam and Eve; they sinned and were forced from the Garden of Eden. They were no longer pure, so they could no longer see the Garden, making it lost to civilization. *Right?* Well, not according to the book passed down through Gramms' family. Every religion has its own perception that was passed down by word of mouth through angels and even God himself. Gramms' Bible claimed to know the real story behind it all.

"Why does it have my name in the book, Gramms?" I asked.

"If it was your responsibility to guard the secret of the Garden, would you give it to the Angel, to the Fallen, or keep it to yourself?" she asked.

"I wouldn't give it to the fallen angels. They are demons, Gramms," I replied.

"They are not demons," she said irritated. "Have you not paid any attention to the stories I tell you?"

I felt bad for saying it, but if it kept my parents together, then I wouldn't stray into the stories she told. "Yes, but it's just a book, Gramms. There's no evidence, no proof. It's time for me to grow up and realize that it's all just a story that never happened. There was one God that created everything, and his Adversary is the Devil, not the Dark Mother."

"Well, you have four more years to decide," she replied, finishing the bow in my hair.

"What happens in four years, Gramms?" I asked.

I waited for her to answer. She had never mentioned anything special would happen on my eighteenth birthday. I felt a chill in the air, and the hairs on my neck pricked up. She had grown completely silent and still.

"Gramms?" I asked, looking over my shoulder at her. She was slumped in the chair, barely breathing. "Gramms! Mom!" I started to run off, but she grabbed me by my arm.

"Listen to me, Sophie, your decision affects the entire world and balance of things." Tears streamed down my face as she clutched her chest.

"Mom! Dad! Help!" I screamed, trying to wrench from her grasp to call an ambulance.

"Do not let your mother or father cloud out your own judgment. Believe....oh...what you want... to believe." Her arm let go of mine and fell to the side of the chair as her last breath escaped her lips. "MOM!!!!!" I screamed at the top of my lungs.

They came bounding down the stairs, and I stood there, shaking Gramms, trying to get her to respond to me. Dad pushed me out of the way and lay her down on the floor to start CPR. Mom picked up the phone and called for help.

"This is your fault!" I screamed out. My parents looked over at me. "All she wanted was for someone to listen to her, to believe in what she said. All you two cared about was saving your marriage! She heard you just as I did!"

"Sophie," Dad called out. I started for the door when Mom grabbed my arm. I wrenched loose from her and ran out the door.

I sat out on the front porch crying. The rest of the night happened in a blur. I remember the ambulance coming, taking her away, and then leaving. I disappeared from the house and ran through the various parts of the neighborhood. Every blind turn I took brought me back to the house when all I wanted to do was get away. I was eventually picked up by the police and brought back home.

I remember a calm feeling descending over me, making me immediately comforted, but no clue as to why or what it was. As I drifted off to sleep, I heard voices that weren't my mom or my dad speaking.

"Do you think Michael or Uriel did it?" a manly voice asked.

"I'm not sure. What I do know is that she wasn't supposed to pass until the day before her 18th birthday," a woman replied. *How could these people know when she was supposed to die?* "We need to report this matter as soon as possible," she said.

"Agreed, it looks as if they are playing dirty when it clearly breaks the law. I was sure they found a loophole somewhere, and yet, they're supposed to be the 'good guys.' Humph!" the man's voice replied.

"Shh, not so loud she is stirring awake," the woman hissed.

I felt another wave of a lulling lullaby without words. I caught a glimpse of a shadow in the corner of my room, but I was overwhelmed by exhaustion and fell into a deep sleep.

I sat there, thinking everything over at her grave. Even the days leading up to her funeral felt odd to me. The days went by fast and numb. I couldn't even feel anything to cry. I felt completely deprived of emotions, just as I had felt lulled to sleep that night. There was a large turnout of people who showed up for the wake and funeral. Some I knew, some I had never laid eyes on before. There were some kids from school that came to lend me their condolences. I murmured my thanks to them as they came up and gave their hugs. The only person who didn't move from his spot was Isaiah. He just sat at the back of the room and watched me. Pain was etched on his face. A few of his friends made whispering comments in his ear, but he didn't budge.

He was always quiet, even in school. Hardly a word was spoken to anyone, and it seemed as if the teachers always skipped him for answering questions. We grew up together on the same street, so I have known him since childhood. Gramms took him and a few other kids in when they were younger and orphaned. I didn't know where they would go now. I hoped they wouldn't be relocated to a different town. We were always friends, always close, that is until my mother started taking me to church.

He completely changed after that. I once confronted him on the issue. I was hurt and alone in the world without my friend. I asked him if he was Jewish, Islamic, or anything as to why it offended him that I began going to church. He never replied.

I realized the entire time I had been zoning and staring at him, he had returned my gaze and watched me. It was normal for me to zone out during times when I needed comfort. For a split second, I looked away from him. When I returned my look, he was gone. I looked around the room frantically, but he wasn't anywhere to be seen. It was then that everything sank in. I felt utterly alone, and all the emotions I had been holding back came boiling to the surface.

I was told later that I had a nervous breakdown. It was just a week or two until school was to start back up, and honestly, I had lost all sense of time. I couldn't even tell you the dates if they weren't etched on her grave. Of course, I was treated with exceptional care, and even to this day, I still am. Most people are afraid to bring up what happened for fear that it will cause me to lose it again. I felt like an outcast and still do.

"I know it sounds silly. I know you really read to me from this book. I read it myself, too, while you were alive. I... I don't understand why I can't see what you read to me or even the first page with the poem on it." A tear slid down my cheek as I talked to her. "It's the only thing I have of you, and I can't even read the amazing stories you told me from it. I can only live in the memory of what we shared. The pages are all blank or in a language I can't understand." I sniffed, wiping away another tear. "Gramms, I miss you so much!" There it was, the waterfall release I so desperately needed. I lay on her grave and cried. I was there for hours. The sun went from high in the sky to barely peeking over the horizon, but I didn't care. It was something I had to do. I could've sworn I fell asleep on the grave. I didn't remember walking home, but I ended up back at home, in my bed, waking to the sunrise.

My head throbbed from where I had cried so much at her grave. I went and hopped in the shower. I made sure my blotchy and puffy face was covered with makeup before I made a grand appearance in front of my mom. I walked over to the counter in the kitchen and pulled a mug from the cabinet. I then walked to the coffee pot and poured a steaming, fresh cup of coffee. I sniffed the aroma, and it began to ease the tension in my head and neck.

"How did yesterday go?" my mom asked as she walked in the kitchen behind me, scaring the crap out of me. I jumped, nearly spilling the coffee everywhere. I walked over to the table and sat down.

"It was fine. Something I needed to do," I responded, sipping on the coffee and reading the paperback I left on the kitchen table for my morning read.

"I know it always bothered you that she passed just a few days before your birthday. You were such a strong young woman burying your grandmother on your birthday." She thought she was comforting me, but she wasn't. She was making everything worse again. After Gramms died, Dad left. He couldn't take the emotions in the house anymore. I get a birthday card every year, but he never comes to see me. Mom said he remarried and has a new family now. I can't see how he could abandon eighteen years' worth of love with his child for a new family. It is what it is, I guess.

"It's fine, Mom," I said, dropping my book and downing what was left of my coffee. "Gotta split. I start my job today, and I don't want to be late." I bent down, kissed her cheek, and was out the door before she could protest. My job didn't start for another five hours, but I couldn't sit and listen to her anymore. Just as I was opening the door to my car, she popped her head out of the house.

"Tonight, the church is having a late-night sermon in honor of your grandmother. Do you want to go?" she asked with a hopeful smile. She knew my answer before it even left my lips. I quit church the same night Gramms died. Most people said they saw the light within me die the day she did; a lot of people said I changed when she died. I didn't know, but I wasn't going to disappoint her and let them brainwash me with whatever stories their Bible told.

"I won't be off work in time, sorry. Maybe next time?" I asked as I plopped in my car seat.

She frowned, went back inside, and shut the door behind her. Gramms' Bible tugged at my mind. I dug it out of the bag I snatched from the chair in the kitchen before I escaped to my car. I ran my fingers along the cover of it. The book always brought back memories of her. It smelled old, the pages looked ancient, and the cover was leather-bound. It had a magnificent tree etched into the leather.

I just wished I could read the stories she used to tell me. As I put the book back in my bag, something smacked my driver's window, scaring me. I screamed like a little kid and then heard laughing. I looked over and saw Dean standing there. He had a devilish look in his eye and a crooked grin.

I rolled my window down in annoyance. "You scared me!" I yelled at him.

"Sorry, I thought you were getting ready to pull out. I was wondering if I could catch a ride with you into town."

His eyes glinted in the sun. They were so the most amazing shade of blue-gray. No, I take that back. Blue-gray doesn't even compare to the color they were. It was as if you were staring into the sky itself during the day with the glow of the moon in them. He was new to town and had just moved in up the street a few days ago.

"Do you want to be shown around or just dropped off?" I asked.

"Just dropped off. I met a few guys yesterday and seemed to hit it off with them, so they invited me out to play football with them." I motioned for him to get into the car. He walked to the passenger side and climbed in. I watched as the curtain in the living room dropped, as my nosy mom was probably doing cartwheels over the boy talking to me. I wasn't much into having boyfriends. Don't get me wrong. I looked, but I had so much on my plate that I couldn't tolerate a boyfriend. It would only be a matter of time before he found out how screwed up my life was, and he wouldn't be interested in me anymore.

"Just let me know where to drop you off, and I will," I said, giving a faint smile.

He grinned back at me. There was something that twinkled in his eye that I couldn't quite grasp.

"So, I'm sorry, what's your name again? I'm horrible with names. My mom is always saying I need to have a memory card installed into my brain," he chuckled.

I pretended to smile at the joke, although it wasn't that funny. "I'm Sophie."

"Ah, that's right. I remember now. Making a mental note of it now," he said, putting his finger to his temple.

He grinned, and I half grinned back. He rolled his window down, and the most heavenly aroma filled the car. It was hypnotic and dizzying.

"Is that your cologne I smell? It's...like heaven in a bottle!" I said, breathing in another breath. He stiffened and rolled his window back up. "Was that a hint of lavender and myrrh?" I asked, looking over at him.

"No, it must have been the wind you smelled. I'm not wearing cologne." We were just passing by the recreational center when he told me to pull off there. I saw the boys from school all running around in the field, chasing one another. "You should sit and watch us play," he said, smiling at me.

I nearly choked on my laugh. I was not the kind of girl that sat around watching boys play games.

"It'll be fun," he said, his eyes glinting at me. *Was he seriously flirting with me?* I felt my cheeks flush a bit.

I didn't know why, but I agreed. "But," I started adding to the compromise, "my job starts in a few hours, so I can't stay all day," I said as I made my way out of the car and over to his side.

He grabbed my hand up, and I felt the blood rush to my face and through my body. No one has ever held my hand or shown me this amount of attention before. We walked to the field together, and I could feel eyes everywhere on me. The girls sitting there were watching me in amazement, envy, and hatred. Their eyes burned into my skin. It's not my fault that he's my next-door neighbor, and it wasn't like I was staking a claim on him. I only offered him a ride, but none of this, I said out loud. My eyes flitted back over to the field of boys. Some of them watched him walk with me to the bleachers and kiss my hand as he made his way out to the group. I recognized half of the boys. The other half must be from one town over. One surprise I didn't expect to see was Isaiah among the group of boys. He looked ready to pounce on Dean as he walked over to the group of boys. His eyes danced from Dean to me, and he glared a look at Dean that I had never seen him ever make before. His face darkened, and I could see his fists tighten.

All the boys on the field stood in between Dean and Isaiah. Dean's back was to me, so I couldn't even see what kind of look he had been giving Isaiah back. Someone patted Isaiah's back, and he let go of his stance. It was almost as if they all had conversations in their heads because not a word was uttered. As soon as his body tension dropped, the overcast sky disappeared. *Weird, I hadn't even noticed it cloud up.* I watched him throw his hands up, mumbling something as he stalked off the field. He walked right by me and looked at me. I could see in his eyes he desperately wanted to tell me something. Instead, he turned around and continued walking toward where all the cars were parked.

I wasn't letting him get off the hook that easy. I ran after him as he walked down the road.

"Isaiah!" I yelled.

He stopped in his tracks but didn't turn around.

"What is going on? Were you mad I showed up with Dean?"

I could've sworn I saw him flinch.

"Why don't you ever talk to me? I show up at the field with my new next-door neighbor, and you're ready to beat him to a pulp. Yet, you won't even talk to me."

He stood there with his back turned. I could tell he was breathing hard.

"Please, talk to me. You shut me out completely years ago, and I don't know why! Please, just let me back in. I miss being friends."

I expected him to turn around, run, and kiss me or something.

Instead, he said, "Go home, Sophie. It's not safe for you to be here." He then began walking to his house without another word uttered.

I looked over to the group of boys who were playing ball, and they had all stopped to watch what we had to say to one another. I swear I could see Dean smirking. The rest of their faces were blank and unreadable. I walked back to my car and was about to open the door when Dean appeared out of nowhere, standing there.

"You're not going to let that punk ruin your fun, are you?" he asked, smiling a lopsided grin. He picked my hand up again, but this time I shook it free from his grip.

"I happen to know that 'punk' a lot better than I do you, and if he doesn't think I should hang around you, most of the time, he is right," I retorted back. I climbed into my car and started the engine when he leaned in my window.

"You are making a terrible decision."

He had no smile this time but an ice-cold look that chilled me to the bone. I saw a few of the other boys I knew make their way for my car when he bolted to the other side of the road. A car pulled up. He jumped in and took off with them. *He was so weird!* The boys made it to my car just as the other car Dean jumped in peeled away.

"You okay, Sophie?" Rafe asked as he leaned in my window.

Rafe was another of the foster children Gramms had taken in. He went by Rafe since his name, Raphael, was so outdated. I was a bit shocked, but I was okay. There was just something about his eyes that made me cringe.

"I'm fine, Rafe," I replied, shaking off the uneasy feeling I had.

"Are you sure?" he pushed a little harder.

I smiled, "I'm fine. Don't worry about me."

His eyes didn't release their tense gaze, but he did look away down the road in the direction both the car and Isaiah had gone. As if some invisible command had been called, the boys pulled up beside him in Sam's Jeep, and Rafe jumped in. They tore off down the road in the direction everyone went.

I didn't know why, but curiosity got the best of me. So, instead of heading into town as planned, I followed everyone else. I didn't know how I knew exactly which way they had gone, but I ended up at the same place they did. I parked my car a block up the street and walked down to where I could hear them speak. It was a public playground, but there weren't any children to be seen.

"You're to stay away from her," Isaiah yelled with a tone I had never heard from him. It was dark and angry.

"You know the rules. This is the year, and she is the One." Dean smirked at Isaiah. *The One? The one what?*

"You will not touch her or get near her again!" Isaiah yelled, and thunder clapped.

Odd, that was another weather anomaly that appeared during his anger.

"We can settle this the easy way, or we can settle this the hard way. I'm sure Father will be displeased if we choose the hard way," Dean sneered, sarcasm dripping from the bite.

"He is NOT my father!" Isaiah yelled back at Dean.

Dean just laughed at him.

"Say what you will, do what you may. This is the year, and she is the One. Before she turns nineteen, she will disclose to me what we all have wanted to know for years! The Garden will be ours again soon, Brother. Father has already won one battle, and Mother is no longer remembered. It won't be long until Sophie is the same way!" Dean chided.

Isaiah snapped and charged at Dean. Sam and Rafe jumped in front of him and held him back. I watched as Azazel, Sam's sister, climbed from the Jeep and walked over to the boys squaring off.

"Enough! All you! You stupid asses just busted yourselves out. She heard everything!"

Oh no! She knew I was here. I didn't know why, but I turned and ran from the spot I was standing in back to my car. No sooner had I reached the door handle than someone grabbed me from behind. I prayed in my head that it wasn't Dean who grabbed me, and I heard a chuckle from the one who grabbed me. I was still being held from behind as the vehicle that Dean was in drove by with his face glaring at the group, and then he looked at me with a sly grin. Once the vehicle was out of sight, I figured the arms around me would drop their hold on me, but they did not.

"I told you to go home, Sophie." Of course, it was Isaiah holding me in place. Even though I figured it would be a rough grab, he held me gently. His arms held me by my waist, and I loved the feeling. Warmth crashed through me, and I could feel my cheeks superheated.

"What- what were y'all talking about? What did he mean by 'me'?" I asked.

I heard him sigh, and I looked around at the group that surrounded me, all their eyes looking from me to him.

"Well, are we going to tell her?" Azazel asked. I felt him tense up as she stared at him.

"It's not her birthday yet. You know the rules," he hissed.

"Well, the rules have already been broken by them! We must inform her about what's going on!" Sam yelled.

He sighed again. "Can I tell her alone?"

"However, it is told, whenever it is told, whoever tells her, it needs to be done before he sinks his claws back into her," Rafe said. "Let him tell her by himself. It might be better coming from just him than all of us and everything at once."

"Tell me what? What are y'all talking about?" I was becoming impatient and very quickly.

"Sophie, do you have your grandmother's Bible?" Isaiah asked.

"How... how do you know about that?" I asked, confused.

I didn't remember him ever being over while she had read from the book to me. I doubt she would have read it to them since it was a treasured family heirloom, and they were just foster kids.

"I will explain as we drive to her grave," he said as he let my waist go and climbed in the driver seat. I stood there, dumbfounded. "Get in."

I walked to the passenger side door and looked at everyone else. They all looked serious, so I knew it had to be serious and not some sort of game. I climbed in, and Isaiah put the car in drive. We started for the cemetery while the car remained void of sound.

"I wish you had gone home as I asked you to," he said, breaking the silence. "I figured this one request of you after years of silent stares that you would have at least listened to me."

"You make it seem like I was the one ignoring you! You were the one who quit being my friend and at the right time, too, the time when I needed you the most, the year she died! I had no one to talk to." I blurted it out without even thinking. My cheeks immediately flushed, and I could tell he sensed my embarrassment.

"I had to quit talking to you. It was against the rules for me to have gotten as close to you as I did. I was already chastised by Sam for it." I could tell he wasn't supposed to have said that either.

"Who is Sam to tell you who you can and can't get close to," I retorted back.

"Please, Sophie, just let me get to the cemetery, and I will tell you everything. I promise. If we go in order, it will be better than hodge-podging all over the place with facts." He didn't say anything else, and the look on his face said he wasn't going to. I didn't push it from him.

Oh, my God! Work! "Ughhh!" I groaned.

"What? What is it?" he asked in sincere worry.

"I start a new job today, and I'm late. Great impression for the first day, right? Idiot!" I facepalmed myself.

"I already took care of that," Isaiah said, smirking.

"Huh? How?"

"I knew you weren't going to listen, and what was going to happen. I called in for you while walking down the road. The town knows what today is; you start tomorrow." I stared at him in disbelief.

"How did you 'know' I wasn't going to listen, or for that matter, what was going to happen?" I asked in a whisper.

"You never do." He grinned at me, and I socked him in the arm. He laughed. It was so wonderful to hear his laugh and to hear his voice again.

"I've missed you." It slipped out.

I'm such a moron. It's barely been half a day, just a small conversation, and I was already pouring my heart out to him. I knew my cheeks reddened once more. I heard him sigh. Whatever he wanted to say back to me, he withheld. We pulled into the cemetery, and he drove over to where my grandmother's grave was nestled.

"How do you remember where it is?" I asked, unbuckling my seatbelt.

He didn't respond and got out of the car.

"Don't forget the book," he said.

I fished the book from my bag and followed him over to Gramms' grave.

"Normally, this is mother to daughter, but your mother has chosen the other side as opposed to our side."

He took the book from my hands and threw up his finger as I was about to ask him what he meant.

"Mariam, please assist me."

He was nuts! I hadn't realized how Gramms' death affected him. I was about to interject when swirling blue lights gathered all around me. I began to retreat, but he grabbed my hand and held it. The touch was magnetic and sent a shock through me, but he didn't drop my hand. The blue lights formed into a body, and then Gramms' face appeared.

"If you think this is some sort of joke, it's not funny!" I was pissed, beyond pissed, actually.

"Sophie, listen to him when he talks to you. Nice to see you, Incaendiel." *What? His name is Isaiah, not Inca- whatever she said.*

"You have to be quick, Mariam. They have already sent the snake down to start in on her, the same one as last time. We must not lose her to the other side!" His eyes pleaded with Mariam's.

"Sophie, do you remember the stories I used to read to you from the book?" I stared in disbelief. *This had to be my Gramms.* All I could do was nod. "Do you have the book?" Isaiah laid it on the ground in front of her. "Pick the book up, Sophie, and open it to the first page."

"It's blank. There's nothing in it," I said, picking the book up.

"Just open it, my dear." I obeyed and opened it to the first page.

The page was blank at first, but then letters began to swirl around and appear. I stared in disbelief as they manifested throughout the entire book.

"Remember the last time I was reading to you from the book, and I told you it was important for you to remember the book? Well, this is the reason why. The heavens are at war with their fallen brothers. The creation story and everything I told you from the book is true. Remember the guardians that hold the secret to the Garden of Eden?" I nodded my head. "Well, they are here for the location. Every one thousand years, they come to us searching for it, and the last time nearly got it. So, I assume that is why they sent the same angel back for it once more since you nearly gave in last time."

"What? I wasn't born one thousand years ago. I'm only 17."

"You are a reincarnated soul, my Sophie. Only you possess the knowledge as to where the Garden of Eden exists. Also, you are the key to the Gates of the summit."

I was speechless.

"They thought by ending my life earlier than what it was supposed to have been that they would have had the upper hand."

"Wait, angels killed you?" I was stunned. I looked at Isaiah. "And you...you're a demon?"

He tensed up and glared at me. "We are NOT demons! We are Wanderers, those who chose to fall, but because he requested it!" I made him mad. I had hit a nerve and was really wishing I hadn't.

"So, you're not even human. All this time...you lied to me about who you are! Your name isn't even Isaiah. It's Inca- whatever she called you, but yet, I'm supposed to believe the ones who lied to me over the ones who haven't even tried to sweet-talk their way into my life."

Isaiah looked at Gramms, and she returned the same gaze back. He shook his head and walked away.

"You have to listen to your gut. You are the only one who can make this decision. This family bloodline has lasted as long as it can against the angels. They're getting craftier; they may show a general love interest in you, but I assure you, it is not." Gramms faded away.

Everything was left up to me. *How was I to decide which side deserved the Garden of Eden?* Sure, Gramms taught me the different creation stories than what the church does, but that doesn't mean it's true. It doesn't mean any of this is true. For all I know, there is no such thing as God, no such thing as angels or demons, well, Wanderers. I grew up listening to those stories and didn't want to believe in either side. Apparently, I was an ancient hag that held the key to the Garden, the key to the summit, and to guard both against the angels, which I have no clue why that would be important.

As I walked to my car, the skies began to darken, and I could have sworn I heard laughter in the wind. I reached for my car door handle, and my hand was grabbed. I looked up to see Dean holding my hand, preventing me from getting into the car.

"Well, I see the hag, and that annoying demon found a way to fill you in on everything. So, tell me, Guardian, where is the garden hidden?"

He wasn't smiling but rather sneering at me.

"You all are insane! There is no Garden of Eden, and it's not like I'm hiding it in my backyard!"

He glared at me and pulled me away from the car with strength I had never felt before. I stumbled to the ground and receded back on my elbows away from his face, with him still holding onto my arm.

"You will tell me where it is. I nearly had you pouring your guts out into my lap last time, and this time will be no different. Incaendiel may think he has the upper hand by growing up close to you and getting to know you, but he will not win! You may have been his zygote when he was in the summit, but he left you! He left you for darkness! I can give you light!"

I didn't know what to think. *He left me once before?*

"Oh, I can see those wheels turning. He has left you more than once, more than twice. There are millenniums of the same actions. His Dark Mother will not allow you two to be together. You will never be his!"

He still hadn't let go of my arm and was dragging me away from the car. My heart was thundering with fear. *Where was he going to take me? Was he going to torture the information out of me?*

"Let me go, or Isaiah will-"

"He'll what? Look around. He isn't here. He left you alone in the cemetery just as he did four years ago when they buried the old hag. You're coming with me!"

He was dragging me further to the center of the cemetery. *Was there a portal there or something? Oh God! I was sliding into their delusions now.*

"Let me go!" I screamed without realizing the power it packed.

He temporarily lost his grip, and I snatched my arm from his hand. I bolted for my car, and just as I took the handle, he hoisted me up at the waist. He continued to haul me, kicking and flailing back to the center of the cemetery.

"Isaiah, help me!" I screamed and kicked.

Dean laughed at my efforts and at my plea. We were nearly to the center of the graveyard, and there was no way I could escape his grasp.

"Incaendiel, save me!"

It was meant to be a silent plea, but I realized it was aloud. There was a crackle of lightning and thunder. In front of Dean, Isaiah stood with Sam, Azazel, and Rafe.

"Drop her while you have a chance, Dean." Isaiah stood there with his fists clenched, ready to lunge.

"Four against one isn't much of a fair fight." Dean toyed with them.

"Oh, I can take you by myself," Isaiah spat at him. "Let her go!"

"You can try like you did last time."

Dean grinned at him. Something along the lines of a growl escaped Isaiah's throat.

"It seems Mama's Boy isn't going to let me grab and go this time," Dean said as he sat me down.

Within a split second, Sam was beside me, dragging me away from Dean. Isaiah stood there, staring down his target.

"You want to throw the first punch, or did Mother teach you to fight at all?" Dean smirked and looked at the three standing there. "We win this year, demons!"

With a blink of an eye, he was gone. There's no way someone can just disappear before your eyes. *I was going crazy! They were dragging me into their crazy delusions.*

I started to get dizzy and lightheaded. Everything was crashing down on me, and I had no clue what to believe. I slipped through Sam's fingers and hit the ground. I couldn't breathe, and the ground was spinning. *Was this a panic attack?* I had only heard them described to me. I had never experienced one before. I began choking back the bile rising in the back of my throat in between gasps of air. *It was all true. I can't believe it; it was all true. I was just getting ready to turn eighteen. I can't make a decision like this. This is not a decision for a human to make, let alone one that has barely made it into adulthood. This was the deciding factor of the war between the angels. What if I made the wrong decision?* I vomited and heaved up everything that was in my stomach, which was nothing but stomach acid. I blacked out. I heard murmuring in between the light and dark moments of my lucidity.

"I can't believe you summoned the old woman! What were you thinking!?" I knew it was Sam yelling. "When this mission is done this time, you will not be returning to help. I will make sure of that!"

No, no, you can't take my Isaiah from me. You can't take my Incaendiel.

CHAPTER 3

THE ANGELS GATHERED AROUND, waiting to see what news was being brought to them. Alpha appeared before them, looking at each and every one of them in the eye.

"Our universe is in trouble, children. By creating each of you, I have thrown the natural balance and order of the cosmos out of place. I never imagined my power would be so great to do this. I existed in the dark and brought about too much light. Now, I come before you to ask of you a simple request. Only the strongest and most powerful of you are up for the challenge." He glanced around at all his trophies of power. "Which one of you would wish to oppose me?"

The court remained quiet; not a single angel dared to oppose their master, whom they loved with their whole heart. "I need one of you to love me so much more than the others that you would give up your place here in the summit and become my Adversary. This does not mean you hate me; it just means we oppose one another with Light and Darkness to balance harmony." Still, not a single angel spoke up to take the test. Alpha became angry and impatient from the silence. "If one of you does not choose to do this yourself, I will command one of you to! I can call forth those of you I created with powers none other have!" The angels glanced nervously at one another. They did not want to give up their place in the summit nor become the Adversary of their father.

A melodic voice rang out through the court; it was a voice with such power that it brought tears to the eyes of the angels just from its sound. "My love, do not frighten the children." They immediately all felt safer and out of danger from the threat Alpha had just made.

"None of them will accept my request. What am I to do?" Alpha was perplexed and sat down on his throne. Omega sauntered up to him and touched his face.

She peered deep into his eyes, "You know I love you more than any of our children love you, right?"

"Of course, I know you do," he smiled back at her and touched her face back. A tear slid down her face, and it took him a moment to realize why..."No! I will not allow it!"

"I am the only one who loves you more than any other present in the court, which was your request. I will never hate you was another of the agreement. Why not me? Yin and Yang energies should be the Light and Dark of the Universe."

Alpha thought back to Tiamat and her words to him. She had sealed Omega's fate before him, and he had not even acknowledged it. Of course, the only power that would equal his would be his bride. He sighed heavily, but he knew this sacrifice was needed if he wanted to keep his authority and power over the universe. Without it, he would not rise to power like the others. "You are to take a few angels with you for protection."

"I cannot take our children from their home. They must choose on their own to leave the light and fall into darkness," she said as she walked to the Gate of the Summit. "Who shall go with me?" she asked, looking at all their faces. She could understand the torn look they had. None of them wanted to go and didn't want her to go either. It was heartbreaking for her. These were her lovely children, and she wished they would all go with her. "Do not feel guilty if none of you wish to go with me. I understand."

She turned to walk away when one of the angels burst forth in front of them. "I will go with you, my Omega, my mother. Father may have been the beginning, but you will be the end." She didn't even have to turn around to know whose voice it was. "Samael, my son, do any others follow you?" Samael turned and stared at his brothers and sisters. "Who shall follow?" Many stood still and glanced between themselves, and then another angel stepped forth. "I will join you, my brother." It was Azazel.

Once Azazel had stepped forth, it was easier and easier with the angels' choices until they were at half-and-half. "One thing you must realize, my children, is that this decision is permanent. You will be stripped of the light within your heart, the exceptional light that binds you to the summit. I will always love you all, but you may never return to your home again," Alpha said with a lump in his throat. "I hope your love for me never dies, and you never forget the real reason as to why you aren't here any longer. You all chose to leave. I did not make any of you do it. Therefore, you will be known as the Fallen Ones. You will keep your grace, but you will be forever changed."

Each of the angels that chose to fall nodded to their creator, their father, and they all jumped from the summit. They barreled straight toward the human world without lifting their wings once. The closer they came to Earth without opening their wings, the less light they held in their hearts. Their wings began to burn and blacken as they fell and sped toward Earth. They watched as their lustrous skin began to lose its sparkle. The Technicolor reality they were accustomed to began to erode from their sight. They looked no different from those of the human world, with their luminescent skin gone. The wonderful, silvery, blue eyes they had begun to blacken over to look like the sea during a storm. Their blonde hair turned to a dirty brown like a chestnut stallion. They were no longer the beautiful, graceful creatures they had once been, but they were still beautiful, nonetheless.

Omega was the last to take the plunge. She looked at her co-creator and smiled, "Let us hope it is not you who forgets to love us." She turned away from him, opened her arms, and free-fell through the blackness. Being a goddess and not one of the celestial creations, she did not lose her grace nor her light. She did, however, bury the light deep within herself. Since they were no longer the Alpha and Omega, no longer arm in arm with each other, she decided to take a different name that better suited her new self. Just as her fallen children looked, she too experienced a change of features except her hair turned a shade so black, it put the darkness of night to shame. Her eyes looked like the night sky, and her skin was the creamiest shade of white. She decided her name would be Lilith, the Dark Mother. When she landed amid the scattered fallen ones, they all gathered around her.

"My children, you will never be forgotten nor unloved, but you will never be the same again. It saddens me to see you in the shape that you are, and now, I wish I had not asked any of you to come with me. You will never be as you once were, full of light and iridescent beauty. As your creator, I am ashamed to see that I have caused this irreversible change to you. As your mother, I am heartbroken that I could ask such a thing of you to come with me, even if you fell by choice. Make yourself available to the humans as though you were still in the summit. For the time being, I will be alone."

She turned and made her way towards the Garden of Eden while all her children stood with tears in their eyes. It seemed as if no one was happy over the plunge. They all separated and went to their normal human assignments to watch over them. The mother stayed in the Garden of Eden, the closest thing she had to her celestial home. She spent a lot of time with Adam. He reminded her of the happier times she had when she was in the summit with her Alpha. Adam saw how sad she had become, and it broke his own heart. He began to pay closer attention to her to cheer her up, ignoring his other creator. This made Alpha bitter and jealous. How could she steal what he helped create as well? It enraged him. So, when night fell, he slipped down to the Garden of Eden, removed Adam's memory of the mother, and placed it within the Tree of Knowledge.

Adam awoke to Alpha, giving him a new rule to live by.

"My dearest son, I have watched you sleep and have grown fond of your presence among my favored animals. I have created for you whatever your heart desires to eat and drink. However, the tree that grows beside the Tree of Life is forbidden to touch." Adam looked to the tree Alpha referenced. "This is the Tree of Knowledge," Alpha told him. "Fear nothing in this Garden, but I do bid you a plea. Whoever enters this Garden, if they do not shine like your guardians, do not speak to them. They will deceive you in any way they can think of. They may come in the form of your guardians, or they may come in the form of a beautiful woman, but they bear false love for you. Do you understand?" Adam nodded his head. "Good, now sleep, my son."

When Lilith entered the Garden the next morning, Adam was scared of her. "Why do you shy away from me, my son?" Lilith asked.

"I have but one creator, and you are not him. Who are you?" he asked, stepping away timidly.

"I have only been gone one night, and you do not remember who your mother is?" Lilith asked, pained.

"As I said before, I have no mother, only my father, Alpha," replied Adam. "He said someone might come and stake a claim as one of my guardians."

Lilith's eyes clouded over, and she glared at Adam. "You do not remember me at all!" she hissed.

"I would never forget such a beautiful face, even if you are evil," Adam said, stepping back with a fearful tremble. "Please, leave me be."

Lilith balled her fists and screamed, "ALPHA!" Adam retreated and ran to safety. The Fallen Ones gathered on the outside of the Garden where they could see and hear everything. Alpha descended in a white, luminescent light with his warrior angels at his flank.

"My love, Omega, how are you, my dear?" he asked snidely.

"Why does our creation remember me naught!? What have you done!?" she hissed so loud the earth shook.

"I removed his memories of you. You spent so much time with him in the Garden; he was beginning to love you more than me," he replied.

"You jealous, Cretan!" she screamed. "This was all your idea! You decided to create an adversary, and the only one able to do it was your wife. This was your fault! If you had visited your creations instead of hiding behind your guarded gates, they might have loved you as an equal, but it takes more than just creation to show love!" Lilith paced back and forth in anger. She glared at her lover, her forlorn husband. "You wanted an adversary? Well, now, my Love, you have one! The Earth is MY domain. You can fill it with as many human souls as you wish, but they must be born and not made. It takes both of us to create a human from nothing, and I refuse to help you. This planet will be under my rule. If you try to invade my domain, there will be a war that I'm sure you do not want your children involved in."

"They made their decision when they joined you, my dear!" Alpha shouted in retort.

"This is the only common ground we shall have to meet as it is the direct gateway to the summit. I have seen what the future holds for Adam. You removed me from his mind; therefore, he will become extremely unhappy and yearning for companionship. Since you do not contain the power we do together, you will have to create his mate, Eve, from his rib, sealing me in their offspring. Once they leave this precious Garden, it will be removed from its position and hidden." She scowled at him.

"That's not fair at all, my Love, for you to know its new location but not me," Alpha replied coldly.

"Neither of us will know the new location. I will choose a family lineage that will hold the secret of the Garden. They will keep the location secret to whatever extent they see fit. This family will be called Guardians. Every one thousand years, you may send an angel to search for the hidden location. To gain the knowledge from the family, your angel may take measures deemed fit. However, the slaying of the family is out of the question. Just to make sure no angel steps out of bounds on the journey their FATHER sends them on, I will send one of my Fallen Ones as well to oversee the family's safety." Lilith finished, staring at the Alpha.

"And if my angels are able to get it out of the human, what does that mean?" Alpha asked.

"The Garden becomes your Garden. We will no longer interfere with humanity and shall retreat into the dark as you wish. However, if the human tells my Fallen Ones first, then we will have limitless access to the summit, fallen or not."

"Deal! So, what is it that our creations do to anger me that it would cause them to be banished from the Garden?" he chuckled.

"They eat from the Tree of Knowledge, where you have hidden my memory," she stated pragmatically.

He quit chuckling. "They will never remember they had a mother. I will always see to it that humanity forgets you and sweeps you under the Earth!" he sneered.

"We shall see, Alpha," she said, bowing and leaving the Garden. The light disappeared as well as Alpha and his warriors. The fallen angels gathered around their mother. She still had tears that dripped from her eyes. Everywhere a tear dropped, a weeping willow sprang from the ground. The tears rolled into a puddle, and the earth trembled as a trench formed. Her tears filled the trench, creating a lake.

"I thought he said he would always love us?" Samael stepped forth, asking. "Why did he stand there and mock our fall? It was he who asked us to join you, Mother. Did he ever love us to begin with? He never fought for any of us who stepped forth to stay! Was his love never there!? Or was it just you, Mother, loving us enough for both of you?" Samael slipped to his knees in despair and tears. The other fallen ones all took to their knees as well in tears. The blatant truth coursing through their veins; they would be Godless; they would be without a father that loved them; they would be bastards that he would make sure never saw the light again.

"My son, I shall never know if his love was ever sincere to any of you or even me," she said as one final tear slid from her eyes. This tear, however, did not grow a weeping willow in its spot. It grew a mountain. The mountain rose in leaps and bounds. At the base was a cave entrance, and she motioned all her children to follow her. The cave led to a stairway that descended into dank darkness. The further they walked, the darker it became. She stopped and snapped her fingers. A light arose in the darkness, and they found their own summit on Earth. They called it the Glade.

Unlike the hellfire and brimstone stories that had been told generation after generation, the Adversary did not live in what most people refer to as "Hell." Why would someone so loving want to live in darkness when it had already seized her heart? She succeeded in becoming the Adversary of Alpha through darkness, but darkness attained from his actions, not her actions. He caused her heart to seize up to prevent it from loving anything else ever again.

The Fallen Ones seemed to enjoy the Glade more than they had their home in the stars. Most of them had been archangels and a few sentinels from the other hierarchies, so they didn't get to stay in the summit. They had their daily assignments to attend, spending less and less time in the summit.

"My children, please gather around," she called out to all her followers. "There will be times when you feel yourself slip into darkness." She looked them all dead in their eyes. "This will not be your fault but mine alone. I asked you to fall, to lose your light, and I am the one to carry that burden. The one thing I ask of you is not to let this darkness consume you entirely. I may handle the darkness within my heart; however, you are not as strong as me. If you let it seep into your heart, you will not return from it so easily."

"We will never succumb to the envy and greed that our father has," Azazel stated as she lowered her head.

"That is good to hear, my dear, sweet Azazel, just heed my warning. Your father may have given you the titles of the Fallen Ones, but that is not what he intends to really call you. In my eyes, you are Wanderers, here to explore the darkness and to seek the light. In his eyes, you will become demons, vile creatures that he will convince humanity are against them and not out to help them. You will be viewed as wicked, dark, and evil because of your choice to follow orders. Through the years, you will learn and gain vast knowledge about the difference between the darkness and the light, and I hope they change your outlook on our situation. This is a blessing, not a curse."

"Are there any rules you are to lay down, Dark Mother?" Samael asked, peering up to his sole ruler.

"Yes. You are to never harm a human. If word gets back to me that you have, I will strip you of your grace, and you will roam the earth as one. In the future, one of your brothers will be sent to walk the life of a mortal man. We are to help his cause, for he is deceiving the father and trying to bring the mother back into the light. Afterward, even though he will ascend and be punished, Lucifer will join our ranks."

A hushed murmur filled the ranks of the Wanderers. "Are you sure, mother? He is Second in Command of the Archangels. Why would he turn on Alpha?" Samael asks.

"For one, he is outraged over the situation; for two, Metatron would not accept the task. Your brothers and sisters have not forgotten you, and they are really angry with Alpha. They will do whatever it takes to save your grace and return your light." Lilith responds.

"Mother, how do you know this?" an angel asked, walking from the back to the front. Most of the angels had been silent throughout the whole speech, with the exception of Samael and Azazel, who were first and second in command.

"You already know the answer to that, Incaendiel, as you already know how the future looks with either the failure or success of your brother, Lucifer." She walked to Incaendiel and brushed her hand along his jawline. "And with Sophie."

CHAPTER 4

A nd the Dream Crumbles

"WITH THE WINDOW to my soul open to your eyes, Not a reflection of hopeless dreams. But the reflection of my eyes gazing back at me, As we share our moment of infinity."

I AWOKE with a pounding headache in total darkness. I figured I would be back home, and all this would have been one huge nightmare. That was not the case. I sat up and looked around, trying to focus in the dark to see where I was. I was still in the freaking graveyard.

"Those assholes left me here!" I was irate, scratch that, furious. I tried to stand but still felt dizzy, so I decided against it until the ground quit spinning. "I can't believe he left me again," I muttered.

"Who left you?" The voice in the dark scared the crap out of me.

I glanced around nervously, and my eyes adjusted to the figure that was sitting just a few feet away from me on a bench.

"I hope you didn't imply that I would just leave you in the middle of a graveyard passed out. That wouldn't be very chivalrous of me." He walked closer, but I already knew who the voice belonged to.

"So, what do I call you?" I asked groggily as I tried to stand again. I still wasn't able to stand up.

"Isaiah is fine," he said, reaching for my arm to help me stand.

"Well, you didn't come when I called for Isaiah. You only answered to Incaendiel." He flinched when I said that. *Good, he did have a heart.*

"What all did he tell you about yourself...about me?" He was beating around the bush, and I knew exactly what he wanted to know.

"Well, let's see; apparently, we're angelic lovers, and you left me for our mother. Kind of incestuous if you ask me," I said, beginning to walk away when he pulled me back.

"I didn't leave you!" There was so much emotion behind the simple statement. "You told me to go! You told me that you saw us being together again one day!" He was furious.

He breathed in a deep breath with his eyes closed, and when he opened his eyes back up, his look softened towards me. His hand tentatively reached for my face. I could see he was fighting the urge to touch it, to stroke it.

"You have no idea how hard it was for me to leave you behind."

I hadn't realized that I was leaning in closer to his face, and my breathing had sped up along with my heart. I had never been drawn to anyone like this before. I don't even remember us having this connection when we were younger.

It was crazy to believe that in the brief period of time we had been talking again, that I could think I was in love with him. This was real life, not Hollywood. However, we had always had a connection. When I broke my arm in sixth grade, he was waiting on the porch

33

when I got home from the hospital with flowers, candy, ice cream, and a sharpie. He said everyone in town knew about it. It hadn't dawned on me that my breaking an arm would not have made gossip of the little town of New Salem.

"We're breaking all the rules by bringing up our true selves. I better get you home." He grabbed my hand to tow me away, but the energy radiated through our hands and into my body.

I couldn't bear it any longer. I pulled him to me and threw myself into him. I kissed him lightly on the lips, touching his face, feeling the electricity prick me here and there. He wrapped his arms around me, inviting my kiss, pressing his lips back against mine, and then he pushed me away. I didn't know what came over me. I have never acted this way before with anyone.

"No, no, Sophie! We can't do this. It's breaking all the rules! Please, please don't make me really leave you behind this time. I can't walk away from you again."

The tears caught in my throat. I had never felt this drawn to him, and it was just getting stronger. I wanted him in my arms. I didn't want anyone else to be in them. I wanted to be his, and it felt like he wanted the same thing until he pushed me away. My heart crumbled. *Does he not want to be with me?* I felt the tension slice through the air when I thought it.

"Well, what do you want me to do? Do you want me to give Dean a chance?" He stiffened when I said his name. His fists were clenched. "I would rather just be with you...I don't want to go without you near me anymore. These last four years have been torture! I've had no one...do I?"

"Those are the rules. He has to be given a chance to sway you to his side." His words stung.

I didn't know what love was, but I was pretty sure those electrical sparks and fireworks meant I loved Isaiah.

"We will always have a deep bond. They hope they can break our bond, break you, and bring you to their side. I don't want them to, but it was part of the pact made, and we never break a covenant pact."

"Are you sure he won't try to drag me to wherever he was earlier?" I feared where I might've ended up if I hadn't called out for him.

"He has been reprimanded for his actions today. He's supposed to be a good little boy from now on."

My heart was aching for him. I knew deep down that Dean would never penetrate what we had together. Even if it was just a few moments of a spark, I felt like it was years of love.

As if he knew what I was thinking, "Last time, you knew who we were together and still almost chose him. Our bond gets stronger with every reincarnation but weaker after your eighteenth birthday."

"Why?" I didn't understand why it would get weaker. *Why then?*

He paused. "Eighteen marks the year I left you to fall." He disappeared.

I was left alone in the graveyard. We were only eighteen when he left. *Does that mean that we were all frozen at that age? Were they forever frozen as eighteen years old because they left their other half in the summit? What happens when I turn nineteen?* All these questions I needed answered, and I doubted that he would be the one to answer them.

I walked to my car and got in without any problems this time. I started the engine and pulled out of the cemetery. I hadn't even noticed that Gramms' Bible was tucked away into the passenger seat. I raced home and prayed mom wouldn't be awake waiting up for me. To my luck, she was soundly asleep in her room. I walked to my room and flicked my desk light on. The only answers I could get were bound in the book that lay on the desk. I opened the book and flipped through the pages to the spot where Gramms had left off.

CHAPTER 5

The Fallen Shed Tears

"THE ANGELS GATHER ROUND, as their world decays. Watching and waiting for the end of night and the beginning of day. Bound by oath forgotten within days, left to walk the earth in pain. Twilight locked in eternal damnation, the darkness swallowing their salvation."

"HOW DO YOU KNOW ABOUT SOPHIE?" Incaendiel asked, walking closer to his Dark Mother. "How do you know what her visions saw but not Father?"

"Even though he created me, he put more power within me than he realized. He does not have the power to see into the minds of his angels. I was the one who breathed life into each of you, so I have a connection with you."

"Sophie said that we would be together again. The vision she shared is hazy in my head and becomes even hazier as the days between us grow. What did she mean?"

All the angels stared as he asked the Dark Mother the question. He had no rank to even speak with her. Why was he not put in his place?

"You two share a bond unlike anything I have seen before. Some of the others have a connection with their chosen ones, but not as strong as the two of you do. You two are what we call twin flames. I split your soul when I created you two. You two will be the key to us returning to the summit one day." Everyone in the room sucked in a breath of astonishment.

"How will we be the key? I do not understand." Incaendiel sat beside the Dark Mother. He missed Sophie terribly. All the fallen ones began to weep as his pain radiated and coursed through their hearts. He looked up to the weeping faces. "How do they feel what I feel?"

"You are more powerful than what you believe. You must believe in yourself, my son. You have the power to project as well as take. Go ahead, try to take the pain you inflicted amongst your brothers and sisters." Lilith smiled and looked out to those weeping in sorrow. Incaendiel closed his eyes and breathed in deeply, breathing back the emotion he had welled up. The tears immediately stopped, and all the Wanderers stared at him. No one here, including Samael or Azazel, had this gift or effect on everyone.

"Sophie will be the key to the summit. She holds the power to return us all. That is why when I proposed there be a guardian, your father hid her and will be sending her as the guardian every one thousand years. Each incarnation, he will get closer and closer to receiving the knowledge of where the Garden is. However, each time, you will get closer to getting your twin flame back and us returning to the summit where we rightfully belong. I should have never agreed to the adversary role. I had no idea his intentions were like this." She bowed her head in defeat.

"I know what the human world will think of me, but that is why I slipped back into the Garden as a snake and told Eve to eat the fruit. He cannot hide the truth about me if it is buried within their mind and etched into their DNA. He was foolish to make that tree instead of doing away with the memory of me completely."

"How many incarnations will she endure before we can be together? When will we know that it's the final incarnation?" Incaendiel was full of questions.

"How old are you, my son?" He had thought they were all created at once because they all looked the same age.

"It has been eighteen years since my creation."

"Each incarnation, your bond will grow strong in the beginning, but once she hits her eighteenth birthday, that bond will decrease, making her more susceptible to the angels that pursue her. When she reaches her eighteenth birthday, and that bond doesn't decrease in the slightest, that is the year that we will triumph and return to the summit. She is literally the key to the Gate." All the Wanderers cheered when they heard this bit of information.

"What happens when she turns nineteen, and the other angels haven't been able to squeeze the location of the Garden from her?" Lilith remained silent for a few moments.

"Do you really want to know what will happen to her?" she asked, staring him deeply in the eyes. He nodded. "On her nineteenth birthday, something tragic will transpire to separate the two of you once again. Her soul will return to the summit, where your father will keep it locked up, safe and sound. You will remain another one thousand years without her by your side." Her eyes were dark and gloomy.

"That's not fair! Why doesn't she get a chance at a normal life?" Incaendiel was enraged. Random fires began to surface and cast their hazy heat in all directions. Lilith placed her hand on his shoulder, and the flames receded.

"She is not a human soul. She has but one purpose, and Alpha sees to that."

"That is still dark on his part. She's not just a toy or a tool in a plot." The anger and pity coursed through his body. Most of the Wanderers had trickled out after the fire nearly set everyone on fire.

"My son, this was her proposal and idea to your father."

CHAPTER 6

Why don't you Stay?

"STAY with me through the night, as my eyes slip into slumber. Stay with me through the day as my mind begins to falter. My heart and mind are not one and only deceive each other. For my heart knows what is what, as my mind begins to saunter."

MY HANDS TREMBLED as I marked the spot I was at and closed the book. I knew the notion of my death had crossed my mind when I thought of what might happen when I turned nineteen. I just didn't think that would be the answer. Of course, deep down, I knew I was the one who had made a deal with God, Alpha, whatever you want to call him. The sun was beginning to peek above the horizon. I hadn't realized I had spent the entire night reading the bible.

I rubbed my eyes and went downstairs to make some coffee. I had to start my job today, and with everything weighing on my mind, I honestly didn't feel like working there anymore. *Why bother?* In a year, I would die. There's no need to save for college any longer. My fate was sealed. I wish Gramms had told me this little tidbit of information. She must have known I would find out eventually.

As I walked into the kitchen, I noticed that coffee had already been made, and a steaming cup of coffee sat on the table. I double-checked Mom's room and found that she was still sound asleep. My nerves knotted up, and I walked back into the kitchen. There was no note by the coffee. I didn't know if Isaiah had made it or if it was a notion Dean had in his mind to do for me. More than likely, the latter since Isaiah said he would be distancing himself from me.

Just the thought of him staying away more sent a pain through my heart. It was like someone had their hand on my heart and would squeeze it every time I thought of his love. *See, there it goes again.* It felt like I had loved him for years. I was afraid of this feeling. I knew what happened to girls when they fell too fast and too hard; they would end up hurt eventually.

I picked up the cup of coffee and walked outside. It had been a while since I had sat on the front porch and drank a cup of coffee while watching the sunrise. My mom let me do it right after Gramms died. Of course, it started off as hot chocolate, then tea, and then finally coffee. I was distraught when she died. The wound was barely scabbed over because if I picked at it, it still bled. So, I changed my train of thought to something else. To my dismay, nothing else would come to mind aside from Isaiah. Tomorrow was my eighteenth birthday, and then, apparently, I would begin to forget Isaiah's love as soon as I remembered it.

"It sucks. I know." His voice didn't startle me nearly as bad as I thought it would. I was getting used to them just popping up out of nowhere.

"What if this time...I don't? What if I hold onto us?" He walked over and sat down beside me.

"I doubt it's this time. Every time you have gotten weaker and weaker after your birthday. It's like your soul is giving up on us being together."

He leaned forward and clasped his hands together, looking down at the porch. It must have been torture for him when he quit talking to me four years ago.

"Maybe this time is different?" I reached over to touch his hands, and he pulled them from me.

"Please, don't get my hopes up. Not again." My heart yearned to touch him. I could feel the intense pull to just reach out and touch his face.

"I want to see what we used to be like. Before the fall..." I knew he could let me see it.

"I'm forbidden to show you. It's against the rules."

He sat back in his chair. His leg was shaking like a nervous twitch. I could see that he fought with every ounce of himself to not touch me, to not make that connection. I ignored the rules, besides, they weren't my rules. I had free will; everyone knew humans had free will. I sat my coffee down and planted myself in his lap.

"Please, Sophie." I ignored his plea and leaned in for a kiss.

Our lips touched, and the same magnetism I felt yesterday radiated through my body. I could feel it vibrating through me. His hands couldn't resist me in his lap. They went to my back, pulling me in deeper into him. I could smell his true self. I smelled lavender, sage, and every sweet note mixed in it. He smelled so different than Dean did when he rolled the window down. He smelled exactly like I wanted.

His hands traced my back, and I dizzied under his touch. I wanted so much more. He must've felt this urgency. He pulled me away.

"You're getting me in trouble. Trust me, I don't mind the trouble, but there are rules I have to follow." He pushed a strand of hair from my face.

I love you, Isaiah. I didn't want to say it out loud. I couldn't say it out loud. If I did, my heart knew that would be the day he did leave. I didn't want to tell him, afraid he would leave me.

"Wait to tell me that after tomorrow," he said, picking me up and setting me down in my chair.

Just as fast as he was there, he was gone. *How did he know what I was thinking?*

The rest of the day seemed to fly by. I called the bookstore where I had been hired and told them unfortunately, I won't be able to work this year. I just wasn't ready. They completely understood and said no worries.

The job would be there all year if I changed my mind. Mom took me shopping, exclaiming how proud she was her baby was finally turning eighteen. I wanted to ask her so badly about what was happening, but I didn't know how she would react. Instead, I trudged along behind her from store-to-store shopping for my party tomorrow. She bought me new clothes for school, a new cell phone and an iPod for my birthday, and then we went out to eat. While we were eating, I hadn't even noticed Dean walk up to the table until I heard my mother acknowledge him.

"Hello, Dean. How are you adjusting to the move?" I didn't even move my eyes from my meal.

"It's going. Sophie showed me around yesterday, and I was acquainted with everyone." I lifted my eyes in anger at him. *Idiot!*

"Sophie hadn't even mentioned to me that you two got to know each other yesterday." My mother smiled at me with a smile that said, *once he leaves, you're spilling the beans.*

"I was actually coming over to ask Sophie if it would be okay for me to come to the party tomorrow." He smiled, looking at my mother, working his magic on her.

"The more, the merrier, sweetie. What do you say, Sophie?" She nudged me under the table, and I lifted my eyes to Dean.

His eyes twinkled today and looked different than yesterday. It was as if he genuinely wished to participate.

"Sounds good. Can't wait to see you there." I tried to sound as convincing as possible.

It worked for my mother, not sure if it worked for Dean.

"I'll be there." He smiled and walked away. *Was Isaiah, right? Would he really win my heart over the love I felt right now?*

"He's cuuute!" She smiled at me, hoping I would take the bait of conversation.

"I just don't know if he's my type. He's more of a bad boy type."

I looked off after him as he made his way out the door. He turned and winked at me. I wanted to scowl at him, but I knew my mother was watching.

"Bad boy? He seems like an angel to me." *If she only knew...*

The rest of the day was over before I could blink, and I found myself lying in my bed, unable to fall asleep. I climbed out of my bed and made my way to the window. My room was on the second floor, and occasionally, I liked to sit out on the roof and enjoy the night air. I shifted the window open and climbed out. I sat down and gazed up at the stars.

"Planning to leave me sooner than predicted?" Isaiah was at my side, sitting down with me. I nudged him with my arm. "I didn't take you for a jumper," he chuckled.

"In exactly five minutes, it will be my eighteenth birthday." We were both silent for a few seconds. "I'm glad you showed up. I wanted to spend the last few minutes I had feeling the way I do about you with you." I leaned my head against his shoulder, and he wrapped his arm around me, inviting me to his chest.

"I'm never too far from you. I'm always here watching you sleep, watching over you in general." We fell silent.

"It was you that carried me from Gramms' grave home, wasn't it?" A look of guilt spread across his face as if he weren't supposed to have done it.

"I couldn't leave you there by yourself. It wasn't safe, not so close to the portal they have to the summit." I nodded my head. He has always been my silent guardian angel. He snickered.

"You can read my mind, can't you?" He didn't have to answer from his chuckle. "I knew it. You're the only one, right?" He nodded. "This explains a lot." It was nearly my birthday like 30 seconds left.

"You were the one who took my pain the night of Gramms' funeral, weren't you?" He didn't respond this time, not immediately.

"I gave it back to you little by little until you could handle it." It made sense. It's why I broke down at the grave. The seconds had ticked down to 10.

"Can I have one more kiss?" My eyes pleaded with his.

He was the one who leaned in this time and kissed me softly on the lips. It felt like we lingered there for an eternity. I dizzied under the feel of his lips. He pulled back just as the clock struck 12 a.m.

"Happy birthday, Sophie."

Just like normal, as fast as he appeared, he was gone. What I didn't expect was the pain I felt whenever he left to still be there. I climbed back in my window and lay down to go to sleep. I knew it had to be a fitful sleep because when I awoke, the bedsheets were torn off, and the blanket was thrown in the flow. I never remembered my dreams. It must be some sort of precaution, so I didn't give away any information. I didn't know.

I jumped in the shower and dressed in the new clothes mom had bought me for my birthday. The party wasn't until the afternoon, so I thought it would be a quiet morning with Mom, that is, until I heard two voices coming from the kitchen, along with laughter. I walked downstairs to the kitchen. I could smell the coffee Mom would have ready for me when she beat me to making it.

My blood ran cold when I saw Dean sitting at the table with Mom. There was a personal birthday cake with a single candle on the top of it to the left of him. It was obvious he was the one who brought it. I closed my eyes and sucked in a breath. This was something I had to do.

Mom looked up at me and smiled, "Well, there she is. Dean thought he would stop by before the party and take you to get some breakfast as a present." The look on her face said, *you better accept the offer, or you're grounded.* I groaned on the inside.

"Sounds like fun!" I tried to sound as chipper as I could.

"Just remember the party is at 2. Don't be late. You know it's rude." The warning on her face for being late was more severe than turning down the breakfast.

"Don't worry. I will have her back in time, I promise." He stood from the table with the cake in his hands and lit the candle. "Want to make a wish?"

The one wish that I wanted to wish I knew wouldn't happen because he wasn't a living person. I grinned at the idea of Dean dropping dead. Since I knew it wouldn't come true, I made the next best one. I wished for Isaiah.

We took my car since he didn't have one, obviously. Small talk didn't seem to be his forte, so I started the conversation. "So, how does this work? Do we date until I fall in love with you, forget my love for Isaiah, and then you gain the Garden? Or would I hold out and rather die? Or I hang onto the love for Isaiah, and you lose?" He scowled at me.

"I preferred the other you. Knights in shining armor were your flaw. I have no clue how to woo you now." So, he had been planning on trying to sweep me off my feet the way he had last time.

"You could try to be yourself, for one." I looked over and saw a glint flash through his eyes.

"I don't think you're into the bad boy thing." He wasn't lying there. I have never been drawn to the bad boy pretense, but there was a slight tug when I saw him and Isaiah show down as they did at the ball field yesterday.

"I would rather you be yourself than someone you're not. That's more of a turn-off than you being a bad boy." *Why was I giving him tips? Was this one of his powers? Manipulation?*

"Ah, so you still like being the damsel in distress but under the strong arm of a man?" *How did he know that!? Uh-oh.* I shouldn't have said anything to begin with. I eased the car into park at the diner in town and turned the ignition off.

We walked in and sat down to be waited on. He was actually nice looking. The eyes of the girls I went to school with pierced through me. Jealousy over me was a new thing. We placed our order and sat in awkward silence.

"This would be easier if you acted like you were at least interested in me." I looked over at him. My eyes found his, and an odd sensation tugged at my mind. I did sort of feel a little comfortable around him.

"This is just a lot to swallow in a couple of days. I went from having no attention from guys to being fought over."

I blushed from blurting it out to him. He leaned over the table and placed his lips against mine. I felt an intense feeling rush through my body. It was a simple kiss, but it felt familiar to me.

"If it weren't for this being a mission, I wouldn't use the tactics I have used before. I really am attracted to you, both the real you and the angel you." His thumb brushed the top of my hand. "I have to follow orders. I have to hate my fallen brothers. If it weren't for the decree, I would be doing anything I could to help them get back as well."

He switched seats and sat beside me. He looped his arm around my waist, and my heart sped up. I didn't know which part of me was having this response, the human me or the angel me. He leaned over and kissed my cheek. "You may not remember, but we did have something special once before." He whispered it so softly in my ear. He sent goosebumps up and down my arms.

I felt like I was lost in the moment. I never knew that this would feel so releasing. My studies had always been my priorities, so I didn't swoon over hot guys at school. Our food came, and we ate in silence, but the silence spoke in volumes. I felt a bit lightheaded around him. I guess this was the feeling most girls felt when they were on a date.

We finished our food and walked to my car. He wanted to take me to a scenic lookout. I turned here and turned there, and we stopped at a lookout point off the highway. I put the car in park and immediately felt his arms around my waist, pulling me into him. His mouth found mine, and I invited his kiss in. He moved his mouth to my neck, and I closed my eyes. My body was responding in ways I had never explored before.

His hand snaked its way up to my face and pulled me in for another kiss. I was enjoying the moment until Isaiah's face popped into my head. It was like everything came to a screeching halt. I couldn't do this anymore. Everything in me screamed no, but for some reason, I couldn't resist. *Was this him still?* His lips touched mine. It wasn't the same electric shock as Isaiah's kiss, but it still sent tingles and waves through my body. *So, is this what it's like to kiss another boy, or to kiss another angel?*

As much as I wanted to pull away, I couldn't. I felt guilty. I knew what I was doing to Isaiah, doing to the "us" that wanted to be together again. It was breaking me apart inside, but something still kept me from pulling away. He slipped his tongue into my mouth, which was a big no-no for me, and I still couldn't pull away. He had to be using mind manipulation. This is how he got to the me one thousand years ago. *Was I stronger than her? Could I hold out as long as she did?* I must be stronger because they would have known he had manipulated her.

His hand started to snake up my leg, and I still couldn't protest. *Oh, my God!* He's going to fondle me, and I couldn't even build up the strength to push him off of me. This was not what Incaendiel discussed with me before. This isn't free will. This was against my will. I began to push with my mind for him to stop. I was yelling and pleading for him to stop. I could sense he heard my pleas, but he pressed forward.

His hand slipped from my thigh and moved up under my skirt. His other hand started groping my chest. I couldn't believe it. I was going to be molested by a freaking angel. *What kind of God presides over him?!* He would sacrifice the virtue of an eighteen-year-old to get information for a freaking Garden! A tear slowly rolled down my face as his hand went further, but slowly up my skirt, as if he enjoyed me squirming under his hand. The bad boy thing was a definite no that I should've kept my mouth closed about.

I couldn't take it anymore. I called out with my mind. *Please, Incaendiel!* No sooner had my mind flashed the name that there were tons of people standing around my car. When I looked up, though, we weren't at the lookout any longer. Somehow, he had made me think we were. We were really at the cemetery. The passenger door flew open, and Dean was yanked off me. My door flew open to hands, grabbing me and pulling me free from the trap I had been in.

"Dean, you're honestly using powers against her! Mind manipulation!? Is that what you did last time as well!?" It wasn't Isaiah or Sam yelling at Dean. It was another young man.

"Michael, I'm sorry. I had no idea I was doing it." His eyes bore fear within them.

"I call bull! Father wants to see you as soon as possible. Your trip is over this time!" The one called Michael was furious. He snapped his fingers, and Dean disappeared. I buried my face into the chest of the person who pulled me from the car. I was so lost in the fear I had no idea who it was, but whoever it was, I was silently thanking them for ripping me out of the car at that exact moment.

"Sophie, I am truly sorry for the way he treated you. Do not be mistaken that this was in any way approved in the eyes of our father. Dean will be reprimanded to the highest measure." Michael was sincere in his words.

"It shouldn't have gotten this far, Michael. What if he had gone farther before she called out?! Lord knows what he would have done-" the voice stopped short. Anger tainted each syllable spoken. The voice I knew so well. The voice that sent ripples through every tendon and muscle of my body. My face flushed as I thought of him.

"We honestly had no idea this is what would have happened. Please forgive me, Brother, and forgive those who were a part of the idea, if any exist." Michael didn't act like all the other angels did. He wasn't rude or snide with them. Then it dawned on me.

"Michael...as in Archangel Michael, the angel of strength and courage?" His eyes widened a bit in surprise. "No, it's not a memory. My mother took me to church for a while, and you are in the Bible." His eyes seemed to relax.

"Yes, I am that angel." He smiled at me, and I could feel that he really meant his gesture. Another angel appeared to the side of Michael and whispered into his ear. "Father requests my presence. Zadkiel, will you see to it that no other tries what has transpired today in my absence." Zadkiel nodded while he stared at me. I didn't feel comfortable under his gaze. Michael broke the air, "Until next time." He bowed his head and was gone. Zadkiel had a look plastered on his face that I couldn't shake. His face seemed so familiar, but I couldn't place it.

"I beg your forgiveness for what my ignorant brother has done to you and for the quick departure of our second in command. What is a suitable gesture for this kind of action? Dinner, maybe?" I was about to answer when I felt Isaiah stiffen.

"Are you sure this wasn't planned so you could be the big hero in her damsel in distress situation?" It clicked with me there. The exact words that Dean had said to me.

"I assure you, Brother, that is not-" I interrupted him before he could finish.

"Choose your words carefully." Zadkiel eyed me, and I could see the facade beginning to lighten.

"Tell me, Sophie, what did that kiss with Dean feel like? Did you want more of it?"

I blushed. He made me feel like a whore in front of everyone standing around. I looked from Sam's face to Azazel's face. I didn't want to answer.

"That's all the answer I needed." He smirked at me and turned to walk away.

"I felt guilty for kissing him." I blurted it out, but it stopped him

47

dead in his tracks. He whipped around, walked up to me and was inches from my face.

"What did you say?" His words weren't as kind as before.

"I-I said I felt guilty for kissing him." All eyes were trained on me, a look of surprise crossing Sam and Azazel's face.

"And why did you feel guilty for kissing him? Because he was an angel? Because it was your first kiss in public? Why!?" he yelled. He terrified me.

I was finally able to choke back the fear and squeak a response. "Because it wasn't Isaiah I was kissing."

It was barely a whisper, but everyone heard it, and I felt Isaiah tense even more. His grip tightened around me. I didn't know why until the angel lunged at me.

"You will give us the Garden! You will tell us where it is!"

Sam and Azazel were holding him back; well, struggling to hold him back was more like it. Isaiah never let me go but flew off with me into the wind. I could hear Zadkiel screaming,

"There will be court pulled for this, Incaendiel! Your days are marked!"

It felt as if we were in the air for only a few moments, but we ended up miles away at a lake. Isaiah loosened his grip on me and turned me to face him.

"Tell me you're not lying to deceive the other side. It's not wise to mess with Zadkiel. Tell me!"

He was furious, and I was still scared from everything that had transpired. My eyes dropped from his to the ground from terror. He softened his gaze at me and lifted my chin so our eyes would meet. The eyes that stared down at me were the eyes I loved to see. So dark, like the sea.

"Tell me!" he pleaded, and I could feel his entire body shaking.

Instead of telling him, I pulled him close to me and planted my kiss on his lips. Our lips lingered forever on one another. The magnetic pull and electrical spark that was always there were stronger. He pulled me in tighter and kissed me harder. My body was completely melted into his. His tongue slipped into my mouth, but it wasn't like before with Dean. I wanted it. I craved it. My body asked for more; it needed more. Just as fast and long as the kiss had started, it ended. He pulled away from me. My entire body buzzed, and I could see a faint glimmer of light from his body. His eyes looked at me in surprise. I couldn't understand what he was surprised about. He should've been able to sense my emotions.

"What? What is it?" I asked in confusion.

"You're shining!" His eyes were wide in disbelief.

"Is that normal?" I asked, looking down at my hands. "Maybe it's because you are, too." He looked down at the faint glow of his hands.

"No, this isn't normal. This has never happened before." I was stunned. I didn't know what it was supposed to mean either. "I'm going to take you home before you are late for your party."

"Will you stay?" He closed his eyes, meaning no. "It would mean a lot."

"I have questions that need to be answered. I'm sorry." He picked my hands up and kissed them.

"Where are you going?" I asked, kissing his hands back.

Just the touch of his hands to mine made me crave him more and more. I didn't understand what was happening. People just don't fall in love overnight. It doesn't happen that way, but there was no mistake in the growing euphoria I had whenever I was around him.

"I'm going to send Sam and Azazel to watch over you in case they try to kidnap you and make off to the portal with you."

He grabbed me by my waist, and it took the breath from me. My heart thumped in my chest, and when I looked around, the lake disappeared. We were immediately at my house on the front porch. I turned to face him. I wanted to kiss him again; I needed to kiss him again. Sam and Azazel appeared immediately by his side.

"Watch her. Keep Zadkiel from her. I will be back later." He started to walk away when Sam stopped him.

"Where are you going?" It was a simple question, but it took a few seconds for him to answer.

"I'm going to see Mother." And like that, he was gone.

The other two just looked at me. They didn't just look at me; they looked me up and down.

"What?" I asked, blushing.

"After the party, we all need to talk." Sam was as serious as I had ever seen.

"Will the humans see her glow?" Azazel asked.

"Not like we do. There will be a glow about her, but it will just be like a happy glow. It bringing attention will be a different story. She hasn't had this glow since Mariam died."

CHAPTER 7

F*eel the Burn*

"THE LIGHTS ARE SWIRLING as the heart beats fast. Visions of love from days long past. Hope is mounting as the fear dissipates.

Longing for the old-time ways. Her hand in his, his lips to hers, eternity waited for this moment of burn."

"INCAENDIEL, why have you left your assignment and come back here? You know you're supposed to stay until her nineteenth birthday. She's not safe without you by her side." I had barely made it down the spiraling staircase when I heard her voice.

"It's urgent, Mother," I replied, reaching the last step.

"What is so urgent that you-" she stopped midsentence while gazing at me. "Your light! It's faint, but there. How did you return it?" She walked over to me, examining my faint glow.

"It's the year, Mother." She stared at me wide-eyed.

"Are you sure? We don't want to get our hopes up this time like we did last time." She was watching my face for a hint of a response before I made one.

"The angels are going against the rules. Dean used mind manipulation on her last time and tried this time. She called out to me before he could do it for more than a day. He tricked her mind into it last time. This time, she is stronger and didn't give in."

"What did he try?" She eyed me curiously.

I held back the rage that coursed through me, afraid I would ignite the Glade again like I did so many years before.

"He tried inappropriate things with her, and she called out to me. The other team of angels were in league with his doings and were going to play the damsel in distress card on her."

My fists were clenched tight. It angered me that Zadkiel had been behind the scheme as well. I knew he was a snake, but I never imagined such a high-ranking angel would stoop that low.

"What did Zadkiel do?" She must've read my body language. Hell, she could've read my mind.

"She wouldn't fall for the damsel in distress card, so he asked her if she felt anything while kissing Dean." I paused.

"What did she say?" Mother had grown curious.

"At first nothing, he took it as a sign that they were winning again, but then..." I stopped again. I still didn't want to believe the truth behind her words.

"But what?" She was urging me to keep telling her.

"She said she felt guilty because it wasn't me she was kissing."

Mother turned from me. I knew she was thinking everything over in her head.

"The words mean nothing, Incaendiel. She has to show you she still loves you." Her voice was solemn.

"I whisked her away from everyone and told her that. That's when she kissed me. The same kiss we share every time after her eighteenth birthday has begun, but it was more powerful than I have ever felt it." I waited for her to respond.

"Is that when you began to glow?" Her voice was still unsure of everything.

"Yes, but-"

"But what!" she interrupted once more, this time a little bit angry. She still wasn't happy with my report.

"She was glowing too." She whipped around and faced me.

"You are sure! She began to glow as well?! You must be sure!" She walked over to me, her eyes dancing over my face for truthfulness.

"Yes, I'm sure. Samael and Azazel can attest to it. She's still glowing." I could see her thinking inwardly to herself.

"Do the angels know she is glowing yet? Have they seen her glow?" She was pacing the floor.

"No, but it won't be long before they do. We're going to keep her under our watch until it's time, just in case they try to kidnap her and pry the information out of her."

"Has she remembered where the Garden is yet?" That's a question neither of us have bothered to find out.

"She hasn't told me if she has." She didn't reply to my answer. "Is that a good thing or a bad thing?"

"I don't know my son, but we need the location of the Garden before we can reach the summit. Even with your light restored to full power, the only gateway we can use to get to the summit is the Garden. You have watched her all these years. Has she ever given any indication of where it's located?"

"No. It's been a long time since she has remembered our love since this began. I'm sure even her soul cannot remember, or for that matter, she may have moved it a couple of times as well." Her eyes darkened.

"I hadn't even thought of that." She was thinking to herself again. "From now on, Samael is to report to me anything of importance, and you are to not leave her side. Ever. For any reason, do you understand?" She caught my eyes, and I immediately understood why. I nodded at her. "It's time for you to return. Have Samael keep me posted." I turned to walk away. "Incaendiel?" I stopped and looked back at her. "You know the stakes. You must not get hurt. In your human form, anything can kill you, even if you have your powers. They are to protect both Sophie and you at all costs. Without your union as one, we cannot return."

My blood ran cold. They had nearly killed me last time, and

luckily, it was on my last day as a human. Right before I passed, I returned to my normal form.

"Don't try to save her this time. If she dies, she will reincarnate. If you die...you will not." I swallowed hard and nodded my head.

Mother knew I would do anything to keep my Sophie out of harm's way, but I knew this time it was important. I had to protect her at all costs, but if I endangered myself, it would all be for nothing in the end. I mounted the staircase and popped out at the cave entrance. I wasn't expecting anyone to be standing there, but sure enough, Michael and Zadkiel with a crew of angels stood before me.

"You know you are forbidden to come to the mountain!" My words filled the air with heat.

"We were just waiting for you, Brother. Come, we would like to have a word with you about your concubine if you don't mind." Zadkiel grinned at me. I scowled at him.

"Brother, why do you talk to him with such malice?" Michael shook his head at Zadkiel's actions. "Please, Incaendiel, we do need to speak with you about Sophie."

"I am not going anywhere with you. We can speak here freely of the issue."

I sent a mental alert to all my brothers and sisters below the mountain floor, and there was a tremendous rumble. Behind me stood an army of my allies.

"Now, is that any way to treat a guest." Zadkiel snickered, and his eyes flared at all of us.

"You are not welcome here, Brother of Light!"

Zadkiel scowled at me and raced forward. He grabbed me by the throat.

"Brother of Darkness, do you wish to test my strength?"

His hand gripped tighter, cutting my breath off. It was against the rules to harm one another while we were in human form, but not a word was said to make him stop. What he didn't know was that I retained my powers while in human form. I grabbed his arm, and my hand superheated. He yelled, dropping his grip on my throat. He threw a punch that caught me square in the jaw.

"Enough, you two!" Michael's voice echoed through the valley. I wiped the corner of my mouth, where it had started to bleed from the punch.

"Do you wish to bring war upon Earth? I see your army behind you, waiting for the word. Why don't you say it and get it over with?" Zadkiel was testing me.

53

"That is not my call. They do not stand here to protect me; they stand here to protect our mother, or has Father brainwashed her from your memory as well?" I knew my words would sting.

"She was the one who abandoned us!" He was furious.

"At Father's request. He should have chosen his words better than he did."

I glared at him and felt the heat radiating from my body. I was only in my human form, but my powers were still damaging. I was one of the few angels who kept my power while in human form.

Zadkiel was fuming now. "She left us!"

"You had the chance to follow! You were too worried about leaving the summit or losing your light that you didn't care for her any longer! It was your choice to stay! She loves us all and still does! That's what you don't understand. Father no longer cares about those who fell with her, but she still loves each and every one of you that remained behind!"

"If she still loved us, she would return!" Zadkiel stared me down.

"What do you think we're trying to do? She doesn't want to abandon those of us who were faithful to her and return without us." I wasn't sure if I should have blurted that out. Michael, however, did become more attentive to the conversation.

"How can you return after you fell? You have no light left." His eyes studied me, waiting for my answer.

"Maybe one day, when I know I can trust you, and it's not a ploy to get the Garden, I might tell you. Right now, I have orders."

He stared at me for a few moments. I didn't know if it was the heat boiling beneath my skin or if he knew he and I would truly talk alone in the future, but he seemed to change in demeanor.

"It's time to return to the summit. Maybe we can catch this chat at a different time." Michael signaled for them to follow him as he swooped through the sky.

Zadkiel scowled at me and then disappeared behind the rest of them. I turned to the army that stood behind me. Their eyes watched me in awe. I knew what they were thinking. No one had ever stood up to Zadkiel or tested Michael like that aside from Samael or Azazel.

"Thank you for standing behind me." They disappeared below the mountain, and I knew it was time for me to return to Sophie.

The year ahead of us was going to be treacherous waters. We didn't know where we stood. Lucifer had yet to join our side of things. It had been two reincarnations already since he was forced upon the cross. I didn't know if he changed his mind about things or if he was just waiting for the right time to leave and join Mother. I knew she had been sullen for the last 2,000 years since he didn't immediately fall into rank on our side. Maybe Father knew of his plot to join our side, and he is imprisoned in the summit until he reforms. Either way, the addition of his power to our mission was thwarted.

I arrived at Sophie's house just as the party began. Her mother let me in, and I walked the all too familiar halls of the house. We walked down to the basement where the party was at. Her mother pointed her out to me, and I nodded, smiling, giving my thanks. She looked so beautiful. Her human incarnation was the closest it had ever been to her angel form.

You have no idea how hard it was to refrain from talking to her for the four years I did. Her Gramms, Mariam, was already filled in with everything when we arrived as young children. All four of us stayed with her as her foster children so we could keep an eye on Sophie. Samael claimed we were getting too close to one another and breaking the rules. So, I told Mariam I couldn't be around whenever Sophie was around. She understood the importance and the rules surrounding the situation. She told me not to worry, though, that this was the year that changed everything. I guess she was right.

I made my way over to the present table. I contemplated putting my present there for her, but I didn't want her to be embarrassed in front of everyone after opening it. I would wait until we were alone, and then I would give it to her. I looked around the room at everyone who was there. I recognized everyone from school, which was a good thing. There weren't any party crashers here, so her party could ride along smoothly. I mingled with a few people, joking and listening to the gossip of the town. I still hadn't laid eyes on Samael or Azazel. They were supposed to have been watching her closely.

I slowly made my way over to her. I didn't know if her light would brighten and be noticeable when she saw me. My eyes were trained on her face. She was smiling and laughing, something I hadn't seen her do in a long time. It was like she was at peace on the inside. As if she felt my stare, she glanced up at me. Her eyes connected with mine, and I felt the intense pull to her I had always felt. She smiled sweetly at me and blushed slightly. I always loved seeing the rush of heat to her cheeks. In those few seconds, it felt like the world stood still between us. Nothing else in the world mattered to me except her eyes looking deeply into mine.

I kept my distance the entire time, making sure we didn't stir any rumors among the people at the party. The cake came; she blew out all the candles, and slices were passed around to everyone. I kept to myself most of the time. I didn't know if I would give anything away if I talked to anyone. Everyone was used to me being silent around them anyway. The entire party she kept glancing over at me with her eyes. Her eyes were full of everything that I yearned for. I missed the passion we held together before the fall.

She opened her presents and thanked every person who brought her one. She seemed kind of glum that they ended. I knew she was hoping to get one from me. I smiled to myself. I just knew this was the year. It would be the final year of all this battling over her would to come to an end. Everyone began to slowly trickle away, going home. She expressed her thanks to everyone who had come to the party. Soon, it was just her and me left alone in the room. The music was still playing, and a slow song had begun to drift from the speakers. I slowly made my way over to her, and she followed suit, meeting me in the middle of the room. No words were spoken; they didn't need to be. I took her in my arms and began to sway with her to the music. She laid her head on my chest and breathed deeply. I knew she could smell my scent, the scent that was unique to every angel.

We held each other in the middle of the floor, her head on my chest, my chin nestled on her head. I had waited centuries for this moment. She moved her head back from my chest and looked up at me. I knew what she wanted. It was the same thing I wanted. I leaned in to kiss her when we were interrupted.

"So, this is the reason you didn't want to go out with Dean this morning. You should have told me, sweetie." Her mom stood there, smiling, watching the two of us. Sophie's face went completely red, and I had to stifle a laugh.

"Mom!" I could see from her tomato, red face that she was completely without words in front of her mom.

"You two should go catch a movie together." She winked at me, and I nodded my head back as a reply. I looked down at her face and murmured, "Sounds like a good idea."

"I'll clean up down here. You two go! Have a fun time!"

Her mother had always been a sweet person. It was such a shame that Sophie's father had treated her the way he had. I led her by the hand to the steps and up out of the basement.

"So, do you want to go watch a movie? Or do you want to go somewhere else?" She peeked her eyes up at me and cocked a sly grin.

"Anywhere?"

I sighed, smiled, and shook my head at myself. I opened the

rabbit hole.

"Yes, anywhere."

She grinned ear to ear at me.

She wrapped her arms around my waist and whispered, "Take me to the lake." I smiled.

In a flash, we were there, still standing, holding each other. She moved her eyes to look up at me and smiled. Her light began to glow again. I couldn't resist the temptation this time and leaned down, planting my lips onto hers. No one else could smell her scent but me. I had asked for centuries, but everyone had always denied she had her angelic smell. The lavender crept into my nose, followed by a rosy, floral scent with warm vanilla hues. I shuddered; the smell and the ripples sent goosebumps over my body. My hands roamed every inch of her back and made their way to her face and hair. I slipped my tongue into her mouth and felt the heat of her skin beneath my hands. Her hands searched my back and sides with fierce strokes. I could feel how badly she wanted to go further than just kissing.

I pulled back from her and saw the burning in her eyes. They were smoky and tinged with fire. She was getting closer and closer to her angelic self.

"As much as I would love to ravage your body on this boulder, we have a few things we have to do before we can do that."

It took a few moments before her eyes went to their normal indigo color. I could feel the heat subside, and her cheeks went to a normal color. But what hit me in the stomach was the sad look she gained afterward.

"What's wrong? I didn't mean to sound so business-like if that's what it is." She shook her head, and I could see she was fighting back the tears. "Well, what is it then."

I lifted her chin to see her eyes. Her angelic powers were running rampant. Her eyes looked like an ocean's waves crashing on the beach.

"I was hoping that...well...never mind."

She bit her bottom lip. It dawned on me she had the same look at the party when she finished opening her gifts.

"You were hoping I had gotten you a gift, right?"

She squinted her eyes as if thinking, "How did he know that?" I chuckled and fished the gift from my pocket. I handed it to her, and she took it carefully. She had no idea what was inside the tiny little box. I could sense her heartbeat had hastened. She unwrapped the paper and stopped before she opened the box. I knew she was afraid of whatever would be inside the box. She opened the box and took in a slight breath. It was an ancient bracelet that I modified to look more modern. I had added angel charms to it, but I didn't destroy the originality of it. On top of the bracelet were symbols that only angels knew how to decipher. It was the language of the angels that historians call Enochian.

"I... I remember this bracelet." My heart nearly stopped.

"What?" I asked. It was impossible for her to remember the bracelet.

"I remember this bracelet," she restated what she had said more matter-of-factly.

"It's not possible." It came out in a whisper.

"I gave this bracelet to you." The world around me seemed to stop spinning. *How could she remember that?* After all the reincarnations and being locked up—only Alpha knows where—to not remember anything...how could she possibly remember that?

"Do you remember when you gave it to me?" I knew it was a long shot, but I had to know how far her memory had resurfaced.

"I gave it to you the day you fell." My entire body was enraptured in chills, and I nearly passed out.

"What do the symbols mean?" I asked, barely choking out the words.

"What symbols? It says, 'together forever.'" I jumped up, nearly toppling her over. "What? What's wrong?"

"It's impossible for you to be able to read that! That's the angelic language. Only we angels can read it!" I was pacing back and forth. I didn't know if this was a good or bad thing. "What else do you remember?"

"I remember being summoned forth in front of Alpha and asked to perform a task." Her eyes grew dark.

"What was your task?" I was in pieces waiting for her response.

"He told me to stay away from you. Your agenda was not a holy one...you were trying to steal the Garden of Eden from him." She stood to her feet and began to back away slowly.

"No, no, no. He implanted the evil behind it." I could see it in her eyes, though. She didn't believe in the good in me any longer. "Please, Sophie, I've waited centuries to give you that bracelet. Don't shut down on me, I beg you."

"Why should I listen to you?! Alpha knew how much it tore me when you left me to follow HER! You abandoned me for the dark! Alpha told me if I kept the Garden from you, I would stay in the light even when you would be swimming in the dark!"

"He lied to you, Sophie! God-damn! I shouldn't have given it to you. I knew he had something to do with messing with your memories. I didn't abandon you! You told me to go! This whole thing was your plan! It was your vision! He's turning it around on you. You have to believe me, Sophie."

Tears began to brim behind my eyes. My emotions began to surge through my powers. Fires began popping up everywhere, along with rain tearing through the sky. The forest caught fire and began to slowly cease to exist. I ran my hands through my hair as the rain soaked me. I was defeated. This is why they were never worried about us getting the Garden. They had brainwashed her true self into thinking we were evil, that we were no longer one of them. *How could he do this?! How could he truly abandon his children over a stupid Garden?!*

I felt a hand on my shoulder. "My son, come out of this dark hole you have formed."

I looked up to see Mother standing there. Behind her stood Samael and Azazel, along with Sophie. She was soaked from head to toe from the rain, and her eyes were wide with fright. Samael and Azazel even kept their distance.

"We will never reach the light. Why struggle against the darkness?" My heart was ripping in two.

"What makes you think you will never reach the light, my son?" Mother sat down beside me at the edge of the lake.

"Father has made sure of it. All these centuries of trying to get her to remember my love, he was up there, brainwashing her into believing we were truly evil now. She doesn't remember the vision; all she remembers is what Alpha put in her mind." I sniffed. The tears had already fallen, and just as Mother's tears, a weeping willow stood where each tear fell.

"What your father had not counted on was not her will, but your will. I don't know if you realize, my son, but you are much more powerful than any of your brothers or sisters. Your power mounts the longer you are with her. The two of you are the most powerful combination since your father and me. You must not lose the hope we have clung to for so long. Her true memories will surface in due time." She kissed my forehead and stood.

"I don't know how much longer I can fight the darkness. I don't know how much longer I can wish for the light without it within me. I'm not strong like you, Mother. The more I try to reach the light, the more I am enraptured by the dark. What would happen if I just finally accepted it?" I didn't even look her in the eyes when I asked the question, for I already knew the answer.

"We're so close to home, Incaendiel. Please, my son, keep your head above the putrid waters." She was gone.

No more questions and answers. I sat at the edge of the lake. I didn't move. I didn't want to move. It was hard enough just to fight the black cloud hovering over me. I couldn't look over my shoulder at the three of them standing there. I was ashamed of my actions and too grief-stricken.

"Are you going to take her home?" Samael asked, breaking into my darkness.

I swallowed the lump in my throat and fought the tears back from brimming over again. "Could...could you...I can't right now...I-" I felt a hand on my shoulder. It was Azazel.

"Don't worry, Brother. We will take her home and guard her until you return."

CHAPTER 8

All is Perceived in Darkness

"THE DARKNESS CONSUMES the soul unlit by heavens waking grace. An unlit soul is hard to save from the abyss of fiery rain. Accept the darkness in your heart or forever walk in between. Darkness is just the night of day the light is forever just a dream."

"IS IT TRUE?" Azazel asked as we both got ready for bed.

She was sleeping over with me tonight; Mom was thrilled. I never had friends over anymore. Azazel and I had been close when we were younger. When Isaiah stopped hanging out around me, we drifted apart. I wasn't sure why, but we did.

"Is what true?" Neither one of us had really spoken since the lake. I had never seen Isaiah so upset, so disturbed.

"That Alpha told you we were against those that remain in the summit."

I really didn't want to talk about it. "That's what I remember." I wasn't in a talkative mood and really didn't want to discuss what had caused Isaiah to flip out and nearly burn the planet down.

"Do you believe it?" *Did I believe it?* After hearing Isaiah talk to me and then seeing the Dark Mother appear, I didn't know what to believe.

"I don't know." We were both silent for a few moments. "What did Isaiah mean by not being able to fight the darkness any longer?" I heard her take in a deep breath and release.

"When we fell with Mother, we lost our light. Our light is what kept us pure, kept us from susceptibility to evil. The longer we're from our light, the weaker our fight against the dark is. We've lost many brothers and sisters to the struggle where the darkness won. They were cast out to walk through the world for all eternity, alone. Those of us who remain have fought long and hard against the temptation of the dark. None of us, however, have fought as hard as Incaendiel has against the darkness. It weighs heavier and heavier on him each time you are incarnated. I guess it was Alpha's plan to use you. Our only key into the summit is you, but it is through him as well. If we lose him, we lose all hope. Up until the last few days, the darkness was suffocating him." She stopped for a minute and then looked at me. "And then you came back into his life. I saw the light in his eyes, and then I saw the light radiating from his body. It was casting the darkness aside." She fell silent.

"What did you see today when you reached the lake?" I asked it without thinking.

She looked at me. "Even though he still has traces of his light, there is a dark cloud that has completely engulfed him. The only thing keeping the dark from completely taking over him is his hope and..." she paused.

"And what?" I asked.

"His love for you." I stared at her as she stared back at me. "We all felt his cry. He has always had that sway over us. Whatever emotion he feels that is immediate and unbearable to hold in, we all feel it. Mother felt it this time."

I was silent. I didn't know what to say. *Sorry? Sorry for telling him what my memories told me?*

"We're so close to the light this time, Sophie. We just want to go home! It's a catch-22. The closer we get to the light, the closer he gets to the dark. Each incarnation of yours, I see it consuming him more and more." She paused as if she were going to say something.

"What?" I asked.

"It's nothing. Just a thought, or rather, fear." She shook her head and smiled.

"What?" I asked again.

She sucked in a breath, "I think at the last moment, when we have won and are returning to the summit full of light, he won't. I'm afraid, at the last moment, as the last person to climb the rainbow bridge, he will lose himself completely to the dark. It would be ironic, really, that the one person who could get everyone into the light would be the one that darkness consumes. I don't know. It's a fear I have voiced with Mother." She sat in the chair at my desk, fiddling with her hair.

"What did she reply?" My voice was barely a whisper. I could see her choke back the emotion.

She cleared her throat. "She said...she feared the same thing for him."

I bit my lip, fighting back the welling emotions behind those words.

"So... ahem," I cleared my throat, trying to fight choking on the words. "So, he will make sure every one of you gets through before he lets the darkness subdue him?"

"I don't know. I don't know how any of this is supposed to work. I don't know if he has the actual power to call down the Rainbow Bridge or what. All I know is that it is up to you and him to save all of us Wanderers and to return our light."

"What happens to one of you if you die here on earth? Are you like me? Will you reincarnate?" Azazel wouldn't even look me in the eyes for an answer. "You die, don't you." It was barely a whisper.

"That's enough chit-chat. You need to get some sleep." She offered a smile, but I saw the sadness behind the smile.

I wished I hadn't said the things I had to Isaiah. I was propelling him further into darkness, which was not a good thing. My entire existence on the planet had caused him to slip further into the darkness, nearly surrendering himself to the cold of the dark. He was completely selfless, whether it be to keep me safe or for his brothers and sisters to cross the bridge.

This whole roller coaster of emotions had me spiraling out of control. One minute, I would hate him; the next, love him and then want to die. I wondered if it was my angelic soul colliding with my mortal body as it tried to surface. I slipped under the comfort of my comforter and drifted off to sleep. For the first time in eighteen years, it wasn't just a sound sleep. I began to dream.

I saw myself, but at the same time, it wasn't me. This girl was exceedingly more beautiful than I could have ever been. She stood with Isaiah, but she called him by his real name, his angelic name.

"Incaendiel, you must go with Mother or the others will be lost." She looked at Incaendiel as all the angels lined up to go with Mother.

"Why does it have to be me? Why does it have to be us?" Incaendiel didn't like the idea she had told him, well rather, the vision.

"We share the strongest bond than any other here." She looked deeply into his eyes. "I do not have your strength or your will. I will not be able to persevere as you would. You would never give up on me. I cannot say I have the same state of mind. It has to be you that goes, or I'm afraid our brothers and sisters will be lost to darkness forever." Her eyes darkened with remorse.

"How will I know you will remember us? How can you be sure our love won't die along with my light?" Incaendiel was against the idea from the start. "How do you know you won't die with my light? There are so many things that we aren't sure of, and you just want me jumping with the rest of them." He peered into her eyes. "I could never lose you, Sophie. It would be the end of me. I would strip myself of my grace."

"You have to trust me. My memories will come back from time to time. When it is the final year of my incarnation and time for us to return, I will regain all my memories. Please be patient with me. In the beginning, there will be false memories. I will come around to the light, I promise, as long as you are there by me to guide me." The other angels were lining the edge of the summit to take the plunge. She grabbed him tight and kissed his cheek. "You will never lose me," she whispered into his ear. She felt a tear drop onto her face. "Go, Incaendiel! Go!"

He ran from her and jumped as the last angel. She watched his plunge along with everyone else's. It nearly ripped her own light from her body when he lost his. An angel stood at her side, watching alongside her. She recognized him immediately. Lucifer leaned closer to her and whispered into her ear, "He will never return, and your light will eventually die, but unlike the other angels who are stripped of their light, you will die along with your light."

I awoke gasping for air. Azazel sat forward in her chair. "What!? What is it?" I could see she was alarmed.

"I had a dream," I whispered, gasping in the air.

"Was it a dream, or..." Azazel stopped and studied me. "You had a memory."

I nodded and burst into tears. "It's not going to work. Neither one of us can be saved."

"I don't understand." Azazel stood, walked to the side of my bed, and sat down. "Tell me the memory." So, I sat and went over every detail with her. I hesitated when I got to Lucifer. "What? Tell me."

"He...he told me he would never return." Azazel's eyes grew wide. "And..." I stopped.

"And what!" She was up, pacing the floor, drinking in what I had already told her.

"He said when he didn't return, my light would die." She stopped dead in her tracks.

"No angel's light has ever died!" I stared at her. "Did he say what would happen to you?"

I nodded my head. "He said I would die when his light went out." She stopped dead in her tracks.

Darkness would take over Isaiah, and I would die unless he could fight the darkness and join us in the summit.

"What if I were to stay behind with him in the darkness? Would I die then?" She closed her eyes, and when she opened them back up, tears were in her eyes. The answer was yes. "It's because I'm not a fallen angel, isn't it? You all fell and lost your light. Mine is being sucked away through the darkness of him." I choked back the tears on the last sentence.

Sam appeared next to Azazel and looked between the two of us. "What happened? What did she remember?"

Azazel swallowed, "We need to talk together as a family."

"Is it that bad?" He stared into Azazel's eyes and could nearly see the full story. "We will go at once." He walked over and took my hand. "All of us."

Within the blink of an eye, we were standing at the base of an ancient mountain. He let my hand down and raised his own hands to the sky. Azazel raised her hands as well, and the ground began to tremble. I thought the mountain was going to split in half. Within a split second, millions of the fallen ones, as far as the eye could see, stood around me.

"Samael, what takes precedence that you would bring her here and summon all of us?" It was the Dark Mother. What was it Gramms called her? Lilith, maybe. She appeared from inside the cave and stood before the three of us.

Sam bowed before her. "Mother, we have troubling news." Her eyes searched the crowd around her.

"Incaendiel?" she asked.

"Is fine for the time being, but what lies ahead for Sophie and him looks grim."

Sam glanced at me. I could see the sorrow in his eyes. Not only had we spent the last ten years growing up together, but we also had centuries together.

"Please enlighten us all, Sophie." She looked at me as if she were peering through me.

"It all started with the dream I had," I told them the entire memory, including Lucifer. When I finished, there was a hushed silence followed by a tidal wave of yelling.

Lilith held up her hand, and the crowd hushed immediately. "And you are sure those are his exact words to you?" I nodded. "Well, we are in quite a predicament here, are we not?" She turned towards Sam and said, "When the portal opens, he is the only one who can control it. We have to make sure that the last person that goes through grabs his hand before he lets it go."

"Aren't we going to tell him what is fated in the future?" I asked, and everyone turned to look at me. "I received the memory for a reason. In the entire eighteen years I have been alive, I have never dreamt before. Someone sent me that memory on purpose. We must warn him!" I was desperate, looking from Lilith to Sam.

"Who do you think sent you the memory?" Lilith walked over and lifted my face to her eyes. She frightened and comforted me all at once. It was an odd sensation.

"I believe it was Lucifer. No one else would have known that memory." Lilith studied my face closer and closer.

"I believe you are right. It has been some time now, and Lucifer was to have already joined our ranks. I suppose Alpha's punishment to him carried more severity than I thought it would have. Undoubtedly, he is free and ready to join us, or he would not have sent us the message. Let us prepare for his arrival." She sauntered back into the cave entrance while Sam and Azazel led me down as well. My eyes searched the crowd of angels for Isaiah, but he wasn't here.

As if answering the question that came to my mind, Azazel said, "He's not here. Sam didn't call him. He left him to meditate at the lake."

My eyes dropped to the ground in shame. It was my words that caused his out-of-control behavior.

"It wasn't your fault, Sister; it was Father's."

I watched her catch up to Sam's pace. It dawned on me. These are angels, fallen or not, and unlike humans who blame God for everything, for once, the blame was proportioned correctly. It was entirely his fault, all this.

As we took the last few steps, everyone froze in place. I didn't know if they were going to attack or run from what they saw. I inched closer to the edge of the crowd and peered in between Sam and Azazel. In the middle of the room stood Lilith, and beside her stood an enormous angel with black wings. When I looked closer at him, his skin was the same color as the others, so he was a fallen one. *Which angel had chosen to fall? I thought they all fell at one time. Were there other fallen angels that were new since the big fall?* When his eyes met mine and I saw his face, I knew exactly who it was.

"Lucifer."

CHAPTER 9

The Pain of Memory Gained

"THE MEMORY of a life before can stand the test of time. Even locked away from the soul's undying light can never make the memory drown. The pain of memories will hurt for a while, and in due time go away. What is important is the memory itself and that it never ever fades away."

"SOPHIE, it's nice to see you. God, I've missed you." He walked over and gave me a huge hug. When he pulled me back, he could see the confusion written in my eyes. "Well, I see not all your memories have returned."

"What do you mean by that?" I asked, eyeing him. "Were you the one who sent the dream to me?"

"Yes, it was me. You needed a push back into the direction you were supposed to go. The memory I returned to you was the one our father had me pluck from your mind. He wanted the last few moments you had with Incaendiel before he fell. Of course, I couldn't tell him no. I could only obey. So, I hid your memory, awaiting my release from the tower to return it to you." *The tower? What the hell is the tower?* He could see the questions mounting on my face. "The tower is where the angels are sent for punishment. There is no light, no visitors, only time to think and ponder on what you have done to disgrace yourself. I'm surprised you don't remember it, considering every nineteen years you are imprisoned there away from all the other angels awaiting your next incarnation."

"He locks me away? Why?!" I was hurt and furious. The father in the Bible is nowhere near comparable to the evil of the true father.

"So, you won't lead any more angels astray." He snickered at me and winked.

I could feel my cheeks burn. He wasn't that bad-looking, and no one had ever paid me this much attention while growing up. My eyes danced around wildly between all the faces.

"Sorry it took me so long, Mother. My punishment earned more time than I had planned with the stunt I pulled in Jerusalem." He chuckled.

"Ah, yes, what was it that you called out to your father?" Lilith smiled.

"Why has thou forsaken me," I replied. They all looked at me, stunned. "What? It's in the King James Bible. Everyone knows that line."

"What else is in the Bible that Alpha saw to being made?" Lilith asked.

"There's lots in the Bible. It spoke of the creation story, but far from the one in Gramms' Bible. It did have you sneaking back into the Garden and whispering to Eve to eat the fruit. Wise move on your part. There was the flood with Noah's ark, Lott, and the city of Sodom and Gomorra. Oh, there is also an entire book in itself for Lucifer." I looked over at him. "Did you really go by the name of Jesus Christ?"

"Who knows, maybe that will surface in a memory." He winked at me again. "What story does it tell about me?" He was truly intrigued by having a book of his own.

"It has bits and pieces of your life up until 12 years old, where they lost you at the temple. From there to around 30 to 33 years old, your life was erased. There was nothing until John the Baptist baptized you." I looked at him while he was snickering. "What's so funny?"

"Did the book say I told my parents they should have known I would be in the house of my father?" I looked at him quizzically.

"Yea. I don't get the joke." I looked at the few angels who were beginning to snicker along with him. "What's funny about that?"

"It's a bit of sarcasm. If you remembered what His house did look like, you would laugh at it being compared to a temple. It's an insult on his behalf. I got a couple of floggings for that comment." He chuckled again and reminisced on all the sarcasm he threw at Alpha while he was a mortal.

"What news do you bring from the summit, Lucifer?" It was Samael who asked.

"Everyone is pretty pissed that Sophie remembered Incaendiel. Father told them she would never remember him, and you all would stay as fallen angels. Father also has them convinced that being away from your light for so long has turned you into vile creatures that he likes to call Demons. On another note, Michael has been unusually quiet, especially with that last encounter with Incaendiel here at the entrance to the Glade."

"When did that happen? He didn't report that to me?" Sam asked with a hint of anger on his words.

"It was the day of the party, is all I know. Ask a few of the brothers here. It seemed as if he called them forth as a first in command could." I don't know if Lucifer was taunting Sam or not, but Sam was furious.

"I was told I alone had that power. How is it he can call them forth too, Mother!" He was pacing with fury.

"Calm down, Samael. He doesn't want your position in the infantry. He was surrounded by ten of your summit brothers and felt like he needed assistance." Lilith placed her hand on his shoulder to calm him.

"How does he hold that power without the rank?" I was wondering the same thing as well as everyone gathered around.

"I have kept Incaendiel's power from all of you. His power is far greater in strength, and it uses less of his grace to accomplish. His emotions trigger the most hazardous moments for those who stand around." She looked at me as she said that sentence. My mind flashed back to the burning lake, and a shiver went through me.

"He has known for quite some time about his power over all of you, but all he wishes is to get you home safe and sound and back to your light." She sighed. "Incaendiel's power is what is causing the darkness to seek him out. It wants his power to be used for evil. He has fought this darkness for centuries. If it does not work this time, he will be overcome with the darkness, and we will never reach the summit." Everyone fell silent.

I looked at Lucifer, who returned my look. He will never return echoed in my mind.

"No! This time, we all go home. There won't be a next time." Everyone's eyes fell on me. "How do I remember where the Garden is?" No one answered me. "How?!" I demanded. I couldn't let Isaiah be consumed by darkness all because of me.

The voice that echoed through the Glade was one I did not expect. "You are the Garden. The garden lies within your light." Isaiah stood at the back of the room.

Everyone parted as he made his way to the front of the room. He stood before me without reaching out to me.

"It's nice to see you again, Lucifer. Sorry, I couldn't make it to Jerusalem. You know how much I detest brutality against mankind."

"No problem, Brother. It's good to see you too." He walked over and threw his arms around Incaendiel. "From what I hear, you live up to the name you were given, you little pyro."

He noogied his head, and Incaendiel grinned; they looked as if they had truly grown up as great friends. I don't think I could ever get used to calling him anything aside from Isaiah.

"So how do we get the Garden to spring forth from my light?" I asked, walking over to him.

"The same way Mother and Father created it." He paused, brushing a strand of hair behind my ear.

"How was that?" I asked in barely a whisper.

"Through love," Lilith replied.

"I don't understand. I already love him; shouldn't that be enough?" I was confused by her reply. I loved him; I did.

"You have to surrender yourself completely to him just as things were before. You two must become as One, and the enchantment will break." I understood completely what she meant that time. I flashed back into the car with Dean and shivered.

"Is that why...Dean..."

"Yes." Incaendiel cut me off before I could finish the sentence. His eyes flashed with anger when I mentioned his name.

"Keep your emotions under control, my son, or you will set us all ablaze." Lilith put her hand on his shoulder, but I could still see the tension in his body language.

"It doesn't have to be right now...does it? I mean, as an eighteen-year-old girl, I don't know if I'm ready for...that." I swallowed hard. This was a conversation meant for private, not to be out in the open in front of everyone. Isaiah smiled at me.

"We have until 11:59 the night before your birthday." I nodded. My face flushed, and I quickly changed the subject.

"Am I still in danger from the others?" Once more, I watched Isaiah tense up.

"No, neither of you is free from the wrath of the others." It was Lucifer who spoke this time. "Before I fell, I heard them conspiring a kidnapping. I couldn't tell who it was they proposed to take. It's one reason I took the plunge. That way, you would be prepared for it. The best thing for both of you right now is to stay together and guarded by at least two at all times."

"I agree. Sam and Azazel have made this small town their home alongside Incaendiel. I think it's best that they stay their guards." Lilith spoke and turned to Lucifer. "And maybe a surprise one."

"Whatever is needed, mother." He bowed to her. There was a tremendous rumble, and it sounded like lightning struck the mountain and nearly toppled it.

Lilith turned to Lucifer. "Were you expecting company to join?"

"No, I was not," he said, disappearing in a flash. Incaendiel grabbed my hand, and in a zap, we were at the base of the mountain. Everyone stood around a crater in the ground. When the floating dirt and debris settled, everyone peered at who stepped out of the hole and gasped.

"Michael?" Incaendiel was astonished.

"Now, Brother, that I have your trust, do you mind telling me how we're all getting our light restored." He looked between Isaiah and me.

"Is there anyone else abandoning Alpha and planning to join?" Lilith asked.

Michael teared up and ran to her, throwing his arms around her.

"Mother, how I have missed your face."

It seemed like he wept for hours holding her when he pulled away. I had never known that Michael could be such a softie with his legends of war and his sword of wrath.

"Metatron is on the ropes, but I'm sure he will join as well. All of us dearly miss you." He looked around at all the fallen ones. "We have missed you all. We want you to return home!" The tears glistened in his eyes.

"And this isn't a trick of Father's, sending a spy down to see how close we are to returning?" Incaendiel said with more malice than he intended.

"Do you think I would have given up my light to spy on you?" Michael glared at Incaendiel.

"You have proven to be a trickster before. What's to stop you now? I'm sure you weren't just 'summoned' away, leaving Zadkiel behind." Incaendiel stepped forth as if challenging Michael.

"What he speaks is the truth," Lucifer stated. "No one can lie in my presence, or have you forgotten the gift bestowed upon me, Brother?"

I touched his arm and had him look me in my eyes. "I believe him, Incaendiel." Practice makes perfect. He seemed to melt before my eyes as I said his true name.

No sooner had I said it than there were streaks of light falling through the sky. It looked like shooting stars falling and impacting the Earth. It truly makes you wonder if the streaks in the sky at night are meteors or angels dancing around. The ground shook and trembled to where I could barely stand on my feet. Incaendiel grabbed me by my waist to steady me. A mass of angels walked forth. The one in front was astonishingly perfect in every way. He was toned in the spots he needed to be and muscled in the others. He looked like a Greek God stepping out of a movie.

"It's nice to see you, Metatron." Lucifer walked over and hugged his brother.

"Well, when Michael left, we noted his seriousness. There have been many talks over who would help and who wouldn't. Not to mention our conversations we've held in private. This cause must be far greater than the one Father has in store for us all." His gaze slipped over to mine, and his eyes twinkled. "It's nice to see you again, Sophie. It has been far too long that Father has kept you all to himself."

I shuddered at those words. If he meant keeping me locked away, as Lucifer had said, I can't see how that was keeping me to himself. He looked over at Incaendiel and bowed.

"What are the orders, Brother?"

I heard Sam grunt behind me and mutter something under his breath.

"I am not first in command. Orders come from Samael, not me," Incaendiel said as he stepped aside and bowed to Sam. Sam's angry face melted away, and for once, I saw him smile at Incaendiel.

Just thinking his name sent ripples throughout my body. I saw he had the same effect when I thought his name as goosebumps prickled on his arms. What astonished me, even more, was the voice I heard back in my head.

"It does me too."

I looked at him; he smiled and winked at me. Each day was more of a surprise with him and the bond we share.

"Have we always been like this?" I thought directly to him.

"Yes," he replied.

"Ah, realizing you two have telecommunication for the first time. It's so cute!" Lucifer flapped his hand in front of his face as if he were going to cry like a chick in a movie. "I'm so proud of my babies." He pretended like he was going to cry, covering his mouth with the tips of his fingers.

We laughed at him. I see why everyone liked him. I wish I could have known him as Jesus. I heard a giggle in my head.

"That was funny!" I nearly laughed out loud.

"Now, now, you two. It's not polite to telecommunicate about people behind their backs," Lucifer chided.

Metatron turned his attention to Lilith. "So now what, Mother? I'm surprised Father hasn't had a tantrum yet finding out his best angels fell from the light."

As if to prove his point, a lightning storm ensued. A bolt dropped right in front of Incaendiel and me. We both jumped back, and his hand gripped mine, preparing to bolt to safety.

"Well, Metatron, I think he just realized." Lilith laughed and pushed the lightning storm away from the mountain with her hand. "First thing's first, we need to devise a protection team for Incaendiel and Sophie. With Alpha losing some of his top-notch angels, he will be more devious than before. The plan we had earlier needs to be reinforced. Samael and Azazel, you will keep your detail as close as possible to the two of them." They nodded in agreement. "Lucifer, I want you at least within a mile radius of those two in case they need your assistance." He nodded in agreeance. "Metatron and Michael, I want you two to keep your radius within the bounds of the town. Alpha only knows who will be sent next to strike, and they need to be thoroughly protected."

She looked over at Sam and Azazel. "You two need to drop the human bodies and take back your angelic forms. You are more susceptible than humans. You can cast a glamor over your wings so no one will see them. Incaendiel has to remain human until the last moment as it is, I don't need you two to be in the same amount of danger."

"Why would he be in danger?" I asked.

All eyes trained on me.

"Angels in human form are not impervious to death. I'm surprised your last incarnation on Earth hasn't surfaced as a memory yet. It would show you better than what I could tell you." She looked over at Incaendiel, worried. "In order for the Garden to surface correctly through her, she has to have all her memories, or it won't work."

"If I'm not mistaken, Father has her memories locked away from her. Someone will have to retrieve them for her to remember," Lucifer said as he walked over to me. He looked me in my eyes, peering deeply within. "They do not exist in her mind."

"How are we going to do this then?" Samael blurted out.

"Everyone, relax. I told you I wouldn't fall from the light without having a purpose," Michael stated.

He reached into the bag he was carrying and retrieved a jar full of glowing white balls. They looked beautiful.

"I do believe these will help in our crusade." He smiled as he handed them over to Incaendiel.

"It looks like you two have some work ahead. Remember, do not give her more than three memories at a time, or you will cause her brain to hemorrhage. These are angelic memories, not human ones." Lilith looked to us both to ensure we understood. We both nodded.

"So, where are we headed?" Sam asked, stepping forth.

Azazel was at his side. I believe there was more than just brother and sister between the two of them, but I knew it was rude to ask. Maybe it will be in one of my memories.

"The lake. It seems to be the perfect spot for her memories to come forth." Incaendiel smiled down at me.

I returned the smile faintly. I remembered what the lake looked like before we left, and I wasn't sure I wanted to return to that spot.

He bent down and whispered in my ear, "Don't worry. It looks like it did when we first went there." He scooped me up in his arms and took off into the night sky.

We landed at the lake, and he was right. It looked exactly the way it did the first time we went there. Sam and Azazel took posts on opposite sides of the lake. Incaendiel disappeared for a moment, then reappeared with my comforter and laid it down on the ground. He motioned for me to sit, and he took a seat beside me. The close proximity to him sent ripples through my body. I fought back the urge to climb in his lap. A smile formed on his lips, making me blush. He knew what I wanted.

"Not right now. We must get a few memories in first. This jar is slammed full of centuries of memories. It may take the entire year to return them to you. Are you ready?" He turned to me, looking nervously.

I stared at him. Millions of questions ran through my head. "How did you nearly die last time? I want to be told before I remember."

He sighed. "I was afraid you would ask me. It's better if you remember than me telling you."

"Please, just tell me a little?" My eyes pleaded with his.

He hesitated before he spoke. "I was protecting you." Of course, he was. "We all assumed the reason you died on your nineteenth birthday was so Alpha could lock you away. Lucifer confirmed it. I hated the thought of you being locked away from me."

He tensed up. I could feel the anger radiating through him.

"You know you have to love Alpha no matter what, right? It's the only way you can receive your light again."

I watched as a tear slid down his cheek. I wiped it from his face, and he looked over at me.

"I will always love my father. That doesn't mean I will see eye to eye on what he does." He opened the jar and reached in for a memory. "Are you ready?"

I breathed in deep. I wasn't sure if I was ready, but it was the only way for all of us to return to the light. I knew he couldn't last another one thousand years without the light. I had no choice.

"I'm ready. How does this work? Do I eat the ball or what?" He smiled.

He bent down and kissed my lips. My heart skipped a beat, and I felt the heat rush through my body. Before I knew it, I was spiraling down a black hole.

CHAPTER 10

The Garden of Good and Evil

"WALK WITH ME MA' Lady through the garden of chaos and havoc. As your demon of redemption holds your heart, the angel of salvation holds your hand. What is salvation and what is redemption in your mind's eye? Can it be your angel is the devil and your demon is the one that flies in the light?"

WHEN THE HAZE DISAPPEARED, I was in a medieval-type dress. *How did I change clothes, especially into ones that are, shall I say, out of season?* I sat up from the bed I was lying in and noticed the lake had disappeared from around me. From that moment forth, everything was on autopilot. I could think for myself, but the words I would say were from the memory.

I walked to the window and peered out of the gaping hole. I lived in a castle. There were banners and streamers everywhere. The servants dashed around the courtyard, assembling everything for a celebration. *What day is it?* There was a knock at the door, and I left my post at the window.

"You may enter." Wow, me speaking proper and all. The person who walked through the door froze my heart. It was Dean. I wanted to shout at him to leave, to ask what he was doing here. Instead, I said, "Dean, what a pleasant surprise. Pray, tell me, why do you call on me?" He walked over to me and took my hand. He bent down and kissed it. "Such a modest gentleman."

"Ma' Lady, you look stunning. Would you accompany me to breakfast in the grand hall? The king and queen request your attendance for formal announcements of your birthday celebration in a few days." He smiled an earnest smile at me.

I wanted to refuse, but instead, my body replied, "Of course, lead the way, good sir." I roped my arm through his, and he escorted me to the grand hall.

We settled into our seats to the left of my mother. I looked around at the grand assemblage of people. It seemed as if kingdoms from around the world had made their way for the celebration of my birthday. *Which birthday is this, my eighteenth or my nineteenth?* The servants began serving everyone their food. My plate was stacked full of every type of food imaginable. I couldn't eat all that, and my body agreed as I nibbled on the food.

The king, my father, stood to make his announcement. "I would like to thank all of you for assembling for the celebration of my daughter Sophie's nineteenth birthday. Two moons from now, we will celebrate both her birthday and her engagement to my future heir, Dean, Prince of Eden."

My mouth nearly dropped open. *Engagement! Was he serious? I didn't want to marry this piece of crap!* My face betrayed my mind, and I smiled as the applause went through the air. He took my hand and kissed it once more. I cringed inwardly. *This was so wrong. Where was Incaendiel? Have I pushed him completely away?* Just as if it were on cue,

Incaendiel made his way to our table. He was dressed as one of the servants. He looked directly into my eyes, and my heart fluttered. This was a real reaction as I felt Dean tense beside me. I could feel the sparks between us as we gazed at each other.

"More wine, Ma 'Lady?" He held up the wine pitcher, and I nodded. He topped off my glass of wine and turned to Dean. "More wine, good sir?"

Dean scowled at him and flicked him away with his hand. I watched him proceed with the queen and king next. Once he was finished serving the royal table, he returned the same way he had come and smiled at me.

"The first thing I will do as heir to the throne is send that servant boy to the gallows." I tensed up after Dean said that.

"You will do no such thing!" I said it a bit louder than I had intended.

My mother cleared her throat, motioning me to lower my tone in front of the men. I glared over at Dean,

"If you harm him in any way, I will call the wedding off and have you sent to the gallows for treason. Do not forget, I know the real reason you seek my hand in marriage. Just know it will not work. You can try all you want, but it will never work!" I hissed under my breath. "Mother, Father, is my attendance still required at this moment? I feel a bit flushed and need a walk through the garden to cool off."

"Very well, Sophie. If you feel ill, let a servant know. Don't pass out in the rose bushes again."

Mother was a bit cheeky with her last statement, but I ignored it. It wasn't rude for the princess to excuse herself from the table, but a guest of honor sitting there had to remain there through the entire feast, which could last for hours.

I snaked my way through the empty castle corridors until my feet hit the grass of the garden. I removed my shoes and sat them at the door. I stepped through the door and out into the garden. I immediately felt the warmth of the sun wash over me. I closed my eyes and drank in the warmth. When I opened my eyes, Incaendiel stood before me. I grinned ear to ear.

"I was hoping you would follow me."

"The queen felt as if an escort would be proper considering your last faint in the roses." He smiled at me, and my heart somersaulted.

"My birthday is in two moons, are you going to attend the celebrations as well?" His smile turned into a frown.

"You know I cannot, Sophie."

He looked so sad. I wanted to profess my love to him but was unable to. Apparently, this Sophie loved him but didn't admit it to him. I reminded myself that in this lifetime, Dean had his hooks in me until the last moment. I couldn't help but stare at him. I knew he was my love. Something tugged at the edge of my mind, something evil and foreboding. A memory hit me hard, a memory from this time period. My brain felt as if it was going to bust as it surfaced.

"I told you not to consort with him. He is the Devil in the flesh. He is here to turn you to the dark side!" Dean hissed at me.

I stared off after Incaendiel as he left the corridor we had been standing in. This was nearly a year before now. My heart would beat faster around him than I had ever experienced.

"Then maybe I am a child of darkness as well," I replied.

He grabbed me by my hand and whipped me around to look at his face.

"You are not of the dark! You are a child of the light! Remember that!" He threw my hand back down to my side and breathed in a deep breath. "This is important, Sophie. He will lead you down the wrong path. He will draw you into the darkness, and the Lord will not forgive for that!" He towed me down the hall back to my chamber room and bid me goodnight.

I snapped back from the interlude and grabbed my head. Incaendiel grabbed me before I hit the ground. "Are you okay?"

His eyes searched mine. They were so sincere in their concern. *How could he be evil?* He was far more angelic than what Dean was.

"I'm fine. It's just Dean trying to get into my head."

He tensed when I said Dean's name, and I could sense his jealousy over him. It felt nice to have a quarrel over my hand. Before Dean came along, no others had voiced interest in me.

"Sophie, you realize this is more important than just gaining your hand in marriage." He was always so serious.

"Yes, I understand that the cosmos are out of balance, and you want to get back into heaven. I know!" He always found a way to irritate me and break me from the bliss I sank into whenever he was around.

"Do you?"

He stopped and turned to look in my eyes. I guess my eyes told him what he didn't want to hear.

"Just don't let him get too close. He's deceiving you to get what he wants, not what's best for you." He left. He left me standing out in the garden just as the rain started to roll in. I remember feeling the pain shoot through my heart. I hated it when he would leave me alone. I had always felt like a piece of myself was missing. This must have been the part of myself that absolutely loved him trying to break through to the surface.

The memory flashed forward to the night before my nineteenth birthday. Dean was escorting me to some play that he had reserved tickets for. We took the horse and carriage out of the castle. We traveled for what seemed like hours when it should have only been an hour's way out.

"Dean, where are we going? We are far out from the city where the play should have been."

I looked at him in the light from the lantern. His face was blank and sinister. From how dreadfully dark it had become, I could only imagine how late at night it could be.

"Mother and Father will disapprove of me being out so late."

He finally looked over at me, but the look in his eyes was more frightening to me as opposed to the lashing I would get being out so late with a man.

"Tonight is the final night, Sophie. You will give me what I came for. I have been patiently playing with you for a year now. I always get what I want." He sneered at me in the dark.

My heart raced with fear and panic. I thought I would pass out from the sheer fright he gave me.

"Dean, turn this carriage around and take me home!" I tried to sound harsh, but I know it came out meek and as a whisper.

"You will do as I say, Princess!"

His words filled me with a feeling I had never felt before. Terror ripped through my body as I made a break for the carriage door, but he grabbed me by the waist and held me down on the floor.

"Where is the Garden?"

His voice sent dread through my body. It was no longer compassionate or angelic. It was dark and eerie.

"I-I don't know where the Garden is! I swear!"

No matter how much I struggled, he was ten times stronger than me and had no problem holding me down.

"You will tell me where it is if I have to beat it from your dead body!"

He was more than terrifying at this moment. I knew deep down he wasn't lying about what he would do.

"I don't know where it is! I can't tell you something I don't know!" I glanced around the carriage, but there was nothing I could use as a weapon.

"We have but a few minutes until it is 12 at night. You have to tell me where it is or suffer a death you have never imagined before."

It was almost as if his voice pleaded with mine. Tears streamed from my eyes. I knew I was going to die tonight. I didn't know where the Garden everyone asked me about existed. I had never been there; how was I to know where it was? It existed millenniums ago when God created the world. I wasn't there!

"Dean, please, I don't know where it is! Please, let me go! I want to go home! Please, just let me go home!" I pleaded with him.

His eyes looked like they softened to my plea.

"You want to go home?" He asked with such sincerity that I genuinely believed he was going to take me home.

"Yes," I whispered through tears.

"I'm sorry, Sophie. You're going home, not just the one here on Earth."

He put his hands around my throat and began choking me. I couldn't get a breath in to scream for help. Tiny dots started floating in my vision, and I went down a tunnel. *This was it. He's going to choke me to death! How I wished I had listened to Incaendiel. Where is my knight when I need him?* As the dark started to swallow me, I threw out the last plea I had, which was really a reconciliation of my heart. *I love you, Incaendiel!* I felt the weight of Dean pulled off of me. I choked and gasped for air. No relief came to my lungs. I lay there gasping for air, but not a single gasp let air in. He must have crushed my windpipe. Images blurred in and out in front of my face. I saw Incaendiel lean over the top of me. There was blood on his shirt and on his hands.

I could hear through a tunnel a whispered voice, "Sophie, Sophie, come back to me." A hazy heat engulfed me as I realized the carriage was on fire.

"Go!" I choked out in a raspy voice that could have only been a whisper.

The world was caving in on itself around me. He didn't move. I could see the fire start to burn his clothes. As my vision went black, I saw a set of hands pull him from the carriage, and then there was nothing.

CHAPTER 11

aving Grace

"ONCE UPON A MIDNIGHT BLUE, I sat and gazed at a world untrue. Through mine eyes and through his soul, I saw the story of the world unfold. Tears of strength and pain seep down, as the memory of the flesh is sound. And as my eyelids flutter open from fear, the arms of assurance surely are here. Swiftly we will be pulled from one another, as dawn emerges with wings a flutter."

I AWOKE, choking and screaming. I gasped for air, fearing that the memory had turned into a real consequence. Tears were streaming down my face, and I realized Incaendiel had been holding me. I turned and cried into his chest. I heaved the tears out, trying to find my voice.

"It was horrible! I don't want to see any others! Please don't make me relive any more of them." I cried, and he rocked me in his arms. "How could I have been so stupid to trust him! I didn't think angels were allowed to murder humans. It goes against their nature!"

I could still feel Dean's hands around my throat. It explained his nature to me when he first came back, why he was so indignant. My head thumped tremendously, like someone had dropped an anvil on it. Incaendiel didn't move. He just sat there and held me until I had cried the entire memory out into his shirt.

"Please, Incaendiel, please don't make me see another one."

I could feel him swallow hard. I knew he didn't want me to suffer anymore, but there was no choice.

"Sophie." He was choking back tears. "Please stop begging me not to do what you know we have to." His voice quivered, and I knew it was from him choking back the emotions welling.

Everything I felt, I knew he felt as well. Everything I thought, I already knew he thought. So, everything I experienced in my memory, he did as well.

I felt slightly dizzy and out of sorts.

"Do we have to do them back-to-back, or can I get a break in between them? My head really hurts."

He stroked my hair and wiped the tears from my face.

"Of course, we can wait in between them. I had Lucifer bring you some food. You need to eat in between the memories."

He sat me up and motioned over to the food and drink setting there. The sun was just peeking above the horizon. I had forgotten it was nighttime when we had come out here. Waking up in the darkness must have triggered a real-life panic attack as I felt my breathing going back to normal. The food came into my view, and I could smell fresh pancakes and coffee. It turns out Lucifer had gone to a late-night breakfast joint and got takeout for two. We both sat there, silently eating and drinking the coffee. As the sun peaked higher above the horizon, it cast enough light onto Incaendiel that I could see his face. He was a wreck. I could only imagine what I looked like.

"So, you felt everything I did as though you were experiencing it." I looked over at him, and he flinched.

"It's not the first time I felt it. I should have followed you two once you left the castle. I was given orders not to. I never forgot what happened that night. When he showed up with you at the rec center, I wanted to choke the life from his body. If Samael and Rafe hadn't been there, I would have. He was dangling his stake on you once more in front of me, and I could do nothing about it."

He swallowed a drink of coffee, and I watched as he fought back the anger building from thinking about Dean.

"How many times have you tried to save me from dying?" I regretted asking as soon as I did.

He nearly choked on his food. He was silent as if battling whether he should tell me or not.

"I've never gotten as close to saving you as I did last time. Mother was not happy that I intervened at all, especially since I nearly died with you in the fire." His face took on a dark shadow.

"You know it wasn't the fire that killed me, right?" I asked, looking over at him.

He just turned away from me.

"I know. That bastard choked the life from you. He wasn't even punished for it. Mother was furious. I swore if I ever had the chance to get even with him over it, I would."

I reached over and touched his hand. The electricity calmed my heart. He was taking in deep breaths. I knew the anger was still fresh from the ordeal. I understood why he was so angry to have seen Dean show up at the field the day I drove him there. If it hadn't been for Sam making him walk away, he really would have killed Dean.

"Incaendiel?"

He looked over at me, and just hearing his name, he melted into my eyes. He leaned in and kissed me. The heat coursed through my body. I pulled away, though, fearful he was going to thrust another memory into me.

His voice came to me in my head, "It's okay. I just want to feel you in my arms. You're not ready for another memory."

I let him pull me back in and kiss me. The power between us surged through my veins. I could feel my heart beating and thought it would explode out of my chest. This feeling I had never experienced. I was eighteen and had never kissed a boy before him.

"Did you stake a claim on me at school? Is that why I was never asked out on dates?" I heard him chuckle and groan over the question.

"Do you really think I would let someone weasel you away from me? You were mine." I could feel the smile from the words as he wrapped his arms tighter around me.

"I love you."

It kind of slipped out in our silent thoughts. He immediately pulled away. I was confused as to why he pulled away after I told him I loved him. It felt like a knife stabbed me in the heart. I was pouring my heart out to him in every way I thought possible.

"What's wrong?" I asked. He didn't reply to me. "Incaendiel?"

He got up from where he was sitting and walked to the edge of the lake. Lucifer dropped in right after he got up. He looked me over, and the look in his eyes was all I needed to confirm I looked like crap.

"So, I can see the memory was hard on you." He sat down beside me. "That was the worst one because it was the most recent." He glanced over to Incaendiel. "Not to mention, it was the most horrific. Father found it funny that Dean took your life into his own hands. He promoted him for the deed. A lot of us angels objected, but he threatened us with the tower to keep quiet."

Lucifer looked down as he sat with his legs drawn up but apart. He could pass as a regular human in his mannerisms. Then again, at one point, he had been human.

"Not that it mattered to me since I was already locked away."

He looked over at me as I sat silently watching Incaendiel. He touched my hand, so I would glance up at him.

"What's wrong, angel?"

I knew I was an angel, but the way he said it tugged at something that I couldn't grasp. I shook the feeling off.

"I did something that upset him," I said, sipping my coffee and setting it back down.

"Was it during your head chats?" *Wow, he was rather good at knowing things.* "It's a gift." He laughed.

"Touché." I chuckled back.

My eyes trailed over to Incaendiel. He just sat there staring off into the water. I heard Lucifer sigh beside me.

"What?" I asked, returning my attention to him.

"It's not my place to tell you." He followed my gaze over to Incaendiel.

"Tell me what?" He had piqued my interest.

"What is it that you tell him in your mind but never out loud?"

I was confused. Most of the things I told him in my mind, he already knew because he was reading it.

"I will give you another hint. What was the plea you called out to him your last incarnation before you died?"

I thought for a moment, not really wanting to recall the choking part. "I told him I love you." I glanced over at him, but he was ignoring our conversation.

"He can't hear us talking, another gift of mine." He smiled at me. "Have you ever told him out loud how you feel?"

"He knows how I feel. He reads my mind and can feel it from my emotions." *That couldn't be the reason why, could it?*

"But have you ever out loud told him I love you."

I thought back to the moment at the lake. I could have sworn I told him then, but I didn't. I only kissed him, showing him how I felt. It sank in.

"No, I haven't." My eyes dropped to the ground, and my face reddened.

"You will when the moment is right. He must realize that it's a different lifetime and that you need time to say it out loud. It has been quite some time since you two spoke openly about how you felt with one another."

He stood up and looked over at Incaendiel. He was still sitting at the edge of the lake.

"I'm going to go scope the area again. I hope you enjoyed the breakfast."

I nodded, and he smiled, pleased. His eyes lingered on me for a moment, and I watched him fly off. I returned my attention back to Incaendiel. *Is that what he really needed? Did he need to hear the human me tell him how much my soul loves him?*

I stood from my seat, a bit shaky, but I stretched it out. I walked over to the edge of the lake and sat down beside him. He didn't look at me. I touched his hand, but he tucked it away from me. Even though I wanted to tell him, I was nervous as hell to try and say it out loud.

"Incaendiel?"

He didn't look at me; apparently, that doesn't have the same effect on him anymore. I scooted over and plopped myself down in his lap so he would have to look at me.

"Will you please look at me or acknowledge me?"

It took him a moment, but his eyes finally met mine. They were so gray and dismal. The vibrant blue they had been was now dim. I searched in his eyes for a sign of life. He was shut down. I leaned forward and kissed his lips, but he didn't return the gesture. I kissed his cheek, then his forehead. I kissed his chin and then his jaw. I made my way down to his neck and kissed it. I could feel him shiver beneath me. I placed my hands on his face and made him look me in the eyes. His eyes looked so lost, so empty. It was my turn to save him. "I-"

"Incoming!" is all I heard.

I didn't even get to finish my sentence when he picked me up from his lap and sat me down on the ground. He made a dash for the jar, screwed the lid on it, and blinked it away. The sky was littered with angels. My heart dropped to my feet when I saw Dean in front of them all. Sam and Azazel were at my side like a blur. Incaendiel stood in front of us, looking at the army that came for us.

"Well, well, isn't this lovely." Dean smiled that sly grin of his. "So, Sophie, do you remember me now?" My blood ran cold as I flashed back to his hands around my neck, choking the life from me. "Ah, so you do. Hopefully, this time, I can feel your life leave underneath my hands without any interruption." Incaendiel clenched his fists. *Where was Lucifer?* "Waiting for reinforcements? I fear they won't get here in time to help."

He laughed, but it didn't last long as the ground began to quake. I nearly toppled over into the lake, but Azazel grabbed me before I fell in. Lucifer, Metatron, and Michael stood before us alongside Incaendiel.

"There are my fallen brothers. Tell me, how does it feel to lose the light? It must have hurt giving up such an essential part of your being," he snickered.

"It's not the first time I have gone without my light," Lucifer replied coolly.

Dean scowled at him. "Father will love it when I bring you back to him to imprison."

"Are you that daft? You can't bring us back to the summit. In order to cross the threshold, we have to have our light!" Metatron barked.

I could see the entire fleet of angels shiver from the sound of his voice. Even as a fallen angel, they still feared the power the first in command held when he was used to being in charge of them.

"What do you want, Dean?" Michael asked, annoyed.

Even when he was surrounded by the fleet of angels in the sky, he didn't seem too fearful. He had his hand on the hilt of his sword. I guess that's what made him the angel of war and strength.

"A few things, actually. One, Father wants the jar you stole from his cabinet before you fell." Dean glanced around. "I see it has already been hidden." He glared at Incaendiel. "Two, I either want Incaendiel or Sophie. I can either take one of them by force, or you can give one of them up freely."

"Is that all?" Metatron mocked.

"That's not all I want, but what I want doesn't matter to father. Are you going to comply?" He looked between us. Incaendiel backed up and grabbed my hand. "Oh, blinking will be pointless. We have a barrier up; no one gets in, and no one gets out." Panic surged through me. We were trapped with the end result being either Incaendiel or I was going with them.

"Let me go with them." I could feel the anger from him.

"Are you crazy? No! I will not allow it!" Men are always stubborn.

"If they kill me, I will just reincarnate again in one thousand years. If they kill you, you die forever, and they win!" I could still feel his anger, and it was intensifying.

"No! I can handle them."

"Incaendiel, please, just let me do this."

"No." He looked over at Lucifer. "Lucifer, make sure everyone gets in the water and stays under the water." Lucifer glanced over to Incaendiel.

"You can't. They are our brothers!" He was pleading with him.

"I have no choice. If they take either one of us, it's game over forever; we will never see the light again. I can't have that on my shoulders. I will not be the reason why my brothers never returned to the light. At least when you die in battle, you get an honorable burial in the sky. Just do as I ask, please!"

Lucifer couldn't argue. Metatron and Michael had already gotten in the water with Sam and Azazel.

Lucifer looked at me with pain in his eyes. "We have to get in the water." Fear tore through me.

"N-n-no. I-I can't! I can't swim! I panic in the water! Every time, I nearly die from stupidity!" I looked back at the water and could already feel myself drowning. "Please, please, please!" I pleaded, but Lucifer picked me up and carried me out into the water.

It was up to my neck, and I already felt as if the water was rushing into my lungs. Tears of fear were streaming down my face.

"Incaendiel, I can't do this!"

He turned around and looked at me.

"Yes, you can."

He nodded for all of them to go under. I sucked in a breath just in time as Lucifer dove under the water. My heart thudded in my chest, and I immediately felt the need to go up for a breath. Lucifer wouldn't let me move. That's when I felt it, the heat. The water in the lake began to superheat, and I strained through the water to see why. Incaendiel had started a firestorm above the water. If I didn't drown in the water, I was going to boil to death.

If you could cry underwater, you would have seen streams of tears coming from my eyes. I was inconsolable. That was when it happened. I lost all control of my breath and sucked in water. I began struggling in Lucifer's arms. I needed to get to the surface, or I would drown. Apparently, Incaendiel wasn't finished. Lucifer wouldn't let me go. I could feel my lungs slowly fill with the lake water. Everything went hazy in my vision, and I felt myself going down a black tunnel. It was the same black tunnel I had gone through when Dean choked me to death. It was a similar death, but water induced this time. It was funny and ironic to think how being choked, drowned, or suffocated all felt alike.

I didn't remember Lucifer lifting me up from the water or rushing me to the side of the lake. What I do remember is coming too and spitting out two lungs full of water. I was gasping for air and still felt the memory of my last death creeping up on me. I was thrashing about, trying to fight off the impending death. I coughed and coughed but still couldn't get a breath. Two hands grabbed my shoulders and set me up to where I coughed and heaved more water out of my lungs. I sat there and sobbed. There was no grand life flashing before your eyes as they made it out in the movies. There's just death. I finally opened my eyes and saw it was Lucifer who held me in his arms. I looked around for Incaendiel. I was desperate to see his face. Panic shot through me, and I tried to get up to run for him. *Where was he?* Lucifer held me in his arms and wouldn't let me go.

My eyes came into focus, and I looked around me. It looked worse than it did yesterday when he set it on fire. Everything was burned to a char. There were wing imprints on the ground where every angel that had been killed had lain and died. I scanned around my surroundings and found Sam and Azazel knelt over a body. I felt my heart stop from fear.

"No!" I screamed.

I tore from Lucifer's arms and ran, stumbling over the rocks. I cut my feet fairly well, but I didn't care. I had to get to his side. I knelt beside him. He wasn't breathing, and he wasn't moving.

"No, no, no, no!"

I rocked back and forth, crying over his body. Sam and Azazel looked at me with tears in their eyes. I looked down at his chest, and right beside a scar was a puncture wound the same size and shape. Dean. He had stabbed him again and got away. He had to have pierced his heart. I threw myself on top of his body, sobbing. I covered the wound with my hand, trying to stop the blood from pouring from it. I began to do chest compressions, but all it caused was more blood to pour from the wound. *Why didn't they just let me die? It was over. There's nothing we can do anymore.*

My chest started to hurt. Not an emotional hurt but an actual searing pain. It grew in intensity, and it felt like my heart was being ripped from my chest cavity.

"AHHHH!" I screamed, grabbing my chest.

Lucifer ran to my side as I doubled over, barely catching a breath.

"What's wrong with her?!" Lucifer screamed as I thudded to the ground.

He knelt beside me as I convulsed in sheer agony. It felt like my body was on fire!

"Her light is dying. There's nothing we can do," Sam said, holding my thrashing body.

Azazel sucked in her breath and squeezed her eyes shut as the tears came pouring out.

"There has to be something!" Lucifer rumbled.

He grabbed my hand, but my convulsions ripped me from his grip. He picked my body up and held me to his chest.

"AHHHHH! IT BURNS!!!!!" I screamed. The pain was so unbearable.

I felt the life leaving my body. Death had always been a touchy subject with me, especially since Gramms had died. *Who would have thought at eighteen I would be dealing with my own?*

"INCAENDIEL!!!!!!" I called out with every ounce of energy I had.

The light was fading out as the pain grew more and more intense. In barely a whisper, I said out loud, "I love you." *My firefly.*

CHAPTER 12

***L**ove can be Stronger than Death itself*

"YOU DIED for me to live today, but you didn't know that I would die with you. I cried out your name in pain, and with my final breath confessed my love for you. Our bodies touched one last time, I breathed out life and you heard my cry. You returned to me but the time was nigh, now my heart will never be thine."

I DIDN'T KNOW if it was her call out to my soul rising to the burial in the sky or if Mother found a way to heal me, but as soon as I heard her scream out my name, her parting words to me, I was sucked back into my body. I sat up and looked down at my chest as the wound began to heal on its own. That was really weird; in human form, we didn't have this power. Sam and Azazel stared at me wide-eyed.

"You're supposed to be dead! We saw you die! It's impossible!" Azazel exclaimed in shock and doubt while tears still streamed from her eyes.

I looked over to my side and saw Sophie lying in Lucifer's arms. She wasn't moving, and from what I could tell, she wasn't breathing.

"What happened?!" I demanded.

I tore her from his grasp. I wrapped my arms around her as I pulled her into me.

"When you died, her grace died. She screamed and convulsed. She yelled out your name right before she took her last breath." It was Lucifer who answered.

I ran my hand over her face. This couldn't be happening. There were too many times I had held her lifeless body in my hands. This time, there was no coming back. She was gone forever. I bent over the top of her crying. I howled out to Father.

"How could you! How could you kill one of your children!"

I felt the dark circling me, suffocating me. I didn't care if it overtook me now. *What was the point of fighting any longer?* Father won. We would never receive our light back now. I didn't care. I had sacrificed so much for my brothers and sisters in the hope that they would return to the light, with or without me.

My tears fell like a rushing river. Foliage sprang up all around me where the fire had leveled it. Storms tore through the lake as rain, hail, and whirlwinds popped up. I felt a hand on my shoulder, one I knew all too well.

"Incaendiel, my son, do not let it overtake you. It is not hopeless yet." Mother always showed up during one of my fits.

"How can you say that? Her grace is gone! She can't return!" I stared down at her as my tears fell and dripped on her face. "She's...she's dead!" I heaved out. "This is all my fault. If I hadn't left the summit, she would be fine. Everything I have been through, we did for everyone else. She wouldn't have had to have gone through everything that bastard of a father has put her through. All this was for a plan we thought we would succeed with in the end. It's bullshit!"

I stared up at the darkening sky filled with lightning. It was a cue that he heard what I had to say.

"All you have to say for yourself is a damn thunderstorm!"

Mother backed away from me as I started to talk to Father.

"You think that you are so perfect and everyone should bow down to your feet. Your lost children pine after your love, and all you do is rewrite us as demons into the minds of humans! The only evil person in existence is you! You locked her away in a tower and made her suffer unbearable deaths I wouldn't wish on anyone. You're the true monster of evil!"

Lightning crackled down in response.

"You do not scare me anymore! Your lightning bolts mean nothing to me!"

The lightning storm receded, and as my emotions came under control, the sky returned to blue. Everyone stared at me, baffled by my outburst at our father.

I looked down at her face and brushed the hair away, tucking it behind her ear. It was a simple gesture I have always done, but now it was the last thing I could do for her. I put my forehead to hers and cried more.

"I'm sorry, my love. I lost you, my other half, the only thing that made me whole. I'm sorry. I should have listened to you. I couldn't bear the thought of you being taken by them. I didn't expect what happened to unfold."

I rocked her body in my arms.

"I would take it all back if I could. Everything! I will not let you die in vain!"

I lay her body down, leaned down, and kissed her lips once more. My soul beckoned to her. I sat there on bent knees and placed my head in my hands. My mind reached out to the empty space and pleaded with everything I held inside as power.

"Please, don't leave me! Please, come back to me!"

A blinding flash lit the entire valley, and everyone had to shield their eyes. Most would have thought Father was making a grand entrance; however, the light didn't come from the sky. It came from my heart. Every time I watched her die, every time I had to endure her leaving me, it came out like an explosion. The raw energy of the light was sending nearly everyone toppling over. Azazel grabbed onto Sam and shut her eyes from the blinding light. A tidal wave of energy went off in the valley. The ground trembled, and the mountain near the lake began to topple from the blow. With a final burst, it disappeared. I fell to my side in exhaustion. Everything went black once more.

When I awoke, I was back in the Glade. I had a horrible headache, but it didn't feel anywhere near the amount of heartache that throbbed within my shattered heart. I shut my eyes and lay my arm back over the top of them to keep the light out. I didn't want to live. I just wanted to lie here and die so I could be with her.

"I saw you wake up. You can't fool me." The voice sang throughout my mind causing me to bolt upright in my bed.

My eyes searched the room for the owner of the voice. My eyes stopped when they rested on hers. She stood up and walked over to my bed. This had to be a dream, or I was hallucinating.

"No, you're not hallucinating. I'm real, and I'm alive." She smiled down at me, stroking my hair.

What now? She can read my thoughts without me telling her?

"Yup."

Wow, there went privacy.

She giggled. She leaned in closer and planted her lips on mine. The same wonderful electricity ignited between us. She pulled away and bent down to my ear and whispered, "I love you."

It sent a frenzy through me, and I pulled her in closer, kissing her, running my hands all over her. I sat up and flipped her beneath me, pinning her to the bed and kissing her deeper. She returned every mad kiss with a more rushed one.

There was no way this was real.

"It's real, my love."

The sound of her voice in my head made my heart throb. I kissed her, trailing my lips from her mouth to her neck. She was practically tearing my clothes off when someone cleared their throat.

"Ehem, don't mind me over here in the corner." Lucifer chuckled, and I saw her face redden.

Oh, how I feared I would never see that look on her face again. I pried myself from her with every ounce of willpower I had. I groaned inwardly as I pushed my dirty thoughts of her aside.

"How long have I been out?" I asked, looking between the two of them.

"Almost a week," he replied. "You nearly depleted your grace, returning hers to her."

I touched her face and murmured, "It was worth it."

"You two go beyond any angels I have ever witnessed. Even Mother is baffled; no angel has ever healed themselves in human form. Father is furious!" Lucifer laughed.

"I bet he is," I said snidely. "What about her memories? I blinked them here before they could touch them. Were they able to get in and find them?"

Lucifer and Sophie exchanged glances. "There's only a little under half a jar of memories left for her now."

"What do you mean half a jar!? I only used one!"

I was furious. Without those memories, the hope was still not there.

"There's only half a jar because most of them returned to me when you returned my grace. I don't know how you did that, but you did." She smiled at me and then punched me in the arm. "You could have told me I met Lucifer while he was Jesus! No wonder he gave me those crazy looks when I was referencing the Bible. He thought they were my memories."

"I couldn't tell you what you didn't know from your own memories." I pretended her punch hurt and rubbed my arm, smiling wickedly at her. "So, now what? I'm sure Father wants my head on a platter for the damage I did back at the lake."

Lucifer's face grew serious. "There have been rumors that he requested you to be punished for your actions. Mother has been thinking it over." His face looked grim.

"Oh, I should be punished for defending myself against a fleet of brothers that he sent to kill me, but his army doesn't answer for the maiming and killing of humans." I puffed and shook my head.

"You know Mother is more honorable than Father, but she does know your actions were warranted from self-defense. Not to mention, as you said, they were sent to kill you and had succeeded." He looked at Sophie. "The bond you two share is the most powerful bond I have ever seen. She called out your name, begging you back. You were dead! I watched as you returned to her. It was remarkable!"

Samael walked into the room and looked at me solemnly. "Mother wishes to see you since you have awakened. Sophie, you are to stay here." He looked over to Lucifer. "You too."

I stood and walked over to Samael. I turned around, smiled at Sophie, and then proceeded through the door. Samael walked in utter silence. I wasn't sure if that was a good thing or a bad thing. We entered the throne room where Mother went during the day to watch the world. She sat in her chair made from a large lily and lily pad.

"My son, I see you have finally awakened. You slept so long; we were fearful you wouldn't wake back up."

She stood from her chair and walked over to me. She wrapped her arms around me, and I could feel her love radiate through me. Again, I didn't know if this was a good thing or a bad thing.

"You may leave, Samael. We have much to discuss." He nodded and left the room.

"Did the others explain the reasoning behind my actions at the lake?"

She nodded, but her face still did not show the warmth I expected.

"I will accept whatever punishment you deem fit for my actions then."

She stared into my eyes. Her eyes were always so hard to read, and I was certain mine were to her as well.

"You have received punishment enough for your actions. I do believe being killed was punishment enough."

She opened the door behind the throne and walked out into the open field that lay beneath the mountain. The Glade was named for its lustrous gardens and fields that sprang up beneath the mountain base. None of the fallen ones knew if the cave spiraled down and then up or if the fields and meadows really did exist below the Earth. I followed her through the meadows as she walked. I had no clue what she meant by telling Samael that she had much to discuss with me if she hadn't intended to punish me for my actions.

We came to a clearing in the meadow where there was an enormous weeping willow growing. It looked as if it held up the sky here. She sat under the willow tree and motioned for me to do the same. I walked over, sat down beside her, and looked around our surroundings. Never had I been to this portion of the Glade; Mother normally didn't let anyone through the door. I wondered why she let me come with her this time...

As I watched the meadow, it began to change from the summery scene it was suspended in into an autumn one. The leaves on the trees began to turn from green to yellow to a beautiful shade of reddish-orange. Each one that fell was caught by the breeze and carried to the center of the meadow. Once every flower had disappeared from the meadow, it began to grow insanely cold. The wind began blowing and howling with snow falling everywhere around. It blanketed the meadow, covering the pile of leaves and fields in thick blankets of powdered ice. Everywhere in the meadow, the seasons changed from one to the next, except for under the willow tree we sat.

"Oftentimes, I come out here and watch the seasons change before my eyes. It's so much more beautiful seeing them change, as if the world was spinning through them that fast. It reminds me of how time is different in the summit as opposed to here on Earth. I have kept this part of the meadow to myself, for it reminds me of who I really am as opposed to who I have become."

I watched her as she spoke. She never talked to us children about herself and the darkness, not since the fall she hasn't.

"There were times I would come out here and cry a river that would wrap around the entire Glade. It has been many years since I have felt the urge to cry over leaving the summit behind."

Her eyes began to mist over.

"There were more important things to cry about than leaving the summit this past week."

As her tears fell, they found their way to the river that was rolling along the edge of the meadow.

"We all feared we had lost you, Incaendiel. I felt Sophie's cries for you. I appeared moments before your soul returned back to your body. I watched her last few moments, her dying breath call out to you, and tell you she loved you. I saw your soul fight against the claws of death to return to her. I have never seen an angel capable of doing that. You are the first one to die a mortal death and then actually return back. Even Lucifer left his mortal body before they plunged that spear into him."

I didn't know if her eyes looked at me in admiration or fear, but she stared at me. She stared long and hard.

"I thought the darkness had completely engulfed you when you found her dead. I saw it swirl your body and grow thicker, darker, and impenetrable. Your grace burst through that darkness and nearly exploded the valley. There has never been an angel with your power. You restored her grace and part of her light. Those are powers neither Alpha nor I have."

She fell silent.

"What does that mean for me?" I asked timidly.

I didn't know if I wanted to know the answer. She didn't answer me immediately. I could see that she was pondering on it herself. When she looked at me, a tear fell from her eyes.

"I believe it means that you are truly his adversary, not I."

The words stung.

"There is no way I love the father more than you do, Mother."

She bowed her head.

"You called out to him in a fit of rage. He heard your plea to him. No angel has the power to call out to him the way you did." She paused. "In order to understand the light, you have to first understand the darkness. You have been battling the dark for many, many years. I have watched you overcome it numerous times. Never once did I know that the darkness was already within your heart. The dark cloud we have always believed to have been engulfing you, sucking you in, was truly you emanating the darkness that was already within you."

"If that is so, then how am I to return to the light? No one that holds darkness in their heart can be a child of the light." I felt the world crashing down around me.

"You are different. You use the dark to seek the light, which is an old and wise power. The universe at one point in time was nothing but darkness before your father had light spring forth throughout it."

She turned to me and peered deeply into my eyes, into my soul. I could feel her eyes piercing my insides.

"You are the darkness, and Sophie is the light. Together, you two are a force the world has never before seen. Apart, the two of you cannot survive without one another. You two are the true yin and yang energies that have kept the universe from falling in on itself."

"What about the fear of the darkness consuming me? I heard you all speak of it."

I was confused by all she was telling me.

"Our fear has always been that at the last moment, the darkness would overtake your light. I thought it meant your actual angelic light."

She stood up and looked out across the valley.

"Well, what light could it possibly mean?"

I had no idea what her riddles spoke.

"We have to keep the darkness from engulfing Sophie."

This was something I already knew.

"Of course, we have to keep her from the darkness. She isn't a fallen one. But what does that have to do with anything?"

I was becoming slightly irritated with the banter between us. She smiled at me.

"I know my riddles have always worked your nerve. But listen closely. An angel of the light can never be engulfed by the dark. They turn evil. They turn into the creatures that your father convinced the world that we are."

"What does that have to do with my light?"

She smiled once more.

"Sophie is your light."

I stood there frozen. *What?*

"Sophie is your light in the dark. She is the one saving you from the dark. Without her light, we are all doomed. We will, one by one, turn into those hideous creatures. She is the beacon of hope for not just returning to the summit but for survival."

I stood there thinking to myself. *If the dark existed within me, how could I keep her from the dark?*

I knew what I had to do without even trying for an answer. I didn't like the idea, and it tore me in two to make the final decision.

"Make sure Lucifer gets the rest of her memories into her."

I started to walk from the meadow.

"Where are you going, my son?"

She was confused, and I could hear it in her voice.

"You said I had to keep her from the dark, right?"

She nodded her head with her brows furrowed.

"I'm the dark."

Her eyes widened in the realization of what my plans were.

"But we need both of you to get the portal open!" She called out to me.

I took a deep breath. "We will open the portal, but I cannot be around her in the meantime. Not while she is receiving more of her angelic memories. The more memories she receives, the less human she becomes."

"What if she needs you? What if we need you?"

I had never seen Mother so torn before.

"I'm just a call away. She knows how to reach me."

I walked through the entrance we had taken into the meadow and back into her throne room. I made my way through the corridors and snaked my way up the staircase. When I was far away enough to where she couldn't run for me to make me change my mind, I called to her.

"Sophie?"

I waited for her reply.

"Where are you?"

I sucked in a deep breath as I walked.

"I have to keep my promise to you."

"What promise is that?"

I didn't know how I was going to force the next few words into a sentence.

"I have to go away for a while. Lucifer will be with you to protect you."

"Why?! You can't leave me behind, Incaendiel. You can't leave me!"

Her pleas were tearing my heart in two.

"I have to. It's the only way to keep you safe."

A tear slid down my face.

"I'm safe with you! Please, Incaendiel, nothing good ever comes from us being apart. You promised me you would never leave me!"

"You're not safe with me right now! You're getting closer to your angelic form and becoming less human. I must stay away. Until you are fully prepared to open the portal with me, I cannot be around you. I'm sorry!"

Tears rolled from my eyes. This was the hardest thing I think I could ever do, leaving her. It was something I had always promised her I would never do; the reason I was at her side each time she died a human death.

"Sophie, I love you...I just can't be with you."

No response was even harder than her pleas. I understood, though. I understood that she was hurting. She needed to understand this was the best thing for her.

CHAPTER 13

I f you Love Them Set Them Free

"WHERE HAVE you gone my love, when you whispered to me forever? When will I see you my love, when you said you would leave me never? You have gone away from me, tearing me down to a brittle house of cards. My heart lays in pieces.... what am I to do now, my love?"

HE'S GONE. He's gone! He left me here. I can't believe that he thinks he is a danger to me. Why would he think that? He saved me! He returned my grace and light! I died, and he brought me back from the abyss. I ran through the corridors and up the spiral staircase. I saw him as he told me he loved me, and then he was gone. I threw myself on the ground in tears. My heart was breaking. *He can't leave me. I need him. I need him now more than ever.*

All the years of memories came flooding to my mind, bringing me to my knees. It was always him begging me to stay. It was him telling me how much he needed me, how much he wanted me, how he would never leave without me. I always turned away from his love. *Is that what he is doing now? Is he turning away from my love?* I needed answers and had no idea who to ask. I lay my head down on the grass, brought my knees to my chest, and cried. I cried like I had never cried before. I felt abandoned. I felt utterly alone. I felt like I had been flying on cloud nine, and the cloud was ripped from my feet. I plummeted deep into my pain.

He can't leave me. He promised me! A hard-learned lesson of "promises were meant to be broken" was not what I wanted to fill my head. I don't know which hurt worse, the pain from my light dying or the pain from my heartbreaking. If you could die from a broken heart, this would be the moment of my final death. I knew, in reality, I wouldn't die, but so many famous people had died from heartache and heartbreak. Deep down, I felt like he didn't want me. Out of all the years of him staying away from me, it was easy to convince myself this was the reason he left. He didn't want me. It was the only feasible answer.

I felt myself gathered up into arms. It wasn't the arms I wanted. It wasn't his arms. I was carried down the spiral staircase and into the room I had run from to stop Incaendiel. I was laid down on the bed. I didn't speak. I didn't move. I was numb to everything. Every voice I heard didn't have emotion in it. Every sound didn't have the same luster to it. The world to me was becoming as dead as the feelings I held within me.

"We have to take her home before she kills us all with gloom!" Sam yelled.

Even his yelling voice didn't have the same effect that it had before.

"There is no way we can take her back home in this condition. Every human in the town will weep for no reason and continue to do so until she stops crying!"

Lucifer's anger wasn't as angry as expected.

"Well, what do you propose we do? Drag him back here? He cloaked himself! Not even Mother knows where he is!"

He wanted to hide from everyone. He wanted to make sure no one would drag him back to me. My heart sank lower in my chest. I heard Lucifer groan.

"Quit speaking like that in front of her, or she will kill us all from despair!"

How can my emotions affect them the way they are? There's nothing special about me. I wasn't like Incaendiel. Just thinking about his name makes my heart ache more. I felt my body sinking into the bed as if it were mud. I wanted to be completely numb. I didn't want to feel this pain. It wasn't real. It had to be a dream. Incaendiel wouldn't leave me behind. He had never left me behind in all our years fighting this battle. The tears began to roll from my eyes again. It was like it was on a timed sprinkler system. I couldn't control them.

"The only person ever able to take away her pain is the one that left!" Sam shouted at Lucifer.

They both looked down at me, but I ignored their stares. Lucifer sat down beside me and stroked my hair. Sam scowled and walked out of the room. Everything grew quiet around me. I saw Lucifer's lips moving, but no sounds escaped them. The silence was engulfing me, suffocating me. I couldn't bear it any longer. I sat up from the bed and bolted out the door. I topped the staircase in seconds, it seemed, and dashed from the cave.

I ran. I ran the way I did the night Gramms died. Mom was so angry and hurt when the police brought me home. I didn't care, though; I had to run, just like I do now. I ran, expecting to tire out, but I didn't. It was as if I had some new energy that I had never before possessed. I didn't know where I was running to. My course changed every so often when I thought I was close to stopping. My feet had a mind of their own. I wasn't breathless; I wasn't tired. I felt free for the first time in a long time. Each step I took seemed to gain a few extra feet. The terrain whipped by me in nearly a blur. I closed my eyes and trusted my feet to take me where I needed to go. The air on my face blew so fast it was exhilarating. When I finally opened my eyes, I was no longer running on the ground. I was flying.

I felt like I was millions of miles up in the air. I pushed forward, and my wings flew with such speed that it took my breath away. I loved it. I soared and tumbled through the air. When my tears fell from my face, they fell as rain across the land. Even in the excitement of my newfound wings, the despair that ran through me still coursed through my veins. *Where could he have gone?* I flew for miles and landed at the lake. Once again, he had used his powers to grow the foliage back around it. I looked around the entire mountain for him, but he was not there.

I flew back to the edge of the lake and sat down. I was stupid to have a sliver of hope that he would be here. He wouldn't have gone anywhere we would have thought to look for him. The tears started again, wisping their way from my eyes down my face. Each one dropped into the lake, making tiny waves and rippling out across the lake. I closed my eyes and breathed in deeply. *When would he come back for me?* I missed him terribly. I felt like my entire life was ripped from my hands. I knew this was what heartbreak felt like. It had to be. My heart throbbed the same way when Gramms died. The sad part was that he didn't die; he just left.

He was my protector, and he left me vulnerable. I wasn't sure which hurt worse, the fact that he left me when I needed his protection the most or that he left me when the love between us had begun to intensify. Go figure, the moment I gave myself completely to someone, gave them my heart, they just walked out of my life. I understood there was more to the entire situation than just an eighteen-year-old's first romance, but that's exactly what this is. My soul may be millions of years old, but right now, it was trapped in a body that wasn't even a measurement on a ruler compared to it. I may remember a good portion of my past lives, but they didn't compare to my experiences in this one.

How long will I have to wait for his return? Will he ever return? Will he just let me die on my nineteenth birthday and say screw it all?

"How could you even think that one!?"

I sucked in a breath as the tears wanted to fall. Just the sound of his voice in my head made me want to ball up and die.

"Sophie, I love you, do not doubt that. I just can't be around you; I can't be with you right now. I'm dangerous to you."

I wanted to answer him, but even the voice in my head quivered with sadness. I closed my eyes as another tear slid down my cheek.

"You can't be with me, or you don't want to be with me?"

Silence filled my head. My heart yearned to hear his response, to hear his voice in my head.

"Please, come back to me."

I wished the fantasy I had played out in my head would have happened; a hand would brush my cheek, and I would open my eyes to see him. When I opened my eyes, there was no one there; there was no comforting hand upon my cheek. I was utterly alone. His voice was gone from my head. How I longed for it to speak to me again, but I knew he wouldn't unless I really needed him. Somehow, I knew he felt my heartache and pain. *How could he deal with what I felt? Is this what he felt all those years when I let the other angels get close to me?*

I sat by the edge of the lake for hours. I didn't want to leave. This was our place. This was where all the moments that meant something between us had sparked. I could feel him here, and that's all I wanted. The day turned quickly into night, but I didn't budge. I didn't sleep. I just sat there and numbly stared out at the lake. The night felt like an eternity in the darkness. I sat there and thought of our last day at the lake, the moment when I was going to tell him out loud how I felt. I was so nervous, so scared of saying it out loud. Of course, I knew how he felt for me. We are bound by eternity with each other. But the hesitance of that moment, of the utterance of those words, was because of this very moment. I was afraid of being alone. Now, look at me.

I watched the stars reflected in the lake water. I hoped to see him hovering above the trees in the background. I turned quickly, thinking I might catch a glimpse of him somewhere. There was no such luck. He never came to kiss me goodbye or tell me in person that he was leaving, yet he wanted to hear the words I love you out loud. This slightly angered me, and I enjoyed the anger. I guess I was going in the order of the chart for grief. I didn't care.

I sat there all night. The sun began to peek out behind the mountain, signaling dawn. I didn't move. I felt someone walk up behind me, but I didn't care who it was. It could have been Dean for all I cared because I didn't care. The person sat down beside me. It wasn't him which sent my heart further into pieces.

"Did you sit out here all night?"

Of course, it was Lucifer. It seemed like he stalked me everywhere I went. If I didn't know any better, I'd swear we had a thing going on in the summit. I didn't answer his question. I sat there quietly.

"Sophie, you have to snap out of this. You're going to grieve your grace away!"

I didn't respond to him. As a matter of fact, it had been an entire day since I had said a single word out loud to anybody. I felt his hand on my shoulder, and it angered me.

"Sophie?"

"Leave me alone!" I shouted and pushed his hand from me.

My voice echoed powerfully through the mountain. I figured he would have flitted away, but he stayed put.

"Why don't you people ever listen? I didn't want to be a part of this in the beginning. I was dragged into it. I couldn't even live a normal life growing up because of this whole mess! The only people who have ever shown interest in me was a conniving, bastard angel and Incaendiel. Where are they now? Nowhere to be seen. I couldn't even have a normal experience as a human while on Earth. Everything has always circled around this damn year! I'm tired of it. I'm tired of being told what needs to be done and how it should be done. I'm tired of feeling like I was abandoned. I'm tired of always grasping but never fully receiving him into my arms. We can finally be together after my eighteenth birthday, and he runs away! He leaves me!"

The tears poured from my eyes. It was centuries of pent-up anger, frustration, envy, and disappointment. My heart did more than just ache; it hurt.

We sat there for a while in silence until he was able to pry me away. He carried me home and put me in my bed. Somehow, they had cast a glamour to make my mom think I had been in bed sick with the flu or something the entire time. School was starting the next day, and everything had to seem like nothing in my life had changed. I stayed in bed even though mom pestered me to get up. I had no energy. I felt like the life had drained from me. The day turned quickly into night, and I didn't feel like starting school at all the next day. Mom agreed it would be best for me to stay home as well.

Night turned into morning, and the days just seemed to flutter by. I never once moved out of my bed. I had missed the first week of school, but I didn't care. I didn't need school. Soon, Mom began to think I had mono and requested for an in-home tutor until I felt well enough to go back. I would lay in bed and stare out the window while the teacher would drone on and on over the studies. The weeks turned into months, and I spent each day in a fog.

"Sophie, I don't know what's wrong with you, but you need to snap out of your funk. Get out of bed, shower because the good Lord knows you need one, and come down for breakfast. It's not a request." I pried myself from the bed and trudged to the shower. The hot water didn't even soothe my broken soul.

When I appeared downstairs, Mom had me a plate of food and a cup of coffee sitting on the table. I grimaced and sat down. I picked up my fork and rolled the food around the plate.

"So, are you going to tell me what's really going on?" she asked, peering over her cup of coffee at me. I was silent. I didn't want to talk about anything. "Sophie, he's just a boy. These things happen."

"You wouldn't understand."

My eyes never left my plate.

"You went on a date with Isaiah, and since then, I haven't seen him around. I understand. I thought you two were going to hit it off as well. That boy was always wrapped around your finger when you were kids."

107

She sat her cup down and touched my hand lying on the table.

"Your first heartbreak is always the hardest. I know he was your first boyfriend, but you have to get through this, sweetie."

It took every ounce of willpower I had in me not to break down and cry. She wouldn't understand the true reasons behind everything. She didn't believe in the family Bible and would have me committed if I told her the truth. I mumbled that I was fine and excused myself from the table. She watched me stand from the table with worry written all over her face. I had to get outside. I needed air. I stepped outside and closed my eyes, breathing in deeply.

"You should have expected the pep talk. It would have been easier."

Lucifer sat reading a copy of Socrates' Philosophy on the porch. I walked over and sat down beside him.

"I didn't think she would have remembered it." I sat there, brooding. "So, what happens now? How do I do the school thing when I've missed so many days?"

He closed the book he was reading and chuckled. "The school thing will be easy. There will be five of us there to protect you. Since Sam and Azazel are first and second in command and, of course, well known at the school, they kept to the same roles they had. Metatron, Michael, and I filled in as transfer students. There will be around the clock protection from at least one of us, so Azazel persuaded the Secretary at the school to insure it. There's still time for you to return and continue on as a normal student."

"What about Dean and the other angels?"

He stiffened when I mentioned their existence. It was as if he had forgotten until now.

"Dean is already causing mischief at the school along with four others as well. As long as you stay away from them and don't get sucked into their lies, you will be fine."

He smiled at me.

"Why are you so nice to me, Prince of Darkness?" I laughed, and he playfully socked me in the arm.

It was the first time in forever I had a smile form on my face.

"Someone has to be. Who better than the compassionate, all-loving son," he murmured as he looked me in the eyes.

He brushed the hair from my face.

"The one that protected you while you were locked away in the tower."

His thumb brushed alongside my jawline, and my heart skipped a beat. I spiraled into a dark hole.

"Incaendiel will return for me. I know he will."

My voice was more reassuring than what my heart and mind were. Lucifer stood before me. His eyes danced in mine.

"He will never return," he said.

"Why do you keep saying that?! He will return! He must return! Or, as you said, I will die!" I began to tear up.

"You misunderstood my words, my darling. I didn't say if he didn't return, you would die. I said if he did return...you would die."

My eyes searched his face for a lie. No one could lie in his presence, so did that mean he was incapable as well?

"You do not speak the truth!" I yelled.

He reached out with his hands and pulled me into his chest.

"You know it is true, Sophie. You just must believe it. His darkness will consume you. It will consume us all!"

It felt nice to be in someone's arms. It felt even nicer that they belonged to Lucifer.

"What if I wanted to die for him to regain his light?" I asked.

"No! I won't let you!" He shook me when he said it.

"His darkness is my fault. I promised him his return. I promised we would reunite. I promised."

I broke down crying.

"Not all promises can be kept, my darling," Lucifer said as he swept me up in his arms.

He wiped away my tears and then kissed me.

I snapped back from the black hole with a pounding headache. "Did you slip a damn memory in?"

His eyes widened in surprise. "No, I didn't. What did you remember?"

I thought back to the memory and looked at him. *Did I really betray Incaendiel with Lucifer? I couldn't have!* The waves that had been rolling in on me when Incaendiel left crashed on top of me. I felt like throwing up.

"What did you do?! Take advantage of me alone in the tower?! Try to get the details from me where the Garden is?! You snake!"

He looked at me bewildered, and then it sank in what memory I had.

"You...saw us...didn't you?"

He looked down at the ground when he asked, his cheeks flushed. I smacked him across the face.

"How could you use me like that?"

I was sad, angry, and confused all in one.

"I didn't use you. We spent 2,000 years together in that tower together. What did you expect to happen?"

I couldn't look him in the face I was so guilty.

"You were guilty then, too, just so you know. You always told me once Incaendiel returned, you would be with him, not with me."

He touched my hand.

"It can still be like that. Until he returns..."

I jerked my hand away. I didn't know what I wanted or what I wanted to do. There was a piece of myself that was drawn to Lucifer. Not a strong magnetic pull like with Incaendiel, but a connection.

"You just want to pick up where we left off? Like there hasn't been any type of change? Incaendiel will return. He will return to me here on Earth, and he will make it back to the summit with all of us. I'm not yours, Lucifer. I was not created alongside you. I'm not Sophia!"

I was sure of his return. Lucifer dropped his head. I knew that last line would hurt him most of all, but I didn't care.

"When you recover more memories, let me know. We will talk then. Otherwise, just don't speak to me anymore."

He blinked away. He was hurt. I had hurt him. I hurt him the way Incaendiel had hurt me. *Did he know? Did he know about my betrayal?* Just thinking the word sent a wave of nausea and despair through me. I had to go somewhere, anywhere. I couldn't let anyone see me in the mess I was in. I hadn't slept in months; I was an emotional wreck, and I needed space from this whole situation.

I walked to my car and hopped in when the passenger door swung open. Michael climbed into the seat beside me.

"We have much to talk about, Sophie."

He looked over at me, and his look wasn't friendly in the least. I looked down at his lap, and he was holding my jar of memories.

"What are you doing with that?"

I didn't understand why he had the jar. Apparently, I no longer needed to be spoon-fed the memories; they just leapt into my mind.

"Drive to the lake."

It wasn't a request but rather a demand.

"What's at the lake?" I asked.

I wished I hadn't pissed Lucifer off. I sent a mental cry to him, inquiring about the lake. I didn't know if it was just a thing between Incaendiel and me or not.

"Just drive."

He stared out of my windshield. I had an eerie feeling with him. I didn't feel safe. Nonetheless, I put the car in reverse and backed out of the driveway. I steered the car in the direction of the mountain. The car was silent. I took quick glances over at Michael as he sat there staring out the window.

"Why do you have the jar of memories? I don't need it to get them back. I've been having memories return on their own."

He didn't reply.

"Why won't you talk to me?"

He turned and glared at me, and then he smiled a sly smile.

"It was so easy to fool you all. Even Metatron honestly thought I had fallen to help. He's so stupid."

My heart stopped. *No! He couldn't lie in front of Lucifer.*

"There are ways around Lucifer's gift."

It was as if he knew what I was thinking.

"Incaendiel timed it perfectly. The best thing he did was leave you. It returned your angelic grace. I waited until you were completely broken in half. I followed you flying through the skies the day he left. You're faster than I remembered, but I kept up pretty well."

He followed me? So, the odd sensation I was hoping to be Incaendiel was him.

"Since you're nearly a complete angel again, I can force-feed these memories to you and not worry about your brain exploding. Once you remember each and every one of them, I'm taking the Garden for myself."

No! Incaendiel, wherever you are, you need to get your ass back here. This is serious! I was half hoping he would answer back, but he did not.

"Do you think Incaendiel would come for you? He abandoned you. And Lucifer!" He laughed. "Lucifer was so stupid to fall for you."

He knew? My face must have shown surprise.

"Everyone in the summit knew. We could hear you two from the castle, for Christ's sake." Then he grinned. "Or should I say for Lucifer's sake?"

So, it was more than just kissing. We...actually... Oh, come on, Sophie, your angelic soul is older than freaking eighteen.

"Lucky for me, Lucifer, and you don't have the same connection with your mind as Incaendiel. This will go off without a hitch. I told everyone you needed privacy with your memories and requested me to help. Perfect plan. No interruptions and Lucifer's too busy sulking to pay it any attention."

I realized what he had done.

"You sent me that memory of Lucifer to have me make him leave!"

He laughed in my face. I was so foolish. *What if I were to drive the car off the road? Would it buy me enough time to make it to the cave?* As if answering my question, a sharp object pointed at my side.

"Do anything stupid, this goes through you, and we do this all over again in one thousand years. Got it?"

We topped the last hill, and I turned the car into the parking lot. The lake was a good three-mile hike. Michael grabbed my hand and blinked us there. Dean and four others were there as well.

"Did you put the stakes in the ground as I said?" he asked, turning to Dean.

"They're all ready." He smiled smugly at me.

"Good. Tie her down."

I panicked.

"Tie me down? What?! Why are you tying me down?!"

Dean and one of the other angels grabbed my arms and towed me over to where I saw the four stakes driven into the ground. I struggled against their grips. Even with what strength and power that had been returned to me, I couldn't fight them off.

Where was Incaendiel? He should have shown up with me being in danger. They threw me to the ground, which knocked the breath from my lungs. I tried gulping down a breath as they tied my hands and feet to the stakes. I pulled against the ropes, but they didn't budge. I was stuck.

"They could kill me, Incaendiel! Where are you!?"

There was no answer to my call. My heart sank further into my chest.

"I thought you loved me!"

Michael walked over to me, holding the jar.

"Well, are we comfortable?"

He sat down beside me and unscrewed the lid of the jar.

"So how shall we do this? One at a time, or all at once. I myself prefer all at once, but you are still human. All of them at once may kill you, and then we would be back at step one again."

He reached into the jar and drew out one of my memories.

He smiled a sly grin. "Oh, I do believe you would like this one indeed."

He crushed the memory in his hand and placed it on my forehead. I convulsed a little and then went down the familiar black hole.

CHAPTER 14

Will Help Ever Come?

"SAVE ME! I cried out thrashing in my chains. Release me from the hold this pain has over me. Swoop in and carry me away on wings of hope. Take me to your place of safety in the heavens abode. Why must I go through this without a hero to cut me loose? I guess this time the hero isn't coming, so it's up to me to save me from doom."

I AWOKE, screaming. The group of angels that stood around me laughed. He had already given me at least ten memories back-to-back. I had truthfully lost count. I was sweating from the pain the memories were causing in my head. I turned my head heaving. I vomited up stomach acid. Even with that many memories poured into my head, the jar still looked untouched.

"Are we ready for another one?" Michael asked while he reached for the jar.

"No, no, no, please!" I cried.

I honestly didn't know if I could handle another memory. I could feel something trickling from my nose. I was getting a nosebleed. They were causing my brain to bleed. My knight in shining armor still had not shown up to save me.

"If you want to kill me, just do it already!"

He laughed at my plea.

"Killing you is not in my nature. Making you suffer is a different story."

I glared at him.

"Well, since you can't handle another memory right now, maybe you can handle some manhandling. It has been a while since we passed you around."

He bent down, brushed my hair away from my face, and tried to rub my jaw as if it were affectionate to me. I jerked my head away from his hand.

"If you touch me, Incaendiel will-"

"He will what? Is he here yet? Have you not pleaded with your mind for him to come to rescue you?"

He eyed me as I glared back.

"Ah, you have. Poor, poor Sophie. You have truly been abandoned. He's not coming for you." He sneered, and all the angels laughed.

"What did you do to him?" I glared up at him.

He matched my glare.

"Let's just say he's not making it anytime soon."

My heart sank. He had to come for me. He promised he would. Then again, I promised him a lot of things that I broke a long time ago. *Is that why he hasn't shown up? Is he making me suffer for my betrayal?*

Michael bent over me and smacked me across the face. I closed my eyes and sent my mind to a different place. He laid blow after blow against my fragile body. I squeezed my eyes shut and made myself project from the place. I must've passed out. When I awoke, Michael was sitting next to me, crushing a memory. My entire body burned and hurt.

"Back to sleep we go, my sweet."

He pressed his hand to my forehead, and down the rabbit hole, I went again.

I was at the summit. Alpha had pulled me in front of him as court was initiated.

"Sophie, you have been charged with treason. The sentence is normally stripping you of your grace and light and letting you roam the earth for eternity. However, I have a far better plan for you. Since your treason was trying to help the fallen ones return, then you certainly will."

I glanced around at my brothers and sisters as I stood shackled in front of Alpha. Not a single one announced their distaste for his ruling. My eyes caught Lucifer's eyes, and he nodded his head.

I returned my look to Alpha. "I accept my punishment."

"Good, you will return to earth every one thousand years to the family of what your mother has called Guardians. On your eighteenth birthday, I will send one of my angels down to rescue you. Your brothers and sisters who have fallen will try to prevent that from happening."

I knew it was a lie. I had my vision that he didn't know about. I knew the real reason behind it.

"Will you influence my decisions while I am in human form? They do have free will."

The question struck him oddly. I could see it in his face.

"Of course, you will have your own free will."

He studied my face.

"When do I start my punishment?"

I was eager to find Incaendiel and return them home.

"Your punishment starts immediately and lasts until either side succeeds. It's up to your human decision how long your punishment shall extend. On your nineteenth birthday of each human life, you will die and return here. The second part of your punishment is to remain locked in the tower in between incarnations."

Everyone gasped. No one had ever lasted that long in the tower. They had never known anyone to be punished to that extent.

My eyes caught Lucifer's as I breathed in deep and heavy. His eyes didn't flicker. He just nodded.

"How soon is immediately?"

I was sucked back out of the darkness. The pain in my head was unbearable. I was dizzy, and the entire sky was spinning. Michael's hand was resting on my bare thigh. He was making circles with his finger. I couldn't even speak or scream out in protest against him, touching me again. I was too tired to do anything.

"Check her pupils. Make sure she isn't going comatose or anything," Michael ordered.

Dean bent over me, lifting my eyelids, and peered at my eyes. I stared back at him. I didn't know if they dilated or not. He just stared at me.

"Well, are they dilating?"

"I can't tell. I think we need to give her a break."

It was odd for him to take my side. I couldn't move my head really to see what all happened. I know that Michael jumped up and grabbed Dean by the shirt.

"I'm the one in charge here. You do as I say."

I tried to focus on all the other angels. They were standing a few feet away from me. The looks on their faces read that they didn't agree with Michael's tactics. I wondered if they... touched... I couldn't even finish the thought in my head as the tears began to brim behind my eyes. Michael and Dean were still gone out of my sight, and the others began to talk.

"If Lucifer or one of the others show up, we're dead!"

I had no clue what their names were. I was never introduced, and I can't remember any of the angels' names.

"Well, what do you propose we do? We can't let her go, or HE will kill us!" another replied.

"That is if Dean doesn't kill him first. Dean has nearly killed Incaendiel twice."

They were wrong. He succeeded the second time.

I licked my lips and tried to cry out to them. It came as a croak from where my throat was so dry.

"Please, let me go."

They just stared at me. I could tell they were on the ropes about what to do. One of them walked over and took out a knife. I flinched away from the blade, and he held up his hands as surrender.

"I'm just going to cut the ropes."

He took the knife to each stake and released my limbs from them. My body thudded to the ground. I had no sensation in my limbs. *How long had we been here?* I slowly rolled over on my stomach and tried to find something to cover my body with as a safety net. I groped at the ground until I felt a blanket draped across me. I looked up and smiled.

"Thank you, Brothers."

It came out as a whisper, but they nodded their heads. They disappeared. The jar of my memories was within my reach, and I grabbed it. I couldn't move anywhere, and I heard the voices of Michael and Dean returning.

What am I going to do? I was frantic. I had nowhere to hide and couldn't hide if I tried. I could barely move. Their voices were getting closer and closer. I closed my eyes and wished with all my might to be in the Glade. The strangest sensation surged through my body, and when I opened my eyes, I was in the Glade. I blinked. I couldn't believe it, *I blinked! But where in the Glade was I?* I looked around and saw no one. I was in some sort of closet.

I tried swallowing to alleviate my throat so I could cry out for some help. It was still bone dry.

"Help," I whispered. "Help."

It came out a bit louder as I croaked it out.

"Help! Help me! Someone!"

I was frantic, with tears coming down my face. I felt no safer than I had with Michael. I tried to move, but my body still groaned against it. *Oh no, what if Michael comes here looking for me? Did he know I blinked away? Does he think I just ran away?*

"Please, someone..." I was in tears. I couldn't even lift my arm to bang on the door in front of me.

The room began to spin again. I was going to blackout again. Lucky for me, I knew it wasn't a memory since I held them in the jar in my hands. The door squeaked open, and I heard a familiar voice.

"Sophie, is that you?" It was Sam. "Guys, I found her!"

He bent down to pick me up when he noticed there was a blanket wrapped around me. He peeled it back to reveal the blood and bruises left behind by Michael's torture.

"What happened to you, Sophie?" Azazel and Lucifer appeared at the door behind him.

Lucifer took one look at me and nearly crumpled. I had no clue what I even looked like. *Had Michael beaten me more while I was in and out of consciousness?* Lucifer pushed past Azazel and Sam and lifted me. He carried me out of the closet and laid me down gently on the bed.

"Who did this to you?!" he demanded.

I opened my mouth to tell him, but the words didn't want to come out. Azazel and Sam stood behind him, waiting for my answer.

"WHO?!" he yelled.

"It was Michael," I croaked out.

Lucifer's eyes went dark.

"Michael has been with us the entire time searching for you!" He was angry. "Who was it?!"

"No, no! I know what he told me." Tears fell from my face. "I know who I saw. It was Michael! He made me take him to the lake. Dean and four other angels were waiting there for us." I was crying and losing the

balance of consciousness. "He forced memories into my head. He...he..."
I cried.

I couldn't say it. The room began spinning again, and convulsions
followed. I foamed from the mouth as my eyes rolled back into darkness.

As I came too, I heard hushed talk.

"Are you sure she said it was Michael?"

It was Metatron speaking.

"Yes, she said it was Michael." Lucifer looked solemn.

"What all did he do to her?" Metatron stood from his seat. "Why
didn't Incaendiel come to help her? What is going on!?" He slung his
chair across the room, furious.

"I don't know any more than you do." Lucifer looked over at me,
and our eyes locked. "What I do know is someone is going to pay for
this." He pulled his eyes away from mine and back to Metatron. "Does
Michael have the power to create doubles of himself?" The room fell
silent.

"I don't know," Metatron replied.

"What if the Michael that fell was a double? The real Michael hung
back in time to strike."

"That would explain why there was a Michael in two places at once."

The room began to spin again. I leaned over the bed and vomited.

"Go help her. We will talk later, Brother."

Metatron left the room while Lucifer walked over to me. Every bone
in my body ached. I felt like I had been pushed down a flight of stairs.

"You took quite a beating. Do you remember any of it?"

He took a wet washcloth and wiped my face.

"All I remember is the agony from the memories he was forcing into
my head while I was tied down."

He picked up a cup and leaned it toward my mouth. I had been
craving a drink of water for forever, it seemed.

"What else happened?"

I didn't want to answer him. I shut down from that point.

"Sophie, tell me. What did he do to you?" His eyes gazed into mine.

My bottom lip quivered. "What you all did to me while I was locked
away in that awful tower."

The tears streamed down my face. He squeezed his eyes tight.

"I apologized to you years ago for acting that way."

He wouldn't look at me.

"Well, that's what happens when the memory hits you. So, does the
pain and anguish tied to it." He flinched away from my words. "Were
you in on it with me from the beginning, or did you just use me to report

to Father?"

He got up and started to walk out of the room.

"Did you think I would fall in love with you? Did you care for me? Or was I just another conquest?!"

He spun around, and I saw the fury in his face.

"I never meant to hurt you. I never used you to gain anything. It was your idea for me to report to him your treason. This was all your idea!"

He punched his fist against the wall.

"God dammit, Sophie, when are you going to realize that I truly do care about you? Does it take getting tortured for it to be even talked about?"

The room fell silent.

"Something has happened to Incaendiel."

Lucifer looked over at me with fear in his eyes.

"Why do you say that?"

"Because when I called for him, he didn't come."

Lucifer went to leave the room.

"No!"

He stopped in the doorway.

"Please, don't leave me alone in here."

It came out as barely a whisper. He turned from the doorway and walked over to my bed. His lips landed on mine, and there was a familiar feeling that soared through me. It wasn't the same feeling I felt with Incaendiel, but it was a feeling, nonetheless.

He pulled away from me and kissed my forehead.

"I will be back, I promise."

Every sensation inside of me rose, wanting to believe the words he spoke, but I knew they weren't true, and I was right. I waited in the room for three days, but Lucifer never returned. It was an empty promise, just like Incaendiel had promised.

My strength returned to me, and I finally urged myself out of the room. I found Azazel on the other side of the door as a guard. She looked at me in surprise as I walked out.

"You shouldn't be walking around!"

"Where's Lucifer?" I asked.

"The hunting party hasn't returned yet," she replied.

"Hunting party?" I didn't understand.

"They went to look for Incaendiel."

I swallowed. Lucifer is going to risk his life for the woman he loves to bring back the man she loves. *How did my life ever end up in a love triangle like this?*

There was a commotion coming from the spiral staircase. Azazel pushed me back into the room, and I heard it lock. I tried to listen through the door to what was being said on the other side. It was all drowned out by the competing voices. I sat for what seemed like hours, waiting for someone to come and release me from the room. I felt like I was locked away in the tower all over again.

Finally, I heard the key turn in the door.

"Lucifer?" I called out.

My heart dropped. It was Michael.

"Lucifer!"

"Do we really have to have this conversation again? He's not coming."

He walked slowly towards me like a cat would stalk its prey.

"Tell me, Sophie, how does it feel to be responsible for the deaths of both of the men you love?"

No, no. He was lying. They were not...they couldn't be. Michael's face melted away, and before me stood an angel that I could not place.

"What?" I was speechless and filled with dread.

"Confusing, I know, but I couldn't have them hunting my scent. If they caught wind of it, I would never succeed in this mission." He breathed in deeply. "Mmm, it's good to be the real me again. I hate shifting into the goody-two-shoes Archangels. Their compassion eats right through me." His grin was pure evil.

"Who...who are you?"

I narrowed my eyes at him studying. His demeanor felt so familiar, yet I couldn't place him.

"Why, Sister, it pains me to know you don't remember your dear, old brother, Beelzebub."

My eyes widened. I didn't remember the one I was supposed to remember, but I did remember the one the Bible spoke of. He was an evil demon.

"Ah, I see you remember at least some portion of the name, whether it be human memory or angel. Now, back to business."

"Azazel!" I yelled out. "Sam!"

No one came.

"There's no one left, Sophie. You are truly and utterly alone. Now, to finish what we started."

He held the jar of my memories up. I backed away, squeezing my eyes shut.

"I can't do it anymore!"

I picked up a knife lying beside the bed and held it out at him. He laughed at me.

"Are you really threatening me with a knife?"

The tears ran down my face in slow trickles. *I love you, Incaendiel. We will be together again, just not this time, not this incarnation.* I lifted the knife above my head to plunge it straight toward my heart.

"No!" Beelzebub cried out as he saw me lifting the dagger.

I closed my eyes, bracing for the pain from the piercing blade, and thrust my dagger down. Instead, I felt a hand grab mine. I opened my eyes and nearly melted into the floor. Incaendiel stood before me. He knocked the knife from my hand and kicked it away. His face was filled with such pain that I had to stifle the cry, wanting to slip out. Lucifer rounded the corner just as I threw myself into his arms. Sam and Azazel had subdued Beelzebub with ropes. I buried myself deep into his chest. He pulled me in closer and closer. I opened my eyes and saw Lucifer's face. The look he had was heartbreaking. My heart felt like it was tearing in two. I squeezed myself tighter into Incaendiel's chest. He blinked me away.

CHAPTER 15

Mistakes of the Heart

"IS my love enough for you? Will you make me leave when you know what I've done? I never meant to hurt you...But I know what's done is done...Can I ever make it up to your heart? To let you know that you're the one I want? I have always loved you from the start...our existence could never be you without me, please forgive me my love...I love you from the bottom of my heart!"

I WAS afraid to open my eyes or to release the hold I had around his waist. I was afraid he would disappear or that I would be back at the lake. I had longed for his return for so long that I never thought it would happen. Tears had fallen and soaked the front of his shirt without me realizing I had been crying. He wrapped his arms tighter around me, and I felt so safe, so loved. His touch felt so real that I couldn't fight the fear any longer. I opened my eyes and found his eyes staring back at me.

"I'm sorry, Sophie. I'm so sorry. I tried to get to you. They had me in a barrier I couldn't break. I felt and saw everything they did to you."

His eyes grew dark, and I felt the anger that rippled through his body.

"I shouldn't have left you alone. I should have never left at all. My trust in others puts you in danger."

I flinched when he said the word trust. I felt the burn come to my cheeks. He lowered his eyes. He already knew what I wanted to tell him. This mind-to-mind thing sucked big time.

"Incaendiel...about Lucifer..."

He didn't even let me finish. He scooped me up in his arms and kissed me. No kiss in the world could compare to this one. It's like our bodies became one. My face flushed with heat as he moved his mouth to my neck. I felt so alive in his arms.

"Does he make you feel like this?" he asked through deep breaths.

"Does he make you feel like this?!"

He startled me to where I couldn't answer out loud. I shook my head no.

"Do you want him, or do you want me?"

This is the first time I wanted to say I want you...but deep down...I didn't know.

"Never mind what he said about me returning. This has to do with your feelings for me and your feelings for him. This will not work if your heart is not completely mine!"

He walked over to me and brushed his hand alongside my jaw and chin.

"The only thing I care about is getting you back to the summit. I don't care if you choose him over me in the end. The love between us has to be real for it to work."

I threw my arms around him and kissed him. I didn't wait for him to make the moves anymore. I slipped my tongue in his mouth and felt his arms tighten around my waist. I ripped his shirt from his body and ran my hands along his chest. My mouth moved down his neck to his chest. When I opened my eyes, we were suspended in the air. My toes danced across the clouds.

I pulled him closer to me, leaned in, and whispered in his ear, "You should know by now who my heart belongs to."

I flew away with him fast on my heels. I zipped through the clouds with him laughing behind me. I took a dive for a river below and raced him down. Before we touched the water, he grabbed my hand and opened his wings. *Was he still in his human form?* He didn't look any different than before, but it was too dark to see anything. He pulled me in close to him and just held me.

"Please, don't ever leave me again," I whispered.

"If I told you I wouldn't, would you believe me?" he asked, stroking my hair.

"I felt a part of me die when you left. I knew you said you loved me, but my heart felt otherwise." I began to choke on my tears. "I expected you to show up at the lake that first day, then the second, and then I knew you would blink into my room." I swallowed the lump in my throat. "I was so scared you had left me forever, especially once Lucifer... it ran through my mind that's why you didn't come."

He pulled me deeper into his chest.

"Nothing in this world, jealousy, anger, nothing, would keep me from saving you if I hadn't been captured."

I wiped away my tears and prepared myself mentally for the next question I was going to ask him.

"Do you think Lucifer's feelings for me are real?"

He tensed under the question.

"Why would you ask me that?"

His voice sounded more like he was hurt instead of angry.

"Maybe he was the one sent by Alpha to snake me away. He keeps telling me you will never return, that your darkness will kill me."

I felt his body shudder with anger.

"What memories do you have of him?"

His voice was husky.

"I had him go to Alpha to turn me over for treason. My punishment is this reincarnation thing and imprisonment in the tower in between." He landed us down on the ground.

"What happened while you were imprisoned?"

I didn't want to think of it. I didn't even want to say the words.

"I was tortured for information..."

I couldn't look at him from the shame.

"Who were the ones that tortured you?"

I closed my eyes.

"Please don't make me tell you."

He walked over and took me in his arms.

"They will never hurt you again."

I knew his eyes wouldn't lie to me.

"Who were they?"

"Too many to remember their faces. I remember Beelzebub and..."

I couldn't say it.

"And who?!" He demanded the name from me.

"Lucifer."

He dropped his hands from my waist and turned around. I saw him run his hands through his hair.

"But..."

"But what!" he snapped.

"When he was locked in the tower with me, he changed. He told me how he regretted doing what he did to me, but it was necessary so that they wouldn't find out about the plan. We..."

I couldn't finish the sentence.

"Say it."

There was no tone, no emotion.

"After some time, we developed a relationship. We made love."

He picked up a boulder and threw it across the river. It landed on the other side, exploding into tiny rocks.

"It never came close to what you and I shared, and after being locked away in that tower for millions of years, it was the only emotion I had received. I craved it."

"The angel who tortured you, you decided to develop a relationship with."

He was angry.

"I thought it best to tell you myself than someone else."

I swallowed back the tears welling. I knew he felt betrayed. I had no excuse.

"What's happened between you two since I've been gone? Sneaking behind my back again?"

I didn't know what to say. I didn't want to answer.

"Tell me, Sophie. What am I up against? A kiss on the cheek, on the lips, some tongue, groping your chest, what?!"

"Why are you asking me this?!" I cried.

Hot tears fell down my face.

"You said that being locked up for millions of years without emotion from anyone was your excuse."

He moved in close to me.

"And!" I yelled.

"What do you think I did the entire time we have been separated? Do you think I've been screwing Azazel or any of the others?"

It dawned on me why my betrayal hurt so badly. He remained faithful to the end.

"I'm sorry, I really am. I never meant for any of this to happen the way it has. I ruined our lives together. I ruined us, I know. Just let me fix it, please!" I begged him.

I needed him to say it was okay. I needed him to say everything was fine. He was silent. I knew what he wanted to hear.

"It was just a kiss on the lips."

He dropped his head.

"When I had the memory of us in the tower, I smacked him afterward."

He looked up at me with a hint of a smile on his lips.

"We need to find out if his actions are truthful or if he is here to deceive us as well."

"Right now, we need to put some more memories in you," he said, lifting my memory jar out of his pocket.

I froze. I didn't want to do it.

"No," I said flatly.

"We have to, Sophie. They won't hurt nearly as bad since I'm putting them in you."

He walked over to me and tucked my hair behind my ear.

"You trust me, don't you?"

His eyes said he needed to hear the words.

"Yes, I trust you. I'm just not too thrilled since my brain nearly exploded last time."

I trudged along behind him as he pulled me into a cave.

"Is this where you have been hiding?"

"It's surrounded by nothing but quartz. No one can sense us here."

"Before we get down to the memories, what happened to you?"

He sighed.

"I was flying out to the Glade. When you had sat for nearly two days at the lake, I couldn't stand to be away from you any longer. Four angels that are new to the mission down here captured me. They had a rope crafted from unicorn hair; the only thing powerful enough to contain an angel. They tied me up and threw me in the cave. I couldn't move, I couldn't blink. All I could do was lay there and yell for help. I wanted, no, I needed desperately to get to you. You were drowning in grief, and it was my fault. I needed you to know I didn't really leave you, even if you felt as if I did. I would never really leave you."

He caressed my face.

"Did Lucifer find you?"

He nodded.

"Does he have visions?"

He squinted his eyes and nodded.

"When I told him I thought something was wrong with you, his eyes widened with what I thought was fear. I think he saw you in a vision. He left right after it."

I left out the part where I begged him not to leave me alone, but I knew he could read it in my thoughts.

He reached out and cupped my cheek in his hand.

"I will never leave you alone again. I shouldn't have left the first time. I was just worried about me being dangerous to you. I didn't think it was dangerous for you without me by your side."

His eyes lingered on mine, and I thought I was going to explode. I wanted his touch so badly. He sat down then motioned for me to lie down on the blanket he had brought. I did as I was told and laid my head in his lap. My heart was thumping in my chest. He brushed my cheek with his hand to calm me. He reached for the jar, which was emptier than what I thought it would be.

"Are you ready?"

I nodded nervously, and he reached into the jar. He pulled a memory out, and I watched him crush it in his hands as Beelzebub had.

"I love you, Sophie."

He placed his hand on my forehead, and down the black hole I went.

This, by far, had to be the oldest memory I've recalled. The scenery was ancient in itself. I looked down at my hands and saw man hands. This isn't right. Why do I have man hands? I felt my chest and there were no breasts. I felt my crotch, and sure enough, there was an extra member there. I was standing in the middle of a field full of sheep and lambs. Am I a sheep farmer? Another young boy right around my age came sauntering up the field to me.

"Are you ready to choose which lamb is to be sacrificed?" he asked.

127

Sacrificed? Why am I sacrificing a lamb?

My voice deceived my questions, "Yes, Brother, and how about you? Have you harvested your best grains?"

He smiled and nodded.

"I hope Father will be pleased with our selections."

He threw his arm around my shoulder, and we walked down the hill to the tiny little cabin we lived in. Mother was ringing the dinner bell, and we needed to go eat before the celebration that night. The lamb I had chosen was tied to the house. We washed our hands in the bucket at the porch and proceeded through the door for dinner.

"At, at, did you boys wash your hands?" Mother asked.

She was so beautiful. She looked just as Lilith looked.

"Yes, ma'am, we did."

I was the one speaking to her.

"Alright, sit down and eat up. You have a celebration to attend to."

My brother and I sat and scarfed down all the food mother provided for us. We helped her pick up the dishes for the dishpan and headed outside. I ran for my lamb while my brother went for his grains. I couldn't even stop myself or look away as I slit the lamb's throat draining it of its blood. I then skinned it and cleaned it up nicely for the offering. I looked over at the altar we had set up, and it looked spectacular. It had a gourd full of food setting there. His spread looked amazing with freshly baked bread and freshly plucked fruits and vegetables.

"He is sure to love your offering, Brother."

He smiled back at me.

"It surely won't top your offering. He always loves the blood sacrifices."

Something about the way he said it nauseated both me and the memory me. My Brother rang the altar bell, and there was a loud, thunderous clap from the sky.

"My favorite young brothers. How are we today?"

That voice sounded so familiar!

"We come before you, Jehovah, and offer up to thee these gifts. I bring gifts of the Earth, by grain, and by salt, I offer up to thee my hard work."

This can't be the story I think it is.

"And I offer up to thee the first newborn of my flock," I said as I raised the meat and bowed my head.

I laid the meat on the stone table, and lightning struck igniting it.

"My decision has been made."

And then the voice was gone. No, it can't be!

"Of course, he would choose your offering, Abel, Father always does. What a wonderful, early birthday present."

That means he's Cain. He didn't look angry after Alpha had chosen my offering.

"It looks like a storm is coming, I will help you gather your sheep in the field."

No, no, don't go with him. My body didn't listen to me. It followed him automatically.

"You remember the creation story Mother and Father told us last year on your eighteenth birthday?"

This is not happening!

"Yes, Brother, it was a sad story for the Mother of Creation."

They herded the sheep down the hill.

"Abel?"

I turned around to look at Cain.

"Where is the Garden at?"

"I don't know what you're talking about, Cain. Your garden is right there beside the house. What Garden do you mean?"

Cain started to advance toward me.

"The Garden that was hidden from Jehovah, from our father, Alpha. The Garden only you know the location of. Where is it?"

Terror ran through me, and it was the terror of the moment.

"I don't know, Cain."

I stumbled backward and fell over a rock. The rock kicked up from the dirt as I tripped back on it. I hit my head, and it dizzied me. Cain was standing over top of me with the rock in hand.

"You have but one more chance, Brother. Where is the Garden!?"

I shook with terror. I already knew how this ended.

My voice answered, "I will never tell you where the Garden is."

Cain dropped his head as if I had failed a test. I felt and heard the sickening crack as he beat me with the rock. Everything went black.

My soul arrived at the summit, and I stood before Alpha.

"Why would you not give Lucifer the location of the Garden?"

Lucifer, that snake! He had betrayed me.

"I did not recognize Lucifer in the face of the young boy I grew up to call Brother. I thought it was one of the fallen ones, so I held back."

Alpha eyed me suspiciously. Lucifer stood by his throne with his head bowed in shame.

"Tell me, Lucifer, how do you feel tainting that young man's hands with blood? He loved his brother Abel. Because of you, he will be forever remembered as Cain, son of Adam, who murdered his brother."

Lucifer flinched at my words and stalked off.

"Throw her in the tower. It is time for the second part of her punishment."

Alpha flicked his fingers. Metatron and Beelzebub escorted me to the tower.

"I am sorry for this punishment, Sister. Maybe Father will not hold out with it as long as we think," Metatron spoke, looking into my eyes.

I knew he was part of the revolution to get our mother and fallen brothers and sisters back into the summit.

"Do not feel pity for her, Metatron. She made her decision when she committed the act of treason."

Beelzebub was always an ass.

"Before you lock the door, let me have a word with her alone."

It was Lucifer stalking up. He pushed me into the room and shut the door.

"How dare you speak to me the way you did in court."

He was pissed.

"You took the assignment of killing me. You, of all people! I thought I could trust you! But you are just part of their scheme."

I was furious. He grabbed me by the jowls, pushed me into the wall, and stared into my eyes.

"Don't forget who is on your side in this," he hissed.

He let go of my jowls, and I backed up to the tower wall.

"Are you allowed to come check on me?" I asked.

"I will be by every so often to make sure they don't harm you. I can't make promises, though."

CHAPTER 16

D own the Rabbit Hole

"HAVE you seen the white rabbit? The rabbit of purity and change? I fell down the rabbit hole once more and my fall chased him away. The colors twisted and changed, the swirling time I felt engulf me. How long until this feeling wears off and the white rabbit becomes the dream I chased away?"

IT ALWAYS SUCKED coming out of the rabbit hole. It felt like a drunken hangover. What was worse was the sense of paranoia that would wash over me. I had a heightened sense of fright when I came to this time that wasn't the paranoia's fault. I was alone in the cave. *Had they found us?* I peeked out the entrance of the cave, listening for signs of the angels. I didn't hear anything. I heard a flutter of wings and watched a figure descend. Their back was to me, but their wings were beautiful. The overcoat of feathers was black with the undercoat, a mixture of grey and black. They had a lustrous sparkle to them. When the person turned around, I was surprised who was standing there.

Incaendiel stood smiling at me, shirtless, in his true form. The silent question I had asked while we were barreling through the skies was answered. I knew exactly why he took on his true form as well. He had dropped his human form...so he could protect me. He motioned for me to come out of the cave. My eyes stayed glued to his body. He looked so different in his angelic form. Just as Metatron had been, he was toned and muscled in all the right places. His black hair seemed to shine in the night sky. As I got closer to him, his eyes were like a dark ocean gazing at me.

Every muscle in my body twitched and quaked under his gaze. My heart was beating faster than I had ever felt it beat without his touch. I felt like I had inhaled euphoria when he gazed at me. His touch sent waves instead of ripples through me. There was nothing more powerful than his touch to my skin. His lips touched mine, and I felt the Earth tremor beneath the exchange.

"Hello, beautiful," he murmured as he pulled back.

So, this was what it was like to kiss him in his true form. I could only imagine how it would feel when I was in my true form as well.

"Soon, your mortal body will melt away. You have been changing in leaps and bounds with your memories."

He stroked my hair with his hand.

"Even your hair has begun to change to the fiery, red hue it once was."

I glanced down at my hair. It had once been a dull mix between red and brown. The shine it had to it looked like magic.

I couldn't speak in his presence. It was so captivating and thrilling. I felt like I was looking at him for the first time.

"Is this what it was like when we were together before the fall?" I murmured, dazed, as he picked me up in his arms.

I felt his breath on my neck and felt like I could just pass out.

"Yes," he whispered.

It was a simple reply, but it flowed through me like warm water. He could sense that every word he spoke teased my humanity; it was written all over his face.

"This is just all too fun," he murmured through a grin.

He sat down and pulled me into his lap. He wrapped his arms around me, and it was the warmest feeling I've ever felt. I felt so loved, so protected. His eyes seemed so much brighter, staring down at me. No more worry or stress existed in them.

"So, what memory did you have this time?"

The words came out as if they were hymns of a lullaby. *I won't be able to focus around him like this.* I struggled to form my words.

"Did you know I was Abel?"

His eyes widened in surprise.

"We didn't even know Alpha sent you so soon, especially not as a boy," He contemplated on it. "This makes perfect sense. Who was it that was Cain?"

"Lucifer was given the task, as we had preplanned. Alpha was angry that I wouldn't give up the Garden to him. I told him I thought it was you all trying to pry it from me. I had to find a way to buy some time." I paused. "I believe that's when he started removing my memories."

His eyes went dark. I could tell he was thinking things over.

"Lucifer is one of us. He is not against us."

"It still doesn't mean I have to like him. He tried to betray one of his own Brothers by taking the very thing that keeps him alive."

His arms tightened around me. I loved the feel of it.

"I love you, Incaendiel. I don't tell you this enough. I can see why your faith in my love wavers, especially since I have betrayed you before."

He wouldn't look at me as I made my statement. I pulled his face to mine.

"I love you, my firefly."

His eyes sparkled, and he leaned in for a kiss.

We were interrupted by a voice. "I wondered if I would find you two here."

It was Lucifer. Not so great timing on his part. I could feel Incaendiel stiffen beneath me.

"Mother wanted to know how close you were to finishing the memories."

"Not sure, Cain. They don't come as easy as everyone thought they would."

I know my sarcasm bit into him.

"You knew what the agreement was when you stepped up to the plate."

He glared at me. I can't blame him. I had both of them wrapped around my finger at one point in time. Now, I felt like I had toyed with both of their hearts.

"Watch your tone, Brother. Do not forget whose side you fight on." Incaendiel didn't hide the venom as it fell from his tongue.

"I bet she hasn't even told you everything from her memories." His eyes were dark, but I could see the pain behind them.

"She told me everything. Why would you think she would hide it from me?"

Lucifer's eyes widened in surprise. I bet I would receive a memory about this one. I probably told him I would never speak of the affair.

"So, you agree that her safest bet would be to be with me?" Fire erupted around Incaendiel.

"Ah, so it's still a touchy subject with you," he sneered.

"Enough, you two." I couldn't believe how they were acting. I looked at Lucifer, "Especially you."

"You can't tell me the kiss we shared meant nothing to you." Oh boy. I put my hand up before Incaendiel even moved.

"Of course, it meant something to me. Yes, it tugged at a part that was buried in me."

I couldn't look over at Incaendiel's face. I could only imagine the look that sprawled across it.

"But that doesn't mean things haven't changed since I was reunited with Incaendiel. You knew what would happen when the time came."

"How about we make the decision easier for you."

Lucifer grinned wickedly at Incaendiel.

"We don't have to fight to prove our love to her. We don't have to fight to knock one another out of the ring. When the time comes, she will choose on her own the one she wishes to remain with."

I can't believe he said that.

"Incaendiel, I have already told you my choice. It's you!"

He looked over at me, and I could feel the pain in his eyes radiate through my body.

"As I said, when the time comes, you will choose the best road to take."

Did he know something I didn't? I wish my memories from when we were together would resurface.

"We were just about to start another memory from the jar. She doesn't have many more left. It seems for every single memory I give to her, another is sucked from the jar automatically."

"How many memories does she have left to receive?"

Lucifer looked over at me with what seemed like a nervous twitch.

"She has six left," Incaendiel replied. "These must be her actual angelic memories. She had her first memory of being mortal."

I sucked in a breath. I looked over at Lucifer, who still had worry written all over his face. Something was wrong; I could feel it. There was something he wasn't telling me, and he didn't want Incaendiel to find out about it.

We walked back into the cave, and I sat down on the blanket with Incaendiel.

He lifted another memory from the jar and asked me, "Are you ready for another one?"

I glanced at Lucifer as he shifted his weight from one foot to another.

"Yes."

He crushed the memory and touched my forehead.

I was in the tower. I sat against the wall crying. I was completely alone, and the pain of the loneliness tore through me. The door popped open, and Lucifer was thrown to the floor. My heart skipped a beat.

"I didn't know what they had done to you. I was afraid they had cast you out."

Lucifer was beaten and bleeding.

"Why did they beat you?!"

I ran to him and touched all the spots bleeding.

"They believe I'm in on the uprising against Father. They tried to beat the information out of me." He grinned wickedly. "They didn't get a thing from these lips."

I helped him walk over to the bed and sat him down.

"It's getting more and more dangerous. I don't know how much longer there is before they completely catch us in this charade."

I sat down beside him, and his hand touched mine.

"They will not find us out. Our mission will work."

He was always comforting. The room grew silent.

"Tomorrow, I will be sent back again to Earth."

He nodded. We had grown so close together. Will us being together have any effect on my love for Incaendiel? Was this the reason it hadn't worked yet? Was I growing farther away from him and closer to Lucifer? I truly did care for him. It wasn't a connection like I had with Incaendiel, but it was a connection. The silence between us grew and along came an awkward hush to the room.

I found Lucifer's hand on my face, followed by a kiss. During our last moments together, he wanted to show his love for me. Was this so I would choose to return with the others? Why wouldn't I return? The passion between us mounted and mounted. He was on top of me, kissing me all over with my body pulsating against his. He lifted me into his lap and layered my neck in kisses. It was the most intimate moment we had ever shared. There was passion behind our touches, passion behind the kisses. His hands roamed my back to my chest, and I dug my nails into his back.

As we both reached that final moment of bliss, a light burst from between us, knocking us off from one another. It was so bright we had to shield our eyes. When the light disappeared, we both stood and walked slowly back over to the bed. The sounds we heard terrified us both. Lying in the bed, wrapped in a blanket, was a beautiful little boy.

"Damian," I said as I picked him up.

I bolted upright with my vision coming into focus. I looked from Incaendiel to Lucifer, whose eyes dropped to the floor.

"What did you see?" Incaendiel peered at me.

I was breathing hard from fear. I didn't want to tell him. I couldn't tell him. I glanced at Lucifer. The look he had said I had to tell him. Everything in me screamed not to tell Incaendiel.

"I was in the tower." I stopped.

I can't do this. I stood up and ran from the cave. I opened my wings and took off into the sky. I didn't know if either one of them followed me, if they both did, or neither did.

I flew faster and faster. I whipped through the clouds with tears pouring from my eyes. *How could I have done that?* I have a son. I had a son, and he was at the summit. This was why Lucifer was fighting so hard for me. We have a baby together.

I landed on a mountaintop and plopped down. I felt so ashamed and guilty. The last few days didn't amount to what I felt right now. This was the ultimate betrayal. I couldn't tell him. I couldn't, but I knew I had to. There were footsteps behind me. I didn't turn to look to see which one of them it was. I felt like dirt. Actually, I felt lower than dirt.

"What did you see?" Incaendiel asked as he sat down beside me.

"Why did you follow me? You shouldn't have followed me!" I cried.

The guilt and pain surged through me.

"Whatever happened, whatever you two did, I forgive you. It doesn't matter now."

He touched my hand, and I jerked it away.

"It does matter because this I can't take back and just say sorry about it. I can't just look at you and tell you sorry for it."

I didn't even look at him. I just stared into the blackness below the mountain.

"Damian is your son, isn't he?" The question hammered into me. "I heard you murmur the name before you woke up. There was so much love and affection behind it. The kind of love only a mother can show her child."

He swallowed hard.

I broke down. "I'm so sorry." I cried in heaves.

He wrapped his arms around me. It didn't take the guilt from me. I would never be able to forgive myself for this one. *An affair was horrible enough, but a baby? A baby I can't even remember. Where is he? Is he okay? A mother should never forget having a baby.*

"I can see why Lucifer would be protective over you. You two share something that we do not."

I looked up at him as he sat there quietly. I could tell he was thinking about it.

"No! This does not mean I will choose him over you! It is my choice! No one else's!"

I tried to say it strongly, but it came out in blubbers.

"This isn't even about him or me any longer. It's about your baby. You can't abandon him."

Tears began to trickle from his eyes.

"Do you still love me?" I cried, dropping my head in my hands.

"Nothing can ever stop me from loving you. We will always love each other even if we can't be with each other."

He choked on the last few words.

"No! I will find a way. I will find a way to fix this! I swear! I can't leave you. I don't want to leave you! Don't you understand? When you fell, you took a part of my heart, a part of my light, a part of my soul! I'm not whole without you. That's why it would never work for Alpha. Even if they were to get out of me where the Garden was, even if I remembered that it lay within me, I couldn't give it to them. The only person I can give it to is you!"

The words came out before I could even think them. The words were true. Out of all the memories that had been plucked from my head, deep down, they couldn't find that one. They didn't know the secret my soul had, the secret both of our souls shared. We were created as One, and only as One will the Garden be brought to life.

"How many memories are left in the jar?"

I sniffed back the tears. I had cried so much that nothing else would come out.

"Four."

"Let's get them over with then."

I stood from the edge of the cliff and held my hand out for him. Every emotion ran through me with my gesture to him. A simple gesture, but right now, it meant the most. He looked at my hand and up into my eyes. My heart skipped around in grief. I knew he wasn't going to take it. A wave of anxiety rushed through me. His eyes locked onto mine, and I fought back the newfound tears that wanted to roll down my cheek. He reached out and took my hand.

CHAPTER 17

What is Love?

"IS it better to have loved and lost when both of the loves stand before you? One holds your heart in his hand while the other one holds your soul in his heart. How can you choose between love and destiny, when normally they're hand in hand? How can you choose between those you love, when both are good men...?"

WE ARRIVED BACK at the cave, and Lucifer was sitting beside the river. I was still full of so much shame and guilt that I couldn't even look at him. I walked into the cave, hoping my silence would make him leave. He remained by the edge of the river. I didn't know if he was expecting a showdown between Incaendiel and himself to unfold, but I knew Incaendiel wouldn't hurt him. The only person truly hurting in all this was Incaendiel. A selfless act for his brothers and sisters turned into a situation where he had lost me to another angel.

Right now, I wish Beelzebub had, in fact, killed me at the lake. A selfish note on my part, but this whole love thing sucked and was too much for an eighteen-year-old human to deal with. Even with an angelic soul, it was unbearable for me to think about what I was doing to both of them. Both of them loved me unconditionally. Deep down, I loved both of them as well. The bond Incaendiel shared with me was overpowering, but it didn't change the fact I had surrendered my heart to Lucifer while locked away in the tower. It was an act that resulted in another life form being created, a selfish act that swarmed my heart with betrayal, guilt, and shame.

My human mind pleaded with me. I couldn't take care of a baby. I didn't know how. I believed my angel self was different, but it was such a big pill to swallow. I just wanted to wither up and die. I didn't deserve to be at the summit. These actions were not angelic actions. I deserved to be in the dark for the rest of my days. Incaendiel would never let that happen, nor Lucifer. I felt that was the only result that would take away the despair I held within.

"You don't deserve anything running through your head."

Incaendiel touched my chin and lifted it to his face.

"Don't ever think about it again. You don't understand what you are wishing for yourself."

I knew he was right, but in a way, I knew otherwise as well. I walked over to the blanket, sat down, and eyed the bottle of memories. Four little balls remained in the jar. Four. I picked the jar up and stared inside it at the memories. If it hadn't been for Alpha, I would already know these things instead of having them thrust down my throat. That is the worst punishment that could have been planned. This was a punishment I, in fact, deserved most of all.

I reached inside the jar and plucked the four balls of light from within it. I stared down at my hand. I glared at the memories. Why they were so important to the entire situation was beyond me. It was my fault everyone was going through what they were right now. Both Lucifer's and Incaendiel's hearts were breaking because of me. They didn't know who

I would choose. Lucifer hoped it would be him. The funny thing is, Incaendiel hoped the same thing. I didn't want to leave my other half.

"What are you doing?" Incaendiel asked, sitting down beside me.

I looked at him. I couldn't think what I was going to do, or he would stop me. I crushed the memories in my hand.

"No!" he yelled.

It was too late. The black hole engulfed me, and the last four memories were going to be forced in me whether I wanted them or not.

I sat in a garden that was so enchanting and exhilarating. I had never before seen foliage or trees that grew in the manner that existed here. Incaendiel walked to my side and wrapped his arms around me.

"Father will be displeased if he finds us here in his beautiful haven for life."

I smiled at the thought of being chastised over such an innocent act.

"This place is so wondrous. Mother knows I came here. I asked permission." I looked over at him. "She knows you are here too."

I grinned at him. He planted his lips on mine, and the garden melted away from around me. I knew I would never feel what I felt in his arms, under his gaze, under his hands. He always touched me in ways that sent me into shock. He captivated my heart and soul.

All the angels had been created with a partner. Samael had Azazel, and I had my Incaendiel. Mother told me we were special. She had mixed us with an extra drop of love that no one would ever comprehend. Forever seemed like a minute to us in our time, and being together forever was always our intention. We could never get past the touches or the kisses. The magnetism that drew us in together was so strong, and the electricity frightened us both. We settled for just holding each other and emanating our love for one another.

Of course, all the other angels had their romances that went farther than just kissing. Some of them had produced creations from their love. We were afraid of what we would create together. We could feel the raw energy that poured through us both. Mother had told me it was the energy of the cosmos. She joked once, saying that we gave her and Father a run for their money. She was always eager to see what we would create.

The timing was never right in our hearts. Whenever we were frenzied together, one of us would always draw back. We were truly afraid of the power we held in each other's arms. Mother told me it was natural, and when we were truly ready, it would pass. I wished we were ready right now. I craved him for more than our passion. He had always pulled back more than me. It was understandable. He had power inside that he held back. I could feel it through our bond. This power had such magnitude,

141

and I could understand his fear of what it could do.

The other angels didn't understand what the worry was about. Samael and Azazel picked at us over our abstinence from one another.

"It is welcomed under the eyes of Mother and Father. Why hold back? You should be embracing it! It feels amazing!"

Azazel had always told me of her and Samael's relations. I envied their romance.

"It's just not the right time. We both have to be ready for the power."

She shook her head and giggled.

"If I didn't know any better, I would think you two are young lovers instead of the age you are."

Angels didn't age the way mortals did. For every 10,000 years, we gained a year. Since we were created by Mother and Father, we skipped a few thousand years of growth. All the angels had expressed their jealousy over us being together. They said Mother had favored us when she created us to be with one another. I never cared what they said. It was Incaendiel who took it to heart. Fighting in the summit was never allowed, but when we were sent to our charges on Earth, they always found a way to nitpick at him. Lucifer had always been the worst. Of course, he had Sophia, but she stepped away from him and decided to roam the Earth in search of herself. It broke his heart, and he took it out on Incaendiel.

I overheard him one day chastising him.

"You can't even be a real man and step up to the plate with her. Always pulling back at the last minute. She deserves an angel worthier of her love than you!"

"You will never understand my sacrifice for her, Brother. Just let me be."

He walked away from Lucifer.

"One day, Incaendiel, she will be taken from your arms. I can't guarantee whose arms she will end up in."

Incaendiel just walked away. He never looked back or retorted to the comment. I found him later at the fountain of bliss. His eyes were always dark until I walked near him. They always lit up like the morning sun.

"There you are, my firefly. I have been looking everywhere for you."

I leaned in and kissed his lips. His eyes fluttered closed like butterfly wings.

"Come, let's take a walk through the garden. Mother granted me permission again."

The garden was always our escape from the other angels. This is one reason why they say we were their favorites. We were the only ones given the allowance to walk through it. We held each other's hands as we roamed the rolling hills and valleys. There was such sheer beauty here. I knew if we were to ever share a moment like the others, it would be within the Garden of Eden.

I dropped his hand and ran from him, laughing. He always enjoyed the cat and mouse game. I had gained quite a bit of distance between us when I looked back. He was gone. I turned around in time, enough for him to land in front of me, wings open, and for him to close his arms around me.

"Caught you," he whispered into my ear.

"You always cheat!" I giggled.

"You know you love it when I do," he murmured, putting his chin on my forehead.

We stood there embracing. It was moments like these I knew I would never forget. I could never forget the love that radiated between us. Even if my memories were to be erased, I knew that he would be the only one to ever hold my heart in his hand.

"I love you, my firefly."

The garden melted away, and I was staring over the side of the summit. The pain tore through my chest like none other I had ever felt. I stood and watched his wings turn from the lustrous, silvery-white we both shared into dark gray and black. His light began to slowly fade from his body and was replaced by a dull hue like that of the mortals on Earth. My Incaendiel, my firefly, had fallen with the rest because I had asked him to.

It felt like a selfless gesture. I fully intended to help them all come back to the light. The vision I had showed me we would succeed in it. Lucifer walked up beside me and whispered in my ear, "He will never return." I turned to him, and my fury flew through my eyes.

"Don't EVER say that to me again," I hissed at him. "You don't know what I do."

His eyes narrowed at me. I turned away from him and continued to watch Incaendiel descend until I didn't see him any longer.

"Do you care to enlighten me on your affirmation?" he asked.

"How do I know I can trust you?"

My eyes burned into his, daring him to buck at me.

"Because right now, I'm the only person you have."

His words cut me like a knife. He was right. The only other people I could have told had fallen as well.

"What I will tell you is treason. If you get caught up in the plan, you

will be punished as well. Do you understand?"

He smiled at me.

"Like you said, IF I get caught."

I fought with myself on the inside on whether I could really trust him or not. I caved and told him everything. He listened to my vision in its entirety, and I explained how Incaendiel fell to make the vision come true.

"If what you say is true, we have much work that needs to be done. We will plan out a strategy and gather as many angels as we can for the cause."

My eyes widened.

"As discreetly as we can, I might add."

I thought everything over.

"Once you have everyone you can find in on it, you have to go to Father and report the treason you have found. You have to turn me over to him."

"He will lock you away in the tower, and then it will never work."

He shook his head against the idea.

"The plan will work. My punishment is going to be what brings our brothers and sisters back home. You must trust me on this."

He sighed and looked at me. The look in his eyes disagreed with everything I was proposing.

"Ok, I will go to him once he returns from the Garden. Mother requested his presence not long ago."

Lucifer's face dissolved from my view, and I was shackled to a wall. There was enough chain for me to scoot close enough to the window to see what was happening outside of the stone walls. Metatron and Lucifer sat talking quietly amongst themselves, occasionally glancing up at me in the tower. They must be talking the plan over between themselves. They stood from their seats, and the door in front of me opened.

"Your first round on Earth is starting. I will be sent along with you to possess the body of your brother. My actions will not be accountable for whatever happens while we are on Earth."

Lucifer stood before me with Metatron at his side.

"Who are we going to be?" I asked, looking between the two of them.

"Father has a raw sense of humor right now. He is sending us to be the sons of Adam and Eve. He hopes sending you as a boy will throw the others off the scent. If they find out, he hopes it will piss Mother off to a boiling point. He said she brought it upon herself."

Lucifer shook his head in disgust.

"When are we leaving the summit?" I asked.

"We will be leaving in a few moments. I thought it best to clue you in on what's going on before you're thrust into the middle of it." Lucifer looked at me. "Are you sure you are ready for this?"

I was silent for a moment.

"Whatever brings them back, whatever I have to do to succeed in that, you have no doubt I will do it."

I had never been so sure in my life. I can't believe how, over the years, they broke me down, broke my soul down. I was so strong and sure of myself then. Now, I was weak and crumpled. Incaendiel was right, not for himself, but regarding me as well. I couldn't have lasted another thousand years in that tower. They would have completely broken me then.

The chains faded away, but the tower remained. In my arms, I was holding a baby. He was the most beautiful sight I had ever seen. He wrapped his hand around my finger, and my heart broke. Everything I had wanted and craved with Incaendiel lay in my arms, and he didn't get to share it with me. I felt guilty and ashamed of the baby, but it couldn't break my love for the life I had created.

Lucifer had walked to the other side of the room and sat. I had no clue what was running through his mind. I knew he loved me, but he knew that I was to be with Incaendiel in the end. The baby changes everything now. I want my firefly, but how can I just leave this beautiful baby behind? It was a decision I couldn't make, and it needed to be made. I held him and kissed his head. He cooed in my arms, and it brought tears to my eyes.

The tower door swung open, and Metatron walked in with a look of despair written across his face. I knew what he wanted before the words left his mouth.

"No!"

I held the baby away from him. He wasn't going to take him. He was mine!

"I'm sorry, Sophie. Alpha gave the order."

He walked toward me.

"No, you can't have him! I won't let you take him!" My eyes pleaded with Metatron. "Lucifer, do something!" Lucifer didn't move. He sat facing the same wall he had been staring at for hours.

Metatron advanced forward and gently took the baby from my arms. "I will make sure he stays safe. You have my word. I promise no harm will come to him. My soldiers will assure that."

He looked from me down to the baby.

"What did you name him?"

"Damian," Lucifer *answered without removing his eyes from the wall.*

Metatron's eyes met mine, with tears falling from them. He turned around and shut the door. I ran to the door and pounded on it. I cried my eyes out.

"Why didn't you do anything!? You just let him take him!"

I was broken and mad.

"You should've known they wouldn't let us keep him in here."

His voice was solemn and mute.

"You could have still stopped him from taking him! You could've fought for our son! Instead, you just sat there and let him tear him from my arms!"

Lucifer flew up from his seat and pinned me to the wall.

"You keep blaming me as if it's my fault. All this is your fault! You and your precious demon! "

"You will never amount to the man that Incaendiel is! You are nowhere near the angel is he is!"

"Well, how about I just take care of him for the rest of us?! How about I just take him completely out of the picture?! Father would be pleased with the notion, and then you can stop acting like such a selfish brat!"

He pounded his fist at the wall beside my head.

"I hate you!" I screamed.

As soon as I uttered the words, everything went black.

CHAPTER 18

F_irefly_

"*I WALK in the shadows craving the light of truth and when dawn emerges, my inner demons shall die and my immortal soul will be lifted into the infinite unknown to start again with wisdom gained from the dark crevices of life unfolded in the pages of flesh and lament. I am a phoenix of the Black dawn and soon I will soar high with wings of rebirth as Ashe dwindles from my enlightened emanation of truth and understanding.*"

"YOU LET her crush all four of them!"

Lucifer was fuming.

"I didn't know what she was going to do! She didn't think it!"

Like he had any right to talk to me in such a tone. I knelt over her body as she convulsed. Foam ran from her mouth. Blood poured from her nose. Her body finally fell still. Her breathing slowed, and the memories took. I breathed out a breath of relief.

I looked up to Lucifer, whose worried eyes calmed over.

"We need to talk," I said to him.

"Talk about what?"

The guilt written on his face didn't make me feel much better than I did.

"She needs to go with you. She needs to return to the summit before the portal closes."

Lucifer's face dropped.

"Why can't you bring her through the portal?"

"I can't come with you all."

He looked solemnly at me.

"Why can't you return with us, Brother? Are you damning yourself here? None of this was your fault! All that happened was part of a scheme." He bit his lip. "Well, almost everything. You must return with us."

"I can't. It's not a choice of mine. It's just what it is." I took a deep breath in. "There is darkness in my heart."

Lucifer slid to the ground against the cave wall in disbelief.

"I am no longer a child of the light. I will always be a starchild. It's not that the darkness won and overtook me. I have always had darkness in my heart. Falling from the light only made it completely overtake my heart. I'm not like the others where it engulfed my soul. I was born with it. However, the light will never return to me like it will everyone else."

I looked over at Sophie lying on the ground.

"I don't have the heart to tell her. I'm waiting until the last minute, and once she goes through, I'm closing the portal."

"There is nothing Mother can do to help?"

Lucifer was grief-stricken. It finally sank in the real sacrifice I gave when I fell.

"No, we have already spoken of it. The light of mine everyone was afraid of the darkness engulfing wasn't my angelic light."

I looked over at Sophie and back at Lucifer.

"It's hers."

His eyes met mine, and he understood what I was telling him.

"You have to promise me that when I give you her hand, you will never hurt her again. You will never let anyone hurt her again, and you make sure she never steps foot back into that tower."

"I thought you said, in the end, it would be her choice."

Lucifer looked over at her. His eyes were full of doubt.

"She would never allow it."

"She must return with you. She will die here. If she is left behind, the darkness will subdue her, but she won't be like me. She will be like the others that the darkness took."

I walked over to him and made him look me in the eyes.

"You two have a family to take care of. There are more important things than me. You must make her see the truth in that. Damian deserves to have his mother. He deserves to have a happy life, not to be caught in the middle of this catastrophe were all in."

"No one will ever understand how you truly are an angel of high authority. I used to be one of those angels. I know I treated you horribly in the summit. Sophie...she opened my eyes to what your true nature is. Even without a rank, you still make decisions based on everyone as a whole. I am honored to have flown with you as your brother. I swear to you, I will never stop searching for a way for you to return to the summit."

I knew it was an impossible task, but I knew what his word meant as well. I nodded at him.

"Well, isn't that touching?" Beelzebub stepped to the entrance of the cave. "Brothers bonding over the whore they share, the whore everyone shared." He snickered.

We both jumped up and stepped in front of Sophie, still unconscious on the ground.

"Aw, such sentiment. Both of you protecting the love of your life, not knowing if she loves either of you back."

Lucifer ran to her side while I stood in front of Beelzebub.

"Remember what I told you earlier?" I asked Lucifer.

He looked at me, puzzled.

"You take her hand; you protect her with your life!"

He nodded. I tackled Beelzebub to the ground. Lucifer scooped Sophie in his arms and darted from the cave. I watched him spread his wings, and he was gone within seconds.

"Letting your wife go with the angel she was sneaking around with; you are a brain teaser."

Beelzebub and I circled each other in the cave.

"I've wanted this showdown since they told me what you did to our brothers at the lake. They call you selfless when you murdered your own blood!"

"It had to be done. They got their strike in."

I narrowed my eyes, glaring at him.

"Yes, but it wasn't successful, for here you are now."

He returned the glare.

"Oh, it was successful, alright. You are just misinformed about the power I share with my mate. It was she who brought me back from the battlefields of death!"

He scowled at me.

"All the more reason to kill her and be done with everything. Screw the Garden! This entire ploy has been nonsense that Father should have realized millenniums ago." He sneered at me. "Since she has been whisked away, I guess your death will have to substitute. I hope you made your peace with her." He lunged at me, and I stepped aside, darting from the cave.

Once I was out in the open, I opened my wings under the power of the moon. Darkness was always my ally. It had always empowered me. I thrust my hands in the air and clenched my fists. Beelzebub ran to me, and I brought my arms down. I bared down with all my might, forcing my power to come to the surface. I was engulfed in flames. She had always called me firefly, her pet name for me. My powers were limited in the summit. I needed the dark to bring my powers to full strength. Once I fell, my powers were uncontrollable. I learned to tame them under Mother's guidance.

When Beelzebub saw the fire surrounding me, he tried to stop in his tracks but slid and landed on his behind. He scrambled backward.

"Your eyes. Your eyes are even flames!"

This was the first time I brought my power to full strength. I was always afraid of it, afraid of the dark consuming me, making me evil. I now fully embraced my true self. I will always be a child of darkness seeking the light. This will always be my true nature. I glared at Beelzebub. The anger that flew through me was replenishing. I remember the fear, the panic, and the agony he had put Sophie through while he forced her memories into her. The terror she had when he stripped her naked and touched what didn't belong to him. How he could do that to a human, whether she had an angelic soul or not, was beyond forgiveness.

The voice I heard next I didn't even recognize as it trailed from my lips.

"You will return to Alpha. You will tell him that you all have failed. They will return to the summit. If he sends more of you, they will die. Anyone who opposes me will die! I am the true Adversary of Alpha. Heed my warning and go!"

He scrambled to his feet and took off into the night sky. The power that surged through me felt freeing. I had been holding it in for so long, afraid that I would never see the light because of it. Well, now, it is written in stone and has been for a while. I will walk through the darkness and embrace it fully. I am not evil. I am not disgraceful. I am a starchild of darkness sent to make everything right again. I am the balance of power needed in the world. I am the Firefly of Immortality.

I turned around as he disappeared from my sight. Behind me stood Samael, Azazel, and Lucifer, with a good bit of distance between us. Samael and Azazel were stricken with fear. It was written all over their faces. Lucifer, however, his eyes weren't filled with fear, but rather it looked like envy. He bowed to me.

"I am at your will, Incaendiel."

I returned the gesture and nodded in compliance. I let my shield of fire drop and released the energy I had held for power. Samael stepped forward tentatively.

"Do you believe he will return?"

I had no answer for him.

"Beelzebub will indeed return, but against his will. You scared the hell out of him just now, but Alpha will make him fight for his side of the cause..."

Lucifer walked to me, and I knew what he was going to say before the words fell from his mouth.

"The war has now started."

CHAPTER 19

H ell Hath no Fury like a Promise Broken

"PROMISE...SUCH a word shouldn't exist. A common falsehood of pretentious hope that what is said will be accomplished. Promise...a word that can bring empires to their knees. The easiest thing to do and say, is to promise so happiness will forever stay. But once that promise is noticed, and the words have been broken, the reaction of fury...should've been known to raise hell."

WHEN I CAME TOO, I was back in the Glade. Metatron and Michael stood guard by the door. *Where the hell was Incaendiel and Lucifer? Why was I here and not in the cave?* My head thumped as I sat up from the bed. I expected blood to gush from my nose, but as I wiped away at it and looked, my hand was clean. That was not what surprised me, however. My hands had a shine to them. I raised the sleeve of my shirt, and my whole entire arm was glowing white. My hair was a fiery red and two feet longer than what I usually kept it cut.

"What the hell happened? Why am I glowing? Where are Lucifer and Incaendiel at?" Metatron and Michael stared at me. "Tell me!"

"Beelzebub attacked while you were unconscious. Lucifer showed up here with you, asking us to guard you. He took Samael and Azazel with him back to help Incaendiel."

Michael was the one who responded. His eyes still hadn't moved from my body.

"Have you heard anything from them?"

Terror flew through me. *How did Beelzebub get loose?*

"No, they haven't returned yet."

My eyes darted back and forth between them as I was thinking everything through.

"Should we go see if they are okay?"

My eyes trained on Metatron.

"They told us to make sure we didn't leave the Glade, let you leave, or leave you here."

Typical. My mind flashed back to the memories I just received, and I looked at Metatron again.

"Where is Damian, Metatron?"

His face went white. He hadn't expected me to ask about Damian. He had been caught completely off guard by the question.

"You told me you would keep him safe, yet here you are without him. You told me you would ensure the soldiers who followed you would keep him safe, yet they came with you."

His face twitched nervously.

"Where is he?"

I watched him swallow, fighting back the urge to answer. I lost my cool.

"Where is he?!"

"Alpha has him."

My blood boiled, and a fire went through my body.

"You promised me he'd stay safe, and you handed him over to the tyrant who locked me in the tower!"

I walked slowly toward Metatron. His eyes were trained on me and full of fear. I had never seen him frightened before

"He showed up right as I closed the tower door. I had no choice, Sophie. I'm sorry. I'm sorry!"

The rage that coursed through me I had never felt before. It was millions of years of pent-up rage. I knew I was taking it out on the wrong person, but there was no way I could take it out on the one I needed to.

"You betrayed your loyalty to me! I entrusted my son to you!"

Metatron and Michael both stepped back one foot at a time with their hands raised in a calming manner.

"Why should I trust you now?!"

"Sophie, calm down."

The words tore through me like a knife. I whipped around, and Incaendiel stood behind me.

"He gave him to Alpha!" I screamed.

Lucifer stood in the corner wide-eyed. Samael and Azazel stood next to him, glancing at each other.

"I promise you, with every fabric of my being, you will get him back."

Incaendiel walked closer while everyone else kept their distance. *Why were they so afraid? They were all more powerful than me.*

"Take a deep breath and relax."

"How?! How can I relax, right?! Why should I!?" I hissed at him.

I was placing my anger at him, wrong, I know, but he was getting in the way of the perpetrator who deserved punishment.

"You will set fire to the Glade if you don't calm down!"

He advanced another step.

"What are you talking about?!"

He was insane. I couldn't set fire to anything.

"Look down at your hands."

He motioned for me to look.

"I already know they glow!"

I was irate. *How dare he mock my pain at this moment?*

"No, they're on fire."

What? I looked down, and I was filled with shock and dread. Everything I could see that was a part of me radiated flames.

"What?" I breathed out.

Panic shot through me. *How was this possible?*

"Apparently, I'm not the only firebug."

He meant it as a light joke, but it didn't make anything better.

"How...how do I get it to stop!?"

I was panicking. My panic only made the fire grow. I felt like I was going to have an anxiety attack or explode.

"You have to calm down."

He stepped toward me again.

"Stop! I don't want you to get hurt!"

I backed away and watched Metatron and Michael run to the side of the room where the others stood. Incaendiel was now directly between them and me.

"You can't hurt me, Sophie."

He stepped closer again.

"Please, stop! I will hurt you; I know it! Everything I touch turns to shit!"

I stepped back again. This time, he took two large steps and was in front of me. He threw his arms around me, and I could see the fire begin to burn him. He let out a groan of pain, but he didn't turn me loose.

"Incaendiel, stop! It'll kill you!"

He held on to me, the flames burning his skin.

The next thing I knew, we were in the lake. He held me beneath the water as it began to boil slightly. He didn't release me, even as the pain seared through him. Finally, the fire went out, and we burst to the surface of the lake.

"What the hell?!" I screamed.

I was confused and terrified.

"How can I do that? I don't understand!"

He pulled me to the edge of the lake, helping me out. My clothes were soaked from the water, and they felt like they weighed a ton. He collapsed where the lake water met the bank.

"You share the same power I do."

He heaved gasps in and out.

"Is this the power we were both so afraid of? Why we would never..." I trailed off in shock.

He nodded.

"So, what does this mean? What does all this mean?"

I was absolutely miserable, frightened, angry, and bitter; all the emotions that one would go through at this point hit me. The emotions were overwhelming, and I began to cry again. I had never in my life cried this much in such a brief time span.

"What do we do, Incaendiel? Alpha has Damian...he has my son!"

"We need to find out what he has been doing with him while you have been here on Earth."

Incaendiel sat up and grimaced. His skin was still slightly burned but was rapidly healing.

"Another thing we need to find out is what Lucifer knows about Damian."

I hadn't even thought of that. He just got out of the tower. *Why didn't he demand for our son back? Why didn't he try to take him from Alpha?*

"Oh, also, congratulations."

He smiled at me.

"What in the world are you congratulating me for?"

"You're completely restored to your true self. You are now one hundred percent angel, with your light and all. How does it feel?"

He grinned at me.

"It feels...different. It still feels like it's not my life like I'm watching it at a movie theater."

"It will come together for you in the end."

I sat down beside him, and he draped his arm around my shoulders, pulling me in closer to him. Even through the sheer exhaustion, I could feel the intense craving my body had for his. The body that truly had waited millions of years to touch him again.

"So... what now?"

He tensed up to my question. He knew what I was asking about. *Sheesh, I can't hide anything from this man.*

"We have to come up with a strategy. Alpha is mobilizing an army of soldiers to keep them from coming through the portal. Once it's open, we have to get mother through and then you."

"No, I want to help."

He stood up and paced.

"Sophie, you can't help! You could get hurt! You must make it through and find Damian. He's more important than this fight."

"Why do you always have to tell me what to do? You need me, Incaendiel. Our power together will take them out."

"I have to make sure everyone gets through that portal. Once everyone receives their light back, they can protect themselves better. This is the only way. That child needs his mother. Do you want him to spend the rest of his days with Alpha!?"

He was right. There was no use in arguing. *He was so stubborn!* He laughed.

"I'm the stubborn one?"

He held his hand out to me to stand.

"Come on, let's go back to the Glade."

I grabbed his hand, and he pulled me up.

"Everyone is going to be mad."

"Trust me. No one is going to be mad. Scared of you, yes, but mad? How can they be?"

Everyone was grouped together when we blinked back to the Glade. Incaendiel made his way to the front, towing me behind him. Everyone parted and stepped back as we passed. Lucifer stood at the front with Metatron, Michael, Sam, and Azazel. Mother stood with them as they talked in hushed tones. They glanced up and were a bit surprised to see us.

"Everything...good now?" Lucifer asked.

Incaendiel nodded.

"Good. We've been discussing what to do."

Lucifer nodded toward Metatron.

"Right, well, this is how everything is going to pan out. Alpha has prepared the warrior angels for this cause for years. They will be waiting at the portal opening for the moment it opens. They're supposed to rush it as soon as it opens, making it impossible for anyone to get through. Once they are through, they are supposed to take out Incaendiel to ensure it closes back and end the whole thing before it begins."

Metatron glanced between the groups of eyes.

"Well, what do you propose we do?" Incaendiel asked.

"We strike at a time they are least expecting," Michael chimed in. "The element of surprise is the only thing that will get as many of us through before they attack."

"And what is the time they are least expecting?" I asked.

"Now," Michael replied. "They expect us to wait until morning to let Sophie's memories sink in or whatever. They don't expect us to open it tonight."

Now, I was nervous. I looked over at Incaendiel as he went deep into thought.

"Are you sure they won't be expecting us right now?"

Incaendiel looked between Metatron and Michael.

"Oh, they are sure," Lucifer replied.

"How do you know?" I asked.

"I've seen both instances out. If we strike now, no one is waiting, but if we wait, they will be prepared."

I breathed in deeply. I didn't know if I was ready or not, but now I didn't have a choice. I felt a hand slip into mine and squeeze it. I didn't have to look to know whose it was. I was awkward to stand in the middle of a group that knew once we left this circle, we were going to go have sex. I felt my cheeks flush just thinking about the word.

Without warning, Incaendiel blinked us to the top of the mountain. It was relieving that there were no awkward good luck or anything like that. In the back of my mind, I was replaying the lake over in my head. I passed out, so I didn't know exactly what Beelzebub had done to my body.

"Are you sure this will work?" I asked.

Incaendiel stepped closer to me. He rubbed his thumb along my cheek while cupping it in his hand.

"What they did to you...what they did will not affect anything. It has nothing to do with virginity or anything like that."

He ran his hand into my hair and pulled me in for a kiss. I pulled away. I was a nervous wreck.

"Sophie, it will be ok. No one is spying on us. We have complete privacy here."

This time, I didn't fight him as he pulled me in closer for that kiss. His lips brushed mine, and it felt like time stopped. Everything went silent around us. There was no wind, no animal noises. He ran his hand up my back while I wrapped my arms around him. He gently removed the shirt I was wearing, and I could feel his hands shake on top of my skin. Electric shocks bounced from him to me as he pulled me in again to kiss.

I began to unbuckle his pants when he pulled away. We had never gotten this far before, and he was just as nervous as me. Without hesitation, I pulled him back to me, kissing his chest. I could feel the shivers running through his body. I finished unzipping his pants, and he removed them. He used his wings to shield himself from my eyes. I realized then that we had never been naked in front of each other before.

He walked to me and grabbed my hips. He began kissing my neck and unzipping the pants I wore. It was me this time that pulled away, but he pulled me right back. He slipped my pants down, kissing my stomach as he pulled them down. He stood upright and lifted me from my feet. His wings moved aside, and he pulled me to his body. I could feel his wings wrapping around my body like a cocoon as he kissed my lips.

I shivered. My naked body was flat against his. I could feel everything, his muscles flexing, everything! He slipped his tongue in my mouth, and I became hot and frenzied. I pulled him to me as if our bodies weren't close enough. He picked me up off of my feet, and I wrapped my legs around him. This was it. This was the moment I had waited millions of years for. I didn't think our bodies could be any closer while moving in unison.

"I love you," I whispered.

The light exploded around us in brilliant colors. I was finally his, and he was finally mine.

CHAPTER 20

Moment Lasts a Lifetime

A "*I HELD a moment in my hand, the kind that lasts forever. I held that moment tightly so it wouldn't fall away. I held that moment to my heart where forever it would stay. That moment began to falter, that moment began to fall away. But it fell into a heart, where I know it will always remain.*"

THE POWER from the portal being opened was exhilarating, and it sent a rumble down through the mountain. I opened my eyes, and our bodies lay entangled together on the grass. I looked around and saw the same foliage as I had in my memories when we were in the Garden. I didn't want to stop. The feeling we shared at this moment was so intense. He finally pulled me away from his body and caressed my face. He kissed me, and everything melted away. We rushed, putting our clothes back on so no one would see us nude. Within seconds, everyone was out from within the Glade and flying in the sky. We stood in front of the portal, peering in, but we couldn't see through to the other side. Mother walked up to us, followed by the top in command.

"Is it safe?" she asked.

"We can't see in. We don't know what is waiting for us on the other side."

Incaendiel looked grave.

"I will fly in and see if the coast is clear," Sam said.

Everyone stepped back from the portal as he walked up to it. He was hesitant and nervous. He clenched and unclenched his fists, and beads of sweat rolled down his face. He inhaled his breath and disappeared through the opening. We waited. Minutes felt like hours while we awaited his return back through the gateway. Everyone was growing antsy after five minutes had passed.

"I'm going in after him," Azazel said.

Just as she was about to step through, Sam came barreling out of the portal, landing on his stomach. He fell limp against the ground. Azazel ran to his side.

"Samael!"

He didn't move. She flipped him over, and he groaned. We all sighed with relief.

"What happened?!" she cried, checking him over.

"They know we're coming," he uttered before he passed back out.

"Everyone! Prepare to be ambushed. They have found out the plan!" Metatron yelled.

The flyers in the sky paired off and swarmed closer around the top of the mountain where the gates to the Garden sat open.

Incaendiel pulled me behind him along with Mother.

"You two stay behind me and stay together."

His orders belted out in a voice I had never heard. He looked to the sky as the moon came from behind the clouds that stretched across the valley.

"Back up!" he barked out.

Everyone moved away from him. Lucifer pulled Mother and me farther away. I heard a menacing groan echo throughout the valley. I watched as Incaendiel bared down and erupted into flames.

No sooner had he brought his power forth than an angel popped through the portal to challenge him. I recognized him immediately, Beelzebub. You could tell by the look on his face that he was forced to be here.

"Beelzebub, I see your father doesn't care about the warning you delivered for me."

Incaendiel had a sadistic smile splattered on his face. It sent a cold chill down my spine.

"I must do what I'm told, Brother." Beelzebub was holding a sword, pointing it at Incaendiel shakily.

"And I must do what's right."

There were no more words. Beelzebub lunged at Incaendiel, who gracefully moved away from the point of the sword. His hands came down hard on the back of Beelzebub. He hit the ground and rolled away to get back on his feet. He flew up into the sky, and Incaendiel took off after him. We watched as we saw a swarm of flies engulf Incaendiel, but they burst into flames as he erupted a fireball from his body. He was at Beelzebub's throat, choking him and then knocked the sword from his hands. It fell to the ground in front of me, and I grabbed it up. The two came careening back down to the ground, with Incaendiel holding him in a chokehold from behind.

When they hit, the mountain trembled from the impact. Incaendiel held him down with his foot and grabbed both wings. He ripped one of his wings from his back as Beelzebub howled in pain. He tore the other wing off, tossed them both down, and motioned for the sword. I walked it over and handed it to him. I stood frozen as I watched him lift the sword into the sky, and just as he was about to plunge it through Beelzebub's back, he blinked away. Incaendiel tossed the sword into the dirt.

The portal erupted with angels. Lightning flashed through the sky. The battle began. Incaendiel took off into the sky with the others following. Lucifer had dragged Samael's body beside us and stood in front of us all as the warriors pelted out balls of light. I closed my eyes and braced for the blows. When I felt nothing, I opened my eyes back up and gasped in surprise. Lucifer had encased us in a shield of light. I didn't even know he could do that. It was impenetrable. Nothing, and no one could enter it. I watched as he fought the angels that stood at the portal. My heart fluttered in panic. There was no one there to help him. I went to leave the shield when Mother grabbed my arm.

"If you get hurt or die, this will have all been in vain."

Her eyes looked through me, deep into me. She must have seen all she needed to see because she let my arm go.

"This is your choice."

I nodded and picked up the sword Incaendiel had dropped to the ground. I left the shield just as one of the angels shoved a sword through Lucifer's leg. Rage erupted through me. I ran toward them, feeding off the rage boiling under my skin, the rage that was placed correctly now. I raised my hand, and a wall fire shot up around them. It distracted them long enough for me to reach Lucifer. As the wall went out, I raised the sword, swiping it through the air. It caught one of them in their midsection, cutting them in half. The other one brought their sword down on me. I raised my hand, and it melted as it hit the flames that surrounded my body. I swung my sword, which was now flaming at the blade and severed their head clean off. Lucifer lay on the ground, holding his leg as he howled in pain. The sword was still jammed through his thigh. I knelt beside him and tried to touch it.

"NO!" he screamed, trying to roll away from my hand.

"I have to pull it out!"

I tried to reach for it again, and he smacked my hand away.

"Quit acting like a two-year-old!"

This time, I grabbed the sword before he could protest and ripped it from his leg. His scream was louder, and his leg poured blood. I placed my hands on the entry and exit wounds. I brought forth the fire into my hands, searing the wounds to stop the bleeding. I tore a piece of my shirt away and wrapped it around the bleeding hole. He had nearly passed out from the pain.

"How can I protect you if I can't protect myself," he said, stroking my face.

"Well, I guess I will have to protect you this time."

He leaned up and kissed me. I didn't stop him or pull back. I just lingered in the moment, lost. I didn't know what was right or wrong anymore. A part of me wished Incaendiel would fight for me; another part of me knew he wouldn't. I know I felt some form of love for Lucifer, but I desperately needed to be with my other half. I gently pulled away with tears in my eyes, about to tell Lucifer how I felt when we heard a shout from the sky.

"The portal is clear! Go!"

The flying fleet of men who had battled their brothers to make it through the portal rushed the gateway. Azazel and Mother picked Sam up underneath his arms and struggled to get over to the opening. I watched as they walked through with the thousands of others flying in past them. Metatron and Michael swooped down and lifted Lucifer to his feet. They walked him closer and closer to the portal. Incaendiel landed behind me.

"Go!" he shouted at me.

"No, I'm staying with you! I choose you!"

He ran up to me, picked me up in his arms, and kissed me long and hard. I then felt myself put back down on the ground, and a hand grabbed mine.

"Remember what I said, Lucifer!?" he yelled out.

"What?! No! Incaendiel, no, please."

I tried to get loose from the hand that had me, but it had a firm hold.

"I love you, Sophie!" Incaendiel yelled, stepping back as Lucifer dragged me to him, pulling me through the portal.

I struggled and kicked, trying to free his hold on me. We made it through. I looked at Incaendiel and saw the pain in his face for the sacrifice he was giving up.

"I love you, too, my firefly."

The gateway closed, and I watched Incaendiel disappear from my sight.

"No!!"

I dropped to my knees, crying. *Why hadn't he come? Why did he make me go?* I felt Lucifer's arms around me, and I smacked them away. I felt like I was dying on the inside. I heard the moans and groans from everyone around me as they fell to their knees in pain, my pain. Everything crashed around me. My heart ripped in two. I would have stayed with him; he knew that. *Why did he choose for me to go? It was my choice. Mine! It was no one's choice but mine!* I sat there for what seemed like forever, with my head buried in my hands. The angels around me thudded to the ground, screaming from the heartache that tore through their chests. I felt like giving up. I had surrendered my heart to one person, and he didn't make it through the portal.

I heard a whimper and lifted my head. Lying before me on the ground was a beautiful baby boy. He had dark hair and the most beautiful eyes in the world. I picked him up in my arms and buried my face into him, crying. The one thing I had always wanted with Incaendiel was now in my arms and without his father.

"Alpha made off before we could make it to the gates. For now, the summit is ours," Metatron said as those around me gathered to listen.

"And what about Damian?" I asked, looking up at him from the boy in my arms, with tears still streaming from my eyes. "Where is he?"

Everyone remained silent.

"He...I'm afraid he took him with him."

Metatron bowed his head. His promise to me years ago was lost in the wind.

"I am sorry, Sophie."

I stood up with my little man in my arms.

"I will search to the ends of the universe for my son."

I looked down at the little boy sleeping in my arms.

"He has a brother that needs him and a mother that needs him."

I looked up to Lucifer.

"A father that needs him to complete his family."

A tear rolled down his face. I assumed that he already knew he had been my second choice, a forced choice.

Mother held her hands out to hold the baby. I gently placed him over into her arms.

"He's so precious. He looks just like him." She smiled down at the baby, and a single tear rolled from her eyes that she quickly wiped away. Everyone was hurting over him staying, not just me.

"What are you going to call him?"

She looked up at me.

"Xavier."

EPILOGUE

The Darkness Succumbs

"THE DARK finally found a way to creep into my soul. Darkness is all I know; darkness is all I feel. The dark was unbearable, breaking me into pieces. How could I survive in darkness when it felt like I was drowning in an abyss. It was then that I stumbled upon a glint, a hollow reminder of what once was. The glint grew in lumens and that's when I knew, the darkness thrives on the outside, when the light exists within you."

I SAT at the crest of the mountain where the gateway had closed. The hardest thing I could ever have done, I did. I gave her up; I let her go. My entire life and heart I gave up so she would be happy, so she could have the family she deserved. I knew I would walk the rest of my life on Earth, incomplete and broken. As long as she was happy, I didn't care. Her happiness has always been the goal, the reason to live, and the reason to keep going. Now, she will be happy, and she will be in the summit where she belonged.

I sat there for hours, not moving. I just stared over the edge of the mountain. *If I died, would it still affect her? Would it rip the life from her as it did last time?* I sat there, contemplating if I should just slip from the mountain and fall to my death. Her light and grace were completely restored to her, along with part of mine. I was sure she would be able to survive with half of my grace and light as hers. I teetered on the edge, closing my eyes. Her face was the only thing I saw. It was the only thing that put a smile on my face. Her face began to fade and was replaced by darkness, my darkness. The darkness consumed me the moment I fell. My light would never be able to compete with it. I would never return to the light as the darkness swirled through my heart and soul. I would never see my Sophie again.

My head and heart both agreed for once. I looked down and closed my eyes. I could never live without her. I had barely made it as long as I had. I was at the point of giving up on her this time. I tipped forward, ready to plunge into the darkness of the valley, when I heard a noise. I opened my eyes and searched for it: a whimpering, a sound of fear and loneliness. The sound tore through my heart. I ran through the Garden that still stood where we had brought it forth, looking for where the sound came from. Behind a rock that sat where the gateway had opened and closed, I knelt. The breath seized in my lungs, and my heart nearly flew from my chest. I reached down and picked up the source of the whimpering.

My heart melted. In my arms, I held the most beautiful sight to ever be seen. Its eyes were so blue that they looked like the sky when the sun was the highest in the sky. The hair was a tuft of fiery, red hair. As I held it close, it latched onto my finger, drawing my hand in closer to it. It nuzzled my finger. A tear rolled down my face as I looked into the eyes of a baby, my baby — the baby I had always wanted with Sophie but could never bring myself to have with her. The baby cooed, and I pulled it in closer to my chest and breathed. The baby was so beautiful and looked just like Sophie. *What shall I name it? What was so fitting to name the only light left in my life, the light its mother had left behind for me?* I smiled down at its beautiful face, the face of my daughter.

"Luxina."

THE SHINING ONES

THE GUARDIANS OF LIGHT SERIES
BOOK TWO

Kasey Hill

Azoth Khem Publishing
Huntsville, AL
April 2025

PROLOGUE: SOPHIE

I SAT ON BENDED KNEE, both in love and with my heart shattering into pieces.

In my arms, I held the light of the world. In my heart, I left the dark half of my soul abandoned and dwindling away. I substituted lust for love, and in the end, lust won. I was ashamed and broken. I don't know how many ways one's heart can be ripped from their chest and still be able to live, breathe, and function. I sat at the threshold where succumbing to darkness and resisting the light of heaven's gates was imminent. Without my other half, the reason for fighting for all these years, the prophecy seen through my own angelic eyes, I feel like an empty shell. Even with a piece of him sleeping in my arms, I was filled with hatred and bitterness. I wasn't given a choice. They chose my destiny for me. Along with the tumultuous pain also came a deepened sadness and regret at the loss of my first child. Alpha would pay for his misdeeds.

The sleeping baby stirred in my arms, and my motherly nature instantly kicked in. It was my sole duty to protect this child; this miracle granted to me by the supreme powers that be. He was the only piece I had left of the love I left behind in the darkness of the earthly realm. His name was Xavier, and he was the only light left in the dwindling ashes of the angel I once was. There was a reason I was gifted this bundle of joy and happiness. If anyone wanted to get to him, they would have to go through me.

I grinned through my chagrin at the beautiful eyes that stared up at me. He looked just like his father. His dark hair and crystal blue eyes were nothing but reminders of the man I was tethered to. I cooed as I grasped his tiny finger in my hand and rubbed small circles against the back of his palm. I had been through hellfire and brimstone. I had died and was brought back to life. I was lost, but this gift saved what small part of love I hadn't been stripped of. I had feared I couldn't go on without my love, without my Incaendiel. I had feared that I would lose myself by losing him. I feared I would pine away by losing my son to the hands of Alpha. I had reason to live now.

"Mommy will never leave you," I whispered as I kissed his forehead. "And no one will ever hurt you..."

XAVIER

I had often watched my mother stare off into the dark void of the universe. Her eyes would always seem lifeless, and a single tear would slide down her cheek occasionally. As a younger child, I would often run to her and throw my arms around her to cheer her up. She would always look down at me, and I could see her eyes brighten just a tad. She would return the hug by picking me up and squeezing me and then set me back down where she could return back to her forlorn gaze into space.

Grandmother Lilith was the one who took my hand and showed me the infinite possibilities of who I was. Mother rarely stayed in the Summit. She was quite often with hunting parties, looking for my half-brother, Damian. Alpha took him. For what reason, only he knows, but he made sure there was a gap in my family to where we would never be happy together.

Grandmother always told me how special I was. She had never told Alpha, but when she made my parents, she made them different than all the other angels. They both possessed the powers over fire and emotions, and they were both unique. She called them twin flames. I often sat in admiration of the stories she would tell me about my father. He sounded like such a wonderful person and the bravest of all angels. She told me there was something special about me as well, but she couldn't quite put her finger on it, not just yet.

And then my dreams began.

I was three the first time I ever had a dream. Angels don't have dreams, so when I asked Grandmother about it, she laughed it off. It wasn't until I started telling her details about my dreams that she started paying attention to what I was saying. I can still remember my first dream of her...

I awoke in a field. Most would think children would be terrified, but I was not. It was rather strange. I was... calm and at peace. As I sat up from my laying position, I heard a whimper and turned toward where the sound echoed. Just beyond the meadow of flowers was a tree, and a beautiful, shining girl sat there beneath the canopy of leaves crying. She was my age, and her hair was so red it put cardinals to shame. I walked cautiously to her so as not to frighten her anymore. I stood at the edge of the mound that the tree grew upon and waited for her to acknowledge me there.

She glanced up, wide-eyed and backed away from me quickly, tripping backward. I ran over to her and reached my hand out to her to help her to her feet. She was hesitant at first but smiled, taking it. An explosive bright flash illuminated the valley and sent us careening back to the ground. We set up from the ground, and the entire valley had been leveled to dust. She started to cry. I held up a finger and smiled. Grandmother taught me how to grow plants with my powers. She said I was just like my father.

I put my finger on the ground, and it began to glow as green grass spread all around us. The wheatgrass popped back up as well as the wildflowers in the meadows. The only thing that had stood untouched was the willow tree behind us. Everything else I restored back. When I finished, I stood back up and looked at her, smiling at me. Neither of us spoke a word to one another. We just stared as if we both were in awe of the other. I held my hand up in the air while she just watched me. Grandmother had been working with me on controlling my fire powers. I lit my hand on fire, and she was startled for a moment. She smiled at me and lifted her hand in the air. She did the same thing, lighting her hand on fire.

We giggled while staring at each other. She placed her hand against mine, and a small light began to shine between our palms. The flames died down as the light grew brighter, and soon, the entire valley was lit up like the sun. We gaped in awe at the colors that flowed around us. The sparkling lights danced throughout the sky. We locked our eyes and grinned at one another.

I STARTLED awake in the Summit as Grandmother shook me. I

had fallen asleep in the Garden again. I looked around at the newly sprouting flowers and foliage. A couple of the higher-ranked angels stood by her side as she stared at me both in awe and fear.

"What happened, Grandmother? What is wrong?" I asked her.

She motioned for the others to leave us to talk. They went on their way, and she sat down beside me.

"You met someone in your dreams this time, didn't you?" she asked me.

I nodded.

"Tell me, who was it?" she asked, craning her neck.

"I don't know her name. We didn't speak to each other," I replied.

She smiled. "So, you met a girl. What was she like?" She brought her legs into a cross-legged position and leaned forward, putting her hands under her chin to listen.

"She was... beautiful," I whispered, looking off into space. "Her eyes were a marvelous green, almost like emeralds but more exquisite. Her hair was like fire, even though it doesn't compare. Her skin was like milk with drops of honey mixed. And when we touched hands, the sky exploded in swirling colors and dancing lights... she looked like Mom would have at our age, I suppose..."

I looked at Grandmother, who sat there both alarmed and serene. "What is wrong, Grandmother?"

"Nothing, Xavier. When you two finally talk... I would love to know her name," she replied, smiling. "Anything else you can remember about her?"

I thought for a moment. "Oh, she shines just like us," I replied.

Grandmother stopped mid-smile while it slowly faded.

"Who is she, Grandmother?" I asked.

"I... I don't know, Xavier," she replied in a distant tone, staring off down to earth. She snapped back to my face and smiled big at me. "Your mother should be returning tonight. How about we make her something special?" she asked.

"Alright," I grinned. I loved making Mother presents. However, Mother never returned that night. In fact, she didn't return for a long time.

My dreams of the girl with the red hair started happening more frequently as I grew older. We began speaking with one another and soon, I learned her name was Luxina. I went to Grandmother the moment I learned her name, just as she had asked, and she frowned.

"Xavier, there isn't a single angel in the Summit whose name is Luxina," she replied.

I grinned back. "She doesn't live here in the Summit, Grandmother. She lives on Earth with her father," I replied.

I received the same wide-eyed stare from her that I did when I first told her about Luxina. She remained silent for a few moments as we laced flowers together in the Garden of Eden. She took me there quite often and would tell me stories about my mother and father and how in love they had been.

"THE GARDEN WAS ALWAYS THEIRS," she replied once, with a mischievous smile. *"And one day, it will be yours and your soulmate's as well."*

"But I don't have a soulmate, Grandmother," I replied.

"You do. You just haven't found her in your waking world," she replied with a smile.

NOW, as we sit here, that smile has faded into one of worry, wonder, and confusion.

"Has she ever told you her father's name?" she asked.

I shook my head in reply. "But," I started.

"But what?" Grandmother asked hurriedly.

"She says at times I look like him when I smile," I replied. "How the light twinkles around me."

Grandmother swallowed hard. "Continue with our little project, Xavier. I will return in a moment."

She returned... but she was different after her return. She no longer spent time with me in the Garden as we had always done. She began to avoid me altogether. It broke my heart. I know others in the Summit looked at me vastly differently than any of the other angel children. For one, my father was Incaendiel, the most powerful angel created. The other... well, I didn't age the way one would think angels should age. They may say they are five years old or eighteen years old or one hundred years old, but that is just by human standards. Angels age quite slowly, so for those that are only a year old, they are truthfully one thousand years old in angelic years. I was different, though. My age rapidly sped by even when compared to that of human years. I am seven years old as of today, but I look sixteen in human years. I never knew if those in the Summit feared me for who my father was... or because they didn't know WHAT I was.

But it didn't stop my dreams. In my dreams, my age didn't matter.

Who I was didn't matter, for she loved me, nonetheless. I was beginning to feel tired more often and caught myself sleeping quite frequently... and she was, too... I often wondered if it was because of our unique aging because she aged as quickly as I did by angel standards. Perhaps just as humans, we hit growth spurts that tire us out.

I lay in the Garden, oftentimes dozing but never fully sleeping. I am never bothered in there, for it belongs to me. Grandmother told me so. Very few angels held the power to enter without permission. So, quite often, I slipped off into the Garden just to sleep among the wondrous plants growing in there. I closed my eyes, thinking of Luxina, smiled, and drifted off into my peaceful sleep.

I awoke in a field. The warm sun beamed down on my face as I rose from my lying position and glanced around. Fields of summer wheat laced the earth along with wildflowers in bloom. The heavenly aroma of lavender and jasmine intoxicated me as I perused through the field. I held my hand out, brushing the tops of the flowers and wheat stalks feeling each tickle the palm of my hand. A breeze slightly blew around me, lifting the sweet notes and carrying them in the wind. A tickle of cherry blossom passed my nose, and I breathed in deeply and closed my eyes, trying to capture the voluptuous fragrance and commit it to memory.

She was nearby.

I opened my eyes and scanned the area, trying to catch the gleam of her red hair in the beating sun's rays. A smile crawled across my face as I saw her playing peek-a-boo behind the willow tree that stood in the middle of the field. Light audible giggles drifted on the wind, tingling my ears. I loved the way she laughed.

I began my slow trek towards her as she popped in and out from behind the tree. When I was close, I crouched and sneaked up to the side of the tree she didn't peer around. As she popped her head around the tree, I crept up behind her as she looked confused out toward the field. I grabbed her by her hips, and she let out a yelp, causing me to laugh at her fright. She playfully smacked me.

"Where have you been, my sweet Firefly?" I murmured as I brushed her hair from her face.

"Battling the darkness that threatens to swallow my existence," she replied.

"It will never take you as long as you are by my side," I said, running my thumb along her lips.

"I believe you," she whispered breathlessly, staring deeply into my eyes. "I just wish we didn't solely meet in the meadow. I want to be with

you in the waking world."

She took my hand in hers and kissed my knuckles lightly.

"One day, my sweet Firefly..."

I planted my lips on her forehead and rested my chin against her brow. It was moments like this I wish I could live in my dreams. Stay in this place with her. The tree we sat below... it always called to me in a whisper, an echo from years past. A familiarity. I had never stepped foot on earth, but the forlorn pull of this tree was full of love and heartache.

"Father is moving us again," she whispered. *"He hasn't told me where, but there is a dread to this move that I cannot shake."*

"Why do you feel dread?" I asked, running my fingers through her hair.

"I fear... I fear for our lives."

I pulled her away from my chest and gazed into her eyes. I could see the storm brewing behind them and feel her terror.

"Know this, my firefly: if anything were to happen to you, I would search the ends of your world for you and bring you back safely. Always remember my words to you. Through the mountains and over the sea, the firefly will cease to be. Over the valley and through the meadow, the firefly exists in the shadows. Fly away, firefly, until we meet again. Maybe next time, it won't be a dream that I get to hold your hand. If you were to disappear from our safe haven, and not meet as we have for years, I will come for you, do you understand? And my hand will pull you back into safety." I whispered it a bit harsher than I wanted.

The sun began to set in the meadow, which signaled the end of our meeting. I held her tightly, fearing it was truly our last time together, before the stars blinked her away from me. However, unlike before, when I immediately awoke as well, this time it was different. I had no idea how to will myself awake either. It always ended at twilight.

I watched as balls of fire emerged in the sky and plummeted to the earth, striking and exploding. The blowback from the impact hit me in barrels of wind. I watched as the mountains around the valley caught alight as they rained down on the meadow. One barreled straight for the center of the fields, and I quickly ran behind the willow tree to brace for the close impact. The wind tore around my body as the ball fire struck the heart of the field. I dug my feet into the ground and wrapped my arms around the trunk of the willow, burying my face in the bark.

When the wind died down and the loud earth-shaking sounds dissipated, I peeked from around the tree to witness the devastation. Everything had been destroyed. I looked at the sky and saw a sneering face staring back at me. Its mouth opened in a huge grin, and the sounds *of its evil laughter filled my ears. I covered them, but even my hands couldn't prevent the voice from piercing my senses.*

"Oh, what a precious sight you are," it hissed. "Soon, you will be mine, for all creation is MINE! You are never safe, even in your dreams, young firefly!"

I snapped from the dream in a panic, gasping for air. Swarms of angels surrounded me in fear. Metatron stood before me extending his hand out to help me to my feet.

"What happened? Why is everyone here?" I asked, dazed.

His eyes glanced around the Garden and back to me. I followed his eyes and saw that the same devastation to my field had happened right here in the Garden... and there was nothing but dust left.

"Fireballs rained down on the garden all around you as you screamed," Metatron replied in a barely audible whisper. "You called out for help, but no one could wake you."

I placed my hand on the ground in agony. I had destroyed my safe haven in the Summit. Not even my powers could bring it back. Or had I?

"I need to speak with Grandmother," I murmured.

Metatron stiffened at the request. "She has sworn off all visitors and requested no one to be allowed in to see her."

"I NEED to see her," I said, walking up to him. "My life... our lives are in great danger!"

"The only danger around here is you, Xavier," he retorted.

"It was Alpha!" I barked louder than I intended.

Gasps filled the empty Garden.

"Please, Metatron. She is all I must turn to. Mother..." I swallowed the lump back, forming in my throat. "Grandmother would know what it means."

"I will pass her the message, but I am afraid that is all I can do," he replied guiltily.

It was days before she would see me. Metatron came for me the day she granted my request to go before her. He led me to her throne room and left us to speak alone.

"Why do you call on me when I have asked for no visitors," she asked coolly.

"Grandmother, why have you changed in demeanor toward me?" I asked.

"I haven't changed, dear one. I have just simply been in retreat to think," she replied. "So, quickly, tell me what you need to tell me and be on your way."

"You used to spend every day with me. You used to look at me with admiration and not with the same stares I receive from everyone else here. So, beg my pardon, but you have indeed changed, Grandmother," I replied.

"Well, what did you expect!" she hissed. "You destroyed my Garden. My first creation of thriving life!"

"It was not I who destroyed the Garden," I replied.

"Oh, it was you, you, and your differentness. Your dreams seized your powers and nearly leveled the Summit!" she yelled.

"Again, it was not I. It was Alpha," I replied.

She laughed. "Do you honestly think I would believe that?"

"It is the truth. He spoke to me at the end of my dream. He told me he was coming for me!" I was outraged she wouldn't believe me.

"If I knew the tower could contain you, I would lock you away in it! You are a danger to us all, Xavier!" She stared at me without any emotion. "You are just like your father!"

"Yeah, my father was the one who saved you all! My father is the reason you get to rule from the throne you sit so 'modestly' upon, Grandmother. So, telling me I am just like him is nothing but a compliment to my ears." She pursed her lips. "If I am such a bother, I will leave."

"Good, you were starting to riddle my last nerve," she replied, rubbing her forehead.

"No one in the Summit will have to worry about me 'damaging' it or bringing them to destruction, chaos, or ruins. And if my mother ever returns, tell her she can find me with my father," I replied, turning away to leave.

"Xavier, you cannot leave!" Grandmother ordered.

"Why stay?" I asked, as I whipped around to face her. "The only person who ever loved me more than all who stood around her sits here and treats me like I am a disease! My mother loves Damian far more than she does me, or else she wouldn't have spent all my growing years chasing after him. I have no one here! They all fear me! They all hate me! They all wish I didn't exist! They all wish for me to be locked away like my mother was for millenniums!!! Including you, Grandmother. So pray, tell me, why?! Why should I stay?" I asked as tears streamed down my cheeks.

She didn't utter a word. I didn't know if she was fighting back emotions or if she truly had nothing to say.

"That is all the answer I need, Grandmother."

I left her throne room. Metatron walked nimbly behind me as I dashed for the records room.

"You are forbidden to be in here, Xavier. You know the punishment! Mother will—"

"Will what?" I asked, interrupting him. "Lock me away in the tower that won't keep me? Oh yes, she's already said she wished she could right before I told her I was leaving, so she didn't have to worry about me anymore, nor do you."

I rummaged through the files and couldn't find what I was looking for. I tore down boxes and threw scrolls aside.

"What is it you seek?" he asked apologetically.

"I need to know where my father is so I can go to him. None of you wish to keep me around, including Grandmother. Mother is never here, always off traipsing the galaxy looking for her precious son. I can't do this anymore. I don't belong here," I replied, throwing scroll after scroll on the ground.

"That isn't true," he said as he placed his hand on my shoulder. "We are just afraid of your powers. The gifts that your parents passed to you."

"Well, you don't have to fear them any longer," I replied.

My eyes landed on the Book of Life. I walked over and stared at it. It glowed golden hues and listed every creature ever born into existence and their current location.

"It is forbidden to look in that book, and you know it!" Metatron hissed.

"Well, then maybe purgatory would best suit me, right?" I asked as I flipped it open.

"Xavier, stop!" a voice hissed.

I turned around to see my mother standing there.

"What are you doing?!" she asked angrily.

"I am leaving. I am going to my father. No one wants me here nor needs me here," I replied, scanning through all the names.

"I w—"

"You!" I laughed. "You are never here! You care more about Damian than your son, who sits in pine for you every day! The son you abandoned so you could seek out the half of the family that makes your family with Lucifer whole! I haven't seen you in so long, I lost count of the days. Hell, I lost count of the months!"

I continued looking for my father's name as she stood there gaping at me.

"What? Oh, did I hurt your feelings? I am sorry, Mother. I am a rotten son. I am a terrible angel who no one here likes, including Grandmother, who wishes to lock me away in the tower that you called home for so long," I seethed.

"What?" she asked breathlessly.

"Oh, you heard me! I went to her because of my dreams and—"

"You have dreams?" she asked.

"Well, if you were around longer than just a few moments in time, you would know this, but yes, Mother, I have dreams," I replied in disdain. "I am treated like a leper here. I hate it here!! I hate the stares! The whispers! The laughter behind my back! I hate that Grandmother, the one person who I thought loved me, now wishes I never existed. I never did anything! Do you all think I want to be different? Do you all think I want unique gifts? I am a pariah! The laughingstock of the Summit!"

Mother and Metatron both stood quietly as I finished searching the book for his name.

"Why isn't he in here?!" I yelled as I threw the book to the floor and kicked it away.

I slid to the ground in tears. Mother walked over to me and sat down beside me. She placed her hand on my shoulder, and I yelled, "Don't touch me!"

"No one can find your father, Xavier. He has powers that hide him from everyone," she stated softly.

I sobbed into my hands. "Why doesn't anyone want me?"

"I want you!" she cried.

"No, you just want something that reminds you of him. You don't want me. You want a memory," I replied, wiping my nose on my sleeve.

She looked like someone punched her in the gut.

"You feel that?" I asked. "Because that is what it feels like to be me every day, knowing that truth. Knowing that I am not what is important."

I stood from my seated position and headed for the door when Metatron stepped in front of me.

"Go ahead," I said. "Lock me away. I don't care. I won't escape. Why would I?"

Metatron threw his arms around me and squeezed me into his chest. "I wasn't able to keep my promise to your mother about Damian, but I will never leave your side, Xavier. That is a promise I will always keep, even if it is to myself."

"It doesn't matter," I replied. "Alpha will find me and take me just as he promised."

He pulled away from me with his hands firmly planted on my shoulders.

"What?" he asked.

"It's why I requested to speak to Grandmother. But she doesn't care either way. She would be glad to be rid of me even if it was to him," I replied.

"What do you mean?" Mother asked, standing to her feet.

She began to glow red as her anger bubbled.

"In my dream, Alpha was the one who rained down the fireballs and told me he would find me because I was his creation. He finds all his creations," I replied.

She turned to Metatron. "You promised him just now, and you *will* promise me that *nothing* and *no one* will *ever* take him! Do you understand me?!" she hissed.

"Yes, Sophie," he replied. "You have my word."

"You failed me once, Brother. Do not fail me again!" she said as she hastily walked off.

"Where are you going?" he asked.

"To see, Mother. She has some explaining to do!" she yelled as she erupted in flames.

"I need to make sure she doesn't burn down the Summit. Will you be okay for a few moments alone? Promise not to run away?" he asked.

I nodded. He walked me from the room and took off after Mother. I walked through the center of the Summit as all eyes trained on me. I could hear the whispers. I could feel the fear.

"There you are!" I heard a familiar voice yell out. "Where you been, buddy?" Lucifer asked as he threw his arm around me.

I never liked Lucifer. Had it not been for him, my family wouldn't be in the shambles it is in right now.

"Around," I murmured.

"Where you off to?" he asked.

"The Garden," I replied, as I shrugged his arm from around my neck. "And no, you do not have my permission to come along."

"Fair enough," he replied.

I walked numbly to the Garden and sank to my knees, crying. It was nothing but burned rubble. Every part of my soul cried out as I sat there on my knees in agony. My gut had been true. Grandmother did hate me, and I haven't the slightest idea as to why. I leaned forward and put my forehead to the ground as I sobbed out all the pain: the pain of not having a mother, the pain of not having my father, the pain of being lonely. Luxina popped into my head, and I cried even harder. Would I ever see her again since our meeting place had been destroyed? Would I ever hold her hand again? Swipe the hair from her face? Kiss her forehead?

I pounded the ground I lay upon and felt the earthquake beneath the blow. I rolled over to my back and peered up at the twinkling stars that hovered above my precious abode. I just want to be loved. Is that so much to ask for? I know... I know I have darkness in me, just like my father. And everyone is terrified of that darkness, but they don't make the darkness any better than what it is. Everyone, that is, besides Luxina. She is the light of my world, the flashlight in the dark, the lighthouse in my storm. I no longer fear my darkness whenever I am with her, for her light outshines it.

I felt something tickle my hand and looked over at it while wiping the tears from my eyes with my other hand. A firefly had landed on my hand. I stared at it as it sat there with me in my misery and grief. It was beautiful. I looked past the firefly, and my eyes widened. There was green grass beneath my hand. I carefully sat up so as not to disturb the creature that graced me with its presence and looked around the Garden. It twinkled as lights danced around, touching everything that had been destroyed and healing it. Every blackened, charred spot returned to its luscious green state. The flowers budded and bloomed. The trees sprouted their leaves. The animals returned to graze. I stared in astonishment at the renewed Garden.

"You are just like him, you know?"

I looked up to see my mother standing there.

"Your father," she started, with a smile, "your father was remarkable. Anything destroyed, he could return to its original state of being. Especially when he cried out his pain."

The firefly flew from my finger and circled her, landing on her outstretched hand. She nuzzled the creature, and it took off into the breeze. She walked over to me and sat down beside me, admiring the Garden.

"This was my favorite place," she said, gazing around. "Mother gave it to me and your father a long time ago."

I sat there silently, just looking around at the still-growing Garden.

"Xavier," she began, "you are loved, my son. I love you more than the stars, more than the moon, more than myself even. You were the only thing that kept me going when we returned to the Summit, and your father stayed behind. I needed you. I wanted you more than anything in the world."

I sat there and listened as she cooed at me, running her fingers through my hair.

"You look so much like him," she said, smiling. "Some days, I stop myself from calling you by his name. And you two brood the same way. I always wished I could reach inside his heart so he could feel and know how much I loved him. I wish the same for you."

"Then, stay with me," I said. "Stay with me this time instead of leaving with the rest of them. I need you, Mother. I need you here with me!"

Her eyes dropped from mine.

"I know it is selfish of me to say, but you have a son here that needs you. You have a son here that has no one left to love him. If you love me, you will stay with me!" I begged.

I watched a tear slide down her cheek.

"It's not that easy, Xavier," she whispered.

"It is, Mother. It is that easy!" I replied harshly. "Let Lucifer go alone this time! For once, pay attention to your child begging for your love."

"I can't," she replied.

I nodded, holding back the welling emotions.

"I'm sorry for you, then," I replied.

"Why?" she asked, confused.

"Because I won't be here waiting for you next time. I won't be like Father. I won't wait around hoping and wishing and wanting for you to realize that I am important."

I could see the knife stab her in the heart with that last statement.

"Please, just let me be," I stated.

I stood up and walked further into the Garden. I sat there until the sun filled the Garden, and then, I sat there longer.

"It isn't fair of you to ask her to stay."

"It isn't fair of her not to stay," I replied. "It isn't fair that she treats me the same way she did Father."

Grandmother sat down beside me and watched as the sun rose.

"I see you fixed the Garden," she said.

"It appears as though I did," I replied.

I refused to look at her. Everything I had ever held on to so tightly I let go of when Mother left the Garden.

"Your dark cloud is circling you today," she said.

"And so it is," I replied unfeelingly.

"Xavier, I—"

"Oh, what? You're sorry?" I asked, cutting her off. "It's a bit late for that, oh, Dark One."

"I didn't mean what I said to you yesterday," she replied.

"Oh, I'm sure you didn't. But don't worry, Grandmother. I don't have a hit list with names, so you are safe from my reign of terror everyone thinks of," I spat.

"I broke you, but I can fix it," she began.

"No one can fix this now," I replied. "I received all the answers I needed yesterday. So, just let me sit here and allow this wound in my chest to fester."

"Xavier, you are letting the dark consu—"

"Consume me? The darkness is me, just like Father. All that you all ever cared about was getting back here, whether it meant he was to be sacrificed or not. Of all people, YOU KNEW he wasn't coming back. But you let everyone believe he was."

She was quiet for a moment.

"Your mother asked me what I thought she should do. If she should stay, or if she should go and continue to look for Damian," she stated.

"And what did you say?" I asked, looking at her.

"I told her she should stay," she replied.

"Did she?" I asked.

She shook her head. "No, she left this morning with the rest of them."

I nodded my head and held back the tears.

"It's always nice to feel second best in life," I said, holding back the tears threatening to spill.

"I am here for you," Grandmother cooed.

"Are you? Or are you going to lock yourself away again? Belittle me when I come to you about my dreams?" I hissed.

"I am sorry. I was upset about the Garden being destroyed," she replied.

"Yeah, and wouldn't even acknowledge the fact that I didn't do it. Everything is always my fault!" I fumed.

"That was unfair of me, I agree. I am sorry about that. I should not have acted the way I did to you or said the things I did to you," she replied.

"Oh, you mean like locking me away in the tower?" I asked.

"I don't know why I said those things," she replied, thinking deeply. "I wasn't myself."

"Alpha is coming," I said flatly. "He is coming for me. He knows about me. No one could stop him from taking Damian, so no one can stop him from taking me."

"He will not take you!" she seethed. "You are not HIS! You are MINE! He will NOT have you!"

"He destroyed the meadow Luxina and I would meet in," I stated. "The fireballs were in the meadow."

"What else happened in the dream?" she asked.

"The normal part. We met and spent time together. She told me her father was moving them again, but she had a bad feeling about it this time," I replied.

"And you said she ages just like you, right? That you two have aged and look the same age?" she asked.

"Yes," I replied. "We both look like we are sixteen even though we are only seven years old."

"When did the dream change this time?" she asked.

"Twilight approached the field, and normally, we just wake up after saying goodbye. She disappeared, but I didn't wake up this time. Instead, huge balls of fire plummeted down and burned everything. When the last one fell, and the dust settled, there was a face in the stars laughing at me. That's when he said what I told you before," I replied.

"Do you know if he knows about Luxina?" she asked, a bit alarmed.

"I don't know. Who knows how long he had been spying on us," I replied.

Metatron appeared at the doorway of the Garden.

"Excuse me for a moment," she said.

I watched as she whispered to him, and he nodded and bowed to her, leaving the doorway. He returned moments later, and I read his lips as he said, "He hasn't moved yet."

She smiled and thanked him as he left the Garden. She walked back over to me and resumed her seated position. I eyed her, wanting her to break her silence, but she didn't.

"You know a secret, don't you?" I asked.

She glanced over at me, worry streaking her brow.

"I can't tell you, Xavier. I can't even tell your mother what I know," she replied.

"Well, what do you know?" I asked.

She sighed heavily. "One day... just not today."

I nodded my head. "Okay," I replied quietly. I debated back and forth with myself for what seemed like an eon before I spoke again. "Grandmother?"

"Yes, child?" she replied.

"I want to see my father. Please take me to see him," I asked, my voice trembling.

"Xavier, I know nothing about your father since we left the Glade. I don't know if..." she began.

"If what?" I asked.

"I don't know if he has moved on from your mother and found someone to start a family with again," she replied.

"He doesn't know about me," I said. "He deserves to know about me."

She looked at me long, hard, and deep. She breathed deeply and exhaled. "Alright. I will take you to him. *But* he is not to see you!" she hissed.

"Yes, ma'am," I replied, grinning.

She took my hand in hers, and before I knew it, we were on earth. I didn't know where we were, but we were here. She motioned for me to be quiet as we watched a young man walk down the back alley from a diner. He carried two platters of food in Styrofoam boxes. *So, he has moved on to another family,* I thought solemnly.

He turned around quickly, and Grandmother cloaked us. I watched him as he stared in our direction, squinting. He felt our presence. He began to jog over to a car and hopped into the driver's seat. He was gone in a flash. Grandmother blinked us to his house, as he pulled into the drive. He ran inside and later emerged with a young redheaded girl. My heart quickened as I struggled to see her face. That hair... her hair was exactly the same as Luxina's hair. The car lights were turned off, so I couldn't see her face. He ran inside and grabbed a few bags, throwing them into the backseat and sped off.

"Well, we spooked him," she said. "Was that enough to satisfy your need?" she asked.

"The girl with him... her hair... she looks just like Luxina from behind," I murmured, walking to the car speeding off.

"Xavier, it is best to leave things alone," Grandmother warned.

"I can't," I whispered, as I sped off toward the car.

I followed them for miles as they passed from state to state. I had to know for sure. I had to know if it was her. It would make sense, so much sense. Mother and Father were created as twin souls. Luxina and I could be an exact replica of them! It was early dawn when they reached their destination. He led her inside a quaint tiny home, and I stood outside watching, cloaked. I had to see her face, just one moment, to know it was her.

"Xavier!" Grandmother hissed, as she spun me around. "We must return. We have been gone for far too long, and the longer we are here, the more dangerous it is for us!"

I turned to the house and watched as my father exited the front door. I swear it was as if he were staring directly at me.

"Can he see me?" I whispered.

"No, nor can he hear us. I have powers of my own, you know?" she replied curtly. "We must go. You saw him. You must not interfere with his new life."

I nodded. "Okay, Grandmother."

Just as she blinked us away and back to the Summit, the front door opened, and the red-headed girl stepped out into the sunlight. Her hair was covering her face and just as she went to brush it out of her way with her hand, we were back in the Summit.

Grandmother grabbed me by my shoulders and shook me. "You must NEVER do that again!" She stared at me. "Do you realize the danger you are in while on earth? Alpha..." She stopped.

"I know, and I am sorry, Grandmother. My mind got away from me," I replied, ashamed. "I promise to never do it again if you ever take me back."

"We don't even know if this Luxina person is in league with Alpha. She could be another one of his..."

"Another one of his what?" I asked.

Grandmother stared past me, and my eyes followed her gaze. It was Mother.

"Sophie, what are you doing back so soon?" she asked. "Did you find him?!"

Mother glanced back and forth between Grandmother and me.

"No," she sighed. "But I have come to realize," she began, staring me in the eyes, "that I have spent far too long on this mission and not enough time with my son, who is right here."

I smirked back at her. "Oh really? So, just like that, you think it is more important to be here with me and not hunting for your precious Damian?"

"Xavier, I know I am not perfect. I have never claimed to be. I never thought it would take this long to find Damian. But I have recognized what a lost cause it is and ask for your forgiveness," Sophie replied.

I shook my head violently. "No, no, no!" I screamed. "You don't just get to walk back into my life and act as if nothing ever happened. You don't get to act like my mother when you haven't been one for the last seven years!"

"Xavier," Grandmother cooed, interrupting. "Give it a chance. You mi—"

I quickly intercepted her sentence and cut her off. "I might what? I might find that I have a lot in common with my mother? I might find that she cares more for me than I realize? No, the only person who ever gave a morsel of love to me was you and even you abandoned me!"

"I did it to protect—"

"Protect me? Protect yourself? Who are you protecting now, Grandmother? You would all rather Damian was here as opposed to me! The precious prodigal son that was stolen away from my whore of a mother," I spat.

"That's not fair!" Sophie yelled, with tears welling in the brims of her eyes. "I love you no more nor less than your older brother! I just want my son back!! Why is that hard for you to understand?!"

"Because I am standing right here! I have always been standing right here! Waiting for you to return. Waiting for you to acknowledge me for more than a mere moment before leaving me to return to your hunt! I wanted a mother that loved me. I wanted a mother that wanted me! But I only got one that wanted what she didn't have and spent an eternity looking for it!" I started to walk away but stopped. "Don't give up looking for your precious Damian now, Mother. You're going to need a son after today because I no longer see you as my mother. You were just the woman who spawned me. I have no family."

"Xavier!" Sophie called out as I walked away.

"Let him be," Grandmother replied quietly as I entered the Garden.

Everything I walked past instantly died on spot. My emotions were rampant and killing the Garden once more.

"You know, you're a selfish brat!" a voice seethed in the distance.

"I did not grant you permission to enter, Lucifer. So please, leave," I replied through gritted teeth.

"You don't scare me, little boy," Lucifer said, spinning me around by my shoulder.

I landed a punch square in his jaw, and his eyes blazed at me. He reared back to sock me when I lost control of any hold I had on my power. He grabbed at his throat as the earth blackened beneath his feet. He coughed and wheezed and spat dust in the air from his lungs as they slowly filled with burning decay as he began to incinerate and die from the inside out.

"Xavier! No!" Sophie called out as she ran to me.

I was too far gone. I turned my gaze to her, and she stopped in her tracks, gasping. However, I am her child for a reason, and my powers came to be from her and my father. She pounded her fist onto the ground, and a line of fire blazed in a path straight to me, encircling me in a hot, fiery crater. I was too distracted by the heat to hold my power over them any longer than I had. They both gasped as the air hit their lungs and spat and sputtered until the oxygen normalized in their breath.

"We have to lock him away as Mother suggested," Lucifer bellowed. "His powers are advancing and in such a dark way!"

"No! I refuse to let my son suffer the way I did for centuries. Anyone who tries will have to answer to me!" Sophie seethed. "Do you want to test me as well, Lucifer?" Her eyes lit with fire as she stood her ground in between Lucifer and me. She glanced back at me as her hands blazed and returned her glare to him.

"You chose this wretched waste of space over finding Damian! Just like you chose his father over me repeatedly. I believe it is time you learned a lesson of your own," he smirked and snapped his fingers.

Angels surrounded Sophie at the command of Lucifer. However, they weren't the everyday angels that lived at the Summit. These were the wayward angels that had turned dark, called The Forsaken. Flames engulfed Sophie as her powers bloomed with fury.

"Do it now!" Lucifer hissed.

From nowhere, a weighted net fell over top of her. She hit the ground with her fire snuffing out. She was completely powerless. She struggled under the net, but it was futile. She was trapped.

"What is that?!" I yelled, running to her aid.

Lucifer snagged me and held me with one of his hands as I struggled to free myself.

"It's a net made from unicorn hair. The only thing strong enough to bind angelic powers," Lucifer sneered.

"Take her to the tower and mark the door so no one can enter. We can't have mother dearie chasing after us," Lucifer laughed.

Two of the Forsaken picked up Sophie and wrapped her in the net so she couldn't escape. Lucifer pushed me off to two others standing there, and they held me still.

"Oh, and Beelzebub, be careful with her, would you?" Lucifer smirked. "We still need her for our plan."

"No problem, Brother," Beelzebub replied.

"One of you needs to grab Lilith as well," Lucifer barked at the rest of the Forsaken standing there.

"Sir, she fled the Summit already," one replied.

"We will hunt for her later, then," he hissed in anger. "As for you," he said, motioning to me with his pointer finger. "Alpha is going to have a field day with you. There won't be any need to experiment on you. You are already dark, just like your father."

I struggled against the two Forsaken holding me back. When they wouldn't let go, I seared their hands with my powers, and they howled in pain, letting me slip free. Freedom was short-lived, however. Lucifer scooped me up in some sort of bag I couldn't escape from.

"No use in trying, kiddo," Lucifer snorted. "It's designed to render you powerless."

"What do you want with me? Why are you handing me over to Alpha? I have never done anything to you!" I asked, scratching at the cloth on the inside of the bag. He jostled me as he walked.

"You should already know. Alpha has my son, Damian. Alpha wants you. It's a fair and even trade to me. Why settle for a half-blood angel when he can have you? He wants you more than Damian."

"Why does he want me so bad?" I demanded.

"Damian only has half of your power. He only has your mother as his parent. You are Incaendiel's and Sophie's child. He is going to be pleased with the efforts we have concocted." Lucifer stopped. "We have one more stop after sending him to Alpha. We must pay Incaendiel a little visit. Alpha says that he has another just like Xavier with him, but it is unclear as to whose spawn she is," he dictated to those around him. "She is to be unharmed and delivered in a loving condition. Her name is Luxina."

Luxina! No! Why does Incaendiel have Luxina? I couldn't believe my ears. My father was with Luxina. *But they have no clue who she is, which means Alpha doesn't either.*

"Grandmother was wrong," I whispered.

"What are you mumbling?" Lucifer asked, irritated.

Before I could answer, someone else spoke. "Do you have Xavier?" a younger voice asked.

"He is bagged and tagged," Lucifer replied.

"Excellent. Alpha will be pleased with this news," the voice replied.

"It won't be long, son," Lucifer said.

Son?!

"Do not call me that! You don't deserve nor have the right to refer to me as your son. Alpha is my father," he replied.

DAMIAN!

Firefly: The Half-Blood Angel
Introduction

XAVIER AND DAMIAN MEET

"LET ME GO! I want to see him!" I yelled, struggling inside the bag.

"Shut up!" he yelled back at me. "You will come to find my terms more pleasing than that of which Alpha has planned for you. At least when I trade these two lab rats for your freedom, he won't be experimenting on you any longer," Lucifer retorted to Damian. "Your brother—"

"Don't you dare talk about my brother as if he is yours! You hate him. You have freely admitted your loathing of him, of which I am sure the feeling is mutual. However, you will not speak ill of him in my presence. He is innocent of your hatred. He is my—"

"Lucifer. Damian. Welcome back!"

"Hello, Father," Lucifer replied, dropping me to the ground still wrapped up in the bag.

Where the hell are we? I thought to myself. *We traveled for such a brief time to get somewhere.*

"Now, let's see what goodies you have brought me," he said, opening the bag.

I stood up and faced my nightmare. There he was, the voice and face of my every nightmarish dream.

"Alpha," I hissed.

"Hello, young Xavier. It is nice to finally meet you," he replied, with a sly grin. "I have been, shall we say, watching you in your dreams for years."

I didn't say a word.

"That beautiful, young, red-haired beauty of yours… do you know who she really is?" he asked.

"I'm not telling you anything," I seethed.

"Xavier, I am God. I know everything. There is nothing you know that I don't already," he said. "However, there are things I know that you do not. Like for instance, do you know why you have special powers? I do…"

* * *

I AWOKE TO DARKNESS. I went to move, but my arms were shackled to the wall. *What is this?* I tried to break them, but they were indestructible. I remembered what Lucifer had said about the net and grimaced. I was trapped here. The light flipped on, and my eyes blurred, trying to adjust. I heard footsteps and looked up at a silhouette standing before me.

My eyes began to clear. Before me stood a red, curly-haired teenager with freckles. He looked just like me except not. I looked around him at two of the men standing behind him. I recognized them immediately as part of the troop that kidnapped me.

"Do you know who I am?" he asked.

The voice.

"Damian," I replied.

"So, you were paying attention while in the bag," he mused.

"Help me!" I pleaded. "Help me escape, brother!"

"Now, why would I do that? Soon, our sister will be here, and we will be one happy family!" he laughed.

"Our sister?" I asked, confused.

"In due time, Brother, in due time, you will learn. But for now, we have some tests to run on you."

"Tests?" I asked, shaking my head, trying to understand. "What do you mean tests?"

"Alpha has a plan for us all," Damian replied, pacing in front of me. "We will be the elite, the strongest angels in the heavens. Far stronger than our parents, be they Lucifer or Incaendiel." He stopped pacing and bent down in front of me. "This is going to hurt just a bit."

He jabbed a needle into my neck and pushed the plunger, and my skin began to crawl with fire. My blood boiled, and I howled in pain.

"What is this!!!" I screamed in agony.

"It's what Alpha likes to call Heavenly Hellfire. The old bloke doesn't understand the meaning behind the name, but that's a later discussion with him," Damian replied.

My body began to convulse, and I hit the ground, foaming at the mouth.

"It's killing me," I strangled out.

"No brother... that is where you are wrong!" Damian laughed maniacally. "It's making you stronger. It's making you like me." His eyes grew black and then went back to their original color.

"What are you?" I hissed.

Pain rippled through my body, and I screamed. It felt like pure fire ran through my blood.

"I am something no one can ever be!" he said defiantly. "But we can be this together! We can hold the power over the angels and start our own allegiance where they bow to our feet. Wouldn't you love that? Wouldn't you love for people to look at you with respect instead of disgust just because you are different from them? This is our escape."

"What would you know about being mocked," I asked, rolling over in my own vomit.

"You think they took kindly to me in the Summit? No, far from it, Brother. They treated me like a leper. I had powers they didn't understand. But Alpha, he loved me, nonetheless. I went through what you are now. It only burns the first few times. By the fourth treatment, you will be strong as an ox!"

"I don't want to be anything like you! You're a monster!" I screamed.

"Is that any way to talk to your older brother, Xavier? I saved you!" he yelled. "I saved you from your own personal hell. We heard about your dreams. We heard how all the angels were terrified of you and wanted nothing to do with you! Here," he said, turning in a circle, "it's like you are Alpha himself."

He smiled a twisted smile.

"I don't want to be like Alpha," I choked out as I vomited more foam.

He knelt in front of me again. "You will be thinking differently soon."

He stood back up and barked an order. "Unchain his one arm and give him a cot to sleep on. That's no way to treat family, especially one so highly magical."

The two Forsaken didn't budge.

"Now!" Damian bellowed.

"He may present a threat unchained," one of them replied.

"Trust me, he won't have the strength to fight back."

He left the room, and the two Forsaken walked over to me. I tried to move away, but Damian was right. I didn't have the strength to fight back.

"If Lilith finds out what is happening here, she will have all our heads on a platter," one of them seethed.

"She can't do anything to us. Besides, why would she care? She hasn't cared for how long now over Damian?" the other retorted.

"This is HER special angel. Everyone in the Summit knows how fond she is of him. She was the one who raised him. She will kill us all!" the one replied.

"Just do your job. Father will see to it that Lilith does nothing to anyone who is in on his plans. I trust Alpha, as should you. If he knew you were doubting his plans, he would skin you alive! So, hush!"

"What are his plans," I murmured.

"In due time, young one. I know you are going through pain, but it will be over soon," he replied.

I blacked out.

When I came to, Damian was standing over me.

"Good morning, Brother. Still in pain?" he asked.

The burning was mild now.

I shook my head.

"Excellent," he said as he plunged another needle into my neck.

The liquid coursed through my veins, but he was right. It didn't hurt nearly as badly as before.

"See, that's not so bad. If you can promise not to run away, I will unchain your other arm," Damian said, smiling. "I would like to properly hug my flesh and blood."

I nodded.

Two new men walked over and unchained my arm left chained to the wall. I rubbed my wrist where the shackles had been. Damian walked over to me and stood before me. Rage tore through me, and I grabbed him and twisted his arm behind his back. I grabbed a short blade sword from the table and held it to his neck.

"Let me go, and I will let him go," I stated.

"We can't do that," the two said as they walked to him.

I let go of his arm and kicked him into the two Forsaken. I picked up another blade and stood in a fighting stance. Metatron and Michael taught me sword fighting and battle techniques.

Damian composed himself.

"You want to play, is it?" he asked.

He picked up a sword and twisted it around in his hand. "Let's play."

I ran toward him, and we began to dance around in a circle. He would thrust at me, and I would block every advance. I did a roundabout kick and caught him square in the jaw. He wiped the blood from his lips, and his eyes turned black.

"Wrong move, Brother," he replied menacingly.

He tore through the room, swiping the sword through the air like a fan. I blocked each advancing strike until he knocked one of the blades from my hand. I used the other to parry the attacks until it was flung from my hands. He cornered me with the blade pointed into my chest.

"I could end you now, but Alpha wouldn't be happy!" he sneered. "I wanted us to be a family, but it seems you can't do that. Chain him back up!" he commanded. "And when does our sister get here?!" he demanded.

"Soon, Lucifer is on his way with her now," they replied.

"Give him another injection. Maybe he will pass out from a double dose. We wouldn't want him poisoning her mind. We need her to be a fresh, clean slate." He tossed the sword down.

They shackled me back to the wall. I winced as the needle hit my neck, and they pushed the fluids through with the plunger. I glared at them. There was no pain. Either I had become immune, or it had already fused with my blood. I didn't know yet."

Damian walked over to me. "This was fun, Brother. Maybe another time we can finish what we started."

I spit in his face. He wiped it off and walked over to the door. "Spend your days in the dark in here. That's all you are. A ball of darkness, just like your pathetic father," he said as he flipped the light out.

I hated the dark.

DAMIAN

I WAS A CHILD BORN OF LIGHT and raised in darkness. I have known but one father, the All-Father, and he has raised me in accordance with his laws. My real father, a deceptive fiend, joined ranks against the only person who has ever shown me gnosis in its purest form. My mother, a whore monger, chose darkness over her livelihood in the Summit. The All-Father, Alpha, was my god and my savior,

I was pushed into training as soon as I could walk. The war among angels was imminent, and I was to be prepared to face off if necessary. If this meant killing my own parents, then so be it. They were of no use to me. They had joined the army of the Dark Mother, Lilith. She was a twisted snake that chose to fall, that chose to disobey the All-Father, her husband. She was a poison to humanity that needed to be eradicated, along with all the angels who chose to leave with her. They were the epitome of evil and disobedience.

Alpha had chosen me to be his right hand, his leverage in the holy war. I spent every day training with the elite in the Summit. Michael and Metatron taught me sword and combat fighting. My chosen weapon had been the long sword.

Ever since I was old enough to make memories, I could remember everyone in the Summit bending over backward to help me. I was the prodigal child, the spawn of Sophie and Lucifer, two of the most powerfully seated angels in the Summit. That was until I began to develop powers. They were unlike my mother's powers. Where she could set things ablaze, I could freeze things in their place. Solid blocks of ice would spring forth whenever I was emotional. Blizzards would pop up whenever I was angry. Everything would freeze over when I was sad. Everything means exactly that, everything. Even the angels within a distance of me were affected and turned into blocks of ice.

My main trigger? My mother. I wanted to be with her, but Alpha told me I was too special to meddle in the affairs going on in the mortal world. Truthfully, he didn't want me kidnapped and warped by the fallen angels, including my mother. I was too special to be warped. Alpha had a plan for me. He said my parents wouldn't understand the potential I was faced with. I was given a divine gift from the cosmos that held power even he didn't possess. They would be jealous of me. I believe he was right, too.

However, when I think about my formidable years, I am the one jealous. All I ever knew was training and battle tactics. I didn't know love. I didn't know empathy or sympathy. Alpha treated me like a soldier, not a son. And then, my mother had a child with Incaendiel. Of course, I never got to meet him. Alpha whisked me away from the fallen angels returning to the Summit, so my pure angelic nature wouldn't be tainted by their darkness. I still envy my brother, though. He was able to grow up with our mother.

I wanted everything he had. He had my home, the Summit. He had my mother, Sophie. He had Grandmother Lilith. He had it all while I was left with Alpha. I was never allowed to call him Grandfather. I was never allowed to call him Father. I was to only address him as Alpha. He hid me from the world, depriving me of any social interaction I could succumb to... and then experimented on me.

I no longer loved him. I no longer respected him. But I needed his attention and approval. I craved it. It was the only attention I ever received. When the injections began, it wasn't long after Mother had gone to Earth. I was growing unusually fast, and he wanted to test my blood against other strains of blood to see how compatible they were. He wanted to make a legion of angels just like me. Except, they really wouldn't be angels. They would be more like angel spawns that went horribly wrong.

My brother and I had one thing in common, though. We both want to get rid of Alpha. I had to keep the façade up long enough to where I could divulge my plan to Xavier about bringing down Alpha before we brought Luxina in here. However, Lucifer is thwarting my efforts, and it will only be a matter of time before she is here as well. If Alpha found out that I had been a traitor in his midst, he would dispatch me himself.

I watched my brother in stealth as he sat chained to the wall. It was fun being able to take him on in battle. He was a fighter. He proved himself to me, and I knew when the time would come, he would help me take down Alpha. I just had to keep up this façade long enough to be able to crumble Alpha to his knees. There was no doubt in the world that he cared nothing for me. I was a weapon, a disposable tool for him to pick up and play with. When the time would come for either Luxina or Xavier to surpass me in strength and agility, I am most definitely sure that he will kill me. So, I fake it as much as I can fathom. I fake the evil. I fake the strength. I don't need additional strength. I received all I needed when I was made from my mother. The only thing these stupid injections did was turn me darker, cynical, and mostly apathetic about everything.

I was much more like Xavier than he realized. I spent my life wanting things I could never have as well. Most likely, Luxina is the same way. We all come from a broken family that had no one to blame but Alpha himself. So, we must take him down at all costs.

"Damian," Lucifer called out, as he walked down the corridor to where I stood watching Xavier. "Ready to go, bud?" he asked.

"I am not nor have ever been your *bud*. Got that, Lucy?" I replied, brushing past him.

"What is your problem with me, boy?" he bellowed.

I stopped in my tracks and cracked my neck. I balled my hands into fists and whipped around to face him.

"Boy?" I asked coldly.

"Yea, *boy*," he reiterated. "You think you're a man, but you're not. You think you are Alpha's prodigal son, but you're not. You're *my* son, *my* flesh and blood. You *will* show me respect."

I squeezed my closed fists even tighter, and they cracked under the pressure.

"Or what?" I asked, glaring at him with all the hate I could fathom.

"Or I will have to teach you a lesson. I will teach you a lesson, and when I am done… I will teach that same lesson to your pathetic excuse of a brother," he replied, jabbing his finger into my collarbone.

"Big mistake," I replied, as I looked at his finger and back up to his face.

In one short, fluid movement, I had him pinned against the wall with his arm pulled up and twisted behind his back.

"Don't you *ever* threaten *me* or my family again, do you understand?" I whispered heatedly in his ear. "I will have no problem killing you and watching you die a slow and painful death."

I released my grip on him and turned to walk away. Two guards stood at the end of the hall, waiting for my signal. Lucifer rubbed his wrist and stretched out his arm as they smirked at him.

"Let's go get my sister," I stated, walking through the exit.

The Valley of the Shadow of Death: Nephilim Rising Introduction

INCAENDIEL

PROLOGUE

I LOOK INTO THE EYES of my child, my daughter, and the world crumbles around me. A piece of myself had been momentarily lost to the light where I could not walk, where I could no longer go. A piece that was my light, the only light that I had left in this darkness. I had to release it; I had to let it go where it needed to go for survival. The light is fragile within chaos. The chaos of darkness would have consumed it, consumed her. She would have become one of the fallen that walk these lands full of discontent and hatred for all things living or immortal. Humanity had been spoon-fed a word for these fallen ones, the fallen angels, my brothers. Alpha had dripped into humanity evil lies, calling my forlorn brothers demons and monsters.

I fought the darkness as long as I could. I had to fight it. It was the only way to save my brothers, my fellow fallen ones. It was a battle that I hadn't won from the start. Darkness lived within me before I fell. There was no consumption once my light left during the plummet to Earth. It existed as an equal to her light, a natural harmonic balance. Our Yin and Yang energies complemented each other. When I took the plunge from the Summit, I never imagined the plan we had created would fall through. Yes, our plan was to return those who had fallen back to the Summit and return their light. She would have never guessed that my fall would have left me desolate and defeated. My light would never return. The darkness won what rightfully belonged to it, my soul.

It surprised me to find this hidden piece of light left behind. The light never belonged in the darkness, and soon, I feared the pit of doom would swallow it. However, this time, I couldn't give it up as easily as I did last time. Granted, it wasn't easy to offer up the light of my life, the love of my life, the other half of my soul to another angel to care for, but she had a family. It wasn't fair of me to take her away from the one thing she had always craved with me. I let her go. This time wouldn't be so easy. I held within my arms a truth that I couldn't just hand over to anybody, not without a fight. I would fight to keep this existence of hers and mine safe and out of harm's way. I would fight to the death anyone who would try to harm my light, my Luxina.

I flew from the mountaintop, holding her carefully in my arms. Her tiny wings would never be able to catch her if she were to fall from my arms. I landed on the ground at the entrance of my home. It was new and old all at the same time. I had lived here for millions of years, but now I would live there alone. Well, not exactly alone, for I would have her at my side still. This little child will be the only thing that gets me through the hard years for me ahead. I walked through the entrance to the Glade and made my way down the spiraled staircase. It was so empty, so abandoned. Thousands of fallen angels once resided in this home with our Mother. Now, it was just Luxina and me.

She looked so much like her mother it was uncanny. It's almost as if the cosmos left a piece of her with me that would stay with me forever. A piece of her I could keep free from guilt and not have to give up. I carried her to the room her mother stayed in most often and laid her on the bed. She cooed her baby talk, and I couldn't help but let a happy tear fall from my eyes. I curled up on the bed beside her, letting her grab my finger and pull it to her mouth. At that exact moment, I felt as if I had everything that I would ever need, even if the other half of my soul was gone. This little girl was all that I would ever need.

Her little mouth opened wide, stifling a yawn, and her eyelids drifted heavily shut. I wrapped my wing around the two of us to cover her and keep her cozy. She drifted off to sleep, and I lay there watching her sleep in my arms. The picture of perfection wrapped tightly in my protective arms. I would never let anything, or anyone harm her. To hurt her would mean death, and I would see to it that they suffered tremendously. I closed my eyes, and her mother's face haunted my mind. Our last embrace, our last kiss, so much love, and so much loss. I opened my eyes back up. I doubt I will ever sleep again, not without her by my side, not without my Sophie.

CHAPTER 1

"DAD, DO I REALLY have to start a new school this year? I'm old enough to where they can't tell anything." Luxina sat in the car as I walked around and opened her door. "Please! I liked my old school. That's where my friends are!"

I sighed and shook my head.

"You know we can't risk staying in one place for too long. People get suspicious of not only you but of me as well." I stood there patiently waiting for her to unbuckle her seatbelt and get out of the car.

"You're paranoid! Ugh!" she groaned as she stepped out of the car. She had such a fiery spirit that matched the flaming locks that draped her body. I chuckled.

"And you're stubborn."

I shut her door back and walked her up the school steps. I knew this was the part she hated most. It didn't bother her to make new friends or get acquainted with people; she was a natural. It was the first day when I had to finish signing the paperwork for her enrollment. This is the eleventh school and the eleventh state we had been to since she was old enough to enroll. Word was that Alpha escaped from the Summit and took a massive fleet of angels with him. I knew who their target would be. Me. I opposed him; I was the reason everyone Alpha had turned his back on returned to the Summit.

"Dad, stop thinking. You're frowning, and your face will freeze like that in your old age." Luxina giggled at her joke.

I swooped my arm around her and noogied her head. She pushed me off, straightening her curly locks.

"Trying to have me make a bad impression on the first day with wild woman hair?" Her sarcasm and jokes reminded me so much of her mother.

Before we stepped through the entrance to the school, I stopped to have the talk again. "Remember, keep your wings cloaked at all times. Make sure you keep your shine under control. If anyone asks, I'm in the military, and you're a spoiled brat who gets whatever you want."

"You mean aside from being able to stay at the schools I wished to."

I narrowed my eyes and frowned at her. She loved irking my nerves on the first day.

"Dad, you don't have to worry. I got this."

Yeah, that's what I thought when she was six, and she decided to show her wings to a little boy in class. *That* was a fun phone call. I ended up having to go and buy a fake pair of wings from the store to produce as the "wings" she showed to him.

We continued through the entrance, and I walked her to the office. A nice young woman met us at the desk. Her eyes lit up when she saw me, and I watched as she messed with her hair to make sure it was straight. Humans always amused me.

"Yes, may I help you?" Her accent had a deep southern tone. I have no clue why I chose to live in Alabama this year.

"Yes, I'm Mr. Graham; I'm here to finish the enrollment paperwork for my daughter, Luxina." She appeared to be a little shocked. My boyish looks always threw them off when I introduced her as my daughter. "I have good genes." I flashed my grin at her, and she blushed.

"Here is the paperwork. We just need a few things to finish up. We received her transcripts, and from her grades and classes, we have placed her in advanced classes." She smiled in approval at Luxina. "You are a very bright young woman." Luxina blushed and dropped her head. She was always self-conscious when it came to compliments about her. "Let's see, we need her birth certificate, her social security number, and a few of your John Hancocks, and we're all set."

I fished her forged birth certificate and social security card out of my wallet and handed them to the secretary. I went through hell trying to get them for her. Finally, I had to use my "powers of persuasion" on the clerk at the courthouse to make up a birth certificate. With the certificate, it was easier to snag a new social for her. I reported she was born at home, and her mother died during the labor. She made copies of both and handed them back. I finished signing the paperwork and slid it back over to the secretary. She looked over everything and placed a stamp of today's date as received. She then went to the computer and printed a piece of paper up, handing it to Luxina.

"Here is your schedule. Do you need a map of the school to find your way around?" Without waiting for a reply, she handed over a map to Luxina. Luxina smiled and murmured her thanks. "I hope you have a good first day, sweetie. Welcome to Decatur, Alabama." She smiled and then looked at me. "It was nice meeting you." I nodded and walked from the office with Luxina.

"I'll be here when the bell rings." I hugged her, and she made her way through the crowd of teenagers.

In reality, she was much younger than everyone thought she was. All angel babies were born in the Summit and adhere to the aging principle there. On Earth, apparently, it was different. She was born on February 6, 2009. She should only be ten years old right now. Luckily, her growth spurt hit in the past couple of years. Most blame it on the hormones when children grow quickly. When her age started rapidly changing, I started bouncing her around from town to town. When she hit around puberty age, her aging slowed again, and it was easier to maintain what her age was. Her birth certificate went from 2009 to 2002, making her seventeen with her birthday coming up.

I made my way out the front entrance of the school when I felt an eerie feeling of someone watching me. I looked around but didn't see anyone. There was a straggler teen making his way up the steps, but other than him, no one else was around. I made my way down the steps when the young man bumped into me. He looked up at me, and I stopped in my steps. His face looked so familiar, though I had never met him before. He had crisp blue eyes, red hair, and pale skin.

"Excuse me," he mumbled, as he continued through to the school.

I continued on my way to my car. *Why did he look so familiar? Maybe his parents were people I went to school with in New Salem.* I nodded, agreeing with the thought. *That had to be it.* I started the car and made my way back to the house. I didn't have to be at work for another couple of hours.

The first couple of years were rough. I was taking care of a baby by myself and trying to work two jobs to save up money. Of course, then, I didn't really need the money. We lived at the Glade, but I knew we couldn't live there forever without the renegade angels looking for us. I saved up enough money from working to where we would always have a decent amount in savings in case we ever had to run. So far, we have been lucky.

As she grew older, the questions started to come. Where was Mommy? Why wasn't Mommy with us? It was hard explaining to a four-year-old the circumstances that surrounded the situation. I told her Mommy was on an important mission, and I didn't know when she would be able to return. I have waited for the question to come up again. I started the car and sighed. I hoped she wouldn't ask me again. This time, I wouldn't be able to make up a story; I would have to tell her the truth. I partially explained the events surrounding Alpha and the renegade angels. She knew the gist of it.

I made my way home with the same eerie feeling I had at the school. Maybe Luxina was right, and I was becoming exceedingly paranoid. I pulled into the driveway of our house and switched the car off. I checked the mail to see if any bills had made it to me yet, but the box was empty, so I made my way inside. I closed the door behind me and went to the kitchen. I put a pot of coffee on and scrounged up some breakfast. It was too obvious for me to remain in my angel form, so I took on the human form I had once been and reassumed the identity of Isaiah. I had coached Luxina to do the same to help hide her identity better. I poured myself a cup of coffee and stood at the window in the kitchen, peering out into the garden Luxina had grown over the summer when we first moved here.

"Whatcha looking at?" I nearly dropped the cup of coffee from my hand when I turned to the voice.

"Lucifer, what are you doing here?" I was immediately on alert looking out the window for any other angels that may be lurking.

"It's just me here," he said, putting the picture down he held in his hands of Luxina. "Who is that?" he asked. I was too startled to answer.

"What are you doing here?" I asked again.

"I wish I could say it's a pleasure visit, but it's not." He walked around the house, looking at all the decorations. He stopped when he came to a picture of Sophie. "Has she been by to see you any?"

"You know the answer to that. I haven't seen her since that night." I set my cup of coffee down, walked into the living room, and sat down. Just when I thought I could get past everything that had happened that night, he showed up at my house. He took a seat in a chair across from me.

"You look good." He was beating around the bush.

"Look, if you've come to ask if I know anything about the location of Alpha, you've come to the wrong place. I haven't heard from or seen anyone since that night." I stood as I heard the oven beep, signaling my breakfast was ready.

"That's only part of the reason I'm here," he said, following me to the kitchen.

"Oh yeah, well, quit beating around the bush and get to it then." He was so annoying when he didn't come right out and say what needed to be said. I pulled the food out of the oven and set it on top of the stove. I started for the refrigerator to get some drinks.

"I'm looking for my son." I stopped in my tracks. *What?* I turned around to face him.

"What do you mean you are looking for your son?" He walked to the table and sat down.

"When we returned to the Summit, Alpha had taken off with a fleet of angels...including my son." I sat down at the table, flabbergasted.

"Do you even know what he looks like? Or, for that matter, where exactly he might be?" I could've passed by this kid one hundred times while I have been here on Earth.

"We've been searching galaxies for him. We always catch a faint sense of him, and then it disappears." He fiddled with a coaster I had on the table.

"By we, you mean Sophie and you, right?" It still stung saying her name aloud.

He sighed. "She misses you, you know?" I looked down at the table. "Mother misses you as well. Xavier keeps them company, though."

I picked my head up and looked at him, puzzled. "Xavier? Who is Xavier?" The look on his face showed he made a slip of the tongue.

"Wow, I feel like kicking myself in the behind now." He shook his head as he realized what slipped from his mouth. "Xavier is...your son." I know the look on my face had shock, surprise, and disbelief written all over it.

"Impossible," I stammered.

"No, it's true. When the portal closed, she found him lying right beneath where it had been. It's actually quite remarkable. He's unlike any angel we have witnessed before. He's been—"

"Growing and aging, unlike any other baby angel." This time, his face showed shock.

"How do you know that?" I walked to the picture of Luxina and picked it up. *Twins?* "Incaendiel, how do you know that?" I held up the picture of Luxina to him.

"Because this is his sister."

His jaw dropped, and he took the picture from my hands. He stared at the picture as if looking at it for the first time. He smiled. "She looks just like her mother." He handed it back to me, and I put it back on the shelf. "Does anyone else know about her?"

I shook my head. "I've been bouncing from town to town so no one could find me or her. I'm surprised Mother doesn't know." I looked back over at him.

"If she does, she hasn't told us. Our main focus has been looking for Damian."

"What does he look like? I might have seen him in one of the towns I've lived in." We sat back down at the table.

"We're not for sure. We only know him as a little baby. If he has the same growth issue as...the twins do, we have no clue what he would look like right now." I nodded and glanced down at my watch.

"Crap! I'm going to be late for work." I ran to get my briefcase from my bedroom. I came back into the kitchen and looked at Lucifer. "Um, make yourself at home. I'll be back after Sophie, I mean, Luxina gets out of school." *Now he has Sophie on my brain. Great! It took me ten years to get her off my mind. Now she's back on it again. Not only that, but I have a son I have never met before...*

Just as I was about to step out the door, the phone rang. I walked over to it and answered it, "Hello?'

"Mr. Graham, we're calling in regard to your daughter, Luxina." *Wonderful! What has she done now?*

"Yes, is anything wrong?" *I was going to beat her if she showed her wings to anyone again!*

"It seems she fainted in class. She's been in the nurse's office for about twenty minutes. She asked us to go home." My heart thudded.

"I'll be right there." I hung the phone up and then dialed the office. "Hey, Margie, it seems Luxina fainted in school, so I won't be coming in today." The call went briskly with her offering her condolences and saying she hoped she felt better.

"Do you want me to ride along to keep you company?" Lucifer grinned. I rolled my eyes. Today was not my day.

"Sure," I said with fake enthusiasm, opening the door of the house.

We walked to the car and drove off to the school. We rode in silence, and the time passed quicker than expected. I put the car in park and walked to the office. The same secretary sat there smiling at me.

"She's through there," she said, pointing to a small hall with a room at the end. I walked to the room, and Luxina was lying on the nurse's bed asleep.

"Hi, you must be her father," the nurse said, extending her hand to me.

"Yes, do you know what exactly happened?" I asked, shaking her hand.

"She was in gym class and fainted, is all we were told. I figured the first day of school at a new school was a bit much for her." She smiled apologetically. "You can sign her out at the front desk. She woke up after fainting, but she went back to sleep." I nodded and walked to the desk to sign her out.

When I came back to the nurse's office, Luxina was sitting up on the side of the bed. The color of her face didn't look good, but that's not what sent the dread through my spine. Her eyes looked frightened.

"Come on, peaches," I said, holding my arm out.

She stood up using my arm, and I wrapped it around her. She walked slowly and groggily out of the school. We went to walk down the steps when she nearly hit the ground again. I picked her up and carried her to the car. I sat her in the backseat and ran around to my door, hopping in.

I put the car in drive and pulled away from the school. "What happened?!" I shouted.

"A boy...in gym class..." she trailed off. Rage erupted through me.

"What boy? What did he do to you?! Did he hurt you, touch you, what?!" I gripped the steering wheel.

"No," she replied. "He showed me his wings."

CHAPTER 2

I SLAMMED ON THE BRAKES, and the car came to a screeching halt. "What do you mean he showed you his wings? How old is he? What's his name? What does he look like?" I pelted the questions out. Lucifer placed his hand on my arm.

"She's still lightheaded. For now, save the questions."

"No! I must find out right now what's going on. We don't know if it's a renegade angel in human form or what! Luxina," I turned around in my seat, but she had passed out again.

I slammed the car into drive and sped to the house. I threw the car into park and jumped out. I scooped her up from the back seat and walked her into the house. Lucifer ran and grabbed the door. I laid her on the couch in the living room. I looked her over to see if he had done anything to her. It makes no sense why she keeps passing out. Is she frightened or just completely unraveled that more of us exist?

"Lucifer, wet me a washcloth, please. They're in the bathroom. I have to get her to come to so I can see what he's done to her." Lucifer ran to the bathroom and came back with a cold washcloth. I placed it on her face, patting it in circles, trying to get her to wake. She opened her eyes groggily.

"Daddy?" she asked. She must not remember me picking her up from school. *What the hell did this boy do to her?*

"Yes, peaches, it's me. Do you feel like sitting up?" She shook her head, and I could tell the slightest movement of her head sent dizzying waves through her.

"Sweetie, do you remember anything about this boy?"

"At first, he seemed shy. He wasn't talking with the other kids. I thought he was new like me. I started talking to him. It seemed we had a lot in common. He said he had bounced from town to town as well. I asked him his name, and he skirted around it." Lucifer brought her a glass of water from the kitchen, and she sipped on it.

"What did he look like?" I asked patiently.

"He had blue eyes, the bluest eyes I had ever seen, pale white skin, and red hair."

My heart dropped to my feet. That was the kid from the steps that morning.

"He pulled me to a part of the gym where no one could see us. He said he knew who and what I was. I told him I didn't know what he was talking about. That's when he flashed me his wings. He said they were coming for me. No matter where we went, no matter how far we ran, they would find us." I panicked. *What the hell can we do?* "He said he had a message for me to give you."

"What did he say?" I was on full alert now.

"He said to tell you that he said hi. Damian and Alpha say hi."

"Damian!" Lucifer yelled. "He's trained him to be an angel hunter?!" Lucifer began to pace. I sat down on the floor where I kneeled beside her.

"Daddy, who is Damian? Why do they want us? What does this have to do with us?" She was in tears.

"Do you feel up to packing?" I asked. She nodded. "Good, go pack the necessities as I told you. Pack all the pictures of us in the house. We have to leave." She rose from the couch, uneasy at first, but she steadied herself and made her way to her bedroom.

"You have to tell her what's going on. How much have you told her about everything?" I just looked at him. "You haven't told her anything. She couldn't even sense he was an angel, Incaendiel! For Christ's sake!"

"She wasn't ready to know."

"That's not an excuse! She was in danger today and didn't even know it. She needs to know everything, including who Damian is to her!" He was right.

"What do you mean who Damian is to me? What is he talking about, Dad?" I closed my eyes and breathed out. She had walked back in without us knowing. "Dad, who is Damian?"

There was no more hiding it from her. "Damian is your half-brother." Her eyes went wide.

"I have a brother, and you didn't even tell me!" I looked at Lucifer with a "thanks a lot" look. "When were you going to tell me? Is that why Mom left? To have another family?" She looked at Lucifer. "What do you have to do with any of this? Who are YOU?"

"Lucifer is Damian's father." She teared up.

"My mom left us for you!?" She was angry and hurt. "And you! You didn't even think this was important to tell me?! You are my father! You're supposed to protect me, and by protecting me, you need to tell me everything! How could you not tell me this?" She walked over to Lucifer. "Where is my mother?"

"She's off looking for Damian. We've been searching for him for years. He was stolen from us." Lucifer looked nervous. He didn't know what to say. Hell, I didn't know what to say.

"So, this entire time, she has been looking for him. Ten years! She couldn't pop in and say hello. Sorry I abandoned you with your father!" She flopped down on the couch, crying.

"She didn't know you existed," Lucifer said.

"Oh, yeah, that makes me feel even better." She eyed me. "What else have you not told me?"

I sighed. I guess it's time to tell her everything. So, I sat down and told her the entire story beginning at the fall all the way to the portal closing. She cried through the whole time. When I finished, she eyed Lucifer.

"You're the reason she left. If it hadn't been for you, I would have my mom. This is all your fault!"

"No, Luxina, this is all my fault. Don't blame him. Your mother could have never survived without going back to the Summit." She collapsed in my arms, heaving out tears.

"You shouldn't have made her go. I'm fine. She would have been fine, too." The tears welled behind my eyes. *How can I explain to her that she had a family when she's part of her family?*

"Damian needed his mother. This was before I knew about you. I found you after the portal closed. It wouldn't have been fair to keep his mother from him."

She flew off the handle. "Oh, so it's fair that you kept her from me!"

"That's not what I meant. We had no idea that we were going to get you out of this in the end, nor your brother!"

There are moments in life where you smack yourself and think, I shouldn't have said that. At this exact moment, I was kicking myself.

"What do you mean my brother!? You said Damian was born long before I was." I looked to Lucifer, who turned and walked to the kitchen. *Gee, thanks for the help.*

"I found out about your brother right before I picked you up from school. He's your twin." She sat there quietly and red-eyed.

"When will I be able to meet him?" I knew the question was coming.

"Right now, we need to leave and find safety. Then, we will talk about what we can and can't do."

I stood up and ran to my room. I packed a few changes of clothes and walked back through to the living room. She still sat on the couch with the truth of her life sinking in. I felt like a terrible father as if I had let her down. Lucifer stepped outside when I went to pack, getting the car ready to bolt.

"You ready?"

She nodded and stood from the couch. She picked up her duffle bag and walked to the door. I stopped, grabbed the two pictures from the cabinet, and stuffed them in my bag. I heard her open the door and step outside.

"DADDY!" she screamed.

I dropped my bag and ran to the door. As I walked out the door, I was struck from the side. When I regained my vision, my eyes swept across the yard. Beelzebub stood with the boy she named as Damian. He clutched her to his side, holding a knife to her throat. My hands were wrenched behind my back and zip-tied. I looked over my shoulder to see who it was, and my heart crashed. It was Lucifer.

"What the hell, Lucifer?!" I flexed my arms, but the ties were stronger than I thought.

"Alpha promised to return my son if I helped capture your daughter." His face was solemn. Anger flew through me, but he placed a knife against my throat. "Don't think about it, Incaendiel."

"Well, since we all know each other here now, let's get down to business." Damian snickered. I already hated that kid. "Father wants your daughter, and from what I hear, she should be a nice little firebug to add to his collection." He walked over to Luxina. "Hello, Sister. Since now you know the truth, no hard feelings about earlier." She spat in his face, and he smacked her. "Is that any way to treat family?" He turned back to me. "Lucifer, or should I say 'Dad,' is going to make sure we get away without you hunting us down so soon. What would be the fun in that?" In the blink of an eye, they were gone.

"If I let you out of these ties, do you promise not to kill me?" I was enraged and just nodded my head. He cut me loose, and I socked him in the face. I kept punching and kicking him until he fell to the ground.

"I only promised not to kill you." I kicked him once more and made my way off the porch.

"You will never find her, Incaendiel."

"You don't know me too well then, Brother." ·

I jumped in my car and drove it until it ran out of gas. I handed the keys over to a homeless man. "Do what you want with it. The title is in the glove box."

I walked to an empty alley and then blinked to the Glade. I dropped my human form and took back my angelic one. I walked to the crest of the mountain, and with every ounce of power in me, I willed the portal open. I stepped through and closed it behind me.

"Metatron!" I yelled out.

My voice echoed through the Summit. All the angels stopped and stared. A figure barreled in front of me from the sky, landing with a loud thud.

"Incaendiel, how the hell did you open the portal? How are you here?" I grabbed him up by his shirt.

"Who all was in on it?" My eyes flared flames.

"No one! I swear. We didn't even know what was going on. I swear." I saw fear flash over his face and dropped him to the ground.

"Where's Sophie? Where's my son?!" I boomed.

"Lucifer locked Sophie in the tower and took off with Xavier." He backed away.

"You were all supposed to protect her, to protect whatever was mine, or did you forget who returned you home!?" The ground shook beneath my feet. "Where's the tower?!" He pointed off to the home that once belonged to Alpha. I flew to it, and the closer I got, the tower came into view.

Metatron flew behind me. "You can't open it. We tried!" I landed in front of the door. I pushed on it, and it didn't budge.

"Where's the key?!"

"Lucifer has it," he replied.

I placed my hand around the cracks of the door and pulled with all my might. The wall around the door began to crack. I pulled harder, and the door gave, breaking a hole in the tower. I stepped through the opening, and there she was, slumped against the wall. I ran over to her and lifted her face to mine.

"Sophie?" She opened her eyes, and a tear slid down her cheek.

"I must be dreaming," she murmured. Her head drooped again as she passed out. I lifted her off the floor and carried her out of the tower. Metatron stood shaking. "Where is Mother?!" I howled.

"When Lucifer went haywire, she fled and hid. She was afraid he would hand her over to Alpha." I swallowed back the anger bubbling up.

I looked at all the angels gathered around me. "I freed you from the purgatory Alpha sentenced you to. I now need your help. He has taken the one thing in my life that left me with any sense of purpose. Who of you will stand with me?" I looked around at all the faces. No one spoke up. "Who will stand with me!?" I yelled louder, and still, no one answered. "I see where loyalty lies with you all." I began walking back to the portal where the mountain was.

"Wait, Incaendiel." Metatron ran up behind me. "I will stand with you." I turned around with Sophie's arms still draped around my shoulder.

"I will, too," Michael said, stepping forth from the crowd of angels.

"We will, too," Samael said as he and Azazel stepped forward. One after another, angels stepped forward, just as we did when we took the fall with Mother.

"Thank you all." I summoned the portal open, and we all stepped forward and back onto Earth. The difference this time, they kept their light. We all descended into the Glade, what was once everyone's home who stood with me. I laid Sophie down in the room I once shared with our daughter. I returned to the meeting room, where everyone waited for a plan of attack.

"How did you know about Xavier?" Azazel asked.

"I didn't until Lucifer told me about him." Everyone looked puzzled.

"How did you know he took him then?" Michael asked.

"Metatron told me when I arrived. I didn't call you together just to save my son. They took something from me that meant the world to me. The only thing I had left of Sophie in this world. They took my daughter." Michael's eyes went wide, and everyone looked shocked.

"You have a daughter?!" Azazel asked, bewildered.

"When the portal closed, I found her just outside of it. She is Xavier's twin." The room fell silent.

"We have twins?"

The sound of the voice sent chills through my body. I turned around, and Sophie walked through the group of angels. My heart thumped in my chest, and anxiety overwhelmed me. The world stopped around me as she made her way to me.

"What does she look like?" she asked.

"She looks just like you," I murmured.

I wanted to touch her face, to take her in my arms, but I didn't know if I was still allowed to do that. I broke my gaze off her and brought my attention back to the group.

"Does anyone have a way to track Lucifer? I left him in Alabama, and I don't know if he's still there."

"We've heard rumors that Alpha was holed up in Alabama. We don't know if he will trade off locations now that he has been found out or if he will stay and fight." Michael pulled out a map of the state. "Where were you living when they found you out?"

I pointed to the map. "We were living in Decatur."

I could feel Sophie's gaze on me. I couldn't look at her. I was too ashamed. The one person I thought I could trust her with, the one person who was supposed to take care of her and protect her, broke his vow to me.

"Michael, Samael, and Azazel, you're coming with me. We're going to stake out Decatur for any signs of them still hanging around." Metatron's orders came out in the same voice I remembered him always using. He looked over at me. "We will get your kids back. You have my word."

At this point, his word meant more to me than any other person in this room. They took off out of the room and went on their way to Decatur. The other angels made themselves at home once again as they had so many years ago.

Sophie remained in the same spot. I kept my back turned to her. I couldn't look at her face. It pained me knowing she was locked away in that tower again, and it was all my fault. I leaned over the table the map was laying on and traced every part of Alabama in my head. I figured she would leave the room or say something, but I knew she was waiting for me to say something. I bowed my head and took a deep breath.

"I'm sorry, Sophie." I turned around to look at her. Her eyes were trained on me, but they held no emotion. "I didn't know Lucifer would do what he did." I wanted to walk to her and throw my arms around her.

She walked from the room silently. I closed my eyes and inhaled deeply. I followed her back to the room I had placed her in. I watched her as she stared at all the pictures I had on the wall of Luxina as a baby. I cleared my throat. "She looks just like you now."

"What did you name her?" Her voice sounded so familiar and yet, like a stranger's voice at the same time.

"Luxina. She was the only light left in my world of darkness." She touched the picture of her. "What does Xavier look like?"

"He looks just like you. I think that's what made Lucifer lose it. He loved Xavier, and then he started to change. He became angrier and jealous of him. I don't know what sent him over the edge that last day, but he locked me away in the tower and left with Xavier." I watched as a tear slid down her cheek. She looked over at me. "I could have stayed, and none of this would have ever happened."

"It would've eventually happened. Lucifer wants his son back. He doesn't realize what Alpha has turned him into." I walked over to her and wiped the tears from her cheeks that kept coming in multiples. "I would have never let him take your hand if I knew he wouldn't protect you as he promised me."

I pulled her into my chest, and she heaved in sobs. I cradled her in my arms. She pulled back, wiping the tears from her face. I wanted to kiss her so badly. I craved her arms around me, her body around me. Being this close to her brought back the same magnetic pull I had always felt with her.

"Is it too late?" she asked, looking up at me.

"Too late for what?" I was confused.

"For what we had to still be?"

I didn't even bother to answer. I scooped her up in my arms and planted my lips on hers. I expected her to pull back, but she fell deeper into my embrace and kiss. This is what I missed. This is what I lay awake thinking of every night. I had my Sophie back, but look at the cost. I broke away from the kiss with my heart wrenching in two.

"It is too late," she said as she stepped back from me. I pulled her back to me.

"No, that's not it at all."

"Then what is it?" Her eyes pleaded with mine.

"There's a little girl that stole what was left of my heart that needs to be found. I can't do this knowing those monsters have my baby girl."

LUXINA

CHAPTER 3

PULL IT TOGETHER, LUXINA! Never had I ever had to give myself a pep talk. Then again, I had never been kidnapped by renegade angels. They were the lowest things on Earth, the true definition of demons that had been passed down by the human bible. I awoke shackled in a stone room and smiled to myself. They must think that I don't have any training with my angel abilities. I tried to blink away, but nothing happened. *What the hell?* I tried again with the same results. I didn't understand. I tried to break the shackles, which was pointless. All that got me was two bruised wrists. I turned around and pulled with all my might, trying to get them to break from the wall. Nothing gave; nothing broke, so I slumped against the wall.

"You won't be able to break them," a voice said from the far wall of the room. It was dark, so I squinted to see who the voice was.

"How do you know? Who are you? Why do they want me?" I tried to sound strong in my words, but my emotions were slipping out.

"I know because I've tried. They have unicorn hair melted in the metal. We can't escape unicorn hair." I heard his chains begin to clank. He walked from the dark corner he had been sitting in to where the slight crack of light came into the room. "I'm Xavier. I would shake your hand, but as you see, I, too, am shackled to the wall. As to why they want you, I have no clue. What's your name?" He sat down in the light so I could still see him. It wasn't enough light to completely illuminate his face, but his voice sounded kind and caring, almost as if I had heard it before.

"My name is Luxina. How long have you been here?" I, too, sat down against the wall, still watching him.

"It's hard to say the amount of time I have been here. Barely any light filters through here, and I'm not used to Earth's hours of light. If I had to guess, I've been here all summer."

"Who had you kidnapped?" I still can't believe Lucifer betrayed those in the Summit. I mean, when you think about it, you honestly can't blame the guy. He was trying to get that asshole of a brother of mine back.

"I was kidnapped by Lucifer. They're handing me over to Alpha for the release of Damian." I heard him snort in anger.

"That's exactly why they kidnapped me!" A few moments of silence went by. I didn't know what else to ask or say to him, and I assume he felt the same way.

"Can I ask you something?" His voice, the more I heard it, the more it sounded familiar to me, like the dreams I had growing up.

"What do you want to know?"

"Do you remember me?" I felt like the breath was knocked from my lungs.

"Um, not really. Your voice sounds familiar, but I can't really see your face."

"We've played together in our dreams since we were babies. Mother told me there were no angel babies in the Summit with the name Luxina, but here you are." I could hear the smile in his voice.

"I'm not from the Summit. I was born and raised on Earth by my dad." Every hour away from him, I missed him terribly.

"Is your dad a human?" I chuckled at the question.

"No, he used to be an angel at the Summit. He took the fall when the Dark Mother did and, long story short, sacrificed his angelic light for the others to make it back into the light."

"Your dad is Incaendiel, right?" His voice sounded like it perked up a bit.

"Yes."

"Damian is your half-brother, too, right?"

At first, I was a little stunned to hear that he knew that. "Yes."

"Your mom is Sophie."

"Ok, now you're scaring me. How do you know all this?"

"Well, apparently, you're my sister as well. Your parents are my parents; aside from I've never met my dad." My jaw dropped. I had only just learned about either of them even existing. Now, I have met both of them?

"How do I know you're not lying to trick me? How do I know you're not feeding me this crap to get close to me and find out information for them?!"

"You have to trust me, Luxina. No one in the Summit aside from me knew about another angel named Luxina. We've had a connection in our dreams for years. There must be a reason why. My mother and father are the same people you named. They didn't have kids until that portal was opened and closed. They found me in the Summit, where the portal closed. I've never met my father; I've only heard about him. My grandmother told me about him every day."

"I don't believe you. You're just trying to get under my skin and find out information for them. Stop talking to me!" Tears had started to fall. I had only learned I had a twin brother this morning, and now, he wants to lay claim to that title. This had to be a trick. The angels in the Summit would not have let him be kidnapped. I heard his sigh, breaking me from my thoughts.

"When you were three, we met in a meadow in a dream. A beautiful meadow I have never laid eyes on. At first, we spoke no words to each other. We just stood and stared at each other, frightened of one another."

"Stop."

"I walked closer to you, and you backed away. You tripped and fell backward. I reached for your hand to help you stand, and our powers collided, leveling the valley."

"Stop."

"I stared you in the eyes, and I told you to take my hand. You would always be safe with me in the dreams. I kissed you on your forehead."

"Stop! That's enough! Quit trying to use my dreams against me! You are not the little boy I have been meeting in my dreams. It's not possible!"

He went silent. I was silent. *How could they take such personal thoughts of mine and try to use them against me to gain my trust? It's horrible!*

"Through the mountains and over the sea, the firefly will cease to be." I looked at him as he continued. "Over the valley and through the meadow, the firefly exists in the shadows." My breathing got faster. There is no way anyone knows this poem. "Fly away, firefly, until we meet again. Maybe next time, it won't be a dream that I get to hold your hand." My heart was racing. *It can't be. He can't be the boy in my dreams.*

"How do you know that poem?" I retreated as far as I could to the wall I stood before.

"You're my firefly."

"You can't be him. He's not real, and you certainly can't be my brother."

"We're more than just that, Luxina. We're soulmates. The Dark Mother told me that we must be like Mom and Dad. We were created as one soul and split, and only a tremendous amount of power could have created us."

"Aw, isn't that sweet? The two of you are getting reacquainted." The lights flickered on, and Damian walked in. He glanced over at Xavier. "I should have known everyone, including our grandmother, would have favored you over me."

My eyes fell to where Xavier sat, and I sucked in a sharp breath. It was him, the boy that existed only in my dreams. Dad always told me that he wasn't real but just a dream. I held onto the belief he was real. He had to be real. His face and heart always called to mine. Whenever I was with him, him sheltering me from the world, I felt safer and a little more. My heart fluttered when his eyes met mine.

"Father has plans for you two. Of course, I don't know what they are," he turned to face me and smiled, "but he said I could do whatever I wanted with you two beforehand, aside from killing you, that is." He walked closer to me and ran his finger along my jawline. I moved my head away from his touch, cringing. His touch disgusted me.

"Don't touch her." It was a simple statement, but I could feel the emotion behind the growl that escaped his lips. It sent shivers and chills down my spine.

"The one in chains decides to give me orders. That's quite funny." He walked over to Xavier and backhanded him. I watched as he pulled against the chains, standing up against Damian. I could see the fury in his eyes. "If you weren't so goody-two-shoes, we could've been best buds, but no, you're a mama's boy."

"Don't forget your place, Damian, and mind the words you say. My mother is your mother as well."

"Yeah, and look what she did. She left me and my father behind, my real father, to go screw yours." I could see the anger building in Damian's face as the words left his mouth. The boys stood staring each other down with equal looks of hatred.

"Alpha tells you lies! Our mother has spent the last ten years searching for you. She has spent more time looking for you than what she did raising me! If anyone should be jealous of the other, it would be me. I'm a bigger person. I love my brother no matter what! I wished every day for your safe return!" *I don't think I could ever love Damian.* "I can tell you this, though: you lay another finger on her, and you won't have to worry about mother loving you anymore."

His eyes pierced into Damian's eyes. My breath caught in my lungs. Aside from my dad, no one has ever stood up for me in that way. I watched a wicked grin tug at the corners of Damian's mouth.

"Unlike our stupid mother, she can be broken down. Father has thought this through better than what he did last time." He turned back around to face me. "I will be seeing you soon." He walked to the door and left, leaving the light on. My eyes trailed back over to Xavier, who was wiping the blood from the corner of his mouth.

"Are you okay?" I asked. It came out with more concern than what I thought I felt.

"I'll live. He hits like a girl." I couldn't help but giggle. He just stared at me. "I can't believe it's really you," he murmured.

I could feel the heat rush to my cheeks. Boys never looked at me like that; either that or I never noticed they did. He continued to stare at my face with wonder in his eyes.

"I can't believe you remember the poem. I used to lay awake at night and run it through my head repeatedly. For the longest time, I thought you were a ghost that haunted my dreams, and here you are."

A smile formed on my face as I looked at him. He was gorgeous. Black hair and the prettiest blue eyes I had ever seen, he was a picture of perfection. I couldn't tear my eyes off him, and it seemed he had the same problem. I snapped my focus back to the problem at hand.

"What do you think he means Alpha thought this through better this time? How am I unlike our mother? How am I weaker?"

"I can only speculate the meaning behind that. Mom devised a plan to help the others return from the fall. The love our parents shared went beyond space and time. No matter how many angels Alpha sent or how many times she incarnated, the only person who had her heart, in the end, was our father." I thought back to the story Dad had told me earlier. I hadn't realized how much of a romantic story it was.

"Well, what about Lucifer? He won over her heart, and he's on their side." I watched as fury flashed through his face.

"Lucifer was not always on their side. He became so engulfed in finding Damian he didn't care what the cost would be. He may have stolen a slight piece of our mother's heart, but our father was the one person that she would level the universe for." *So, there is still hope for their unison.* A warm feeling rushed through my heart hearing that.

"So, how am I different? How am I weaker?" The statement still troubled me. I know I'm a strong-willed person. I take that back; Dad says I'm stubborn and act just as my mother did.

"Our mother and father got a chance to exist together in the Summit before the fall. We have not. We have only met in dreams. We do not share the same bond they do because we have never touched one another. Our bond has not been forged yet; therefore, you are weaker than our mother and more susceptible to the charm of Damian." I cringed at the sound of his name.

"I don't believe that the last part is true. Damian gives me the creeps." I got the heebie-jeebies just thinking of his face. Not that he wasn't good-looking, he had all the charm in that department he needed, but I could feel his sinister side. "What happens if Damian does get under my skin?"

He looked at me, staring at me. "The war would start, the official war, and you would be on their side while I fight for this side. In the end, ultimately, if I cannot save your heart...I must..." He couldn't even finish the sentence. He just looked at me with tears glistening in them. "It won't ever come to the latter, so there's no need to say it." He offered me a warm smile, but I could tell he forced it past the emotion welling in him.

I wish I knew what it felt like in real life and not in dreams, what it was like to touch his hand. I remember the power we shared in our dreams. Could it be any more powerful than that? The more I looked at him, the more I knew he was right. I could feel his heartbeat along with mine. I got lost in his eyes every time they met mine. I could never get over the way he looked at me, as if I was the only person in the entire world.

"What's the other alternative?" He stared at me.

"Have you ever heard what came after the creation story?"

"No, just the search for the Garden." He frowned at me. I bet he was running through his head why on earth didn't our father tell me more.

"After Lilith, our Grandmother Omega, left the Summit, Alpha no longer had the power to create human life the way they did together. Without the combined power of them together, his creations came out mutated, vile, and malevolent. That's why Eve was created from a rib as opposed to the way Adam had been made. The mutations were savage beasts that roamed the earth with blood lust. He had long been experimenting on several types of creatures, trying unusual ways to breed them. He branded them all as demons."

"Yeah, Dad told me that Lilith warned them that he would make the Fallen ones out to be evil as opposed to just fallen angels," I remarked.

Xavier nodded. "The first to be made was what you call vampires.

Their thirst for blood outnumbered the animals of the planet that thrived. Alpha tried to destroy the savage monsters and dispatched a sentinel army of his first in command. There were a number of Seraphims, Cherubims, and Thrones sent down to take care of the problems that the beasts were causing. It turned into a blood bath. Alpha had tried making humanity stronger and more agile in his attempts by himself. It increased their strength, but it came with a consequence. The blood lust that frenzied them made incisors develop whenever fresh blood was around. They dropped the army one by one, turning them as well. The angels that were turned didn't become the frenzy of creatures that had turned them."

"What happened to them afterward?" I asked.

"The angels were to become known as the Watchers. Disgraced by their new state of being and unable to return to the Summit, they went underground to what is now called Stygia. They hid from the sight of their Father, damning themselves to the darkness for what they had been made into. When they finally emerged from the darkness and were sensitive to the light's power, they vowed they would hunt down the creatures that had made them the way they were, half-angel half-demon."

"What happened next? Did he send more angels to fight them?" I asked.

"No. Since the best of Alpha's angels couldn't thwart the actions of the humans with fangs, he created another type of horror. He took the blood of hellhounds and created what we know as werewolves. The beasts not only had a blood lust as their enemy, but they killed in more numbers. Not only did they drink the blood of their kill, but they ate the bodies as well. Unpleased by his efforts in creating these creatures, Alpha cursed the beasts in three ways. The first way, whoever survived the malicious attacks of the beasts became one as well. They would shift during the full moon into their form, as opposed to remaining the beast like the originals were, cursing them further into damnation, being neither human nor beast. The third curse was that they all would bear the mark he would later call the Mark of Cain. The Mark of Cain is a blessing and a curse all in one. Whoever tries to harm the creatures would be struck down by hellfire."

"How awful," I murmured.

"I'm sure you have heard some version of Lott in Sodom and Gomorra, right?"

I nodded my head.

"Well, the stories circulating aren't nearly as close to what really happened. There was a band of werewolves running rampant through the valleys. They were growing closer to the city of Sodom and Gomorra, leaving a trail of bodies in their wake. The city had started gathering the virgins of the city as an offering to the beasts so they would go unscathed. Grandmother caught wind of what was happening and dispatched a few of the Fallen Ones to the city. They went to every house, warning them that their actions would lead to hellfire and brimstone. None wanted to listen to their warnings. Lott was the last house they were to go to. They convinced him of the danger of sacrificing his daughter to the monsters and the impending doom of the city."

"Is that when they decided to leave?" I asked.

"Yes. They fled as the monster struck the center of the city. The girls had been gathered in the center, and instead of killing their offering, they stole their offering for breeding. This made Alpha angry at the city for their stupidity in offering virgin women to these beasts. He poured down the fire on the city as Lott and his family ran."

"Then how did Lott's wife turn into a pillar of salt?" I asked.

"Trailing on their heels were a few stragglers that were still scoping the city out for fresh meat. The Fallen Ones tried their best to keep the stragglers from reaching Lott's family. One slipped away and went nipping at the feet of Lott's wife. She went to smack the beast, turning around to fend it off from herself and before her hand brushed the beast, she was struck by the hellfire and turned to a pillar of salt."

"So, what happened to the werewolves after Sodom and Gomorrah?" I asked.

"The Fallen Ones were eventually able to drive the non-shape shifting beasts to the end of the earth, but not before they met their sworn blood enemies, the vampires."

"What happened when the two different species came into contact?" I asked.

"It was war in itself from the frenzy of the two different bloodlines colliding. Neither could kill the other, something Alpha had never expected when he created them. Their blood only combined, making a more problematic creature than what they had been dealing with. When you take two immortal creatures and mix their blood, one with no heart and the other with a heart, you create an undead creature. The dead began to rise in numbers, warrior creatures that only had primal instinct and couldn't think for themselves."

"Zombies?" I asked flabbergasted.

"Modern culture dubbed these horrors as zombies, but the truth of them has trickled away through time. The Fallen Ones spent years eradicating the vile things from the earth. It was after the slaughter of these unnatural creatures that they finally drove the two enemies apart. They drove the rogue vampires into what we now know as the abyss and the rogue werewolves into Tartarus, where they remained as what they had been created from: hellhounds."

"Wait, but there are still legends of werewolves. Like, among the Native American tribes, they have the Wendigo and Skinwalkers," I replied.

"I will get to that part in a bit. Let me tell it how it happened," Xavier said with a smile.

"Ok," I replied.

"What these beasts left in their wake was catastrophic, but apparently, not catastrophic enough for Alpha. He found the rogue Fallen Ones that darkness had consumed and offered them a deal. If they would help him out when it came down to the final war of the Summit, he would restore their light. These Fallen Ones had been called the Forsaken and such from their name; you can imagine they were more than eager to accept the deal. The Forsaken were to be known as Greater Demons. They later kidnapped humans, feeding them their blood and created minions for themselves, the Lower Demons."

"So, even though Alpha had abandoned them originally and was the cause of them turning dark, they fell right into rank with him?" I asked.

Xavier nodded. "As they patiently waited for Alpha to declare the official war, they became antsy and bored. They decided to start experimenting the same way Alpha did. They took the blood of the Seelies they caught and mixed it with their blood, creating sirens and mermaids. They were as beautiful and lustrous as angels were but nasty and deadly as the vampire, and demon blood coursed through their veins. Once satisfied with their marvelous success, they moved on to the werewolves that inhabited Tartarus. When they mixed their blood together, they created what are known as shapeshifters. These shifters weren't as savage and mindless as the other werewolves were but could shift into anything they wished at any time during the moon cycle. They were like their human half-breed counterpart, but more powerful and deadly since the demon blood coursed through their veins with that of the angel blood."

"So, they are the legends I spoke of?" I asked.

"Yes, and when Alpha found out what his First in Command of the Dark Army had done, he punished him, but even though it was done without his say, he welcomed his children of darkness with open arms. He took the blood of these creatures, the damned, the children of the night writhing with demon blood, and created an elixir with it. He waited for millenniums for the right angel to prove their worth to him, to receive the elixir and become more than just a first in command. Then, to his delight, Lucifer and our mother gave him his final wish. Neither of them could refuse to hand over the baby because they were locked away in the tower. He began experimenting at once on Damian. He didn't mutate or morph because he was already an angel. Instead, he became an angel with demon blood searing through his veins, darkening his heart."

"How do you know all this?" I asked.

"You learn to listen when there is nothing to do except be chained to a wall," Xavier replied.

"Well, what does all that have to do with you and me?" I asked, terrified of his response.

"Because we're different than other angels. He either wants to inject us, then take our blood and use it for Damian or inject the same elixir in us to see what we change into."

"Why? Why are we so different from the others?" My bottom lip had started to tremble.

"We're basically demi-gods."

"How can we be demi-gods? You mean, like Hercules, right? Well, Hercules was half human and half God in the myths. We're not!" I stammered.

"We're not demi-gods in the sense of myths. We're demi-gods in the sense of power our parents had in our creation. We're half-angel and half-god, something no one has ever witnessed before. Something Alpha is extremely interested in."

"So, what do we do? I don't want him taking my blood for Damian, and I certainly don't want to become some...THING...a laboratory experiment where I end up growing fur, fangs, and can sing songs like Disney characters." I started to rattle my chains and pull on them. I wanted to get OUT of this place. They were not going to use me as some sort of hypothesis where they don't know the outcome's answer.

"Luxina, calm down! It's going to be all right, I promise. You can't get out of those chains. I have already told you that." He was talking calmly and patiently to me. Well, no, he was talking at me.

"Don't patronize me! We're stuck in here and could become monsters and you want me to calm down!" I started breathing deep gulps, trying to stay calm while he just watched me have my nervous breakdown. "What are we going to do then?" I asked breathlessly.

"The only thing we can do... wait."

CHAPTER 4

I AWOKE from the dark voids of my eyelids. I didn't even remember falling asleep, let alone having a dreamless sleep. I have never experienced sleep without some form of dreaming involved. The dreamless sleep wasn't what captivated my attention; it was the banging of a door as it flew open and hit the wall behind it. I fought the urge to drift back off to sleep as I watched two men drag a body into the room. I could tell it belonged to a female by the black hair that silhouetted the face it hid. I watched as they walked her body by her feet and head to a cot that sat in the corner. I didn't remember the cot being in here, so undoubtedly, they must have come in here once before and brought it in to set it up.

They shackled her hand to one side of the cot that had chains binding it to the floor and wall. They laid her gently in the bed and brushed her hair off her face. To my relief, they stalked out of the room without paying me any attention and shut the door behind them. My eyes trailed back over to the woman sleeping on the cot. Words couldn't describe the beauty that she held. Her black hair had a shimmer to it like the sun hitting glitter. Her skin was the creamiest pale I had ever seen. My gaze drifted from her to Xavier as a feeling gnawed at the pit of my stomach. I glanced in between them noticing they had the same hair color, the same pale skin. *Is this my mother?* I wondered.

"Xavier." He didn't move. *Had they drugged us somehow?* "Xavier," I said a bit louder. He still sat slumped against the wall, asleep.

"Xavier!" I hissed, and he stirred. I watched as he fought to open his eyes groggily and look at me. "Who is that?" I asked, motioning my head to the bed. His head shakily trailed in the direction I pointed, and he bolted upright.

"Grandmother! Grandmother, are you ok?!" Worry and fear streaked across his face.

"That's our grandma?!" I breathed. That's when I noticed how similar she and my father looked.

"This is not good, this is not good at all," he murmured and thought inwardly to himself. "Who knows what Alpha has planned or what he intends with all of us."

The woman he called Grandma began to stir on the bed. She sat up from the bed and rubbed her head as if it were sore. When she lifted her eyes, they met mine and went wide. She then turned her head and looked at Xavier. "Xavier, what are you and your mother doing here?"

"She's not my mother, Grandmother, she's not Sophie," he replied.

"She looks just like her!" she exclaimed.

"This is the girl I told you about from my dreams. This is Luxina, my twin sister." The woman stared over at me wide-eyed.

"Are you sure? No one knew you had a sister. Are you sure this isn't a trick?" She glared at me, and I returned the glare back.

"It's not my fault you all abandoned my father and me here once you went back to the Summit. Ten years. It's been ten years, and not a damned one of you checked on him. You didn't make sure he was ok or see if he was still alive. You left us!" I didn't expect that to roll out, but all the emotion I had been holding back since Dad told me everything boiled under my skin. "How hard would it have been for someone to come look in on him? Make sure that he was ok after everything he did to get you back to the Summit." Tears streamed down my face.

"It was too risky to leave the Summit. We didn't know what Alpha had planned once he escaped." She was calm and collected.

"No, it was too risky to check on him, where you would have found out about me, but it wasn't too risky to look for that filthy brother of mine, Damian. The golden boy that everyone put up on a pedestal to find. The one who kidnapped me from my father! I don't even know what happened to him after he blinked me away. I have no clue if he is alive or dead. I have been the lost child of the light for years, and my father spared me the reasoning behind it. I see it now. Even if you were to know about me, I wouldn't have abandoned him here in this forsaken world to go with you all. The 'all-knowing' power didn't know about me. How do we know you're not the trick? You should know everything! You should be able to still feel his emotions. Why don't you?!" Xavier stole a glance at me and then looked back at Lilith sitting on the side of the bed. No emotion fluttered in her face, no retort, nothing.

"Grandmother, are you ok?" Xavier asked, peering closer at her. She didn't move or respond. She just stared blankly ahead. "Grandmother?"

She turned away from our eyes and rolled on her side on the bed. She didn't respond to his repetitive name-calling. Soon, he fell silent and looked at me. I couldn't quite grasp if he was mad at me or not. He just sat there and stared at me.

"Maybe she's right," he spoke softly.

"Right about what?" I asked back.

"Maybe you are a trick of the mind." The breath caught in my throat. It felt like a hammer hit my heart as I heard his statement.

"Me, the trick of the mind. ME! How do I know you're not!? That brat brother of yours dragged me away from my father. How do I know you didn't have a part of it? How do I know if anything you told me is real?! How do I know you're not Alpha disguised and my real brother, XAVIER, isn't locked away somewhere else? Someone drugged me so I wouldn't dream so that I couldn't communicate with him. How do I know you didn't?"

"I refuse to answer your questions. Grandmother is right. You're not her." I was baffled. A moment ago, he was trying to break his chains to go after Damian and now he doesn't want to believe who I am.

"Apparently, we're not the twins. Twins would know one another. Earlier, you had me stupefied into believing you were him, playing on what I had just been told by my father, Lucifer, and Damian. Now...now I don't even know who I am. Since I'm not who I'm supposed to be then what would you care if Damian draws me to his side? I'm nothing special to anyone but my father."

I sat back with tears glistening in my eyes. I didn't care anymore what may or may not happen. Maybe none of this was real. Maybe this whole room was an illusion. All he did was stare at me, and I wanted him to stop. I flicked my hand to the light bulb, and it sparked and blew to where there was darkness in the room. It was the darkness I was accustomed to by being around my father. He showered me in love, and if darkness existed in his soul, then love existed in the dark.

I slipped back against the wall and sank. No one would understand what we have been through for the past ten years. We were always on the run, moving from town to town so no angels would find us, and now look. I've been captured and thrown into a room where both people in here are trying to tell me I'm not who I am. If it weren't for the fact that I'm only ten years old but look like a teenager, I would believe them. I know when I was born, where I was born, and to whom I was born, and no one can tell me any different from that.

"How did you make the light bulb blow?" the voice called out in the dark. I didn't want to answer; I was done talking. "Could you turn it back on? I don't like the dark." His voice sounded meek and guarded.

"Maybe you wouldn't be afraid of it if you hadn't lived your entire life in the light. I'm used to the dark, and it doesn't bother me. You got to live in the Summit. You got to experience the actual touch of the light. Me, I've been shrouded in darkness my whole life. I'm my father's light, the only light he needs. If I'm not the person you thought I was, and you're not the person I thought you were, why should I care?"

"Please." I have never met anyone who could be this afraid of the dark. I flicked my hand, and the bulb sprang back to life with a new energy current. Xavier sat in the corner, hunkered like a little kid.

"There, happy now?" I rolled my eyes in irritation.

"How can you do it?" he asked.

"Do what?"

"Live in darkness for so long." I had never thought of this to myself really. It was just a natural thing I was accustomed to.

"Apparently, I didn't deserve to be in the light as you."

It was a simple answer, but it packed a punch deep within. *Is that what I really think?* Dad always told me I was a gift to him, that I was the light he couldn't have back. I love my dad, but it really wasn't fair to me. I had no choice. I have never had a choice about anything: where we lived, who I could hang out with, nothing. Xavier stared at me as I sat against the wall, pulling my knees to my chest. Of course, I was right. I was being punished for what my parents did. I wasn't supposed to have been created. There wasn't supposed to have been any light left once everyone returned.

I have never felt this lonely and unhappy before. Sinking into depression has never been my thing. I have always been happy and bubbly, but locked away in this room without my dad, everything was sinking in for face value. I wasn't supposed to have been created.

"Why do you think you weren't supposed to have been created?" I looked over to the woman sitting on the side of the bed, staring at me.

"How do you know what I was thinking?" I asked, biting back the tears after hearing the phrase said aloud. She stared at me, the same stare that Xavier had been giving me. "I didn't say that out loud. How did you know I was thinking it?"

"Just because no one knew you existed doesn't mean you weren't meant to exist. You are right; you are the shining light keeping your father afloat. Without you, he had no reason to live. You gave him that tiny ray of hope that one day, you two would come to the Summit. You two are more alike than you think but total opposites as well: you being the light, he being the dark. If I had known you were born, I would have held you as I did all the other grandchildren I have been given. I'm sorry no one was there for you besides your father. He did an excellent job alone, though," she said, winking at me.

"Grandmother, don't let her get into your head. It's what they want," Xavier piped up. "She will deceive you in any way she can, especially by mimicking the powers of people." He glared over at me. "You may fool others, but you will not fool me."

"Well, I see things went south faster than what I expected," Damian said, walking through the door. "Since you're no longer overly fond of our dear sister, maybe you won't mind if I take her for a little while." He walked over to me and smiled. He reached his hand out and stroked my cheek. "Let's get you out of these chains, shall we?" He removed my manacles and pulled me gently along behind him.

"What are you going to do with her?" Lilith asked.

"Shh, it's a secret." He grinned ear to ear. My eyes flitted from her face to Xavier's face. There was no expression on his, just a blank stare. "Come now, sister, we wouldn't want to keep Father waiting."

He led me from the room with Lilith protesting against my departure. The corridors were gloomy with barely any light filling the space. In the rooms we passed by, I heard screaming and moaning as people shouted out with what could only be torturous pain.

"Those are the ones caught that defy Alpha," Damian said as I shut my eyes, trying to drown out the screams. He led me up a flight of stairs and snaked his way through more halls while I kept my head down, trying to fight off the sounds of the screams erupting from each room we passed. Finally, we arrived at a door at the end of the hall, and we walked in without knocking.

"Father, I brought Luxina to see you," Damian said, shutting the door behind us. The room felt empty and cold. My eyes grazed over all the empty walls and landed on the desk sitting in the middle of the room. Behind the desk sat an old man with silver hair and a smile splattered on his face.

"Hello, Luxina. I have waited ten years to meet my new granddaughter. If you're anything like your parents, you must be a star on the rise. I have never come across two angels that had the power they did, and I must say, I was astonished as well as surprised to learn that their power created you and your brother." He got up from his desk and walked over to me. He placed his arms gently on my shoulders and looked me over. "You are a radiant child." He smiled and then drew me in for a hug. "Now, I bet you're wondering why I went to the lengths I did to bring you to see me. Your father has been angry with me for years, and I doubted he would bring you to me for you to meet me. I hope they have been treating you properly. If anyone has stepped out of bounds, let me know, and they will be punished."

He motioned with his arms to a chair that I can only assume he wanted me to sit in. I obliged and sat down as he walked back around to the other side. Damian took a seat on the wall away from the table. I nervously glanced between the two of them. Neither made any indication they wanted to hurt me or cause any type of torture that I heard as I passed through the halls.

"Is that all you wanted was to see me?" I asked boldly.

"As I said before, I had never come across two angels with the power that your parents share. I wanted to see firsthand what kind of power lay dormant within their children. You and your brother are special; I hope you know that. Neither of you are full angel, human, or anything. You are, how should I say this...you are higher ranked than the Seraphims in the Summit. I'm sure you have heard of demi-gods." Well, Xavier was right about one thing. I nodded my head. "Well, we can't call you a demi-god because you aren't half-human. I have decided to call you two fey."

"Fey? Like in faeries?"

"You are far more superior to faeries. Legend says that the fey were direct creations of the Gods of the mythos, placing them among earth as faeries. It's partially true; they were created by Gods. Even your parents do not know there are other powers as abundant as your grandmother and me, but there are. Where we come from, we haven't the slightest idea, but we exist. However, what separates you from the faeries on earth is that you were created by two angels that had the powers of Gods. Your grandmother created your parents with, as she said, a bit more love added. In truth, she mixed part of her power in with them. They both were our favorites. We always allowed them into the Garden to roam and have fun. They were so light-hearted, but both deadly with their power. When your father fell, it felt right that they be split apart. That much power together was too catastrophic for them to even grasp. It saddened me to learn that your mother was part of a revolution against me. I'm not so bad. She suggested her own punishment and took to it. I was never mad with her or with your father. It was quite the opposite watching these two combine their powers together to complete the task they set out in the beginning to accomplish.

"When they created you two, I was baffled with the product. I could feel the power radiate through the heavens when you two sparked into being. I knew immediately what you had become. You are more than just angels with godlike powers. You are lower-level gods, in between demigods and gods. The angel blood that runs through you is just as remarkable as the godlike powers that do. You are fey, and your children's children will be as well. You two were created for each other just as your parents were, but you are more powerful than just simple twin flames. You two will change everything in this universe together, and I want to be there to witness it."

"That's all...you don't want anything from us?" It was stupid to ask, but I was curious.

"Actually, now that you have asked, there is something you could do for me. I would love to examine your blood, see if it can be replicated or if you are one of a kind spontaneous creation."

"No." I was flat with my answer.

"I would never hurt you, child. Look at your other brother, Damian. I have done no wrong by him." I glanced over at Damian sitting somberly in his chair. He gave a halfhearted smile, but I could see something eating away at his thoughts. When our eyes connected, it was as if I could hear him tell me not to do it.

"No, I don't want to be a laboratory experiment."

"Well, with your permission or without your permission, I will either get what I want from you, or I will cause you days of pain with my own injections to make you more...powerful." Xavier was right. He would turn us into something else.

"My answer is still no. I know more than what you think about all this. You will not get my blood. If you had the power to duplicate us, you would have already. For all I know, you want to take our blood for him," I said, motioning to Damian, who looked tired and weary.

"Well, I see cooperation is not in the works here. Damian, take her back to the cell and have the men start immediately working on her. I want the results documented and blood work each day after the injections." Alpha looked over at Damian who at first looked as if he were to say no as well. He glanced at me once more, and I could definitely see the noticeable pain in his eyes that time.

"Yes, Father, as you wish." He stood and walked over to me, tugging at my sleeve to stand.

"Excellent." Alpha flicked us away with his hand. Damian pulled me from the room, and we started back down the halls.

"I'm sorry, Luxina." It was the only thing he said to me, and I didn't respond. I knew he had no choice but to listen to the only person he knew as a father. I would obey my father as well.

When we returned to the room, there was a bed set on the side of the room I had been in. I watched as Lilith looked me over to see any signs of trauma while I had been gone. Damian bent down, picked up a manacle, and laced it back around my wrist.

"I'll be the one to check on you each day." He held my hand and squeezed it lightly then let it drop to my side.

I sat down on the bed as he walked from the room. I didn't know how these injections were going to go. All I knew was he wasn't getting untainted blood from me. I looked over at Lilith, who sat nervously on the bed. My eyes skimmed over to Xavier, who still hadn't moved from his seat.

"You were right, Xavier," I whispered.

"Right about what?" he asked. Two men walked into the room, pushing a cart with syringes on it. I looked from the cart and back to him.

"Lie back on the bed, and this will go smoother," one of them said. I obeyed and lay back on the bed. I felt the sting of the needle as they injected one of the syringes. They followed suit with four more and then left the room.

"Luxina, what are they injecting you with?!" Lilith hissed. I couldn't answer. I was already beginning to feel the dull ache wash over me. "Luxina!"

I drifted off into space. I didn't pass out. I was aware of everything. I could hear my name being yelled at to get my attention. I couldn't respond when I tried to answer. It wasn't as bad as I thought it would be. I began to drift deeper into an unconscious state. My name became less audible until it felt like I was in utter silence and complete darkness.

CHAPTER 5

AT FIRST, it felt like a bee was stinging me. I figured the men had come back in and were giving me more injections. The bee sting feeling grew in intensity to where it felt like a knife was digging into my arm. The pain started radiating from my arm and through my body. It felt like I was being stabbed repeatedly. A hot sensation filled my body along with the stabbing. I felt like I was being thrown into a crematorium, and fire was searing my flesh. I knew from biology that once the fire burns your nerves, the pain subsides before you die. In my case, the hot, fiery pain didn't leave. Instead, an icy hot feeling enveloped me as well. I felt like I couldn't breathe. I tried to swallow, but it felt like hot coals trickled down my throat instead of saliva. It felt like lava sprang from my tear ducts as I cried the pain out.

I writhed in pain. There was no relief from it, no momentary give to the searing flesh. I thought I was going to die from sheer agony. My body started to convulse, and I felt my hands flailing against the wall hard. I don't know if I was actually hitting the wall or not, but even the sensation in my hands didn't register a new pain. The burning, stabbing pain overwhelmed any of my other sensory functions.

I didn't know how long the pain had lasted, but it finally began to subside. My eyes opened and burned in the light above me. A blurry shadow hovered over me, and when I finally focused, Damian was bent over me, mouthing words. Apparently, my senses hadn't come back yet. I tried to sit up, but the world felt like it was raining hellfire around me when I lifted any limbs to move. My hearing started to return in a low, shrill hum. It grew louder and shrill, as if someone were blowing a whistle. When it reached normal hearing capacity, I realized it wasn't a whistle but my own screams being muffled.

"Luxina!" Damian yelled. He touched my arm, and pain shot through it, sending another scream from my lips.

"Stop touching her! You're making it worse!" another voice boomed out. I couldn't recognize the voice through all the pain and ringing in my ears from my own screams of anguish.

"I have to make sure she stays conscious. She wasn't supposed to have a blackout like that! Luxina, it's Damian. Say something, anything!" I tried to respond, to croak something out, but even my throat was so dried out and hoarse from the screaming it didn't want to cooperate like everything else. "She can't do these injections. They are literally killing her."

"What do you freaking care?!" the voice yelled out again.

"She's my sister. I care!" Damian yelled back. "I'm going to Father at once to report this. I will return in a few minutes." He looked down at me. "I'm going to bring you something to drink." He felt my forehead. "She's burning up! How many did they give her at once?"

"They gave her four shots."

"Four! Were they purposefully trying to kill her? I'll be back!" he yelled and stalked out of the room.

My head throbbed, and my body was so tired and weak. I couldn't even will myself to sit up. I remember when I was little, I got into a nest of fire ants. The pain from their bites didn't even compare to the agony I just experienced.

"Luxina, can you hear me?" The voice I didn't recognize was speaking directly to me. "I'm sorry. I'm sorry I said those things. Just hang in there." It had to be Xavier talking to me. I still couldn't answer back. Even the strain of thinking sent fiery ripples through my body. "Grandmother, is she going to be ok? What can we do? She won't make it through another round of those injections."

"I don't know what we can do. We have no way to stop them unless Damian convinces Alpha otherwise." Her voice was faint in my ears. My chest heaved up and down, trying to gulp down fresh air to fill my burning lungs.

There was a commotion in the hall, and two men hovered over top of me again. "You can't give her anymore! You will kill her!" Damian yelled, pushing them away from me. I watched as one of them pinned him to the wall.

"Are you going soft already, Damian? Maybe we should give you your dose sooner. Your angelic blood is fighting it off sooner than last time." The one remained hovering over me, smiling insidiously down at me.

"Leave my sister alone!" Damian yelled, and the other man pulled him out into the hall and shut the door.

The one that remained bent over me. "This will be fun. You're a fighter. Your blood is stronger than what we thought so Alpha said to up the dose."

"Leave her alone, Abaddon!" Lilith yelled.

"Oh, Mother, you cast me out in the darkness and made me this way. I thought you would enjoy my behavior." I felt the sting of another needle and whimpered. "Shh, little one, just let it run its course." He thrust seven more needles into my arm, and the fire took my body over again.

"Please," I managed to croak out. "Please stop." I knew my begging would be futile. I heard the screams of those they tortured with these injections. I knew there was no relief from it.

"Be a good little girl now," he said and left the room. Damian burst back in the door.

"Luxina, stay with me. Fight the darkness!" he yelled into my ear. It was too late, though; the darkness was beginning to swallow me.

"Find my father," I managed to say before I was totally enveloped in the darkness and pain.

Stories from the bible poured into my mind. The fiery abyss of despair described seemed like a cakewalk compared to the fire that blazed through my veins. It makes you wonder how much accuracy was written in Revelation of how those would be treated if they didn't succumb to the God of the Old Testament. How many souls believed they were truly cast into the lake of fire to burn until God decided they had met their doom and washed their souls clean of the livid waters? It wouldn't come to me, the relief of cool waters. I had made my choice, and I was sticking to it. I had defied Alpha. He would make me pay for the defiance. I felt powerless, mortal, and human. I didn't feel like a god or an angel. I couldn't stop this from happening to me.

An eternity of pain is what it was described as. Who could save me? Who would jump in this burning lake of torture to rescue me? The darkness of my unconscious mind dissolved, and I opened my eyes in the lake of fire. I could see it. It was as real as it was described in Revelation. I could feel the boiling water cooking me as if I were food undercooked and not yet done. The tortured screams I heard earlier filled the lake, and I could see their faces, the faces of the damned. Their skin was melting away. And I believed if mine could melt away, some sort of relief would envelop me. Without nerve endings, you can't feel pain!

I turned my face from the lake and saw dragons filling the water with their putrid fire, sustaining the heat in the lake. I watched as creatures filled the lake with gasoline to keep it burning hot and wild. Is that what the lake was? Pure gasoline? I began to choke as I convinced myself I was gulping down gasoline instead of the boiling water. I felt my throat and lungs incinerate. Death at last! But death did not come to me. I sat choking on the fire and gasoline. Each breath I took in felt shorter and shorter, and I assumed I would suffocate as opposed to burning alive. Still, I kicked and thrashed about in the water, sucking more and more of the burning liquid down my throat.

I was locked in this nightmare, the pit of eternal damnation. "You could end this pain," a voice called out in the lake. End the pain? Yes, I want to end the pain. "I just need your blood." What? My blood? No! No! "Then continue to suffer." The fire seemed to grow larger and hotter after the voice left. Had Xavier been tortured this way? If so, how is he still alive? Did they believe me to be weaker than him, more susceptible to giving in? I smiled inwardly. I lived my life in darkness. The dark is my best friend, the only love I know. The dark is what soothes me, the only thing I have ever been accustomed to. I am the light in the dark. I am the candle of freedom that burns bright no matter how fierce the wind blows trying to snuff it out. I am strong. I do not bend. I do not break.

"I will not bow!" I yelled out from the molten lake of lava. "I will not break!" I yelled louder, screaming with what breath was left in my lungs. "You will not make me falter. I will not fall! I am stronger than you are! I am not your child! I am my father's child! I am a firefly!"

The pain lasted and was intense, but I coped with the agony from it. The lake started to dissolve around me, and darkness swept across me once more. The dark was blissful. Through the dark, I saw a light develop.

It began to grow brighter and brighter. When I reached the light, my eyes focused on a face.

"We have to get you out of here." Xavier leaned over me, trying to break the manacle shackling me to the bed. I looked over to where he had sat and saw the holes in the wall where he had pulled himself free.

"How..." I whispered breathlessly.

"You are not the only one who is your father's child," he replied. He heard me at the lake. Was he there, too? I didn't see him there. How did he hear me?

The shackle clattered to the floor, and I felt lifted in his arms. "Wait, wait, where are we going? We can't leave grandmother." The words trickled from my tongue.

"There's no time. You need to leave before they kill you," Lilith said. "I will be fine. Go!"

I had no time to argue. I felt the cool rush of wind on my face. I opened my eyes and saw we were in the air. My arms wrapped tighter around Xavier, who in return, tightened his grip around me. "Where are we going?" I croaked out.

"We're going to Stygia, the only place we will be safe," he replied.

"What about the Glade? My father? That's where he will be..."

"No, they will search the Glade. Whoever stands against Alpha to turn you over will die. We must find power. The Watchers were the strongest angels. They can handle whatever he sends."

"What if they won't help us?"

"They will help us." He sounded so sure of himself.

The frigid air against my skin felt like heaven, but the burning poison coursing through my veins still had me balled up in pain. I began to drift back into the darkness, and the fire returned like a nuclear bomb being dropped on me. I felt myself free-falling through the blackness, and then I thudded.

"Luxina! You must stay awake! You're thrashing about!" I couldn't help but drift off into the void. The burning lake returned, and I could see a figure standing above the fire. The picture of Dante's Inferno doesn't compare to the monstrosity that stood before my eyes. The figure had the head of a bull and the body of a horse. Its tail whipped at me like a lizard tail striking me and tearing the flesh from my body. I howled in pain.

"Do you think you can escape me?" the voice boomed. "Every time you close your eyes, I will be there!"

An icy cold gripped me, and I began choking. The lake vanished, and I pried my eyes open trying to suck in air. My lungs filled with water, and my eyes stung from seawater piercing the tissue. I thrashed in the water, trying to get to the surface to cough the water from my lungs. Hands grabbed me by my waist, and I fought with all my might to be loose from them. They felt hot, unnatural against the cold of the water. Within minutes, I was on the shore of a beach, coughing up the salty water that had infiltrated my lungs.

"Are you ok?" a voice echoed in my ear. I could barely breathe, barely see, and all my senses were distorted. I spit mouthful after mouthful of water out. "Luxina!" the voice shouted. The hot hands returned to my body, and I smacked them away, trying to fight them off. The hands felt like the poison in my veins, burning me from the outside in. "Luxina, stop! It's me!"

My brain started to register everything. I had thrashed around in Xavier's arms, and he lost his grip, dropping me into the ocean. His hands felt unnatural on my skin. "Why are your hands so hot?"

"You're burning up with fever! Your body is registering it as hot, but they're really colder. We have to get you to Stygia." He picked me up in his arms, the torturous heat back on my skin. I expected to feel the cold rush of air, but the wind was seized from my lungs. When I blinked my eyes and reopened them, we were no longer at the ocean but at the entrance of a mountain.

"The Glade," I breathed in relief.

"No, this isn't the Glade. It's the entrance to Stygia, where the Watchers and Nephilim are. Belial should be here." He walked through the cave entrance and deeper into darkness. I fought with all my will to stay awake. I knew what would happen if I drifted off into the black of my mind.

A voice echoed through the passageway of the cave. "Announce yourself and say why you are here. Trespassers are not welcomed too kindly."

"Baphomet, we need to see Belial right away," Xavier replied, struggling to hold me in his arms.

"You know the rules. You must first send for admittance before just showing up. There are rules—"

"Baphomet! Take us to Belial. Alpha has poisoned her blood with demon blood injections. If we don't get the toxins removed, she could die!" Xavier pushed past Baphomet, winding down the dark tunnel. I felt a swift gush of air as Baphomet swooped past us two.

"Follow me. He won't be happy about this."

We were led through tunnels and passageways that zigzagged and winded downward. My ears began to pop, so I knew we were descending faster than the air pressure could keep up. We soon found ourselves in a cavern that was lit by torches. I looked around and saw at least twenty to thirty people standing around. My vision was starting to duck in and out with tiny white spots floating around. There was a rush to my head and a tremendous pain that wrenched me from Xavier's arms.

"Please, someone get Belial!" Xavier shouted as he leaned over me.

"What's wrong with her?" I heard a woman's voice ask.

"Baphomet, you know the rules. They are instituted for a reason," another voice chimed.

"I didn't have a choice, Ozael. He said Alpha had poisoned her blood with demon blood. Watchers or not, rules or not, we are still angels and bound to protect one another!" Baphomet yelled.

I began to convulse again. I could feel my body thrashing and kicking, lashing out at anything close to me. "We have to hurry," Xavier urged. Foam began to pour from my mouth, and my body stiffened.

"How long has she been having the seizures?" another voice echoed through the cavern.

"A day. Damian said they overdosed her with the injections," Xavier replied to the voice.

"How many did they give her?" it asked again.

"Twelve," he replied.

"Belial, is it too late to do anything?" the woman's voice asked again.

"I don't know. We will do everything we can for her, though. She is the daughter of Sophie and Incaendiel," Belial replied. I felt a hand brush my hair and a slight prick in my arm, and I fell out into the dark abyss.

The fire was tolerable this time. It burned, but it was nowhere near the pain I had felt while in the Lake of Fire. I looked down at my searing flesh and saw that the flames were beginning to die down and flicker. My skin's busting, oozing blisters were beginning to diminish in appearance, and my skin was returning its original shade of creamy ivory. Soon, I found myself drifting off into a somber state of darkness. No pain, no agony, just sleep, and sleep I did.

INCAENDIEL

CHAPTER 6

"ANY NEWS?" I asked as I walked into the gathering hall. Metatron and Michael stood bent over maps strewn across the table. They looked up with a grimace and shook their heads. I sighed heavily. It had been three weeks since they had taken Luxina. There wasn't a sign of her anywhere. None of those we had captured for information were speaking, either from fear of what Alpha would do or for fear of what I might do when I heard the news. Alpha had disappeared into thin air once more, and we had no leads on his whereabouts aside from the ones we had when we started the hunt.

"Don't give up hope, Incaendiel. News will pop up soon," Michael offered, as I paced back and forth at the table. It was easy for him to say. It wasn't his child that was kidnapped by an insane, tyrannical dictator God. I leaned over a chair and gripped the back of it with my hands. I was beyond irritation or aggravation. I was sinking into a hole I didn't know how to swim in, the hole that I had fought so many times in the past, the dark abyss from which there was no return from.

I felt a hand sweep over my back, and I regained my wits. It was the hand of salvation that has always pulled me from the fathoms of the deep. I looked up into Sophie's eyes and was overwhelmed with emotions.

"Come," she motioned with her head. "Take a walk with me." She started through the doorway, leaving me staring after her.

"Go. As soon as we have news, we will come for you," Metatron said.

I nodded my head and walked from the room, following the weaving trail her light left behind in its wake. I found myself twisting through the corridors and popping out in the throne room Mother used to take refuge in. I followed the luminescence through the door behind the throne and popped out in the meadow. The one and only time I had been here was with Mother ten years ago.

I found Sophie sitting beneath the tree in the middle of the meadow, watching as the seasons went through their abrupt changes. She sat mesmerized in wonder as she watched the leaves brown and fall, the snow cover the ground, and then the sunshine reappear, melting away at the snow-covered banks.

I sat down beside her and pulled her close to me, wrapping her into my body. We sat in silence, watching the ebb and flow of the seasons before us. "I never imagined this would turn out to be how our existence would unfold," she said. "We have to find them, Incaendiel, but we cannot blame others for the result not being what we want to hear." She always had a way with her words with me.

I turned my attention to the ground where the river cut through. Maneuvering its way from the water was a snake. It didn't move too fast, but it wasn't a hesitant slither as well. I stood from my sitting position and began to walk to the serpent. When we came within a few feet of each other, it stopped moving and stood up as if in a strike position. I went to smack it down, but no sooner had I reached my hand toward it, it had disappeared. I turned to walk back to Sophie, and there it stood in a strike pose behind me. It was taunting me as a cobra would taunt its prey. I picked my foot up to stomp it, and once again, it was gone. I turned in a circle, looking for the creature, when I heard a startled gasp from Sophie.

I spun around to face the tree we had been sitting under, and there, in front of Sophie, taunting her in a strike pose, was the snake. Even though she had let out a startled cry, she looked serene and composed. It looked as if she were staring straight through the snake as if she was hypnotized. It proceeded to curl up her arm when I ran to her, and was about to smack the snake away when she threw up her hand in protest.

"No, Incaendiel. It's Andromalius," Sophie said in a monotonous tone. "He is telling me about the kids." She touched my hand, and I was frozen in place.

"Hello, Incaendiel. I hope I find you well today. I'm here to deliver some good news and some bad news. The good news is that Xavier was able to escape from Alpha with Luxina. The bad news is that Alpha used injections on her, and we are currently pulling the demonic poison from her blood." Andromalius was precise, with no emotions in his voice.

"Injections? What the hell was he doing to my daughter?" I was furious.

"Calm, Incaendiel. We are reversing any and all of its effects. She did the hardest part already by not accepting the injections and rejecting them with her mind. Once we get her stable, we will wait until the coast is clear and then deliver them to you."

"No, there will be no waiting. We will come to her at once." I began to pace in my mind although my body remained still.

"You cannot come here, Incaendiel. It will draw too much attention. This way is better for all of us," Andromalius replied.

"Well, has the group at least considered our proposal to join the Guardians of Light? It will be a war the world has never seen." I wasn't sure of what his answer would be, but there was a slim chance of them joining.

"We will be holding council here in the next few days once we get all the poison out of your daughter's system. Right now, we have seven healers pulling it out, and three of them hold seats on the council. As soon as we come to an answer, I will come in person to deliver our answer. Do not give up hope, Brother. The odds are in your favor as of now."

The snake retreated from Sophie's arm and slithered back to the river, disappearing into the water. I didn't know what to say or how to respond to the information he gave us.

"There was word in Evermore that Alpha had been concocting potions and injections to combine the powers of the wicked he had created." She sat staring where the snake had disappeared into the water. "He experimented on Luxina, but not Xavier...why? Who knows how long that monster has been giving Damian injections?"

"We don't know for sure he has been," I replied, trying to coax her out of her trance.

"Are you seriously trying to say he acted the way he did because he truly loves Alpha?" Her words were bitter and angry. "All you care about is finding your daughter. You don't care about my sons at all, even if one of them is your flesh and blood. You don't care!" She stared at me with hatred in her eyes.

"Oh, you're making this out to be my fault? Whose lover was it that kidnapped one of the kids and helped kidnap the other kid after locking YOU in the tower? Don't turn this on me, Sophie. Every move I ever made was to protect you, to keep you from harm, to keep you from dying! I stood on the edge of the cliff that night and was going to take the plunge. I couldn't bear living without you, and you couldn't stay with me! The darkness would have seeped into you. You weren't strong enough to hold it off. So, I sacrificed us for you to stay alive.

"Just as I was about to slip over, I heard it. I heard her cry. She saved me. She gave me a reason to keep going. She's all I have had for ten years. You have been surrounded by a sea of angels. All I have known has been mortals. I had to hide her growth anomaly and move from place to place. But that doesn't matter to you, does it! All you're worried about is getting *your* sons back. The son you couldn't even bring to meet his father. If you had visited me or sent someone to give me a message, you would have known about your daughter.

"Do *not* try to make me out to be the bad guy in this situation. We are both equally hurt, and we both want our kids back. Right now, we need to stick together and not blame each other." I was harsher than I meant to be, but I believe she got the point.

"Lucifer was right about you. All these years...you have changed." She stood up and made her way from the center of the field to the exit door. I remained behind, sitting beneath the willow.

Had it truly been too long for us to recover what we had? I had spent millenniums trying to get her to remember who I was, to remember our love, and was met with obstinance. I finally broke through to her to find out she not only had been having an affair with the same angel who tormented me for years, but also had a son with him. How in all this did I come out to be the bad guy? I sacrificed my love for her to live. I brought her back from the dead, something we are forbidden to attempt.

She was blind to see the extent Alpha had manipulated Damian into being. He was, after all, the one who took Luxina. She wasn't there to see the look on the kid's face. It was pure hatred and evil. It was almost as if he blamed Luxina as if she were a torturing device Alpha used against him. I can only imagine what he was put through by Alpha to turn him into what he is, but it was no excuse for his actions. Lucifer, on the other hand, was just doing what I would have done to get my child back. Even so, what they both did was unforgivable in my eyes.

I sighed and stood up. So much had changed in the last ten years, and there was no end to it still. My life had been unraveled in the blink of an eye, and I made the wrong decision and trusted the wrong person with the other half of my being. I'm sure she hated me for handing her over to Lucifer, but I knew it was the only way for us to survive. She had to go to the Summit. I couldn't let the darkness turn her into what I am.

I still don't understand what we were, what we had been crafted into. I have yet to see another angel with our powers.

As I crossed the field, there was a shift in the atmosphere in this field of dreams. Something was off, and I could feel it. I turned back around to face the willow tree in the center of the field. The leaves had begun to change colors, and one by one, they slowly floated to the ground. This I had never witnessed and was fairly sure it wasn't supposed to happen. The breeze stopped blowing, and it felt like time had come to a standstill.

The ground began to tremble beneath my feet. The earth broke open beneath the willow tree, and it caved into the molten core that flowed beneath it. The field started to burn, and smoke filled the area. The skies darkened, and lightning crackled through the air. The last remnants of the tree sank into the magma, catching fire and disappearing. The lava began to overflow onto the hill and slowly trailed down the field, catching every plant on fire.

I ran to the exit of the concave and pushed through the building. I was met with a handful of concerned eyes as I burst through the door.

"Everyone must get out now! The mountain is going down!" I yelled.

We all dispersed, running to the different tunnels and signaling everyone to get out as fast as they could blink. We all made it to the top just as the mountain exploded and erupted into a volcanic plume of fire. I searched frantically up top for Sophie. I began to zig-zag in between all the others.

"Sophie?! Has anyone seen Sophie?!" I yelled frantically.

Everyone stood in silence as the answer came to me. She wasn't here. I turned back to the mountain and walked closer. It felt like a bomb had gone off, and I was caught in the shell shock aftermath. I felt arms on me, and I shrugged them off as I walked closer to the burning mountain. Arms wrapped around me, and I fought them off. I was soon overcome by dozens of arms and pulled to the ground. I heard a frantic yell erupting through the crowd and tried to drag myself closer. I knew it was her scream. *She was in the mountain!*

I hadn't noticed I had been crying until I felt the wetness on my chest. I hadn't known I had been the one screaming until my hearing was restored.

"What the hell happened in there?" Metatron yelled, shaking me. "Did you set the Glade on fire?! You could have killed us all! And now Sophie..." he trailed off as he saw my face. I could only imagine what I looked like at that moment. My heart was tearing in two all over again. For the last time, the final time, I had lost her...forever.

"It wasn't you," Michael stated as he loosened his grip on me. I shook my head. "Then what was it? Are there Alpha's doings?"

I shook my head again. I knew what this meant. I knew deep down what had happened. "It's Mother..." They all dropped their hands off me.

"What do you mean it's Mother?" Samael spat through gritted teeth.

"We were in the concave. Andromalius came to us with news."

"What news did Andromalius have?" Metatron asked.

"They have Xavier and Luxina. Alpha injected her with demon blood, and they were pulling the poison out." I swallowed the lump back in my throat.

"What about joining us as an alliance?" Michael asked.

"They haven't met yet. The healers are the council members. They said give them a few days."

"What does this have to do with Mother?" Samael asked again, more annoyed.

"The willow died in the middle of the field and fell into the core. It set fire to the concave and erupted the entire mountain. The concave was Mother's sanctuary. Something must have happened to her. This mountain is part of her."

Everyone grew silent. "Alpha has her," a voice from the back of the group called out. Everyone turned to see who said it, although Incaendiel already knew who it was.

"How do you know Alpha has her?" Samael asked viciously.

"Do you honestly doubt my visions, Brother?" Gabriel called out as he made his way to the front of the line.

LUXINA

CHAPTER 7

I OPENED MY EYES, and blue lights swirled all around me. My vision was still blurry and dimmed in and out. I could still feel the faint touch of fire coursing through my veins. I tried to lift my head and sit up, but it felt like I was tied down. I began to panic.

"She's awake," a voice called out.

"Well, put her back to sleep, Aislinn," another voice replied.

"I don't know if I can, Camael. No one has ever broken my sleep state before," Aislinn replied.

"Well, we need to do something fast. I cannot work on her unless she is completely under," a different voice replied.

"Irisael is right. Her eyes have blood spots in them, which means severe trauma that needs to be healed soon. Sanarael, can you help Aislinn put her back under?" Camael asked.

"I'm no Raphael, but I can try. It may take three of us to do it," Sanarael replied.

"I will help. I can induce a heavier sleep for her." How many people were in this room with me?

"That's perfect, Somniel!" Aislinn exclaimed.

I saw three people surrounding me. I couldn't make out their faces through the blur, but the glow they had around them was spectacular. I saw a rainbow aura, a baby blue aura, and a pale, yellow glow about their bodies. I blinked my eyes rapidly, trying to clear the haze, but with each eye blink, my vision grew darker and darker. Soon, I was in total blackness once more. Instead of it being a calming black as it was before, I felt my chest tighten in panic. I was afraid of this darkness. This was something I had never experienced before.

Dad had always taught me there was nothing to fear about the dark walls, but something about these walls sent panic and fear through me. I fought back with every ounce in me. I felt a hand touch my skin, and it felt like a blowtorch was cutting through my skin. More hands fell over me, and I screamed in my head from the pain.

"What's happening?!" Camael shouted.

"Something's going wrong. Her body is sucking the poison back in instead of pushing it out. I have all my power trained on her, and it's not helping anything!" Irisael yelled.

"Alpha must have her locked in some sort of hallucination. These injections show her what her deepest fears are. Luxina!" Aislinn yelled. "Luxina, whatever it is you see, it's not real. Do not be afraid!"

The darkness grew more tormenting. Fires began to pop up and surround me in this hallowed space of air. The flames licked at my skin, burning me as they had done in the lake of fire. I was never going to get through this. The injections were permanent. I could feel them seeping into my heart and killing my grace. My chest grew tighter, and I couldn't breathe.

"What are you doing here?!" I heard Camael yell.

Oh no, he found me! I knew it had to be someone that Alpha sent. They had tracked me here through the connection in my mind. With each tormenting thought that passed through my mind, the fire grew brighter, stronger, and more heated. My blood felt like it was boiling, and I felt that at any moment my entire body would explode.

"We will fill you in later. How long has she been thrashing like this?" the voice asked.

"She just started when we tried to put her back into her sleep state. We can't work on her conscious, and the sleep state is inducing a hallucination from the injections," Aislinn replied.

"Let me help," the voice stated.

"If we add any more healing waves, it could destroy her body," Irisael retorted.

"Then back off and let me do it," the voice replied.

"Do not step into our territory and boss us around," Camael retorted.

"Do you want her to die or live?" the voice boomed. It sent ripples and shivers through my spine.

In the flames, a face began to form. A hand reached out and grabbed me in the flame. The hand burned into my arm, and I howled in pain. The arm yanked me closer to the flames, and I peered through the fire at who had a hold of me. I felt the breath leave my lungs as I stared into eyes that looked like a reflection of mine.

"Mom?" I asked.

"Let Raphael heal her!" Sanarael yelled.

I was sucked from the flames and darkness. The hand that had held tight to my arm was being pulled along with me, still burning into my skin. It wasn't as bad as the eyes that burned into mine. She mouthed words to me, and I struggled to understand what she was saying. I was being pulled further and faster through the hollow black.

"I can't understand you!" I cried out to her.

Just as the light began to approach, words formed in the air. "This is all your fault!" She released her grip on my arm, and I watched as I was sucked away from her. She never took her eyes off me.

I erupted through a cloud of smoke, and light surrounded me. Sunshine as far as the eye could see covered a valley in warmth. It wasn't the cold, burning warmth of the fire. It was peaceful and serene. I felt it fill me on the inside. As hard as I tried, I tried to let it take my anxiety, but those words and her voice chilled me to the bone. She hated me, and I didn't even know why. I had never met her, and she didn't even know about me. Why would she say those things to me?

Sorrow filtered in through the warmth, and I found myself balled on the ground, crying. The one person I wanted to meet, wanted to love, hated me... Why? What had I done that was so terrible she would hate her own daughter?

"Luxina, sweetie, come back to me," a voice echoed through the valley. I knew the voice, and it swelled my heart to hear it. "Come back to me, sweetie."

"Daddy? Daddy! Help me, Daddy! Save me from this perpetual hell! I can't take it anymore! I'm not strong!" I cried and cried.

"Come to me, sweetie. Follow my voice."

I listened to the echo throughout the valley. My eyes fell on a cave at the bottom of the hill from which I stood.

"Follow my voice."

I walked slowly to the cave, hesitant that I would succumb to the darkness.

"Daddy, I'm scared!" I pleaded.

"It's ok. Follow my voice," he replied.

"How do I know it's not a trick?" I cried. My breath heaved in and out in terror.

"Follow your heart, sweetie."

I walked through the cave and found myself lying on a table. I walked over to myself and analyzed my body. My skin had grayed, and there were red blisters all over me. I swallowed the lump that formed in my throat and choked back the sobs. "I'm so scared," I whispered. "What do I do?" I reached out to touch the cold arm that lay on the table.

I bolted upright, gasping for air. Tears blurred out everything around me. I once again felt hands and arms around me, and I fought with all my might. I struck out with my hands, landing blows against the person in front of me. I would not be taken again. I refused to be taken.

"Honey, it's me. It's me!" I heard crying out through the noise. The arms wrapped around me and pulled me in. I breathed in deep, and the smell hit me, the smell of a meadow, of flowers, of sun.

"Daddy?" I cried out. The arms tightened around me, pulling me in closer.

"Yes, baby, it's Daddy," he replied.

I felt the splash of tears on my face. I threw my arms around him and clung to his chest.

"I was so scared," I whispered. "I didn't... I thought... I thought he had me again," I sobbed. "I tried to be brave. I fought him for so long. I didn't want to give in," I cried.

"You did what most could not do, Luxina. You did not bow to him and his torture," he replied, choking on his words.

"Xavier?!" I yelled in panic. "Where is Xavier? Is he ok? Is he safe?" I asked in bewilderment.

"Xavier is fine. He's waiting with the others."

"Mom... where is she? I saw her..." I cried.

"You saw her?" he choked.

"Yes, in the fire. She said... she told me this was all my fault! I don't understand! Why does she blame me? What did I do wrong?" The sobs heaved out.

"We will talk later about that," he replied.

"Incaendiel, we're not sure if all the poison is out of her system. We weren't able to finish the healing process." I looked around for the face of the voice, and my eyes fell on a beautiful woman with long, flowing, blond hair. Her eyes were purple, and a faint glow of yellow rounded her pupils.

"That's the least of our worries right now. With everyone showing up here, Alpha will be alerted, and he will send out his warriors." I looked around for the voice, and my eyes fell on a man. His eyes were piercing blue but with a red glow to the pupils. His hair was black as night. They both had markings on their skin that resembled tattoos. I looked around at everyone in the room and noticed for the first time that all the angels had these markings as well. Everyone but my father and me had them. I couldn't recall them being on Xavier either. What did these markings stand for?

"Can you keep Xavier and Luxina here?" Incaendiel replied.

"Yes, we can shield them, but the rest of you, I'm afraid our shields can't withstand that much angelic power in one place," Belial replied.

I looked up at Dad wild-eyed. "You can't leave me here!" I protested.

"We will come back for you. Right now, it's not safe for any of us to be here." He brushed the hair out of my face.

"Please, Daddy, don't leave me here," I pleaded. I wrapped my arms around him and clung to his side.

"You will be protected here, and it won't be for long. We must make sure all the poison is removed before you leave."

CHAPTER 8

IT HAD BEEN A DAY since Dad had left us in the care of the Watchers and Nephilim. I paced quietly waiting for him to return for me. They were nice to both Xavier and me and provided the protection they had promised. I replayed over and over in my head the last few things I could recall from my dreams when I was injected with that serum. The one memory of my mother hurt the most. *Why is it my fault?*

I asked myself that over and over, but I couldn't come up with an answer. Xavier thought it was Alpha playing a ruse. I don't think that. It felt genuinely like my mother. Her anger and her words made my heart hurt. I wanted to know my mother so badly, and now, she is blaming everything that has happened on me.

As we sat waiting through the day, we had someone pay us a visit. I had never met her before, but her eyes were an amazing color of purple.

"Hello, Luxina. It's good to see you up and about doing better," she said, as she walked into the room.

"Thank you," I replied with a smile. "I was out of it when I was brought here, so I don't know anyone's names. Who are you?"

She smiled. "I am Sophia," she replied. "I came to talk to you about what happened when Alpha had you captive."

"Sophia? You were Lucifer's mate, right?" I asked, sitting down.

She nodded grimly. "Yes, I was. I left him not long after the Garden of Eden exile of Adam and Eve. I came here to be with my brothers and sisters that weren't allowed to return to the Summit. I pleaded with

Lucifer to join me. He told me no. He had something he had to take care of before he could join me."

I watched her face as she told me her story. I could see the pain in her face when she spoke of him.

"What would you like to know?" I asked.

"Everything," she said, taking a seat beside me.

Xavier joined us from across the room.

"What did he inject into you?" she asked.

"We aren't entirely sure. All we know is it's supposed to be a concoction of demon blood," Xavier replied.

"Did he inject you as well?" Sophia asked Xavier.

He nodded.

"Why didn't you tell me?" I asked.

"It wasn't important," he replied. "I didn't react like you did. The first injection was painful, but the ones that followed were not."

"What did Alpha tell you, if anything, about what you are? What did he call you?" Sophia asked, glancing between Xavier and me.

"He never spoke to me about what we are. All I know is we are like demigods," Xavier replied. Their eyes turned to me. "Did he tell you anything?" Xavier watched me as I dabbled back and forth, deciding whether to answer or not.

"Yes, he said we were called fey," I replied. Sophia laughed heartily.

"He told you that you were fey?" she asked.

"Yes. I asked if it was like faeries, and he said no, that we were what created faeries." Sophia still grinned at the joke, and I had no clue what it was.

"You two are not fey," Sophia chuckled. "Alpha lied to you, Luxina. The fey are broken into two segments: The Light, which are called the Seelie Court, and the Dark, which are called the Unseelie Court. They were created from the Old Gods of Atlantis. They are literally the faeries of the myths, alongside the nymphs and sprites. Those that are of the race were created by an old God that goes by the name of Enki."

"Enki? Like Enkidu from Egyptian lore?" I asked, growing more curious.

"I see they still teach about ancient civilizations among the humans," Sophia smirked. "Yes, that is the same Enki. He frowned on Alpha when he went to Dragonazi for help to create all the 'evils' of the world."

"Why haven't any of the angels ever been told about the others? The other gods? We have always thought it to be Alpha and Omega," Xavier interjected.

"Omega, or Lilith as she goes by now, wanted to clue all the angels in on it. Alpha refused. He believed they would turn their backs on him and take to the other gods and goddesses. He has always been a jealous god, so jealous he thought he needed an adversary."

Sophia paused, flitting her eyes between us.

"I never imagined Incaendiel would have become his true adversary. Lilith never had it in her heart to go against Alpha. However, when she created your parents, when she added the special and extra ingredients, she awakened an incredibly old power. Once I left Lucifer's side and banished myself to Earth, I came to Lilith, my mother, where she confided in me a secret. Even Alpha didn't know about the secret. When they created the angels, all of us, they used their power alone in doing so. When it came to creating Sophie and Incaendiel, she mixed a few ingredients together and molded them within their bodies before they brought them into existence."

"Angels weren't just 'thought' into existence? They were molded like humans?" I asked, confused.

"Yes and no. Humans were molded from the dust of the Earth, where they return when they die. Angels were molded from the dust of stars," she replied.

"So, what were the ingredients she used in making our parents?" Xavier asked.

"She took the feather of a phoenix to give them power over fire. The Seelie court offered up a bit of their faery dust to create an enchantment."

"What kind of enchantment?" I asked.

"No one knows for sure. Neither of your parents ever dared to venture to the Seelie realms because of how precious they are and would be coveted to keep, especially by Mab," Sophia replied.

"Who is Mab?" I asked.

"The Dark Queen of the Unseelie court," Sophia replied.

"What else did Lilith add to make our parents?" Xavier asked.

"Lilith traveled to the deepest fathoms of the universe and found a star, an old star, the first and largest star to have leapt into existence. This star was a sun in another galaxy where other gods and goddesses ruled over their intelligent creations. These civilizations were dying off as their sun began to fade. The solar system was being abandoned in search of life elsewhere to cohabitate with other life forms."

"Aliens!" I interrupted. I blushed from the outburst.

"Yes, what humans call aliens were these other civilizations. Lilith went to the galaxy before the sun began to supernovae and grow cold to take the power the sun was relinquishing into the universe. She added this power into her moldings and then, alongside Alpha, poured life into them. She had once asked Dragonazi what the oldest creations that existed above gods were. He told her only those born from the power of the universe hold more power and are above the gods. He told her they were called Ntidus Assis, the Shining Ones. Only the wisest of gods knew how to rehabilitate this old form of power. She sought out dozens of the crones and sages until she found her answer and made your parents."

"Who is Dragonazi?" I asked.

"An old, old God that Alpha had sought help from prior to Lilith taking the fall as his adversary," Sophia replied.

"So, he gave her the idea to make our parents? And in turn, their power made us?" I asked. "What else did this power make?"

"The gods used to take this power and add a slight drop to their human creations. This is where Indigo, Crystal, and Rainbow children come from; they are earthly star children. You two are Stellar Star Children, as well as your parents; always created in a pair to reproduce...twin flames."

I sat back and drank all this in. *Shining Ones? Could it be that was why Alpha feared my dad?*

"Is that why the injections wouldn't take?" I asked. She nodded. "What about Damian? He is half a shining one, right? They must continuously dose him because he burns through it. Is there such a thing as half a star child?"

"I haven't looked into it that far, but Damian is Sophie's son. I would have to consult Dragonazi for a definite answer. What I do know is we need to get Damian away from Alpha as soon as possible before the injections do take. Part angel, part star child with demon blood...that's a scary thought. Who knows how much longer his blood can fight off the injections?"

"Will the Watchers help us? I mean, not just to save Damian, but also to take down Alpha for good. For too long, he has destroyed everything that was dear to me. My parents spent millennia apart; Xavier and I were kept apart for ten years because of him. Now, he has Damian and tortures creatures for their blood to experiment with. He's a monster!"

I hadn't realized how angry I was with Alpha until this very moment, but I truly despised him.

"I will hold council with the others and give you your answer by dawn's first light. It will take more than just us Watches to take him down. If agreed upon, we have a lot of work creating an alliance of fighters against Alpha."

I drank everything in. I sat with everything spinning around in the void of my mind. Dad had always told me how manipulative Alpha was. I rolled everything over in my mind so far that I had been taught.

"Sophia, if you don't mind, I need more information," I said, still staring out into space as I spoke. "My father has always spoken of the evil that Alpha was. He said he used propaganda to insinuate wars on earth, but I need more details than that."

"Are you sure you are ready for this information download?" she asked. "It's a bit more than what most people hear their entire lives." I nodded my head and glanced up to her, locking my eyes on hers. "Very well." She took a deep breath and exhaled. "Humanity has always been preyed on by Alpha. Lilith really pissed him off when she snaked into the Garden and told Eve to eat the fruit of knowledge. He has worked consistently to not only keep humanity from learning of the Goddess but also so humanity wouldn't know how evil he was."

"I'm sure your father taught you about the Illuminati and the Luminari brotherhoods, correct?" Sophia asked. I shook my head. "Well, I will tell you two different stories of who they are. One story society believes them to be, the other is who they really are. To get to these stories, I must also go into the story of Atlantis. I mentioned Atlantis earlier, but I didn't think of going into the story.

"Before the birth of Lucifer born flesh as Jesus, there existed this place called Atlantis. It was said that their civilizations were powered by a god other than Alpha. A hod older than he and more powerful than he, the God Enki that I told you of. This made Alpha sorely angry. The gods who had created this place of wonder in the world were given permission to do so by Lilith, who had domain over Earth after the fall. The same gods who gifted your parents with their sun's energy are the same ones who created the inhabitants of Atlantis. Many believe that they may have been the actual extra-terrestrials from the solar system abandoned after the sun died.

"These people were beyond any advancements of the humans that lived here on earth. However, their presence sparked creativity in the humans of Earth. The Mayans created the temples and all the structures of their civilization. The Egyptians built their pyramids and other iconic statues. The influence wasn't noticeable at first. With each advancement of nations, Alpha became increasingly jealous. The influence this society had over his creations made him angry. He thought only he should be able to persuade his creations.

"Word got about in the cosmos, and Enki knew Alpha would try to destroy the city of enlightenment. They withdrew the civilization from the world and buried it deep in the depths of the earth. When they withdrew the civilization, the influence that was held over humanity dissipated. This took Earth from the fourth dimension of existence into the third. The power the gods had in this world came to neutrality as they saw that Alpha would do whatever he wished to do.

"Alpha thought he could pull all the free-thinking humans back to his side when he sent Lucifer to the world to walk as Jesus. Lucifer did the opposite. Instead, Lucifer influenced his followers to break farther away from Alpha and closer to the Goddess. Instead of being a poster boy for Shamballa, he fronted Agartha. The two of them together created the Brotherhood of the Snake. Shamballa, being that of the Illuminati, is the Red Dragon, and Agartha, being that of the Luminari, is the Yellow Dragon. This enraged Alpha, so he worked quickly to make amends for it. He made sure the authentic teachings never made it into the minds of man.

"Shamballa, the Illuminati, want a government-controlled world. When the government controls the world with the access point directly connected to religion, world domination is shown. The withdrawal of Atlantis really hurt the ebb and flow of free thinking. However, those connected to the divine oneness of the Dark Mother were able to lift the veil of truth from their eyes. Those that were consciously aware of what the Illuminati were monopolizing from created factions. The Rosicrucians were born and later grew into the Freemasons. They were led strictly by those of the fallen.

"The Illuminati retorted by using the inspiration that Atlantis had on Egypt and exploiting the iconic symbol of the all-seeing eye with the pyramid. They also labeled the Luminaris with that of Alpha's name to confuse the followers who sought the feminine divine. Alpha then labeled the Illuminatis as Omega, even though their energies were masculine. Agartha was clearly seen as solace and sanctuary for the Atlantean priests who were seeded and dispersed. At long last, they took refuge among them before the Illuminati could wipe out the Kumaras for good. Without their influence in the world, there would be absolutely no way around the Illuminati.

"With the rise of the Illuminati, Alpha was able to manipulate and plot against the Dark Mother. With Eve taking a hit by eating from the Tree of Knowledge, women were slowly pushed to the back part of the brain as opposed to being superior to men. They were looked at as taints;

they were the cause of their departure from the Garden since submission was lost to them, thanks to Lilith. Women were the reason man was damned. Ultimately, the influence Alpha had over men and how a woman was perceived enabled Alpha to have the priests delete the Dark Mother from existence in the Bible. He then had them perpetuate fear in humans by making the adversary evil and only there to bring down the salvation of man. It was never the plan of Alpha for Jesus to die on the cross. Lucifer was supposed to escape the confines of the soldiers, but he remained behind to be selected to die for his rebellious teachings.

"It has become harder and harder for Alpha to remove the Dark Mother from humanity." Sophia stopped and grew silent.

"So, what you're telling me is that Alpha has personally persuaded lore throughout humanity to destroy grandma from existence in the human world? How did he personally do it? The angels just influenced through touch and thought. Did he literally come down to the humans?"

"Alpha has taken many guises over the years, unbeknownst to the Dark Mother. He has always had his finger dipped into humanity. He would be an advisor to the Presidents of the Nations, or he would be on the council that elects the pope. Anywhere he could possibly influence man to control HIS religion, he was there advising away. The Bible of humanity was written by man but guided by the word of him. He has literally corrupted humanity by instituting the Illuminati and heading it himself."

"So, in order to completely take Alpha down, we would also have to eradicate the Illuminati... right?" Sophia nodded. "What else?"

"We will have to once again embark upon the war that was started millennia ago before Eve was ever brought into existence. We must eradicate any beast or any creature he has made to symbolize the fear that makes humanity cling to religion. We must break down all mythologies, all dogma. We must take out his foundation for existence to weaken him and make him vulnerable. Do you understand what that means?"

I nodded. "We're going to need reinforcements. We will need every fallen angel that was returned to the Summit, all angels willing to fight against him, and more," I said, gazing at her. Our eyes locked, and I could feel the information exchange between our silent minds. "Do you think both the Seelie and Unseelie courts will help us?"

"We will see, Luxina. Right now, we all need our rest. In the morning, the council meets and will decide the point of action.

CHAPTER 9

MORNING ARRIVED as I waited impatiently for Sophia to bring us news of what the council had said. I had odd flashbacks from my time with Alpha and the lake of fire he had thrown me in. *Why did he need me so badly?* I shook my head and cleared my thoughts when they landed on Damian. I could vaguely remember him leaning over me and asking me if I was ok. Xavier stood beside him, arguing for him to stay away. I could see the frantic look in Damian's eyes. He knew what it felt like. He had been tested on the same way and didn't like it. He helped Xavier escape with me...

"A penny for your thoughts," Xavier murmured, breaking my concentration.

I smiled weakly. "I was just thinking of Damian."

His face fell a bit. "Oh," he replied.

"We need to save him, Xavier. He is our half-brother. He doesn't deserve the treatment he has received from Alpha. He was forced through what we were as well. We have to..."I paused as Sophia entered the room.

We both abruptly stood in her presence.

"News from the council?" Xavier asked.

She stood solemnly. "Yes, but you aren't going to like it."

"Tell us," I implored.

"The Council agreed to join the cause on one condition," she stated, pausing for a moment. She looked between us and sighed. "They will only join in if both the Seelie and Unseelie courts agree to fight in league with us. If either oppose, then we will not be joining the rest of the Guardians to fight against Alpha."

"Well, that's good news!" I exclaimed.

"No, it isn't," Xavier sighed. "The Seelie court hardly lets any creature in that isn't pure fey blood. It would take a great amount of bartering with them."

"Well, what about the Unseelie court?" I asked.

"Oh, they would love to have us there," he replied. "But it's like the Hotel California. You can check out anytime, but you will never ever leave unless they allow you to."

"Xavier is right," Sophia stated. "And between the two of you, they would never let you leave because of how special you are."

"Why?" I asked.

"Because you are a beautiful creature that they don't possess in their realm," she replied.

"Well, it's a chance we are going to have to take," I blurted.

"Absolutely not!" a voice yelled out.

I sighed heavily. "Dad! We can do this!"

He wrapped his arms around me. "I just got you back from that twisted monster. I won't let you walk into a den of even more devious creatures than that of Alpha. I will go," he replied.

"Incaendiel, you mustn't," Sophia argued. "They would keep you as well!"

"They could try. I have had my fair share of dealings with the Unseelies for centuries. They know me and would listen to me. However, the kids are new specimens. They would want to keep them," Dad replied. "But, before anyone goes on any adventure, there are more important tasks at hand that must be seen through."

"Like what?" I asked.

"Like spending time with you and the son I had no clue I had," he replied, looking over at Xavier.

Xavier's face clouded over. "This is more important than catching up. Grandmother was left with that insane lunatic!"

"Mother can hold her own," Dad replied. "I need this."

"There is a chamber off to the right down the hall where you all can spend some catching up time together uninterrupted," Sophia said. "I am going to tell the council the decision was made to implore the fey for help."

Xavier, Dad, and I walked to the chamber that Sophia had directed us to. Xavier took a seat in the corner while Dad and I sat down beside each other. He looked as if he hadn't slept in weeks. It dawned on me...

"How long have I been gone?" I asked.

"Two weeks," he replied.

"What?!" I exclaimed. "Two weeks? It felt like just a couple of days!"

"That's how Alpha manipulates you. He puts you in that room, and you have no sense of reality," Xavier replied.

Dad looked over at Xavier. "I'm sorry."

"For what?" Xavier asked.

"For not being there for you. For not being there to save you. For not knowing you ever existed when, of course, you existed. There are grudges being held for not being told about you that I must deal with myself, but I am sorry no one ever told you about me. I am sorry they never let you see me. It's my fault," Dad replied.

"How is it your fault?" Xavier asked smugly.

"Because I am dangerous to you. Just like I was dangerous to your mother. I have... darkness in me that will never leave. That darkness will harm anything that is bright around me. Once this whole war is over and Alpha is defeated, I plan to send Luxina to stay in the Summit," Dad said.

"What?! No! I am not going anywhere without you!" I replied defiantly. "I am fine! My light is fine! You are not blanching me, Dad! I refuse to go," I said matter of fact. "Refuse."

"Where is my mother?" Xavier asked. "They locked her in the tower was the last I saw of her."

"When we were at the Glade, there was a fire. The entire mountain was destroyed by Alpha's hellfire. I don't know if she just didn't make it out or if Alpha has her. If what Luxina saw while she was out of it is true, then Alpha has her... and he is running experiments on her as well."

"We have to go back!" Xavier yelled, jumping from his seat.

"Where you two were is a fortress!" Dad yelled back. "No way in and no way out! You were lucky once. I am not risking your lives to take you back to save people. That is what the council and the fey are for."

"You can't tell me what I can and can't do, *father,*" Xavier sneered.

"Enough!" I exclaimed. "Xavier, listen to Dad. Dad, stop being bossy. We are going to get everyone back! But we must have a plan, like Dad said. We can't run back into a trap."

"Whatever," Xavier replied, storming out of the room.

Dad went to follow, but I stopped him. "Let me. He will listen to me," I said.

Dad gazed at me and smiled. "Just like your mother."

I left Dad behind in the room as I went to look for Xavier. I found him looking at maps in a large library.

"What are you doing?" I asked.

"Looking for where we were so I can go back," he said, walking over to another map.

I followed him and lightly touched his hand. Shock waves of energy ran through me, and I nearly toppled from the surge. He caught me as I was about to fall. I laid into his chest and peered up at him as the energy between us intensified.

"Please, don't leave my side," I whispered.

I saw his face crumple as he leaned in for a kiss and whispered. "Never, my firefly."

Alarms sounded all around us. "Oh no," I breathed. "They're here."

"Take the children to the river, now!" Sophia barked as she ran through the room.

Five Watchers surrounded us and led us out of the room through dark passages and corridors. Before long, we were locked inside a room and were being guarded.

"What's happening?" I demanded. "Where is my father?!"

"When it is safe, we will let you leave. For now, just make yourselves comfortable," one of them replied.

He looked different than Sophia. His skin color was different. "Why don't you look like the other Watchers?" I asked.

"Because we are the Nephilim. We are the offspring of those who were cast out from the wars. The Watchers protect us as they always have. Our parents are both angel and mortal," he replied. "We are the abominations Alpha tried ridding the world of. When the council pledges the allegiance of the Watchers, we pledge our allegiance to our forefathers as well and join them."

I sat thinking quietly to myself when it dawned on me. "Xavier, hey," I said, nudging him. "We can get into the Seelie court."

"What?" he asked, trying to follow.

"Sophia said that Lilith went to the Seelie court for enchantments to make Mom and Dad. We have a touch of Seelie running through our blood. They would let us in," I whispered.

"You heard Dad. Neither of us is going. He is," he replied.

A knock sounded on the door. The Nephilim guards took out their weapons and stood in front of us to protect us.

"It's Sophia, let me in!" she yelled.

They unlocked the door and opened it. Sophia ran in and yelled, "Close it back!"

She had a look of bewilderment on her face.

"Where is my dad?" I asked, standing from my seat.

She looked at me sympathetically. "They took him. Alpha took him. They were looking for you. Lucifer..." she trailed off. "We must get you out of here. The river is just through the back gates," she said, walking to the middle of the floor.

She removed the carpet that laid on top of a door.

"Follow this passage until it ends. Take a boat across the River of Styx and get to the Seelie and Unseelie royalties. Tell them what is happening. Plead with them, beg with them, offer them riches, but do not offer anything of yourself to them. They will try and trick you; they will try to make you stay in their courts." She motioned for the Nephilim I had been speaking with to walk over. "Go with them, Praeziel. Protect them with all your will. They will need it."

She didn't give us a chance to protest. She pushed both Xavier and me through the hidden trap door. Praeziel followed, and she shut it back. We heard the lock locking it in place, and the little bit of light that came through the boards disappeared as she laid the carpet back over top of it. We heard a loud bang as the door burst open to the room we were in.

"Where are they, Sophia?" Lucifer demanded.

"You will never find them, love," she replied.

"Oh, but you are mistaken, dear Sophia," Alpha said.

"Let the other child go, Alpha. You are going to kill him with your experiments," she hissed.

"Oh, I beg to differ. It seems as if the last injection has held out far longer than any other I have given him. Pretty soon, I will make a permanent one and bend you all to my will!" he exclaimed.

Damian! We are too late to save him.

"Damian, come here, son," Lucifer called.

"Yes, Lucifer," Damian replied.

"Kill everyone in this room, especially her," Lucifer spat.

"Let's go look for the other two," Alpha said. "They can't have gotten far."

There was silence as everyone left the room.

"Damian, you don't have to listen to them. You don't have to do this!" Sophia pleaded.

"Scream," he said.

CHAPTER 10

"WE HAVE TO GO BACK and help her!" I protested as Praeziel and Xavier pulled me along in the tunnel.

"We have to do what Sophia said," Praeziel replied.

"We have to help—"

"No! I will not disobey orders from my mother!" Praeziel yelled.

I went silent and stared at him in disbelief.

"Yes, Sophia is my mother. My father wanted nothing to do with me after I was born. He tried to sacrifice me, and she intervened. Alpha had told him to do away with the filthy Nephilim, and she saved me. So, as much as I would love to save her right now, she left me with one final wish. To keep you two safe and make sure you got to the Seelie and Unseelie Queens to pray for help."

"Which one are we going to first?" I asked.

"The Seelie court, of course. We will ask King Oberon and Queen Titania for their allegiance and then follow up with the Unseelie court if Alpha hasn't already beat us to it," Praeziel replied.

"Are they nice?" I asked as we trudged along in the dark.

"The Seelie court caters to humanity. They are the light to the dark," Praeziel replied.

"How do we get there?" I asked.

We reached the end of the tunnel, where the mouth opened to a river that had a boat.

"Everyone, climb on," Praeziel ordered.

Xavier and I climbed on while he pushed the boat and jumped on as it left the dock.

"We must find a meadow of white ash trees. They are the portal into the Seelie realm," he replied.

"In school, we studied Robert Frost. The teacher told us that the largest meadow of white ash trees was in Isle of Mann," I stated.

"Then that is where we have to go," Praeziel replied.

The water forked off into three sections, each of which was an assorted color stream. There was an ocean blue stream to the left, a black stream down the middle, and a golden stream to the right.

"Do you know which one to take?" Xavier asked as we grew closer.

"Of course," Praeziel replied. "The one down the middle leads you to the mortal underworld. As you know, when mortals die, they do not go to the Summit. The one to the right is a special river that leads you to the Garden of Eden. Our cave was built right where Adam and Eve left the Garden once they were banished. The river to the left is our passageway out of here."

At the mouth of the river stood two large beings dressed in black robes, holding scythes. They crossed the scythes, and the boat stopped.

"Who dares to enter the mortal realm from this entrance?" one of them asked.

"It is I, Praeziel, sent by Sophia herself to serve and protect the Ntidus Assis in their journey to the Seelie courts. We had to take this path since the conclave was under attack," Praeziel stated boldly.

"Passage granted," the other one said.

They lifted their scythes, and the water started flowing once more. The boat lurched forward, and Praeziel bowed to the two figures as we passed through the gates to the mortal world.

Once we were out of earshot, Praeziel said, "Lucky for us, Alpha doesn't have complete control over everything in this universe."

"How does he not have control over them?" Xavier asked.

"They are older than Alpha. They are Guardians of Death. They govern what Alpha cannot touch. He cannot interfere with humanity's souls. Even he is limited in power," Praeziel replied.

We drifted in silence for a while. The scenery was gorgeous as we entered the mortal world. It was nearly technicolor like the Summit was supposed to be. My mind began to stray, and I couldn't help but think of Damian.

"Praeziel?" I asked.

"Yes, Luxina," he replied.

"Will you help me save my brother?" I asked. "He is being forced to do what Alpha wants him to do. He doesn't do it out of free will. Alpha controls him with the same injections that they gave me. We must rescue him from Alpha and detox him the same way I was detoxed before it becomes too late to save him. I don't want to lose him to darkness. This darkness... it isn't like the darkness my father has. It's malevolent like those that are Forsaken but worse."

"The reason it is different from that of your accustomed darkness or even that of Forsaken is because it isn't angelic at all. Omega, your grandmother, requested from the Seelie Queen, Titania, an enchantment for her elixir to make your parents. Well, we have been doing surveillance on Alpha for a while. He too went to the fey, but not Queen Titania or even King Oberon. He requested court with the Unseelie Queen Mab.

"At first, she refused his request. She didn't want to have any part in the destruction of the natural order of the oldest universal power." He nodded to both Xavier and me. "When she didn't give him what he wanted, he began to kidnap Unseelie fey and drained them of their blood. However, the blood wasn't sufficient on its own. So, he went through them one by one, draining the Unseelies of life. The Queen of Air and Darkness couldn't bear to see her beautiful court dropping like wildflowers starved of water. So, she granted him his request. She withdrew one pint of her own blood for him to use.

"However, there was a price for him to pay as well. If he were to fail with the amount of blood she gave him, he was to never return to the Otherworld. He had to remain a prisoner of the Unseelie court for the rest of his days. There would be no more blood offered than the pint she gave him as well."

"So, he traded his freedom, his godly powers, to create a serum to mutate us into monsters?" I asked flabbergasted.

Praeziel nodded. "And he is close to perfecting it. Your brother doesn't have much time left before the injections don't burn through his blood anymore. When the injections stop burning, that means they are working."

"What if the injections only burned once? What if they only initially burned, and you didn't feel anything for the rest of them?" Xavier asked.

"Then that means they were successful," Praeziel replied, narrowing his eyes at Xavier. "Why?"

"When he gave me the injections, the first one hurt, but I was so angered by the second injection, I felt nothing. I don't feel any different, though... so are you sure it means they worked?" Xavier asked.

"You may be different. You are full blooded Ntidus Assis. The injection might not work on either of you at all. Your brother, however, is not full blooded. He is a half-blood. So, he is in more danger than either of you ever will be," Praeziel replied.

"How would we know it did work on us?" Xavier asked, with a hint of fear in his voice.

"If it did work, we will soon find out at the Seelie court. They detect anything in your blood that is malevolent," Praeziel replied, with a tad of worry on his face.

"What?" I asked. "Why that look?"

"They may put a kill order on him if he does have demonic blood in his veins. He poses a threat to their realm," Praeziel replied. "They make you swim in a lake of purity. If the water stays the same, your blood is clean and pure. If it turns black, it means your blood is tainted."

"So, what does that mean?? We were both injected with the serum," I asked.

"Yours was burned out of your blood. Him," Praeziel nodded toward Xavier, "I'm not so sure if it was or not."

"Is there a way we can test that theory? How would we know he still has the serum in his blood?" I asked.

"Not all Nephilim live at the conclave. Some live very mundane lives. I would have to put in an urgent call to a brother who works in a laboratory in a hospital. He would be able to view the malformities under a microscope," Praeziel replied.

"Alright then, first stop is mundane city," I stated.

"There is another way," Praeziel said. "But it isn't a pleasant one; however, it wouldn't involve interrupting the mundane life that the Nephilim lived."

"What is it?" I asked impatiently.

"There is an oracle that lives as a hermit. She is powerful beyond her years. We have protected her entire lineage, which dates back to what is referred to as biblical times. She can sense the presence of angels, demons, and alike. However, we haven't called on her family in years. She may not even know about the war at all. It's a risky chance," Praeziel replied.

"What's her name?" I asked.

"She goes by Starfire," he replied.

Our boat crested a bank, and we all disembarked into a meadow. I had spent my entire life living in the mundane world and never took the time to appreciate my surroundings. I stopped and smelled the flowers and watched the bees buzz. As we walked, the area started to become remarkably familiar. I looked over at Xavier, and he had a wide-eyed look of surprise. I followed his gaze, and in the middle of the field stood a burned tree. I knew that tree.

"Where are we?" I asked nervously.

Praeziel smiled. "I see you two recognize the field. That must mean you have dreamt of this place. This is one of the few holy places on earth. Not many, including angels, know about its location or even what it is called."

I looked around and noticed there were graves far off in the distance. I never remembered seeing them while meeting Xavier here.

"What is this place called?" I asked.

"פוטר של שדה," Praeziel said in Hebrew. "Potter's Field. This is where the bodies of angels are buried."

I ran toward the graves. I had to see for myself. I crested the top of a field and gasped. There were miles and miles of graves to be seen.

"All these angels were…" I couldn't finish the statement.

"Yes, they were all killed during the war. Their spirits departed to the burial in the sky, Akashar, similar to that of Valhalla," he replied. "We must get a move on. We have a ways to go before we get to where Starfire lives."

We began to walk by the graves that were unmarked. My soul cried out for each and every single angel that had risked their lives on either side for a cause from greed and vanity.

"Does anyone know who is buried here?" I asked.

"In the Summit, there is a room that lists every angel that has died in battle and gone to Akashar," Xavier replied. "I have, um, sneaked in there a few times out of curiosity."

We walked quietly and solemnly past the graves. I couldn't believe the numbers that had been buried. We were always told that there was an infinite number of angels, and it looked like hundreds of thousands had been buried here. I glanced over at Xavier, who was watching my face, and I could see it bothered him how upset I was over this.

"Why don't we just fly there?" Xavier asked, interrupting the silence.

"Several reasons," Praeziel replied. "One: When you're in angel form, you can be tracked. Two: Since you can be tracked and not cloaked, you put her at risk of being killed, which is not what we want at all. Three: I can't fly. Half mortal, remember?"

"Have you ever lived among the mundanes?" I asked.

"When I was of age to take care of myself, Mother granted me permission to live a normal life in the city like other Nephilim," Praeziel began. "I had lived so long in the conclave that being around those who weren't Watchers or other abandoned Nephilim felt... wrong. I often had panic attacks. I hated the train that ran above my apartment. The crowds gave me anxiety. I had to limit what I could say to people. Mundanes aren't supposed to know anything about our world other than their religious beliefs. I returned home about a year after living among humanity. I didn't belong with them nor conformed like my brothers and sisters have."

"My mundane great-grandmother knew, though," I stated. "She was the one who told my mother about all this."

"That was because she was part of the lineage that Sophie had been reborn in over and over," Praeziel replied. "There are certain humans who are personally clued in on everything by us. There are some that figure everything out on their own, kind of like Starfire. The rest, they are clueless to the war and mindless drones that listen to the teachings that Alpha has plastered across the world through the Illuminati."

We reached the end of Potter's field, and the sun began to set. I took one final look behind me at all the graves we passed and said a little prayer for their souls. So many had died fighting this stupid war. *How could Alpha subject his creations to this type of finality?*

"We will make camp here and start our journey in the morning," Praeziel said. "Unlike you two, I need sleep as opposed to having it as a luxurious passing of time."

* * *

PRAEZIEL LAY SLEEPING while Xavier and I sat up, unable to sleep. We were only able to think about what we had to do.

"It's getting chilly out," I remarked as my breath began forming crystals in the air.

"Yea, it's unusual," Xavier replied, narrowing his eyes and looking at our surroundings.

Before we knew it, we were ambushed by a bunch of figures in cloaks. They restrained us all, and one stepped forth and removed its hood from its head.

"Gwynevere," Praeziel shouted. "What do you think you are doing? I am on a mission. I am with these two to protect them to get to Starfire, and then from there, we must go to the Seelie court. What do you want from us?" he asked.

"That's exactly what I want with you. See, the Dark Queen has heard about your little travels and wants to meet with you before you see Titania and Oberon. We figured you wouldn't come along without protesting, so we thought we would take you along to see her ourselves," Gwynevere replied.

The troop walked us to a moonless part of the forest. Nightshade shrubs created a path that split through the forest. Misshaped trees grew along the tops of the shrubs. As we walked forward, the atmosphere began to change around us. I could feel an energy buzz as we crossed dimensions. Cypress trees and tall sycamores set a path to the Unseelie Queen's castle.

"I thought unless we were bearing gifts, we wouldn't be allowed in?" I whispered to Praeziel.

"This is different than you requesting court with the Dark Queen," Gwynevere replied. "You were invited."

Weeping Willows stood in front of the castle, and their tree limbs peeled back as we entered through the gate of the Dark Queen. When we entered the castle, festivities were commenced. The castle was lavish in food and drink. All the Unseelie fey were merry with laughter. However, we didn't stop in the common room.

"The Dark Queen wants to hold court with you in her throne room," Gwynevere informed.

We took stairs up a tower and entered the courtyard where the Dark Queen sat upon her throne. She was gorgeous to the eye. She had dark burgundy hair and racy blue eyes. Her skin was fair with dark red lipstick. Her nails had been groomed into talons. Her dress was magnificent, wrapping her in just the right spots. It shone luminescent under the fire glow in the throne room.

"I thought she was supposed to be a hideous dragon?" Xavier whispered to Praeziel.

"Well, when I have noble-blooded visitors, I like to dress down for them," the Dark Queen replied.

"Apologies, Dark One," Praeziel said, bowing. "They are not accustomed to etiquette outside of what they have been taught."

"Ah, but you have young Nephilim. Tell me, how is your dear mother Sophia these days? I haven't seen her since, well, since Christ hung on the cross," she mused.

"I wish I could tell you the truth, Dark One, but the truth is I do not know. When we left the conclave, it was under ambush by Alpha and his men. I fear my mother did not make it," Praeziel replied.

"Do not fret, young one. Your mother is fine," the Dark Queen replied, winking. "Now, as for you two… down to business, young Shining Ones."

"What do we owe the honor of your courtship?" I asked, bowing.

"Smart girl," she replied. "I wanted to meet the children of Incaendiel and Sophie. I did offer up some of my own power in their creation, so it was only right that I get to witness the power of their offspring."

"You offered up your dark gifts to my father's power, didn't you?" I asked.

She nodded. "The twin flames had to be balanced. Titania and Oberon offered their light gifts to Sophie, and I offered my dark gifts to Incaendiel. But with darkness came absolute power. He is stronger and ultimately indestructible as opposed to Sophie," the Dark Queen stated. "One of my most prized possessions, I'm afraid." She smiled. "I would have kidnapped him long ago, but the world needs him. My greed has its limits."

"So, all you wanted was to meet us?" Xavier asked.

The Dark Queen nodded.

"Ok, we met, so we will be on our way," I said.

"No," the Dark Queen replied, looking over Xavier, mesmerized. "He's a delectable little creature, and he will do just fine as a trophy in my gallery of exotic blooded creations. He bears his father's powers and is mine to keep."

"Over my dead body," I shouted, heated with a twinge of jealousy. I walked towards her with flames bursting from my hands. I hardly ever used my powers since we lived among humans, but they were as strong as they ever could be as I protested protecting Xavier from the Dark Queen.

"On second thought," she said. "You will make a fine addition yourself. Guards, take them both captive," the Dark Queen announced.

"You can't do this!" I shouted. "We are protected by Seelie enchantments! It runs through our blood."

"I can do whatever I want," the Dark Queen replied. "I helped make you; thereby, I own you."

"Alpha will destroy us all unless we stop him. He doesn't care about any creature in the universe. He is bringing about the apocalypse. He is making an army undefeatable. He has enslaved every type of creature there is to make this serum, including Seelies like yourself," I protested.

The Dark Queen nodded. "Why do you think I have taken you captive? I intend to offer you two to him as part of a negotiation. If I offer you up to him, the bargain is he will stop slaying Seelies while performing lab experiments for his serum."

"Don't you get it, though? It's not just about us. He is creating an army for a larger reason, a larger spectrum on the scale. Earth is just a pawn for him. When the apocalypse is over and gone, he's got bigger fish to fry. Think about that! You will be the cause of the destruction of the entire universe, including yourselves! Our side is the side that you need to be on." I was irate.

The Dark Queen frowned as she pondered over everything I had said. "I will make a bargain with you. I have but one request. I want a present. Bring me my present, and you can have your freedom. You fail at bringing me my present, and I will enslave you and turn you over to Alpha," the Dark Queen replied.

"What do you want?" I asked.

"I want the Garden of Eden. We created it, and we want it back," the Dark Queen replied.

"I don't have the authority to just give you the Garden of Eden. I would have to speak to Lilith. She is the guardian over its threshold," I replied.

"You need not worry about Lilith anymore. Lilith is not on your side," the Unseelie Queen remarked with a dry smile.

"What does that even mean?" Xavier asked.

"It means that she has joined forces with Alpha once more," the Dark Queen laughed.

"I don't believe you. No, Grandmother would never do that to us. She would never trade off her children. She loves us too dearly to do so," Xavier replied.

"It is true. Fey cannot lie and have no intention of doing so. However, they never tell you the whole truth so they can sway you with their own truths," Praeziel replied.

"The boy speaks the truth. No Fey, whether Seelie or Unseelie, can speak mistruths. We may be benevolent and mischievous, but we cannot lie. Therefore, it lies solely between you two. Would you give up the Garden of Eden to save yourselves and the universe? Or would you refuse me my gift and bring about the turn of the apocalypse?" The Dark Queen asked, grinning.

"What if we were to make this deal with you, and it is the same deal that the Seelie court wishes to make for them to join alliance with us?" I asked.

"I will add additional terms to the bargain. If you are to give the Fey the Garden of Eden back, it will be for both courts of fey. Neither side will have any say over it more than the other side. It will be fair share," she stated.

"Grant us to leave to speak with the Seelie Court, and once we speak with them, we will give you an answer," Praeziel requested.

"You have three days, Praeziel. And then dear Gwynevere will be coming for you again," she grinned wickedly. "I have one more request," she said before we walked through the throne room.

"Yes?" Praeziel asked.

"Your brother Damian," she started. "You must kill him if the serum adheres to his blood."

"Why?" I asked.

"Alpha would be my prisoner then, for there wouldn't be evidence of his success," she replied. "He doesn't know that it bonded with Xavier nor that it bonded with you because you act differently than Damian."

"Wait, what?" I asked, surprised. "It has bonded with us both?"

She nodded her head. "Your blood has extracted the benefits of the serum and rejected all the negative anomalies. However, your brother Damian isn't a full-blooded Shining One. His blood is more susceptible than yours. Unless you save him soon, he will be a lost cause," she replied.

"We need to go then," I said boldly.

I began to walk to the exit when two Unseelie guards blocked my path.

"What now?" Xavier asked.

"We aren't just letting you go so you can skip out on my agreement," the Dark Queen replied. "I will be sending one of my own with you."

The Dark Queen motioned, and the one named Gwynevere stepped forward.

"Go with them to the Seelie court and ensure their safety," the Dark Queen said. "Make sure Oberon hears them out for this task as well. He can be problematic."

"Yes, ma' lady," Gwynevere replied, bowing.

"Now, you may leave," the Dark Queen stated.

As we left the castle, Gwynevere led us down a path we didn't take to the castle.

"Where are we going?" Xavier asked.

"Seelies have portals throughout their realms that can jump them from place to place. She will be taking us to the gates of the Seelie court through her realm," Praeziel replied.

"Well, at least we don't have to get Starfire involved now, and her protection will be unbroken," Xavier stated.

Praeziel grimaced and looked at Gwynevere.

"You haven't told them!?" she asked.

"I told them what they needed to know to get them there," he replied.

"Wait, what?" I asked. "What are you two babbling about?"

Praeziel sighed. "Your powers are not activated yet. You haven't been trained. Starfire is your trainer. Your parents were never trained. They have untapped potential, even as deadly as they already are."

"Wait, so how can she train us?" Xavier asked.

"Your Seelie enchantments must be activated. There is a reason her name is Starfire. She holds the power to unlock the gifts the universe gave to you. All you lack is the starfire activation. You have the power of the sun resting in your bodies. She can bring it forth," Praeziel replied.

"What could we possibly do with that?" Xavier asked.

"No one knows. You have been a myth until Sophie and Incaendiel came into existence," Gwynevere replied.

"Wait, what about Damian? He is a half Shining One. Can Alpha activate that part of him after the demon blood adheres to his blood?" I asked.

"We don't know," Praeziel replied.

"When we were being held captive, and Luxina was rejecting the injections, Damian was concerned for her," Xavier said. "He only acted like he hated us when others were around until they gave her four doses. It's all been an act. Could it be possible that his Shining blood is doing what ours is doing, and Alpha doesn't know?"

"Yes and no. If Alpha gives him the wrong injection, it can turn him completely demonic. Since he doesn't know about the blood bond, he keeps changing the serum up," Gwynevere replied. "He has to report daily to the Dark Queen."

"What does she really look like?" I asked. "I know it was a façade of what she looked like to us."

"She is a dragon. One of the oldest in creation. One that no one was able to take down. Oberon helped her disguise herself by giving her Seelie blood. This is how we know it does work. She was created from Seelie enchantments and became ruler over all things dark and unnatural," Gwynevere stated.

"Then all the Unseelies... where do they come from?" Xavier

asked.

"The same place Nephilim came from," Praeziel replied. "Mortal bloodlines."

"So Seelies took on human mates?" Xavier asked.

Both Gwynevere and Praeziel nodded.

"We are here," Gwynevere stated.

I looked around, surprised.

"We didn't travel long," I replied.

"We walked through several portals, but you were distracted talking," Gwynevere giggled. "You ready? This leads us to the Isle of Mann. From there, we go through the Seelie portal to the castle."

"We're ready," I replied.

CHAPTER 11

WE DISEMBARKED the portal at the Isle of Mann. Gwynevere walked us over to a row of white ash trees that lined a path.

"There is the entrance," she said, pointing straight down the path.

"Aren't you coming with us?" Praeziel asked.

"No," she said, shaking her head. "Unseelies like me are shunned from the court. The king could have me locked up for even breaching the gates."

"Yes, he can," a voice shouted.

We looked back to the path we were supposed to take, and a manly creature stood there. I could only assume he was a Seelie.

"Ramon," Gwynevere stated. "What do we owe the pleasure for you greeting us outside of the portal?"

"King Oberon and Queen Titania learned of your journey here and requested we meet the lot of you here and bring you in personally," Ramon replied.

"Another escort," I replied, rolling my eyes. "Fine, we will come along."

"We will see you when we are done speaking with the court nobles," Praeziel said to Gwynevere.

"No," Ramon stated. "She comes too."

Gwynevere's face turned fearful.

"I must have your word that she is to remain unharmed and released at the end of this meeting, or she does not come with us," I said.

"I cannot guarantee any of that. I do not have the authority," Ramon replied.

"No, it's ok. I will go," Gwynevere stated.

"You don't have to risk your life," Praeziel replied quietly.

"I have to do this, love," she said, brushing his face with her hand.

"That explains a lot," Xavier whispered in my ear as we crossed the threshold into the Seelie realm.

* * *

"YOUR MAJESTY, here are the travelers as you requested," Ramon said as he led us into the noble's hall.

"Excellent, Ramon. Good evening, travelers. How may I help you?" King Oberon asked.

He had a pinkish hue to his skin and was much, much younger than I imagined him to be. Queen Titania sat silently to his left and watched on. She was a beauty! She reminded me of the Dark Queen, except all her colors were pastels.

"We have come to ask the Seelie court to stand alongside the Watchers, the Nephilim, and the angels of the Summit as we battle Alpha in his apocalyptic war," I replied.

King Oberon laughed. "You want us to join forces against Alpha? We have no quarrel with Alpha."

"He has slaughtered numerous Seelies, and you say you have no quarrel with him?" Gwynevere objected.

"Quiet, half-breed. I don't even know why I told them to allow you in court. Guards, take her outside of the castle," Oberon ordered.

"Is that the way you treat your subjects?" I asked. "How are you considered the light and Queen Mab the Dark Queen? Your duty is to protect humans. Humanity needs you before Alpha sets the apocalypse into motion. Are you going to let your loyalty to Alpha outweigh the needs of the world, including your own?"

"The Seelie realm exists out of space and time. Whatever Alpha does, he does to his own timeline, not ours," Oberon replied cheekily. "So, I will do whatever I want."

"Let's go, Luxina. At least we can still hold up our end of the bargain with the Dark Queen and give her the Garden," Xavier replied.

Oberon abruptly stopped laughing. "The garden?" he asked. "What garden?"

"The Garden of Eden. We are exchanging it with the Dark Queen for our freedom. She has agreed to cooperate with us, unlike you," I replied.

"Out of the question. She does not deserve the garden. Give it to me," he demanded.

"No. Bargain is the Garden will belong to all the fey whether they be Seelie or Unseelie, full breed or half-breed," I replied.

"I forbid it. We created the Garden—"

"And you gave it away. We own the Garden now and can do what we want with it. Lilith bequeathed it to us," Xavier stated.

Oberon's face turned four shades of red. "Guards, seize them!"

Xavier and I both activated our fire shields and stood on either side of Gwynevere and Praeziel. The guards retreated from us. Fire glowed around us. Xavier's eyes were a shade of golden amber, and I could only imagine mine were the same.

"We came to you peacefully and would like to leave peacefully. You have no quarrel with Alpha; well, we have no quarrel with you. We can either leave together or we can leave fighting. The choice is yours!" Xavier shouted. "We are the Shining Ones. We are older than you no matter how long ago we were born. You granted us life. You granted us protection. You cannot break your oath!"

"Enough!" Queen Titania shouted. "Stand down," she yelled at the guards. "I have seen and heard enough. We will stand alongside you against Alpha."

"But dear," Oberon began.

"That is final," she hissed at him.

"Thank you, Queen Titania," I replied, bowing. "We shall be on our way."

"Before you go," Queen Titania started. "Gwynevere, dear."

Gwynevere shakily walked up toward the queen. "Yes, ma 'lady," she replied with a curtsy.

"You are welcome back here anytime," she said, smiling. "In fact, all Unseelie from henceforth will be welcome here. It is time we end our own blood feud."

"Thank you, ma' lady," Gwynevere replied, grinning.

We left the castle in merry spirits.

"We did it," I stated. "I can't believe we did it. We have both Seelie and Unseelie courts as an alliance, which means the Watchers and the Nephilim will stand by our side."

"You still have to make good on your promise to Queen Mab," Gwynevere warned.

"Do we have to do it in person?" I asked.

"Yes, you do," the Dark Queen replied.

We all turned in surprise to the sound of her voice.

"Ma' lady," Gwynevere replied, bowing. "We have restored the alliance with the Seelie court, and all Unseelies are once again welcome in front of the nobility. They agreed to fight alongside us for the cause against Alpha. We now own the Garden." She gave the full report and stood back up.

"Excellent news," the Dark Queen replied. She looked at me. "I underestimated all of you. You have our allegiance. You had it from the beginning. Although it would have been a fun game to turn you over to Alpha, we needed you. We can only twist our words to gain what we want, and we did. Do we have your word on the Garden of Eden?" she asked.

"Only if you keep your word about sharing it with all Seelies," I replied.

She snapped her fingers. "Done. It was marvelous meeting both of you. I must, however, return to my realm. You two still have another stop to make. Don't forget about Starfire," the Dark Queen said, winking at Praeziel.

"Thank you, ma' lady," he replied, bowing.

And just like that, she was gone in a flash.

"We should camp here tonight," Praeziel said. "It will be safest right outside the Seelie court realm."

"The last time you said that we were kidnapped," I replied jokingly. "So, since we now have everyone's allegiance, what next?" I asked.

"I must call a Tribunal. We must gather all the Nephilim and prepare them for the uprising against Alpha. It has been long since overdue," Praeziel replied and sighed heavily. "Yea, though I walk through the valley of the shadow of death, I shall fear no evil..."

FIREFLY: THE HALF-BLOOD ANGEL

THE GUARDIANS OF LIGHT SERIES
BOOK THREE

Kasey Hill

Azoth Khem Publishing
Huntsville, AL
April 2025

CHAPTER 1

I HAVE A SECRET. Secrets are something hard to keep. I was a secret that came to light. My mother had an affair with my father, and here I am. However, that's old news. Water under the bridge, so to speak. I never came to know nor love my mother and father. I came to love Alpha as my sole parent. But love is a fickle thing. It can come and go as it pleases, and now, I hold nothing more than loathing and apathy toward Alpha. Whether he knows it to be true is undoubtedly the question. Still, that is not my secret, either. My secret is simple. I am not evil.

I have done horrible things in the name of Alpha. I didn't care. I had no one else to guide me, and I felt that he was guiding me in a way I needed to go. His rhetoric, his law, seemed right and true. I was his little monster, and I enjoyed it. However, I came to learn he was hiding something from me, something that would change my life forever.

I grew up abnormally because I, myself, was not a typical angel. My mother was special, like her twin soul, and they held powers not seen in any other angel ever created by Alpha and Omega. I had no guidance, and Alpha knew only to use those powers for his own gain. For those differences, I did not age the same as other angels would. I aged expediently into my late teens, where it halted. That was when the more challenging training came, and I found myself forced into training even when I did not want it. Alpha had his reason but never divulged it to me.

I found out later. I found out when he swept me away and told me we had to leave the Summit. The Fallen Angels were revolting and reclaiming their places in the purified world he had created. Most believed his actions for requesting someone to oppose him was to create a balance in the world. It was not. He needed to eliminate those who were poisoned and would not follow him to the end with his plans. Those who chose to fall with Omega were the poison, and those left behind were the pure. It was a culling, so to speak. He believed those who remained behind were loyal to him and none other. He was wrong.

There were active members of his angel fleet who were working with those who fell to return them to the Summit. My mother and father were among those angels. Ultimately, in the end, they fell as well to join Omega in her war against Alpha. Even with all of this, I was still Alpha's loyal little soldier. It would be years later that I found out a piece of information that sent my blood to boil. I had siblings that Alpha never told me about.

I had come to learn that I dream, and angels do not dream. At least, typical angels do not. I was far beyond normal. It was within these dreams that I found my siblings. It was always the same place. There was a field in the middle of nowhere with a tree at the center. It was so peaceful and serene. I had been walking these fields for years until, to my surprise, two others joined the place. I hid away from them, envious of their connection. I learned their names while there: Luxina and Xavier. There were times I had nearly come out of my hiding spot to introduce myself to them, to get to know them, but I was cowardly. They hardly knew about each other except in their dreams, and even then, they only knew each other's names. They did not know they were born as twin flames like their mother and father were. So, I sat, and I watched them from afar. I grew fond of them both.

To my horror, Alpha had gained the ability to spy on my dreams along with me. It was then that he became something different. He became distant and malevolent. He locked himself away from me, and it was then I realized I had no one. We had been hiding out in the old Chernobyl buildings, long ago abandoned. I had no idea he was inventing a new race, a new breed of angel. And it was going to start with me.

I traveled with him to the Unseelie Court, where Queen Mab gazed upon me in amazement and desire. She listened to Alpha as he wagered with her, never removing her eyes from me.

"I will give you what you want on two conditions," she replied as Alpha stood by eagerly waiting for her demands. "The first one will be that if you are to succeed, I get to keep this one as my payment," she said, motioning her eyes to me and smiling deviously.

"What is your second condition?" Alpha asked.

Her smile grew wider and even more sinister. "My second condition is if you fail, you yourself will become a prisoner of my court. You may never leave, and you will lose all godly powers you have ever gained. You will, of course, be very well taken care of. However, you pose a threat to all. You have two years to complete the trials."

"That is ludicrous. I would never wager myself for power. You would have to be a fool to strike such a deal," Alpha huffed.

"Well, then you don't get what you came for," Mab replied, holding up a vial of blood. "This is what you wanted, of course, right? A vial of pure blood. My blood?"

Alpha stared at the vile as his face twitched and darkened.

"This could be yours if you are willing to pay the price," she said, twisting the vile back and forth, almost as if she were enchanting Alpha.

"You have no authority over me," Alpha stated. "What makes you think I wouldn't destroy you here and now for the endless amount of blood to gain from your dripping carcass!"

"You cannot harm me," she replied, raising an eyebrow and grinning. "I am older than you and was made by gods that ensured I could never be harmed by gods lower on the spectrum than what they were. Try all you might, you will die before ever touching a hair on my head."

Alpha gulped. I had silently stood by, watching the two of them bicker back and forth. Free of Alpha sounded like a blessing. If he failed, I would be free of his tyranny. Free.

The Dark Queen glanced in my direction as if I had spoken it aloud. I looked around in terror, hoping Alpha had not heard either.

Do not fear, my little Shining One. He cannot hear you as I can.

I was a bit fearful and shocked. I looked at Alpha, who was lost in thought while making his decision.

I can hear you, too? I asked.

Of course, young Damian. You have special gifts like your mother, your brother, and your sister. You have an enchantment that needs finished sealing, however. You need to escape Alpha and find your brother and sister and join them on their quest. Together, all three of you will be able to save the world, she replied.

What quest? They haven't even met yet, I replied.

All in due time, young one.

"My patience is growing thin, Alpha," Mab seethed. "What shall it be?"

Alpha spoke finally. "I will agree to your conditions."

The Dark Queen laughed maniacally, turned over an hourglass, and looked back at Alpha. "Tick tock, Alpha."

Since that meeting, I have been tortured with various injections. The Dark Queen did not tell him it would be harder for my blood to adhere to the magic since I was not wholly a Shining One. And there were dangers if it did succeed. I may become something completely evil like those vile creatures he had created in the beginning. I didn't want that. But I had no one to stop him from trying them on me.

I lay in agony for days after the first series of injections he created. Hell wasn't even a description that could bring the pain I felt justice. My body rejected injection after injection. With each injection, he would lock himself away, trying to perfect the serum using as little of Queen Mab's blood as he could. He synthesized it to make it last longer. I came to learn that I was not the only one he was using them on as well. He had been taking lower demons created by the Forsaken and experimenting with them as well. They were once humans with just a trace of angelic blood in their systems. Many died at the hands of Alpha. But he didn't care. He wanted this, and whatever Alpha wanted, Alpha received.

I never wanted to be a test dummy. They had to drag me, kicking and screaming, to the chamber to be administered the injections. I fought with everything I had. I froze some of those who dragged me away with my freezing ability. I fought many off in sword combat, killing many of them. I was always outnumbered and always subdued. After so many times of trying to fight, my spirit broke. I eventually began to allow them to lead me to the testing chamber. They would shackle me to a bed while I endured the burning lava injections. Quite a few times, I came close to death, and I begged for mercy to feel the cooling feeling of the abyss envelop me and carry me off to the angel's potter's field. I always recovered at the last minute and would cry for days after wondering what I had done to deserve everything I endured.

The only thing that kept me going and kept me fighting to survive was Luxina and Xavier. I had to keep them from Alpha's grips, even if it meant I was subject to his torturous methods. I knew one day we would be able to meet and greet. I could get to know the family I never had growing up. And I would kill anyone that tried to hurt them.

My only solace and escape were my dreams, where I got to see them. If I could see them, I knew they were safe. They had yet to meet as well and only graced each other in their dreams. The first time I saw them, the power they emitted upon touching each other's hand was monumental. I envied their connection, but I was not jealous of them. They were perfect together. Alpha, at one point, wanted me to do what he had done with Sophie and Incaendiel for all of those years. He wanted me to get Luxina to try and love me, severing her connection with Xavier and becoming less powerful. That's where the twin flames gain their strength, with the connection with their twin soul. I would never do that. I could never do that. However, everyone thinks I am an evil little sentinel for Alpha. If it keeps everyone else I love safe from Alpha, I will let them think that until the day I die.

I remember the day that Lucifer finally made it to Alpha. He didn't even fight his way here. He found one of the sentinels of the Forsaken and bartered his way here, promising Alpha Luxina and Xavier in exchange for me. I immediately hated him. I stood by Alpha's side and glared at him with all of the hate in the world as he proposed to bring Xavier first and then Luxina for Alpha's disposal. All the while, Alpha listened, never intending to let him have me in return. I tried to stop them. I disguised myself and tried to interfere before it was too late. I pretended to be one of the hunting pack that looked for me days on end. That's when I met my mother. I may not think of her much as a mother because I wasn't raised by her, but I could see the good in her heart and the love she had for me.

There were times I would go back to the Summit with them and would watch how she interacted with Xavier, and it made me hate myself. She sacrificed the love for her one son to find the one that was hopeless. Xavier suffered at my expense. Whenever I would catch Sophie alone, we would talk about how much she adored Xavier and also how much he despised her. He felt abandoned by her in her pursuit of finding me. It was I who convinced her to stop searching and return to the Summit to be with Xavier. She needed to protect him from Lucifer because the plan was drawing to a close. If I had acted sooner than later in convincing her to go back and give up, he would not have been harmed by Alpha. There would have been ample time to hide him away. The day came for Lucifer to steal Xavier away, and there wasn't anything I could do to save him without exploiting myself.

I watched as he put our mother in the tower like Alpha had done so many times. It was the same tower I had been born in that he and Sophie were held prisoner in. I already had plans on breaking them out long before Luxina arrived in Chernobyl. What I wasn't expecting was them to dose me along with the others. It made me weak and vulnerable. I had to listen to what I was told without exception. The mind control substance he gave me bent me in ways I couldn't escape until it wore off. I met Xavier long before Luxina arrived, and he already had a steady hate for me. Why wouldn't he hate me? I was the reason he grew up without a mother. She was always looking for me instead of being by his side. I would hate me, too. Our first encounter was less than astounding and not at all what I had imagined meeting my brother for the first time. His pure hatred for me made me falter each time I was in his presence. At times, the injections broke me, and I found myself at his throat, trying to kill him as he egged me on with his venomous words. There would be no doubt that if given the chance to kill me, he would try with all of his might. He had no compassion, just as I didn't. Again, something that can be laid to rest on my shoulders.

When Lucifer came to Alpha ready to go in for Luxina, I wanted to head the party that brought her in. I wanted to keep her as safe as possible. Alpha agreed to let me go, but not before another one of his cocktail injections. I remember slapping her at some point and felt terrible after the injection began to taper off. She was held for a few days before Alpha brought her to his office to meet with her. I expected her to hate me, but I could feel the sorrow and compassion leach from her to me. She wanted to save me. She wanted to truly save me and everyone from the clutches of Alpha. I remember how her heart sank as we walked through the halls, and she heard the cries of the creatures Alpha had been running experiments on. He would inject them, morph them, take their blood after it mutated, and then kill them if they weren't of any use to him.

I witnessed her defiance in front of Alpha when he asked her to join his side. I had heard so many stories of Incaendiel when it came to Alpha, and it was one of the few moments I was glad she had her father's temper and spirit. She would need it to survive the injection. The ones he gave me were vastly different than the ones he had planned to use on her. Even the ones Xavier was subjected to were different than the ones she had. She was receiving almost pure blood from Mab and a cocktail mix of all of the mutt creations he had made.

I watched the moment she struck a nerve in him, and at the last minute, he added an injection that I was unaware of what the contents were. That was until he injected her with them all. He had created an injection that he called Heavenly Hellfire. He gave it to those who refused to cooperate with him. It must have been one of the injections he gave me in the beginning but twice the dose. He could bend the mind to his will through the injections. He wasn't counting on her defiance being even stronger than the injections.

When the Heavenly Hellfire failed, he gave her a series of injections to kill her. Her will to live was just as strong as her defiance. I watched her writhe in agony, and they just kept the injections coming. When I tried to help, when I tried to stave them off from injecting any more of the serum into her, they caught me in the neck with one. It burned through my body, searing every nerve ending I had. I reached out to Xavier with my mind before they pulled me out of the room.

Get her to Stygia. Find Sophia. Quick, before she dies. She will be the only one to end this war, and Alpha's reign of terror will come to an end. I will find you, and we will stop him together.

A flicker of acknowledgement rolled across Xavier's face, and I watched through the window of the closing door behind me as he broke the chains free from the wall and swooped her from the place to safety. I, however, was unable to escape to help them. Instead, I was subjected to beatings and torture. I had injections over and over until my body had gone numb and my soul had gone limp. There was hardly any fight left in me. All I could do was think over and over that Xavier had made it to Stygia in time to save Luxina.

I sent him to Sophia for a very specific reason. She knew what to tell them. She knew what to explain to them about what we were. I had come across her once before, and we began to meet in private. She had a plan to help thwart Alpha, but it wouldn't work unless all of the Shining Ones were together. She herself had been to see Mab and knew more things than I could imagine about what we were. We were more than just meager angels. We were almost gods, and together, we were more powerful than Alpha.

It had been several days after Xavier and Luxina had escaped that Alpha came to me in the dungeon. I was chained to the ceiling, suspended off the ground to where my tip toes just barely grazed the floor. He watched me as I spat blood from my mouth. I had just recently been tossed around the room, and my wounds were still fresh.

"You disappointed me, son." His words fell flat as he pulled a chair up and sat down in it. "You helped them escape, and I know you did. What I don't know is how? And most importantly, why? Why is my best soldier turning against me? I raised you. I gave you everything you could ever want. And this is how you repay me. You throw it back in my face!"

He composed himself and watched for my reaction. I gave him absolutely nothing.

"I have half a mind to feed you to those mutts starving in the cell across from you, but I need you, unfortunately. You have one more chance to prove yourself worthy of me. You will be going along with Lucifer and me to Stygia to get your siblings back. I need all of you together. Are you going to follow my wishes, or are you going just to hang here until your body gives out?" he asked.

I quickly ran everything through my mind. I had to go along. I had to help them escape before he could recapture them. There was no choice.

"I will go with you," I replied.

"Excuse me?" he asked indignantly.

"I will go with you, *father*," I replied once more, emphasizing father for him.

He looked pleased with himself and made a motion with his two forefingers. Asmodeus emerged from the shadows and walked toward me. He released a lever from the wall, and my chain came bounding down from the ceiling. My legs were so weak that I hit the ground with a thud. I could barely feel any of the muscles in my body. Asmodeus walked over and unshackled by bound wrists.

You need to run as soon as you can. Alpha will kill you if this plan falls through, he thought.

I had no idea he knew I could read his thoughts, or anyone knew for that matter. I acknowledged him with my eyes as Alpha watched us. He pulled the chains from around me that had landed in a heap on my legs. I shakily stood stretching out my still numb limbs.

"Mark my words, boy. You fail me and do not kill who I tell you to kill. . . Well, you can imagine the rest," Alpha stated, turning on his heels, and left the dungeon room with Asmodeus close behind. "We leave at dawn."

I spent all night trying to devise a plan for Xavier and Luxina to escape safely. I hated the thought of having to kill others to protect them, but I have to act like I am on Alpha's side, or else they won't have anyone to help them any longer. I cleaned up all of my cuts and applied a poultice to my bruises when I was back in my room. I winced with each touch as the cuts burned with the herbs.

My door opened, and I thought it was probably Lucifer coming to check on me. However, it was not Lucifer. It was the last person I ever thought I would see walk through that door. It was my mother, Sophie. She ran to my side and threw her arms around me.

"My boy, my sweet, precious boy," she murmured through silent tears of joy.

I winced with pain as she squeezed my broken ribs.

"What have they done to you?" she asked, looking me over and fretting.

She picked up the salve I had been applying and began to gingerly treat my wounds as I stood there in both shock and disbelief. Her fingers worked nimbly over each of the wounds I had until they reached my face. She stopped short and just stared into my eyes as I stared back.

"What are you doing here?" I asked, still confused as to what I was seeing.

She set the jar of salve down on the table, pulled a chair out, and sat down, clasping her hands while leaning forward.

"Alpha attacked the Glade, where a fleet of angels were set up planning an attack to get Luxina and Xavier back," she began. "Before the mountain fully fell, I was grabbed and whisked away to here by Lucifer. He told me he had you three here together all safe."

"Why haven't I seen you before today then?" I asked, stretching a shirt over my head.

"I wanted to see all of you. I wanted to rescue all of you. However, I was chained in a room until I could prove that I wasn't here to stop Alpha. I agreed that it would be safer for all three of you to stay with Alpha than risk trying to take you from here without any help," she explained.

"So, you stood by while they gave Luxina injections? How long has it been since you have been here? Were you here when Xavier was receiving his injections as well? Why didn't you stop them?!" I seethed.

"I was not here for the injections Xavier received. And I was receiving them myself when Luxina arrived," she replied softly. "When Luxina failed to bow to Alpha during his head games, he doubled my doses of Heavenly Hellfire. I made a connection with Luxina and may have said things that were... not truthful to her. I blamed her for my current predicament. The child I had yet to meet, and I was cursing her for defying the one person we all defied after the fall."

Sophie looked away, ashamed.

"I could hear Incaendiel calling out her name to pull her out of that nightmarish place we were stuck together in," she said as she began to weep again. "I said horrible things to him as well prior to the Glade coming down. I'm not even sure if anyone knows I am alive."

I ran my hand through my hair, frustrated.

"Why are you here?" I asked again heatedly.

"I just told you—"

"No, why are you in my room?" I yelled. "Did you think you could come in here and just sweet-talk your way into me calling you mother and collapsing in your arms in tears because you had finally saved me from the evil monster I have called father since I was little?"

She looked a bit stunned at my choice of words.

"My brother and sister are being hunted down like wild animals, and you're sitting here playing tea party with Alpha instead of helping them.

You're a terrible excuse for a mother, and you are no mother to me. Please, leave my room," I ordered, pointing in the direction of the door.

"But, I thought," she began, confused. "You don't want to be taken from Alpha?" she asked.

"Not at the risk of my brother and sister falling into his clutches again. They are more important than me. What kind of brother would I be to allow them back here to be tortured more by that devil in disguise? I would be no better than you or Lucifer."

I stared at her long and hard.

"Lucifer," she started when I cut her off again.

"Don't get me started about that pathetic waste of space. You're honestly going to sit there and defend him when he was the one that orchestrated the entire kidnapping plot of both of your children. I am not more important than two lives." I held my door open for her to leave. I looked her dead in the eyes and said, "You will never be my mother, and Lucifer will never be my father. I don't have a family. Had it been my decision, you would have died in that mountain."

Dumbfounded, she just gave me a nod and left the room. I slammed the door closed behind her and threw myself backward on my bed, landing on my back. I would never understand her rhetoric of thinking. Had she been totally brainwashed? I stared at the ceiling for quite some time before another knock came on my door.

"For the love of all that is holy," I muttered, standing to answer the knock.

I opened the door, and yet another face I despised stood before me. Lilith, Omega, whatever you want to call her, loomed in the doorway before letting herself in the room. She walked around the room, lifting things up and setting them back down. I watched her, completely unaware of what she was trying to accomplish. She unscrewed the lightbulb in the room, and once she was satisfied with whatever search she was doing, she sat down in the chair my mother had just left not too long ago.

"Hello, Damian. We have yet to formally meet," she stated after a moment of silence.

"I'm Damian. You're Lilith. We have met now, so you can leave," I replied hastily, motioning to the door.

She studied me with eyes that were unfamiliar. A glimmer of life floated through her eyes before they glazed back over. She swallowed, slightly clearing her throat before she spoke to me again.

"When you leave to go with Alpha on this trip, you must escape him once Xavier and Luxina are safe," she declared, unwavering in her lack of emotion.

"I already know. He plans to kill me if his plan fails," I replied, annoyed.

"You could only wish for death for what he has planned for you after it fails," she whispered.

"I just spent days being strung up by my arms with my feet barely touching the ground to stand up. I'm sure whatever it is, I can handle it," I retorted.

"You have such a fighting spirit. If I didn't know any better, I would swear your father was Incaendiel instead of the lousy one that brought you forth," she remarked, fire blazing in her eyes.

"That is something I can agree with," I replied with a wicked grin. "My father is a piece of crap that deserves nothing more than to be doused in gasoline and dropped into the lake of fire."

"Now, since we are on the same page," she decreed, careening her neck and smiling, "let's get down to the matter at hand. All three of you need to be as far away from Alpha as possible after this raid ends. Unless you can absolutely convince him that you had nothing to do with their escape... "

"I don't know how many times I have to stress to you people that I don't care what Alpha does to me as long as Xavier and Luxina are safe," I barked, exasperated. "I hate repeating myself over and over."

"For the power of the Shining Ones to work, to put an end to Alpha, all three of you have to be together," Lilith urged. "You weren't supposed to have become. I never imagined that Sophie would succumb to weakness in that tower. So, when Luxina and Xavier were born, they were not born with the full power they should have had. You are the missing piece in all of that. You have to make it to them and join them. Or else, all of this will have been for naught."

"If I wasn't supposed to exist, I wouldn't," I snarled. "What makes you so sure it's me that wasn't supposed to exist and not one of them?"

She eyed me, pursing her lips. I could see I struck a nerve. Everyone knew about how my mother had me and what she did. She had betrayed Incaendiel. So, most think I wasn't supposed to exist because of that. Had Sophie never been in the tower with Lucifer, I wouldn't exist here because she would have never been tempted. However, it doesn't say anywhere that twin souls have to be born at the same time, so it is quite possible that I am supposed to be and Xavier not. However, either way, it doesn't change anything. I will protect him either way.

"Why are you helping us when you are joining forces with Alpha?" I asked suspiciously.

"Because out of everything I have made in this world, Sophia and Incaendiel will be the one thing I cherish the most. In extension, you three are also my cherished creations. I will not see my creations destroyed. If it comes down to it, Alpha will have to destroy me in the end and then figure out how to rebuild the universe alone. I have never stopped loving Alpha. He is my other half no matter how screwed up he is. It was inevitable for us to come back together."

"What do you suggest I do then?" I asked.

"What we all have been telling you to. Run."

CHAPTER 2

ALPHA ASSEMBLED an army to raid Stygia. Every demon was armed with a sword and instructed to kill anyone who attempted to interfere. The Shining Ones, Xavier and Luxina, were to remain unharmed. If Incaendiel happened to be there, he was to be taken alive as well. Lucifer and I were to head the mission, and Alpha came along to observe. As we waited for the rest of the soldiers to fall in line, Lucifer tried to make small talk with me.

"Your mother told me she came in and saw you last night," he lamented, loading himself down with weapons.

"Yup," I replied curtly.

"She said it was groundbreaking," he raved.

"I'm sure for her it was," I snidely retorted.

"Everything we do, we do for you, Damian," Lucifer reasoned.

"I'm sure you do everything for me and not for yourself," I returned curtly.

"One day you will see," he stressed, falling off from his sentence.

"One day you will see what a piece of-"

"Fall in, soldiers!" Alpha commanded.

I glared and repositioned my chest armor. Everyone else readied themselves.

"Off we go!" Alpha ordered.

He was seated in a chariot pulled by four horses. A red one, a black one, a white one, and a pale gray one pulled him along like he was the antichrist himself. His chariot shot off into the air, and we all lifted up in flight alongside him. It didn't take us long to make it to the entrance. That was the one beautiful thing about flying. You could get anywhere you wanted in the blink of an eye. I'm sure we looked like we were flying into the apocalypse had we been seen by others heading toward Stygia. Alpha must make a grand entrance wherever he goes. It's quite nauseating as opposed to get in and get out, getting the job done without showboating victory.

I found it odd that there were no guards standing to prevent us from entering. Were we walking into a trap? Alpha paid no mind to the fact there wasn't anyone guarding the place and marched right in. No sooner had we breached the entrance than alarms sounded, echoing throughout the underground facility. We watched as they all scrambled into their positions. The demon fleet began their assault on those that made an appearance and soon were fighting their way through the Watchers. Lucifer, Alpha, and I broke off into one of the side tunnels. I had no idea where we were going when the fighting was taking place in the main corridors.

"Do you know where she would go?" Alpha asked Lucifer.

"She has her own private quarters. We just must follow this path and go through the maze. I know the way there. I have visited her a few times," Lucifer replied.

"Good. She will surely be the one to hide them and send them off to safety," Alpha droned.

"Who?" I asked, unsure if my gut was tugging me toward the right answer.

"Sophia, of course," Alpha proclaimed.

Oh no. Not Sophia. We followed Lucifer through the maze of tunnels below. He weaved through them as if he had been here more than just a few times. He seemed to know them like the back of his hand. How long had he been seeing Sophia? Did he know that she had filled me in on details in prior meetings? I know Sophia was his bound soulmate who left the Summit long after the Fallen Ones had chosen to side with Lilith. Had he been still coming to see her even after declaring my mother as his true love? If he had been, it would have been pretty crappy on his part. As much as I dislike Sophie for her errors in judgement calls and choices she has made regarding Luxina and Xavier, she didn't deserve that type of treatment.

We arrived at the door that Lucifer said would be her quarters. I expected Lucifer to break the door in himself, however, that was not the case.

"Damian, you go in first," Alpha requested.

I knew it was not a request, but moreover a demand of compliance. I nodded my acknowledgement of his request and busted through the door. I caught a glimpse of her putting the rug down just in time over the escape hatch in the floor. They were safe for the time being. I held my breath, hoping that neither Lucifer nor Alpha had seen what I had.

"Where are they, Sophia?" Lucifer demanded.

I let out a sigh of relief by mistake and then looked to see if either had been watching me. Alpha eyed me curiously, but he didn't say a word.

"You will never find them, love," she replied.

"Oh, but you are mistaken, dear Sophia," Alpha decreed.

"Let the other child go, Alpha. You are going to kill him with your experiments," she hissed.

"Oh, I beg to differ. It seems as if the last injection has held out far longer than any other I have given him. Pretty soon, I will make a permanent one and bend you all to my will!" he exclaimed.

"Damian, come here, son," Lucifer called.

I had to keep my composure even though my blood boiled just at the mere thought of having to acknowledge him calling me son without refuting it.

"Yes, Lucifer," I replied.

"Kill everyone in this room, especially her," Lucifer spat.

"Let's go look for the other two," Alpha said. "They can't have gotten far."

As they left the room, I spoke silently to Sophia.

I was going to use this opportunity to escape, but now I can't. I'm not going to hurt you; just play along, ok?

She nodded.

I'm sorry, but I have to kill them, I motioned to the Watchers standing in the corner.

Do what you must, she replied.

I watched as they laid their swords down and sacrificed themselves for the cause. I made their deaths swift, and it broke my heart knowing that there were so many that would die for this cause.

"Damian, you don't have to listen to them. You don't have to do this!" Sophia pleaded.

"Scream," I said.

She let out a bloodcurdling scream, and I smeared blood all over her from the others I had slain. She lay still on the floor in case anyone came in to do body checks. I had lost my opportunity to run by saving her. Had I not done what I did, they would have found Xavier and Luxina by following me. I walked from the room with blood splattered all over me and caught up to Lucifer and Alpha ahead in the cavern. I hoped my plan worked, or else I would be the body lying in blood on the floor when Alpha got done with me.

"Well done, son," Alpha remarked, patting me on the back.

We made our way back to the main cave entrance, and bodies lay mangled everywhere. Demons stood around chattering while others were scouring the rest of the cavern to see if there were others that had not escaped yet to slay. There was one person that stood hooded with their hands bound behind their back. Asmodeus held him firmly by the shoulders.

"We found Incaendiel, sir," Asmodeus stated.

"Good, that means the kids aren't too far gone. I want this place searched top to bottom. Every person alive I want questioned until death succumbs them. I want those two found and brought to me. That's an order!" Alpha bellowed.

"What do we do with him?" Asmodeus asked, nudging Incaendiel.

"Damian, escort our fearless leader here back to our quarters. We have much to discuss, Incaendiel and I," Alpha demanded.

"Yes, sir," I replied.

Asmodeus handed Incaendiel over to me, and I blinked him into the very dungeon they had held me. I placed the shackles tied to the wall on his wrists before I cut the ropes away from his hands. I removed his hood, and all he did was glare at me. Thousands of thoughts swirled through his head. *Where were Luxina and Xavier? Where was Sophia? How many were dead? How can I kill him and escape out of here?*

"They're safe and will stay safe," I whispered.

His face contorted in a confused, angry glare.

I looked around to make sure we were still alone. "We will talk more later," I assured him as I left the dungeon.

Just as I closed the door, Alpha appeared before me.

"The prisoner is secured," I reported.

"Good, good," he replied.

He studied me long and hard. I didn't know if I was dismissed or if I was required to stand there until he walked away.

"You did good today, my boy," he praised, clapping his hand on my shoulder. "Return to your living quarters and await further instruction."

"Yes, sir," I replied and brushed past him as fast as I could.

I didn't like how he was studying me lately. I felt insecure, as if my poker face was going to break. I believe my face may have shown some flicker of guilt at some point by the way he had been watching me and surveying my actions closer than usual. It wasn't much longer after I had made it back to my room that four of Alpha's lackeys busted in and dragged me off to the injection chamber. I kicked and lashed out the best I could. I caught one of them in the eye with my fist and another in the mouth with my foot. They never would take me without a fight.

"I did what I was told! I killed without thought!" I screamed as they tossed me onto the metal table and locked me into place. "Why?!"

"Because you failed the mission," Alpha replied, walking into the room and holding the injection himself.

"I killed. I brought Incaendiel back here like you asked. What more could you want from me?!" I spat.

"The twins were not secured," Alpha lectured monotonously.

"They were gone when we got there!" I protested. "There wasn't any way for me to find them with the tasks you had given me!"

"I do not believe that," Alpha seethed. "You knew where they went, and you didn't tell us."

"Please," I pleaded. "Please don't inject me!"

"Weak. Weakness is all I see in your tears," he said coolly. "I had such high hopes for you when you were born. Now, you're a sad, whining, pathetic little boy, and I need to fix that."

I shook the table, trying to free myself, jerking as hard as I could at the straps. I howled and pleaded for someone to help me, but no one came to my aid. Alpha jabbed the needle deep into the side of my neck, and the pain exploded as he pushed the plunger down, releasing whatever toxin he had in the syringe into my bloodstream.

"Now show me what kind of soldier you are. Only the strong prevail," he taunted before exiting the room and leaving me to writhe in pain.

The room went dark, and fire erupted through my veins. I screamed until my throat began to crack and bleed from being dry and hoarse. I could taste the blood as it drained down my esophagus, threatening to strangle me. I had experienced these injections so many times that I no longer blacked out from the pain and felt every single nerve ending pop and die as the hellfire surged through my veins. I prayed for death, but to whom I prayed was questionable. To me, there was no god. There was a power-hungry mongrel that called himself God to the humans. But to me, to an angel, an Elohim, a Shining One, I had no god any longer. So, I prayed to death itself, fate, everything that controlled the life and death cycle of angelic beings. The universe, maybe?

I guess I could consider myself lucky that I didn't have to witness Alpha's face billowing in the flames of the Lake of Fire like Luxina did. I had my solitude to endure the pain. I was accustomed to being alone for so long that I felt comfort in the fact I was alone during this, and no one could see my torment to pity me. Pity is one thing I refuse to accept from anyone. Pity shows that you were indeed weak at one point. Pity reflected your character of not being able to overcome struggles. I didn't need pity. I didn't need understanding. I didn't need anything from those who did not empathize with how I felt at that moment. No one was raised solely by Alpha and believed him to be a true father only for him to rear his ugly head and show you how demoralizing he was. Alpha broke whatever love I could feel for parental figures. That's what abuse does to the mind. He had abused me so much that love was most likely impossible for me to experience.

I never could tell how long I lay in writhing pain until it finally subsided. I'm always in a windowless room without a clock, but I'm sure that it was a couple of days this time. Asmodeus came and unbuckled me from the table. I rolled over and vomited up frothy yellow mucus. He scooped me up and carried me to one of the dungeons that had a small window that let light in. He had made up a bed for me against the wall, so I didn't have to lie directly on the floor. Since this was my punishment, he placed one of the shackles on my ankles whether he agreed with it or not. He picked up a ladle from the water bucket and slowly gave me some water to drink. I drank it slowly so I wouldn't choke or immediately heave it back up. The water burned my searing throat at first, but it soon became a soothing, cool rush down my throat. Asmodeus always took care of me after the injections. I don't know what I did to garner his sympathy and empathy, but he was the one person that I never complained to receive it from.

"I'll bring you some food down at dinner time," he assured as he left the room, locking it in place behind him.

"Thank you, Asmodeus," I croaked, barely audibly.

I scooted the bed as close to the window as I could and collapsed into a dreamless sleep. I don't know how long I was asleep before I awoke to a tray being shuffled across the floor with food on it. I walked to the tray near the door and had to lie on my stomach and stretch my arm out to reach it. My fingers grasped the edge of the tray, and I pulled it closer to me. I picked it up and let it sit on my bed. I stared at the tray, wondering if starving myself could gain me a faster death than Alpha's torture. I walked over to the window and punched one of the glass panes out. A cool breeze filled the room, and I closed my eyes, breathing in the scent of the wildflowers growing in the field. The sun was shining brightly while birds chirped and bees buzzed obliviously to my plight. A butterfly happened by, and I reached out of the window for it to land on my hand.

"Queen Mab, if you can hear me, please, save me," I whispered to the butterfly.

It took off from my hand as if to hand-deliver the message personally to the Dark Queen of the Unseelie Court. I walked back over to my bed and scarfed down the food so I wouldn't have to bear the taste of the gruel that was sent for me to eat. Besides, if I wanted to live through these next few weeks, I needed my strength. No sooner had the thought escaped my mind than the doors busted open with the chain gang. Alpha's little gang circled me as if I had anywhere to go. Two tackled me to the floor, with me swinging punches while the other two tossed the chain over the bar in the middle of the floor. They brought the shackles over to my hands and clamped them down over them. They removed the shackle from my foot while two of them hoisted me into the air. Once I was dangling with my feet barely grazing the floor, one of them landed a punch squarely in my ribs. My body absorbed the punch, and my ribs cracked instantly under the pressure.

I gasped in excruciating pain as my lungs struggled harder for air.

"Is that the best you got?" I wheezed, taunting them.

One of them let out a cackling laugh and produced a whip that had an electric charge at the tip. He flicked it once at my body and ripped through my skin with a searing heat. The pain that accompanied the burn was excruciating, however, I never let anyone know if they hurt me. They don't deserve that satisfaction.

"Come on!" I yelled. "More!"

CHAPTER 3

BY THE TIME THEY LEFT the room, the sun had set, and I was a bloody pulp. My wounds oozed and dripped onto the floor below me. I could hardly breathe. Not only had they broken my ribs on one side, but they came in on the other side and cracked them as well, quite possibly puncturing my lung. I could be dead by morning for all I knew. I was to hang like this until Alpha told them to let me down. I was well familiar with the tactic. This time, however, it was more gruesome than all the other times. There was no mercy, and I was never beaten to within inches of life, either.

My nose bled from where they broke it, and I had slash marks all up and down my torso and back from that whip, as well as across my face. The whip was new. They hadn't used it on me before. The door to my cell opened, and Asmodeus rushed in. He untied the chain from the wall and let me down as easily as he could. I definitely couldn't breathe now and shook my head, moaning and choking on air as I gasped. He lifted me back up to the pose I was in and tied the chain back off.

"Boy, I told you to run. You're always thinking of everyone but yourself." He cursed and kicked the water pale that was long empty.

"I couldn't run. I would have led them straight to Xavier and Luxina," I rasped. "Besides, Sophia didn't deserve to die. It was either save her and the twins or run selfishly." I wheezed, and my skin around my ribs sunk deep within as each breath became shallower than the one prior. "I need to tell you something," I began.

"No, don't you dare! I don't need to hear it now. You can tell me tomorrow. You're not dying tonight!" Asmodeus protested.

"I wanted to tell you thank you for your kindness when you don't need to offer any to me," I continued, ignoring him.

"I wasn't always this thing I have become," he said. "I was once a beautiful angel, and I chose to fall with Lilith. I let the darkness consume me. No fault but my own."

"You're still an angel," I croaked. "You may have darkness, but you're still an angel."

He looked up at me with tears threatening to spill. I had never seen him show any type of emotion regarding anyone prior to now.

"Don't you give up," he choked out. "Stay strong. They won't be back tomorrow. They believe you will die tonight. But you show Alpha that no one dictates when you die but you! Incaendiel may not be your father, but you have his will and his fire!"

"How is he?" I inquired through wheezes.

"No one has gone to his cell since he was brought here, and most likely, no one will. Alpha wants to leave him there to rot," Asmodeus scoffed.

"Well, that just won't do," I sniggered.

I sent myself into a violent coughing fit that made it feel as if my ribs burst through my skin.

"That's enough talking for you now," Asmodeus fretted. "I can try to let you down again and get you comfortable in bed."

"No, it will kill me. The blood won't fill my lungs this way. But thank you," I panted.

"I will be back to check on you periodically throughout the night," he said. "Try not to die on me, man. Ok?"

"No promises," I joked.

He frowned, turned on his heels, left the room, and closed my door behind him. I spent a good portion of the night struggling to breathe and trying not to die. As promised, Asmodeus popped in every so often and offered me small sips of water to keep me hydrated. By morning, the pain was tolerable enough, and my breathing good enough for him to let me down from the chain and then help me over into the bed. As soon as my body touched the bed, the pain shot through me, and I drew in ragged breaths. Asmodeus was dismissed quickly when Lilith entered the room. She carried in her hands the herbs and poultice I had in my room, along with a bowl of water and a washcloth. Asmodeus bowed to her and left without a word. She walked over to my bed and set everything on the floor beside me. She pulled a chair up to the bed, reached down in the water with the washcloth, and wrung it out.

She dabbed the cloth on all my oozing wounds, and I winced as she cleaned them. She worked methodically and had me cleaned up with the salve and herbs applied within minutes. They burned more than usual, but my flesh wounds were deeper than all the times before. I gritted my teeth as she stuffed some of the herbs into deeper wounds. She watched me with curious eyes, but she never spoke a word as she doctored me. By the end of the process, I was drifting off into an exhaustive sleep, praying that I wouldn't have any dreams.

"So, you dream just like the twins?" she asked as she wrapped me in bandages.

"Yes," I managed to croak out.

"What else can you do?" she asked.

I dropped my hand to the floor and searched for the water bowl she had been using to clean me up with. I dipped my finger into the bloody bowl of water, and it instantly froze into a solid block of ice.

"Fire and ice. What a deadly pair," she declared. "That all?" she prodded.

No, I replied with my thoughts.

"Well, well, well," she crooned, lifting an eyebrow. "And I assume Alpha doesn't know?"

"That's right. He knows about the ice but not about the telepathy," I uttered. "Some things are best kept secret."

"So, you were the reason he was able to attack Xavier in his dreams?" she asked.

I nodded. "He hijacked me in my sleep. I received lashings for not telling him about my power."

"Why haven't you run away from him? You have had ample opportunities. Why do you stay?" she countered.

"When I'm not being tortured, I am being controlled by the injections. The moments I have to myself where I am not experiencing either, I have other lives to consider if I were to flee," I maintained. "Not to mention he can track me whether I am cloaked or not."

"How so?" she asked.

"It has to do with the injections. Most likely, a tracker was injected. He told me I would never be able to hide from him."

She leaned in close and whispered in my ear, "We will get you out of here. And when we do, you run, and you don't stop running. You find Luxina and Xavier, and you don't stop looking for whatever can destroy him until you have found it. Understand me?" she stipulated.

I nodded. "Yes, ma'am," I conceded.

"Now you hush up with that ma'am crap. Call me Grandmother if you wish. I am your grandmother as much as I am the twins' grandmother," she responded with a smile and wink.

"Yes, Grandmother," I answered with a hint of a smile.

I felt comforted around her. A warmth radiated from her that I never experienced with Alpha. All you felt around him was a cold despair that wrought you to your bones. She stood to leave when I caught her hand. Is this what unconditional love feels like? A love that you didn't have to fight to win the affection of? A love that came with no strings attached, no fulfillments to be made. Pure, unadulterated love?

"Will you stay?" I begged. "Until I fall asleep?"

She smiled at me and squeezed my hand. "I thought you would never ask," she cooed.

By the time I had awakened, she was gone, and the sunlight poured through the window. I struggled to sit up in bed. My body was a mess. Aches and pains popped up in places I didn't even remember being hit. My ribs screamed in resistance, and my lungs ached for deep breaths of air, but I managed to sit straight up in the bed. I moved my feet off the side of the bed and tested the strength of my legs. They were still wobbly, but I could stand without hitting the ground. I hobbled over to the window of my cell and looked out as dark clouds began to cover the sky. I could smell the rain in the air as it drifted into the window.

Tiny droplets began to fall, splattering my face as they hit the concrete slabs of the tiny window. I crouched to the floor beside the window and just watched as the storm brewed. Lightning crashed, and thunder rolled as the rain fell harder. The harder it rained, the darker my mood became. Or was it vice versa? Did I wake up in darkness? Did it matter? Gale force winds tore through the tiny meadow beside my window. Much to my astonishment, the rain turned to ice and snow, and within minutes, snow began to pile up outside of the tiny window. Ice began to form around me in my cell, and I watched it crawl its way up the walls, freezing every inch of the cell into solid ice. Everything, except me.

A pounding came to the door.

"Damian! Damian, you must stop!" Lilith yelled through the frozen door.

I ignored her as the storm outside grew heavier and the winds picked up to hurricane force levels. It was at that moment that my own questions were answered. It was me.

23

"Damian! You're going to kill us all!" she pleaded through the door.

What do I care if everyone dies? Everyone that was here was now on Alpha's side. There was no chance for me, for Xavier, or for Luxina to live through this hell. Maybe it would be better this way. I am no longer a threat to anyone. No one is a threat anymore. The world is saved.

"The world is not saved! Alpha isn't susceptible to this power of yours. You're killing everyone but him. You're just doing him a favor and taking lives and spilling blood that should be on his hands and not yours. Please, you must stop!"

I couldn't stop it. They all deserved to pay, even if it didn't affect Alpha. I could take him out easier without his minions around.

"Damian! Incaendiel is here. Luxina will never forgive you if you kill him! He is innocent in all this! He has been the one trying to defeat him from the beginning. You kill him, and you kill whatever chance this world must be saved."

That was the only thing that could stop me. She was right there. I couldn't kill Incaendiel. I couldn't take him away from Luxina. I looked out the window, and the snow began to pitter out. The dark clouds began to move away, and the sun slowly came back out, shining as brightly as it had been earlier. The ice began to melt from the walls, and the water pooled around my feet. The door to my cell swung open, and I expected the chain gang back in here to chain me up once more for my little temper tantrum. Instead, it was just Lilith who stood there.

"They won't be back," she assured. "May I come in?"

"Oh, there's a choice now?" I retaliated.

"Fair enough," she answered, walking in. "So, what was all that?"

I shrugged my shoulders. "I didn't even know I was doing it until you came along."

"Alpha has no idea it was you who froze hell over," she mused, sitting down in the chair beside my bed. "And I plan to keep it that way."

"He must know it was me. It's not the first time I have used my powers," I corrected.

"Yes, he has seen ice come from your hand and be directed at a target. However, the ice crept up and covered everything, unlike your normal ice blasts," she proclaimed, pursing her lips and knitting her eyebrows together. "We need to keep it that way, too. No more freak ice takeovers, no matter how much you hate us all."

"I don't hate you all," I retorted. "I'm just tired... I'm tired of this twilight I am stuck in. Half between heaven and half between hell... the darkness that comes in waves... the loneliness and isolation. I don't want to do this anymore. I can't do this anymore. Always fearful that I will be beaten and tortured. Afraid that one more injection is all it would take for me to be a puppet forever to Alpha. Afraid that one more injection and I could kill the two people I care most about than myself. That's what he is going to have me do. In the end days, I will be the one forced to kill Luxina and Xavier."

"When the next opportunity comes up, you must run. Don't think of anyone you are leaving behind. Don't worry about the deaths that will come at the cost of your escape. You must GO!" she pleaded.

"And what then? Be hunted down by mutts? Lead them straight to the people I want to protect," I snapped. "Every way this scenario goes, I lead him to the very people that need to be as far away from him as possible."

"You're going to have to take that chance. If they do follow you, Xavier is trained to fight them off by your side. Fight and don't stop fighting. Even in the end, when all hope seems lost, don't stop fighting!"

"I don't know if I can promise that," I whimpered in choked words as tears threatened the backs of my eyes.

"Don't promise. Just when the time comes, and you will know what that time is in that very moment, you fight!" she repeated.

I nodded, accepting her words. She stood from her seat and walked to the door. "I don't know when or how long it will take, but we will get you out of here." With those last words, she left the room and shut the door behind her.

CHAPTER 4

THE SEASONS CAME and went as I sat in the dungeon I was cursed into. I had lost count of the days once the beatings had begun again. I had just recovered from the broken ribs when Alpha sent the chain gang back in. I guess Lilith could only have so much say in what happened to me while I was here in Alpha's clutches. I never did get broken ribs again, though. I did, however, receive the sharp end of the whip countless times. Whoever created that whip was first on my kill list when I busted out of this prison cell. My body was littered with scars from the bites it left with each strike. They hardly ever fed me. Asmodeus would sneak me food whenever he could, but even that was sparse. If this was Alpha's idea of breaking me, he had no idea what it would take to break me into a conformed soldier completely.

One thing I was allowed to do in between the beatings was read. I asked Lilith to bring me the books from my room down to the dungeon as well as grab me new ones from the library wing. She was the only person I allowed in the room to see me. I had not seen Sophie since the last day in my room, although Lilith had told me many times that she wished to see me. I never acknowledged the thought, so she never stopped by. The last I saw Lucifer was when he told me to kill Sophia. That I will never get over. Sophia was his soulmate, his one true half. His black heart held no bounds regarding the women in his life. He was as much of a monster as Alpha was.

I picked up the books lying around my bed and thumbed through the pages I had memorized. I had read through every book of mythology I could get my hands on. There had to be an inkling of research on what it meant to be a Shining One. I would scan through the pages and set the book aside, picking up another to take its place. Nothing. I could never find anything. I tossed the books to the floor in frustration as I balled myself up on the bed, tucking my arms deep under my armpits. In these moments of solitude, it wasn't hard for my thoughts to drift to Luxina and Xavier and wonder how they were faring, staying safe from the hunting parties Alpha executed. In truth, those two were the only things keeping me going at this point.

I sighed heavily and looked at the window that was now boarded up. Alpha had them board it up today as if taking away my one piece of time mattered. I still had my memories of sunshine, of wilderness, of rainstorms. He could take away the view, but he couldn't board up my mind. I hadn't seen anyone all day long and hoped that it meant there wouldn't be any torture for the day. Just a moment of respite is all I needed. My eyes were heavy, and I had staved off sleep for so many days, fearing the moment they closed, I would be strung up once more to endure the whip. I closed my eyes and drifted off to sleep for the first time in days.

Harrowing images flooded my mind. I watched as Alpha rode through the sky in the chariot he had used to fly to Stygia. It was being pulled along by the same horses as before. A red one, a black one, a white one, and a pale gray one. Something tugged at my mind from scripture. It dawned on me what the significance of those four horses meant. They were the horses of the apocalypse. War, famine, pestilence, and death. Below him in the valley, hordes of creatures crept, slithered, crawled, and bounded in one massive black wave toward the angel fleet that was stationed on the corresponding side of the valley. Fire and brimstone rained from the sky, exploding as they hit the ground below. Those standing in the wake of destruction burned to crisps, leaving an ashen body, or were struck down into pillars of salt that blew away in the wind.

The advancing mass of creatures had draugrs, werewolves, vampires, demons both greater and lower, and whatever other mutts Alpha had created in his laboratory using stolen Seelie blood. I watched, waiting for Lilith or Lucifer to appear at his side, but neither of the two was there. Sophie was nowhere to be seen as well. However, Incaendiel stood at the forefront of the army of angels who all stood waiting for his command to charge against the stampede hurtling toward them. The ground broke free beneath the angel army and flames tore through the sky as they all fell to a burning grave.

I tried to move, but I stood waist deep in a tarry, black pit that I struggled to free myself from. I looked to my right and left, and stuck alongside myself I found Luxina and Xavier struggling to free themselves as well from the hot, oily substance. No matter how much we struggled, we just sank deeper without breaking free. Alpha arrived at the pit with a laugh.

"Join me and be free," he yelled, laughing maniacally.

"Never!" I seethed.

"Then die, young Shining Ones." Alpha stared at us emotionlessly. His eyes were like bottomless pits, cavernous and oblique. It was a look I had never witnessed before in his cold, dead-set eyes. He had completely gone off the deep end and most likely had planned something even more terrifying than the nature of the apocalypse. I heard the sound of a gong and a loud crack in the air. I watched in frozen horror as molten lava came racing toward us across the valley, burning all the creatures he had made. From behind us, water crashed through the valley. The universe seemed to implode on itself as bits and pieces of planets and asteroids rained down around us, along with the fire and brimstone. Every star in the sky seemed to supernova and explode all at once, and just as he had sparked the universe into existence, he began to dismantle it.

New beings swarmed the air. They had the wings of angels and the grotesque, disfigured faces of animals. No doubt, these were more of Alpha's experiments. When they opened their eyes, they shone like the sun. He had done it. He had created his muddled shining ones that were half demon, half shining one.

"If I can't have what rightfully belongs to me, no one will," Alpha bellowed. "I will just start over and do it the right way." It was then that the lava and waters reached Luxina, Xavier, and me in the pit just as we reached for each other's hands.

I woke from the dream, choking and gasping, fighting the air around me with all my might. My senses finally came to me as my surroundings materialized around me. I was safely tucked away in the dungeon. Well, as safe as safe can be compared to that nightmare I just had. I sat up on the side of my bed and ran my hands through my sweat-riddled hair. Was that just a nightmare? Or was that something more? Is that what the end will look like? I stood up and began to anxiously pace the floor.

A gentle breeze filled my room, and I looked at the door to see if someone had entered it while I was lost in deep thought. No one had opened it, and the window couldn't let enough air into the room to cause that building wind in the room. Papers I had been writing on began to blow around the room as well as the books I had tossed casually to the floor earlier. I held my hand up to my face to protect it from anything that might strike me from the whirlwind forming in the room. A translucent, window-type thing appeared before me, and a little old woman stepped in from the most marvelous oasis you could imagine.

"Hello, Damian," she greeted. "I'm Starfire." The hole she stepped through stayed up behind her as the winds ripped around the room. "Come with me, child. I can keep you safer than Lilith can."

"Who are you?" I marveled incredulously. "How do you know who I am?"

"I'm the Oracle, and time is running out. Your dream was much more than just a dream. You got a taste of what the end of days looks like for every being that exists in this universe," she postulated.

"How do you know that?" I refuted. "How do I know this isn't some trick?"

"I told you. I am the Oracle. I have seen what you have seen, and I am the only one who can give you and your siblings what you need to defeat Alpha. Come with me," she repeated, extending her hand.

"Are they there? Luxina and Xavier?" I stammered. "Are they safe?"

"They are close, but they are not here yet," she replied. "They will arrive safely in due time, but you, I am afraid if you don't escape soon, there will be no end of days for you to see." Her face was grave as she spoke the words to me. "Please, take my hand and come with me."

I shook my head. "I can't. I must save Incaendiel first."

"You have to stop trying to save everyone before there's no one left to save," she rebutted.

Why does everyone keep telling me that? It is so frustrating to hear it over and over.

"Once he is safely away from Alpha, I will come to you," I promised. "I will make it!"

She frowned and shook her head. "You, my child, have a heart bigger than the universe. I will see you soon."

She turned to walk back through the slice of world that floated in the room.

"Wait!" I yelled.

She turned around with a look of hope on her face that I may have changed my mind.

"If I don't make it, if I don't get to see them again, tell them I did everything I could to keep them safe. And I'm sorry. I am so deeply sorry."

"Tell them yourself," she replied with a smile, stepping through the translucent hole.

It disappeared from my room, and the wind died down, dropping everything to the ground it had been tossing about. One of the books dropped open, and I picked it up to close it when the title header caught my attention.

⟨⊕⌐⌐⌐⌐⌐⌐⌐⟨

I HAD STUDIED every ancient language, and this was the original language of them all. The title was in Enochian, my own language. The angelic alphabet wrapped its letters across the pages of the book I held. I couldn't help but smile, knowing that this was a gift from the Oracle who had just left. I poured over the pages, reading as much as it offered about what I was.

The Shining Ones were an old race of Elder Gods who died out prior to the big spark of the universe referred to as the big bang. They were a superior race who had powers beyond any god or goddess that existed within the realm. They had faces that shone as bright as the sun, eyes that glowed like burning stars, and they glowed like a raging wildfire from their own internal flames that burned through their bodies. Their wings were as bright as gold, and their skin as white as snow. They always came in pairs as twin flames.

The prophecy foretold of a special birth of three that would wield powers of both fire and ice to rule the universe as one. Any and all lower gods that stood in their way would be made to bow to their powerful majesty. The three special Shining Ones who were to be birthed would be unstoppable as a trio but would ultimately bring the balance of the universe together after many failed attempts of power-hungry gods. With the birthing of the special trio, they were given powers as a pair. The one that wields fire and the one that wields ice would be the rulers of the new world order as part of the new God and Goddess quartet. The third Shining One would ultimately be absorbed by the twin since they were never meant to be three of them in the end.

Humanity has all but wiped out the very notion and idea of the Shining Ones after church rose to power through the manipulations of the god they worship as the one true god. While the church holds its grasp over the world, so does the lower god who helped create it.

The Shining Ones were called by many names, such as the Anunnaki, Elohim, and even angels. However, the names do not give these carefully crafted beings the justice they deserve. Angels were created by gods and goddesses and do not contain the power of their masters. However, Shining Ones are above the class of gods and goddesses, and to be rudimentarily referred to as an angel is an error. These great beings comprised the original seven members of the Council of El prior to their dying off.

I closed the book, and it vanished into thin air. It was only for my eyes, it seemed. The words of Starfire echoed in my mind, of her urgent pleas for me to join up with Xavier and Luxina. The three of us together was the only way to stop Alpha. She was right. But there were so many things that were left out. How could the twin flames not be meant to be with one another? Xavier and Luxina were supposed to be together, not Luxina and me. Did that mean that Sophie and Incaendiel were never the true god and goddess to be? Just the ones responsible for the creation of the new world order? And what was the whole absorbed thing? Is Xavier truly not meant to exist?

Thousands of questions rolled through my head as I processed the information overload. There would absolutely be no way Luxina or I would absorb Xavier. So, what then? Is that why the world ends in the apocalyptic dream? Because we are still all together, and it isn't just Luxina and me? The realization of my thoughts sank deeply in, and that's when I knew for a fact that we were all doomed. There was no way we could defeat Alpha without this key fact.

The door opened, and Alpha's chain gang walked in. I groaned inwardly and shut my eyes, waiting for them to tackle me to the ground. I slowly opened my eyes and noticed they had just congregated around the door. They didn't come bearing chains, either.

"Alpha wishes to see you," Mammon stated, swinging the door wider for me to follow them.

I walked over to them, and two led in front of me with two behind me as we climbed the stairs from the dungeon. I walked the familiar halls with a mind heavy with knowledge. The fate of the universe, the fate of myself and siblings, all of it swirled around in my head. We passed by the doors that had been barricaded, and bricks now stood mortared in place as the screams of the beasts within the walls echoed through the hall. It was always hard to drown those sounds out of my head. At times, they haunted my dreams as well as haunting my every waking thought.

They led me down the all too familiar hallway to the door behind which Alpha sat at his desk. The door opened, and the two who stood in front of me parted ways. I walked alone into the room. Alpha had his usual demeanor he donned while quietly studying me as I walked to a chair and took a seat. There was a long moment of silence between us. I could only assume he was trying to think of the right words to say or the right question to ask. I stared back at him unblinking, hoping that my poker face was as believable as it had always been.

"You look terrible," he finally spoke.

"I suppose I do," I remarked. "I'm sure you already knew of what my condition was prior to bringing me here."

He smiled a sinister grin. "You are quite right, my boy. You are quite right."

He tapped his forefingers together as he contemplated his next words to speak to me.

"I have a small task for you," he said, leaning back in his chair and resting his feet up on the desk.

"And what would that be?" I asked.

"I want you to be the one to speak to Incaendiel. Get whatever information you can out of him. He hasn't been seen nor touched the entire time he has been here and locked away just as you were. It's time someone goes in to try and break him." Alpha replied.

"What makes you think he would talk to me?" I asked. "He most likely hates me. I know he despises Lucifer and equally despises you. I'm your pawn in all this. What makes you think he would tell me anything?"

"Because there's more to the way Incaendiel works than just being fueled by hatred or rage. He is methodical. The ringleader of all. He says jump, the others ask how high. He is superior to them all, and they acknowledge that. Everyone except you, that is. I believe he would talk to you," he replied earnestly.

"What? You want me to go now?" I asked.

"Yes," Alpha replied, a bit agitated. He composed his face and, with a smile, said, "The sooner, the better."

He was trying to sweet talk me into doing his dirty work is what all this was. I nodded and stood from the chair.

"And Damian," he started.

"Yes, sir?" I asked, stepping to the door and opening it.

"Don't fail this time," he stated venomously.

"I don't know what to base pass and fail with you anymore. So, I will try, sir, to not fail you," I retorted, closing the door behind me.

Alpha's escorts waited for me outside of his doors, ready to rush in at a moment's notice. I saw the tension ease from their shoulders as I walked out of the door, closing it behind me.

"Take me to Incaendiel," I ordered.

They looked at one another hesitantly.

"Do you really want me to open that door again and have him tell you?" I asked, aggravated.

They exchanged glances and led me from Alpha's door back down toward the dungeons.

CHAPTER 5

"BEFORE YOU GO IN, Damian, there is something we would like to say," Mammon began. "We didn't sign up for this. Alpha assigned us this detail. And you know the punishment for disobeying his orders. You say the word, and you won't have to stay to suffer anymore."

"Why does everyone want to help me escape?" I asked, shaking my head.

"Because you will become our new leader one day," Mammon replied.

He slipped a blade in my hand. I looked down at the gift and then back up to meet his eyes. I nodded my head, slipped the blade into my pocket, and pushed the door open to Incaendiel's dungeon. It was dark in the room, with hardly a sliver of light coming from the boarded-up window across from where he was chained. I flipped the light switch on in the room, and he squinted through the blinding light. Recognition registered on his face, and a glare replaced the once confused look. He looked at the door, I suppose waiting for more people to follow me in. When I walked closer into the light, his look of anger faded away to pity. It was then the questions started pouring from his mind. *Were they feeding him? Were they torturing him?* He took notice of the scar on my neck the whip had left behind. A moment of insecurity struck me, and I didn't want to do this. I didn't want to report anything to Alpha that was said. But I had to report something. I squared my shoulders and walked over to Incaendiel. I pulled up a chair and sat down, staring at him, his stare equally matching mine. And then his thoughts changed. *I wonder what Alpha wants him to do to me?*

"Nothing," I replied.

I watched as he processed what I had just done. His face went from surprise to confusion and then to downright bafflement. I tried to act casually and leaned my chair back lifting the legs off the floor and looped my arms behind my head. It was kind of fun playing cat and mouse.

"I know. It's confusing. And no, Alpha has no idea," I replied with a confident grin.

I watched the realization hit him. "You can read minds?" he asked, a bit unbelieving.

"Yes, but I haven't always been able to. I'm sure it is something that has to do with the experiments that Alpha does on me," I replied with a shrug. "It may have been the connection with my siblings that triggered it. I will never know. All I know is that one day, I could hear the thoughts of every person who stood in the room with me. Some may think it's a curse, some a blessing. I find it to be a useful asset in times of war."

"Your mother and I could read each other's minds. It might have something to do with that," he offered.

"She is not my mother," I replied heatedly.

I tried to compose myself.

"Why do you say that, Damian? Why do you speak of Sophie in such ill regard?" he asked.

I hated it whenever anyone mentioned Sophie being my mother. I looked at his face as he read me. He had no idea that Sophie was even alive or that she had turned out to be on Alpha's side. He had no idea what he was protecting from Alpha she was trying to fork over. I couldn't tell him that. I couldn't be the one to break that news.

"She may have created me with my father, but neither of them will ever be my parents. They will never understand me. They will never understand the endured torture I have been put through while being with Alpha."

He nodded in understanding.

"You know, Luxina and you have that temper thing going for yourselves. She gets angered and explodes into fire so easily. I can't imagine who she gets that from," he said with a chuckle.

"From my understanding, she gets it from you," I replied with a smirk.

"What does he want with me, Damian?" he asked.

"The same thing he wanted with me. The same thing he wanted with Sophie, and the same thing he wanted with my brother and sister," I replied. "He wants to build an army of new angels."

"I thought he no longer had the power to create? He can't just go around injecting people, hoping the injections take. And I certainly hope he doesn't think we can procreate a new race for him," he said, still not knowing everything that I do.

"He isn't going to do any of that," I replied with a sincere, concerned look.

"What are his plans?" he asked.

I looked around the room and leaned forward to him, the chair legs settling softly on the floor. "Once our blood accepts these injections, he plans to use Lilith at his side to create a special race from our newly formed blood. The creations won't be mindless anymore because he has Lilith at his side now. However, they thought the original werewolves and vampires were horrible in the beginning, but these new creatures, these new angels he wants to make… they will destroy everything." I stared at him with bewilderment and fear.

"Why are you helping him?" he asked. "Why do you fear this plan but still help him?"

"I have no choice," I replied, straightening up and returning to my position in the chair I had been in. The nonchalant, not caring attitude washed back over me, and I had to play it cool once more.

"We all have a choice, Damian," he replied. "There has to be a reason you are helping him."

"Who says I am truly helping him?" I replied with a sly grin.

"You helped him take Luxina and Xavier," he stammered in confusion.

"Incorrect. Lucifer was the one that orchestrated both of those incidents, not I," I replied. "I don't want them anywhere near Alpha."

"Afraid he would choose them over you, and you would be the outcast once more?" he asked, a bit too sarcastic. I appreciated his wit more than he could understand.

"Yes," I replied very quietly and simply. "And they don't deserve that as a punishment."

I watched as he processed everything I had said. He was beginning to realize that I truly wasn't just some soldier for Alpha that was manipulated my entire life. He was seeing me for me.

"You care for them, don't you?" he asked, squinting at me suspiciously.

"Why wouldn't I? They are what I am missing in life. They are my blood," I replied. "I keep everyone at arm's length. I don't wish to get close to anyone. It's been my thing since I was a youngster. Alpha never showed me what love is. He never showered me with affection. He just wanted me to create this stupid army of his. However, I have seen the way Luxina looks at me. She looks at me with love, empathy, and sorrow. She doesn't see me as a monster. At least, she didn't until the attack of the Watchers. I have no idea what her thoughts of me are at this moment. She could hate me for all I care. All that matters is that she and Xavier stay safe and as far away from Alpha as I can keep them."

"So, when you took her from me, all those things you said. Your cold demeanor... that wasn't you?" he asked.

I shook my head. "The injections Alpha gives me make me vulnerable to mind control. I must do whatever I am told. Lucifer struck a deal with Alpha to deliver both Xavier and Luxina to him in exchange for me. Alpha took the deal, but he won't hold up his end of the bargain even if he still had them in his grasp. Alpha needs us."

"Mother created us. She can create more of us. Why does he need us in specific?" he asked.

"Because the Unseelie Queen will no longer help him, nor will she aid Lilith in creating more of the Shining Ones. I also don't foresee Lilith remaining in the end," I replied, shifting in my seat. "She is the key to it all..." I was about to tell him everything I knew. He needed to know from beginning to end what was going to happen. To hell with Alpha. He could return me to the dungeon if he wished to. This was what was important.

"How?" he began when the door busted open.

Lucifer walked in, grinning from ear to ear. "Ah, son, starting early, are we?" he asked, walking over to me. "Did Alpha give the orders to start on him?"

"Yes and no," I replied, settling my chair back on the ground and standing up. Why was he always ruining things? "We were just having a small chat. I needed to know where my siblings might be hiding and who, but their father would know that answer. However, you interrupted."

I reached out to Incaendiel with my thoughts. *I will return to speak with you again. I have a lot to fill you in on before things get so out of hand that they cannot be controlled. There will be another visitor, and after they leave, I will be back to free you.* He looked at me and nodded with his eyes, acknowledging what I had told him through telepathy.

"Well, does he know where they are? Do we need to force it out of him?" Lucifer asked, grinning madly.

"He doesn't know," I replied, walking to the door.

"And you believe him?" Lucifer shouted.

I spun on my heels and pinned Lucifer against the wall. I wanted to take him out right then and there, but I knew I wouldn't be able to make it safely from this place if I did. "Do you question my authority?" I demanded, glaring at Lucifer. "He doesn't know."

I could see the fear settling on Lucifer's face, and it was most satisfying. I hoped he could feel the hatred I had for him leach from within me and flow through his body.

"That is not how you talk to me! I am your superior, and I am your father! You will respect me!" Lucifer bellowed.

"Respect is earned, and you do not have a single respectable bone in your pathetic existence," I retorted.

"Is that why you're in here? Buttering up to Incaendiel in hopes he would adopt you as his?" Lucifer demanded.

"At least he proves to be a better father than you ever have," I seethed. "Now, leave the room and do not bother the prisoner. Alpha wants him to remain untouched and unharmed. Those are orders!"

I stomped from the room with Lucifer hot on my trail. No one met me on the other side of the door to lead me anywhere. I pushed forward as fast as I could to get away from Lucifer before I sank a dagger into his heart.

"I'm not done talking to you!" he yelled down the hall, his voice echoing and bouncing off the walls.

I turned on my heel and faced him, clenching my fists and calming myself before he knew about my power.

"What do you want?" I demanded through clenched teeth.

"You need to change your attitude toward me and toward your mother!" he roared, pointing his finger and jabbing it in my chest.

I grabbed his hand and twisted the finger that jabbed me until I felt it cave and break under my grip. I pushed him with his broken hand against the adjacent wall from us and gripped it even tighter.

"You listen to me!" I yelled. "You will NEVER be my father. She will NEVER be my mother. You brought my brother and sister here for Alpha to do to them what I have been subjected to for years. I do not hate them. You may hate those two, but they are innocent in all this, and I will not stand by and watch you and everyone else wreck what I have left in this world on a power trip! My advice to you is to stay away from me because next time, I won't hesitate to drive a blade so deep in your chest that no one could pry it from your lifeless body."

As the words left my mouth, I pulled the blade I had been given and threw it to the ground. He watched with fearful eyes, not knowing where

I had gotten the blade.

"You are not my superior. You're just another pawn in Alpha's chess game. And the next time you interrupt me when I am doing what I was told to do, I will no doubt kill you for insubordination."

I released the grip I had on his now crushed hand and continued my way up from the dungeon and headed to Alpha's office. I opened the door without even knocking, and Sophie and Lilith were sitting around his desk. They all turned to look at me, surprised to see me in the office.

"I was unable to perform my job," I stated curtly to Alpha. "Lucifer interrupted me while I was speaking with the prisoner and turned everything personal. I will have to go a second time to get whatever information you need."

Alpha motioned me in the room, and I closed the door behind me.

"What did Lucifer do to stop your interrogation?" Alpha asked.

"He busted in and asked me if I was there on your orders to interrogate the prisoner, to which I replied yes. He then began to badger the prisoner, interrupting even further. When that wasn't enough for him, he began to drag personal history between the two of us into the interrogation. You can find him down near the dungeons with a crushed hand after he threatened me. I told him his next act of subordination when speaking to his superior would be death."

I relayed everything in my soldier attitude that I had always shouldered.

"I have my boy back," Alpha replied, grinning. "Instruct Mammon to take Lucifer to the dungeons and string him up for his insubordination."

"Yes, sir," I replied with almost a click of my heels.

I began to leave the room when Alpha stopped me.

"And Damian?" he began.

"Yes, sir?" I asked.

"Sleep in your room tonight," he replied as he glanced through papers that were on his desk.

I could only get a brief glance at them before I was formally dismissed from the room. It looked like some sort of mechanism he was building. It almost looked like an iron heart.

As I left the room, Sophie followed behind me.

"Why did you do that?" she asked angrily. "Lucifer just wants to talk to you."

"When will you all get it through your thick skulls that I do not care about any of you, or what will happen to you?" I replied vehemently.

"We just want what's best for you," she replied, trying to tuck a lock of my hair behind my ear.

I swatted her hand away.

"NO, you just want what's best for yourselves. And at what expense? Incaendiel is locked in the dungeon and has been locked away for as long as I have been locked away. You're trying to hand my brother and sister over to the very man that turned me into some kind of killing machine. You are the monster in this scenario. You don't see how well you are playing into Alpha's hand. You never will."

"Incaendiel is here?" she asked, bewildered.

"Oh, your master and mother didn't tell you? See the secrets they don't even tell you? What side are you truly on because obviously, to them, you are not on their side. That makes you expendable. If I were you, I would watch my back. I was sentenced away for not fulfilling a fool's plan. What do you think you would have to do to be locked away and tortured as I was?"

"Which cell is his?" she asked.

I rolled my eyes. "As if you care."

"I do!" she hissed.

"He's in the very last cell in the bottom of the dungeon," I replied. "But don't tell him I sent you."

She nodded and whisked away down the steps. I headed to my room and slammed the door shut. All this drama was getting on my nerves. Why did the angelic realm have to be full of so much malice and hatred when it was supposed to be the epitome of unconditional love?

A quiet knock came on my door, and I opened it, expecting some other person to cause me more agitation. Asmodeus stood there with a plate of food and some water.

"Alpha sent this for you," he said as he walked into my room and set my food down on the tabletop.

I quickly glanced up and down the hall before shutting the door behind him.

"It's good to see you out of that dungeon. You don't deserve that treatment," Asmodeus raved as he wrapped me in a hug.

"We don't have much time before spying ears and eyes come along. I have a plan that I need your help with," I stated hurriedly.

"What is it?" he asked, sitting down in the chair at the table.

"I'm going to break Incaendiel out and leave with him, and I need your help to do it."

He mulled over the idea before speaking. "What do you need me to do?" he asked.

"Incaendiel is expecting a visitor from me to signal him that it's time.

You're to untie his chains so he is at full power," I explained. "We will then fight our way out or die trying."

"That plan has so many flaws in it," Asmodeus replied, shaking his head.

"Please, you are the only person that can help pull this off. Everyone wants me to escape, but I also need Incaendiel to get to safety as well. Please, Asmodeus, help me."

"I will see what I can do. I am sure others here will help you as well. There have been building murmurs within the ranks about how Alpha has been treating you poorly when you have done everything you can for him. There will be riots soon if he hurts you more than what he has," Asmodeus stated.

"Will you come with us? When we escape?" I asked.

"We will see when the time comes," Asmodeus said with an appreciative smile. "Your safety first."

"Do you know what Alpha plans to do with me now?" I asked.

"We haven't heard anything lately. But rumor has it that he has been building the gladiator rink up with new, ferocious beasts," he replied grimly.

"I see," I said. I couldn't stop the defeat from pouring through me.

"You will survive it. You always do," he replied, patting me on my back. "Eat up. You will need your strength."

He left the room, and I sank into the chair he had just been sitting in. This would be my final trial. My final test. This was my life-or-death moment. Once I walked into that gladiator ring, it was either kill or be killed. I have fought werewolves, vampires, and every other concoction Alpha has thrown my way and came out a victor on the other side. This time, however, I was disadvantaged. I was skin and bones. I hadn't trained in nearly a year. I had been beaten and starved almost to the point of death so many times I had lost count of the brushes of death I had.

I stared at the food that was left for me on the table with crippling nausea. I didn't know how long I had before I was tossed into that ring, and right now, I couldn't stomach food. Maybe I could escape before the time came. I knew it wouldn't be possible, though. I had just been granted freedom from the dungeon. I couldn't do anything without being caught in the act.

I picked at the food on my plate and just pushed it away. If it was my time for death, then it would be my time. I would give it my all and fight to the end. If fate had different plans for me, then so be it.

CHAPTER 6

THEY CAME FOR ME at night in the grips of one of the apocalyptic nightmares that riddled my every moment of sleep. I awoke thrashing and kicking, trying to escape the nightmare I had been in.

Damian...

Damian!

"Damian!" the voice called, breaking me from the nightmare.

I glanced around the room, trying to clear my head and understand what was going on. Asmodeus, Mammon, and a few others stood around my bed, each holding something in their hand. Asmodeus held out the gladiator outfit for me to change into. Mammon held the scissors to cut my hair. I stripped in front of them and donned the ridiculous outfits I was forced to wear whenever I fought in these stupid games that Alpha held. Mammon walked up behind me and began to cut all my red, curly locks away until I was nearly bald. The others held out weapons for me to fasten. I had a mace, an axe, a long sword, a short sword, dueling knives, and a bow and arrow quiver. I strapped each of the special weapons all over my body. These weren't your average weapons. They were the size of an ink pen, and when you clicked a button on the side, they transformed into the weapon at hand. Everything, that is, but the bow and quiver of arrows. They then oiled down my bare skin so I would be less susceptible to scratches.

"Are you ready?" Asmodeus asked.

I cocked an eyebrow at him. I most likely looked like death. It had been several weeks since Alpha had allowed me back into my room, and I was just starting to be able to eat and keep food down.

"As ready as I can be," I replied.

He nodded and stepped aside. Two of them led me in front, with two on my sides and two flanking me in case I tried to run. That chance was long past. Asmodeus had begged me every night to flee, but I couldn't. My conscience wouldn't let me leave here without at least trying to break Incaendiel free. I had to do it for Luxina. I was told I was too noble for my own good. That may be it: pride. But I sure as hell was going to try and do what was right. Had I known I would have been subjected to the torture I had endured, I wouldn't have even brought him back. I didn't get a pat on the head or anything for obeying orders.

The gladiator ring was more or less a colossal stadium that Alpha had erected. Those that attended it either loved it or hated it. They loved the death, the chaos, and the gore. Some loved to watch me fight to the death with all these creatures, screaming in the crowd with joy as they got to watch the battles. Others sat quietly, less than enthused by the show. They abhorred the idea that Alpha would go to the lengths that he did for a little entertainment for those in the compound. I was led to the iron gate where I was placed, a gate closing behind me to lock me inside and make sure I didn't try to flee. I would stand there until the gate rose and let me into the arena where I had to ready myself within seconds before they opened the other doors for the mountains of creatures to attack.

I stood silently, readying my weapons on my side, and the gate slid shut behind me. I turned to see the group that had led me to the death rink staring at me with grief, awe, and a mix of emotions.

"See you all on the other side," I smirked.

I could already hear the cheers and jeers from the crowd awaiting the release of the gates. I scanned the crowd through the holes of the gate to see who all sat in the crowd. I saw Alpha on his throne at the center, with Lilith and Sophie on either side of him. Of course, they would be here. I heard the gears creak as the chain began to move, working the gate up so that I could enter the stadium. A hush fell over the crowd as I stepped forward into what was most likely the last place I would ever see.

Normally, there were loud voices yelling out in the air when I came into this place. But not this time. Every person there remained quiet, almost as if it were a protest. I pulled a sword from my side and clicked the activating button. The long sword materialized in my hand, and I readied myself for the onslaught of whatever Alpha had made special for this evening. A rumble came to the ground as they raised all the gates at once. I wasn't prepared for that. Normally, it's one at a time until I have killed them all. Panic flew through me as my eyes swept gate to gate, wondering what to expect first.

The first creature to emerge was directly to my left, and I could smell its breath before I could even see it walk out from the darkened tunnel. A putrid smell filled the arena, mixed with a nauseating gaseous smell, almost like the smell of death in a bottle. I turned my attention to the tunnel, waiting for it to come out into the light. I questioned whether I really would make it out of this fight as soon as it walked from the darkness and out for me to see. It had the body of a werewolf, but this one was much different than the ones I had been used to fighting. It was twice the size of the ones Alpha had been producing for me to fight. Green beady eyes stared me down as it sniffed the air. Drool dropped from its jaws and sizzled as it hit the ground. Most likely, he had altered the saliva to pure acid. Would it eat through my weapons?

I had no time to sit and wonder what would happen as the beast leapt toward me, its muzzle snapping and snarling as it cleared twenty feet in a single bound. The thing was huge, and muscles rippled throughout its body. Patches of fur fell off with each movement of its body, exposing the sickly green color of its skin. Its tail was like that of a lizard and upon closer inspection, its clawed paws were more like hands. I scrambled back as it bounded within inches of my face, swiping with my sword. I tripped and fell to my back, barrel rolling into a crouch. I had cut through the skin right under the eye, and it immediately healed.

"What the—" I muttered as it didn't waste a moment countering my attack with a swipe of its own clawed fingers.

I rolled again out of the way as I saw another one of the beasts emerge from the gate. It spotted me and came careening directly for me. One thing was for sure: they were hungry and most likely hadn't eaten for weeks. I thought back to the hallway I had been led through up to Alpha, where the walls had been sealed with bricks and mortar. The howls that came from the other side... it was most likely these things.

I had to get my head in the zone. Both of those things were closing in on me. I clicked another sword to life from my side and began to fight the one closest to me. Its claws parried the blows almost as if they were made of metal themselves. I swiped with one sword while distracting it and came down with my other, severing its clawed hand from its leg. The beast howled in pain and fury.

"Heal that!" I challenged it.

The second beast was but a bound or two away from me, enraged that I had hurt the other one. Knowing my luck, they were mated pairs. Alpha had a knack for mating pairs of beasts, so he could breed them easier than having to recreate the bloodlines. I glanced at a rope above my head and debated the jump. I clicked the swords off and jumped, grabbing hold of the end. I kicked my legs, swinging myself up on a boulder. I kicked off from the height of the boulder and came down on the back of the beast I had severed the foot off. Midair, I activated the sword and buried it to the hilt in the monstrosity. It gave an enraged howl of pain before it teetered over. I twisted the blade, severing its spinal cord before ripping the blade from its back. As it hit the ground, I plunged the sword through the thing's sternum straight through its heart.

Before I had time to even appreciate the kill, the other monstrous creature roared with a bellowing rage that filled the quiet arena and sprinted toward me. I ran at full speed toward the creature, and just as it was about to pounce on me, I slid underneath it, holding the sword up, and drove the sword deep into its body. I sliced it clean open from the heart down to its stomach. Its innards fell out on top of me, and I was covered in the blood of the fresh kill. The body collapsed, dead to the arena floor. I walked up to the now dead beast and thrusted my hand into its chest cavity. I pulled its heart from the carcass and held it up to the crowd.

"Is that all you got?" I yelled, tossing the heart into the crowd.

Alpha smiled as the screech filled the arena. I turned to the source of the sound and watched as an enormous bird walked in from another of the open gates. Its beak was filled with razor sharp teeth like that of pterodactyls. It towered even taller than the werewolf mutts I had killed. It let out another deafening screech and spread its wings, flapping hard. The gusts of wind nearly toppled me over as it took to the sky. It had the wings of an angel, the body of a dragon, the face of a bird, and instead of just two sets of talons, it had four massive, clawed paws. Is that a... no. It can't be?

It was a mutated form of a gryphon. And, it had a great advantage right now. It was airborne. I sheathed my sword and pulled my bow from my shoulder. I clicked a button, and it spread into a large missile-shooting weapon as opposed to the puny bow it had appeared to be. I loaded one of the arrows and clicked a button on the side of it. It transformed into a huge spear. I drew the string of the bow back and let the arrow fly. It missed the bird mutt by inches. I drew another and another, shooting them as fast as I could. The bird taunted me in the air. It was planning the moment to strike, to swoop down and grab me up with its claws and rip me to shreds. The moment it thought I didn't have any more arrows, it would make its move.

No sooner had I thought the words than the bird swooped down to scoop up its prey. I rolled out of the way at the last minute and instantly readied the bow, releasing the spear into the back of the bird. It screeched in pain as it tore through the bone of its wing. It landed with a thud and turned to face me with a deafening sound that made me nearly grab my ears to drown out the debilitating noise. It ran for me, its tail growing longer and swiping my feet out from under me. It was on top of me, and I used my bow as a shield. It opened its mouth to take a bite, and I shoved the bow in. As it tried to shake the bow loose from its beak, I grabbed one of my swords and clicked it into action. With one sweep, as it brought its head down trying to drive its beak into my exposed torso, I sliced its head clean off. I quickly rolled out of the way as its body crashed onto the arena floor, spraying me with even more blood.

I stood from the ground and looked around the crowd as they sat silently. I picked the head of the beast up and thrusted it into the air. They erupted in cheers of my success. I tossed the head to the side and walked toward the center of the floor.

"Is that all?" I taunted. "I can do this for days!!!"

Alpha, looking none too pleased, just tapped his fingers together as a gong sounded. That was something new. What did the gong mean? Was it over? The ground shook as if an earthquake was splitting the arena in half. No, it wasn't over. It was the sound of hundreds of feet pounding on the arena floor, rushing to the center where I stood. They erupted from the gates all around me. All the creatures I had seen in the nightmare were now careening toward me in the middle of the stadium. Had I fallen unconscious at some point? Am I asleep? I blinked my eyes just to make sure this wasn't a dream. My eyes caught it just then. Within the piles of creatures spilling out, it was the beast that had angel wings and the distorted face with eyes that shone as bright as the sun. It moved in a clunky manner, almost as if it were an iron giant. I backed slowly away as the masses filled every gate except the one I had come through. My back touched the metal gate as they descended in on me. Snarling, drooling, growling, snapping mouths with teeth that dripped acid. Some had wings and were flying while others shot fire from their mouths. I tossed my sword to the ground to admit defeat. Alpha had won. I raised my arms as the crowd went nuts in terrified banter. I was giving up.

I felt the gate behind me shift, and just as the creatures were about to pounce, I was yanked through the gate with it thudding back shut.

"Now, did you really think we were going to let you die in there?" Incaendiel asked.

He dragged me away from the gate and out of the arena entrance, winding through the tunnels.

"But, how?" I began stammering.

"Less talking and more running!" he shouted.

He pulled me along the dark corridors as the sounds of the hungry creatures echoed through the hall.

"We have about three minutes before that gate is lifted and those things come after us," he said as he jerked me from hall to hall.

"How are you free?" I asked.

"Asmodeus is an old friend of mine. He has been filling me in on you for a few weeks. He told me about this, about what Alpha was going to do and how you refused to leave without setting me free," he replied. "Kid, what part of no one cares about themselves as much as they care about you three do you just not get?"

He pulled me down long corridors that I didn't recognize. Were we in a part that I had never been before?

"Where are you taking me?" I asked.

"To freedom," he answered.

He ran at full speed and busted through the wall ahead of him. As the dust settled, I looked around. It was the meadow just outside of my cell. Incaendiel stood blazing in the sun with his wings spread as wide as they could stretch. He looked like what a god should have looked like in that moment.

"Alpha is going to be hot on your trail," Incaendiel stated as he handed me a bag full of weapons. "You need to lead him on a wild goose hunt before you meet up with Xavier and Luxina. He's going to be sending everything he has your way, including those things he made to tear you apart. You have to be fast and remain strong."

"Aren't you coming with me?" I asked.

He shook his head. "I have someone else myself to save before I leave here," he replied.

Sophie.

"Yes, Sophie," he replied as if reading my mind. "Now, go! That's an order! I can take care of myself. There's an uprising. Alpha will have to flee. The Forsaken weren't too happy when they found out about this plan of his with you. You have friends in low places, kid."

"Make sure Asmodeus stays safe," I asked.

"You have my word," he replied. "Now, go!"

I didn't think twice about it. I was gone.

CHAPTER 7

I HAD NO TIME to cloak and run. If I needed to escape quickly and gain ground against the monsters, I had to fly. It began to rain as I took off from the ground, watching Incaendiel disappear back into the fortress we were held prisoner in together. I soared through the sky faster than a bolt of lightning striking, gaining momentum with each flap of my angelic wings. However, no matter how fast I flew, those things Alpha created were equally fast. I heard the screeches from behind me as a fleet of flying mutations pushed as hard as they could to catch up with me. With what bit of strength I had, I summoned the cooling ice from within me, and the rain that pelted down turned into shards of ice that could rip your flesh clean off your bones.

I heard the howls of pain as the ice bit into the skin of the fleet following close behind me. I looked back to see each ice shard buried into the creatures, and they dropped one by one from the sky. Pleased with myself, I returned my attention to what was in front of me. Advancing toward me were more of the giant birds that I had fought in the arena. Their beaks bared their teeth as they screeched and howled with those same ear-splitting sounds that nearly caused me to falter from the sky. I didn't have time to grab any weapons from the bag that was draped over my shoulder. I held out my hand and shot ice spears from my palm. I couldn't even aim. I just pointed and blasted ice at them. They dipped and dodged from the onslaught of ice that I sent their way, still making their way headstrong toward me.

I didn't even think about my next action. I began to spin and twirl my body as I flew closer and closer to them. A whirlwind tunnel formed beneath my feet, and I stopped midair, continuing my spinning until the whirlwind grew into a twister. I held my hands out and blasted the sides of the funnel with ice as it picked up debris from the ground below. Ice weapons formed in the funnel, and the centrifuge suction of the winds pulled the birds into their impending demise. I stopped spinning and pushed the whirlwinds with my ice powers straight into their path. I could hear their screeches as the wind caught them and tore them to shreds with the sheets of icy winds.

Still, behind me, more creatures appeared, almost as if materializing from thin air. I used my palms and shot icy blockades that engulfed each of them one by one, and they dropped from the skies as frozen ice chunks. I continued to fly and shoot the ice as missiles at each of the targets that closed in on me. I was soon flying solo in the air once more and continued my ice storm for clear and safe passage through the skies.

A static filled the air as I forged my way through the falling crystals, immune to their blades of wrath. Even as the wind tore past me and the precipitation shot out at damaging speeds, silence fell all around me.

"Damian..." a voice whispered in the wind. "Damian!"

My eyes quickly surveyed my surroundings to see where the voice was coming from. It was a haunting, hollow voice.

"Damian!!" it bellowed. The sound echoed throughout the sky as I pushed forward harder and faster.

"Damian... you can run, but you can't hide from me..." the voice taunted me as I raced to find safety. Thunder rumbled, and lightning crackled all around me in the dark skies.

"I will always find you, Damian. There is nowhere you can go. Nowhere you can hide. No one that can keep me from getting to you. And when I get to you, you're going to wish you had never been brought into this universe." The voice was smug, no doubt Alpha in one of his disillusioned states. "Just when you think you are free of me, I will be there to take your life myself. When you think you have won, I will be right there to show you your failures. You're mine, Damian. And if I can't have you at my side, then no one shall have you!"

A bolt of lightning careened through the air and struck me as I tried to dodge it. I was free-falling through the sky, half-conscious from the blast. One of my wings was torn and would no doubt need a long time of healing. I flexed with all my might but could not catch myself from somersaulting to the ground. My body went around and around as I grew closer and closer to the ground below. Tree tops came into view, and I hoped with everything in me that I could latch onto a branch before I thudded to my demise.

Almost as if by answer, as I came crashing through the trees, their limbs reached out, embracing me, grabbing me, and helping me slow down. I landed in a mound of moss with a softened thud. I lay there staring up into the canopy of trees, breathing deeply and rapidly as I tried to calm myself down from the adrenaline rush that had seized my body during the fall. All the trees erected back to the straightened trunks they had been before I descended. I sat up and checked the damage on my wing from the lightning. It was bleeding and burned badly, but I wouldn't lose it. I opened the weapon's bag to see if Incaendiel had stuffed any bandages in there for just in case purposes.

"I can fix that right up for you," a melodic voice rang out.

I looked around the trees to see where the voice had come from. My eyes rested on the last person I thought I would see anytime soon.

"Aren't you a little ways out of your kingdom?" I asked, standing to my feet.

Queen Mab moved from her shadowy spot in between the trees out to where I could see her better.

"I heard through the grapevine a certain Shining One needed my assistance. However, by the looks of things, I believe you have everything covered on your own," she replied with a sweet smile.

She looked different than the last time I had seen her. She looked my age as opposed to the middle-aged woman's body she had used when Alpha and I took court with her. She always had the most remarkable and astonishing features, no matter the body she assumed.

"So, the butterfly carried my message to you," I said, walking closer to her. "It's about several months too late."

"I'm afraid it wasn't safe for me to come directly to Alpha's keep and take you away. But as I can see, someone did, in fact, help free you. Incaendiel, I presume?" she asked.

"Yeah, he was one of the last people I thought would help me bust out of there. I was sure he hated me for what I did under Alpha's control," I replied.

"Walk with me, love," she cooed, extending her arm out for me to loop mine through. "You have lots to learn about your friends."

I hesitated and looked around the field I had landed in. It was either go with her and have a little bit of protection from Alpha or wait here and see what other things he sent after me. I looped my arm through hers, and she walked me through the woods. Everything transformed before my eyes, and soon, we were surrounded by trees that had beautiful blooms falling from the branches. This must be the passageway to her court.

"Incaendiel is an old soul that my gods helped create," she murmured, passing by all her plants. They all reached out to touch her as she moved past them. She petted them as we walked. "Therein, you are much like me, as he is. You were born of the same universal power except far more superior."

"How are we more superior? What makes us so special?" I asked.

"You know how there are tons of angels that Alpha and Omega created?" she asked, turning us to walk through a field of nightshade. The field peeled back as we walked through and closed behind us with each step we took. "Well, I am like that. We are the angels of our gods. The three of you were made with the power of the universe, not the power the gods possess. That is why starfire burns through your veins."

"I don't have fire in my veins, though. I have ice instead," I replied.

"Yes, because you are unique. I'm sure you have already stumbled across the prophecy in your studies," she presumed. "There must be a balance of power. You are the perfect complement of power to Luxina's fire."

"Then why wasn't I born as her twin flame? Xavier is her counterpart, not me," I replied.

"Who says you aren't her twin flame? They don't have to be born at the same time, you know?" she mused. "And you also know what must happen in the end. You know Luxina and you must absorb him with your powers. When you absorb him, you will each share a part of another with each other. She will have a touch of ice to her fire, and you will have a touch of fire to your ice," she explained.

I watched as her castle materialized down the path from us. Guards stood around the gates, armed to the teeth. Were they expecting a battle?

"That will never happen. It can't happen. I won't do it," I replied. "In the end, we will all survive."

"If you do not do it, then the nightmare that riddles your dream will become the future. In order to save the universe, there must be sacrifice."

"Why can't I be the sacrifice?" I asked heatedly. "Why him?"

"You already know the answer as you have read it, and I have explained it. Xavier wasn't supposed to have been birthed. When Sophie and Incaendiel separated after raising the heavenly portal, the power of their creation was split in two as well. It was just supposed to be Luxina. Xavier was an accident. A fluke in the grand design. Finding the Garden of Eden wasn't the plan Omega had devised. That was just part of the game she played with Alpha. The real goal was to have Incaendiel and Sophie raise the heavenly portal. Only those two could have accomplished it, for they are gods greater than her and Alpha. She had to test their power. It was a rather cruel joke she played as well, making Incaendiel believe his darkness would kill Sophie if she stayed behind. But she couldn't keep them together. They were far too powerful together to control than they were apart. The whole sex part for to raise the Garden, well she wanted them to create Luxina. She is not as innocent as many believed her to be."

She walked us into her castle and led me to her throne room.

"That last part doesn't surprise me," I replied. "We are all just pawns in their game."

"You are wise beyond your years, young Damian," she crooned as she sat down on her throne.

"So, what now? Do I stay here?" I asked.

"You may stay the night to recoup and mend your wing, but I am afraid the courts cannot protect you from Alpha," she replied gravely. "However, there is another option, but it is rather perilous."

"I'm running from danger. It makes sense to head straight into it as well," I chided.

"The Otherworld is a vast place outside of space and time. It has realms of its own buried within the magic that keeps it from collapsing in on itself. Alpha may be able to travel into the Otherworld; however, he cannot travel everywhere. Not even we Seelies travel into the realm of Shadows and Nightmares. It is nothing but darkness, and its name holds truth. It is where nightmares thrive. The ones that leach into your mind late at night are those that try to escape from the depths from which they were cast. There is no goodness that exists there. Unimaginable creatures creep and crawl much like those that Alpha has created with mutations."

"Is there any type of magical aid that can help me once I cross over into this place?" I asked.

"There are very, very few things, but I can arrange for those that may aid you to be delivered for your journey. I will also include instructions on how to use them as well."

"Thank you for your kindness," I replied. "It is much needed and much appreciated."

Queen Mab motioned for one of her guards and whispered into his ear. He left the room and returned with another Seelie.

"This is Nautila. She will lead you to your quarters for the night. Rest well, Damian, for the future does not bring sleep for you," Queen Mab instructed with a dismissing hand.

Nautila curtsied before me, led me out of the throne room, and through the grand hall.

"Are you hungry?" Nautila asked.

I knew better than to eat faery food. They could trap you here with a single bite or drink of food.

"No, thank you," I replied.

She smiled as if she knew what I was thinking. "Queen Mab does not wish to keep you here as a slave. You have much to do to save not only your universe but our realm as well. Please, have something to eat."

She motioned me to a bountiful table of fruits, cheeses, and loaves of bread. There were chalices full of all kinds of meads, milks, and waters.

"Can you tell me what is ok for me to eat?" I asked nervously. "I know even though you can eat the food, it doesn't mean certain things will not harm me."

She nodded and gathered some food on a plate for me. She placed some bread and cheese on the plate, skipping the fruit. She grabbed me a chalice of water and led me off from the room. The castle buzzed with fey both sleeping and awake. Some danced merrily as music was played, while others sat in groups listening to sonnets being recited. It was amazing the candor they had, knowing they may be wiped from existence.

Nautila wound up a stairway and banked to the left down a long corridor. She pushed a door open on her right and led me into a quaint room. She sat the plate of food and chalice down on the table at the door. I looked for a lamp but then realized there wasn't any type of artificial lighting here. She smiled, guessing I was looking for lighting. She walked over to a makeshift lamp and opened a door in it. She gently blew inside of it, and dozens of fireflies lit up inside it. She closed the door, and the light grew brighter.

"Thank you for your hospitality," I said graciously with a bow.

"Is there anything else you may need?" she asked, leaning her shoulder seductively against the door frame. "Lonely?"

I eyed her as she stood before me at the door. She was petite and wearing a dress made from moss and flowers. Every inch of her clothing clung to just the right parts of her body, adding a mystifying allure to her. How do I respectfully decline this?

"I am fine. Again, I thank you for everything," I replied with a smile.

She curtsied and left the room, closing the door behind her. I expected to hear a lock come down in place, as I had always heard in the dungeon. I didn't hear a click. I walked to the door and tried the knob, and it opened freely. I reclosed the door and slumped down in the chair at the table. I eyed the food, both hungry and nauseated. I picked up a bit of cheese and some bread and nibbled at them. I drank from the chalice of water until it was empty. I hadn't realized how thirsty I was. I tried to think of the last time I had eaten and drunk something, but my mind was so jumbled with the events of the day that it was a futile effort. As I set the chalice back down on the table, it magically filled with more water just as cool as the water I had drank. They thought of everything here. Never-ending food, never-ending water; it was a neverland of wants and needs.

A wave of exhaustion overtook me, and I threw myself on the bed near the open window. It was soft with moss and ivy for a blanket. I lay on top of the moss and stared out of the window. The sky dazzled with its own little solar system of stars and planets. Unlike on Earth, where you can't see the planets, just bright dots in the sky, the planets were up close here and marvelously breathtaking. It felt as if I was back at the Summit all over again.

I remembered how the galaxy sparkled and lit up everywhere with stars and dust particle clouds hued in blues, pinks, and purples. The sky here was not dark but a dark shade of pink and purple. A moon rose gallantly through the sky, a light bluish glow illuminating it. It was peaceful, serene. I sat waiting for the door to bust open and guards to rush forward to bring me to some torture chamber as I had been accustomed to it for so long. However, no one came, and I was able to lie in bed in a somber state.

My mind wandered, and I found myself thinking about the prophecy, about what the Dark Queen had told me. There was no doubt that Lilith was as sly as Alpha and equally manipulative. She was his other half after all. But, to subject Incaendiel and Sophie to the lies she had was unforgivable. Even as much as she helped, she couldn't be trusted in the slightest. Did she know about the prophecy and what the birth of Luxina and Xavier meant? If she had just let Incaendiel be with Sophie, would there be this issue at hand right now? I felt like I was grappling with my own fate when, in fact, I was grappling with the idea of life without Xavier. I thought back to Queen Mab's words, and they made complete sense. Xavier is the dark half of Luxina's soul, an extension of everything she felt, thought, and existed to be. Did he know it? Had he figured out that he wasn't supposed to exist in this life?

I remembered watching them in that field in our dreams. The first time they ever met, when they touched, it leveled the field with power. Luxina's power was trying to reattach, but the momentum of the touch instead made the power reflect itself back. I sighed heavily. I didn't like this prophecy, and if we didn't do as it dictated, then the apocalyptic vision I had would manifest in the end. In that vision, we all three stood before Alpha but were powerless against him. Would we three be selfish enough to end everything, let the universe crumble in on itself just to exist as we were born? It was unfair to ask us to do such things. It was even more unfair to lay all this on Xavier's shoulders. I couldn't blame him one bit if he chose to let the universe end. Luxina and I wouldn't even flinch at that decision and would try everything we could to reverse the possible outcome of the end times. But if he chose to do it... If he chose to sacrifice himself for the good of the universe, he would need to be immortalized in some shape or form. He wouldn't even be given a grave at Potter's Field because his soul would just be absorbed.

I have become so tired of the power trip of the gods and the mess they have created with everyone involved. People I love dearly are having to make life and death decisions like kings and queens. We were kids, and we're faced with things that shouldn't even be thought about. Our creators were supposed to be gods, and they acted as mortals would with greed, envy, and jealousy, almost as if they were the epitome of the seven deadly sins themselves. Their selfishness was the downfall of this universe and the reason it was caving in on itself. Their selfishness was causing all of us grief and despair. We shouldn't have to turn on them to make things right. They should know how to do it themselves.

I closed my eyes, but not for long. My thoughts drifted off back to the arena, back to those creatures all swarming me. The iron giant angel that Alpha had created. Was that the diagram I had seen in his office? Were they able to syphon from my blood the magic to bring those things to life? There would be no stopping them if they were let loose. My eyes did not mistake the shimmering glow of metal. And if they were made of iron... I remembered Queen Mab telling Alpha that he was unable to harm her. Could those things destroy the Otherworld as well? Is that why they were so damning to us, to Luxina, Xavier, and me? Because we were a superior race to the fey but made by the same power, just an amplified amount, is that why those things could destroy us?

I thought back to the enhanced werewolf Alpha had created and the dripping acid saliva. Maybe there was more to it than it being acid. Maybe... oh no! I bolted upright in my bed and clamored to get up. I opened the door of my room and ran down the long corridor. I wound down the stairs, bounded through the great hall, and entered the throne room where the Dark Queen rested.

"You're in danger, and you need to flee to safety. All you," I stammered.

Queen Mab smiled. "I have already sent all those in the Unseelie court to Titania and Oberon for safety."

"Why did you stay behind? You are in danger!" I yelled. "You need to go!"

"I promised you some things that you need prior to voyaging through the Nightmares and Shadows realm," she replied. A guard walked in carrying my bag. "Ah, right on time, Ceri. Thank you, join the others."

The guard nodded and disappeared down the hall.

"Here is your bag of weapons and also the weapons I promised you to help," she said, handing me the bag that Incaendiel had given me. "We modified the swords you had in there. They are now encased with iron and silver."

She stood from her throne and began to walk through the long hall. She turned around and motioned for me. "Come along, Damian. I will show you where the entrance to the realm is, and then I will be on my way."

I followed her down the long hall where guards lined the walls. These guards looked different compared to the ones I had seen when we first arrived. They were dressed differently.

"These are my foot soldiers, my warriors," she replied. "They are specially trained in unique battle techniques."

I hope they are. If I was right about Alpha's creations...

The howl came with a deafening crack through the air of the castle.

"We must hurry," Queen Mab stressed, grabbing my arm and towing me faster through the castle.

We exited the keep with her little army of warriors on our heels. I could hear the pounding of the feet of the creatures Alpha had sent into this realm. He was starting a war that he intended no one to survive.

"There are vials of poisons in your bag, as well as silver flakes, and a special powder I blended from Forget-Me-Trees to make invisible creatures appear to you. They forget why they are invisible when it is used. There are several other things with the instructions, just as I promised."

We were running as fast as we could down the path.

"Take the next right, Damian. And may the universe keep you safe. This is as far as I can go. I must get to the safety of the Seelie court," Queen Mab said, pointing down a path up on my right. "Go, my boy!"

And with a shove of her hand, she sent me in the direction of the path to the Nightmares and Shadows realm of the Otherworld.

CHAPTER 8

I WAS LOST in total darkness, wandering a road that I had no clue where it ended. They didn't call this place the Nightmares and Shadows realm for no reason. It was exactly that. It was even harder keeping track of time in this place than it had been in the Otherworld. The darkness stretched on for miles with the crackle of lightning and the rumble of thunder here and there. With each step I took, the ground slightly glowed underneath my feet, almost as if the road itself was alive. That's exactly what I needed right now, to be swallowed by a living creature disguised like a sunfish. However, I pushed forward. Those things Alpha had created knew absolutely zero boundaries regarding their own mortality or lack thereof. They would follow me in here and wreak havoc upon me and anything else that was in their way.

Streaks of blue cut across the sky that I could only surmise were shooting stars in the desolate abyss that hung above me. Voices swirled around me, almost as if ghosts of the past tiptoed around down here. It almost looked as if memories in my head were playing on a screen as I walked through hazy forms of people. Every evil thing I had ever done played on repeat through the sky for me to watch. The length of Alpha's control over me haunted me as I was forced to remember everything I had done to Luxina and Xavier. I saw my face with my eyes blacked over as I whisked Luxina away from Incaendiel. My face as I fought with Xavier after Lucifer brought him to me. I tried so hard to be nice and loving, but Alpha and those injections turned me into a monster.

That's what I was and most likely still am, Alpha's little monster. I don't want to be. I want to be good. I want to be pure like Luxina is. The deeper I walked, the more scenes unfolded before me of every single little thing that had happened to me. Was there ever a time that I had more than just an inky black depth to my soul? Did I ever have a technicolor to me that separated me from the weapon Alpha had been molding into me? I had learned my lesson, whether at fault or not, for the assailing attacks I had inflicted upon masses in the name of Alpha. But were those bridges burned long turned to dust and able to rebuild back? Or are they still burning in anger and hatred toward me?

It felt as if no one would ever know me for who I truly was and not the puppet Alpha had made me into. Even Incaendiel had his doubts about me. He would continue to have those doubts, too, until I could prove myself to him that I was worthy of the light and not the suffocating shadows that grappled with me internally. No amount of hiding would ever erase the damage I had caused throughout the universe. There were so many silent sorrows lost in the yesterdays of my existence that I didn't even know what tomorrow promised me. There wasn't a promise of forgiveness, a promise of love, or promises of wholeness.

If there were any moments that could have meant something, they were now gone. Pieces of chaos were all that was left, blowing on the wind from the aftermath of my storm. Could I ever prove myself to Luxina that I was more than this creature I had become? Would she ever love me for me? See my true inner light? Could she see the colors that existed within me that I could not even see?

Damian, the voice whispered. I looked around to see if anyone was following me. It was nothing but darkness as far as my eyes could see.

Damian, come for me, it whispered again. I began to panic just a bit. The voice sounded like Luxina's voice, but I couldn't be sure. Was she down here? Was she hurt?

"Luxina!" I called out. "Luxina, where are you?"

Daaaamiannnn, the voice sang. *Come for me, Damian. I need you.*

"Where are you?" I implored, a sickly anxiety building deep in my stomach. "Why are you here? Tell me where you are, and I will find you."

And then, I saw her. She was about fifty yards out, standing in the middle of the path I was walking. I began to run to her, but the more I ran, the further away she seemed to be.

"Luxina, run to me," I urged out. "It's not safe here."

No, it isn't, she whimpered, her voice caught up in the violent winds that began to tear at the foundation of the road. *Save me, Damian.*

"I'm trying," I sputtered, breathless and desperate.

Save me before it's too late. Save me before I turn into stardust floating through the universe, she wailed, her voice distant and distorted.

I ran hard and fast, inching closer and closer to her outstretched hand. A sword sliced through the middle of her chest, and blood spilled down the front of her torso.

"No!" I screamed, stumbling and hitting the ground.

She fell to her knees and dematerialized, bits of dust dispersing all around me.

Damian, another voice called out.

Panic now riddled every breath I tried to suck in as my heartbeat quickened with every gasp. My chest tightened in fear as I looked for the owner of the voice because I knew it too. My eyes scanned around the darkness, looking for Xavier.

Damian, why do you hate me? he warbled. *Why do you want me to die?*

"I don't want you to die," I cried, pounding the ground before me.

You are the reason Alpha wants me. You are the reason Alpha has me, he argued.

"No," I whispered. "It's not real."

Save me, Damian. Save me before Alpha kills me. Save your brother from eternal damnation, he crowed.

I glanced up to see Xavier standing ten feet from me. His hand reached for mine, and I lifted mine from the ground, stretching for his hand. He was dragged backward by an invisible force. He clawed and clamored, trying to break himself free.

Damian! You must save me! he hollered. *You must save Luxina!*

He was pinned to the ground. I scrambled to try and reach him, but the distance between us grew in leaps and bounds the harder I tried to reach him.

"I'm trying!" I screamed, my voice cracking from the pressure of the words exerted on my vocal cords. "I am trying so hard to keep you safe. I am trying so hard to save you both."

Damian, help us! he screamed.

I looked up just in time to see his head lopped from his body and roll across the grass, stopping inches in front of me. Blood sprayed me as my hands shook with fury and pain. I tried to wipe the blood from my hands and face, but the more I wiped, the more it seemed to spread and stick. I frantically smeared them across my clothes, and it seemed that nothing I did was helping. I put my fists against my ears, squeezed my eyes tightly shut, and let out a guttural scream as I rocked back and forth. When I had no breath left to continue, I opened my eyes. Xavier had dematerialized. I looked at my hands and clothes, inspecting them for blood, but not a drop was on them.

I felt like I was suffocating.

What are you doing, boy!

"It's not real," I mumbled, crying into my fists.

Did you think you could hide from me? I always know where you are. You can never hide from me! the voice yelled, the voice of Alpha.

"This isn't real," I repeated. "This isn't real. This isn't real."

You are nothing more than what I have made you to be. You will always have evil in you, no matter how hard you fight it. You will always be a creature. You will always be my monster.

"No!" I shouted. "No, I will not! I am not a monster!"

You think you are so smart. You think you are stronger than me, but you are nothing but a weak, little boy that will always search for people to love him. Not a single person will ever care for you. You are unlovable. I made sure of it. I have left you riddled in scars that leave you hideous to look at. I have turned your heart black and cold to anyone that dared to save you from me. I made sure that you couldn't slip through my fingers. I made sure love could never save you.

"No!"

Love is weak. Love isn't real. It's an illusion that pulls you into an imaginary land of wonder. It will begin to fade until it completely disappears, leaving you in writhing agony, leaving you in a pit of anguish that you can't breathe in. Do you think she will stay once she sees you for who you really are? She will go away. She won't want you when she sees the monster deep within.

"No, you're wrong. Love is patient and kind and everything that she is," I barked back.

Do not quote my scripture at me, boy! There is nothing but a cold, empty decay in you. And you will only ever feel it as it eats away at you, as it eats away at everything you love until there is nothing left but darkness and ruin. You are nothing but a monster, a soldier in a war that ends in death for those you hold tightly to. You are MY monster, and you will obey your Master!

"I won't let you win," I refuted. "I will always fight against you. You will never own me. You never did!" I shouted.

Laughter filled the air. Thousands of creatures swarmed me as I pulled my sword to fight them off. I didn't even look as I slashed and hacked through the barrage of monsters that came at my left, right, front, and back. A mountain of bodies formed around me as they increased in numbers. When I began to pay attention to what I was fighting in the darkness, I dropped my sword and pushed my way through the bleeding bodies. They weren't the creatures I thought. Angels lay in heaps around me. My face reflected in their armor, and I could see the black eyes of death staring back at me. I howled in rage. No matter where I ran, Alpha would be there. I was a monster trained to kill. Even the monsters in my head were real and heavily trained to kill me. There was no escape. There was no respite.

I heaved and heaved all the contents of my stomach to the ground, then dropped my sword with a clatter, falling to my knees. I bent over, placing my head to the ground, wallowing and crying in defeat. A tug came at my arm.

"Mister?" a little voice asked.

"Something else that isn't real," I asserted to myself.

I looked down to see an exceedingly small child-like being standing beside me. She was dressed like one of the fey, but her skin color was a dark shade of blue.

"Oh, I am real alright," the itty-bitty thing replied. "Why are you here? This place isn't for you."

"I have to be here," I explained.

"But you walked into the Bog of Damnation," she replied. "If you stay here, you will surely die. It turns every one of your nightmares, grievances, and fears to life until you can't handle it anymore."

"What?" I asked.

I looked around as my eyes came into focus. The darkness that had encased me began to slowly fade into some form of watery grave.

"Come with me," she smiled. "I can show you safer places to travel while here in the shadows."

She offered me her hand, and I stood as she led me away from the decaying cypress trees and mosh pits.

"My name is Nillona," she stated. "And you are?"

"Damian," I replied.

"It is nice to make your acquaintance, Damian," she responded cheerfully. "You must be the one everyone has been talking about," she declared as we walked through a small forest.

"What do they say?" I asked.

"That you're going to save the universe," she replied. "That you are important, and everyone should make sure you make safe passage through here on your journey."

"Is that so?" I asked.

"Mhmm," she squeaked.

"What makes them think I am anything more than a monster?" I asked.

"Because Queen Mab helped you escape into the realm," she replied. "Although we live in an untethered part of the kingdom, a lot of us do respect Queen Mab's decisions in her rule."

"Why do you live here and not in Unseelie court?" I asked as she led me in what seemed like circles through the woods.

"Those who live here do not wish to be forced into a governing rule. We aren't all pure evil. There are some creatures here that are the essence of evil, but the others just want to exist without being told what we can and cannot do. We were all once loyal followers to Mab until she started her own personal war with the Seelie court. Bickering is not becoming of fey," she replied quietly. "So many of us retired to the shadows. Shadows aren't always bad. They are just a subtle reminder that light now exists."

"You are a very wise little girl," I mused.

"Well, I may be small, but I am not a girl," she rebutted. "I am 362 years old. I have seen and heard things as well as taught things."

She gave a soft giggle as my face flushed.

"My apologies, little lady," I digressed.

"No need for apologies, lad," she insisted. "No use in fretting over little things."

She led me to a tiny, quaint village tucked away safely inside the forest. Cottages with smoke billowing from chimneys sat spaced apart with gardens in between each. Many of the villagers sat gathered around a fire, singing and dancing, when we came walking up. A few of them had instruments that they gayly played. Silence filled the air as they paused the merriment and stared at me while I equally stared back.

"He is not to be harmed," Nillona instructed those sitting within hearing distance. "Make sure everyone knows, or there will be consequences."

They all nodded their acknowledgement of the declared immunity of my head on a platter.

"Not to be harmed? Would they harm me if not for your protection order?" I asked.

"Oh, yes. We are Gwyllion. We are normally tricksters, but tonight, we shall be hospitable," she replied smiling. "Please, sit and eat with us. I promise you. We will not poison you."

I nodded my thanks and squatted beside the fire, warming my hands up by the crackling embers. I couldn't help but feel a nagging sensation tug at the back of my brain. Could I really trust them? They were pretty upfront about what kind of fey they were but ensured that they meant no harm. However, I couldn't help but think that I would wake in the morning being handed over to Alpha.

"You're nothing but skin and bones," Nillona said. "Here, eat up and get some fat back on you."

Correction, I could wake up being eaten. She handed me some sort of dish that I could only guess had meat on it. My stomach turned just looking at the food. I looked over at the other Gwyllions as they used their bare hands to pick the food up and tear into it. Juices dripped from the mouths that they chomped loudly from. I swallowed the nausea building and set the plate down.

"I can't eat, but thank you," I replied.

"Mind if I have it?" a chubby Gwyllion asked.

"Knock yourself out," I replied, pushing the plate to him. Nillona eyed me. "I haven't eaten much in so long that the smell of food makes me sick to my stomach."

Her eyes softened. "So, the rumors of your torture are true as well?" she asked.

I nodded. "Alpha used me to do his dirty work, and whether I was to succeed or fail, I was punished to the full extent."

"That explains all the hideous scars," she said, pointing to my face. "A face only a mother would love," she chided.

I didn't expect her words to bite, but they did. I had never been self-conscious before, but knowing that I was now littered with scars made me feel tiny.

"I didn't mean no harm," she cooed. "It was a terrible thing to say, and I apologize."

"It's ok," I replied. "I am just starting to come to terms with how awful I must look."

"Whoever chooses to love you will love you for more than what you look like on the outside. My understanding is that you have a heart of gold. That will be the breadwinner with any decent woman," she gushed, nodding in agreement with herself. "Anyone special in your life? A girl waiting for you?"

"Maybe, maybe not," I replied.

"Well, which is it. Out with it," she prodded.

"At this moment, I don't know. She doesn't know a lot of things and probably just sees me as the monster I was made to be," I replied.

"If she thinks of you as a monster, then she is a monster herself," Nillona stated. "It is mighty fine what you are doing for the creatures of the universe that have neither helped you nor defended you in the years past. We all owe you a debt for what you are doing."

"What exactly am I doing?" I asked, still not knowing what the rumors were swirling around. "What have you heard through the grapevine, so to speak?"

"Why, bringing down Alpha, of course," she replied. "It has been many a year that he has stolen fey from the Otherworld and used the blood from their corpses to run experiments on humans."

"On humans?" I asked, sitting forward. "That I did not know."

"Aye," she replied. "He has been turning humans into creatures of darkness, his Children of the Night."

"What kind of creatures has he made?" I asked.

"Vampires, for starters," she began.

"Everyone knows about the vampires," I replied, shaking my head.

"No, young one. You know about the vampires he made trying to make humans. You don't know of the vampires he has made using humans. It isn't right, I tell ya. Poor souls. Trapped in darkness they are. The sunlight burns their skin to a crisp if exposed. If they stand in it too long, they burst into flames," she said. "Plus, the only thing they can eat is blood."

"What else has there been?" I asked.

"The easier question is what has there not been," she replied grimly. "He took the werewolves and changed humans into those as well. Unlike the full moon shifters, these ones shift into wolves whenever they want to or whenever they can't control themselves. Sometimes their anger makes them shift against their will."

"So, he just kidnaps mortals and subjects them to his tests?" I asked. "How could I not know this?"

"He has been doing it for centuries, love," she replied. "Long before you were ever born."

A few of the Gwyllion were whispering amongst themselves motioning to me, which undoubtedly made me uneasy.

"They want to know if you will demonstrate your power for them," Nillona disclaimed. "We heard tell that you have special powers no other angel has."

I picked up a cup in front of me that had water in it and dipped my finger in it. The water began to turn to ice instantly. The Gwyllions murmured and chattered quietly amongst themselves. I removed my finger from the cup and dumped the lump of ice onto the ground.

"So, the legends are true?" Nillona asked. "You really are one of the Shining Ones."

I nodded my head in affirmation.

"And the young woman you were speaking of, she is the one from the prophecy too, right?" she asked.

"Yes," I replied. "But I have been mirrored as a monster to her by Alpha, so she probably hates me."

"Word has it that she was adamant about saving you from Alpha and even asked Queen Mab to help as well," Nillona mused.

"Really?" I asked, a bit baffled.

"Aye, especially after Queen Mab said you would need to be killed if Alpha's injections were successful on you," Nillona responded.

"The only thing she told Alpha was if he was successful that I belonged to her," I replied.

"That was so Alpha wouldn't have you as a weapon. However, she knew Alpha had no intention of turning you over to her. That is why she executed a kill order in case your injections did turn you into a beast," she hissed.

"Well, I guess it's a good thing I escaped him then, huh?" I asked.

"That's enough chit-chat for one night," Nillona said, abruptly standing to her feet. "Let me show you where you can rest your head for the night."

I stood from the ground and followed her to one of the tiny cottages at the end of the row of houses.

"This one is empty. You can stay as long as you would like," she said with a nod to her head.

"Thank you, it is much appreciated. I can't stay too long, though. I don't want to put you all in any danger," I replied graciously.

"We can handle our own. You need not worry about that," she said with a sharp nod of her head and turned on her heel, walking away.

I ducked into the cottage that was about a foot too short for me to stand straight up in. There wasn't much to the place. It had a bed, and that was pretty much it. I took my weapons bag off my shoulder and tossed it on the bed, and my body followed. I had no clue how long I had been walking in this place before she came along, but I knew I was tired. I feared sleep more than I feared dying here. There was no telling what kind of dreams I would have after experiencing what I did in the Bog of Damnation. Everything had felt and looked so real... just like the apocalyptic dreams I had.

My skin crawled just thinking about those visions of how the end played out. I rubbed my hands up and down my arms, feeling each and every bump, scar, and scab from what Alpha had put me through. My thoughts roamed to my conversation with Nillona regarding how I looked now with the scars riddling every inch of my skin. They would never go anywhere and always would be visible to everyone. *A face only a mother could love...* she was right. The few times I had caught sight of myself in a reflection, I looked absolutely hideous. My once smooth, creamy skin was now littered with pink whip marks from my abuse at Alpha's hands. Sometimes, the whip would peel my skin back, so there were large lumps of flesh that had to heal that way, leaving jagged edges on some of the scars. Whether it was real in the bog or not, the things he had said to me were true. He had made me unlovable by making me unbeautiful. Luxina would never look at me as she does Xavier. I am not beautiful in the least now. I am an eyesore to gaze at.

A girl waiting for you? I never even considered if Luxina had any type of feelings toward me at all. The few times we had any interaction, I was under the duress of Alpha. If I had shown her any type of compassion or empathy, or even if I had shown her that I was not evil, had she seen it? She must have. *She was adamant about saving you.* Why would she want so desperately to save me? The only thing I could surmise is to protect the universe. Could it be more than that, though? Could she have suppressed feelings for me? Feelings she didn't even acknowledge because she knew what happens when you abandon your twin flame?

Sophie did a number on all of us regarding the psychological destruction she caused by not staying true to Incaendiel. We all walked on eggshells, wondering if this was really the path that fate had spelled out for us when it came to whom we loved. In the end, Sophie chose Incaendiel as her one true love, and he made her go to protect her. Lilith's cruel punishment to keep their power apart had damaged this family in ways that it would be a miracle to mend the bonds. *Family...* Did I think of them all as my family? Could there be a time in the future when I can look to Sophie as my mother? My creator? I guess only time would tell at this point.

I sighed deeply while closing my eyes, trying to do anything but think of Luxina, but it was a failed attempt. There was no doubt that I had always loved Luxina, but it had always been a protective sort of love. I had never wanted to intercede between Xavier and her. However, I can't help but wonder if I had always had an interest in her. Alpha was pushing me to do to her what he had done to Sophie for all those years. Had he known this whole time about the prophecy? Had he done what he did with Sophie and Lucifer to bring about the prophecy? It was nauseating to think he would have done this all on purpose just to have us as a war machine for him. However, knowing the truth about Luxina and Xavier now, I can't help but to look deeper into how I feel about Luxina, developing Alpha's original plot without intending to do so.

I can't help but wonder if she will or does feel the tug at her heartstrings for me as well. Can she truly give up Xavier to be with me? Most likely not. Who would sacrifice love just to save me, to save the universe?

Could it be possible to be in love with two people at the same time and be able to choose one over the other? She was adamant about my safety... did she love me? If they were presented the prophecy, would they eagerly climb aboard? Would one fight it and the other accept it? Which one would fight it, and which one would accept it? So many questions swarmed through my mind. When Luxina is told about the prophecy, would she choose me out of obligation or because she really wanted me? That was the million-dollar question. I had no idea if she would ever love me in the capacity she had loved Xavier, even after finding out that Xavier was just the dark half of her soul made sentient. There's also the possibility she could resent me for having to give him up. There's also the possibility that she would choose not to choose me in the end.

How do you tell someone that the person they love is really their shadow self and it was a cruel joke of the universe for her to love him? Was it a joke, though? Incaendiel had grappled with his darkness for so many years, nearly succumbing to the darkness many times. Was she given a chance to love the dark half of herself, so she wouldn't be so easy to slip into the inky black depths of the abyss in her mind?

I tossed and turned, unable to fall asleep after plaguing myself with every question imaginable to think of to further my anxiety over the situation. I laid my head on the pillow, and my feet hung off the short bed. Feelings for Luxina were growing in me that were unstoppable at this point, and I didn't know how to slow them down. It wasn't hard to feel them once they began to blossom. Luxina was breathtaking. Her eyes could stare straight into your soul. I rolled to my side and began to drift off. Sleep was arriving, whether I wanted it, needed it, or wanted nothing to do with it.

Screams erupted from outside of the cottage that ripped me from my half-dozing thoughts and had me grabbing for my weapon bag, tossing it over my shoulder. I pulled a sword from within and walked to the door. No sooner had I reached the door handle, it popped open, and Nillona was standing there.

"The trackers have found you," she panted, alarmed. "You need to go!"

"I cannot leave you all unprotected," I protested, stepping through the door and outside. "They are here because of me. I will fight to protect those who showed me hospitality."

"It is a noble notion, young Damian, but it is you we must protect, even if we die trying," she refuted hastily. "Now, take this map." She handed me a folded-up piece of parchment paper. "Slip off behind the trees and keep running in a straight line. You will come across a riverbank. Follow the riverbank east. The map will show you everything you need to know to maneuver through the shadows and how to get to where you need to go. Use this to light your way as well," she said, slipping a rock into my hand.

"I can't thank you enough," I replied with a bow, slipping the paper and rock into my pants pocket.

"Go, Shining One. And when there are those that ask you how you were able to manage through the Nightmares and Shadows, you tell them. You tell them Nillona of the Gwyllions helped you. You honor my name," she spouted, pushing me off into the woods.

"You have my word," I replied in a shout as I took off into the woods.

I did what she said. I stayed in a straight line as I ran through the woods, branches whipping me in the face. Vines seemed to reach from places unknown to snag me and try to pull me down. I pushed through it all. I ran with every ounce of energy I had, escaping the screams and howls of pain coming from the village behind me. They were dying for me. They were dying to save the universe, and I had to make sure that people knew exactly who it was that helped me, just as Nillona asked. I wouldn't let anyone who helped me and perished die in vain. The universe would know each name and would worship them for eons to come.

The trees opened directly in front of a river just as she had said they would. I pulled the map from my pocket and folded it open. Not only had she provided me with a means of traveling through this hellish place, but she also gave me a tiny rock that glowed in the dark. I had wondered what the rock would do when she thrust it into my hands. I adjusted the weight of the weapons bag and held the light over the paper. She said to head east. I scoured the map and a tiny, red x appeared on the map with "you are here" written underneath it.

"Show me east," I stated.

Little red dots began to emerge on the map to the left of the x on the page. I turned in the direction the map led me, and as I walked, the x moved. The dots closest to the x would disappear and new ones would appear in the forefront. I looked closely at the name of the river listed on the map I was following. *River of Sorrows* was what it was called. *I wonder what that meant?* I know how the Bog of Damnation was dangerous. I wonder if this place was as dangerous. I glanced at the river, but it just looked like a normal river to me. I shrugged my shoulders and continued what I had been doing.

I scanned the map, looking for landmarks that were named that I would come across following this river. All along the river were strange names for specific spots. There was *The Hanging Tree, Dead Man's Leap,* and *Bleeding Hearts Forge.* It dawned on me what the river really implicated, and I came to a complete stop. It was a suicide river. I slowly turned my head to look closer at the running water and quickly snapped it back, squeezing my eyes shut. Bodies piled on one another all along the riverbank, the boulders in the river, and some floated freely along the river current. This was where the fey came to kill themselves. How could I not have seen the bodies the first time? Did you have to be aware of what the river was like in order to see them?

I breathed deeply, slowly letting the air out of my lungs and gently breathing back in. I tried to calm my nerves and made myself trudge forward, keeping my eyes on the path ahead of me. I had enough images of bloated, dead bodies to keep me awake for centuries now, added along with the creatures Alpha made and every single other thing that plagues my mind.

I stayed on the path that the map pointed out to me, walking closer to the first place on the map, which was called *The Hanging Tree.* Voices began to whisper in the wind, and for a moment, terror took hold of my stomach as it knotted, remembering how the Bog of Damnation had drawn me in. I glanced up from the map briefly to see translucent lines of fey heading in single file lines to the riverside. Up ahead was a tall, incredibly old tree. The base of the trunk was at least fifty feet wide, and its branches reached tall into the dark sky, almost as if touching the clouds from below. The whispers turned into an audible lull as they sang the saddest song I had ever heard as they marched forth to the tree.

THE TREE TWISTS high
The tree twists low
Follow me,
Follow me, oh
Down the forgotten path
Of nameless peace
To the hanging tree
Where a necklace
Of silvery fire
Hoists you up over

A deathly mire
No screams come out
As you descend
From the hanging tree

I WATCHED as they disappeared and reappeared hanging from the branches of the tree. Their bodies swung back and forth in the wind. I stood, horrified and yet mystified, at the grandeur of the entire scene. Their song called to me in a bittersweet memento of a certain promised death. Death... I wanted death. I craved death like a butterfly craved the sweet nectar produced within the buds of wildflowers growing in meadows. I craved it like a caged fox craves the sweet escape of captivity to run boundlessly free, jumping and twisting in the air, running after the butterfly. I had craved it for so long I could taste what it felt like. The sweet reprieve washing over my body as it slowly turned to stardust in the wind.

I don't know what it was that snapped me from the lull I had been placed in. It sounded like someone calling my name to get my attention. As I snapped back to lucidity, I stood upon a branch of the Hanging Tree with a noose wound tightly around my neck. The tree had called me to death, and I had blindly followed the path it had rolled out before me. I tore the noose from around my neck and jumped from the tree branch, thudding to my behind on the muddy riverbank. I scrambled back over to the path as fast as I could. I searched for the map, hoping I hadn't dropped it, and it floated away in the wind. I patted myself down and pulled the map out from my pocket. I didn't even remember putting it in there prior to climbing the tree.

I briskly walked from the tree and continued on down the road, putting distance between me and my near, ill-fated brush with death. I now understood why Queen Mab had declared this place dangerous. It wasn't so much as creatures as the actual realm trying in a whole to dispatch whoever didn't belong here. Nightmares and Shadows was a ravenous creature in itself. It was starved of fresh blood and was pushing as hard as it could to get me to take my own life here. Twice now, it had nearly succeeded. Had I not been pulled from the Bog of Damnation, I most surely would have taken my own life then as well.

More quiet voices floated to my ears as I saw the fey spirits pour from the woods, rushing as quickly as they could to the river and throwing themselves into the murky depths. I waited for each of them to surface, but none ever did. It explained the bodies upriver where the water was shallower than what it was here. Their song grew in volume as I struggled to ignore it.

WE'RE MARCHING on
Down to the river
We move as one
Down to the river
The noose hangs low
Down at the river
The water runs cold
Down at the river
Our souls shall roam
Down by the river
Forsaken ashore
Down by the river
Our bodies are drawn
Down through the river
Time won't move on
Down through the river
We're marching on
Down to the river
We move as one
Down to the river...

THE SONG CONTINUED, and it soon became amplified by the growing voices of the dead. I quickened my pace so I wouldn't get lost in the soulful songs and follow them along into the cold waters of death they disappeared into. How long did this river go on for? Did it just end, or did it turn into a waterfall? The map gave no indication of how far or how long I was supposed to follow the river. I didn't even know where I was supposed to be going. She just told me to follow the river. Follow the river to where? No one told me where I was supposed to go while in this realm.

A peaceful serenity overcame me. I could hear sweet sounds floating in the air like the sound of rain in the mountains during a summer storm.

AAAAAAAAAHHHHHH, Aaaaaaaaaaahhhh

I LOOKED for the source of the melodic notes and saw Luxina standing near the riverbank, swinging from a tree branch, feet kicking back and forth in the air.

"Luxina?" I called out.

She looked back at me and smiled, giggles erupting in the breeze. Her mouth opened, and the beautiful notes I had heard poured from her lips.

AAAAAAAAAHHHHHH, Aaaaaaaaaaaahhhh

I WALKED CLOSER TO HER, drawn in by everything. The sun beat down on her hair, and it looked like tendrils of fire whipping back and forth as her hair blew in the breeze. Her smile drew me in, and I felt compelled to watch her, leaning against the tree she swung back and forth from.

AAAAAAAAAAAHHHH, Aaaaaaaaaaaahhhh
My love did search
High and low
To find me here
Safe from woe
He soundly kissed
My parted lips
Long blue and cold
And now we hold
Each other's hand
And safely tread
Upon the land
Where snares nor foes
Can end our love
Until love's true kiss
In death.... we part
Now my love
Does waste away
In a small
Shallow grave
And love did fleet
As he sank so deep

And softly dreams
In death so sweet...
Aaaaaaaaahhhhhh, Aaaaaaaaaaahhhh Aaaaaaaaahhhhhh,
Aaaaaaaaaaaahhhh

I FELT SO ENTRANCED with her song as I leaned in to kiss her lips smiling sweetly. I was jerked back at the last moment, landing on the ground below. My eyes instantly searched for Luxina to see if she was harmed or safe when I came to realize a siren sat upon the river bend of the forge. I had been entranced by one of those cursed things Alpha's minions had created by mistake while goofing off with Seelie blood and demon blood. I glanced over my shoulder and was surprised to see Nautila standing behind me.

"Queen Mab should have known better than to send you into the Nightmares and Shadows realm alone. I'm surprised you aren't dead yet," Nautila hissed, pulling me to my feet. "Or perhaps that was her plan?" she asked, raising an accusing eyebrow.

"Nautila, what are you doing here?" I asked, bewildered to see a familiar face.

"It looks like I am saving you," she smirked. "That's what I am doing here."

"No, what are you doing in Nightmares and Shadows? How did you even find me?" I asked as we walked.

"My family is from this realm," she replied curtly. "I, however, found this place to be distasteful for my liking."

She handed me the map and the stone light that Nillona had given me.

"That still doesn't explain how you found me?" I asserted again.

"I ran across the Gwyllions' village. It's another quick way to get to the main city here, Caudir. That city is where the dark market is, and I do a lot of trading there. Nillona sent me in this direction, telling me you were probably already dead. For an angel, you sure can be tricked into illusions easily," she mused.

"Of course, her sending me this way was a trick. I should have known," I muttered, walking along with the map, seeing where we were.

The map had an ex on Bleeding Heart's Forge. "Oh, that explains everything," I hissed.

"Nillona did not send you here to trick you into death. If she wanted to kill you, she would have left you in the Bog of Damnation," Nautila replied. "You're headed in the right direction," she belted, annoyed as I watched the map and the path in front of me.

"Right direction to where?" I asked exhaustedly. "I don't even know where I am supposed to be going, let alone where I have been."

She smiled. "Silly, you are looking for the end of the shadowland. There will be an exit portal there that will take you wherever you wish to go. All you must do is think of the place or a person, and you are there."

"Well, that would have been nice information to know prior to being tossed in here," I replied, irritated. "Are those creatures still looking for me?" I asked as we walked.

"I have no idea," she answered. "They were gone from the Gwyllion village by the time I happened by."

"Were they able to ward them off?" I asked.

"Gwyllions are pretty adept at fighting off attacks," she replied. "Most of them were ok. There were just a few that didn't make it. There's a rule about fey. If they are attacked by an animal or attacked by a bug, they die from the interaction. Our bodies build a neurotoxin that kills us within a few hours. The poison is what killed them."

"It doesn't change the fact they were injured and put in harm's way due to trying to keep those monsters from mauling me. I hate knowing there are people dying for me," I admitted. "I don't deserve that. I am not worthy of that type of loyalty."

"You don't give yourself much credit, handsome," she teased.

I felt the heat rush to my cheeks. I wasn't used to that type of response by my body in the least. Insecurity was something new that I had to find a way to get around. I was not handsome in the least now, not with all these scars that riddled my face.

"Do you know the way to the portal without this map?" I asked her, changing the direction the conversation may have headed.

She shook her head. "You need that map because the portal is never in the same place for long. So, the map will lead you to it wherever its new resting place is for the day."

"Oh, that is just perfect!" I shouted sarcastically. "Knowing my luck, one day I will be right near it, and the next it will be back where I started."

"Don't say such things of bad luck here, or they will manifest," she warned urgently. "This place makes your fears, anxieties, and nightmares come to life. It's why mostly fey travel these plains. We are pretty much joyous beings."

She frowned immediately after saying that, considering we were traveling beside a suicide river. She hooked her arm with mine as we continued to walk by the river.

"Don't look. Don't listen and act like the river doesn't exist," she urged. "Don't even look at the map to see where we are. Just keep your eyes on the road ahead of us."

"What is it?" I whispered. "It can't be worse than what I have already experienced. I was almost hanged at that tree."

"This is much worse, and as long as they don't catch your attention, it won't lure you in," she declared. "You don't want to know what it is, and it's best you remain in the unknown. You are far more susceptible to the temptation of this river."

"Why?" I asked.

"Do I really need to explain it to you?" she hissed. "It's called the River of Sorrows. You're not exactly a jovial person. You have too much darkness swirling within you."

So, for once, I listened, and I kept my eyes straight ahead and muted out the sounds of the world around me.

CHAPTER 9

WE HAD TRAVELED for what seemed like days. Nautila steered me clear of any of the enchanting elements that the shadowland possessed. We grew closer to the dark markets and cities of the shadows, and she indicated she knew a place where we could stay and get much needed sleep. I had never traveled through the Otherworld and witnessed their cities, villages, or markets. I had only ever been to the Unseelie Court Kingdom. There was nothing to compare to how the dark market operated here. However, I knew whatever they were doing wasn't allowable in any sense in either of the courts of the Otherworld. It also made me wonder what business Nautila would have had in the market. It couldn't be Mab approved, and if it was, what on earth would Mab desire to gain from a market she bans to other Unseelies for use.

It wasn't long after venturing into the dark market that my questions were answered. All around us, there were diverse types of vendors that sold unspeakable things. People bartered with enslaved fey here. Those from the Seelie court were of a higher price than those of the Unseelie court because of their pure blood. I saw exotic forms of food being cooked, sold, and served tableside at vendor shops. There were weapons shops, tailor shops, everything imaginable here.

"Do not make eye contact with any of the vendors here," Nautila warned, wrapping herself in a cloak and raising the hood over her head.

"Not all fey here are as kind as Nillona was to you. Some of them would sell you to the highest bidder or worse, make a deal with Alpha for your head."

I nodded, acknowledging her warning as she handed me a cloak. I quickly put it on and kicked the hood up over my head. We maneuvered through the crowds with person after person bumping into us. I often caught stares from people who saw my face and flinched away from their view. I would tug the hood down further, but it kept sliding up. The deeper we moved into the crowd, the more the stares came to follow me across the courtyard as we walked.

"Ignore the sideways glances. You look fine," Nautila whispered, linking her arm with mine.

She tugged at me as we made it to a tavern. She pulled me through the doors and then scampered off to find the innkeeper. I stood near the door in a corner so as to not attract attention to myself until she returned with a key.

"They only had one room to share, so it looks like we are roomies tonight," she teased.

"Lead the way," I replied, holding my hand out in gesture.

She scrunched her face into a smile, grabbed my hand, and led me upstairs where the rooms were located. She found the door with our number on it, opened it, and stood aside for me to go in first. I brushed past her into the room. It had one bed, a table and chair on one wall, and a sofa couch against another wall. A small, curtained window was on the far side of the room that overlooked the market below. I briskly walked to the window and pulled the curtains shut so nobody could look into the window. She followed me into the room, closed the door, and slid the lock into place. She removed her cloak and set it on the chair. She fluffed her hair out as I slid my cloak off as well, tossing it on the couch. She stretched her arms out and stifled a yawn.

"You can have the bed," I offered. "I will take the couch."

"Now, that doesn't sound fun," she mumbled, puckering her bottom lip. "You can lie with me. I don't bite."

She climbed onto the bed and patted a spot beside her. My eyes trailed her body as they had the night in the Unseelie court room. I hesitated a moment before I relented and crawled in bed beside her. She let out a soft giggle of triumph. She propped herself up on her elbow and stared down at me.

"You're still a pure one, aren't you?" she asked teasingly.

"What do you mean pure?" I responded, not understanding the question.

"You've never been with a woman, have you?" she asked.

My face tightened in anger and humiliation. "That's really none of your concern or of importance at this moment," I retorted.

"Ah, so you haven't," she giggled. "That can change tonight if you want."

She went to touch my chest when I snatched her hand in midair.

"Not going to happen," I replied, standing up.

I moved over to the couch and sprawled out on it.

"She must be really special to you," she spoke softly.

"It has nothing to do with anyone else. I am simply not interested," I replied.

"Is it because I am a fey?" she demanded. "I can change my appearance for you. I can be whoever you want me to be."

I looked over as she began to transform into different women she must have come across paths with. Her final form landed on that of Luxina.

"Is that better?" she asked, her voice sounding just like Luxina's.

"You may be able to look like her, but you will never be able to be her," I declared.

"What makes her so much better than me?" Nautila demanded, shifting back into her own form.

"It's not that she is better than you. It's something you wouldn't understand," I stressed back.

"It's that stupid prophecy, isn't it? If not for that prophecy promising you to one another, you wouldn't think twice about her and would lie with me tonight," she insisted.

"If there wasn't a prophecy, I wouldn't even be here right now. I most likely wouldn't even exist," I muttered in return. "So, the prophecy is the last reason for me rebuking your advances. I am simply not interested."

She stood from the bed and huffed, left the room, and slammed the door behind her. It didn't bother me. I just hoped I hadn't hurt the poor girl's feelings. I was used to solitude and being alone. I think there was more than it having anything to do with Luxina. I don't like having company. I don't like to be bombarded with questions and jives. I sighed heavily, wondering what my refusal to be intimate with her would bring me eventually. Would she hand me over to someone who would sell me to Alpha? It was doubtful but also a very real possibility. She simply wouldn't understand why I refused her. Of course, it has absolutely nothing to do with her. She is beautiful, her body is objective, and she is as nice as they come, but that doesn't change the fact that I am hideous and a monster. What would she possibly want with me when she is gorgeous, and I am a disgusting looking thing?

I had my doubts that even Luxina would love me after everything I had done and how I look now. *A face only a mother could love...* Nillona was right. No one would love me. They would use me for their own pleasure and superficial gains, but at the end of the day, they wouldn't love me. They wouldn't be able to get past the outer shell to learn about what's inside of me. So, even though she made advances against me, Nautila only wants to take pleasure in relations with an angel. It has nothing to do with me as a person on the inside. It has to do with me being a powerful entity.

Nautila had been gone for quite some time. I was just about to go look for her when a commotion broke out on the other side of the window. I peeled myself from the couch and walked over, pulling back the curtains to peer out and see what was going on. Nautila burst through the door of the room with frightened, wide eyes.

"Demons are in the market looking for you," she blurted.

She ran to the window beside me, and we looked down at the groups of dark fey gathered as a handful of the sentinel demons of Alpha's army slowly walked through, surveying the vendors' tables. I watched as they looked around at their faces, removing the hoods of those that were cloaked. Dark fey stood frightened at their tables, unable to move or escape to somewhere safe. They tousled some of the dark fey around in the crowd until the streets began to clear out. They all piled into shops up and down the courtyard so they could escape from the Forsaken.

"We are looking for the Shining One," one of them bellowed. "We know he is here. We will leave everyone unharmed as long as he is turned over to us."

I watched, frowning as they moved table to table, storefront to storefront. They weren't going to stop searching until I was found. There would only be bloodshed until I was turned over if they didn't get answers soon.

"What do you think they want with you?" Nautila whispered.

I dropped the curtain, stepped away from the window, and began to pace.

"I have no idea," I replied. "There could be a number of reasons. There was an uprising in the demonic ranks when I escaped. They could be either friendly or foes."

"I can find out for you," she mumbled.

"No, the best thing to do will be to wait it out until they leave," I remarked.

"What if they don't leave? What if they start killing fey one by one?" she asked.

"If they start doing that, then I will reveal myself. I won't let any more people die to save me," I hissed.

She watched me carefully. I'm not sure if she was reading into anything I said or trying to determine if I was really worth all the hassle of keeping safe. Either way, she climbed into her bed, and I followed suit, lying back down on the couch. I lay there sleepless for hours, just waiting for something to happen. I thought the door would bust open or something, and they would drag me to the courtyard to kill. Different scenarios played in my head until there was a thunderous sound outside. It was startling enough to wake Nautila from her sleep. We both slowly walked back to the window and peeked through the curtain to see what was happening in the marketplace.

"Damian!" one of the demons shouted. "We know you are here. It's time to show yourself, or these innocent fey will die one by one."

"It's a trick," Nautila refuted. "They won't hurt anyone."

She was interrupted as another thunderous sound rumbled through the courtyard. They were blowing up the shops one by one. I grabbed my weapons bag and tossed it over my shoulder, then picked up the cloak she had given me, tossing it over my back. I tied it and flipped the hood up.

"You stay here. Thank you for all you have done for me," I said as I opened the door to the room.

"I can help," Nautila replied. "I was trained to fight in battle. Queen Mab thought I was too pretty to fight, so ordered me to the castle."

"No," I replied. "This isn't your fight."

I left the room, closing the door behind me, and started my way down the steps. Dark fey lined the walls, watching me descend to the tavern below. No one spoke a word as I walked past each of them, but they did lower their heads in some form of respect. All these fey knew who I was and had refused to tell the demons where I was. I had to pay my gratitude and keep them from dying aimlessly for Alpha's stupid cause. I walked through the door of the tavern and out into the middle of the market. Dozens of dark fey parted ways for me to make it through the crowd and to those who were demanding my head on a platter.

"I'm here," I called out from the crowd, stepping out into the open space between the dark fey and the demons.

I looked from face to face at those who stood before me searching for me. I didn't recognize their faces, so I could only surmise they were not friendly but foes.

"Well, well, well," the ringleader spoke. "If it isn't the prodigal son."

"I'm sorry, have we met?" I asked.

"I am Raum, commander of 30 legions," he snarled.

"Oh, you must not be too important then. Those that Alpha takes council with I know personally," I jested. "So, obviously, you have no authority to demand my name in crowds without punishment."

"Because of you, thousands of demons have been pitted against one another. One side fighting for Alpha, and the other fighting for you. You are a poor excuse of existence, and it will be my privilege to kill you on sight as ordered by Alpha," he sneered, pulling a sword from the sheath on his side.

"You can try," I replied, arrogant and smiling.

I tore the hood from my head, unraveled the cloak from my body, and threw it on the ground beside me, wielding two large swords that I had activated while he was distracted talking. I spun the swords over the tops of my hands and readied them in combat stance.

"Are you sure you want to do this?" I asked.

He grinned deeply. "It will be my pleasure to be the one to rip your beating heart from your chest."

I leapt with agility and brought my swords down on him. I pushed him around the market with blow upon blow as I laid down an assault of weapon mastery. I saw the fear creep into his eyes as he parried and blocked as fast as he could.

"Alpha didn't tell you he was sending you to your death, did he?" I asked as I pounded him with blows. "I bet he also forgot to mention that I was trained by the best of the best for combat fighting, something even you are not entitled to."

My sword caught his arm, and he grabbed it with his free hand. I had him backed into a wall with no escape. The other demons that had been burning down the shops were now standing behind me as I held my sword to his throat.

"We can do this the easy way, or we can do it the hard way," I declared. "The uncomplicated way is you letting me go and living in the end without your buddies here dying along with you. You leave the shadows and report to Alpha, telling him you found nothing here. The hard way is I kill you and then take out those standing behind me. Alpha still doesn't know I have been found, and these hospitable dark fey will still be safe and sound from future attacks."

He laughed. "You will never be able to run and hide from Alpha. He owns you!" he sneered.

"Last chance," I replied through gritted teeth. "What's it going to be, boys?"

I looked back at those who stood behind me. A couple of faces looked back and forth between one another nervously but still held their swords ready for attack.

"The hard way it is," I sneered.

Raum pushed me off and sliced his blade through the air. I ducked and twisted around, my foot catching his feet and taking him down to the ground. I brought my sword up and over my head and crashed it down on his neck. His head rolled for about five feet before it stopped, his hollow dead eyes staring back at me. I turned my head to the others and glared. At some point, you would think stupidity would disappear and be replaced by fear. These idiots were not the case. They lunged toward me. I picked my swords up and fought them off. One sword parried and blocked one of them while the other sword concentrated on the other. I kicked out with my foot, catching one behind me in the chest and knocking him to the ground.

"That's enough!" a voice yelled.

We all stopped to look at the one who had shouted for our attention. One of the demons had slipped off when I wasn't watching and had Nautila with a sword at her throat. I glared at him as he brought it up closer to her neck. Her eyes widened with fear.

"She's not part of this," I growled. "She is just an innocent fey like everyone standing in this marketplace. Your fight and qualm are with me. Let her go."

"Ah, you see, this one has a thing for you, though," the demon replied, sniffing her hair deeply. "I heard her telling the girls in the tavern that she had planned to get you as hers one way or another."

"She is still innocent and not worth killing for me," I protested angrily. "I am not worthy of bloodshed. Why do you lay down your lives for Alpha when he sent you here to die!?" I bellowed. "Are you that blind? Do you not know when he is sacrificing you, or are you too bloodthirsty to realize you are being used?"

"I sacrifice myself in the name of Alpha as all his army should," he testified.

"That is such a shame," I maintained. "If you can take me alive or dead, you can try. But, let her go. She has no part of this."

"Soft on this one, aren't you?" he jeered, grabbing her by her jowls.

"I just don't want people dying for me," I replied.

"You should have thought about that when you were Alpha's little minion," he seethed. "Her blood is on your hands."

He swiped the sword across Nautila's throat, and she choked, gasping for air as her mouth filled with blood. She thudded to the ground, eyes wide open and blood leaking from the corner of her lips. Anger tore through me.

"I suggest any other fey that is willing to aid the Shining One go quietly inside," the demon spoke aloud.

They didn't spare a moment and clamored as quickly as they could from the marketplace back into the shops that weren't burned down.

"What's your name?" I muttered.

"What?" he asked, confused.

"What is your name?" I annunciated.

"Zepar," he replied. "But why do you want to know?"

"Because I want to know what to carve in your dead body as I send it back to Alpha with a message," I sneered.

I held my swords out and spun around quickly, dispatching the three demons who had stood around me earlier, fighting. Their heads rolled across the ground landing at Zepar's feet as their bodies thumped to the ground.

"Alpha won't stop with us. He will just keep sending more of us to find you," Zepar laughed. "Kill us. Kill one, and two shall rise in his place," he hissed.

"Well, then I guess I will just kill all of you until there is no one left but Alpha," I remarked, swinging my sword around, preparing it for my assault on his body.

"You can take us out, but you will never defeat what he created just for you," Zepar replied. "You will not live to see the end of the world."

He blew a whistle in the air as I ran toward him, bringing my blade up and over my head, slicing it down the middle of his body. He crumpled in halves to the ground, blood spraying me as he fell. I lifted Nautila's body from the ground and carried her to the tavern door, laying her gently down. She shouldn't have died. Her death was now on my own hands. Even if I hadn't been the one to take her life, she was killed because of me.

The dark fey began to pour out from the shops they had taken refuge in and stood around me in a circle.

"You are the brave Shining One who everyone has been talking about," one of them asserted.

I nodded my head.

"We will stand by your side," he replied, putting his arm across the middle of his chest. "The dark fey will fight your fight. Alpha will pay for his crimes against all fey."

They all stood around me, each placing their arm over their chest and bowing to me. I bowed my head in acknowledgement of their loyalty.

"Damian!" a familiar voice shouted through the crowd.

I looked around, and my eyes landed on another fleet of demons who were heading into the market square. I searched the faces to match the voice I had heard call my name, and my eyes stopped on the face of Asmodeus. The dark fey stood around me and readied whatever weapons they had on their sides to fight against the new wave of demons advancing. I motioned for them to lower their weapons.

"Asmodeus," I replied, walking up to him.

I kept my distance, unsure of whether he had finally turned against me and was here to drag me back to Alpha or not. I didn't have to give it much thought as he wrapped his arms around me in a bear hug.

"You are a sight for sore eyes," he murmured. "I was afraid we wouldn't get here in time to stop Zepar and Raum's gang."

His eyes rested on the bodies of the demons lying on the ground. He cocked an eyebrow.

"I was trained by the best," I replied with a shrug.

"Well, they were the least of your problems. Those things Alpha created are on their way here. Zepar released the call to signal where you are," he replied.

"We must leave here, then. These fey do not deserve to die," I said.

I turned around to all those who stood behind me. "Seek shelter. Lock your doors, bolt them, and make sure they are impenetrable. There are far more things to fear than the shadows here, and those things are on their way to this very place. So, go. Hide!" I instructed them.

They nodded and began to file away into the shops quietly. I returned my attention to Asmodeus and those who stood behind him. "You all need to leave as well. These things… they are unlike anything of Alpha's I have fought."

"No," Asmodeus protested. "This is the one time we will not listen to you. We will stay, and we will fight them alongside you. And if we die, then so be it. But you will not face them alone anymore. Half of the demons split in two. Those that side with Alpha, and those that side with you. We plan to meet up with Incaendiel and the rest of the angels to join forces."

"So, he is, ok?" I asked. "Incaendiel?"

"As far as I know, he is. I haven't heard if he has been recaptured or not," Asmodeus replied.

"And my- I mean Sophie?" I asked.

He shook his head. "Sophie is a lost cause to all but Incaendiel."

A howl ripped through the air, jerking us away from our

conversation. Those that stood with me all faced the other direction. We all readied our weapons, waiting for the beasts to rip through the courtyard. The sounds seemed to come from all sides as we all followed the sounds, turning around and around as the creatures circled the market, ensuring none of us escaped.

"You ready?" Asmodeus asked, scanning the openings between all the buildings that stood around us.

"Are you?" I answered.

Werewolves burst through the buildings, snapping, snarling, and growling. Their fangs dripped the same acid that those from the gladiator ring did. The fighting began. The sounds of swords ripping through flesh and howls of pain filled the air around us as we tore and hacked our way through the ferocious group of beasts. However, no matter how many of them we slaughtered, more poured in around us.

I caught notice of several types of creatures making their way into the market square. They were all the same ones that I had watched emerge from the tunnels prior to Incaendiel yanking me behind the gate. None of us would make it out of this alive, that was for sure. We were outnumbered by thousands. I looked around at those who stood by my side, fighting. They fought with me, for me, and because of me, and if they had a choice, they would die with me. I would never let them do that, though. I am not worth the lives of others and never would be.

Arrows tore through the sky, catching the creatures left and right squarely in the center of their heads. They dropped like flies one by one as mountains and mountains of arrows rained down around us. Some were fiery arrows, while others exploded upon contact. I looked to the tops of the buildings, and the dark fey who had hidden away in their buildings stood on the building tops, aiding us in the fight. Fireballs were flung from catapults, exploding in molten lava balls burning the creatures to a crisp. Bombs were released that, upon impact, poisonous gas crept upon the beasts, and they gasped, dropping to the ground hacking and frothing at the mouth.

Cries and shouts erupted from the building tops as the dark fey began to be attacked by creatures that flew. The winged beasts flew around, snatching them from the buildings, ripping them apart in the air, and tossing the carcasses to the ground below. I used my icy powers and began to shoot ice spears through the air taking them down one by one as those who were able to use their own arrows to take them out of the sky.

"We need to get you out of here!" Asmodeus shouted, fending off attacks from his left and right.

"I can't leave them behind defenseless," I replied, turning my ice powers to those who were on the ground.

One of the creatures shot out a flaming torch of breath that I quickly threw up an ice shield against. The ice slowly melted from around us as more and more of them appeared, breathing fire.

"When are you going to get it through your head that without you, there is no end to Alpha?" Asmodeus hissed. "Now, you need to get out of here while we hold them off. We have enough assistance from the dark fey to keep them from following you."

"Where am I supposed to go!?" I shouted. "Do I just appear out of thin air to Luxina and Xavier and expect them to welcome me with open arms?"

"You have to do what you have to do!" he yelled. "They will know. I am sure the message has been gotten out to them. They have a fey with them who has been helping them. She must know something about what is happening. The entire universe is buzzing about it! Everyone is antsy and can feel the war brewing like a storm."

"I left you behind once," I replied. "I won't leave you behind with certain death."

"You've been like a son to me," Asmodeus replied, placing his forehead against me. "And I would rather nothing more than to die protecting you as such."

"Why does everyone I care about have to die for me?" I protested. "This shouldn't be the way things are!"

"Things don't always work out as we hope," Asmodeus replied quietly. "But we must push forward with what we are given. I was once an angel that darkness stole. I won't let that same darkness take you and claim you. Now, go! Run! And don't stop running for anyone until you get to where you need to be."

"And where is it I need to be?" I replied, refusing to accept his words. "What if I belong nowhere?"

"You belong!" he yelled. "You belong! Don't ever let anyone make you think that you aren't worthy of respite, or worthy of love, or worthy of existence. You don't let anyone tell you that you are a monster! You aren't a monster! And you deserve the light more than most of us ever have!"

He pushed me from the center of the fleet toward an opening that was free from any of the creatures.

"Go, Damian!" he shouted. "I will see you again."

I backed away slowly, still unsure if I should leave them. I couldn't leave them. I couldn't leave Asmodeus to die. I couldn't, and I wouldn't.

I summoned my power from deep within, and ice rained in sheets from the skies, driving the Forsaken helping me further back to the buildings. They had to duck inside and take cover from the assault of daggers that fell from the sky. I screamed. I howled in anger. Power exploded from my core, and blue lights swirled around the square as torrential freezing winds swarmed the creatures. The lights swirled around them as they began to gasp and choke, starved of air.

No sooner had the beasts collapsed to the ground, suffocated, more creatures began to pour into the square. I could fight them all day like this. I planted my feet, preparing for the onslaught, when a yell erupted throughout the rumble of monsters.

"Damian! Go!" Asmodeus bellowed.

I scowled in frustration. I gave a quick look at the creatures and then to Asmodeus. He and the other demons stepped out in front of them as they rushed to the center of the marketplace, and they began fighting the beasts off for me to escape. I turned and ran through the opening that still remained free from the growing carnage. I slipped through the alleyway between the buildings and ran off into the shadows as they rapidly overtook me, encasing me in a shroud of inky black protection.

CHAPTER 10

I STILL HAD THE MAP and pulled it from the bag around my shoulder. I picked up the stone, and it lit up in my hand, illuminating the area around me as I walked. It was nothing but the road I had been on for miles. I looked at the map, and it told me where I was located. *Wandering Road* was what it showed to me.

"Great," I muttered to myself. "I bet this road makes me walk and walk without ever reaching my destination. Another cruel joke from the realm."

I quickly scanned the map to see if I was close to the portal. To my luck, I was close. If I didn't get lost by following this road, then I would make it there within a few hours. However, the tricky nature of this place was sure to slow me down for sure. I just hoped I would reach the portal before it jumped to another place. I was tired of traveling. I was more than tired. My heart, body, and soul were exhausted from this place, exhausted from the predicament I had come to find myself in. I was ready for it all to be over with.

If this was what mortals believed hell to be like, I would quickly agree. This place was worse than Sheol. I had always found it amusing how the mortals stuck to their beliefs of eternal fires and damnation when no such place had ever existed. The Lake of Fire spoken of in their written texts was an illusion that Alpha had created. Quite honestly, there was no such place as heaven either. There was no eternal resting place in the sky where you got to sit with God at his throne. Much like death for angels, mortals just dissipated into the universe and released their energies back to it. The Summit may be quite like what they believed heaven to be, but it was solely the home for angels.

What mortals didn't understand about their god, about Alpha, was that he didn't care about anything but for them to worship him endlessly. That was the only thing Alpha wanted for everything he had created, which was for it to worship him. Nature, angels, mortals, and even those vile beasts, his only wish was for them to bow to his power. I remember the days we sat in the Summit and watched the mounting war between the angels of the Summit and those that had fallen to the Glade. Alpha enjoyed the negative energy he had sparked between them all. However, he despised Incaendiel for his lack of worship. For even as the Fallen Ones fought heavily against the angels of the Summit, they still loved their father creator. All of them loved Alpha except for Incaendiel. He had grown a hateful disposition toward Alpha that developed a depth no other had.

Mortals had called this adversary Lucifer. There was a story where God had asked him to love mortals more than he loved God and Lucifer refused. That's not what happened at all. We all knew that Omega was the one that chose to fall, and we all knew Incaendiel was the true adversary of Alpha. It was quite humorous knowing that he was created to take over power once Alpha and Omega grew powerless and turned back into stardust. He would win in the end, whether Alpha liked it or not. Incaendiel was the rightful god over the galaxy. He wouldn't be as conceited about it either.

I watched my footsteps appear on the map as I continued walking down the road. This contraption was unique and very handy. It was too bad that it only worked for the Nightmares and Shadows realm. It would prove to be quite useful elsewhere, like searching for Starfire. I let my thoughts drift to Luxina, and I wondered where they were at this very moment. Were they safe? Were they fighting off monsters as well?

Everything seemed to become a deafening silence around me. I hadn't even realized I wasn't making any noise as I trudged along the path. My feet fell silent against the road no matter how hard I stomped them. I stopped for a moment, looking in both directions of the road. I listened intently for any type of sound. The paper map in my hand didn't even make a noise as I rustled it. Something was off. Why were there no sounds here? I looked at the map to see if the name of the road had changed. I panicked slightly. There wasn't anything on the map at all. It was just a blank sheet of paper.

I folded it in half and then opened it again to see if there would be any change on it at all. There was nothing. There was no red x marking where I was on the map. There weren't any places listed, no forests, no red dots of where I had traveled from and toward. It was as if I had walked into a part of this place that didn't even exist in the land. I didn't know what to do. Do I keep walking and hope that the map reappears? Should I turn around and go back the way I came and hope that the map comes back? There were so many options and so few right answers as to what I should do.

I sat down in the middle of the road in defeat. Even if I traveled back the way I came, there was no guarantee I wouldn't become even more lost than I am right now. The road was called the *Wandering Road* for a reason. You wandered lost on it. If I stayed right here, maybe someone would happen along and tell me where I was and what I had to do to get back on course to my destination.

I lay down in the dirt and stared up at the dark sky where meteors had begun to fall again. They were beautiful streaks of pinks, purples, and blues. Even though this place was a black hole, it did have some beauty to it. Even the *River of Sorrows* had an elegance to it. Even though it was a heartbreaking place of fey suicides, it still had a beautiful symbolic meaning behind it. No one escapes the throes of death, and fey live for hundreds of years. Sometimes, suicide may seem like the only answer they have for escape. The spirits there showed they gained a semblance of peace because they did not reincarnate back into a young fey again. They were stuck in a limbo type state of being without having to experience life all over through another set of eyes.

Maybe that is what it would be like for me. If I were to die, I don't think I would drift off to the land of the fallen angels at Potter's Field. I believe that just like the gods releasing their energies back into the world, I would, too. I would float through the universe endlessly as stardust until it was used to mold another being. Maybe the stardust would have some sort of conscience like most believed souls to have. Would I float around like a spirit in the vapid space of the universe? Mysteries of death have always captivated me.

My mind soon replayed the day over, and I was now thinking of Nautila. She was another person who died innocently because of me. If I had let her come with me to fight, would she still be alive instead of being caught off guard and dragged outside by Zepar? She hadn't even fought back with him even though she had said she was trained. Did she act as a martyr and let her death fuel the dark fey into joining the war? They had pledged their loyalty quickly after I had avenged her death. Could they see that I was compassionate?

As always, my thoughts drifted off to Luxina. I wanted to see her, to hear her voice. I wanted to know she was protected and that whoever protected her would swear her life over theirs. That was the type of protection she needed. All these people were dying for me, and I wasn't worthy of such selfless acts. But she was. She deserved people to die to protect her. I need to be there to protect her. I needed to make sure these creatures would never hurt her. How do I get to her, though? I sighed deeply. I closed my eyes and pictured her face in my head. Her red, fiery hair wrapped around her face where her green eyes shined back brightly at me.

The sounds of crickets filled my ears, and I opened my eyes to see if there was something growing closer to me on this road. My eyes looked directly up into the night sky where stars shone brightly, and a full moon hovered just above the canopy of treetops. I sat up, looked around me, and saw that I was in a thicket of bushes. I pulled the map out that I had tucked away to see where I was at in Nightmare and Shadows. How did I move when I didn't move at all? When I pulled the map out, the red x was back, and I was somewhere in a place called The Netherlands. I stood up and scratched my head. This was a map of places on Earth. I glanced back and forth where I stood, and sure enough, I was surrounded by regular trees and growing foliage.

"I must have walked into the portal and didn't even know it," I murmured to myself. "But why am I here?"

I heard voices off from where I stood and quickly squatted in the brush so I wouldn't be seen by whoever was walking toward me. It could be anyone at this point. I focused on the thoughts of the people who were advancing toward me.

What does she want now? I heard in my head. *I wish she would just leave me alone. She always wants to talk. I don't have anything to say to her. People seem to die around us all the time. We aren't worth it. She just keeps pushing on.*

Is that Xavier? I tried to peer through the brush to get a look at who I was hearing in my head.

If I must hear any more about the need to save Damian from Alpha, I will rip my ears from my head. It's always Damian this and Damian that. Then, she wonders why I am in a bad mood. Maybe if she cared more about me than she did him, she would see the pain that I am in as well. She is so self-centered.

They were within range of me to hear the spoken conversation they were having.

"Did I make you mad at me or something? It's been a year of these conversations," she asked Xavier.

I could feel the pain and torment that she felt regarding him. He must have been pushing her away for quite some time, jealous over me. So, the Unseelies did not lie when I was told that she wanted to find me.

"You didn't do anything," he replied heatedly. "I just don't want to talk."

I watched as he walked away through the trees back to wherever they had come from. How could he leave her there alone and in such pain? I watched as she fought back the tears threatening to spill down her face. I imagined what it would feel like to brush the tears away while caressing her face in my hands.

I stepped out from the brush without thinking. My heart raced, and my mouth went dry. I needed to let her know I was here. I needed to comfort her. I needed to take her fears away. But most of all, I needed to protect her.

"Give him time, Luxina," I spoke softly into the night air.

Her eyes landed on me, and I could see and hear all the questions that bubbled beneath her surface. Deep within those questions, I felt what I needed to feel from her. It might seem trivial to most that I needed this type of response to know that I was accepted by her and possibly even quite loved. But it was the most soothing experience my weary soul could feel after my travels. After experiencing everything I had felt in the realm of Nightmares and Shadows. What the *Bog of Damnation* and the *River of Sorrows* had put me through regarding my growing love for her. I felt her heart flutter...

THE VALLEY OF THE SHADOW OF DEATH: NEPHILIM RISING

THE GUARDIANS OF LIGHT SERIES
BOOK FOUR

Kasey Hill

Azoth Khem Publishing
Huntsville, AL
April 2025

PROLOGUE

IT HAD BEEN A YEAR since we escaped Alpha. Xavier and I hid in the realms of the Otherworld as we made our journey to find Starfire. Praeziel was our guide, along with Gwendolyn, as we hopped from portal to portal, trying to find the oracle's cloaked cabin. We have traveled far and wide, often crossing the same places twice, looking for her. By the time we had reached her last known place of existence, she had already fled to seek safety and refuge from Alpha. My understanding has been that Alpha knows about her and has for quite some time. It has been his plan to find her so she can help him with Damian like she is to help us.

Praeziel doesn't know much about how she is going to help us. The only thing he knows is that she is the key to unlocking our full potential. My guess is that it has to do with the faery enchantment that was placed upon our parents when they were created.

I find myself every day wondering if my parents are both okay and if Damian is being tortured anymore. We know for a fact that Alpha is still running tests and creating new species of demons. We have happened across a few of them along our travels that we had to dispatch. Damian's altered blood is now the key to these creatures, whether Alpha has perfected his serum or not. After my visions with the injections, everyone began to wonder if my mother, Sophie, had actually died or not when the Glade fell to ruin.

After we visit with Starfire, that is when the real battle of minds and wits begins. Alongside Praeziel, we will have to convince the Nephilim to join ranks with us to help defeat Alpha. We gained alliances with Seelies and Unseelies and even mended the bonds of discrimination amongst their ranks. A new world order is coming to pass, but only if we are able to defeat Alpha in the end. If we can stave off the apocalypse that is brewing, ending the heavenly war, we will, without a doubt, be able to forge an unbreakable alliance to keep the Children of the Night and the Forsaken in the abyss with all of the other monsters Alpha created throughout time.

CHAPTER 1

"WHERE COULD SHE BE?" I asked as I loaded my arms with firewood.

Xavier and Praeziel had been slowly building us a fire for the night with what sticks we could scrounge up from the area. I dropped the firewood beside their circle of stones and dusted my hands off on my pants. A chill had filled the air, and I rubbed my arms. We were far from any trail in a remote area of the wooded hills in Europe. We had traveled through so many faery portals that I didn't even know which country we were in this time. Gwendolyn had gone to hunt us some food to roast over the fire and hadn't made it back yet. It made me nervous whenever she went off by herself. We could be ambushed at any moment of the day, and we are better in numbers. Xavier and I were the only safe ones from harm. Alpha would have Praeziel and Gwendolyn killed on-site. I couldn't live with myself knowing more people had died trying to keep us safe from Alpha.

"Gwendolyn not only goes out to hunt but to ask local fey if they have heard of anything from the trees, plants, or animals as to where she may have gone," Praeziel replied, jabbing a stick into the fire and kindling it into a roar.

"I wonder if we keep tripping her senses, and she believes we are the danger that Alpha poses," I commented, hunching down beside the warm flames.

"That could very well be," Praeziel replied, leaning back against a tree stump.

Xavier sat quietly, picking at blades of grass, lost in thought. If only I knew what went through his mind… somehow, he was able to put a block up so I couldn't hear his thoughts anymore. It happened after the escape from Stygia. I'm sure it had to do with meeting our father for the first time. Or maybe learning his mother had died. Actually, it could be a number of things, but it doesn't make the loneliness I feel any better.

"I'll take first watch tonight," Praeziel stated as he watched me yawn.

"Oh, I'm not even tired. I'm just cold," I replied with an appreciative smile, rubbing my arms again. "I don't ever recall being this cold. Where are we?" I asked.

"We are in the Netherlands," Gwendolyn replied, appearing with rabbits, squirrels, and some bird attached to strings slung over her shoulder. Her hunting bowstring rested across her chest with her quivers on the opposite shoulder, along with the prey she had hunted.

"Any word?" Praeziel asked.

"Possibly," she replied as she plopped the dead animals down in front of her. She pulled out a blade and began to skin the animals to prepare them for the fire. "I spoke with some of the river nymphs, and they heard tale that Starfire is on an island out past Australia. It's a few days' journey from here."

"That's good news, right?" I asked, looking between her and Praeziel.

They both nodded quietly and returned to the silence of the night. Xavier didn't make a sound nor acknowledge Gwendolyn's return. I could watch the air around him darken and shroud him as he thought deeper and deeper to himself.

"Xavier," I spoke aloud. He glanced up to me, bewildered, looking around. "Let's go for a walk," I said with a small smile.

"Don't stray too far," Gwendolyn ordered. "The hills around here are treacherous, and you could find yourself in a hole made by trappers."

"We'll be careful," I promised as I stood up and held my hand out to Xavier to take.

He stood along with me and walked over to me, but he didn't take my hand. His demeanor toward me had changed ever since we went to see the Dark Queen. He hardly talked to me anymore. He never held me while we slept, and any type of physical contact was put to the back of his mind. I don't know what I did to make him angry with me or to change in regards to me, but a sinking feeling always blossomed in my bosom whenever he refused my hand.

"A penny for your thoughts," I said, as we strolled silently through the trees.

He still didn't speak, and I sighed. "What's wrong, Xavier? You never talk to me anymore. What's going on in that head of yours?" I asked, peering up at him in the little bit of moonlight that breached the tops of the trees.

"I just don't have anything to say," he replied.

"Did I make you mad at me or something? It's been a year of these conversations," I asked, prodding deeper.

"You didn't do anything," he replied heatedly. "I just don't want to talk."

And with that, he stalked off back the way we came to the campsite and left me alone in the dark. Tears threatened to spill as I once again felt as if my heart was going to break in two.

"Give him time, Luxina," the voice called out in the dark.

I jerked my head around, trying to scan anywhere I could see in the dark. I knew that voice. Only one person would call me sister. Damian. But how did he find us?

"How would I not find you? You're my blood," the reply came to the silent question in my head.

I still couldn't find him in the dark, inky black of night. Was he here to steal me back away to Alpha? Was he here to kill me as he had killed Sophia?

"No and no," he replied.

I heard a twig snap, and I jerked my head in the direction it came from. There, in the low glow of the moon, I saw the red curls split through the dark trees. I was too far from the campsite to yell for help even if he did intend to hurt me. I had no weapons on me, either.

"I can sense your fear and anxiety. I assure you, sister, that I am not here to hurt you. As a matter of fact, I am here to help you put an end to Alpha's reign of terror," Damian said as he stepped into the light, and I could see his face.

I scanned it deeply, looking for a twitch or a tell-tale sign of him lying. I didn't find anything. My insides wrenched against each other as I grappled with my own fears. Could I trust him? And even though the past could clearly show I could not, something tugged at me as my heart thumped that said I could indeed trust him.

"Were you followed?" I asked, scanning the area from where he appeared in the dark.

"No. I slipped out undetected, and I am cloaked. No one, not even Alpha himself, would be able to find me by tracking my wings."

He stopped short of me with his hands clasped behind his back. I wonder if he has a weapon? As if to answer the question in my mind, he brought his hands around and showed they were indeed empty.

"I don't want to be Alpha's soldier any more than your father did," Damian stated, staring into my eyes. "I just want to be with those I care about. Not with someone who just uses me because I have special blood."

Funny enough, I believed every word he said. Even so, I had to be hesitant. I had to be sure.

"You killed Sophia. You killed Praeziel's mother," I said dryly.

"No, I did not. Sophia is safe and hidden away. I pretended to murder her to satisfy Alpha. Trust me, Luxina, she is safe and well with the Watchers that are left," he replied quietly. A few moments passed as I just stared him in the eyes. "You believe me, don't you?"

His voice was different from most of the times we talked. He sounded needy, as a child looking for approval from a parent would sound. The harsh undertones in his speech had filtered away, and a soft tone had replaced the voice of the boy that stole me away from my father. I took a deep breath and let my gut take control... or was it my heart?

"Oddly, yes. I believe you," I replied, stepping toward him. I reached my arms out to hug him, and he flinched away. I could see the terror in his eyes.

"I just want to hug you."

"Why?" he asked, looking closely at my hands, examining them for weapons.

"Because that's what people do when they care about one another," I replied as I wrapped my arms around his shoulders.

He didn't know what to do. I could tell he had never been shown affection by Alpha. He hesitated as he lifted his arms and placed them around my shoulders as well. The hug deepened, and his arms tightened around me as tears slid down his cheeks.

"I always knew you were in there, somewhere," I said as he silently sobbed into my hair.

"Alpha is so close to making the injections the right way, and I am so scared of the monster I would turn into," he cried out in breaths.

"We won't let that happen," Praeziel said, startling Damian and me from the hug.

Behind me stood Gwendolyn, Praeziel, and Xavier. I don't know how long they had been there watching. I didn't even hear them walk up. I am horrible at this whole stealth and hunting thing. Damian quickly swiped at his face, drying the tears so no one would see them.

"So, everyone is in agreement that Damian stays with us?" I asked, looking face to face.

Gwendolyn and Praeziel nodded. Xavier didn't even acknowledge the question. He just stared angrily at Damian and me. He scowled and stalked off back to the campsite alone.

"I will talk to him," Praeziel stated and sighed, heading back to the campsite as well.

"Good luck," I mumbled.

"As I said," Damian began. "Give him time."

"Easy for you to say. You haven't gotten the cold shoulder for a year now," I replied, more heated than intended. "Sorry. It just annoys me how he is acting so childish."

"He has every right to act childish," Damian replied softly and wisely. "He just lost his mother, and he doesn't know where his father is. There's more, but it's his business to bring it to light, not mine."

"The mother part, maybe. The father part, not so much. The first time he met Dad, all he did was sit and talk angrily, then glare at him. He blames everyone for growing up without a family to call his own," I said as we meandered back to the campsite.

"Don't we all," Damian whispered in reply.

I felt a pang of guilt. He and Xavier were alike. Neither grew up with their mother nor father. One grew up with Lilith, and the other grew up with Alpha. They were closer to being twins together than Xavier and I were.

"Well, I am here now. I will always be here," I replied as I took his hand in mine almost as if by instinct. "And when this is all over, you can live with us. My dad would love you as his own. You know that, right?"

He chuckled a bit. "Oddly enough, yes. I do know."

I squinted at him, wondering exactly what that meant. The last I knew of him meeting my father was the day he kidnapped me for Alpha. Based on that alone, there was no way my father would adore him, as I had stated, without getting to know the real him first. I mulled on it and let it go without prodding him further. By the time we had made it back to the campsite, Gwendolyn had the food roasting across the fire, Praeziel was watching the perimeter, and Xavier was sitting alone at a tree away from the fire. Damian dropped a bag at the tree line and took a seat near me at the fire.

"Dinner is almost ready," Gwendolyn stated, pinching the animals as they roasted. "You hungry?" she asked, looking at Damian.

A frown quickly hid the developing look of shock Gwendolyn had as she averted her eyes and looked back to the fire. I followed her gaze, looking at Damian more carefully. I nearly gasped. He was just skin and bones. Red scars littered his face as if he had been beaten with a whip. His eyes sunk in with black rings underneath them. Anger coursed through me, and steam began to rise from my skin. Damian stepped back, confused as to what he did wrong to spark such a response from me. A quick glance around the fire alluded him to the answer when no one would look directly at him. Once he realized it, he smirked a bit.

"To say I'm starving would be a bit of an understatement," he replied with a laugh.

The tension in the circle broke, and sympathy washed around everyone. I had recalled my fire back within before I burned the trees down around us. I had gotten better at controlling it with the help of Gwendolyn and Praeziel. They taught me a few calming tricks. Dad had always tried to help me, but he never could get it right. He still had troubles himself reeling in his own fire. I guess we all just had a temper with a short fuse, which is why.

Gwendolyn picked up one of the sticks that had a roasted rabbit on it and handed it over to Damian.

"Thank you," he replied as he took the stick from her.

Hungry eyes stared at the food, but his face also looked a shade of green as if the thought of food was revolting. That could be a very real possibility. I know they taught us in physical education that when the body is starved, food can make you sick.

"Take it one bite at a time," I coaxed.

He looked at me, and for the first time, the strong eyes I remembered seeing for the first time a year ago had disappeared. Before me sat a boy with puppy dog eyes, hoping that his weakness didn't make him actually weak.

"Luxina, here you go," Gwendolyn said, holding out a stick with a bird roasted on it.

"Thank you," I replied with a smile and glanced over to Xavier. "Hungry, X?" I asked.

He didn't answer me. I rolled my eyes as Gwendolyn reached over to him a stick with a squirrel on it, and he took it without offering a thank you or anything. I felt a hand brush my shoulder and knew it was Damian, reminding me again to give him time. Something tugged at my heart, and I brushed the feeling away. I stole glances at Damian as he took small bites of the food he was given. He had only eaten a small portion of the rabbit when he set it aside, propping it up against a tree, so he didn't get it dirty.

The circle was silent as everyone ate but didn't ask the lingering question in the air.

"How did I get away from Alpha?" Damian asked aloud. He smiled and chuckled a bit as we all looked a bit confused at him. "That answer is simple." He stood from his spot and stretched out his cramped legs and arms in the air before returning to his seated position. "Incaendiel helped me escape."

We all gawked at him. The question we had needed an answer to, and we finally received it. Alpha did have him. That's why he hadn't come for me.

"Is he ok?" I asked a bit too eagerly.

"He's alive." Damian wouldn't look at me. It was all the answer I needed. He may be alive, but he wasn't ok in the least bit of sense. "Alpha won't kill him. Trust me. Lucifer has tried to persuade him to let him perform the deed. He needs all of us," Damian replied. "And as for the mind-reading, no, it isn't your imaginations. I can read everyone's mind sitting around this campfire."

I glanced at Xavier to see if that bothered him. If it did, it didn't register with him. He sat silently, eating the food Gwendolyn had given him. He tossed the finished carcass off into the tree line, fixed his sleeping gear on the ground, and rolled over to go to sleep.

"I think Xavier has the right idea," Gwendolyn purred. "We should all get some rest."

"I have the first watch," Praeziel replied with a smile. "I called it already."

I had an extra bag with sleep gear in it that I had been toting in case one of ours was damaged in some way, so I tossed it over to Damian. He caught it and nodded his thanks. I put my sleeping bag on the ground where I had been sitting, unzipped it, climbed inside of it, and zipped myself back up in it. The warmth of the bag enveloped me, and I snuggled deeper down into it. Damian stretched his out right above my head and just sat on top of it. His eyes looked so sunken in with the little light the glow of the fire emitted.

"How long has it been since you slept?" I asked, propping my head in my hand.

"Who says I sleep?" he chided.

"Because you are one of us. You sleep and most likely have dreams as well," I replied softly.

He was quiet for a few minutes. I sighed in exasperation. Looks like they both will only let me in so far. I rolled onto my back and stared at what few stars I could see through the canopy. I often wondered what the universe looked like from the gates of the Summit. I bet it was breathtaking. The beautiful lights of the stars dancing throughout the galaxy. The purple and pink particle clouds floating through space while comets shoot by.

"It is just that beautiful," Damian said, breaking me from my thoughts. "And I haven't slept in weeks, months before that. Not since Alpha began the torture..."

And it was back to silence. I didn't know what to say. I could only imagine what they had done to him. His own father... I drifted off to sleep with everything tumbling through my head. Damian was here. Damian was here safely. My father helped him escape. Alpha torturing him. What was he trying to get out of him? Did he know where we were, and Alpha knew? Was that what Alpha wanted from him? Maybe he stopped taking his injections.

CHAPTER 2

I KNOW I HAD to have a fitful sleep for anyone observing me while I dreamed. My dreams were terrible, horrible...

* * *

FIRE AND BRIMSTONE rained from the sky. People I had heard of were being burned to death or turned into pillars of salt where they stood. Alpha led a chariot through the sky pulled by four horses. Each horse was a distinct color. Red, white, black, and a pale gray color. The valley under him darkened as millions of werewolves, vampires, demons, and other creatures he had created ran forth, ready for battle. I stood powerless as I watched my father lead the advancing angels into the developing war of the heavens. A pit formed below their pounding feet filled with draugrs, the zombie creatures made from werewolves and vampires. I watched helplessly as they tumbled into the pit, and it filled with fire. I waited for my father to emerge from the pit. I was running to him. I was running to pull him free. But I was held back. I was trapped in tar. No matter how much my feet pulled and pulled at the thick, oily substance, I just sank deeper and deeper. I looked to my left and saw Damian and Xavier struggling just as I was in the pit. Alpha arrived with a cheerful laugh of triumph at our plight.

"Join me and be free," he yelled, laughing maniacally.

"Never!" Damian seethed. *"Then die, young Shining Ones."*

Alpha stared at us emotionlessly. It was almost as if something had snapped within him. He felt nothing now. It was then that we watched his plan unfold. We watched him snap his fingers, and the valley filled with lava from one side and water from another. Asteroids rained from the sky along with the fiery brimstone that had been pelting down. And I watched as the universe burned to ruins. The stars exploded in the sky. The air we breathed became toxic, and I gasped for air.

"If I can't have what rightfully belongs to me, no one will," Alpha said. *"I will just start over and do it the right way."* It was then that the lava and water reached Damian, Xavier, and me in the pit.

* * *

I WOKE UP SCREAMING, gasping for air that readily filled my lungs. Tears streamed freely down my face. Hands were on me, and I fought them. It was Alpha. I knew it. He had found us. Damian had led him here. It was all part of a plan.

"Luxina!" Damian yelled as he tried to fight my arms down to my side. "Luxina, it was just a dream!! Open your eyes!"

I pried my eyes open without realizing I had been squeezing them shut from fear of what it would look like around me. I was in my sleeping bag, and Damian was above me, shaking my shoulders. I thumped my head back against the ground and let out an exasperated sigh.

"It was just a dream," I choked through tears.

Damian scooped me up in his arms and squeezed me tightly. "No," he whispered. "It was the beginning of the end."

The sun shone down on us, and the morning rays peeked through the treetops. I pulled away from him and looked deeply into his eyes. I could see the fear. I could see the agitation. I could see everything that I was feeling reflected back at me.

"That's why you don't sleep," I whispered softly.

He nodded.

"What's going on?!" Xavier demanded as he rounded the corner and shot to the middle of the campsite.

I hadn't even realized that there wasn't anyone here except for Damian and me.

"We heard screaming," Praeziel stated as he rounded the bend right behind Xavier. "Are you ok?" he asked, eyeing Damian.

"Yeah, sorry. I, uh, had a bad dream is all," I replied. "Damian was just trying to wake me up."

Xavier glared at Damian as he stomped wordlessly back off into the woods. Praeziel just released the breath he had been holding. I knew what he was thinking. He had trusted his gut with Damian until he heard my screams. He nodded in our direction and turned to follow Xavier back into the woods.

"What were they doing?" I asked Damian.

"I have no idea. All I know is that they left at dawn, and that is the first I have seen them since," Damian replied as he went to untangle himself from my arms.

"No! Please, don't," I said as I wound my arms tighter around him. "I... you... it's just comforting." I was silent for a moment. "It's peaceful in your arms. I can't explain it. I feel calm around you. I can't imagine being without you right now, with Xavier being the way he is. You feel like home, and I don't ever want to know what that doesn't feel like... Please, just stay with me for a bit."

"Always," Damian whispered, tightening his arms around me. "I won't ever leave you."

We stayed like that for a few minutes until he pulled away, and I let him this time. I stared up at his face and wanted to cry. The fire's light showed little compared to the light of day. His entire face was sunken in. He looked like a walking skeleton. At some point in the night, he had removed his shirt to try and get comfortable, most likely. His chest, stomach, shoulders, and everything were skin and bones with large healing scars all over. I went to touch one, and he grabbed me by the wrist before I could touch him. His grip was tight and hard before he realized he was squeezing my arm too tight. My hand had begun to turn a deep red-violet when he released my hand.

"I'm sorry," he said sheepishly, rubbing his hair. "I don't like to be touched."

"No, I'm s-" He put his finger to my lips as he shushed me, looking around.

"We need to leave. Now!" he hissed, scrambling to his feet.

Xavier, Praeziel, and Gwendolyn all came bounding into the campsite.

"We have to go!" Praeziel yelled.

They all began to break down their things at the campsite as I struggled out of my sleeping bag. Damian helped me out and got it rolled up for me. He ran to his bag and rolled it up, stuffing it into the duffle bag I had given him last night. I stuffed mine into my bag as well and glanced to see that the other three had taken notice of his appearance as well and were staring at the marks on his back as they scrambled to stuff the supplies in their bags. Damian pulled his shirt on and reached into his pocket. He pulled out something that was as small and as slender as an ink pen. He pushed something on the side of it, and it transformed into the hilt of a sword, then metal materialized into a point.

"What is it?" I asked as I slung my pack on my back.

"Werewolves," Damian replied as the others slung their packs on, too.

He lifted his bag and the duffel bag I had given him from the ground and scanned the area.

"Where is the next portal?" he asked in a nervous but commanding tone.

"Just through the brush," Gwendolyn replied, pointing in the direction behind me.

He tossed me the bags, and I fumbled, catching them. "Get to it before they pick up all your scents," he demanded as he stood his ground.

I bent over, picking the duffel bag up from the ground and balanced the load in my arms. "You're not staying behind!" I refuted. "You're coming with us!"

"I can't let them find you!" he yelled back, turning to glare at me. "You have to go now!"

"NO!" I yelled back.

"This is not a debate!" he shouted. "They can follow you into the portal. It doesn't stop them."

"Then, I will stand and fight at your side," I replied stubbornly. "We just got you. We aren't leaving you behind!"

"Luxina, get into the portal with Gwendolyn," Praeziel demanded. "Xavier and I will stay behind and help."

It was then that I heard the sounds that Damian had heard in the dead silence with his fine-tuned ears. I could hear the pounding of feet through the brush. The trees pushed back, cracked, toppled, and swayed as the herd of werewolves stampeded toward the campsite. Their snapping and snarling jaws could be heard, and their howls and growls grew louder.

Praeziel threw Xavier a sword from his side as he wielded a bow and arrow. Xavier twisted it in his hand with ease. It was then I saw they were all right. I had no battle skills. Dad had never taught me to wield a weapon. I was untrained. Damian, Xavier, and even Praeziel had all been trained in combat style. Gwendolyn most likely had been trained as well, but she was going with me to protect me from the other side of the portal. At the thought of her name, I felt her hand grab my wrist and pull me off in the opposite direction of the assailing enemies. We had breached the portal door when the first wolf tore through the brush and bounded toward Damian. I watched as he sliced the head of the beast cleanly off before three more crashed through the brush surrounding them all. Everything disappeared from view as we crossed into the portal.

Gwendolyn placed herself between the portal and me, waiting for anything to come trampling through it. The anxiety and anticipation were killing me as I waited behind her. It seemed like an eternity. The silence between us grew deeper and deeper as she waited for something to come flying toward us. When I thought I couldn't wait any longer and was about to run back out, Xavier stepped through the portal. He was covered head to toe in blood. I gasped and ran to him to inspect him for injuries.

"It's not my blood," he finally said.

I looked into his eyes to see if there was any life in them in the heat of the moment. I wrapped my arms around him, and the static between us grew. He pushed me off and walked off behind Gwendolyn. Praeziel walked through next, covered head to toe in blood and gore as well. Gwendolyn let out a sigh of relief and ran to him, throwing her arms around her.

"Don't you ever make me leave your side again. Never again!" she said as she hugged him deeper.

He returned her hug, wrapping his arms around her. "I cannot make that promise, and you know it."

I waited for Damian to appear, but he didn't. I began to panic.

"Don't worry," Xavier said before I could ask. "He's fine. He went to search for the den. They were sent by Alpha. So, he must kill the rest of them and then hide his scent." His eyes lingered on me for a few seconds as if he wanted to say something more, but he didn't. He turned and walked to the stream off to the left of the portal to clean himself up. Praeziel went with him as well to wash up.

I released the breath I didn't even know I had been holding. Xavier and Praeziel had just finished cleaning off the blood and guts from their clothes and bodies when Damian finally stepped through the portal. He was covered in even more blood and bits than they had been. I sighed in relief as soon as I saw him. My breath caught in my throat as I looked into his eyes and saw the golden glowing light from them. He looked majestic. I had never seen that before.

"I followed their tracks for a couple of miles. They ended in the middle of a field. It was as if they had materialized out of thin air," he said as he walked to the river to join the other two in washing up. "It doesn't make sense."

I watched as the blood pooled in the water from the three of them washing. And just as quickly as I looked, it disappeared. I looked at Gwendolyn in confusion, hoping she could or would explain.

"Nature here takes care of itself. It purged the river of the blood and sent it back to your world. The Otherworld is a special and unique place. Things that do not belong do not settle here," she explained.

I nodded in understanding. The guys were getting their clothes back on and picking their weapons up, along with the duffle bags they had.

"Let's get a move on," Praeziel stated. "We have a three-day trip to make it to Sable Island."

"Sable Island?" I asked, a bit confused. "I thought we were going to Australia."

"No, she's on an island off of Australia," Gwendolyn replied. "Most of the journey will be through the Otherworld. So, we should be safe for the time being."

I lifted my canteen from my bag and shook it. "Is the water safe for us to drink?" I asked Gwendolyn.

"This river is, yes. But always ask, so you don't accidentally drink from the poisoned ones," she replied.

I filled my canteen, and everyone else followed my example. I handed Damian the bags he had tossed at me before taking on the werewolves. He put the duffle bag over one shoulder and carried the other in his hand. Gwendolyn took the lead of our little group and led us through the forests. Xavier followed behind her with Praeziel on their heels. I hung back and walked with Damian as he took in the sights around him.

"It's beautiful here, isn't it?" I asked, looking around at the different trees and plants.

Flower petals drifted in heaps from the trees, making it look like it was snowing flowers. The aroma in the air was sweet, with a hint of death. Although they were pretty to look at, you must never touch them.

"It really is," Damian replied in awe, looking around.

A full bloom drifted down intact, and he caught it in his outstretched hand. He handed it over to me, and I felt my cheeks warm.

"Thank you," I replied, tucking it behind my ear.

"Don't mention it," he replied with a smile. His face darkened a bit. "Next time, please do as I ask. I don't want you getting hurt."

"Train me?" I asked. "I want to help, and I don't want to be useless. Dad never trained me, and I feel like a damsel in distress. You had diligent militant training."

"Why doesn't Xavier teach you?" Damian asked. "He's had ample opportunity."

"I don't know," I replied with a shrug and looked at my feet. "He hardly talks to me. What makes you think he would train me? Sometimes, I feel as if he blames me for everything that has gone wrong in his life."

"When we make it to Starfire, I will be happy to train you," Damian said.

I gave a smile that would normally be accompanied by a girlish squeal of delight but refrained from drawing attention to us. Autumn leaves now fell in heaps as the flowers had. Where the air had been warm and inviting, it now had a crisp chill to it. You could feel the impending immortal sleep for the trees to come. However, in this part of the woods, it would be forever in a perpetual autumnal state. The trees were consistently "dying off" while never fully dying. It was a rather sad notion.

The wind picked up, and dust swirled around our feet and up our bodies, bringing flower petals and fallen leaves up and over us. The sun in the sky began to grow dark as the moon of this world eclipsed it. I glanced ahead to catch Xavier's face to see if he was affected by the sights as much as Damian and I were. He seemed to walk unphased through the mesmerizing scenes of the Otherworld. He seemed more like a soldier now than the caring boy I had met in the meadow. Where light once filled his eyes, darkness now rests. It was almost as if he lived in the shadows now. Everything that had mattered was left in a city of dust that had already capsized into the wind. I just wish he could find the peace he needed. A place above the shadows that drowned him in silent sorrows. Everything he lost in the yesterdays had just damaged his tomorrows. I miss the colors of his soul that shone so brightly to me…

I returned my attention back to my walking companion, who had grown silent. I guess there's no more privacy with him around. I'm sure he was prying into my thoughts as we walked in silence.

"I was not," he laughed, breaking the quiet air.

I giggled alongside him. "Oh, now I definitely know you were." I laughed heartily, and it felt refreshing to have someone to joke with.

"I do have a question for you, though, one that that isn't related to training or anything I have been thinking about for the past, I don't know, thirty minutes?" I said as we watched the season begin to change slowly. "How long have we been walking? Time seems to stop in here."

"I think it's actually been an hour," he chuckled. "And what would that be?" he asked, quirking his lip up in a side grin.

"How did they find you?" I asked. "Aren't you cloaked like us?"

His eyes pinched together in a frown. "Yes," Damian replied. "But they can track the scent of my blood because of the injections. Blood smells blood."

"You're not one of them, Damian. You're not a monster," I replied heatedly. "It's not your fault what Alpha has done to you."

"It may not be my fault, but I am part monster until the injections can filter out of my blood. That's how I knew they were there. I could smell them," he said. "Blood smells blood."

"How can they come through the portals?" I asked. "I thought only the fey could access them. That's why Gwendolyn has led us everywhere in the Otherworld."

"They were made from Seelie blood, remember?" he replied. "So they can follow us through the portals."

"Even the original werewolves and vampires were made from Seelie blood?" I asked. "I just thought the creatures made after were made from the blood."

"That's what he wanted everyone to assume. He tried to make humans with the aid of Titania and Oberon. However, the Seelie blood mutated the humans he attempted and created vampires. The werewolves were made from hellhounds, which are a special breed of wolf from the Otherworld. Everything always comes back to the Seelies," he explained.

"So, we aren't safe anywhere from anything that has to do with Alpha," I replied.

"No, we are not," he said, sighing. "Next time I ask you to do something, please do it without arguing. You could have been hurt back there. That is the last thing I want for you."

"I was afraid no one would stay behind to help you and would have left you to fend those beasts off by yourself," I explained.

"I could have taken them. I was thrown into the arena with werewolves as part of my training. It was like the gladiator battles except I was the only one tossed in," he replied.

Up ahead, Gwendolyn had come to nearly a full stop when Damian and I paid closer attention to our surroundings. It was dead quiet. The wind did not blow, the animals did not make noises, and even the tree branches had fallen silent. The hairs on my neck stood on end, and every nerve ending lit up with anxiety and panic.

"What is it?" I asked.

Gwendolyn held her finger up to tell me to be quiet. The panic was rising in the back of my throat. Before I could even protest her, I felt myself jerked from my feet, and I thudded to the ground with a yelp. I was dragged backward while I clawed at the ground, trying to get a grip on something to stop whatever was pulling me. A scream escaped my lips, and I rolled over to see what had a hold of me. However, there wasn't anything there. I felt a hand on my arm, and I halted in midair. I looked ahead of me. Damian had snagged my arm and had his foot firmly on a small boulder on the path.

"Hurry up!" he shouted as Gwendolyn came running to my side.

"What is it?" I screamed, kicking, trying to release my foot from whatever held it.

"I'm not sure. It's cloaked to even me. It must be from here, though. There was no way anything could have tracked us after we walked through the Forget-Me-Trees of spring. Whatever this is must be from the Nightmares and Shadow realm of the Otherworld," she replied.

"Look in my bag," Damian shouted. "There is a vial of dust. You must expose him with the dust to see him."

Gwendolyn scrambled through his bag, looking for what he said to grab. She pulled the vial from the bag and poured a handful of dust into her palm. She blew it in the direction that whatever had me would have been. The creature began to materialize. The grotesque thing in front of me couldn't even be described in words. It had tusks like a walrus, it was as tall as a troll, and it had one eye like a cyclops.

"I'm losing my grip," Damian urged as his foot slipped a bit from the rock he had wedged it against.

"I don't know how to kill this thing," Gwendolyn replied. "You're going to have to use your power."

"I can't use it without risking burning the woods down or catching you all on fire here," I retorted.

"It's your only chance!" Gwendolyn yelled as she retreated back to a safe point.

"Let me go, Damian!" I shouted.

"I'll be fine," he replied, not releasing his grip on my arm that was slowly slipping through his sweaty hands.

Before I could even summon forth the fire from my belly, a tunnel of flames flew straight toward the thing that had my leg. It dropped me immediately as the flames engulfed him. I looked back to see Xavier funneling his powers at the creature. It dropped to an ashen crisp at my feet as Damian pulled me back onto his lap. I stared at the thing, afraid to move. I looked back at Xavier as he withdrew his flames and smoldered under the sun. His eyes burned the same color Damian's had when he had walked through the portal after fighting the werewolves.

"How did you do that?" I asked in disbelief.

"Praeziel has been helping me learn to channel the flames into a usable weapon," he replied with a superior smile.

Enraged, I stood to my feet. I watched as Praeziel and Gwendolyn retreated as I felt the steam rise from skin.

"Is that what you two were doing this morning? Training?" I asked heatedly.

"Well, yes," Xavier replied. "We do it every morning."

I turned my gaze from him to Praeziel. "Is there some reason you feel it isn't necessary to include me in anything at all? You have been training him with his powers, with his fighting, but you haven't attempted once to include me in anything."

"I didn't think it would be necessary for you to train," Praeziel replied, a bit shaken.

"Why? Because I most likely won't be in the 'final battle?' Don't you think it would be necessary for me to be able to protect myself and others at all? What would have happened had Damian not been there to grab my arm at the last second? He struggled to keep me here. He struggled alone. Not one of you even bothered to run for my other outstretched hand to help pull me to safety. Gwendolyn's only offer is for me to torch the whole place and everyone standing around, hoping that you all survive. So, I ask again, Praeziel, why do you feel it isn't important for me to even learn the basics of defense when I am at a disadvantage between the two guys that were raised with a sword in their hand?"

Silence fell over the group, and Xavier lost the grin that had painted his face a moment before. No one answered me as I stared at each of them in the circle as if they had a secret that I wasn't allowed to know.

"I'm not a fragile flower. I have powers that need to be tamed just as much as these two do. I'm tired of being an afterthought when it comes to anything that has to do with saving this universe. Do you know what my nightmare was? I was trapped and unable to help anyone else and had to watch every person I cared about die before my eyes. If you want to leave me vulnerable, fine. I will find someone who will train me the decent way."

I stood from the ground and dusted my outfit off. I picked up my duffle bag and headed toward the closest portal to the mortal world I could see.

"Where are you going?" Xavier demanded.

"Anywhere but here with you all," I replied.

"You can't enter without my help," Gwendolyn stated softly.

"Newsflash, I have Seelie blood running through my veins. I can go anywhere I damn well please," I shouted as I drew closer to the portal.

"Fine. No one wanted you here anyway," Xavier yelled. "They wanted to leave you with Mab and do this journey with just me, but I told them to bring you. This is why. You're a spoiled brat."

I couldn't stop myself. It was all coming out, and I just couldn't stop. I snapped around to face him.

"Coming from the one that has everything handed to him on a golden platter. The one that had training at his disposal. The one who lived his life in the Summit. Yes, it must be so difficult to be you. Poor you. Your mother wanted to look for our brother instead of being around you. Well, guess what? I didn't have our mother, either. Damian didn't have our mother. And before we could even meet her, she was gone. And the ONLY person in this miserable universe that gave a damn about me is in the clutches of Alpha. My father, the one who does love me more than life itself. The one that selflessly has taken care of me for years. So, yes. I am *totally* the spoiled brat here. I'm the spoiled brat that has been left defenseless against ANYTHING! If you would take the silver spoon out of your mouth and stop pointing fingers at everyone, you just might see that."

My face was hot and red. Xavier's nostrils flared with anger. "Just go!" he demanded.

"Gladly, but one thing you must know before I do leave," I started as I turned back to the portal, not even sure how I knew what I was about to say. "All three of us must meet Starfire, or she won't help any of us. We all must be there. So good luck on your hunt for nothing."

I stepped through the portal and landed on a sandy beach. There was nothing but sand and water for miles. I turned around to find trees upon trees behind me. There was a huge mountaintop with a pillar of smoke coming from it. Someone must be here. Maybe they can help me hide out until the end of the world. Even as I thought the words, I just sat on the ground in defeat as tears began to bubble to the surface.

"Your father was right. You do have a temper," Damian said as he sat down on the ground beside me.

"What are you doing here?" I asked, swiping at the tears and wiping them from my face so he wouldn't see them.

"I couldn't let you wander off on your own. What kind of a protector do you think I am?" he asked, nudging me lightly with his arm.

"I was sure you would be tagging along with the others to who knows where," I replied.

"Right now, they're arguing about whether you were right with everything you said," he said. "You're right, at least I think so. They should have been training both of you, not just singling one out to be the greatest of all."

"They were most likely training him to kill you, and they knew I wouldn't," I replied.

"Fair enough, but still not fair to you," he remarked back. "I think you have a greater chance of taking me out than anyone."

"Oh, I do?" I asked with a choked laugh, still wiping the tears from my face that flowed relentlessly.

"Yes," he replied. "There's no way I could ever hurt you. Not to even protect myself." He wiped a straggling tear away.

We both stared at each other as that familiar feeling began to stir once more in my belly. I quickly stood from my seat on the ground and pointed off into the distance where I had seen the smoke wafting up.

"Who do you think that is?" I asked.

"Most likely Starfire," Gwendolyn replied. "I'm surprised you found the right portal. I would have taken us through so many different ones that it would have taken much longer to reach her. Impressive job."

She offered me a smile, an apologetic one. I nodded an affirmation of apology accepted. I watched as Xavier and Praeziel stepped through the portal as well. Xavier scowled at me and refused to acknowledge me after that point. So much for true love, eh? Damian snorted. Eavesdropping again, I see.

I can reply as well, but only to my favorite people, he replied in my head. I smiled and felt the tension melt from my shoulders.

"So, are you three ready to meet the game-changer?" Praeziel asked.

"As ready as I ever will be," I replied and began to head the group to the smoking mountain.

CHAPTER 3

WE HAD BEEN WALKING for hours and had come no closer to the base of the mountain than what we were when we landed on the beach. The sun beat down on us in the unforgiving, growing palm trees. I had nearly finished the canteen of water that I had filled from the river while in the Otherworld. We slogged on down the path we were following when we came across a boulder I knew for a fact we had already passed.

"We're going in circles," I said, dropping my gear to the ground and plopping down under the shade of a palm tree. "She must have some sort of glamour or force field up."

The rest of the group followed suit, dropping their gear to the ground and sitting down under some shade. I watched them pull their canteens from their bags and drink. I licked my parched lips and gave my canteen a small shake. It had maybe a sip or two left in it. I needed to save it for when I needed it. I stuck the canteen back into my bag when I felt a nudge. I looked over, and Damian was holding his canteen out for me to take a drink.

I shook my head in protest. "You're going to need it," I said, pushing it back toward him.

"Well, it won't do us much good if you die from dehydration," he replied, handing it back to me again.

I took the canteen from him, sighing, knowing that arguing would be futile. I took a swig and handed it back to him. He put the cap back on and placed it back in his bag. We all sat examining our surroundings until Xavier broke the silence with the question we were all thinking.

"So, what do we do now?" he asked. "We can't uncloak our wings, or else we would alert everyone to our location. We can't keep walking in this stupid circle, or we will drop off like flies."

He was right. We were stuck in a situation we had no way out of. As the chatter came for ideas, my gaze lingered on the path we had been on. I stared and stared until a glint of sunlight seemed to bounce off an imaginary wall. I blinked a few times to see if my eyes had been playing tricks on me. The glint was still there. I stood up and walked over to the area that had a slight light reflection to it. I could feel the energy buzzing from it. The hairs on my arms stood up when I got close to it, almost as if it were an electrical current. Dad had taught me how to pick up electrical fields when I was little. He didn't want me getting zapped by fences or walking straight into a power plant. I reached out to touch the wall and was zapped hard by whatever it was Starfire was using as a ward. I fell on my back, and the wind was knocked further out of my lungs.

"Luxina," I heard through a tunnel. There was a ringing in my ears, and all I could do was see the blurred faces over the top of me. I could hear nothing but loud bells. I couldn't even move.

"She isn't breathing," another voice garbled. Hands were on me, pressing my chest while someone else blew air into my lungs. "Stay with me!" I heard voices calling out. "Luxina!" The voices were desperate.

The sounds of the surrounding area came into focus, and I coughed, choked, and gasped for air. Xavier and Damian knelt over me with bewildered faces. I continued to cough and gasp until I felt the air in my lungs become normal.

"What were you thinking?!" Xavier shouted at me.

"I saw the light hit a wall," I squeaked out as I sat up. Pain tore through my body. "What happened?" I asked groggily.

"You were electrocuted by whatever Starfire has up as a ward. You died!" Xavier shouted. "Don't ever do anything without checking with us. Next time, we might not be able to bring you back," he huffed and stalked off down the path.

"Don't wander too far," Praeziel called after him. "This could be a maze."

All he did was flick his hand to dismiss Praeziel and disappeared from view around the bend.

"I really didn't mean for that to happen," I stammered, apologizing. "I thought Starfire was just an oracle. How does she have magical wards up? Wards that electrocute you at that."

"She has to have the aid from warlocks," Gwendolyn replied as she wrapped my hand in a bandage.

I was confused as to why she was wrapping my hand when I glanced down. It was burned badly.

"The ward must react to any type of blood that isn't pure angelic," Praeziel offered as he saw the confusion on my face. "All three of you have the injections still swirling in your blood."

"Then, how do we even get to her?" Damian asked.

"I don't know. I wasn't expecting this at all," Praeziel replied. "We will rest here until we can come up with some sort of plan."

Damian nodded and looked at me as Gwendolyn finished the wraps on my hand. A faint memory of him and Xavier bent over me after Alpha gave me the injections came to mind.

"Get away from her," Xavier had said. *"She's my sister, too!"* echoed in my mind.

This time, however, they worked side by side to ensure that I was ok. In the haze I still felt from the electrocution, a very faint memory came to light. It was during one of our dreams Xavier and I had together when we met in the meadow. I remember running and tumbling through the flowers when I caught a glimpse of someone else who was there. But as fast as I saw the person, they vanished. All I remembered was red hair, curly red hair, peeking out from behind the tree in the middle of the meadow. Damian's eyes met mine, and they held a moment of vulnerability.

You were always there, weren't you? Watching us, making sure we were safe... I thought to him.

Yes, he replied, then stood, turned in the direction Xavier had gone, and followed him.

I wished my dad was here. He would know what to do right now. I sat helplessly and hopelessly, waiting for Damian and Xavier to return. I watched the force field shimmer as the sun set on the horizon. Fireflies began to emerge, and their floating lights made me miss my dad even more. We got our nicknames from Mother. She called him Firefly. He called me Firefly. Xavier and I called each other fireflies. There had to be more to the nickname, though. Fireflies didn't flit around with fire in their wake. And when we do use our powers, our eyes glow like the sun... like fireflies...

"Maybe..." I thought out loud instead of to myself.

"Maybe what?" Praeziel asked as he began to work on a fire for the night.

"Nothing. It's just a stupid afterthought," I replied.

"Maybe it is, maybe it isn't," he offered.

"We were called fireflies for nicknames because of our fire power. But what if that isn't the real reason for the nickname? We're the Shining Ones... we have to be able to harness the glow from the inside out without fire being used," I explained.

Praeziel stopped what he was doing and stared at me. "That might actually be the answer," he murmured, lost in thought.

"What might be the answer?" Xavier asked as he and Damian popped back up.

"Luxina, explain it to them," Praeziel stated and got up from the fire he was building. "I need to find Gwendolyn." As always, she had gone off to hunt for food.

"I was watching the fireflies' glow and thinking about our nicknames being fireflies. Whenever you two have used your powers, your eyes glow this bright golden color as if the sun were to burst through your eyes. We must be able to harness the power of our fire without bringing it forth and using it," I explained to Xavier and Damian.

They both took a seat beside me and mulled over what I had said. Xavier was the first to speak.

"How do we do that, though?" he asked.

"I have no idea," I replied, slumping and propping my chin on my hand.

"Yes, you do," Damian said quietly.

"What?" I asked, not understanding where he was going.

"Remember the apocalyptic nightmare you had the other day?" he asked.

I nodded.

"We were together in the dream, but we weren't close enough to save each other, right?" he asked.

"Right," I replied. And then the idea struck me. "We have to be together to activate it."

Damian offered his hands to both Xavier and me to hold. We each grabbed his hand and then grabbed each other's remaining hand. Energy erupted through us. This was far greater than the sensation I felt whenever I held Xavier's hand. This was something else. I could feel the energy jumping from Damian to Xavier and then to me and continuing around and around in a circle. Our bodies began to glow, and we were lifted from our seated position on the ground into the air as lights began to swirl around us like a twister. I looked at Damian and Xavier's faces and saw their eyes glowing as I had earlier in the day. Light orbs materialized from our kis and slowly moved toward the center of the circle we had created.

27

They joined together, forming one large ball light that shot straight into the sky and exploded. The now dark island was lit up like the sun was up. The night became full day as the light show erupted into a full spectrum of colors swirling above. I felt the energy receding, and we slowly floated back to the ground and released one another's hands.

Praeziel came bounding up behind. "What was that?!" he shouted as Gwendolyn caught up to him.

"That was the Shining Ones," an unknown voice replied.

Our heads jerked in the direction we had heard the voice come from and saw a tiny, quaint woman standing there with a giant man at her side. She couldn't be but maybe five feet tall while her escort was at least seven feet. He towered over us, staring hard into our faces.

"Don't just stand there. That light show you just put on will alert every single creature that speaks, and word will get to Alpha where we are. Come now," she said and turned around to walk through the force field that had electrocuted me.

"Wait!" I started to shout and watched as she passed through it easily.

"The field is down," she said as if to answer my forming question. "Now, come along." She glanced at Praeziel and Gwendolyn. "All of you."

We followed her, and once we passed through the barrier that had been up, our eyes widened in surprise and awe. It was an oasis inside the barrier. The whole island was apparently a glamour. We could see for miles as we stood upon a cliff. There were waterfalls and jungles. A rainforest went on end throughout the valley that lay below us. Rainbows filled the sky as birds danced through the clouds.

"Where are we?" I asked, breathlessly taking in the sights.

"This place is called Lightshade. It's home to all warlocks," Starfire replied with a shimmering grin. "It never gets dark here. There is always sunshine to remind the warlocks that peace exists. They weren't always privy to this place. Before they banded together to escape the clutches of the mortal world, they lived in darkness. The place they used to call home was nothing but an abyss. It was called Shadowmaw. Alpha had cursed them into hiding. When my family found them, they offered them an oasis away from people and Alpha, where they would never be found again. We took Sable Island and helped them put up a glamour so no one would be able to find the island on the seas again. From there, they built this paradise for their children to grow and learn what they can do with their magic."

"It's beautiful!" I breathed.

"Follow me, and I will show you where I live," Starfire stated as she began to lead us down a winding path from the cliff.

Exotic flowers I had never seen before bloomed on either side of the path and seemed to have a glow of their own as we traipsed down the hill following behind Starfire. Purples, pinks, and blue foliage lined the pathway, and it almost looked as if they reached out for us as we passed by.

"Will any of the plants here hurt us?" I asked as I examined the exotic breeds bending to touch us.

"No, unlike the plants and water in the Otherworld, nothing here is dangerous," Starfire replied. "A lot of these plants themselves possess magical powers that, when ingested, help aid the warlocks with their magic. Some are herbs that we use to treat illnesses or aid in magical workings. Then others are just for beauty." She stopped to smell some type of rose bush that was growing off to the right of the path. It had unusual color blooms on each stem that were colors I had never seen before. "Sometimes, you just need a little beauty in your life to remind you why you're important to the grand design."

As we walked, I continued to ask questions. "Did all the warlocks come here from Shadowmaw?"

A grim expression filled her face. "No, they did not. There were many who stayed behind. The idea of leaving behind their dark magic was too much for them to bear. So, they stayed," she replied sadly.

We rounded a bend, and there was a quaint cottage on the edge of the path that Starfire walked up to. She motioned for all of us to walk inside with her. From the looks on the outside, there was no way we would all fit in there comfortably, but once we stepped inside, we realized magic was still at work. Inside the cottage, it looked like a mansion. Rooms upon rooms were stacked with different things. She had a room full of magical books and another room that had a chemistry set constructed, most likely for making potions.

"And you're still just an oracle?" Xavier asked with a chuckle.

She shrugged her shoulders. "What can I say? I like to dabble in magic," she laughed. "I have plenty of rooms for you each to have your own instead of having to double up. There's plenty of food and water available in the kitchen and pantry. It has been a busy day, and I am sure you all are very tired after traveling as much as you have been. Pick a room and get rested. We have very little time to doddle. You have one more adventure to set forth on before I can begin to train you fully."

With that last comment, she retired to her own room and shut the door behind herself.

"Well, I don't know about all of you, but I am starving," Gwendolyn said as she started down the hall toward the kitchen.

We all rubbed our stomachs in agreement as they growled. My eyes scanned the rooms as we made our way down the long hall toward where Starfire kept her food. I was well-accustomed to a kitchen since I grew up mostly acting like a human child. Everyone began to pick through the pantry to find something to eat. She had everything you could dream of in there. Fresh vegetables, meat, dessert. My mouth salivated as I eyed a plate of macaroons. It had been so long since I had delighted in sugar that I nearly pushed people out of my way to get to the plate.

"You know sugar will kill you one day, right?" Damian asked, chuckling.

"Then, I will die happy," I replied as I stuffed two macaroons in my mouth at once. "Try one," I mumbled through the crumbs that escaped my lips as I talked with a full mouth.

"And I believe I lost my appetite," Xavier replied.

I made a face, and everyone laughed. We gorged ourselves sitting around a table merrily. Food was slim pickings while we had been journeying. It was mostly foraged berries, if there were any, and whatever we could find for meat. Starfire had pallets of berries, cheeses, loaves of bread, everything I missed while searching for her. We all cleaned up the mess we had made and headed up the stairs to find a room to crash in. A sudden panic overcame me as I realized this would be the first time in a year that I wouldn't have company right beside me in a circle around the fire. As Praeziel and Gwendolyn slipped off into the rooms they had chosen, I stopped Xavier as Damian entered a room at the end of the hall.

"Mind if we bunk together tonight?" I asked, not trying to sound too desperate.

He glanced between the bedroom he had chosen and me as if debating what he should do.

"Not tonight," he replied as he went to walk into his room.

"What did I do?" I asked, stepping closer to him. "If I said something or did something that was out of line or that offended you, please, just let me know. I don't like being locked out, and you have had me shut out for so long now…"

"I can't do this right now, Luxina," Xavier said, stepping further into the room.

"Why? Why are you shutting me out? What are you afraid of?" I demanded.

He was quiet for a moment before he answered, closing the door. "Every time we are close together, people die."

The door closed in my face, and I felt the tears welling behind my eyes with a knot of anxiety building in my chest. All the doors were shut with people behind them, not fearing things the way I did. I had never spent a day in my life alone. I always had my dad, and when I was taken, I had Xavier. And even when I didn't have him, I still had the comfort of having Praeziel and Gwendolyn around the circle with me. I walked numbly to the room in between Damian and Xavier and entered it, closing the door quietly behind me. I stared at the inviting bed that called to me to come and lie in it. I couldn't make it there, though. I slunk to the floor at the door, pulled my knees to my chest, and buried my head in my arms, rocking gently back and forth.

Was it true? Am I the reason everyone dies? Had it not been for Xavier taking me to Stygia, those who died or were captured would not have been put in that position had I not been taken there. Was our mother's death my fault as well? How many others have pledged their lives to keep us safe and out of harm's way? We have forged alliances with the fey and with the Watchers. We saw what happened to the Watchers. Would the same fate come to the Seelie and Unseelie courts for aiding us? Will there be no end to Alpha's revenge? How many people and creatures would have to die to stop this inevitable war?

I was too afraid to close my eyes alone. The memory of the nightmarish prophecy still echoed in my mind from the previous night. I sat underneath the window that was enchanted to filter in moonlight instead of the ever-shining sun outside. A light knock at the door jolted me from my thoughts. I stood and walked to the door, cracking it open. Damian stood on the other side with a sympathetic look in his eyes.

"Can't sleep?" he asked.

I shook my head and opened my door wider for him to walk in. "I don't ever want to sleep again," I replied, closing the door after him.

"I couldn't agree more with that statement," he said as he plopped on the bed.

Instead of sitting down beside him, I paced the floor as his eyes watched me go back and forth. A million different things ran through my tired mind. Questions of how we were going to pull this off and pull that off tugged and pulled at me until I was exasperated with everything. I was too anxious to sleep, and even though I was tired, my body wanted to do something else instead of sleep. I turned to Damian, who sat perched on the bed like a cat waiting for attention.

"Train me?" I asked, raising my eyebrow up. "There's no sleep in sight for me. Unless, of course, you want to sleep, then no worries."

He stood from the bed with a smile. "I thought you would never ask," he replied.

We opened the door, and I quietly waited outside of his room while he gathered some weapons from his bag. When he emerged and closed his door behind him, we tiptoed down the hall, made our way down the stairs, and bounded outside into the midday sun. We chose a spot in front of the cabin that had bare ground, so we didn't mess up any of the grass or plants and also in case someone came searching for us.

"Alright, what first?" I asked as I placed myself in front of him.

"Let's start with the basics first. Hand to hand combat," he replied. He held up his hands, palms facing outward. "I want you to punch my hands."

"Easy enough," I said.

I squared my body off and threw alternating jabs into his hands.

"Not bad," he said. "For a three-year-old." He laughed and ducked as I threw a punch at the side of his head. "You must anticipate your enemy. Have you ever played chess?" he asked.

"Yeah, Dad taught me when I was little," I replied. "How does that help in punching?"

"Hand to hand combat is like a chess game. You must plan for what your enemy will do five steps ahead of you. You must learn their maneuvers and use them against them. Swing at me again."

I did as instructed, and he blocked my arm with his hand.

"Now block mine," he said.

He swiped at me, and I mimicked the move he made, knocking his punch away before it could land anywhere.

"The best offense is a good defense," he said with a devilish grin. "Alright, I am going to hold my hands up again, and you're going to punch at them. I want two left jabs and one right."

I nodded. He held his hands up, and I delivered the two left jabs and the right jab.

"Again," he demanded.

I obliged. Two left jabs and a right.

"Again!" he demanded.

Two left jabs and a right.

He swiped his right hand out, and I ducked out of the punch.

"Again!" he demanded.

Soon, we fell into a rhythm. Two left jabs and a right, swoop, duck. By instinct, after I ducked, I lifted my leg and swung it around. He caught it in midair and chuckled.

"Can we hold off on throwing other body parts into this? We must get you mobile before we start the fun stuff." He grinned in delight. It looked as if teaching me really brought out the spirit that looked broken when he first arrived. "Ok, so next. We are going to Tango while you throw jabs. Jab, step; jab, step; jab, step, swoop, duck, then jab. Got it?"

"Uh-huh," I replied with a nod.

I jabbed with my left hand while stepping forward with my right foot, and he mimicked my steps. This time, he advanced toward me while I threw my jabs. We practiced this a few times until I was moving with grace.

"Faster!" he demanded.

We moved back and forth in the circle we had made. I would advance punching, and he would push back. He caught me by surprise and tossed out a punch I wasn't expecting. He caught me in the cheek with it. I didn't stop, though. I kept going, and the next time the surprise punch came, I was ready and blocked it, delivering a blow of my own to him.

"Nice!" he exclaimed. "Now, you can throw in those legs."

We quickened our pace with the jabs, ducks, feet moving, legs kicking. I was having fun. Why hadn't anyone done this with me before?

"They looked at you like a girl that needed protection as opposed to an angel warrior like you are," he replied.

"Well, they should know better," I said, still jabbing and moving. "What did they expect me to do? Sit by all pretty-like on the sidelines, hoping no one came my way?"

"Pretty much," he replied with a small shrug of the shoulders. "I mean, they had the best intentions at heart. They just wanted to keep you safe. A promise that Praeziel made to Incaendiel."

"What's next?" I asked.

"Ready to learn backflips?" he asked in reply, stripping his shirt off.

"Um," I was able to get out when he lifted off in the air, sailing backward, and landed steadily on his feet.

His skin glistened in the sun as sweat beaded along his torso. That was clearly a distraction to me. I shook my head a bit to get my mind back in training. Instead of a back tuck like he did, I did a standing back handspring back tuck. He cocked his head to the side in confusion.

"I did gymnastics at one of the schools," I replied with a proud smile.

"You're just FULL of surprises, aren't you?" he asked, a stealthy grin spreading. "Alright, utilize everything they taught you in gymnastics.

Cartwheels, back tucks, back springs, all of it. Don't forget to keep your feet moving, jab, parry, block, and duck."

"Got it, teach," I replied, throwing a jab his way.

We moved around the circle, almost as if we were dancing. The moves were so rhythmic and methodical. I could read his body language and ascertain what his next move would be to appropriate my next move.

"You were right," I said, a bit breathless. "It is like a game of chess."

I threw a punch, and he ducked down, kicking out his leg and spinning it toward me. I jumped over it and did a backflip out of the way. He was on me no sooner than my feet hit the ground, and I ducked out of the way of his swooping arm. I spun my leg around and caught his legs, knocking him from his feet. He didn't land on his back, though. Instead, he barrel-rolled into a crouch. We ran at each other, throwing jabs, parrying, ducking, neither one of us landing any hits.

"Oh, I enjoy this," he remarked, swinging his leg at me as I tucked and rolled, kicking out with my leg.

"This is so exhilarating!" I exclaimed.

"Of course, it is. It's in your blood," he replied.

He picked up two of the small pen-like things he had when he fought the werewolves. He clicked a button, and they burst into swords.

"Ready for some weapons training?" he asked.

"I thought you would never ask," I replied with a laugh.

He walked the sword over and handed it to me.

"Sword fighting is terribly like hand-to-hand combat with the exception you are using an object and not your hands. So, you throw the sword the way you would your hands. You use the sword to parry as you did with your hands. And of course, duck."

I nodded in acknowledgment. He brought his sword up with both hands on the hilt. I positioned my hands the same way.

"Now, swing your sword at me," he stated.

I did as I was told and swung the sword around, bringing it down over my head at him. He parried the sword with his.

"Nice form!" he praised. "Now, again. Except this time, come from the other side. It will be left, right, left just like with your jabs."

I planted my feet firmly apart and swung the sword the same exact way but in the opposite direction, and it landed neatly on his parrying sword. I repeated. My moves became faster, and soon our feet were moving the same way we had during the hand-to-hand combat.

"Do you have two smaller ones?" I asked. "This one is large and tires me out really quickly. Maybe two smaller ones I could move with agility."

He lifted two of the pens from his pocket and handed them to me. He clicked the button on the side of the sword, and it capsized back down into the pen-sized instrument it had been. I clicked the buttons on the sides of the ones he handed me, and two medium-sized swords appeared. I balanced the weight of each in my hands.

"These feel much better," I said, testing them in the air.

"It's because you're a double hander," he replied.

"What's that?" I asked.

"You work better with a weapon in each hand."

I lifted the swords in my hand and leapt toward him. I came down on his sword, and he pushed me back and then proceeded to bombard me with his sword. I worked my blades smoothly and carelessly, getting swifter as I parried his attack. He ducked down and swooped his leg that I jumped over. We continued. I moved my hands like I was painting the sky. I would duck, weave, bombard, parry, and repeat.

We each took a step back and clicked the swords back into place. I went to hand the swords back to him when he raised his hand, shaking it.

"Keep them. You earned them," he said breathlessly. "I haven't had a sparring buddy in a while, and you best even the greater demons. I was putting in effort in that last five minutes."

"Well, thank you... I think." I grinned in satisfaction. "Now, what about my powers? Can you teach me to hone them?"

He walked over to me and turned me around to face the opposite direction. He put one hand on my stomach and his other hand on my arm.

"You feel it from there," he said in my ear, shivers erupting over my body. "But instead of letting it burst through your whole body, you channel the flames to here," he said, running his hand down my arm to my fingertips.

My heart raced as his light touch stopped on my hand. His voice was light and sweet, caring.

"Give it a try," he whispered.

I felt the burn in my stomach and felt the heat rise from my skin. "What if I hurt you?" I whispered in return.

"You can't hurt me," he replied as his hands cooled to freezing temperatures.

My heat ran up through my chest, through my arm, and out of my fingers. A torch of fire sprayed from my hand, and I panicked. I didn't know how to stop.

"Now, bring it back gently," he whispered.

I pulled the fire back in the way Praeziel had shown me and stopped when the flames reached my hand. He ran his cold hand through the fire before I could protest.

"See," he said. "You can't hurt me."

I watched as his hand danced in the ball of fire in my hand. I glanced out of the corner of my eye at his face. It was so intent, but yet so serene. He turned toward me and caught my eye. We were caught in a gaze for just a moment before he broke it. He dropped his hands from my body as the fire disappeared in my hands.

"Well, you passed the training. I would give you a card, but I'm fresh out," he chided.

"She did more than pass training," Starfire said, walking out of her door. "She learned what her blood was meant to do. The power that rests inside all of you is so much more than just fire and ice." She gazed at me hard. "Would you like to spar with a few of my men? Show them what you learned? They won't take it easy on you."

I saw a flash of irritation cross Damian's face. Was he jealous?

"Sure," I replied. "Will they be using magic?"

"Of course," she replied with a grin.

She snapped her fingers, and a young man materialized in front of me. He was about my age. He was olive-skinned, with dark cat-like eyes. His hair was spiked with metallic green. He wielded two swords in his hands. I brought my swords out and clicked the buttons. He grinned at me when his swords burst into a purple glow. That must be the magic he uses. I readied myself when he made the first move. His blades sliced through the air like butter as I parried and blocked his attacks. I methodically moved around as Damian had taught me. One of his blades nicked my arm, and red bubbled to the surface of my skin.

"Oh, you shouldn't have done that," I said coolly.

I watched his eyes widen in surprise with a hint of fear. I pulled the heat through my body the way Damian had shown me. Except when it got to my hands, I funneled it into my swords. They burst into flames on the blades, and I advanced on my target. I swiped through the air faster and faster, backing him into a corner. I pointed the blades at his throat until he dropped his swords in defeat.

"Now THAT was awesome," Xavier said, breaking the silence of the fight.

I shook the young man's hand before he disappeared as quickly as he had appeared. I walked back over to Starfire, snuffing the fire out on my swords before putting them away.

"Now, you are ready, Shining One," Starfire said with a grin. "Are you ready for the quest?"

She looked around at Damian and Xavier, and then her eyes rested on me.

"Yes," we all said in unison.

"Good, because only you three will be able to go," she replied. "Praeziel and Gwendolyn cannot go where you have to go."

Praeziel and Gwendolyn stood off on the porch with solemn faces.

"We thought it would be best if she told you," Praeziel said.

"Where are we going?" I asked quizzically.

She smiled deeply. "Why, my dear, you're going to Atlantis."

CHAPTER 4

Damian, Xavier, and I geared up for our journey. Xavier and Damian pilfered through the weapons available to take. Damian grabbed his sword, a bow and arrow quiver, and a mace that he strapped to his back. Xavier picked up a sword, a throwing axe, and some ninja stars that worked as boomerangs. I had the swords that Damian gave me. As we packed to leave, the young man I had sparred against appeared within the cottage and bowed to me.

"I want you to take my blades," he said.

He held out the two hand knives that he hadn't used earlier. I examined them closely and saw they wrapped around your hand as brass knuckles would and that the blade curved on the outside of your hand. I picked them up from his hands, and they immediately sprouted the purple haze that he had used. I smiled in appreciation.

"Thank you," I said. "What's your name?"

"My name, I do not know. I was just a baby when I came to the island with Starfire. My parents stayed behind in Shadowmaw. The name Starfire gave me is Reilak. My parents were necromancers, so the name fits," he replied.

"Thank you, Reilak." I bowed my head in appreciation, and he stepped away to stand beside Starfire.

I placed the hand knives around my palms and fitted them over the top of my hands. They were snug like gloves, almost as if they were made specifically for me. Starfire walked around and handed us each a red hat. I frowned, staring at what she gave us.

"What are these?" I asked.

"They're called red caps. They are what merfolk use to swim and breathe in the water. Merfolk are not like mermaids. They actually live quite like humans except at the bottom of the ocean in a bubble-type fortress," she explained. "This is how you will swim to Atlantis. Don't put it on until you are ready to dive into the water, or else you will drown above ground. It gives you gills."

I tucked the cap into the back of my pants. She had given us all new clothes to wear. I wasn't enthused when she handed me an outfit that was leather. When I put it on, it grabbed my body in all the places I had never shown off before. My breasts were noticeable as well as my butt. The top was too short, and my belly button showed. No matter how I tugged it down or my pants up, neither covered that area, and it made me feel a tiny bit insecure.

"What are we looking for?" Damian asked.

"Once you get to the city of Atlantis, you will come to a dome that surrounds the city underwater. You must hold hands to walk through the dome. On the inside, remove the red caps as there won't be water but rather air for you to breathe. Hidden within the grand city is a chalice that has a white powder in it. Put the chalice in this bag," she said, handing us a satchel. "This material is specifically woven to shrink around the contents it holds, making an airtight seal. Water will not get in the chalice, and the contents will not spill out. When you get to the surface, blow on this," she said, handing over a seashell. "It will alert me to send the portal to bring you back."

"That seems easy enough," Xavier replied, taking the shell from her hand.

She looked at him gravely. "Be careful and mindful of whatever you encounter below the waters. The seas are filled with all kinds of creatures that mean to do you harm, mermaids especially. Since the sinking of Atlantis, they have claimed the place as their own. Mermaids were created by Alpha and are not the fairytale creatures you think them to be. If you must, kill them to escape."

All three of us exchanged glances and nodded in unison.

"Alright, Reilak. Make the portal," Starfire stated.

The young boy did a magical dance with his hands as they began to glow the same color purple the knives had been imbued with. He began to circle them around and around, and a translucent whirlwind circle appeared. We gazed through it, amazed. Unlike the faery portals that didn't show what was on the side, this portal showed us exactly where we would be stepping foot. There was rocky ground with waves crashing against it.

"Step through the portal, put on your red caps, and dive deep. Use this," she said, handing us each a necklace with a bright-colored stone on it. "These are special faery amulets and will glow in the dark."

We tied the necklaces around our necks and stepped through the portal. It disappeared behind us, and we found ourselves on a rocky beach area. Off in the distance, we could see a sailboat that I could only assume was used for fishing.

"Where exactly are we?" Xavier asked.

"Somewhere in the Mediterranean near Greece," Damian replied. "Don't you two read mythologies?"

"Yes," I replied. "We also know that the lost city of Atlantis was inhabited by a superior alien race created by older gods than Alpha."

"I see you listened intently when Sophia explained everything to you," he said, smirking. He fished his red cap out of the back of his pants. "You two ready? I don't like being out in the open and exposed like this."

Xavier and I grabbed our red caps from our pants as well, and we all put them on at the same time and then dived into the crashing waves. We began to sink when a slight panic took over me. I didn't know if the red caps were working yet or not, and I refused to drag in a breath of air under the water.

"Luxina, breathe!" Damian exclaimed through the underwater current.

I gulped in seawater and realized to my embarrassment that the red caps were indeed working properly.

"We can talk underwater?" I asked.

"It's all part of the enchantment on the red caps," Damian explained. "Let's go."

We swam, descending deeper and deeper into the ocean waters. The deeper we went, the less I could see the sun shining through the water. When darkness was just about to envelop us, the stones around our necks began to shine a bright, luminescent light. Each of our lights was a different color based on the color of the stone she had handed us. As soon as the dark depths were illuminated with our lights, and we could see again, there were behemoth creatures all around us that made strange noises under the water.

"They're whales," Damian explained. "They won't hurt us."

We swam alongside the massive creatures as they wailed in their language, talking to one another. We swam atop a large underground garden that had flowers with floating petals, long strings of grass, and colorful rocks that glowed like our necklaces.

"It's called a reef. The rocks are called corrals. The flowers are called sea anemones, and the grass is called seaweed. All these things are living creatures," Damian said.

I watched an orange and white fish pop out of what he called a sea anemone and float back in. It kept repeating the action before it came completely out and swam off along with the other creatures among the reefs. I saw things shaped like stars and pointy little round balls.

"Those are called urchins. Don't touch them. They're poisonous," Damian warned. "The other is called a starfish." He pointed to a little creature that looked like a mixed dragon-horse. "That's called a seahorse."

"How do you know all this?" I asked in wonder.

"I read a lot in my spare time," he replied.

Under the sea was a whole other world of enchantment, almost as if it existed apart from the mortal world. All kinds of sea creatures swirled around together, swimming absentmindedly as we passed by. It was just as breathtaking as when Starfire brought us to Lightshade. As we swam, the creatures took note of us and watched us curiously. A tiny little thing swam up to me and stayed beside me as we descended deeper into the water. It was followed by another and then another. Soon, I was surrounded by these teeny, little creatures. They looked a bit like fish, but they had faces.

"Damian, what are these?" I asked a bit nervously as more and more began to show up and circle me as we swam.

No sooner had I asked him than they all bared nasty, sharp little fangs.

"Luxina, swim as fast as you can away from them!" Damian shouted. "They're baby mermaids."

I picked up my speed, and the little creatures nipped and bit at my feet. I pushed myself harder as we all tried to outswim the bloodthirsty things. I felt my hand tugged and noticed Damian had grabbed hold of it and was pulling me faster away from the cloud of mermaids as they viciously snapped and bit, trying to mangle my feet.

"We must be getting close to the underwater kingdom," Damian said. "We have to be on the lookout. There will be all kinds of monsters protecting the entrance."

"If those are baby mermaids, where are the parents?" Xavier asked nervously.

"Let's hope we don't find out," Damian replied. "Mermaids are nastier than Starfire let on. It's why she said if we have to, kill them. They were made from the blood of Seelies and the venom of vampires, then mixed with demon blood. They are vile things and will eat you alive."

"I thought those were called sirens?" I asked as we gained momentum through the waters, catching a natural current.

"Sirens are far worse," Damian replied. "They sing you a song to lull you into sleep and then devour your body as you lay there, helplessly locked in a sweet nightmare."

We topped over a bank of tall seaweed when a glow deep in the water caught my eye.

"Is that?" I began to ask.

"Atlantis," Damian finished. "It's so deep down that no human would ever be able to find it."

As we grew closer to the glowing light, a creepy feeling came over me as if we were being watched. It was the kind of feeling that made my hair stand on end. The water buzzed with an energy unlike any I had ever felt.

"Do you two feel that?" I asked as we grew closer to the kingdom.

"Yes," Xavier replied, looking around in the darkness.

"I don't like this," Damian replied. "This feels off."

We continued to swim, expecting the light to grow bigger, but it was almost as if no matter how fast or hard we swam, the light still remained a reasonable distance off. We slowed our underwater pace and began to take note of our surroundings. There wasn't a single fish or creature that we could see. It was a dead wasteland under here.

"I don't like this at all," Damian repeated.

"Yeah, you said that," Xavier replied nervously. "Woah! Did you see that?"

"See what?" Damian asked, looking around nervously.

"It looked like some huge blanket of darkness that passed by on my left," he replied. "There it is again!" he shouted, pointing to the right of me.

Damian and I caught a glimpse of it. Damian readied his sword, and Xavier and I followed suit.

"What is that thing?" I asked, looking nervously all around me.

"I don't know, but I'm sure it thinks we are dinner," Damian replied slowly edging forward.

I caught whatever it was on my right when Xaiver and Damian yelled at the same time, "It's on my left."

"It can't be. I just saw it on my right," I protested.

We drew closer to the light, and the water around us fell dead silent. There wasn't an air bubble, a ripple, or a current. Damian motioned to his lips with his finger for us to be quiet.

No more talking. Use your thought speech, he commanded.

Ok, I replied.

No argument from me, Xavier said.

In the beginning, Alpha created night and day. He created land and sea, Damian began.

Yeah, we know the creation story, Xavier interrupted.

And in the sea, Damian continued, *held a behemoth that no man could ever survive. He had slain the great god of the abyss, Tiamat, and cast her into the sea, creating what scriptures called Leviathan.*

No sooner had he uttered the name from the scriptures than a howl erupted through the waters. A tentacle ripped through the water as we all scrambled to dodge the assault the beast began to commence. I watched as Damian parried with his sword, but I couldn't bring myself to hurt the poor creature that Alpha had created. Blood soaked through the seawater as they chopped and hacked the tentacles that flew to them, trying to grab them unsuspecting. As I stood watching the boys fight off the tentacles with their weapons, I hadn't realized that one of them was wrapped around my foot. It gave a hard jerk, and I was lifted off through the water.

"Do you think you are worthy of the treasure that lies in wait at Atlantis, you puny little angel?" it bellowed.

"Tiamat, wife of Drac?" I asked.

The leviathan stopped the assault, and the boys swam up to me and grabbed hold of my hands, pulling me from the grip the tentacle had on me.

"You know who I am?" she asked.

"At first, no. I just knew you were Leviathan until I ran the first name Damian had called you. Tiamat. I remember the story when Alpha created the heavens and the earth. When he created all his angels, the universe began to cave in on itself. He went to the Elder Gods to seek an answer. He came to you. He didn't like your answer but did it anyway. When it failed his power trip, he punished you. He stole you away from your own universe that toppled without you. The universe that was already growing old and dying that you were sustaining. He took you away before you could get all your creations off to safety. Those that were led to safety hid in plain sight here in Atlantis. You continue to protect your people from Alpha. Do you want your revenge? Help us!" I called.

"Who are you?" Tiamat asked, slithering through the water closer to me. "You're like angels, but not. Your blood runs thick with fire and ice."

"We are the Shining Ones," I replied. "The ones you helped create, so in extension, we are your people."

"Ah," she replied with a smile to her voice. "You are Sophie and Incaendiel's children." She looked at Damian. "Except you. You are only half-blood. Sophie's son, I presume?" she asked.

"Yes," he replied.

"What do you seek in Atlantis?" she asked.

"The chalice," Xavier replied. "We were sent by the Oracle Starfire to retrieve it. It's to complete our disenchantment."

"Yes, the enchantment," Tiamat mused. "I told Omega when she made Sophie and Incaendiel to give them all the power and not to hide it. It would have saved a lot of devastation and pain had she done what I said. She feared Alpha would destroy them, so she hid what they were."

"Will you let us pass? So, we can forever take down Alpha and put an end to his reign?" I asked.

"Do you understand what you are getting from Atlantis?" Tiamat asked.

"Just that it's a chalice full of a white powdery substance," Xavier replied.

"It's called manna," Tiamat replied. "A gift from the universe, if you wish to call it something. It is what molded us gods into being. Crafted from the molten lava of the brightest star and doused in the white powder, we were forged."

"Then, how does it help us?" I asked. "Won't that make us…"

"A god?" Tiamat finished my sentence. "Of course, my dear. What did you think you were? Just super angels? Omega made herself tiny little gods to take over once her and Alpha's rule ended. Sophie and Incaendiel were to be the new reigning superiors. They are far more powerful than Omega and Alpha combined. The power within you all is as deep and true as the power of all the remaining elder gods."

"So, you will let us pass?" Damian asked.

"I will let you pass on one condition," Tiamat began. "You are to swear to me that you will do whatever it takes to stop Alpha and bring an end to his rule. When he is dethroned, I may return to my abode."

"We want nothing more than to make Alpha pay for everything he has done to ruin this universe," I replied. "We would be more than happy to restore you to the cosmos."

"Then, you may pass, but I must warn you. The water only gets more treacherous past me. Creatures that have no thoughts live here, and they want nothing but one thing: to eat."

Tiamat moved aside so we could continue on our journey.

"Be careful, young Shining Ones. You are the future, and without you, there is no future."

We nodded to her in appreciation and continued past her to our destination, which seemed to grow no closer the further we swam. Her warning echoed in our minds, and we advanced with caution through the treacherous waters. We had no idea what to expect that laid in wait for us. Damian scoured the waters as we swam along with his weapons in hand.

"Luxina, arm yourself with the dueling swords I gave you," he ordered.

I reached to my sides, unhooked the swords from their sheaths, and clicked the activate buttons. The blades blazed under the water to their natural size, but I still had no idea why these would be better than the hand blades that Reikal had given me.

"The weapons I gave you were a gift from the Dark Queen Mab. She took my regular battle blades and turned them into weapons that specifically fought creatures with Seelie blood. They are made from iron and silver," he explained.

"When did you see the Dark Queen?" Xavier asked.

"After my escape from Alpha, I was unable to come directly to you. He had created monsters that followed me from his fortress. Terrifying things that he made me battle. Incaendiel saved me from certain death, and after fighting them for so long while running, the Dark Queen took me to the Otherworld with her. However, it was just a moment of respite. Those things followed me there. I spent quite a while battling through the Nightmares and Shadows realm," he explained.

"That's why you had the dust in your bag and knew what to do when I was attacked," I said. "Why didn't you tell us?"

"There was no time to fill you in completely on my adventures," Damian replied. "There's still so much more that I need to tell you both, but it can wait until after we get what Starfire needs us to acquire."

"What happened to the Otherworld people?" I asked. "Gwendolyn has been preoccupied for some time and not telling us what is bothering her."

"When we get back, I will tell you the whole story. We need to stay focused on this mission," he replied.

I nodded my okay, and we continued to swim through the dark depths. We came to the end of the bottom of the ocean, and it dropped off into some sort of ravine-type trench. Damian motioned for us to look. We followed his gaze, and in the middle of the trench, the great city of Atlantis stood with a grand dome encasing it.

"Look closely," Damian said as he took a knee, watching the waters.

We all looked intently at the waters surrounding the bright light emitted from Atlantis. It had things swimming around the kingdom as if they were protecting it. As we looked closer, we could see the creatures a bit better. The bottom half of their body was a fishtail, and the top half looked almost human.

"Mermaids," I murmured. "Why don't they look like the babies we came across? These... they look absolutely beautiful."

"If you were creating a monster that was deadly, would you want those unsuspecting of its deviant nature to be afraid of it and run away before it had a chance to tear the flesh from their body? Or would you rather they look majestically beautiful, lure those unsuspecting in, and then tear them to shreds?" Damian asked. "Alpha is a grand chess player. When you think you are five steps ahead of him, he is really ten steps ahead of you."

"So, what do we do? There is no way we can slip in undetected. There are too many of them swimming around," I asked.

"We fight our way through," Xavier replied, readying the sword in his hand.

"I don't think I am ready for that," I stammered, gulping down my welling anxiety.

"You will do fine," Damian replied. "Just do what you were doing with me."

I looked to my swords, unsure of myself, with Damian's words echoing in my mind to reassure me. He motioned for us to follow him, and we began our descent into the trench. We tucked our lights beneath our shirts as we grew closer to Atlantis so we didn't alert the mermaids of our approach. We swam through banks of seaweed to hide our approach to the gates of Atlantis. A sudden jerk brought my attention from watching the circling mermaids to the seaweed we were swimming in. My foot had gotten tangled up in the tall strands of the underwater grass. I worked my fingers against the blade, trying to release myself, but the more I struggled with the vine-like grip it had on me, the tighter the tendrils grew.

"Damian, is seaweed a live creature, too?" I whispered as I struggled to untangle myself.

My finger slipped, and the side of seaweed cut me like paper would slice through a finger. It grew tighter around my ankle, cutting it, and another piece grabbed my other leg. I picked up my swords from the bank side, and a tendril snaked over and grabbed me by the wrist. Damian and Xavier were paying me no mind while they waited for me to get untangled, keeping watch with their backs to me.

"A little help, please?" I squeaked as another blade shot out and grabbed me by the torso.

It was as if they couldn't hear me talking. They floated there with their backs turned to me, not speaking nor moving, just watching. The seaweed clenched tighter around me as more and more blades grabbed my body. The tendrils tightened and cut through the clothing. I began to feel myself being pulled closer and closer into the dark roots of the plants. My bones felt like they were being crushed like a snake eating its prey.

"Help!" I screamed louder than I intended.

Damian and Xavier whipped around; however, the two figures that now stood before me were neither of them. They were mermen. They smiled at me, and terror flooded my body as I counted each sharp tooth that was in their mouths.

"Damian! Xavier!" I shouted, struggling against the iron grip I was held in.

More seaweed snaked around my body and began to cover my face.

"The perfect dinner for us tonight, is it not?" one of the mermen asked the other.

"Oh yes, seaweed with a side of angel. Perfectly delectable," he mused.

Just as the seaweed began to cover my eyes, I watched swords slice through their midsections, cutting them neatly in half. Xavier and Damian stood before me with cuts and scrapes of their own. Their blades worked at the seaweed, hacking me from its briny grips. I gasped for air as the blade that had wrapped around my neck, strangling me, released. I clamored from the shallow grave I had nearly found myself in sushi-style.

"Stay out of the seaweed," Damian muttered.

"You don't have to tell me twice," I replied, equally annoyed. "I thought I was surely a goner. I thought you both were still right here with me. What happened?"

"The seaweed grabbed us like you and dragged us down the trench. Our powers are useless under the water," Xavier replied, slicing the final tendril from my leg.

Deep gashes were left behind from where vines had gripped me so hard. Damian inspected them as Xavier stood to watch for other mermaids or mermen to swim by.

"As soon as we get to dry land, we need to get something on that and bandage it," Damian stated. "What worries me is the scent of blood in the water now. We will be swarmed if we don't hurry."

I nodded, and we swam past the seaweed beds, making sure not to get tangled in them anymore. The wound around my ankle was the worst and stung in the seawater. The pain began to grow to an unbearable stabbing feeling. I looked down at my ankle to see if there was poison or something leaching from it, causing the increasing pain. Hundreds of little baby mermaids swarmed my leg, biting at it like little, tiny piranhas. I screamed out in pain as they bit and dragged their teeth across the wounds. Their mouths were too small to tear much skin. Damian and Xavier swam to my side, swiping at the creatures with their swords, but they were too tiny to do any real damage to them.

"There's too many of them," Xavier remarked as they started swarming him and Damian as well.

I didn't wait to argue about whether our powers worked here or not. I grabbed Xavier's hand with a shattering exertion of power as we touched. I built a fire from my belly, and the water began to boil around me. The boil extended a ten-foot radius, killing any and all those little monsters that swam to us. Within minutes, they had all been boiled away, floating from the depths and upwards.

"We were told to use our power together, and this is why," I stated, examining the damage that was done to my leg and ankle.

"We have problems," Damian muttered.

I followed his gaze and looked around the tiny cavern we were floating in front of. Mermaids by the thousands hissed and snarled at us. We had killed their babies, and they were enraged about it. Damian and Xavier grabbed my hands, and we began to swim as fast as we could through the waters as thousands of mermaids swarmed at us. Pure white light enveloped us as our powers as the Shining Ones burst forth. The mermaids kept their distance, still trying to rip us to shreds, but the light was so bright it burned their skin. We swam at speeds I had never gone with more and more mermaids coming at us, attracted, and yet repulsed by the bright light we emitted. They knew what we were, and they wanted to get their hands on us and feast upon our special blood. We barreled through the water at warp speed with the light of Atlantis growing closer and closer. The sea all around us blackened with the bodies of the mermaids that reached out to grab us, retreating their hands as they burned off in the pure white light.

We were almost to the dome when another sea creature swooped in and knocked us apart. Damian and Xavier were more than twenty yards away from me and from each other as well as we tried to come to our senses from the blow. A massive serpent rose to our left and had nine heads.

"What is that?" I asked in alarm, trying to swim to Damian.

A tentacle came down in front of me, blocking my way as I scrambled quickly backward.

"It's the Lernaean Hydra," Damian called out from the other side.

Another tentacle careened down at me as I swam out of its reach, just as it smacked into the ground. I tried making my way to Xavier, but another arm reached out, slamming me to the ground and blocking me. I was trapped by the monster. Arm after arm swooped down around me as I dodged the assault. Behind me waited a barrage of mermaids to rip my flesh from my bones. There was no escape.

The hand knives that Reikal had given me began to glow a bright purplish color. My hands began to move as if controlled by another person. They danced the way Reikal's did when he summoned a portal for Starfire. The water began to swirl around me like a whirlpool. It began to recede around me as the whirlpool grew larger and larger, driving the hydra back from me. The mermaids screeched in anger as they were pushed back away from me, and Damian and Xavier were exposed to the center with me.

"How did you do that?" Damian asked, removing his red cap to breathe.

Xavier followed Damian's lead and removed his red cap, then pulled the one from my head as well.

"I'm not the one doing it," I replied, motioning with my head toward my hands, which were still dancing.

"Will it move with you?" Xavier asked.

I shrugged my shoulders. "It's worth a shot." I began to walk forward as my hands continued to glide and dance through the air. The water kept receding and would fall in behind us as we walked closer to the dome covering Atlantis. We stood before the entrance as I continued to push the water away from us.

"Grab onto my arms and then run," I instructed.

They did as I said, and we ran full force to the dome as the water began to crash down behind us. We were just at the gates when the water pushed us, and we all tumbled as one through the dome that opened and shut quickly, trapping the water outside of it.

Xavier handed me my red cap, which, oddly enough, was completely dry. I stuffed the cap into the back of my pants, and we all surveyed our surroundings. We were standing on a massive land bridge that looked like it stretched at least half a mile across various motes. The city was a huge circle broken into smaller circles the closer you got to the center. The architectural structures were remarkably similar to the old pillar-style Colosseum in Italy and the architecture of ancient standing buildings in Greece. Two-story buildings jutted out on their own little bridges, creating a tapestry of circular patterns around the center of the city. The streets were inlaid with golden bricks, and statues that appeared to be Greek figures stood along the sides of the streets. It was like glancing at history that had been frozen in time. The city sparkled and glowed underneath the glowing light that hung above the centermost point of the area.

"Textbooks say that the Atlanteans were able to find a power source that wasn't electrical in any fashion to power their cities and hover vehicles," Damian explained as our eyes looked over the marvels of the lost and hidden place.

"They were an advanced civilization is why," I replied. "They came from outer space and lived in a galaxy far from this one. Tiamat was their Goddess."

We walked the empty streets looking for some sign of life, but if there was any, they were hidden away in their homes, away from the windows. The place was a ghost town, even though Tiamat acknowledged that her people were safely tucked away inside the walls of the dome. As we drew closer to the large building at the center of the ancient civilization, a hum could be heard in the air.

"That's the sound of whatever energy they are using to keep this place running," I said, looking for electrical wires. "My only guess is the inlaid gold along the roads is what helps push the electrical current throughout the city like ley lines."

"Did Starfire give any indication where this chalice was supposed to be stowed away here?" Xavier asked. "I mean, we're just walking in a straight line to a place that could probably kill us with electrical currents."

"I believe, if I am not mistaken, that is the inner city, and that is exactly where we need to be," Damian replied.

"I hope you're right," Xavier mumbled as we drew closer to the large, round building.

As we made it to the center of the city, outside of the large dome building was a magnificent landscape. It had growing foliage, flowers, fruit trees, olive trees, nut trees, and so much more. At the very center of the garden, there was a fountain that had an angel in the center of it. The guys swept by me as I stopped to admire the statue. The angel held a sword in one hand and a chalice in the other. I looked closer at the cup, squinting to make sure I saw things correctly. Is that…

"Guys, I think I found it," I said as tons of soldiers swarmed the courtyard we stood in. Damian and Xavier ran back to where I stood, and we faced off against the warriors as they pointed their swords and spears at us.

"Who dares disturb the peace and tranquility of our sunken city?" a voice called out over the crowd of soldiers.

A man and woman emerged as the soldiers stepped aside to let them through.

"What do you want?" the woman asked, narrowing her eyes at us.

Of course, we didn't look peaceful strapped to the gills with weapons.

"We were sent here by the Oracle to retrieve the chalice," I replied, motioning to the cup that the angel held.

"And what makes you think that it belongs to anyone other than our city that you so dare to breach our gates and try to steal it?" she asked in reply.

"We need it," Damian replied. "Tiamat gave us her blessing to retrieve it."

"Ah, you mean the Leviathan that stands guard for our city. Tiamat is no more than a cast aside goddess slew by the god of this galaxy, quickly gaining power he never had in the beginning. She is a moot existence," the woman replied. "So, I ask you again, angels, what gives you the right to take what isn't yours?"

The soldiers took a step closer to us, pointing their weapons even closer at us.

"Because it is as much ours as it is yours," I replied heatedly. "We were forged from the dying sun of your universe. The manna in that cup will bring us to full power to save the universe from the god you so callously speak of who slew your goddess."

"I don't believe you," she replied. "Guards! Dispatch the thieves and toss their dead bodies to the mermaids."

Just as the soldiers stepped another step closer to us, I grabbed Damian and Xavier's hands and willed with all my might for the fire to sprout faster than it usually did. Instead, the bright light shot from our bodies as we rose into the air. The faces of the soldiers contorted into fear, as did their leader's face. They hit their knees and laid their foreheads against the ground.

"We plead for your mercy," the leader begged without lifting her forehead from the ground. "We were brash and mistaken in our bad judgment. We beg for mercy from the Council of El. Take the cup. Take anything that you desire, oh Shining Ones."

We descended to the ground below and released our hands. The Atlanteans remained in their positions, afraid to look at us.

"We do not wish to hurt you," I said, kneeling before the leader and offering her my hand.

She lifted her head slightly from the ground to see my outstretched hand. She took my hand, and I lifted her to a standing position.

"Again, apologies, your majestic grace," she said, bowing her head. "We have protected the chalice for many years for the prophetic ones to come and lay claim to it. I had no idea that they would be young ones."

"Prophetic ones?" Xavier asked.

"Yes!" she exclaimed. "Prophecy spoke of the grand emergence of three Shining Ones to bring the evil of the universe to its knees." She glanced from my face to Xavier's face. "Has no one told you about the prophecy?"

"No," I replied. "We just recently learned what we were."

She looked past me at Damian, who stood quietly with pleading eyes. Her eyes acknowledged a silent agreement between the two. I narrowed my eyes at him. He knew something more about this prophecy and wasn't telling us. She turned to me and smiled.

"You will learn in due time," she said with a smile.

She climbed atop the fountain and pushed a button. A platform emerged from the water and raised her to the height of the angel so that she could claim the chalice from its hands. The platform retracted, and she stepped down from the fountain. The entire city went dead. No electricity hum, no lights, nothing.

I looked at her, furrowing my brows.

"The manna powered our city. But, when you defeat Alpha, we shall be able to claim the sea top once more as our home," she explained.

"It's just powder. How does it power your city?" I asked.

"It is more than just powder. It is the soul of the universe where the spark first began," she said. "Now, go! You must hurry. The dome will not open without electricity. It has enough of a charge for one more push open, but you must make it there before the energy exhausts itself."

"Thank you," I replied, taking the chalice from her hands.

I pulled the bag out that Starfire had given us to place it in. As soon as the cup touched the inside of the bag, it sealed precisely how she said it would seal around the cup. I tied the cup to my waist and nodded my thanks to the Atlanteans before we turned and ran toward the gate entrance we had come through. I understood what she meant finally. There was a glass fail-safe sliding into place that would lock us in if we didn't get to the outer dome in time. Damian, Xavier, and I pounded down the long bridge, racing the glass seal falling into place. We dropped to our sides, sliding underneath the dome as it locked into place.

"Can we portal from here, or do we have to be seaside?" I asked Damian.

"I'm pretty sure we have to be seaside," he replied. "They must know where to open the portal, and they have never been to Atlantis or know its exact location. They could accidentally suck up the ocean instead."

All the mermaids waited for us at the glass dome, staring at us angrily and hungrily. The Lernaean Hydra still swam around the border of the city as well. I swallowed the lump of fear in my throat as I stared out at the creatures waiting for us to emerge so they could devour us alive.

"Ok, game plan," Damian began. "We open the gate and swim as fast as we can go to the topside."

"Then what? We have no idea where we are in the ocean. Then we swim the rest of the way to the shore?" I asked.

"Well, do you want to return the way we came?" he asked.

"Not really," I replied, exasperated.

"Everyone ready?" Xavier asked, grabbing our hands.

"As ready as can be," I muttered.

We pushed against the dome and were sucked out by the waters and push of air from behind us. I tried holding onto their hands as we somersaulted and spun through the water, but at some point, I let go and was lost in a spiral of water. The mermaids swarmed in on me, grabbing at my body as I struggled against them to free my swords. I clicked the buttons to activate them, and they flashed brightly as if activated by the presence of Seelies. The mermaids backed away slowly from me, seeing the glint of silver. They scowled at me as they parted slowly, creating a path for me to make it back to where Damian and Xavier rested with their swords drawn as well. It was then that the Leviathan swam in, grabbing as many mermaids in its mouth as it could fit. The Lernaean Hydra howled in a rage, almost as if the mermaids belonged to it. A fight ensued between the two gargantuan creatures as we swam as fast as we could the way we had come to Atlantis initially. Everything sped past us in a blur as we held hands and used our powers to propel us through the waters. We made it to the reef in record time and continued until we met a wall and swam upward. We popped from the water, snatching the red caps from our heads so we could breathe the fresh seaside air.

"Hurry, blow on the shell," Damian demanded, looking around on guard for something, anything, to attack us.

I patted myself, realizing I was not the one that had the shell. "Xavier, do you have it?" I asked.

He fished around in his pockets and produced the shell. He put it to his lips, and we all expected a loud trumpet-type sound, but nothing came.

"Did you do it, right?" Damian asked, turning in circles.

"Well, it didn't exactly come with instructions, Damian. She said to just blow into the seashell when we were ready to return," Xavier replied, irritated.

"Do it again!" Damian demanded.

Xavier put the shell to his lips again, huffed in a lungful of air, and blew as hard as he could at the end of the conch. Still, nothing happened.

"I don't like this," I remarked. "What if Alpha got to Starfire?"

"There is no way Alpha could have gotten into Lightshade," Damian replied. "Hair brain over there just isn't doing it right."

Xavier tossed the conch to Damian, who fumbled with it and nearly dropped it. "Well, then you do it, genius."

Damian did the same maneuvers that Xavier had tried, and still, nothing happened. I had an idea after Damian turned red in the face for a third time trying to summon the portal. I lifted my hands that still had the blades snugly fit to them. I waved my hands like Reikal did and pulled my power from within and up to my hands. The knives began to spark bright purple and yellow flames. In front of us appeared a portal remarkably similar to the one Reikal had summoned up, but a bit different. It glowed the same color as the sparks had been, but it wasn't translucent. However, we could see to the other side and saw Starfire, Reikal, and Gwendolyn all sitting around a table talking.

"How did you do that?" Xavier asked.

"Well, if my father could do it, then why can't we?" I asked with a smile.

We stepped through the portal, and it disappeared behind us as those who sat around the table stopped their conversation and looked over at us.

"About time you got back," Starfire said. "We were about to send a search party for your bodies."

"We tried to use the seashell, but it didn't work," Damian replied, handing it back to her.

She laughed. "That was a ruse. I apologize for my joke. I wanted you to use your powers to get back, which I see you finally caught on." She motioned to the bag wrapped around the chalice on my hip. "Is that it?" she asked.

"Yes," I replied, handing the satchel over to her. "We almost weren't allowed to take it. And whatever we needed it for needs to hurry before the people of Atlantis die from not having it."

Starfire nodded, opened the satchel, and carefully pulled the chalice out of the bag. "Excellent," she whispered. "Now, I must get to work on making you the elixir to drink to strip the Seelie enchantment from you."

Starfire stood from the table and ducked into a room to the right, closing the door behind her. Gwendolyn and Reikal sat silently at the table, staring at us.

"You three look... well," Gwendolyn remarked.

"I'm sure we do," I replied, shaking my head. "Where is Praeziel?"

"He left earlier. He went to round up the Nephilim that are willing to fight for the cause," she replied quietly.

"I'm sorry I didn't tell you about your home," Damian spoke softly. "I had no idea you didn't know about what had happened in the Otherworld."

She smiled with appreciation. "It's ok, but thank you."

"Well, I am going to go change out of these wet clothes," I said, breaking the small silence.

Xavier and Damian glanced down at their soaking wet clothes as well, noticing they were leaving puddles on the floor.

"We better go change as well," Xavier remarked, glancing at Damian.

"See you back in a bit," Gwendolyn replied and continued whatever conversation she had been having with Reikal prior to our arrival.

The three of us all headed up to our rooms, ducking in and closing the doors behind us. I pulled the wet pants down and kicked them off into a corner and slipped a warm, dry pair on to replace them. As I was pulling the shirt over my head, I got stuck inside of it. Of course, the shirt would trap me inside of it. It was practically glued to my body already. Once I was able to get it up and over my head, I tossed it over to the wet pants and then slipped a dry shirt on. I slipped my feet back into the comfortable boots I had been wearing and opened my door, heading back downstairs.

I was the first to arrive back at the table. You would think boys wouldn't take as long to change their clothes. It was a possibility that they were exhausted and lay down to sleep. I mingled with Gwendolyn and Reikal at the table and joined in with the chatter they had going, releasing the built-up tension from the day's events from my shoulders as I sipped warm chamomile tea.

Starfire emerged from the room that she had been in with five bottles in her hand.

"It's ready," she said, setting them on the table.

CHAPTER 5

"WHY ARE THERE FIVE?" I asked, staring at the bottles.

"Three are for you three. The other two are for your parents," she replied. "They need their enchantments taken away as well. As soon as they find me, they will be given their elixirs as well."

"How do you know they will find you?" I asked.

"Because I know everything, dear," she replied with a small tug of a smile to her mouth. "I am the Oracle, the all-seeing and all-knowing."

The boys emerged from upstairs no sooner than Starfire had explained everything. Both of their moods were different than what they had been before they went to change. Xavier looked. . . crushed. That was the only way I could describe his face. I looked at Damian, and his face had the same grim expression.

"You two, ok?" I asked.

"Yes," Damian replied, changing the expression on his face to a light-hearted one.

I glanced at Xavier, and he gave a half-hearted smile in return as well. I knew something was wrong, though, and if I had to beat it out of the two of them, I would eventually find out what it was. Starfire pushed the three vials of the elixir to the center of the table.

"Drink up," she said with a smile.

I picked up a vial and uncorked the bottle. I thought it would smell horrible, but it actually smelled sweet and flowery. Damian uncorked his as well, giving it a sniff. Xavier just stared at his cup, almost as if he didn't want to drink it.

"You too," Starfire said, pointing at Xavier. "You need to drink it as well, or it won't work for you three at all." There was a look in her eye, almost as if she knew something that Xavier knew, but no one else did.

Xavier picked his vial up and uncorked it like Damian and I had done. He gave it a sniff, and his face seemed pleased at the smell of it.

"Bottoms up," I said, and we all turned the vials up at the same time and downed the contents.

The elixir was just as sweet as it smelled but had a bitter aftertaste to it. I set the vial down on the table and waited for something to happen. I looked over at Damian and Xavier to see if there were any noticeable changes with them as well. They were checking themselves over just as I had. I looked at Starfire, who watched us carefully as we reacted to the potion.

"Nothing is happening," I replied with a shrug, setting the bottle down on the table.

No sooner had the words left my lips than pain tore through my stomach. I doubled over, almost as if I would vomit the contents back up. I wretched and took deep breaths as the pain radiated throughout my body. I heard Damian and Xavier react the same way I did.

"You poisoned us?" I asked in disbelief.

"No, my child. No one said this transformation was going to be easy," she replied, stroking my hair. "It gets worse before it gets better."

I fell to the ground, writhing in searing pain. It felt as if I were back in the Lake of Fire again, and the gasoline was fueling the fire within my veins. I screamed out in pain as the fire burned from my stomach and throughout my entire body. I heard Damian and Xavier's screams alongside mine. Steam rose from my skin, and fire crackled to the top. The more I burned outwardly, the worse it felt inwardly. But no matter how my skin blazed, nothing else in the room caught fire. Almost at the moment I was giving up and submitting to the imminent death from the toxic potion roiling through my veins, the pain began to subside. The nerve endings that had popped and frayed, burning to a crisp, came back to life, and I could feel the coolness of the air sweep over me. I sat up, with sweat dripping from my body and breathing deeply. I still didn't feel any different than I had prior to drinking the ancient substance.

I stood from the floor and dusted off my clothes. I watched as Damian and Xavier did the same, and we all looked at Starfire.

"You are almost ready," she stated. "But before you can move forward, there is one more thing you have to do."

"What's that?" I asked.

She looked at Damian and Xavier, who exchanged glances. "You have to fulfill the prophecy," she replied. "Damian and Xavier already know what the prophecy states."

She placed a book in the middle of the table and flipped it open to a page. My Enochian was a bit rusty, but the header on the page read "Shining Ones." I looked up at Damian and Xavier.

"You both have read this?" I asked.

Damian shook his head. "I have read it. Xavier has not, but he knows the basics of what it says," he replied quietly.

I quietly read through the pages of the ancient language when I reached the part about the prophecy. I slammed the book shut and threw it across the room.

"No!" I yelled. "It lies!"

"It is not a lie, child," Starfire replied. "It is inevitable."

"I won't do it," I replied angrily, looking at Xavier. "There has to be another way."

"There is no other way," Damian said. "You saw the vision in your nightmare just as well as I did. If we don't do it, we lose to Alpha."

"I'm not doing it!" I seethed. "End of discussion!"

I stomped from the room and ran up the stairs to my room, slamming the door behind me. I leaned against the door and sank to the floor below. The words of the prophecy haunted my vision as I squeezed my eyes shut. I buried my face in my legs and cried. This can't be the only way! This is not going to happen! I won't let it!

A soft knock came to the door.

"Go away," I yelled.

"Can I come in, Luxina, please?" Xavier asked on the other side of the door.

I stood from my seated position and turned around, opening the door. He stood there with an unimaginable look of pain on his face. I motioned for him to enter the room. He walked over to the bed and sat down.

"We will find another way," I spouted off before he could speak. "This is not going to happen."

He patted the bed beside him. I sat down and leaned my head against his shoulder. He wrapped his arms around me, placing his chin on my forehead.

"It's not that bad," he replied.

"How can you say that?" I asked. "You will die!"

"I won't die," he replied, gently rocking me in his arms. "I will just become part of you. I am you. I always felt different, almost as if I shouldn't exist. I always thought it was because of my loneliness. It wasn't that. This whole time, it was because I really never was supposed to exist."

"Don't say that," I cried into his shirt. "Your life has meaning! You mean so much to me!"

"And you mean a lot to me," he replied. "That is why I am not upset by this. I will always be a part of you. I will always be there."

"But why? Why did this happen?" I asked. "Why would the universe cause this to happen?"

"It was an accident. When the power of the heavenly portal diminished, and the power between our mother and father was split, our power split as well," he replied.

We stayed that way for a while. Both of us silently cried into one another. I had to absorb Xavier and therein, reabsorb the part of myself that had always been missing. The darkness that my father had to experience that I had never felt. It wasn't like someone had just sucked the darkness away from me. It was sentient. It was a person. And I loved that person dearly.

"Do we have to do it now?" I asked.

"I'm not sure," he replied. "All I know is it has to be done before the final battle with Alpha."

"I want to keep you as long as I can…"

"Soon, you will have me forever," he replied. "And there is no greater gift that I would give than to give you the chance to live."

I buried my face into his chest, and he squeezed me tightly.

"I love you, Xavier," I whispered. "Forever and always."

"You're supposed to," he replied. "You had to learn to love yourself. Our father, when he was created, didn't understand how to love the darkness. He didn't know how to love himself. You were given a gift by seeing the dark of you and being able to love it. You were given the gift of self-love, Luxina. It may hurt in the end, knowing that all what you felt, the power, the love, the moments, was nothing more than moments with yourself and not your other half. But remember the memories. There will always be memories."

We stood from the bed and made our way back downstairs. Starfire had already retired for the evening, so it was just Damian and Gwendolyn sitting at the table, talking quietly. Reikal had already left to go home. Damian's eyes caught mine as I walked into the room, and he quickly looked away.

"You knew this whole time and didn't tell us," I sneered.

He looked down, ashamed. "I was going to do it at the right moment. The last few days happened in a blur. I just couldn't find the right time to tell you."

"The Atlantean leader, she knew, and you asked her not to say anything, didn't you?" I asked heatedly.

"Yes, I didn't want you finding out from a complete stranger in the middle of an important mission," he replied. "I'm sorry."

"I bet you are," I jeered. "That's why you have been buttering up to me so much. Because you read what the prophecy said in full."

"I was not buttering up to you," he replied angrily. "Every emotion I have shown you and experienced has been real and not a ruse. Excuse me for trying to take the time to show you that I wasn't a bad person."

He stood from the table and walked to the door.

"Where are you going? Running away?" I asked nastily.

"You're not my mother, Luxina. Stop acting like her. That's how you get pushed away," he said, walking out the door.

"Well, maybe it would be better if you pushed me away. I trusted you. And you couldn't even share this secret you knew with me. It seems like everyone knew but Xavier and me. How fair is that?"

He stopped short in the door frame. "I'm sorry," he said once more and then left the cottage.

I followed him. "No, you don't get to walk away from this!"

"Luxina, leave me be," he replied through gritted teeth, balling his hands into fists.

"Oh, you're getting angry. Join the club," I shouted.

The heat began to rise through my body, and I got angrier. I didn't want it to stop. I wanted to lash out at everything I could. I wanted to burn everything to the ground. Damian whipped around, his eyes glowing brighter than I had ever seen them glow before.

"You want to blame someone? Blame Starfire. She was the one that dropped the book for me to read before I had to escape a pit of death Alpha had arranged for me. Do you really think that was the one thing that was at the forefront of my mind? I ran for DAYS from creatures you could never dream of. Oh, wait, you did! Those creatures in your nightmare, I fought. Alone. I nearly died. From the moment I have been with you all, I have been staving off attack after attack from countless creatures trying to kill us all. So, excuse me, princess, that I didn't call a timeout to all those things to fill you in on details I had just told Xavier about prior to Starfire handing you that damned forsaken book."

He walked up to me as I searched for the words to reply to him. He grabbed my hands in his, and I looked deep into his bright eyes.

"I did this all for you," he stammered. "Why can't you see my worth? Why must I be blamed for everything that goes wrong?"

He let my hands go and placed his hands gently around my face.

"I don't care what happens to me as long as you are safe. I gave up my life to keep you and Xavier safe. I laid down my sword and admitted defeat in that ring before your dad yanked me from it. If I was dead, you would be safe. Alpha could no longer use you two against me, and I wasn't a threat to your safety." His eyes searched my eyes, pleading with me to believe what he was saying. "But I will never be more than Alpha's little monster to you."

He let my face go and ran in the opposite direction, disappearing into the thick brush. I just stood there, stunned. Is that what he really thought? Was that how I treated him? Keeping him at arm's length and only letting him in when I was vulnerable. Did I really still think of him as Alpha's little monster? No, of course, I didn't. I thought of each time he was at my side, pulling me to safety, sacrificing his own life to ensure that I was protected. It was then that I realized how everything was true. It was why Xavier kept to himself and away from me. I didn't want to save myself. So, Xavier's personality and mood changed. Is that how it worked?

I sat on the ground and pulled my knees to my chest. I waited. I waited for Damian to return. I waited so I could apologize for everything. I needed to tell him. I needed to show him that he wasn't a monster to me. I needed him to know I honestly did care about him. I waited for hours. The sun beat down on me, but I didn't move from the spot I sat. However, no matter how long I sat waiting, he did not reappear. I buried my face in my knees. I screw up everything.

"You do not screw up everything," Xavier said, sitting down on the ground next to me. "You just pushed his buttons is all. He will be back. You will apologize, and he will forgive you."

"No, he won't," I croaked. "I'm too broken to love. I'm too broken to understand. I'm broken beyond repair. This whole mess of things is my fault. There were so many things I could have done differently."

Xavier wrapped his arm around me and pulled me into his chest. "You are not broken beyond repair."

"That doesn't help when it comes from you," I replied, burying my face into his arm.

"He is hurting over this as much as you are," he said, rocking me. "He has to lose a brother."

I hadn't even thought of that. I felt even more horrible for the way I acted, as if I was the only one who mattered.

"Are you sure he will forgive me?" I asked, peeking up at him from his shirt.

"How could he not? I would," he replied with a light laugh.

"And you're ok with everything else?" I asked.

"It makes more and more sense the more I think about it all," he replied. "I came to terms with it easier than either of you did."

"We could still try and figure out a different way," I protested.

"No," he replied. "I'm ready to go home."

"And where is home for you?" I asked.

"Home is in your soul," he murmured.

"How do you suppose we do it?" I asked, trying to picture my body absorbing him, but the vision came out of me eating him instead.

"That I don't know," he replied. "But I am ready when you are."

He stood from the ground and offered his hand to help me up. As I stood from the ground, Praeziel came down the path from the portal at the top of the mountain. I half expected to see an army of Nephilim following him, but he was alone. I wonder if they declined to help fight in the war against Alpha. Xavier and I met him as he reached the bottom of the path.

"I see you all made it back in one piece," he said with a light smile. "Where is Damian?"

"Cooling off," Xavier replied.

He nodded as if he understood. He looked at me with sympathetic eyes. "I take it Starfire shared the prophecy with you upon your return?" he asked.

I dropped my eyes, nodding. "When did you find out about it?" I asked.

"She told Gwendolyn and me after you all departed on your quest to Atlantis. It was then I thought it would be best to go and gather the Nephilim," he replied.

"Were you successful?" I asked.

"They will be here in the morning," he replied with a nod. "Our numbers against Alpha are growing. We have the Nephilim, what is left of the Watchers, and those that made it to safety in the Otherworld."

"Add that to the numbers of angels there are in the Summit, and we have a decent team," Xavier said.

"Let's pray that is so," Praeziel replied. "Something tells me Alpha has more up his sleeve than what we are aware of."

"You happen to be very correct," Damian said as he emerged from the brush. He refused to look at me. "Alpha has made all kinds of new creations. I had just a taste of them in the arena. If my dream is right, he has millions upon millions of these things made and stashed away."

"Ah, Praeziel," Starfire interrupted, stepping out onto her porch. "Right on time. Fill us all in on your little adventure." She motioned for him to come inside.

Praeziel took the forefront, and we all headed toward the cottage. As they started up the steps, I snagged Damian by the hand and pulled him back to me. Xavier stopped and turned around to see if he was needed.

"We will catch up in just a few," I said, reassuring him we were okay.

Damian stepped down from the step he was on and stood before me. I had never paid attention to most details about him. He had freckles across his creamy white skin. His eyes were a penetrating color of blue, but not just any blue. It looked as if I was staring straight into the galaxy. Different shades and flecks of blue popped here and there the closer you examined them. He was much taller than me, almost by a foot. When you looked at his red curly hair, you could see streaks of white mixed into the different hues of fire that grew. His hair was shorter than the last time I remembered seeing it. His skin had small scars that had long ago healed and were just pale patches of skin slightly raised. His eyelashes were long and white and almost seemed to flutter as he opened and closed his eyes.

He never once faltered with his gaze as I took in every part of his body, memorizing them each for the first time. He stood there quietly as I took my hands and ran them down the sides of his neck, almost but not quite touching his skin where the scars of his torture were visible. I looked up into his soft eyes, pleading with my own, searching through them to see if I would know the answer before I spoke.

"I'm sorry," I whispered.

He looked away quickly, and I turned his face back to mine. I wanted him to see that what he believes about himself is not what I believe. I wanted him to read it from my soul.

"You're not a monster," I gently spoke. "You are not what Alpha tried to make you into."

"You say it, but you don't mean it. I saw the way you looked at me. You will never see me for more than what I have been showcased as," he replied, pushing past me.

"I need you as much as you need me," I stated without turning around to see if he even stopped. "I will forever need you."

"That's the problem. You need me," he replied, walking upright behind me to stand, hesitant to continue. "But you don't want me."

He turned swiftly on his heels and walked inside the cottage, leaving me alone with his words. Every emotion I had been fighting since meeting him came rushing to the top. I didn't need to feel him. I wanted to feel him. I didn't need him by my side. I wanted him by my side. It was then that I realized I had been fighting against so many things regarding him. I was afraid of ending up like my mother and choosing the wrong person. I pitied him when he took me from my father, but I felt compassion for him because I knew that he was being made to do it against his will. This whole time I had been fighting this welling, overwhelming feeling inside for him because I honestly believed that Xavier and I were twin flames like our parents. But now, since that is all said and done and over with, I knew what the flutter in my stomach had meant when Damian touched me gently with his hands.

It was simple to realize once I stopped looking at Xavier as if he were anything more than an extension of myself. Yes, I loved Xavier, but there was just an energetic feeling. But within Xavier was a piece of myself that also reflected Damian. Xavier was everything Damian was, and Damian was so much more than Xavier. I watched them from the door as they spoke and easily got along. The piece I was missing from within that would attach so easily to Damian was in Xavier. If I were ever to really genuinely care for Damian, Xavier had to meld with me. It was pretty unfair. Once a sentient being sparks into existence, even if it was never meant to exist, it is unfair to snuff its light out. But, as I stare at Xavier, I can see it. I can see the glamour the universe had put up. A mirror stood before me, and I saw reflected back a dark-haired me. I saw what darkness would look like on the outside. The confidence I lacked. Everything represented by the shadows of your ego.

Both of them looked up and saw me watching them, arms crossed leaning against the door jam. My eyes rested briefly on Xavier, switching to Damian's face, and my stomach knotted and flip-flopped when I reached his eyes. It felt like heartbreak racing through my heart while simultaneously being elated. I turned and walked away from the door out into the small yard that surrounded Starfire's cottage. I started walking without knowing where my feet were carrying me. My walk turned into a jog that quickly developed into a sprint. I was running without a clue as to where I was going. But it felt like that's what I needed to do. Was I running away from my problems? I most likely was, but the exhilaration of the wind whipping past my face made it feel like I was flying, which is what I wanted to do most of all.

I quickly found myself deep in the thicket of the woods. The smell of dirt and plants filled my nostrils, and I breathed the heady petrichor scent in deeply. I still continued my run. I followed a creek and watched as tiny little creatures with pincers buried in the dirt beneath the running water. The creek bed became broader and deeper, and I was soon following along the banks of a river. Birds soared overhead, and fish jumped and splashed back down in the river. I looked across the river, and a family of deer stood there foraging and drinking water. The river picked up speed, and I raced it, my feet pounding the forest floor as I ran freely without a care in the world.

I heard a thunderous roar as the river ended and flowed over the side of a cliff, forming a waterfall. As I grew closer and closer to the edge of the cliff, preparing to jump and dive into the water, I closed my eyes and held my arms out. I was tackled to the ground from the side and rolled with my assailant until we came to a stop in a blanket of moss. I opened my eyes, and Damian rested on top of my body.

"What did you do that for?" I asked, breathless from the running.

"Do you have a death wish?" he asked angrily. "You didn't even look to see what was on the other side of the cliff before you tried to jump."

"I would have been fine!" I retorted. "Why were you following me, anyway?" I asked heatedly.

"To make sure you didn't do something dumb or death-defying," he shot back.

"Why do you care?!" I shouted.

"Because you are all I have," he replied, pounding the ground beside me. "You're all I will have left."

I ran my hands through his hair and pulled his face to mine. "Do you love me?" I asked. "Not like you would love Xavier. Do you love me? Do you want me, or do you need me?"

"I could ask you the same things," he replied.

My heart raced in my chest. My fingers brushed his lips and danced across his face. I knew my answer. I had been fighting it for too long. The fight was now over.

"I-"

Damian jumped from the spot he had been in, hovering over my body. "No," he said firmly. He paced back and forth in front of me. "No," he said again, shaking his head and pounding his fists against his ears.

"Damian, are you ok?" I asked, rising from the ground.

He covered his ears and howled in pain. His screams tore through the empty forest, echoing and bouncing back. I went to grab him, to try and help him, but he grabbed my hands and pushed them away.

"Go!" he demanded. "Go... now!" he squeezed out distraughtly.

"What is it? What's wrong?" I asked in a craze.

I tried to touch him, and he just pushed me off and put his hands back over his ears.

"Just go, Luxina!" he demanded again.

I remembered the promise I had made him after the werewolf attack. *When I tell you to go, just do as I ask.*

"I'll go get help," I stammered. "I'll be back for you!"

"No, don't!" he cried. "It's Alpha... I don't know... I might hurt someone!" he screamed.

"You won't hurt me!" I yelled, grabbing his face to stare into his eyes. "You're not what Alpha made you. You can fight this!"

He pushed me down to the ground and was on top of me. As his fist came down, I rolled out of the way as it met the ground below. I barrel-rolled into a crouched position and waited for him to make another move. I saw him fight whatever force he was grappling with in his head. His fists pounded the sides of his ears, and he doubled over, shaking his head to rid himself of whatever was fighting internally in his brain. Whatever he heard, I could not. I don't know if it was some kind of low pitch frequency he was picking up or if Alpha was talking directly into his brain. But when he turned to stare at me, his eyes had blacked over. He glared and ran at me. He started throwing jabs that I parried and kicked away. My hands moved with precision as his assault came faster and stronger. I did a backflip and kicked out at the same time, striking him in the chest and pushing him back. I landed in a crouch and swooped my leg around. He jumped over it, coming down with another punch. I grabbed his arm, twisted it, and then flipped him over my shoulder. He landed with a thud, swiping me from my feet with his leg. I tucked and rolled as I landed, and his foot barely grazed me as he hammered it to the ground.

We were back on our feet, jabbing and parrying every attempted move by the other. He grabbed his ears again, screaming in pain.

"Leave!" he screeched.

"No, not this time," I replied.

I did a roundabout kick, catching him in the temple, and he went down. He didn't move, and I panicked for a moment, thinking I may have killed him. I ran to him and checked his breathing. I watched as his chest rose and fell and breathed a sigh of relief. Now what? I had to get him back to the cottage and tie him up before he woke back up. There was no way I could lift him and carry him all the way back. I had run a few miles deep into the woods. I looked into my hands and thought of giving another portal a shot. I didn't have the knives Reikal had given me this time, so I hoped it would work.

I reached deep within me and pulled with everything in me, waving my hands as a whirlwind appeared before me. I could see everyone sitting around the table. I grabbed Damian underneath his armpits and pulled him with all my might into the room before dismissing the portal. Everyone jumped from the table and rushed to his side.

"What happened?" Xavier asked. "Were you two attacked?" He looked at the scratches all over my body.

"No," I replied. "We need to tie him up. Alpha hijacked him."

"What do you mean Alpha hijacked him?" Praeziel asked.

"We were talking, and then all a sudden, he started talking to himself, screaming no. He grabbed his ears and told me to leave. I stayed to offer him help. That was when his eyes went black like the demons' eyes, and he attacked me," I explained.

"He was probably a spy this whole time, waiting to get the elixir from Starfire so he could become Alpha's weapon," Gwendolyn remarked.

Fire tore through my body. "That is NOT the case at all! He is not a monster! He is not Alpha's toy! He is suffering! He is innocent!"

Everyone took a step back from me as my skin began to sizzle.

"This is what Alpha wants you to believe. He wants you to think Damian is playing sides so that we will send his weapon back to him. It's not going to happen. Now, grab some rope and tie him up in a chair!" I demanded.

"The only thing that can stop his powers is something that is made with unicorn hair," Xavier replied quietly.

"I have just the thing," Starfire replied, hurrying into a room adjacent to the one we stood. She returned just as quickly, carrying some chains. "These were given to me in case of fail-safe measures." She dropped them on the table.

Everyone just stared at the chains and then at Damian. They didn't like this idea one bit. I didn't like it either, but I sure as hell wasn't handing him back over to Alpha now. And anyone that tried to stop me from protecting him would quickly become my enemy. I grabbed the chains from the table. Xavier and Praeziel hoisted Damian up into a chair. They tied his legs to the chair legs, wrapped the rope around his upper body, and then I placed the manacles around his wrists behind his back.

I pulled a chair up to face him and waited for him to regain consciousness.

"You all can leave if you wish," I stated curtly. "I have this handled."

Praeziel and Gwendolyn left the room. Xavier stayed behind with me as Damian's eyelids fluttered to life. I hoped I would see the blue of his eyes staring at me, but all that was there were the cavernous eyes of an abyss. He glared and tried to free himself of his ties. Once it proved futile, he leaned back in the chair and relaxed with a malicious grin spreading from ear to ear.

"You think you can stop me, but you can't," he stated coolly. "I will be triumphant in the end."

"I want to speak to Damian," I replied calmly.

"You're speaking to Damian," Damian replied. "Although, you may not recognize him with all this power staring at you."

"I want to speak to Damian," I once again stated calmly.

"Damian isn't here!" he hissed. "How are you fairing, Luxina? You don't look well."

I glared at him. It was Alpha.

"Oh, you just realized who is speaking through Damian. This is too fabulous. Now tell me, dear, what was it like when you found out that all along, I had been keeping your real twin flame hostage? Were you angry? Were you sad?" He paused for a minute, and a smile spread across his face. "Oh, you didn't think I knew about the prophecy. Why do you think I was so adamant about getting you and Xavier back here, or should I say you and your split personality?" He turned his head toward Xavier. "Tell me, boy, how does it feel to know that you were never meant to exist and, honestly, really don't exist at this moment? How does it feel knowing you have to give up your life to save the universe?" Xavier stood emotionless, staring at Alpha. "Oh, that's right. Whatever she feels is how you feel." He looked back at me. "Am I right so far?"

I didn't acknowledge a single word he was saying to us. I stared blankly at him with the poker face that Damian uses so well to hide things.

"So, tell me, where exactly are you? Are you really safe? Or are the ones you are with secretly plotting against you?" he asked with a crooked grin. "Can you trust your traveling group? Are they really on your side? Or are they with me?" He laughed heartily. "Oh, how wonderful would it be for you to genuinely believe that the Seelies have pledged their devotion to you. Tell me, how is young Gwendolyn doing? Still catching rabbits for you to eat? Did you ever wonder why it was she that led you through all the portals through the Otherworld, and you could never quite catch Starfire that had never moved once?"

There must have been a flicker in my eyes because his grin spread from ear to ear.

"That's right, Luxina. Starfire has been in the same exact spot for many years. I just can't get through her firewall."

I glanced nervously at Xavier as he chewed on a nail.

"I want Damian back," I stated once more calmly. "I want him back now."

"You're going to have to battle me for him. I have control of his mind right now. Would you like to fight for him? Meet me in the meadow. I won't really be there, of course, but you're going to have to be strong enough to pull him back to the surface." He glanced at Xavier. "Sacrifice one to save the other..."

He smiled evilly at me, and I couldn't help but glare back.

"Starfire!" I called out.

She appeared from her room, awaiting my request.

"Find something to put him to sleep," I said. "Something that will knock him out for a while."

She nodded and disappeared off into the alchemy room. She returned with a potion bottle. Damian smiled and took the potion without a fuss. He immediately slumped unconscious in his chair.

"Ok, one problem down," I said.

"What's the next one?" Xavier asked.

"You know the answer to that," I replied, standing from my chair and looking upstairs. Gwendolyn stood at the rail of the balcony where our rooms were. I wasn't sure how long she had been standing there, listening to the conversation. Her face didn't show any signs of her being caught in the deceptive lies she had been telling us for the past year.

"Starfire?" I asked quietly, not taking my eyes off Gwendolyn.

"Yes, child?" she replied.

"I just need to know one thing," I stated calmly.

"What do you need to know, child?" she replied.

"Have you been here our entire journey, or have you been bouncing from place to place?" I asked.

"I have lived here my entire life," she replied quietly.

"Thank you," I replied without drawing attention to what my hands were doing. "That was all I needed to know." I clicked my knife's button to activate it as soon as I tossed it through the air. It came to life in the middle of the air and landed squarely in the middle of Gwendolyn's chest. It was one of the knives that Damian had specially crafted for him by the Dark Queen Mab. Gwendolyn slammed into the wall behind her from the force of the blow and slowly sat down on the floor. She couldn't even pull the knife from her chest as the handle was made from iron as well.

"Praeziel," she croaked.

Praeziel emerged from his room and, upon notice of her condition, ran to her side.

"Stop, Praeziel," I commanded.

Xavier had already pulled out his bow and arrows and had them pointed at Praeziel. Praeziel put his hands slowly in the air and backed away from Gwendolyn.

"Did you know?" I asked.

"Did I know what?" he asked heatedly.

"That Gwendolyn was working for Alpha?" I questioned.

"She was not working for Alpha," he seethed. "She would never betray me!"

"Ask Starfire where she has lived this entire time, then," I replied. "Ask her if every time we thought we were close to her, she moved. The birds, the trees, nature, telling Gwendolyn when she went alone into the woods that Starfire had uprooted again. Ask Starfire where she has lived this past year."

He looked at Starfire, the answer already ringing true in his mind. Gwendolyn had lied to us all. He looked at her as she wept, the blood seeping down the front of her chest from the blade buried deep within her cavity.

"Why?" he cried, hitting his knees.

"I don't know," she replied quietly.

Blood began to trickle down from the corners of her mouth. Praeziel stood from her side and drew his sword from its sheath.

"I'm sorry," she whispered.

Without hesitation, he cut her head clean from her body. He pulled my knife from her body and tossed it to the floor where I stood.

"I suggest you do it as well," he stated somberly. "If I can do it, you can too. Drive a knife through his heart before this world goes to hell."

He walked back into his room and shut the door behind him. I returned my gaze to Damian, soundly asleep in the chair in front of me. His head had lolled to where it now hung to his chest.

"He isn't right, but he isn't wrong either," Starfire said. "You either must break Damian free forever from the clutches of Alpha, or you will have to watch the world die. There is no middle ground."

"I don't even know how to save him," I replied.

"There is only one way to save him now," she replied, looking at Xavier.

I closed my eyes and breathed in deeply. I wasn't ready for this. There were people he still needed to say goodbye to. Alpha had played the chess game, and I was at the final move. I could either bring my queen out and put her in position to take his king, or I could move my knight, and he takes my king. Sacrifice one to save the other...

"Hey," Xavier said, breaking my deep thoughts. "I already told you. I am ready when you are. I'm just going home."

I nodded. I knew what we had to do. We had to meet in the meadow like we always used to. That is where my ego and shadow self lived. My psyche was whole there.

"Starfire, can you help us slip into sleep?" I asked, tears glistening down my face.

She nodded and left the room. Xavier reached over and squeezed my hand.

"Let's go save the world," he said with a smile.

CHAPTER 6

XAVIER AND I LAY side by side in my bed, our hands intertwined as we waited for the sleep potion that Starfire had given us to kick in. This one wasn't as strong as the sedative she had given to Damian, so we had to drift off to sleep naturally. I moved and draped my arm across his chest. He squeezed me tighter in response. My eyelids began to grow heavy and droop in exhaustion. It had been days since I had fallen asleep. The inky, dark background of my mind washed over me, and I felt myself tumbling down a black hole.

I sat up in the middle of our field. Xavier and Damian were nowhere to be seen. Where were they? I stood from the ground and dusted my clothes off. The grass had grown back from the devastation Alpha had wreaked upon the valley. Our tree stood behind me, green and vibrant with leaves and flowers. The wheatgrass gently blew in the breeze as bees buzzed and birds chirped.

I felt a tap on my shoulder and turned to find Damian standing behind me.

"Beautiful, isn't it?" he asked.

His eyes were still deep pools of black. I looked frantically around for Xavier, but he had not shown up yet.

"Waiting for your other half, I presume," Damian remarked. "Are you sure he will come?" he asked.

"Yes," I replied firmly.

"You put your faith in so many people," he laughed. "I mean, you trusted Gwendolyn. Look at where that got you."

"You're the reason Gwendolyn betrayed us," I retorted.

"Me? Who do you believe you are speaking to right now?" he mused.

"I know it's Alpha talking through you," I replied. "You have to fight him, Damian!"

"No, Luxina," he replied. "This is all me. This is who I truly am."

"No, it isn't," I hissed. "You are not what he made you. You are more than that."

"How do you know? How do you know that I am not evil?" he demanded. "How do you know I won't kill you right here, right now? You don't!"

"Yes, I do know the answer to that," I replied heatedly. "You told me yourself I am the only person that could ever kill you because you would never hurt me."

"That was the weak me," he snickered, grinning. "The strong me thinks otherwise."

I grabbed his face and stared into his eyes. "Come back to me, Damian."

He leaned in close and whispered, "I am right here."

"Leave her alone," Xavier said, walking to where we stood.

"Oh, the faithful lapdog shows his face," Damian sneered. "Ready to dissolve away into nothing?" he asked. "Because that's all you are. You are nothing. Nonexistent."

Xavier's face didn't waver a moment with Damian's words. "There is nothing you can say to me to hurt me."

"No, but I can kill you, can't I?" Damian asked.

"You won't hurt me," Xavier replied. "You won't hurt either of us. You had plenty of chances to do so before. The real Damian, not the one Alpha tries to control. He would never hurt us."

"That you know of," Damian replied. "Tell me, how much do you know about me? Do you really know the pain and torment I faced at the hand of Alpha? Can you feel it? Can you feel every stroke of the whip that burned into my body? No, you can't. You have absolutely no idea what it is to feel what I feel or to know what I know."

"I can," I replied. "I can feel it. I can see it. I know your anguish and your despair, and you are nothing like the person you think you are. You don't even know what you are. You think the world doesn't know, but I do. No one will ever know you as I do!"

I grabbed his shirt and pulled him close to me. I placed my hand on his forehead, and with everything in me, I willed every moment we had ever shared together into his mind. What he felt, what I felt, what happened, the experiences, they all rushed through his mind until he passed out, hitting the ground.

"We don't have much time," I croaked in tears to Xavier.

Xavier and I walked to the tree and stood embraced in front of it. The tree that sparked so many memories between us now would be an empty reminder of the moments I had spent here with Xavier. Never again would I see his face or hear his laugh. I wouldn't be able to reach out to him in the middle of the night for comfort. I would never be able to experience him as a person ever again.

The petals on the tree began to fall and float in the breeze as we stood and embraced in front of it. It looked like our walk through the Otherworld as the Forget-Me-Trees shed their petals all around us. He squeezed me tighter.

"I should have been kinder to you than I was," he said to me as he kissed my forehead.

"I wanted to be pushed away. That is why you did it. It's not your fault," I replied.

"There are so many things I want to tell you," he whispered.

"I'm sure I will find out," I replied in quiet breaths.

He placed his forehead against mine, and our bodies began to burn lightly. I stared into his eyes, and he matched my stare. His eyes began to glow that bright light I had always admired.

"Yours do, too," he said, and I knew what he meant without asking.

His body began to glow brighter, and I could see the same light swirl around me as well. We placed our hands together, palms out, and the energy crash crackled through the air. His skin felt like fire the brighter he burned. I felt myself grow weightless as our bodies began to float lightly above the ground. Lights like the light that shot from all three of us now swirled in tiny orbs around us. His body was nothing but one bright light.

"Never forget me," he whispered.

"I could never forget you," I whispered back. "But what if I can't feel you? I am not worthy of this."

"I am the dark of you," he replied softly. "I will always be there. You just must listen. Listen to my call. I will be there with you through it all."

The entire valley was lit with a blinding white light, forcing me to shut my eyes, and I felt a tearing pain in my body. Everything went dark around me, and I slowly opened my eyes as the burning feeling slowly faded away. Xavier was gone. I stood alone in the middle of the field. Empty but whole. The missing part that I had never known was missing now rested in my soul. Tears spilled from my eyes, and I hit the ground on my knees. Fire sprang to my skin and traveled to the tree we shared. Slowly, inch by inch, the tree caught fire. The petals that had blown so beautifully from the tree before were now ashen petals of regret and shame that floated softly to the ground. Light fires began to sprout in the field as the dry wheat grass caught aflame from the glowing embers. I screamed out in rage and pain. I screamed out in fear and doubt. I screamed out in hatred and self-loathing.

I balled my flaming hands together, pressing them to my chest in anguish. If I couldn't save Damian, I really was forever alone now. It didn't matter if I was whole. I couldn't feel anything that was supposed to signal the completion of my soul. I didn't feel Xavier's presence. I felt nothing but a numb, drowning, sinking feeling welling within my heart. I looked off into the field to see if Damian had woken up yet. He stood in the center of the wildfire blazing out of control in the field, watching me silently. It felt like time stood still or was going by in slow motion. He slowly began to walk toward me, and the fires in the field froze over in his wake. Fire and ice— what a pair. He stopped before me, his eyes still black as death. He would kill me now, but honestly, I didn't even care any longer.

He dropped to his knees in front of me and stared into my swollen eyes. He didn't say a word. He just sat there quietly. The finality of everything was finally sinking in. A tear slid down his face and turned to ice as it dropped to the ground.

"He's gone?" he breathed.

My face contorted, and I nodded yes, tears falling freely down my face while swallowing the lump in my throat. The tears came one by one down his face. He leaned his head against my forehead.

"No, no, not yet," he whispered over and over.

"He did it for you," I replied, choking on the words. "I did it for you."

Silence fell between us as we sat there, forehead to forehead.

"I can't feel him," I cried, my lips quivering. "He's not there. I can't hear him or feel him like we thought."

"I can feel him," he replied, choking on his tears. "I can't," he started gulping air. "I can't be here."

"No!" I cried out, grabbing his face. "Please, please don't leave me too. Don't let me go. There's nothing left but you. Don't leave me! Stay with me, Damian!" I called out to him with everything in me. "Stay with me," I whispered, my heart pounding in my chest.

He stared into my eyes and reached his hand out to my face. He stroked my face ever so softly and gently. His other hand followed suit, and he was holding my face in his hands, gazing into my eyes so intently. "Always."

He leaned in, pulling my face close into his, and pressed his lips against mine. The light exploded between us. A light that was so different from whatever had happened with Xavier and me. Colors swirled around us: pinks, blues, purples. The colors of the galaxy. I knew now what it looked like. I had every memory Xavier had ever experienced tucked away in my mind. He was here. He was me. The dark of me shining the light in the dark like tiny little stars in the sky. A thought that had never occurred to me prior to that. Darkness isn't just about an inky blackness that engulfs you. It holds the key to whatever light is hiding within you, waiting to explode out. It comes first, in waves, and just when you think that is all there is, the light leaps forward as if it were being sheltered by the dark the entire time. It was almost as if the darkness was protecting the light from any harm that it would incur. Darkness doesn't hold you back. Darkness helps you learn to spread your wings and take off into the light like a baby bird.

Our kiss deepened, and his arms wrapped around me tighter and tighter. I was lost in the moment. Everything that I had held back exploded from within me. Ashes rained down all around us, and bits of snow fell from the sky. Our bodies smoldered against one another as they momentarily became one. My hands roamed freely through his curly locks of hair, bringing his face urgently down over and over as his lips met mine fervently.

"I love you," I whispered in his ear, laying my head on his shoulder.

"I have waited so long to hear those words," he murmured. "I didn't even know I wanted you until I knew I was destined to be with you. And the moment it became clear how our future was going to go, I wanted to protect you. I wanted to love you. I wanted to be the one that held you, calmed your fears, and wiped away your tears."

I opened my closed eyes and looked into his. Those piercing blue eyes were back, with a subtle gray hue to them. His red locks had been replaced as well with solid white hair. I looked at my hair strands that fell around my shoulders, and they were the same color. I guess this was one of the traits of what we really were. He took my hand and led me to the center of the field, and we laid down in the middle of it, wrapped in one another's arms. We watched, mesmerized, as the snow, fire, and ash fell down around us. I reached out with my hand to catch a snowflake and saw the blaze of fire glowing on my hand. He touched my hand with his, which was equally glowing with an icy fire.

His fingers intertwined with mine, and he brought our hands down to his bare chest. My fingers roamed the places he wouldn't allow me to touch before. I touched every single scar that was left from Alpha's hand, ever so gently.

"I could stay here forever with you," he murmured, running his hand through my now white hair. "Don't ever let me go?" he asked.

"Close your eyes," I whispered as I ran my hand over his face, his eyes fluttering closed as I touched his skin. "This is what forever will always feel like because I won't."

He opened his eyes to look at me. My face rushed with heat as his fingers traced my mouth. I started to look away, to look at the field, when he gently pulled my face back to his.

"Don't," he said. "Everything is on fire."

"Come morning," I began, "we will be safe and sound."

It felt like forever lying there with him. We laid there in serene bliss, wrapped in one another's arms, crying at times for the loss we both experienced. We watched the day turn into night as the sun slipped below the horizon. Stars erupted in the sky above the burning field as we remained oblivious to the swirling smoke and ruin. The moon rose and set, and we didn't budge a muscle. Our hands rested on one another, and his chin never left my forehead. Every feeling I had felt for Xavier was now amplified twice as much regarding him. Twilight appeared on the horizon, and soon, the rising sun signaled that dawn was approaching. I felt my body growing light and realized the sleep meds that Starfire had given me were wearing off.

"See you on the other side?" I whispered.

"I will be waiting," he replied, kissing my forehead.

I awoke alone in my bed; the spot to my side was still sunken in where Xavier had laid with me hours before. I rose to my feet and made my way swiftly down the stairs to where Damian still sat chained and tied up in the chair I had left him in. I unshackled his hands and cut the rope from his body as he was still sleeping soundly. His face was peaceful and serene, almost looking as if a smile tugged the edge of his lips.

"Should you really be doing that?" Praeziel asked, breaking the quiet of the room and startling me.

"He's fine now," I calmly replied.

"For how long?" he asked.

"Alpha can never touch him again," I replied quietly, brushing his white locks from his face.

"Well, I hope for our sake, you are right," Praeziel retorted, standing to his feet and sheathing his sword. "Where is Xavier?" he asked.

"Xavier... is home," I replied, staring up into Praeziel's eyes.

He nodded, acknowledging what I meant. "The troops are to show up today. We all begin training with Starfire. It is my understanding that the warlocks will be fighting alongside us as well." He turned to leave through the door of the cottage when I called out his name.

"Praeziel?" I began.

He stopped and turned my way. "Yes?" he asked.

"I'm sorry," I replied.

"I know," he said.

"I also wanted to say thank you."

"For what?" he asked.

"For being you," I replied.

He looked a bit confused, and then he smiled and nodded, walking out the door. With strength I didn't have before, I lifted Damian from the chair he sat in and carried him up the stairs to my room, shutting the door behind me. I laid him down gently on my bed and sat beneath his head, stroking his hair. I figured he would have woken up by now. The sedative Starfire had given him must not have worn off yet. I watched him as his eyes rolled back and forth under his eyelids. I touched his cheek and stroked it, rubbing my thumb under his eye and down to his mouth. He began to stir, and for a brief moment, I was fearful that when he opened his eyes, he wouldn't be himself. However, no sooner had the thought crossed my mind than his eyes fluttered open, and I was gazing into the eyes of the universe.

"Welcome back," I murmured.

"Miss me?" he asked, reaching his hand up and touching my face.

"You already know the answer to that," I whispered, tugging at his locks.

He sat up on the bed, repositioned himself, and pulled me into his arms. I snuggled in close, breathing in his scent. I had never paid it attention before. He smelled like a meadow on a warm spring day. He shifted his position and leaned back against the headboard, pulling my body on top of his. We laid there snuggling, drinking each other in.

"Do you think we possess the power to freeze time?" I asked.

"We could try," he murmured.

"Think anyone else would notice?"

"No one but us would ever know."

I smiled at him and gently closed my eyes. Months of mental fatigue and physical exhaustion overcame me as I lay serenely in his arms. How long had it been since I was able to sleep a whole night without nightmares or being awakened by an attacking monster? I couldn't even fathom the number of days. I felt myself slip into darkness, the darkness in me finally at rest. A tranquil sense of calm washed over me as shooting stars and galaxies tumbled through my mind. They were no doubt vivid memories of what I had always wished to see. The viewpoint from the Summit that Xavier had witnessed, that I had witnessed all along. The dancing lights and swirling clouds of color put my mind at ease, and for the first time in a long time, I slept peacefully.

It was just a moment of respite. I was shaken awake by Damian as we heard the thunderous sounds outside. We slipped out of my room and ran down the stairs to the front door. Damian crashed through the door, nearly breaking it from its hinges. Hundreds of warlocks stood gathered outside, looking at the sky. We followed their gaze, shielding our eyes from the bright sun beaming down. Hundreds of meteors pelted against an invisible dome in the sky, crashing and burning upon impact. Stardust rained down from the burning rubble, filling the air.

More and more of Lightshade's people gathered, using their magic to protect their homes. They reinforced the barrier with each militant strike against it. I watched them all nearly deplete their magic and be replaced by another to carry on in their place.

"Alpha," Damian sneered.

"You are quite right," Starfire replied, walking up beside us and watching the sky. "He is angry."

"I took what was his," I replied, my eyes fluttering in Damian's direction. "This is my punishment."

"What can we do?" Damian asked, turning to Starfire.

She closed her eyes and smiled. "What you do best."

We both looked at her, confused.

"Shine."

Damian and I looked at one another, and he took my hand in his. The fiery glow of our souls erupted to the surface. He glowed his icy blue fire while I blazed in red and orange embers. We lifted from the ground, holding tightly to each other's hand. We each lifted our free hand, and light exploded, shooting across the valley. Our bodies grew brighter, and soon, nothing but pure white light was visible to the naked eye. The powerful glow gathered to the top of the sky in the center of where the magic dome encased the valley. Its tendrils slowly crept across the dome, latching onto every bit of magic that swirled above and solidified it in its place. It sparkled and crackled as it wound over and out across the entire paradise. We pushed hard with our light, and the descending meteors began to slow and hover in midair, suspended briefly before bursting into clouds of stardust.

Alpha's scowling face appeared in the sky, glaring intensely at me.

"Parlor tricks," he hissed.

"We're coming for you, Alpha," I replied. "You can try to run, you can try to hide, but we will find you, and you will fall like the ashes of Eden."

He laughed deeply. "Do you think you can take me alone? A handful of Nephilim and Warlocks? A meager fleet of angels. You will still fail in the end! My army grows by the day, and they are bloodthirsty." He smiled, rolling his head and cracking his neck. "Bow to me, and those you love will live in the end. Defy me, and well, nothing will be left to mourn. Not even you two."

Damian shot an icy fireball into the sky, and Alpha's face distorted and disappeared. We descended to the ground below, and those around us watched in awe. As our feet touched the ground, Praeziel walked up to us. He put his right arm across the center of his chest, then took a knee.

"I pledge my allegiance to you," he shouted. "I will follow you to the ends of the earth, no matter how soon or far off that may be."

We looked around at the growing numbers of people that stood in Lightshade. While we had been protecting it, the Nephilim had begun to arrive. One by one, each Nephilim that had entered the valley gathered around us, pledging their loyalty to Damian and me. The warlocks took a knee, yelling their allegiances into the air. We looked around in amazement as they, one by one, each announced to follow us to the end of days.

"We shall fight alongside you as well, young Shining Ones," a voice called out behind us.

We turned around to see the Seelie and Unseelie courts standing behind us. The Dark Queen Mab, Titania, and Oberon stood at the forefront of the gathered fey. All three of them bowed to us, and every single one of their followers followed as well. More and more people began to appear from various portals into Lightshade. The sun eclipsed to cast a shadowy glow across the valley.

"The vampires pledge our allegiance to the cause as well," replied a young man stepping forward. "For too long, Alpha has experimented with humans, turning us into nightwalkers with the vampiric blood of those in the abyss."

"The werewolves do as well," a young woman said, stepping into the front of the crowd. "Alpha has mistreated our kind for far too long. It is time he pays for the crimes he has committed against all."

I was overwhelmed by the support of every imaginable creature that had suffered from Alpha's reign of terror. I looked from face to face as millions stood before us, pledging their lives to stop him.

"We will follow you wherever you go," a voice said behind me.

I turned around and ran toward the voice.

"Daddy!" I shouted as I wrapped my arms around my father's neck.

He hugged me, tightening his grip around my shoulders.

"I have been so worried about you," I cried, tears spilling onto his chest. "I was so afraid that Alpha still had you and was torturing you as punishment to me."

"You don't know how good it feels to see you and know you are safe," he replied, pulling back from the embrace. "I never imagined in all the worlds that you would be so powerful."

"I get it from my father," I replied as he swiped away a falling tear.

Behind him stood thousands upon thousands of angels who had been left in the Summit when Alpha abandoned his throne in the sky. I scanned the crowd, looking for one particular face.

"She's not here," he said, knowing who I was looking for. "I will explain it all, but right now, we have business to attend to."

Damian walked over to join us, and my father patted him on the back.

"It's nice to see you again, kid," he said, smiling. "I see you kept to your word."

"Not quite," he murmured.

Dad looked at him, a bit confused. I knew exactly what he was referring to.

"Where's Xavier?" Dad asked, looking around in the crowd for his face as I had my mother's face.

"That's a long story," I replied gravely. "But for now, just know he is safe, and he is home."

"Welcome, Incaendiel," Starfire said, pushing through the crowd to stand face to face with him. He towered over her like a giant. "We have much to talk about and to do."

"Yes, we do," he replied, nodding in agreement. "It's my understanding you have something for me?"

"I do," she replied. "Follow me inside. I was hoping Sophie would be with you, but that was another alternative move in the vast game of chess."

Dad's eyes lowered. "Yes, I had hoped as well."

"Come now, don't doddle," she said, and we watched the two of them disappear into her cottage.

CHAPTER 7

THE SOUNDS OF SWORDS clashing against one another filled the air as training commenced in Lightshade. They trained in rotations, allowing the vampires and werewolves to train under the eclipse of the sun each day. Nephilim and angels, warlocks and Seelies all spent their days preparing for the ultimate battle with Alpha. Starfire had given my father his elixir, and he painfully drank it alone without my mother to take her dose. She had refused to leave Alpha's side.

Damian and I trained in hand-to-hand combat with one another as others stopped to watch and stare in amazement. We danced in a fiery ambiance as our skin glowed brighter and brighter each day, the haze of our powers never diminishing. We clicked our swords active and began to battle one another, him with his long sword and me with my dueling swords. Our weapons clanked against one another as we worked at a precision speed, gaining momentum with each thrust and parry.

"You had one helluva trainer," Dad said as he watched us.

"I sure did," I replied, smiling at Damian.

"Don't let her fool you," Damian said. "I'm really just hanging by a thread here. She is schooling me."

Dad laughed heartily. I saw a shine in his eyes I hadn't seen since I was a little girl. He liked Damian, not like he had a choice, really. I dropped my dueling knives and pulled on the hand-to-hand knives Reikal had given me.

"That is not fair," Damian said. "Those things amplify your powers."

"Is someone afraid of losing?" I giggled.

"I like a challenge," he mused, cocking his mouth into a side grin.

I readied my hands when a sudden pain tore through my chest. I pressed my fist into my chest, sinking to the ground.

"Luxina," Dad said at my side faster than a bolt of lightning. "What's wrong?" he demanded.

"I... I don't know," I choked out, the pain growing sharper.

It's Alpha, Xavier's voice called out into my head. *We made a mistake.*

"Xavier?" I asked out loud by accident.

Damian narrowed his eyes.

"Xavier? Is something wrong with him?" Dad asked.

My eyes slowly turned up to my dad's eyes. We hadn't told him about Xavier yet, just that he was safe.

"Not right now," Damian hissed.

"He needs to know the truth," I hissed, wincing as another pain tore through my chest. "It might be that!"

"It might be what? Tell me what?" Dad asked.

"Help me carry her inside," Damian said, lifting me up under one of my arms.

Dad grabbed me under the other and led me into Starfire's cottage. They sat me down in one of the chairs while Damian ran to grab me a glass of water.

"What do I need to know?" Dad demanded.

"There was a prophecy," I began.

"What prophecy?" Dad asked, shaking his head.

"The one about the birth of three Shining Ones. Except the third Shining One was never supposed to exist. When I was created, the power between you and mom split," I explained, clenching my jaw in pain. "I split in half. Part of me staying with you, the other part of me staying with mom."

"This doesn't explain anything about where Xavier is," Dad replied.

"Xavier was me, Dad. Xavier was the dark half of my soul," I said, pressing my hand harder into my chest as another wave of pain sliced through.

Realization spread across his face. "So, what happened?"

"I absorbed myself back," I replied quietly. "It happened a lot sooner than what we had hoped it would. But we had to save Damian from Alpha. He had hijacked his mind. It was the only way to save him."

"You sacrificed your brother to save him?" Dad seethed.

"Xavier sacrificed himself!" I yelled. "I sacrificed myself. You of all people should understand. Look at what you sacrificed for Mom! For a lie!"

"What do you mean a lie?" he asked, irritated.

"Ask your mother," I hissed. "It was all a lie. The search for the garden, your darkness leaching mom's light. None of it was true. Your mother played a power trip with both of you."

"Let me guess, he told you?" Dad asked, glaring at Damian. "It's lies, Luxina."

"He didn't tell me. He didn't have to. I know everything he knows. I can still hear the words echoing from the Dark Queen Mab's lips as she told him in the Otherworld," I hissed.

"Instead of arguing over what is truth and what is not, how about we focus on what is happening to Luxina?" Damian interrupted. "You can hate me later, but right now, she needs help."

"Indeed, she does," Starfire said, walking into the room. "Something went wrong with the absorption."

"Xavier told me it's Alpha doing it," I cried out, grabbing my chest as it felt like it was ripping from my chest.

"We know the poison from the injections was removed from Luxina by the Watchers. What about Xavier?" Starfire asked.

"No," Dad replied. "He wasn't dying from them."

"He had already absorbed them," Damian said. "After the first set he received, they no longer affected him."

"So, when she absorbed him, the poisons slowly began to re-enter her system," Starfire stated.

"Why didn't they burn away as mine did?" Damian asked.

"Because she was still transitioning and hadn't fully taken Xavier's soul into hers. The transition is complete now," Starfire replied. "That's why she can hear him now."

"Well, what do we do?" Dad asked. "We can't just let her writhe in pain."

"I'm afraid that's exactly what we have to do. She must filter it out of her system," Starfire said, setting the manacles we had tied Damian up with on the table.

"What are those for?!" Damian shouted.

"You know what they are for," Starfire retorted. "Now, put them on her. Alpha will work her the same way he did you."

"No," Damian replied, outright refusing. "We are not chaining her up. I can handle her."

"Damian," I croaked out. "Just do it."

"No," Damian hissed. "You are nothing like I was. You won't hurt us."

I rose to my feet against my will as if I were being controlled. Everyone took a step back from me.

"Everyone, leave the room," Damian demanded.

I watched as Starfire slowly backed away from me.

"No, no, over here," Damian said, jumping into my line of sight. "Get her out, Incaendiel."

"I'm not leaving this room," Dad replied.

"Just do it!" Damian shouted.

I turned to look at Dad as he walked calmly over to Starfire and stood in front of her as he helped her out of the cottage.

"Hey," Damian spoke softly. "Right here."

I returned my gaze to him, craning my neck as I stared at him. He held his hands up gently as if coaxing me out of a temper tantrum. My body moved forward even though I didn't want to. He stood his ground as I walked closer to him. I reached my hand out to touch his face, expecting him to flinch away. He did not.

"Your hair is white now," I said. I looked around the room, and we were the only ones left in here with the front door shut. "Where did Incaendiel go?" I asked.

"He escorted Starfire from the room," Damian replied nervously.

"Why? I wasn't going to hurt her," I said, walking around the room and touching everything.

"Luxina?" Damian asked. "Luxina, can you hear me?"

Yes, yes, I can! I shouted. But the words did not leave my lips. *Why can't I talk?*

Because someone else is controlling you, Xavier replied.

Who? I asked.

You already know who it is. Just dig deeper, Xavier said.

He was right. I did know.

"Come with me, Damian," I said calmly. "Come with me to where it is safe."

"I'm right where I need to be," Damian replied.

"Safe?" I laughed. "Do you think you are safe here? Safe with Luxina? She killed your brother. She took my Xavier from me, and she will take you from me as well."

"Sophie?" Damian asked.

"Yes," I replied. "It's me. It's mother."

"You're not my mother," Damian sneered. "You aren't anyone's mother."

"Don't talk to me like that!" My voice echoed off the walls with a deafening screech.

The door opened, and Dad walked back into the room. My eyes watched him close the door behind him and walk over to Damian's side.

"Incaendiel, you look so different now. Brighter, glowing," I whispered. "Why did you leave me?"

"I didn't leave you, Sophie," he replied. "You refused to go with me. Alpha has brainwashed you."

"Alpha is our one true father, and no one should come before him," I stated. "Why can't you see that?" My voice was pleading.

"No, Sophie. That is one thing that isn't true. We are our own gods and far more superior to him," Dad replied.

I felt the fury growing in me, and the haze of glowing skin burst into flames.

"She was more important to you than anyone else in the end. Even more important than my precious boy." I lifted my hand, and a flaming fireball formed. "I tried to tell you. I tried to make you see. But you refused to believe that your precious little baby was evil."

"She is not evil!" Damian yelled.

My head jerked to look at him. "She has you under a spell, son. She will kill you in the end, too. You're nothing but a monster to her."

No! He is not a monster! I screamed inside.

"I know her better than you think," Damian replied. "And she would never call me that."

I cackled, throwing my head back. "You are so naive," I cooed. "Alpha was right. You're nothing. You're weak. She has turned you into a mindless drone."

I tossed the fireball in my hand at Damian and struck him in the chest, knocking him to the ground.

What have you done? I whispered to myself.

Another fireball formed in my hand, and I looked at my dad. He stood there, calmly.

"You're not even going to fight back?" I asked. "Too afraid of harming your precious cargo?"

"I don't want to hurt you, Sophie," Dad replied, walking casually to me.

"Liar!" I screamed. "If you had never wanted to hurt me, you wouldn't have made a choice for me all those years ago. You would have come with me to the Summit, or I would have stayed with you at the Glade."

"Mother is to blame for that," Dad replied. "She lied to us, Sophie. She lied to lay claim to power in the little game she played with Alpha. And it just goes around and around, and it always claims us in the end. She wanted to control us. She needed to keep us apart so our power wouldn't overpower her own."

"No," I whimpered.

"Yes," he replied.

He stood before me with pleading eyes. He wrapped his arms around me and squeezed me tightly.

"I love you so much, Sophie," he said. "I never stopped loving you. And when I thought you loved another more than me, my love grew for you in leaps and bounds. Come to me, my love. Come and be with our children."

"Do you love him as your own?" I asked in a whisper.

"I was the one that saved him," he replied.

I felt something snap around my wrists. Damian had slipped the manacles onto my wrists while I was paying attention to Dad. I screamed in fury, and then everything went dark. When I woke up, I was tied in a chair, wrestling with the ropes that bound me. Damian sat in a chair directly in front of me as I had done with him. His head was bent down, resting in his hands. He looked up, tired, and just stared at me.

"Come back to me, Luxina," he whispered.

I'm right here! I shouted in my mind.

"I'm here for a while, so get used to it," I replied instead. "I don't understand why you care so much about her."

"You never will," he replied, annoyed.

"Then, explain it to me," I said snidely. "I have all the time in the world."

"The only person in this room that would understand is him," Damian said, pointing to my dad. "He loved you. He loved you more than life itself. He died and came back to life for you. I watched it happen."

"So, you would die for her?" I asked.

"Over and over and over, again and again, and again," Damian replied. "She saw me for more than a weapon. She saw me for more than just a chess piece. She loved me without condition. You... you chose Alpha over every person that loved you or that you loved. Luxina, she defied Alpha. You know she did. You were punished for it."

I stared at his face, studying him.

He is nothing like me, Sophie thought within. *How can he be so much like Incaendiel?*

"Because he knows right from wrong right now," Dad replied. "Alpha is injecting you with nothing more than mind-controlling substances. He has gained your trust in him through lies. You weren't strong enough to fight it. You aren't at fault for that. But you can't blame innocents for that. Luxina, she is innocent in all his. She is your daughter. That should mean something to you."

"There's nothing but cloudiness in my mind. All I can think of is hating her," I replied.

"That is Alpha thinking through you," Damian replied. "I know more than ever what that feels like."

"Save me," I pleaded. "Incaendiel, save me!"

Dad went to leave the room.

"No," Damian demanded, halting him in his steps. "This is a trick."

A deep laugh emerged from my throat.

"Oh, you were always the smart one," I said profoundly. "Did you know that at any moment I could just simply kill her?"

Damian's eyes widened.

"I love these little games we play too much to do that," I laughed.

Damian stood from his chair, kicking it across the room.

"You give her back," he demanded, yelling into my face.

"Tsk-tsk. Always with that temper," I replied coolly. "I was so sure she would never save you from me that you were mine in finality. But you loved her so much. You came back for her. Do you think she loves you as much as you do her?"

Yes, I do! I cried. *Don't listen to him, Damian.*

"If she didn't love me, she would have never tried as hard as she did to save me from you," Damian replied quietly.

"That is what you think or what you know? Could it be that she was using you as her own little weapon?" I asked.

"Don't listen to him, Damian," Dad said. "He will manipulate you and will use anything he thinks will make you weak."

"Luxina is already his weakness and has been since he learned who she was. Always fighting how he felt around her. Wanting her and her precious Xavier to stay together. I hold in my hand the only thing that will destroy him," I replied. "How do you save her when you couldn't even save yourself?"

Stop it! I shouted at Alpha.

"Join me, Damian," I said.

"I will die before I join you," Damian sneered.

"Then have fun rescuing your precious Luxina from the darkness," I said.

My head slumped forward. I was unable to move.

"Luxina?" Damian asked, running to me.

He grabbed my face in his hands, gently shaking it.

"Luxina?" he asked with growing worry in his voice.

I sat there numbly, unable to respond. He placed my hand to his face, covering his eyes as he sobbed. I wanted to answer him. I wanted to tell him everything would be ok, but I could not speak. I could just stare blankly ahead, aware of everything. A haze began to fall upon my vision as darkness descended in my mind. I tumbled and free-fell through a dark hole, thudding to the ground. I was back at the meadow. There was hardly any light here. The tree where I had met Xavier so many times was nearly burned to a crisp from the last time I was here. It still smoldered from the flames.

I sank to the ground and brought my knees to my chest. I gently rocked back and forth as I fought the panic and anxiety welling within my chest. This had been my greatest fear. Being utterly alone. I looked up to the sky, and the dark blankets that covered it didn't produce a single star. It looked as if someone had painted over it all with a large brush. I buried my face in my hands. I was lost. I didn't know how to find my way back to the light.

Luxina.

I could hear Damian's voice in the wind, but he would never be able to find me here.

Please, Luxina. I can't do this alone.

His voice was but a whisper in my ear. I sat there for hours listening to him plead with me. I tried to follow his voice quite a few times and just found myself back at the tree. I eventually gave up and just balled up on the ground. No one could help me here. No one could save me here. This was worse than the Lake of Fire. At least with the lake, I felt pain. I feel nothing here. It's almost as if I am a ghost walking through Sheol.

"That's a word I haven't heard in a long time," a familiar voice said.

I glanced up to see the smiling face of Xavier. I jumped from my feet and hugged him tightly. I cried into his chest.

"It's you," I breathed. "It's really you."

"Of course, it is me," he replied. "I am you, remember?"

"I didn't think I would ever hear you or even see you again," I replied, sniffling.

"You're not supposed to see me," he replied. "You're a long way away from the light."

"Alpha put me here," I replied. "He is punishing Damian."

"I know," Xavier replied. "I am here to help you get back to the light."

"You can't help me," I said. "No one can save me here."

"You don't ever pay attention to anything, do you?" Xavier asked. "I am the dark half of you. This right here, this is where I stay, in the quiet, dark abyss. But the abyss, it isn't bad. It's vast and deep, but it's not a death sentence. You, you're the light. You're the hope that keeps this place thriving. This place looks to you like a lighthouse in the dark. When the air is thin, and the darkness feels like it is suffocating, you are the call that lets it know that things will be ok."

I stared at him in his infinite wisdom.

"I told you I would be with you through it all. That means the good and the bad. And when things get dark, I am here to let you know that darkness is not forever. Because you make the shadows tolerable."

Luxina! I could hear Damian's voice, which had grown quiet a long time ago.

"His voice is back," I murmured.

"He is leading you home," Xavier replied.

"Where is home?" I asked.

"Where your heart is," he replied.

"Where my heart is…" I whispered. "My heart is with Damian."

"Then follow the sound of your heart," he replied. "It will lead you to the light."

"Will you come with me?" I asked.

"I will walk with you as far as the darkness lets me," he replied.

And he did. He walked with me through the dark as I listened for Damian's voice. Every now and then, it would be so loud, and then the sound would soften to barely a whisper. Xavier walked me through a garden that had all kinds of flowers that bloomed in the night air. White daffodils, azaleas, magnolia trees, and all kinds of white flowers bloomed here, lending some light to contrast the dark. When the darkness started to lift, we walked through a bed of tulips that started off white and then turned to crimson sprouts, and he stopped.

"This is as far as I can go," he said, holding my hand.

"What if I get lost or turned around?" I whimpered.

He smiled at me. "Just follow your heart. Trust your instincts." He bent down and picked up a tulip, handing it to me. I brought it to my nose and breathed in the sweet smell it emitted. It was partially white and partially red, split down the middle. "Tiptoe through the tulips. They are delicate and fragile but persistent and beautiful nonetheless, just like you."

He stood there, watching as I made my way to Damian's voice until I could no longer see him in the darkness.

Come back to me.

I am, Damian. Lead me back home to you.

I walked through more and more tulip beds that turned into a giant field under the light rays of the sun peeking through the clouds. The light became a blinding light, and I shielded my eyes as I continued to walk. I looked back toward the darkness where Xavier was.

Stay with me!

I paused, torn between the two. I looked at the blinding light and back to the darkness.

Stay with me...

His voice began to fade away. The light grew brighter and brighter as I ran headfirst into it.

Always, I replied.

CHAPTER 8

MY EYES FLUTTERED OPEN as sunlight filtered in an open window. I scanned through the room around me when my eyes landed on Damian slumped in a chair, sleeping. It wasn't often I was able to steal glances at him without him turning away from me. I drank in every single aspect of him I was able to see. Even as scars riddled his body, he was the most beautiful thing I had ever laid eyes on. Even if he refuted it himself, he would never be able to sway my made-up mind at how marvelous he looked. His white hair glistened in the rays of sunlight that filtered over him. And those eyes of his... They were remarkable pools of light in which I could spend all day basking in the ambiance of their glow.

I may have been forced to slip into the darkness where all seemed hopeless, but emerging into the light with him at my side was the best feeling in the world. It nearly felt like everything had been but just a dream. I got to speak with Xavier. I desperately needed to know that he was with me, and that question had been answered in the best way possible. I learned more about myself in my short time with Xavier than I had in my entire existence. Darkness was but a metaphor. There was nothing sinister about it. There was nothing about it that would harm me.

I began to stir in bed when Damian's eyes opened. I watched the recognition transform his glazed eyes to vibrant ones of joy and happiness. He rushed to the side of the bed and cupped his hands around my face, peering deeply into my eyes. His eyes wandered and searched every inch of my face as they came to rest on my eyes.

"I thought I had lost you," he murmured. "I was afraid you would never come back to me."

"I will always come back to you. I will always come back for you. I will always come back when it has anything to do with you," I replied, grazing his cheeks with my hand. "I heard your voice, and it led me back to the light. It led me back to you."

He leaned in and kissed my lips ever so gently. It felt like rose petals brushing up against them. I pressed back against his, and the fire built within my belly and bosom. I wrapped my arms tightly around his neck and pulled him deeper into the kiss as his body crashed down onto mine. All I cared about right now was showing him how much he meant to me. He was not a lost soul or a lost cause. He was not a monster. He wasn't Alpha's plaything. He was mine, and I was his, and there wasn't anything that anyone could do to stop it now.

I tugged his shirt off and up over his head, then ran my fingers all along his torso, memorizing every scar as if they were braille on his skin telling me a story. He wound his hand through my hair and flipped me over in the bed, where I was on top, pulling me in closer and closer with each labored breath of excitement. I settled beside him in the bed with his arms wrapped around me, binding me tightly to his chest.

"I could hear everything and see everything when they had control of me," I spoke softly.

"Yeah, I could, too," he murmured in reply.

"You know everything Alpha said to you was a lie, right?" I asked. "You do know I love you just as much as you love me, don't you?"

Damian fell silent.

"Damian?"

My eyes moved to meet his. He just lay there staring off at the wall behind me. I propped myself up on my elbow and gently caressed his chin with my hand, pulling his face to look at me. He couldn't maintain eye contact with me as his eyes gave away what he was thinking.

"I only think of you as one thing. It isn't a monster. It isn't a weapon. It isn't a chess piece. I think of you as beautiful. You're the most beautiful person I have ever met. Even before I knew Xavier was me, I had fallen in love with you. When you showed up at our campsite… I tried to fight everything I was feeling. But I couldn't. The more time I spent with you, the more I wanted to be with you. It was always more than just saving you from Alpha. I didn't want to save you because Alpha could use you as a weapon. I wanted to save you, to set you free."

His eyes locked on mine, and I could see the pain and anguish that Alpha had put him through. I could see how Alpha had convinced him time and time again that no one loved him. Had he waited for us to rescue him? Had he given up on us ever loving him? Had the doubt seeped deep enough that he would always question my love for him?

"I would have rescued you over and over and over again if given the chance," I whispered to him. "You're worth saving. You're worth loving. You're worth everything to me. You're my universe. Feel my love for you," I said as I placed his hand over my heart.

The room fell silent as I waited for him to speak. Everything in me felt like it was dying at once. My heart felt like it could wrench free from my chest and explode. How do you convince someone who feels worthless and loveless that they are the center of your world? That you love them unconditionally? That you see beauty where they believe ugly exists? How do you make them see through your eyes and experience what your heart feels for them?

He gently removed his hand from the center of my chest without a word. He stood up from the bed and walked to the door.

"When you feel up to it, we have training to do," he spoke softly.

He opened the door, walked out, and closed it behind himself. A range of emotions washed over me. How can you go from madly kissing someone to being distant and cold? Tears threatened to slip down my cheeks. I wiped them away, furious. I hated Alpha. I hated every single drop of pain he had caused my family to feel. I was going to make him pay, even if it meant I had to do it alone. He would regret every single moment he made Damian feel worthless and unloved.

I left my room and walked downstairs to the open door of Starfire's cottage. The Nephilim were training with the warlocks, and Damian was their leader. His skin glistened under the rays of the sun as he moved with diligence and ease. They mimicked his moves in unison.

"Nephilim were once powerful beings," Starfire offered, jarring me from my thoughts.

"What happened?" I asked.

"Alpha happened. They are half-mortal. They age exponentially slower than other mortals. They have immortal souls, but they do die. Alpha made sure that their immortality wouldn't last an earthly age. He stripped them of their immortality prior to the Great Flood, hoping they would all perish. Many did. The ones that survived had hidden away in Stygia with their mother. Many years after the flood, some decided to venture back out. They assimilated with humans. Some don't even know they are descendants of angels. The ones that stayed behind lived longer than the ones who did not," Starfire replied.

"Why?" I asked, confused.

"In order for them to retain their immortality, they had to pair up with another Nephilim. That was how Alpha stripped their immortality away. If they chose to take on humans as mates, they would live a human life. The ones that paired up lived forever. The ones that choose no side were met in the middle with death. They aged quite slowly, but eventually, they died. Once Alpha is defeated, they will be able to choose if they wish to be purely immortal or if they want to live mortal lives without being stuck in the middle of the two."

I watched the Nephilim soldiers as they picked up their swords and began to duel. I wondered which ones these were. Were they paired with other Nephilim, or were they paired with human mates? Were they paired at all? I caught Starfire watching me from the corner of my eye and turned to look at her.

"I know what you're thinking about doing," she stated.

"And what is that?" I asked innocently.

"You're going to try to stop Alpha all on your own. Kill him before the battle begins," she replied.

I turned my gaze from her and focused on Damian training those around him.

"He deserves to know that someone loves him enough to avenge what happened to him. What Alpha did to him," I said firmly.

"You know he won't let you go fight Alpha alone," Starfire chuckled. "He won't let you go at all."

I smiled. "That's why he's not going to find out," I replied.

"What are you going to do? Sneak off?" she asked.

"That's exactly what I'm going to do," I replied, shifting my body weight. "And you're not going to speak a word of this with anyone."

Starfire nodded. "Do you care if you live or die trying this?" she asked. "Because I know the answer."

I shook my head, staring back out at Damian. "No, I don't care either way. Just as long as he knows how much I really did love him. That's all that matters."

"Well, you better get a move on then," Starfire replied. "Training will be over soon."

I nodded and gave her a quick hug. I stepped out of the door frame so no one could see what I was doing. I pulled from deep within and summoned a portal. I had been to the compound Alpha had kept Damian. I was a prisoner there as well. I remembered the room they had held me captive in. It appeared in the translucent doorway. I stood there, staring through the open gateway. Could I really do this? Was I strong enough to really take down Alpha? Starfire knew, but honestly, I didn't want to know myself. I was a god now. I should be able to take on Alpha head-on and make it out alive. He couldn't even put Tiamat down. She still existed as the Leviathan. Just as I was about to step through, a voice called my name.

"Luxina?"

I looked over at Damian, standing in the doorway. He was puzzled, and his face gave away every bit of confusion he had. He looked at me and then looked through the portal to see where I was going. His face went from confused to fearful as he registered what I was doing.

"No!" he shouted.

"I love you, Damian," I said.

He ran toward me as I stepped through the portal, and the doorway disappeared behind me. I stood in the darkened room where, a year ago, I had been chained up with Xavier while Alpha tried to turn me into a war machine. This would be my only chance to make everything right again. I had to prove to Damian how much I cared. I had to show everyone that I was willing to take risks. I was not just a pretty face. I am my father's daughter. I had to prove that I was unbreakable.

"Ah, Luxina. You came back after all!"

I turned around to the voice that broke through the darkness.

"Hello, Alpha."

Firefly of Immortality II

THE GUARDIANS OF LIGHT SERIES

BOOK FIVE

Azoth Khem Publishing
Huntsville, AL
February 2026

Prologue

I SAT IN silence as those around me bickered and argued. I had traveled alone to Stygia to hold council with the Watchers. Half of them didn't want to engage with Alpha and half of them wanted to wage the war that had been long overdue. I sighed heavily as I squeezed the bridge of my nose in annoyance. I hadn't a clue as to why they weren't as furious with Alpha as I had been for the past millions of years. My emotions began to run rampant, and I could feel the burn bubbling to the surface. I had repressed my anger and resentment for far too long, and it was ready to rear its ugly head.

"Why is it so hard to decide?" I yelled out, erupting into flames.

Silence fell over the quarreling room as all eyes rested on me. The flames receded as I composed myself. I looked at each face that sat in the room. The scars of war were painted on their skin. Runes of power etched their arms and faces. Their eyes... they told a story that no one could hear.

"You were all abandoned by Alpha. You were left to rot, and for what? Doing your duty? Listening and doing what Alpha told you to do? You were all cast aside because he created something he himself could not destroy. You others," I stated, looking out toward the Nephilim in the room, "you were created from angels, and he turned his back on you, calling you abominations! He loves no one but himself. He must be brought down to the level he deserves."

Glances were exchanged amongst themselves with quiet murmuring.

"Incaendiel is right," Sophia insisted, standing from her seat. "We were made into Children of the Night. Alpha is growing his numbers by the day, and soon, we will be battling replicas of ourselves that are evil, twisted, and manipulated into thinking we are the bad guys. That is what Alpha does; he manipulates others to bend to his will, and if you don't, he will make you one way or another. Look at Incaendiel's poor daughter, Luxina. She stood against Alpha, and he nearly killed her with those injections. We need to stop his tyranny. We need to stop being afraid of the father who disallowed our entrance back into heaven. It is time to stand and fight. When the Seelie courts pledge their allegiance, we shall, too. Both Watcher and Nephilim."

The room nodded as the murmuring grew to a loud hum and turned into boisterous chatter. I nodded to Sophia and smiled. I needed this. Alpha had taken so much away from me. Sophie had been the last straw. My heart sank as I thought of our last words before the Glade imploded. I balled my fists in fury and heartache. I would avenge whatever happened to her.

A loud siren began to echo throughout the war room, and everyone scrambled to their feet.

"What's going on?" I called out to Sophia over the noise.

"Intruders," she yelled back. "Quick, we need to get the kids to safety!"

She began to run down a narrow hall that opened into an atrium. She disappeared down a corridor as I rounded the corner behind her. Hands snatched me from behind, and before I could even react, I felt all my power drain from my body as someone wrapped around my wrists the one and only thing that could subdue all angels, something made from unicorn hair.

Chapter 1

IT HAD BEEN so long since I had seen daylight that I had forgotten what the sun looked like as a sliver of light seemed to find its way into the dungeon I had been locked away in. Time was a moot point, and there was no telling how long I had been left to rot in this cell. This place couldn't have been the place Alpha had been hiding this entire time. That would have been too easy, plus the Watchers would have immediately executed a strike in retaliation for the bloodshed left behind when Alpha captured me. All I have been able to think of is whether my babies were able to make it out safely. I know Sophia would never let anything happen to either of them. She knows more than the rest of us about what they are. She told me how we all are the key to saving the world as we know it, before Alpha completely ruins it all with his new breed of angels.

It is so odd to think of me having more than one child when it has been just Luxina and me solely for the last eight years. I saw the look on Xavier's face. He isn't too fond of me, but from my understanding, he isn't too fond of anyone except for Mother Lilith. She was the one who raised him while Sophie was off traipsing the galaxy for her son, Damian. Just the thought of that little red-headed boy sent both sorrow and hatred through my bones. He was the reason Luxina was taken. However, he was also raised by Alpha without any choice. And the experiments Alpha has performed on him... the poor kid.

As if by cue, the door to this dreary place popped open, and in he strode. You couldn't mistake his fiery curls on his head nor the astonishing blue eyes that shone like the stars. He was his mother made over. He didn't have a single feature of Lucifer about him, except maybe his attitude. I got a closer look at his face. His eyes were sunken in with dark circles under them. He was bone thin, as well. Were they feeding him? Torturing him? I saw a red mark that trailed down his neck and under his shirt that looked fresh and was still bleeding a bit. He lingered at the door as if he were contemplating what he was doing. He straightened, and his demeanor changed. I waited for others to follow, but none did. He was alone, but that didn't erase the cocky smirk from his face as he shut the door behind him, walked over to me, and pulled a chair up sitting down and staring. I stared back, studying his face, trying to read his mind. He was a blank slate. I wonder what Alpha wants him to do to me.

"Nothing," he stated with a poker face.

I know a look of confusion had to spread across my face because he sat back in the chair, placing his arms behind his head as he teetered the chair off its front legs, watching me as if pleased with himself.

"I know. It's confusing. And no, Alpha has no idea," he replied with a confident grin.

My brows shot up, and I tilted my head a bit. "You can read minds?" I asked in disbelief.

"Yes, but I haven't always been able to. I'm sure it is something that has to do with the experiments that Alpha does on me," he replied with a shrug. "It may have been the connection with my siblings that triggered it. I will never know. All I know is that one day, I could hear the thoughts of every person who stood in the room with me. Some may think it's a curse, some a blessing. I find it to be a useful asset in times of war."

"Your mother and I could read each other's minds. It might have something to do with that," I offered. I still didn't understand how Sophie and I could talk to one another silently.

"She is not my mother," he responded heatedly, his eyes dead set on me, roiling beneath the surface with an icy fire.

I watched as he composed his anger and returned his gaze to me. His face once again registered a cool, calm, collected look.

My brows knitted together with uncertainty. "Why do you say that, Damian? Why do you speak of Sophie in such ill regard?" I asked, not understanding why he held so much contempt for her.

He looked away as a moment of sadness washed over his face before he could replace it with the cold, emotionless expression he likes to sport.

"She may have created me with my father, but neither of them will ever be my parents. They will never understand me. They will never understand the endured torture I have been put through while being with Alpha." He looked at me earnestly, and I empathetically nodded my head.

"You know, Luxina and you have that temper thing going for yourselves. She gets angered and explodes into fire so easily. I can't imagine who she gets that from," I added with a chuckle escaping.

"From my understanding, she gets it from you," he remarked with a smirk.

I watched him intently. "What does *he* want with me, Damian?" I asked, gazing deep into his eyes.

His face was solemn. "The same thing he wanted with me. The same thing he wanted with Sophie, and the same thing he wanted with my brother and sister," he answered. "He wants to build an army of new angels."

"I thought he no longer had the power to create? He can't just go around injecting people, hoping the injections take. And I certainly hope he doesn't think we can procreate a new race for him."

"He isn't going to do any of that," Damian confessed with a sincere, concerned look.

"What are his plans?" I pressed, leaning forward as far as the chains would let me.

Damian looked around the room and leaned forward to me, the chair legs settling softly on the floor. "Once our blood accepts these injections, he plans to use Lilith at his side to create a special race from our newly formed blood. The creations won't be mindless anymore because he has Lilith at his side now. However, they thought the original werewolves and vampires were horrible in the beginning, but these new creatures, these new angels he wants to make... they will destroy everything." He stared at me with bewilderment and fear.

I mulled over what he was telling me. "Why are you helping him?" I probed. "Why do you fear this plan but still help him?"

"I have no choice," he replied, straightening up and returning to his position in the chair he had been in. The nonchalant, not caring attitude washed back over him.

My eyes bored into his. "We all have a choice, Damian," I refuted, shaking my head. "There has to be a reason you are helping him."

A mischievous look replaced his poker face. "Who says I am truly helping him?" he teased with a sly grin.

I scrunched my face in puzzlement. "You helped him take Luxina and Xavier," I stammered.

He narrowed his eyes at me. "Incorrect. Lucifer was the one who orchestrated both of those incidents, not I," he countered. "I don't want them anywhere near Alpha."

A snicker escaped my lips, and before I could stop myself, I quipped, "Afraid he would choose them over you and you would be the outcast once more?" a bit too sarcastic. I expected him to fill with rage, but he did not.

"Yes," he murmured very quietly and simply. "And they don't deserve that as a punishment."

It took me a moment to process what he meant by his last sentence. I studied him closer underneath the poor lighting. There were tiny scars all over his face. The sunken eyes I had noticed were more than just sunken, but were hollow and lifeless. The spunk and spirit he had the day he took Luxina had been replaced with bruised and broken. The fresh blood I noticed was now pooling more and had spread further on his shirt, while other spots on his torso began to bleed through. While I couldn't let him know, I truly ached for the treatment he had been dealt.

"You care for them, don't you?" I queried, squinting at him.

"Why wouldn't I? They are what I am missing in life. They are my blood," he remarked, squinting back at me. "I keep everyone at arm's length. I don't wish to get close to anyone. It's been my thing since I was a youngster. Alpha never showed me what love is. He never showered me with affection. He just wanted me to create this stupid army of his. However, I have seen the way Luxina looks at me. She looks at me with love and empathy, and sorrow. She doesn't see me as a monster. At least, she didn't until the attack of the Watchers. I have no idea what her thoughts are of me at this moment. She could hate me for all I care. All that matters is that she and Xavier stay safe and as far away from Alpha as I can keep them."

A warmer look overtook my face. "So, when you took her from me, all of those things you said. Your cold demeanor... that wasn't you?" I asked.

He shook his head. "The injections Alpha gives me make me vulnerable to mind control. I have to do whatever I am told. Lucifer struck a deal with Alpha to deliver both Xavier and Luxina to him in exchange for me. Alpha took the deal, but he won't hold up his end of the bargain even if he still had them in his grasp. Alpha needs us."

"Mother created us. She can create more of us. Why does he need us specifically?" I questioned.

"Because the Unseelie Queen will no longer help him, nor will she aid Lilith in creating more of the Shining Ones," Damian replied, shifting in his seat. "She is the key to it all..."

"How?" I began when the door busted open.

Lucifer walked in, grinning ear to ear. "Ah, son, starting early are we?" he inquired, walking over to Damian. "Did Alpha give the orders to start on him?"

"Yes and no," Damian answered, settling his chair back on the ground and standing up. "We were just having a small chat. I needed to know where my siblings might be hiding and who but their father would know that answer. However, you interrupted."

A voice echoed in my head. *I will return to speak with you again. I have a lot to fill you in on before things get so out of hand that they cannot be controlled. There will be another visitor, and after they leave, I will be back to free you.* I looked at Damian, who was staring at me intently. I nodded with my eyes.

"Well, does he know where they are? Do we need to force it out of him?" Lucifer prodded, grinning madly.

"He doesn't know," Damian responded, walking to the door.

"And you believe him?" Lucifer shouted.

Damian spun on his heels and grabbed Lucifer, pinning him against the wall by the shirt collar. "Do you question my authority?" Damian demanded, glowering at Lucifer. "He doesn't know."

I could see the fear settling on Lucifer's face and nearly grinned. That boy does hate him, and who could blame him? He was dealt a crappy hand by this whole thing.

"That is not how you talk to me! I am your superior, and I am your father! You will respect me!" Lucifer bellowed.

"Respect is earned, and you do not have a single respectable bone in your pathetic existence," Damian retorted, pointing his finger in Lucifer's face.

"Is that why you're in here? Buttering up to Incaendiel in hopes he would adopt you as his?" Lucifer demanded, glaring over at me.

"At least he proves to be a better father than you ever have," Damian seethed. "Now, leave the room and do not bother the prisoner. Alpha wants him to remain untouched and unharmed. Those are orders!"

And with that, Damian left the room. Lucifer scowled in my direction and followed, shutting the door behind him. Once again, I was left in the dark, dank room with everything whirling around in my head. Could that be it? Could Damian be looking at me as a father figure? I processed everything we had spoken about. I believed him. His fear of what Alpha was planning was real. I believed him when he said he was being forced into doing what Alpha wanted. He wanted to be free. If I ever escaped this hellhole, I was going to be the one to free him, too. I owed it to Sophie. I owed it to her memory. I owed it to her soul. She had spent so long searching for him to get him back. I had to save him just for her. She wasn't here to do it herself...

One thing that Damian had said bothered me the most. He spoke as if he had seen the chaos and destruction of the future if Alpha were to succeed in making this new race of angels. He had the ability to read minds; could he see the future as well? Did all of the children have this gift? When did it start? I know Luxina would have mentioned hearing people's thoughts if she could, but I had just met Xavier before I was seized. I didn't even get a moment to speak with him, really. Is he like Damian? Did he have special gifts as well? Does Damian dream like the twins do? These were all questions I needed answers to, and I couldn't even go to search for them. I was trapped here. I knew if I pulled hard enough on the chains that they would break free from the wall, but what good would that do? I would still have to fight my way free. If they captured me once, they could do it again. My only choice was to sit here and wait for Alpha to appear and share his grand plans with me. Damian gave me a taste of what the plans are, and I needed more than that. I needed to see who my visitor would be.

With the sight of Damian, I couldn't help but be consumed with thoughts of Sophie. Grief overtook me as I sat there thinking of the only person I had and would ever love. I had spent millennia trying to convince her mortal mind and heart to love me once more. As fast as I had gotten her back, I had lost her. I agree with Luxina that it wasn't fair of me to let her go. Lucifer wasn't supposed to hurt her either. When I had seen her locked away in that tower, so helpless, so vulnerable, every empathetic fiber for Lucifer snapped within me. After he orchestrated the kidnapping of Luxina, my blood boiled in regard to him.

The last few moments I had with Sophie were… the most painful ones I had ever experienced. Wanting to wrap her in my arms and float off into eternity was thwarted for I had more pressing issues at hand than my own selfish love interests. Our children needed to be saved. What bothered me the most, though, was when Luxina broke free of the nightmares inflicted by the injections Alpha gave to her, speaking of her mother. Her mother blaming her as she burned in the fire. Was it possible that Sophie's soul spoke beyond the potter's field of angels? Our last words together, she was enraged, thinking I only wanted to keep Luxina safe and not Xavier as well. As if I would let my own son be harmed in any way. I had no clue I had a son until Lucifer informed me right before he took Luxina.

The Watchers told me that Luxina spoke of burning in a lake of fire in her moments of lucid talking. Was it possible that Sophie was also in that lake? Could Sophie have genuinely reached out to Luxina? Was Alpha punishing Sophie for Luxina escaping with Xavier? Dozens of thoughts flooded my mind, and I couldn't even escape them. The one that lingered the heaviest, though, was who my visitor would be.

Chapter 2

I SAT UP groggily with my vision zoning in and out from light and then to black. Little flecks of light darted around in the black, and I sucked a gulp of air into my lungs. As my eyes came into focus, I surveyed my surroundings. I had no idea where I was or how I got here. I touched the back of my head and winced in pain, withdrawing my hand that had blood smeared on it. What happened? I tried to focus my thoughts on one single moment, but everything was a blur. The last coherent thing I remembered was chatting with Damian and Lucifer busting in. I tried to concentrate on what we had been talking about, but my mind was foggy.

My eyes still circled the area where I lay. I looked down to see exactly where I sat to see if there were any clues as to how I got here, what I was doing here, or even why my head was bashed in. A soft bed of peat moss with pink and purple flowers growing all around it lay beneath me. My eyes moved out a bit further than where I sat, unfocusing and focusing from my head trauma, and I noticed that there was a circle of stones around the bed of moss. *Circle of stones.... Circle of stones... I know there is....* I tried to think hard and remember what a circle of stones in the forest meant. The harder I tried to think, the worse my head hurt.

"I can fix that up for you, love," a voice cooed in the wind ever so softly.

I whipped my head around, trying to see who it was. My eyes began to unfocus and blur again, with the blackness threatening to take over.

"Do you know how you got here?"

The voice was a female voice, melodic and soothing. I tried focusing again, looking around. My eyes landed on what looked like a small woman. I squinted to try to ease the blurriness of my double vision.

"I can't remember anything," I replied as I tried to stand.

Nausea and dizziness overtook me, and I sank back into the ring of moss. *Ring of moss... circle of stones... fairy circle...*

"Are things coming into focus now?" she asked, stepping closer, but still maintaining her distance.

"You're a fairy," I blurted out.

She giggled. "Aye, that I am. But do you know which fairy?" she mused, chiding.

"If I knew what fairy, I would have said your name," I retorted, irritated and a bit snarky.

"I'm not just some measly sprite or brownie, now. I'm a real faery with some real power in my punch. I'm fey, part of the Seelie court," she offered.

Seelie court... it can't be...

"You wouldn't happen to be the Queen herself, would you?" I inquired, attempting to stand to my feet once more.

"You're a quick one, Incaendiel," she cooed. "Aye, it is I, Queen Titania."

"How do you know my name?" I asked, walking over to her with wobbly legs and a loud thump on my head.

"I know all about you. You're a Shining One, just like your children are. Sweet lad and lass, you have there," she sighed and smiled.

"You've met Xavier and Luxina?" I stammered with mixed emotions.

"Of course, I have," she replied with a giggle. "Come with me, and I will tell you all about it."

She extended her hand to me, but I hesitated for a moment about taking it. The fey have never provoked the celestial realm, never caused any trouble with angels or fallen angels, but they could be nefarious, whether they were Seelie or not. I weighed my options. I could stay here, wherever here was, and try to find some way to go where I needed to go, even though I couldn't remember where that was supposed to be. Or I could go with her, and she might be able to fill me in on what exactly was going on.

I took her hand, and she smiled as she walked me through a meadow. Birch trees wrapped around us as we walked, and either my vision was still weird from the hit to my head, or there was something strange about how our surroundings looked. They look almost... warped.

"That is the portal you see," Titania responded as if she knew what I was thinking. "Birch tree groves are direct portal paths to the Seelie court."

The more we walked, the more our surroundings transformed into a beautiful world. Angels had never ventured into the Otherworld before. We were forbidden. It was a grand sight. Meadows and mountains as far as the eye could see, with skies that twinkled varying shades of light blues, pinks, and purples in a similar fashion to the aurora borealis. Creatures that humans had long since forgotten bounded around the area. A giant cyclops stomped around the mountains in the distance. A harpy flitted around like a hummingbird. A sphinx soared overhead of us, letting loose a deafening roar.

"The world had grown too dangerous for these beasts to survive and not be killed off," Titania stated as if she were reading my mind.

As if on cue, a solid white unicorn galloped in front of us, and I stopped dead in my tracks in the middle of the field.

"Do not fear it, love," Titania chuckled.

"Unicorn hair renders us powerless," I replied, keeping my distance.

The unicorn walked closer to me, and just as I was about to step back from it, it kneeled before me.

"As I thought," Titania squealed. "Hurry, love. Come with me. There is much work to be done."

"What does that mean?" I asked as she tugged me along, away from the unicorn.

As we walked, more and more of the mythological creatures that Alpha had told us had gone extinct after the flood of Noah began to appear. A pegasus flew high through the clouds in the sky, playing with a gryphon. Another deafening roar erupted in the sky as a red dragon breathing fire raced through the sky, holding gold in its claws. A squall followed as a red bird soared above the treetops, landing on one of the birch trees. A feather loosened from its body and floated down to me. I picked it up from the ground to inspect it. Another loud squall followed as it flew to the ground below and burst into flames.

"A phoenix," I breathed in awe. "They still exist." I tucked the feather away that it had left me with.

"You have much to learn, Firefly," Titania giggled.

"Firefly?" I asked, turning to her. "How do you know my nickname?"

"Because I was one of the ones that helped create you, deary," Titania replied with another childish giggle.

As she walked me through the meadow and away from all of the majestic beasts of lore, a castle appeared before us. A mote circled the castle as if it were plucked from the tales of King Arthur. We walked across a drawbridge as the Queen's knights stood guard.

"Good evening, Raul," Queen Titania stated, smiling as we walked through the gates.

Raul bowed to her. "Good evening, ma'lady," he responded.

"Tell me, Incaendiel," Titania began as we continued into the castle. "What do you remember about your time being held captive by Alpha?" she asked.

"To be honest, not much," I replied as I touched the back of my head. "I am fairly certain I was struck and lost my memory. I remember speaking with Damian while I was chained up, and that's about it."

"Ah, young Damian," Queen Titania sighed with a smile. "He is on his own journey as of right now through the Unseelie courts. Such a sweet boy, to my understanding. Very misunderstood because of Alpha's abuse."

"I wouldn't know. The few times I spoke to him are hazy, but he was also one of the people who grabbed Luxina. For his sake, I hope Alpha was controlling him," I replied.

We walked into a grand hall that had a large fountain in the middle. The water sparkled as if it had magic of its own. Queen Titania walked over to it and ran her hand through the water.

"This water is special water," she stated as she played with the falling water streams. "Would you like your memories back?" she asked, peering up at me.

"I would," I answered hesitantly. "How does it do that?"

"You will see," she said and motioned for me to climb into the water.

I walked over to the fountain and began to climb in.

"I'm afraid it will be painful," she warned. "You must fully submerge."

I nodded, finished stepping in, and lay down in the water. As soon as my head was submerged, a searing pain tore through my body. The water began to turn black around me as it leached whatever was in my body out. I screamed in pain, but it came out in gurgles beneath the surface of the water.

"I did warn you," I heard her reply in garbled words.

Memories began to pour in.

***

I was chained to the wall of the dungeon I had been locked away in after Alpha had kidnapped me. Even though there wasn't any way to gauge time in that room, it wasn't long after my capture when the door opened. Alpha walked through the door, and the room lit up. He looked younger than I last remembered him to be.

He pointed up to the bright lightbulb. "Funny how that happens whenever I grace a dark room," he chuckled. "Hello, my son."

I stared daggers at him and tried to stand, but the chains weren't long enough. "Where am I? Where is my daughter? Where is Sophie?" I demanded.

He took a seat across from me, and I lunged, the chains keeping me from reaching him.

A devious grin spread across his face. "Such spirit," he laughed. "I can't imagine where you get it from. Must be me."

I ignored his attempts at father-son bonding. "Answer my questions," I demanded again.

He pursed his lips. "You are in a dungeon in a hidden place away from the rest of your cohorts," he replied. "As for your daughter, I haven't a clue where she is. I was hoping you could answer that question."

I looked down my nose at him. "Even if I knew where she was, I would never tell you," I hissed in contempt.

He was quiet for a moment, studying my face with tight lips. "Why do you hate me so much, Incaendiel?" he asked, shaking his head. "What have I ever done to you that caused so much contempt to rile you in this manner?"

I scowled and sneered at him, "You know what you have done.

He raised an eyebrow as a defensive and innocent look spread across his face. "I have done nothing. It was your choice to fall with the others," he replied. "A moment of free will for you all. I allowed you to choose to stay with me or to fall with your mother. You chose your mother. If anyone should be angry, it should be me that you chose your mother over your father."

"You didn't give her much of a choice, did you? You asked one of us to fall, and when you grew angry, she took our place," I retorted.

A devilish grin lit up his face as if he knew something I didn't. *"She has all of you wrapped around her finger, doesn't she?"* he asked inquisitively. *"She's not the saint you believe her to be, you know?"*

I snorted. *"I have to disagree,"* I replied. *"Everything out of your mouth is a lie and always has been. You promised never to abandon us, and that's exactly what you did. You abandoned us once we fell."*

"Did I? Or is that what she told you?" Alpha asked, cocking an eyebrow. *"You see, son. Your mother and I had a marital spat in the Garden. She was the one who declared war, not I."*

I glared at him. *"Lies!"* I snarled.

His brows shot up. *"Are they? Then why would she be here with me?"* he mused, leaning forward.

Anger tore through me. *"You kidnapped her, too?!"* I demanded, trying to break free of the chains.

Alpha laughed and leaned back in his chair. *"That's what she wants you all to think. She is here out of her own free will. She chose to come back to my side."*

I rolled my eyes in annoyance and disgust. *"And why would she choose that?"* I asked.

He smiled. *"So, we can rule together again, of course,"* he replied. *"And to make sure you don't steal our throne of power."*

"Yeah, ok," I laughed.

As if on cue, the door opened, and in walked Mother. She walked over to me, knelt before me on the floor, and put her hand gently on my face.

I stared into her eyes. I hadn't seen her since the fallen had returned to the Summit. Just as he looked, she appeared a bit younger in age.

"Mother?" I breathed.

Her eyes were warm and inviting. *"My son,"* she replied with a smile.

She stood from her kneeling position in front of me and walked to where Alpha was sitting. She stood by his side, placing her hand on his shoulder.

"So, it's true," I gasped, followed up with a glare.

Her eye twitched nervously. *"Yes,"* she replied, swallowing hard. *"Your father and I have made amends."*

Rage tore through me as I watched the two of them smile like some sort of hand-crafted puppets. I lunged again, and the chains in the wall gave some.

I had had enough of the small talk banter of deception. "Where are my kids?" I demanded.

The door opened, and to my surprise, Asmodeus, as well as a few others, rushed in to secure my chains. Asmodeus held me from the front with his back to Alpha and Lilith. His eyes tried to tell me something, but I had no idea what he was trying to convey to me.

"This might hurt, son," Alpha stated as a needle jabbed into my neck.

Everything went dark. When I finally came to, I was alone once more in the room. How long had I been out? The door opened, and Asmodeus walked in, carrying some water and food.

"You are a sight for sore eyes," I chuckled as he set the tray down in front of me.

"Brother," he smiled as he wrapped his arms around me and looked around nervously. "I haven't much time before they come in to give you another injection. The next injection is THE injection. Alpha will know everything at all times once you receive this injection. It is his mind control one. He can make you say and do things you normally wouldn't do or say."

"Help me, then," I urged.

He withdrew his embrace. "For now, this is the plan. Just go with it. These injections will manipulate your mind, and he will make you think things that aren't real. You will have to decipher what is real and what isn't real." He grabbed the back of my head, put his forehead to mine, and looked deep into my eyes. "Stay strong. Do not bow to him, Brother."

I nodded. Just as he said, as if on cue, in walked another person holding a needle.

"Do not fight it, Incaendiel."

"Mammon?" I asked. "Is that you, Brother?"

"I'm sorry," was all he said as he slid the needle into my neck.

Everything went dark again.

When I regained consciousness, this time, I was no longer in the dungeon. I awoke sitting in a field where a tree stood. A weeping willow. Strange, I thought. Luxina told me about a place like this once before.

Someone stepped out from behind the tree, and I squinted in the glinting sun to see who it was.

"My firefly," the voice sweetly called.

"Sophie?" I asked, scrambling to my feet.

I ran to the tree, and as I grew closer, her face came into view. It was indeed Sophie. I reached her and embraced her, bringing her face into mine and kissing her deeply. I took a step back to look her over for signs of torture or abuse.

"I thought I had lost you," I murmured, pulling her into me and wrapping her in my arms.

"You did," she replied.

When she pulled back, I saw that her eyes were black pools of nothingness.

"What's wrong with your eyes?" I demanded.

She stepped closer to me and leaned into my ear. "Give in to Alpha, and we can be together again," she whispered seductively.

"What are you talking about?" I asked, pulling away from her. "He wants to hurt our kids."

She shook her head innocently. "He doesn't want to hurt them. He loves them just as you and I do," she replied with a loving smile. "He has taken such great care of Damian in my absence."

"He turned him into a monster, Sophie!" I hissed. "He is a devil spawn."

Her loving face mutated into rage as she erupted into flames. "Don't talk about my son in that manner!"

Her fiery hand held onto the tree we stood beside, and the fire trailed upward, burning away the bark and leaves. Ashes and glowing embers fell around us like soft snow. Soon, the field was set ablaze, and we stood among the fire face to face.

"Don't you love me anymore?" she pleaded with her eyes.

"This isn't you," I hissed, grabbing her by the arms and shaking her.

She began to laugh crudely. "This is the real me, Incaendiel. The free me."

The field melted away, and I was back in the dungeon room, still chained to the wall. It was all fake. It wasn't real.

"He will use her against you," a soft voice spoke.

My eyes searched the room to look for the source.

"Mother," I sneered as my eyes landed on her silhouette in the corner.

"Resist him, Incaendiel. He must not control you both," she replied quietly.

"Why are you helping him?" I demanded. "Why are you allowing this to happen?"

"If I don't, he will destroy me along with you," she stated. "And I like existing." She paused for a moment. "And I can't bear the thought of losing you."

I glared at her.

"When Damian comes in here, do not tell him anything important. Do not let him tell you anything important. Alpha will be using you to spy on him," she urged.

"Why is everyone worried about that kid?" I asked.

"When you see him, you will understand," she replied.

She walked to the door and stopped for a moment. "I'm sorry, Incaendiel."

As she left the room, Mammon walked in with another syringe.

"It won't work," I told him.

"I know," he replied as he plunged it into my neck. "That's what we are counting on."

As soon as the dose was delivered, I yanked on the chains hard and pulled them from the wall. Mammon backed into the corner as I stepped past him and walked from the room. I began to wander hall to hall, trying to find my way out of the maze I had become trapped in.

"Incaendiel!" I heard shouted.

I turned to see Sophie smiling. Her smile faded, and a look of urgency replaced it.

"Quick, we must go!" she yelled, holding her hand out to me.

I ran to her and took her hand. She pulled me through the halls like she knew every twist and turn. She stopped in front of a door and pushed it. It opened, and the sun from outside filtered in through the door.

"We're free," she breathed, walking through the open doorway.

I followed her, smiling. "How did you do that?" I asked. "Isn't this place heavily guarded?"

"Alpha trusts me," she replied. "No one batted an eyelash when I went to see you."

Something tugged at the edge of my brain, but I couldn't quite grasp what I was trying to remember.

"I love you, Incaendiel," Sophie whispered as she leaned in for a kiss. "I have always loved you. I will always love you."

Our lips met, and the kiss deepened.

"Where are the kids?" she asked in between lip locks.

"I don't know," I replied.

"Yes, you do," she insisted. "Just tell me so we can go get them."

I pulled away from her. "I don't know where they are."

"Tell me!" she demanded.

"I don't know!" I hissed.

It was then that I realized what this was. It wasn't an escape. It was another fantasy.

"You're not real," I said flatly.

"I am real," she replied with a sinister smile. "I'm just not the being you thought I was."

Her eyes flickered black.

"Alpha is controlling you, isn't he?" I asked.

"Is he?" she asked, toying with me. "Or has this been me the whole time?"

"Sophie," I began.

"My name is not Sophie," she cackled. "Oh dear, Incaendiel. And you believe me to be the one manipulated by Alpha and toyed with. You don't even remember my real name. How long has Mother and Father been screwing with your head, my love?"

"What are you talking about?" I asked, completely confused.

"One word will unlock everything. One name will bring everything back to you," she sweetly replied. "But it's not time for it."

The mirage faded, and once again, I found myself in the dungeon, still chained to the wall. The door opened again. I was expecting Lilith, Alpha, or another stupid fantasy about Sophie to traipse in or even Mammon with another syringe. Instead, it was Luxina and Xavier.

"Daddy!" she exclaimed as she ran over to me.

She immediately started working on getting the shackles off my arms.

"What are you doing here?" I hissed. "It's not safe for you to be here at all! This is what Alpha wants."

"I had to find you!" she protested. "I couldn't bear it if Alpha hurt you or killed you. So we came up with a plan to rescue you."

"Are you two alone?" I asked as the chains dropped from my wrists and I rubbed them.

"No, Praeziel is waiting for us outside the compound," Xavier replied as he helped me to my feet. "We need to get out of here as quickly as we can."

"You two get out now!" I ordered. "I have a few things I need to do first."

*Luxina stopped and turned on her heel. "No, you're coming with us!" Luxina ordered. "Rescue mission for **you**! No one else!"*

"We can't leave without a couple of people!" I protested.

"Sophie?" Luxina asked, crossing her arms.

"Yes, her, among a few others," I replied.

"No one else matters!" Luxina argued. "Now, let's go!" She tugged me by the arm again, but I didn't move.

"We have to at least help Damian," I urged.

"Why?" Xavier smirked. "He's where he belongs."

"No, he isn't," I hissed. "He is most likely being controlled and tortured by Alpha."

"Good," Xavier chuckled. "He gets what he deserves."

"We need to go now!" Luxina ordered.

Just as the words left her mouth, the Forsaken filled the room, grabbing Luxina and Xavier. Hands were on me as I fought them off as they dragged the twins from the room.

"No!" I bellowed.

I could feel the heat and anger bubbling beneath the surface, but I couldn't use my powers even though there wasn't anything on me to prevent them. Alpha walked into the room with a curt smile.

"I knew it would be just a matter of time before they came to rescue you," he said, leaning against the wall.

Rage filled me, and those holding me were thrown into the air as I ran over to Alpha. My fire burst forth on my arm as I rammed it into his chest. His eyes filled with shock as I held his heart in my hand. I squeezed it, feeling its every beat pulsate in my hand before I ripped it from his body, and he slowly collapsed to the floor. I stood in shock at what I had done.

"I did it," I murmured. "I... killed him."

"Or did you?" a voice asked from the door.

I immediately recognized the voice and looked to see Alpha standing in the doorway. My hand began to shake, and I turned my attention to the body lying crumpled on the floor.

"No, no, no, no, no, no," I repeated over and over as my voice began to crack. "Sophie..."

I knelt beside the body of Sophie, who lay in a pool of her own blood. Her eyes were lifeless, and blood trickled from the corner of her mouth.

"I told you to leave with us, Daddy," Luxina said as she walked into the room and touched my shoulder. "It's your fault she's dead."

"I didn't know," I cried as I picked her body up from the floor and rocked back and forth with her in my arms.

"I can bring her back," Alpha offered me.

Tears streamed as I stroked her fiery red locks from her face.

"I am the almighty, powerful God," he continued.

I gently kissed her forehead as I felt what little part of my heart that had held onto her slowly begin to die.

"All you have to do is join me," Alpha said as he bent down beside me. "Join me, my son."

"If you truly loved your children, you would bring her back either way," I hissed through gritted teeth.

Alpha smiled. "You are right."

He waved his hand over her, and a bright light glowed beneath his hand. Sophie gasped for air as she came back to life. I pulled her quickly into my chest and heaved in relief as she wrapped her arms around my neck.

"I do love my children, Incaendiel," Alpha said. "I still love you, my son."

"We could be one big happy family here, Daddy," Luxina offered, smiling at me. "He's not going to hurt us anymore."

I looked at Luxina, and her smile seemed to touch her eyes. I looked at Alpha, whose face was full of compassion, something I hadn't seen in millennia. Xavier stood behind Luxina, smiling as well. My eyes trailed to the door where Damian stood, leaning against the door frame. His face was not a smile, and even though he didn't speak, I could read what they said without needing to hear him.

"Join me, my son," Alpha repeated. "You will have everything you ever wanted."

Damian shook his head quietly with pleading eyes. Luxina's smile seemed to grow wider, and I noticed her teeth. She had a mouthful of razor-sharp fangs. Xavier did as well. I heard a clicking noise emitting from Sophie as I held her close. I slowly pulled away from her to see her smile full of the same teeth as the others.

"Join me!" Alpha insisted again.

"No," I murmured. "This isn't real."

Sophie lunged at my neck, and I snapped awake in a sweat in the dark dungeon room, still shackled to the wall. A lone person sat in a chair across from me. I squinted in the dark to see who it was.

"You will be the reason she dies. You know that, right?" the voice asked.

I sat quietly and didn't respond.

"You will be the reason they all die. Do you really want that, son?"

I glared at Alpha. "Why are you doing this?" I demanded. "Why give us free will if you want us to submit to your will in the end?"

"I didn't lie to you," Alpha responded as he stood from his chair. "I do love all of my children, including you, Incaendiel. You and Sophie were always my favorites."

I rolled my eyes. "You have a funny way of showing it," I grumbled.

"Your mother dragged you all into our marital spat," Alpha contested. "It was never my intention to use any of you for personal gain or as pawns in our ego trip."

"You abandoned us," I huffed. "You said you would always love us and would always be there for us, and you abandoned us."

Alpha swallowed hard. "I know. And I am sorry for that. But there was more to it than any of you know."

"Like what?" I asked.

"Omega... Lilith," he began, "Lilith kept you all from me. When we had our argument in the Garden, and I selfishly talked to Adam about our marital issues, she started a war. She told you everything you wanted to hear. That I no longer loved you and had abandoned you. She hid you all away in the glade and kept you all from me. I didn't abandon you, so to speak. She kept you all away from me and put in your heads that I didn't love you and fostered a deep hatred of me. Did you know she spent time with the rest of your brothers and sisters who remained behind with me?"

"What?" I asked. "What do you mean?"

"When she wasn't in the Glade in her throne room, she was meeting with the others to spend time with them. She kept her relationship with them and kept you all from me so that you would hate me, and in turn, you all would help her overthrow me for the throne in heaven. And she succeeded, didn't she?" he asked. "As soon as your brothers and sisters made it back to heaven, I had to flee, and she claimed my throne. You're not just a pawn in my game. You are a pawn in her game as well for her power grab."

I remained quiet as I mulled over everything he was telling me.

"I never understood why you all were so angry at me until that day... the day you died and came back to life. Who do you think brought you back to life?" he asked.

I glanced up at him questioningly.

"I brought you back," he answered for me. "I couldn't lose my son over the petty fights."

"You sent them there to kill me," I protested.

"I did no such thing, and Dean was punished for what he did to you," Alpha replied.

"What do you want from me?" I asked. "What do you get out of all of this?"

"I get my family back," Alpha answered.

"Why? So, you can torture us as you do, Damian?" I asked heatedly.

"Damian has done unspeakable things for which he gets punished. He has everyone convinced that I make him do the things he does. He does those things willingly, Incaendiel. He manipulates everyone into feeling sorry for him. He is evil, a little monster who I have to keep in check or else he would run, causing everyone heartache and pain. He thrives on pain," Alpha replied.

I leaned forward and looked Alpha in the eyes. "I. Don't. Believe. You."

"I see he has you fooled, too, and you haven't even sat down to talk with him yet," Alpha sighed. "He will use his power of deception to fool all of you. He will kill Xavier, you know? And he will convince Luxina that he is on her side just to use her powers for his own gain. He is a master manipulator and will make you all believe he is on your side when in truth, he is on his own side to take the throne from all of us. You will see."

"Yeah, I guess I will," I replied.

***

I came up from the pool for air, coughing up all the water I had swallowed. I looked at Queen Titania, still sitting there with her hand in the water, waving it back and forth.

"You're not done," she said sweetly.

"How much more can there be?" I asked.

"More than you can imagine. You were trapped there for a long time. You want to remember everything, right?" she asked as she pushed my head back under.

***

"At least he proves to be a better father than you ever have," Damian seethed. "Now, leave the room and do not bother the prisoner. Alpha wants him to remain untouched and unharmed. Those are orders!"

And with that, Damian left the room. Lucifer scowled in my direction and followed, shutting the door behind him. Once again, I was left in the dark, dank room. It had been months of fake fantasies of Sophie trying to persuade me to their side when Damian had come in to talk to me. I didn't know if he had been real or not at first. It wasn't until the voice conversation and Lucifer busting in that I really did realize it was real. And then, she walked through the door.

"Incaendiel?" Sophie gasped as the door opened, and she stepped through. "Is it... is it really you?"

I laughed, "And here I thought it was all real. But the boy was fake, too. It's proven now that you're here."

Sophie ran over to me. "Incaendiel, it's real. This is real. "She stroked my face. "How long have you been here?"

"You should know. You're just him pretending again," I replied snidely.

"What are you talking about?" she asked as confusion spread across her brows. "Who is 'him'?"

"Alpha. You're Alpha, guised as Sophie, trying to get me to bow to him. Trying to get me to tell him things. Well, I'm not. So, you can just disappear. Fade away."

She grabbed my face with both of her hands. "It is me!"

She leaned in to kiss me, and I pulled away. I leaned in, glaring at her. "You're. Not. Real."

She grabbed my face in her hands and pulled me in. Our lips touched, and I could feel the power radiate between us as I always had. There was no questioning or deniability. It was the real her.

"Sophie?" I breathed in disbelief.

"Yes," she cried.

"Quick. Unchain me," I ordered, shaking the chains and looking around.

She stood up, and her face saddened. "I can't."

My brows knitted together. "Why can't you?" I asked.

"I'm not even supposed to be here. He didn't even tell me you were here. I cannot disobey him," she replied, quietly sitting down on her knees.

I rattled the chains again. "Sophie, untie me!" I demanded.

She shook her head. "He will hurt Damian. Every time I disobey, he hurts him."

"I know he hurts him. I saw him earlier. I didn't know why, though," I replied.

"Alpha tells him it's because he's not obeying, but it's my fault," she cried, placing her face into her hands, ashamed.

"Alpha is manipulating you both. We need to get both of you out of here," I growled.

"Sophie!" Asmodeus hissed, walking through the door. "You know you can't be here. You weren't even supposed to know he is here."

Her eyes burned with intensity as she stood up. "You knew all along and didn't tell me?!" she cried. "I should set you ablaze, Brother."

Fire started creeping up through her skin.

"He couldn't tell you either for the same reasons," I replied. "Right, Brother?"

He nodded nervously, and her flames sputtered out. "We have to move soon. I don't know what Alpha has in store for Damian, but he has the gladiator ring set up again for him. He hasn't allowed any of us to see what he has been creating. We have to get him out before Alpha kills him. Alpha knows he is not obedient to him anymore and wants to dispose of him," Asmodeus urged as he paced the room.

"When?" I asked.

"Tomorrow morning."

I quickly ran it all through my head. "Come back then. Release me, then. I will get him out of here," I replied.

"I don't know if that will be in time or not," Asmodeus refuted. He sat down and ran his hands through his hair. "That boy is hanging on by a thread. You saw him," he said, motioning to me.

I nodded. "How long has his torture been going on?" I asked. I inquired, remembering the scars that painted his body.

"Long before he ever helped take Luxina from you," Asmodeus replied. "Alpha went to Queen Mab for her pure Seelie blood to use on him. He thrashed in agony for so long whenever he would receive the injections. When he helped the twins escape from here to Stygia, his punishment was the dungeon, where he was beaten. I tried to get him to run and escape, but he wanted to protect the twins from Alpha. So he remained his lap dog."

"He sacrificed himself to keep Xavier and Luxina away from Alpha?" Sophie asked.

Asmodeus nodded. "When he failed in securing them from Stygia, Alpha sent him back to the dungeon where he was tortured relentlessly. You saw him, Sophie. They nearly killed him," Asmodeus responded.

"I only saw him briefly. He wouldn't allow me in to talk to him, really," Sophie stated.

"The last beating, they broke his ribs, and it punctured his lung," Asmodeus growled, inhaling a deep breath. "I had to leave him hanging overnight just so he could breathe. I have been rallying up the others to support Damian. When the time comes, we will fight to set him free."

I nodded. "I will help. He doesn't deserve that kind of treatment. No one does," I replied.

"That will anger Alpha if you take Damian from him," Sophie snapped. "He will kill us all!"

"No one cares what will anger Alpha anymore," Asmodeus spat. "Of all people, you should be the one who bets for Damian's safety above everyone else. Isn't that why you're here?"

"I have to go," Sophie replied flatly, walking toward the door.

My face fell. "You're seriously going to stay here with Alpha and not leave with us?" I asked. "With me?"

She stopped. I could see she grappled with things in her mind. I had no idea what Alpha had done to her, but he was controlling her in some fashion.

"I love you, Incaendiel. I always have and I always will," she replied, turning to face me. "Where are the kids?"

"Fuck off," I seethed and squeezed my eyes shut. "It's all in my head again. This is all in my head again. It's not real. Nothing is real," I repeated over and over.

"Incaendiel?" Asmodeus asked, breaking my mantra.

I opened my eyes to see him still sitting there. I looked at the door, and Sophie had left.

"Is this real?" I asked, tears of frustration dripping from my eyes. "Because I don't know what is real and what isn't whenever she is around."

"That's how he is trying to break you," Asmodeus sighed. "Of course, that would be his strategy." Asmodeus put his hand on my shoulder. "It's real, Brother. We've got to get you out of here, along with Damian. I made a promise to Damian to help you escape even though the little turd *didn't know I was already devising a way to get you out. But we have to figure out how to save him. That ring will kill him tomorrow. The things Alpha has made for him to fight...*"

"*Morning? Right?*" *I asked, wiping my face on the sleeve of my shirt.*

"*Morning,*" *he nodded and walked out of the room.*

***

Once again, I popped out of the water, gasping for air. Queen Titania sat on the edge of the fountain, still waving her hand around in the water.

"There can't be more!" I pleaded.

"Oh, child, but there is," she replied, pushing me back under water.

Chapter 3

AS MY HEAD went back under water, more of the memories I had lost came racing forward again.

*****

I couldn't tell how long after Asmodeus left when another visitor came to see me.

"Hello, Mother," I huffed.

"Incaendiel," she smiled. "We have much to discuss, you and I."

"What could there possibly be for us to discuss?" I asked. "You are in league with Alpha. You are helping him torture that poor boy. You are helping him hold me captive so he can get his hands on the other two. Did I miss anything? Please, enlighten me."

"I know you must think horrible things about me," she replied softly as she walked in front of me. "I can't blame you for it either. But you must know I have done everything I have to protect you and Sophie."

"Protect us?" I sneered. "How is this protecting us?"

"Alpha would have destroyed you and could have destroyed you easily when you were first created. You two are far more powerful now than he could have ever imagined. I gave you the time to grow and to flourish."

"Is that what you call it?" I asked. I leaned forward and spat at her. "We are nothing but pawns in your game."

She was taken aback for a moment and then recomposed herself, taking a seat across from me. "There are things you must know that I don't have a lot of time to tell you. So just listen," she said. "First and foremost, there is a war far greater than what you have fought that is coming."

"Let me guess, the biblical apocalypse Father had the humans write about?" I asked, laughing.

Her face remained calm, but her eyes showed fear. "Yes, son. That is exactly the war. There is a reason why the Hebrews didn't believe Lucifer was the messiah or son of God. He isn't the messiah. Do you remember the young girl that you were overseeing right before the war broke out?" she asked.

"Yes," I replied. "Eva."

"She is quite special, Incaendiel. She needs to be found and protected at all costs. She is your prophet. She is your messiah," she replied. "She is the key to everything."

"She isn't a prophet," I retorted. "I would know if she was a prophet."

"You have to have your powers activated by Starfire," she reaffirmed. "Those powers activate every single starseed you have ever had charge over. The humans you helped create. You must protect her, understand?"

"Is that all?" I asked curtly.

"When they release you here shortly, you make sure you save Damian before Alpha has him killed," she said. "You cannot leave without him!"

I eyed her suspiciously. "What do you care?" I asked. "What's in it for you?"

"He is my grandchild," she replied. "He doesn't deserve what is happening to him. No one deserves what is happening to him."

I nodded. "I agree with that."

"After you get him to safety, find your brothers and then get to Lightshade where Starfire is," Lilith said quickly while glancing at the door.

"Which brothers?" I asked. "I have a lot of those."

"Gabriel and Raziel." She glanced nervously at the door again. "They have more knowledge for you to help defeat Alpha. I am sorry. I must go now."

She quickly stood from her seat and ushered toward the door.

"Wait," I commanded.

She stopped and turned around.

"What's in this for you?" I asked once more.

She smiled sweetly. "Nothing is in it for me." She turned on her heel and walked nimbly out the door.

"Yeah, sure," I muttered.

Within minutes after she left, there was a deafening rumble that shook the entire building. Not long after the rumble stopped, Asmodeus showed up, running as quickly as he could through the door.

"We have to hurry," he yelled as he clambered to my chains. "Alpha sent for him earlier than expected. It's time. He is already in the ring." He plopped a bag down beside me.

"What's in the bag?" I asked as he fumbled around with the chains.

"Weapons," he replied as he clumsily dropped the key.

"Get me out of these damn chains," I seethed.

"I'm trying! Don't yell at me!" he hissed.

Asmodeus unlocked the clasps as fast as he could, and I stood to my feet and stretched. Every muscle in my body ached from the movement. I hadn't been able to stand the entire time I was here.

"Where is the ring?" I asked as I picked the bag up from the floor, and we began to run from the room.

"Follow me," he replied as we raced through the halls. "There's a whole fleet of us ready to fight on yours and his behalf. We were up all night making these plans."

"I will get him out first and then come back for Sophie," I said as we ran up numerous flights of stairs.

"She is a lost cause, Incaendiel!" Asmodeus urged. "She didn't even try to stop the gladiator fight."

"She probably thinks Damian is strong enough to withstand it," I replied. "He has my vote. That kid has spunk."

A loud gong echoed through the building.

"What was that?" I asked, looking around.

His eyes widened. "Faster!" Asmodeus urged.

We rounded the hall that led to the entrance of the ring. Asmodeus went to lift the gate with the drawstring mechanism. "They cut the rope!" he screamed, grabbing the pieces sliced in half in his hands.

I dropped the bag and peered through the gate and saw Damian backing away up to it as a horde of monstrous beasts filled the arena, all heading toward him. His back was against the gate when I reached for the bottom of it and, with all my strength, pulled it up and held it with one hand as I grabbed him with the other and pulled him through, letting it crash back down into place.

"Now, did you really think we were going to let you die in there?" I asked as he stared up at me, bewildered.

I picked the bag up, then dragged Damian away from the gate and out of the arena entrance, winding through the tunnels.

"But, how?" he began stammering.

"Less talking and more running!" I shouted.

I pulled him along the dark corridors as the sounds of the hungry creatures echoed through the hall.

"We have about three minutes before that gate is lifted and those things come after us," I said as I jerked him from hall to hall.

"How are you free?" he asked, still confused.

"Asmodeus is an old friend of mine. He has been filling me in on you for a few weeks. He told me about this, about what Alpha was going to do and how you refused to leave without setting me free," I replied. "Kid, what part of no one cares about themselves as much as they care about you three do you just not get?"

I pulled him down long corridors that he didn't seem to recognize as his eyes scanned his surroundings.

"Where are you taking me?" he asked, looking around.

"To freedom," I answered.

I ran at full speed and busted through the wall ahead of me. As the dust settled, I looked around. It was a beautiful meadow with a forest just on the other side.

"Alpha is going to be hot on your trail," I stated as I handed him a bag full of weapons. "You need to lead him on a wild goose hunt before you meet up with Xavier and Luxina. He's going to be sending everything he has your way, including those things he made to tear you apart. You have to be fast and remain strong."

"Aren't you coming with me?" he asked, taking the bag from me.

I shook my head. "I have someone else myself to save before I leave here," I replied.

Sophie, he thought.

"Yes, Sophie," I replied, reading his mind. "Now, go! That's an order! I can take care of myself. There's an uprising. Alpha will have to flee. The Forsaken weren't too happy when they found out about this plan of his with you. You have friends in low places, kid."

"Make sure Asmodeus stays safe," he urged.

I placed my hands on his shoulders. "You have my word," I replied. "Now, go!" I pushed him off.

He was gone in the blink of an eye. A searing pain shot through me, and I turned around to see Beelzebub shove a needle into my neck. "Have fun escaping now, Brother," he snickered.

With one quick swipe, I took his head off with my hand. Whatever he injected me with burned through every nerve ending in my body, and I toppled to the ground.

"I have to find Sophie," I murmured.

I stood to my feet but was dizzy. Everything seemed to spin around me. I held the walls and shambled through the building. "Sophie!" I called out. "Sophie!"

Asmodeus ran up to me. "Why are you still here?" he demanded.

"Sophie," I breathed, hardly able to stand while holding my neck.

"What the hell happened?" he queried.

He pulled my hand away from my neck and looked concerned.

"Who did this?" he asked.

"Beelzebub," I replied breathlessly. "I killed him."

"Forget, Sophie. We have to get you out of here and that poison out of your system before it kills you," he said, wrapping my arm around his neck to help me walk.

"Sophie!" I called out.

"I'm right here, Incaendiel," she replied.

I looked for the face to match the voice, but my vision was going in and out.

"Come with me, Sophie," I said. "Damian is safe. You can leave now."

"Oh, Incaendiel," she laughed. "But I like it here."

Hands were on me, and I began to fight them off one by one. I couldn't see anything at this point, and the few glimpses of blurred faces I did see were revolting creatures or black-eyed monsters. Sophie stood off to the side, just smiling and laughing with her black eyes. She waved and walked away from me.

"Sophie!" I yelled.

It seemed like the hands multiplied, and I fought each and every one of them away. I began to run as fast as I could. "Asmodeus, where are you?" I called out.

Where had he gone? Was he mauled by those things, too? I reached the hole in the wall I had made and took to the sky. My wings barely wanted to work, and I was feeling fainter and fainter the more I moved.

Those things were chasing me. With what energy I could muster, I sent a blast of fire out through the sky, striking them down. I didn't make it far before I was struck by something in the back of the head and careened to the ground.

***

I came to the top of the water, gasping for air.

Instead of sitting in her usual position, Queen Titania was standing beside the fountain. "Well, now that you are up to speed on everything, let's get you into some dry clothes," she stated with a smile.

I stood from the water and felt that my energy had been restored, and I was no longer dizzy.

"Did that pull all the poison from my system?" I asked.

"It indeed did," she replied. "This fountain is fed by the Lake of Purity. Not only did the injections distort everything you had seen, but they also caused you to lose your memory of what had happened."

One of the Queen's chambermaids appeared. "Please see to it that Incaendiel is given some new clothes and a fresh bed to rest," she ordered.

"Yes, ma'lady," the chambermaid responded with a curtsy.

"Incaendiel, this is Anika. She will take good care of you until the morning," she stated with a smile. "Then, we have much to discuss."

"Thank you for your kindness," I replied with a bow.

She giggled and scampered off.

"Follow me, sir," Anika said as she began to lead me through corridors.

I watched Anika admire her unique features as we walked.

"You're taller than the Queen," I declared, breaking the silence.

"I am a halfling," Anika responded.

"I didn't think halflings were allowed to live in the Seelie Court since they aren't purebloods?" I asked.

"They are when they are the daughter of Queen Titania," she replied with a crooked grin.

"I see," I said, also with a smile.

"Here we are," she affirmed as she opened a door for me.

She led me into the room and bustled to the closet, pulling out an outfit for me.

"We have had many guests in the Seelie court before, and some of them left behind their belongings," she explained as she laid the outfit on the bed for me. "This should fit you fine."

"Thank you," I replied with a bow.

She snapped her fingers, and a cart pushed by another servant appeared in the room with cheese, fruit, meats, and all kinds of goodies.

"Don't worry," she began before I could ask. "All of it is safe to eat. Nothing will trap you here. Unlike the Unseelie court, Queen Titania doesn't believe in harming free will."

I nodded. "Thank you."

"I will be here in the morning to wake you for your meeting," she replied with a curtsy, closing the door behind her.

I quickly changed from my drenched clothes into the dry ones. I sat on the bed with all of the memories from Alpha's dungeon swirling around in my head. A knock came on the door, and I stood and walked over to open it.

"Gabriel!" I exclaimed.

"The Queen told me you were here," he replied, walking in. "We have wondered where you have been all this time. It's been a year since you left to go and see the Watchers. We all thought you had been murdered by Alpha."

"Tortured more like it," I replied. "What news do you have from the others?" I asked, taking a seat at the small table in my room.

"I haven't been with the others since your departure," he replied, taking a seat across from me. I motioned toward the cart of food for him to get some, but he held up his hand and passed. "It's not safe for me to be out and about with Alpha any and everywhere. I came back to hide out in the Otherworld. I have been here since Alpha tried to destroy me. Queen Titania helped heal me, and this has become my home since then."

"We all wondered if you had made it or not. We were surprised when you showed up at the Glade after it had been destroyed. Did you at least tell the others where you were going?" I asked, munching on some bread and cheese. "So, they didn't worry about us both?"

"I told Metatron and Samael. I am sure Samael told Azazel," he replied quietly. "I don't trust anyone else. I am afraid, and those two swore they wouldn't tell anyone about my location. I'm sure it has already gotten back to Alpha that I am alive and well."

"Everything seems to get back to Alpha about everything. He is always two steps ahead of us," I stated, popping some strange fruit in my mouth. "The all-knowing almighty God," I joked sarcastically.

"The Queen said you got your memories back after taking a dive in the fountain," Gabriel chuckled while playing with a grape.

I groaned. "That water is the devil in disguise," I breathed.

"What memories had you lost?" he asked.

"All of them, pretty much," I replied, taking a sip of water. "I could only remember my brief talk with Sophie's son, Damian, and remembered how much he hated Lucifer when Lucifer came into the room."

"What did Alpha do to you?" he asked, shifting uncomfortably in his seat.

"He injected me with some sort of mind control substance and then made fake fantasies about me being free and being with Sophie," I replied. "He did it so often, I couldn't tell the difference between the mirages and reality. I am sure it would have become more brutal had I not escaped."

Thinking back on everything from the dungeon, realization hit when I remembered who I was talking to. "Lilith came to see me when I was in there. She told me to find you and Raziel. That you had information for me to use to defeat Alpha."

Gabriel nodded. "We do. But we all need to be together before it's divulged because it is a lot."

"She told me I had a prophet?" I asked, a bit perplexed.

"You do. The girl you are in charge of is your prophet," Gabriel replied. "She will activate when you activate."

"What does that even mean?" I huffed, walking over to the bed and flopping back in it. "Everyone keeps saying that like I am supposed to know what it means."

"You haven't had any visions yourself?" he asked, baffled.

I shook my head. "No, I haven't. Everything I have witnessed firsthand," I replied.

"Do you want one?" he asked, cocking an eyebrow. "Do you want *the one*?"

"You can share your visions?" I asked, sitting back up.

He nodded and held out his hand. "Touch your forehead against my hand."

I did as I was told and leaned forward.

I didn't know exactly what I was seeing, but somehow, I knew it was the end of creation. I watched as Alpha rode through the sky in the chariot he had created in the beginning for himself. He hardly ever used it except for special occasions. It was being pulled along by the horses he had created from varying universes, where he had extracted dirt to mold them. A red one, a black one, a white one, and a pale gray one. In the scriptures of humans, these were known as the horses of the apocalypse. War, famine, pestilence, and death. Below him in the valley, hordes of creatures crept, slithered, crawled, and bounded in one massive black wave toward the angel fleet that was stationed on the corresponding side of the valley. Fire and brimstone rained from the sky, exploding as they hit the ground below. Those standing in the wake of destruction were burned to a crisp, leaving an ashen body, or were struck down into pillars of salt that blew away in the wind.

The advancing mass of creatures had draugrs, werewolves, vampires, demons, both greater and lower, and whatever other mutts Alpha had created in his laboratory using stolen Seelie blood. I watched, waiting for Lilith or Lucifer to appear at his side, but neither of the two was there. Sophie was nowhere to be seen as well. However, I stood at the forefront of the army of angels who all stood waiting for my command to charge against the stampede hurtling toward them. Alpha rode by on his chariot, smiling at me as the ground began to quake beneath me.

I scanned the area and saw Damian, Luxina, and Xavier waist-deep in a tarry, black pit, all struggling to break free from it. The ground broke free beneath me, and I jumped, landing on the ground before me as the rest of the angels fell to their burning deaths. I returned my attention to the kids as they sank deeper into the pit, struggling against the tar. Alpha arrived at the pit with a laugh.

"Join me and be free," he yelled, laughing maniacally.

"Never!" I heard Damian seethe.

"Then die, young Shining Ones." Alpha stared at them emotionlessly. His eyes were like bottomless pits, cavernous and oblique. It was a look I had never witnessed before in his cold, dead-set eyes. He had completely gone off the deep end and most likely had planned something even more terrifying than the nature of the apocalypse. I heard the sound of a gong and a loud crack in the air. I watched in frozen horror as molten lava came racing toward them across the valley, burning all the creatures he had made. From behind them, water crashed through the valley. The universe seemed to implode on itself as bits and pieces of planets and

asteroids rained down around them, along with the fire and brimstone. Every star in the sky seemed to supernova and explode all at once, and just as he had sparked the universe into existence, he began to dismantle it.

New beings swarmed the air. They had the wings of angels and grotesquely disfigured faces of animals. No doubt, these were more of Alpha's experiments that he had let loose on Damian in the arena. When they opened their eyes, they shone like the sun. He had done it. He had created his muddled shining ones that were half demon, half shining ones. Above these creatures floated a single angel with black wings I had never seen before. He smiled maniacally and raised his hand. As if he commanded them alongside Alpha, they rushed through the air, heading for me.

"If I can't have what rightfully belongs to me, no one will," Alpha bellowed. "I will just start over and do it the right way." It was then that the lava and waters reached Luxina, Xavier, and Damian in the pit just as they reached for each other's hands.

"No!" I screamed as everything crashed in on the kids and the flying monsters enveloped me.

"What the hell was that?" I cried out as I jumped back from his hand, bewildered.

"That, my brother, is the end of everything," he replied solemnly.

I panted, still feeling the adrenaline from the entire vision. "What do we do?" I asked. "How do we stop him?"

"Now that is the million-dollar question," he remarked, leaning back in his chair.

A riotous commotion erupted outside the castle walls. Gabriel and I shuffled over to the window and saw hundreds of fey pouring in from the meadow.

"Are those Unseelies?" I asked in disbelief.

Gabriel nodded. "What the hell is going on?" he asked, wide-eyed and confused.

We left the room and made our way down to the grand hall, where he led me to the throne room of Queen Titania and King Oberon.

"Ma'lady," Gabriel enunciated, taking a knee. I followed suit and bowed as well. "What is happening?" he inquired.

She fixed her eyes on both of us. "The Otherworld is under attack," she explained. "Those creatures Alpha created followed young Damian to the Unseelie Court. Queen Mab sent all of the Unseelies here for protection."

Oh, no. He's in trouble. "I have to go help Damian," I replied, turning on my heel to leave.

"No!" she pleaded. "Those beasts can come here, too. They have Seelie blood in them. Pure Seelie blood. They will kill us all without your protection."

I was torn. I didn't know what to do. *Do I stay here and protect those who helped me, or do I go help Damian?*

"You stay here and protect us," Queen Mab insisted, walking into the throne room.

I turned to face her. "Where is Damian?" I asked her.

"I sent him into the Nightmares and Shadows realm," she answered nonchalantly.

I was filled with frustration and anger. "Are you insane?" I barked. "That place is the most dangerous place you could have sent him!"

"He will be fine," Queen Mab smiled, eyeing me with interest. "I gave him weapons and a map to navigate through there."

I paced back and forth. "He's just a kid!" I fumed. "And that kid... that kid is important," I rasped. "More important than any of you know."

"I see Gabriel shared his vision with you," Queen Mab mused, glancing in his direction. "Yes, we all know how important he is, as well as Luxina and Xavier. He is on his way to find them."

"Then you know why he needs to be protected at all costs!" I shouted.

"You saw him fight," Queen Mab remarked. "He can take care of himself. He is just like you," she smirked.

"He is only half Shining One," I retorted.

She waved her hand dismissively. "Half or whole. He is still powerful," she replied with a gleam in her eye.

"They are right, Incaendiel," Gabriel interjected, placing his hand on my shoulder. "We need to protect them. Damian will be fine."

"Are you sure?" I asked, piercing his eyes with mine for an answer.

"The vision I had has not changed. So, the future has not altered. This was supposed to happen like this," he assured me.

"Now that we are over the whole do I stay or do I go, do you mind going and killing the beasts?" Queen Mab asked, pointing her finger through the gates of the castle. "I would very much like not to die today."

I agreed silently and made my way out of the castle. I walked to the meadow and stood in the center, listening for any sounds. The wind blew, and every creature I had seen coming into the Seelie Court was hidden away from sight. There wasn't a single sound to be made, and it was eerily quiet. I readied myself, waiting for the beasts to burst through the portals at any moment. A stench filled the air, and I grabbed my face to keep from vomiting. It was rancid and putrid as if rotting meat had sat in the summer's heat for a week straight. A shadow overtook me, and drops of liquid hit the ground around me, sizzling like acid. I turned around, and behind me stood some sort of beast that looked like a beefed-up werewolf. A low growl began to emit from its throat as it bared its teeth at me.

Fire erupted through my body, and I prepared to fight barehanded with the beast. A sword came barreling through the air. I jumped and caught it just as the beast lunged. My hand touched the hilt of the blade, and my powers became one with it as it lit up like a torch. I swiped the sword in a downward motion as my body came down to the ground and cut the beast's head off with one clean stroke.

I examined the sword I had been tossed, and my eyes went wide. It wasn't an ordinary sword at all.

"I figured you could use an extra oomph to your power," Gabriel explained as he readied his own sword, preparing to fight by my side.

"It's *the* flaming sword," I breathed. "I thought Uriel possessed it."

"I stole it," Gabriel laughed, cocking his head to the side and shrugging. "Why do you think Alpha was so pissed at me."

A herd of creatures broke through the brush as if waiting to pounce. Gabriel and I stood side by side, fighting them off, slicing through them one by one.

"There are too many of them," Gabriel yelled as his blade moved back and forth.

"I know," I shouted. "You need to get out of here."

Gabriel shook his head. "I'm not leaving you to fight them alone," he refuted.

"Go!" I commanded. "I got this!"

Gabriel scowled but listened. He disappeared as quickly as he had appeared. The rage built within me as I slashed each monster that attacked. I stopped, and with a deafening howl of my own, I unleashed all of the built-up energy outward, leveling the trees and burning the creatures into ashen embers with one large fireball. As the smoke cleared, I collapsed to the ground as I looked at the devastation I had caused.

"Oh no," I murmured as I looked around the meadow.

Everything was burned to a crisp and destroyed.

"Thank you," Queen Titania said, walking to my side.

"I'm sorry," I cried, looking all around me shamefully. "I... I didn't mean to ruin your meadow."

She smiled. "It is quite all right."

"What about all the creatures?" I inquired, with tears forming. "They were the last of their kind, and I destroyed them."

She touched my hand. "They are safe, Incaendiel. They returned to the Garden."

"The Garden?" I asked, puzzled. "But how?"

"Xavier traded the Garden back to us. It was a part of our universe given to Alpha and crafted to his liking as a gift for letting us reside peacefully in his universe. We sent everyone there as you fought with great bravery against the creatures," she replied. "We helped create you. We know how powerful you are. We knew what we were asking when we asked you to fight against the beasts."

"I can fix it," I offered, looking around and placing my hand down on the ground.

"That's quite all right for now. It will heal in its own time," she chuckled, patting me on the back. "For the time being, we will reside in the Garden until it is safe here in this universe."

I was silent for a moment. "How do I stop him?" I asked, lost. "I am just me."

"Incaendiel, you are a powerful being. You have to believe in yourself. That has always been your problem. You don't have faith in what you can do, and you have always feared your power because it brings destruction with it," Queen Titania replied. "And *they* conditioned you to fear your power. You have to accept yourself. Accept the darkness inside you. Accept the power inside you. You are it, and it is you."

I looked around at what I had done in the meadow. The area was already starting to restore itself with new life.

"Incaendiel!" Gabriel called out. He ran to my side and stopped in his tracks. "Woah," he gasped in surprise. "I have been gone for far too long. When did your power grow to this?" he asked.

"After we fell," I replied quietly.

"Well, I must be on my way," Queen Titania interrupted, making her way back to where the castle had stood. "I can't have Queen Mab convincing everyone she is in charge now, can I?" she giggled and then looked at me. "We believe in you, Incaendiel. Just believe in yourself."

She walked back across the field and disappeared into nothing.

"So now what?" Gabriel asked, facing me.

"The vision is the same, right?" I asked. "Damian is still safe?" I had to be sure.

"Yes," he replied, bobbing his head.

"Then it's time to return to the Summit," I stated. "We have to convince what's left of our brothers and sisters to join me in the fight against Alpha before he destroys us all."

"Will they listen to you?" he wondered, his eyes clouding over with doubt.

"I don't know," I replied. "But I have to try."

Chapter 4

I ARRIVED AT the Summit with Gabriel at my side when Metatron met us at the portal.

"Incaendiel!" he shouted and gave me a hug, picking me up from the ground. "We thought you were dead."

"I would have rather been dead than deal with what I have dealt with," I replied, pulling back from the embrace after he put me back on my feet.

"Alpha captured you at Stygia, didn't he?" he asked.

I agreed silently. "I need to convene a council with everyone. There's a lot that needs to be said, and things have to be brought to light that you would never have imagined."

"Ok," Metatron affirmed, with a slap on my shoulder. "I will gather everyone in the throne room."

I rubbed the spot Metatron had smacked as he walked away, and a loud voice, as if on an intergalactic intercom, erupted through the heavens. "All angels are to report to the throne room for an important meeting immediately."

"I see he still likes to act in charge," Gabriel mused, smirking.

I laughed. "Now, as for you, you need to hang back out of sight and out of my mind until it's time for you to make an entrance. We don't know how well your reception will be with everyone together. Alpha told us all he had dealt with you, and you would never return. Many of our brothers and sisters here didn't fall and have accepted everyone back, but we still don't know who is really loyal to Alpha still."

Gabriel nodded. "Got it," he said as he threw the hood up on his robe, shrouding his face.

"Nice disguise," I chuckled.

I made my way to the throne room at the end of everyone as they filed in and stood waiting. I walked to the front of the room where Alpha's throne stood empty and gazed upon it. I could recall a time when I would gaze upon Alpha sitting on the throne with love and affection. In the beginning, he wasn't all that bad. He was a doting father, as one would expect. He looked fondly at Sophie and me, and Mother quite often told us that we were their favorites. I smirked, thinking how he must hate us even more now as we grew into our powers. He still wanted to control us. He couldn't have a power out in the universe that could challenge his own, and we were the closest it could come. If we had allies, we would be all-powerful. I turned around and looked out at the crowd.

I once again stood before my brothers and sisters to convene another critical meeting. This place was like an estranged relationship to me, even though I had spent my formidable years here prior to the fall. It felt wrong and right, all at once. It was my home once before, but it no longer called to my soul. I didn't have a home anymore. The Glade had been destroyed. I was a real Wanderer now. I lived among the humans for so many years that, at times, I forgot I wasn't one of them, especially once I had started raising Luxina among them.

The roar of voices speaking and arguing among one another about why they were called here echoed and reverberated hard off the walls of the room. The tension and stress that had inflamed my mind and soul already wore heavy on my heart. I stared at each of their faces in solemn musings. Azazel and Samael stood at the front of them all as they had since the day they had all fallen from the Summit. Others joined them, such as Raphael and Michael, as well as Metatron and a whole fleet of those ready to go to battle. My words would be the make it or break it point of the fight to be held between Alpha and me.

"I come before you, once again, my brothers, in hopes you would hear my pleas," I began.

The room fell silent as they waited for me to continue on. "Alpha has yet to be tamed or reprimanded for any of his actions against us all. His betrayal cuts deep into our wounds that we have let fester for millennia.

He abandoned us and then used us as chess pieces in his game of war with Mother. He has upped the stakes in the game. He commands an army of monstrosities that I have personally witnessed myself as I watched young Damian battle against them one after another."

A hushed murmur fell over the crowd.

"These monsters are different than anything I have seen. They are worse than the hellhounds. They are worse than the Forsaken. And they are worse than the Draugrs," I commented. "These monsters are the heralds of Alpha's apocalypse against his own children of light. We must fight them to preserve not only ourselves but also the future of mankind. Quite possibly even the cosmos. For when he is finished with us, he will let them loose upon earth and everywhere else, and it will end in fire and brimstone as he has told the prophets of Revelations."

"There's also the possibility that he does not intend to bring the mortal souls back to Lailah for the Giving Tree in the Summit. He is most likely going to feed the souls to the monsters and give them the everlasting life promised to his devout mortal followers. When he is done with this world and this universe, he will move on to others that he has yet laid waste to and claim them for himself as well. If Lailah has no souls to replenish the Giving Tree, then all life would cease to exist, period," a voice called from within the crowd.

"That is correct," I replied, then motioned with my hand. "Step forward, please, and reveal thyself."

An angel emerged from the crowd in a cloak and came to the forefront where Samael stood, removing his hood.

"Raziel?" I asked, squinting my eyes. "Is that you?"

"It is, Brother," Raziel replied. "And do I have a secret for you."

Azazel snorted, crossing her arms. "Secret? We all know it was you and Gadreel who plotted against Father in the Garden. Mother already told us."

"That is true. Gadreel and I both were accused of the deception of Eve, which in truth is not the real reason we were punished," Raziel replied, looking at Azazel, then back to me. "But I did something even worse than that of Gadreel, who by the way, is still locked in the damned tower as well. Have any of you ever thought to release him?"

"Once we hear what you two did, we will release him," I assured him. "Tell me, Raziel, what is it that you did?"

"Michael knows, don't you, brother?" Raziel asked, turning toward Michael.

Michael pursed his lips. "He gave Adam and Eve his book."

My eyes widened. "*The* book?" I asked.

"It doesn't matter," Michael scoffed. "Raphael and I snatched it from them and tossed it into the sea."

Raziel's face erupted in a snickering grin. "Or did you, Brother?"

Michael's brows knitted together in frustration and confusion. "Out with your point!" Michael demanded. "Or we will throw you in the tower with Gadreel."

"Let him speak," I said to Michael.

"Tell me, Incaendiel, where is your beloved?" Raziel asked, looking around the room.

"She is with Alpha," I replied, gritting my teeth. "It is one of the reasons I stand before you all. I wish to rescue her."

A riotous commotion fell over everyone. There was yelling and shouting against the very idea of risking their exposure to Alpha so he could lure them away.

"As you should," Raziel chimed with wide eyes.

All eyes turned to Raziel.

"What gives you the right to dictate what we shall and shan't do?" Metatron asked, bucking his chest up.

"Sophie has my book," Raziel proclaimed.

"What?" I asked, confused.

"Think long and hard about the last twenty-five mortal years or so," Raziel replied. "What was your charge?"

"Watching over Sophie until she came of age again," I answered, shaking my head, confused.

"And?" Raziel asked, cocking his head and leaning in for more.

"And what?" I replied, pinching the bridge of my nose in frustration.

Raziel sighed, rubbing his forehead with his fingertips. "Your beloved was born into a special family. An old bloodline of hunters. You may remember them as the Magen and then the Order of the Shield. Then, there were the Knights Templar, and finally, what we call them today, the Diakonian Order. Hunters for Alpha."

"What does that have to do with Sophie's family? She was adopted after her birth mother died during labor?" I implored.

"Because her adopted grandmother and her adopted mother were also members of the Diakonian Order," Raziel replied. "Her birth mother was part of the same order."

"I'm not following!" I shouted, exasperated with the back-and-forth banter. "Out with it!"

"The Bible, Incaendiel, where is her grandmother's Bible?" Raziel asked.

"I'm not sure," I replied, with a shrug. "Most likely with Sophie's mortal mother. Why?"

"Do I have to spell it out for you? Are you that daft you can't put the puzzle pieces together? Do you not remember who the sons that comprised the Magen were descendants of?" Raziel asked, flailing his hands in irritation. "What mark do they bear as a birthmark, a symbol of their heritage?"

"The Mark of Cain," I replied, becoming impatient.

"And who was Cain?" Raziel implored.

"The son of… Adam and Eve," I sighed, as the realization of what he was getting at finally clicked for me.

"And when God banished Cain to the land of Nod, Eve took pity on her son and handed him the book of all mysteries of life. My book. The tell-all book. The book with the real story of our creation and our fall. And throughout the years, I have added to it and righted the story of Cain. Cain was a pawn of Alpha's, just as his descendants are. It was Lucifer who slew Abel. So, Cain was imbued with the Mark and sent off into the desert. And each generation of his offspring, whom I ensured survived the Great Flood, passed the book down to their sons and daughters until it ended with Sophie. The family is destined to help put an end to Alpha since he corrupted their bloodline to begin with. Unlike Sophie, who was born as Abel, Lucifer only possessed Cain when he murdered Sophie. Cain witnessed it all and was unable to stop it from happening."

"Sophie's grandmother's Bible is the Sefer Raziel Ha Malakh?" I asked, unable to believe it.

"It is much more than that, my brother. 'Tis much more than that," Raziel grinned madly. "We must rescue Sophie and search out that book. It has secrets in it that none know of and secrets that need to be brought to light. Now, do you mind releasing our brother from his prison like we agreed upon?"

I nodded and turned to face Metatron. "Metatron, go free our brother, Gadreel."

Metatron agreed silently and left the room to retrieve Gadreel from the tower.

"It's funny that you are here," I remarked to Raziel. "Mother told me to find you and a few of our other missing brothers."

"She did?" Raziel asked, raising an eyebrow.

"Yes, she said you all would have knowledge that I would need," Incaendiel replied. "And I do believe she was right."

Raziel's face darkened. "There is a reason I have been missing since Gadreel's capture, Brother."

"Yeah, you didn't want to be locked away with Gadreel," Azazel chimed in.

"No, Sister. It's because I know truths about Alpha and Lilith that no one else knows about," Raziel retorted, worry spreading across his face. "It is why we must find my book. It contains everything. There were pages that were unreadable by the hunter family Sophie had been born into. I couldn't chance Lilith's top fleet finding the book and trying to destroy it, thinking it was all a lie. The text is encrypted, and it looks to read as nonsense."

"What does it have in it?" I asked. "I don't remember seeing pages like that."

"It has *everything* in it, Brother. Every single thing Alpha has ever done. Every single thing Lilith has ever done. The real truth about the Apocalypse to come. There are only two beings in existence that can read it. I am one of them," Raziel answered, shifting his weight to his other foot.

"Who is the other?" I demanded.

"You already know who," he replied.

I began to think back to the conversation I had with Lilith. She mentioned a girl...

"Eva?" I inquired.

"Yes," Raziel responded. "And we have to protect her at all costs once she becomes activated."

"We will get to all of that in due time, Brother. I promise. We have another bigger problem as well," I stated, looking at those in the room as they waited for me to continue. *How can I tell them this without them rebelling against me?*

"Out with it, Incaendiel," Samael commanded. "We have things to do."

"Mother. Lilith. Omega. Whatever you want to call her," I began and stopped.

"What about Mother?" Raphael urged, murmuring following his statement from others in the room.

I hesitated for a moment, unsure if they would believe me. "She is in league with Alpha now," I breathed.

"Lies!" one called out.

"Not true!" another reiterated.

"She would never do that!" a third yelled.

The voices began to clamor in the air, and the deafening roar of anger tore through the room.

"Quiet!" Metatron yelled as he returned with Gadreel in tail. "Let Incaendiel speak. He has never lied to us before. He wouldn't start now."

"How do we know?" one demanded.

"It could all be a lie!" another yelled.

"I said quiet!" Metatron bellowed in his god voice.

The room shook, and the angels immediately hushed.

"Continue, Incaendiel," Metatron stated softly.

"Thank you, Brother," I began, clearing my throat and pushing back the conditioned feeling of fear at the sound of his voice. "When I had been captured by Alpha, Mother came to talk to me there."

The room remained silent as I looked from face to face in disbelief.

"She told me she was by his side for self-preservation, but I don't believe that either," I continued. "Not only did she allow young Damian to be tortured by Alpha and thrown to the wolves to be destroyed, she also allowed him to torture me with some sort of mind control substance he had been using on the children. There were a few other things Alpha told me about her, but now is not the time to go into those."

"For all we know, you could be under his control right now," Zadkiel refuted, stepping forward. "How can we even trust you?"

"Everything was leached from my system when I went to the Seelie Court and stepped into the Fountain that pulls from the Lake of Purity," I assured.

"But *how* do we know you speak the truth?" Zadkiel reiterated, crossing his arms. "Just because you say so? Who else here doubts Incaendiel and believes him to be the adversary Alpha asked us to be all those years ago? Who believes him to be the Great Deceiver? The Silver-Tongued Devil?" Zadkiel asked, waving me off with his hands.

"Alpha warned us about this," someone spoke out.

"He did!" another affirmed.

The crowd began murmuring once again, and I knew I was losing them.

"You bunch turn on one another so quickly," a voice said.

I smiled and breathed out in relief. "Gabriel, Brother. Glad you could make an appearance."

"Gabriel?" others repeated over and over. "He was supposed to have been destroyed by Alpha."

"Alpha tried," Gabriel stated, removing his hood from his face. "But he did not succeed."

"You revolted against Alpha!" someone yelled out. "You are just as deceitful as Incaendiel."

"So did Metatron. So did Michael. So did many of you!" Gabriel yelled, turning in a circle to face them all. "You all fell to help them return to their rightful place in the Summit. Every single one of you who reside in this room revolted against Alpha. It may not have been in the beginning when a lot of them did and fell with Lilith, but you are just as guilty for seeing through the façade Alpha had put up."

Gabriel made eye contact with me and nodded his head. "I have been in the Otherworld for many years, hiding among the fey. The Seelie Court has been quite accommodating for us angels. I was there when Incaendiel swam in the fountain. He no longer has anything in his system that could put you in harm's way with Alpha. He speaks the truth."

"Continue on, Incaendiel," Metatron spoke, putting a silence to all of the chatter with his hand.

"I need your help, Brothers and Sisters," I began again. "I need to keep the children safe, and I need to rescue Sophie from Alpha. If we do not, then Alpha and Lilith will destroy us all. I have only come to you once before, and it was to save my daughter for selfish reasons. But it is more now. More is threatened than just a simple child being taken. These children are special, as most of you have attested to with Xavier here in the Summit. They are different than what we were. They have special abilities that angels do not possess. They are the future. They are the ones who can destroy Alpha."

"Says who?" Zadkiel huffed, with his arms crossed.

"Sophia," I replied.

"Lucifer's old concubine?" Zadkiel snorted, rolling his eyes. "Isn't she also the mother of the Nephilim? Another traitor against Alpha with an axe to grind with him."

"Oh, but she is much more than just a simple angel," Gabriel laughed, harboring his own secrets. "We have hidden truths that none of you know about. We have more knowledge than even Raziel's book contains."

"Like what?" Zadkiel demanded, turning toward Gabriel.

"Like, for starters, we're not angels," a voice said, breaking through the crowd.

"Sophia!" Gabriel exclaimed, running toward her and embracing her. "You are a sight for sore eyes."

"What do you mean you're not angels?" I asked, turning toward her.

"We have a secret that Alpha has kept from you all for years," Sophia began as she walked to the front of the room. "In the beginning, Alpha never told you about the Council of El. They are gods of old. The gods that came before him and the gods that told him you all were too powerful. We are part of those gods. It was true, as not only Gabriel and I had joined Alpha in disguise, but for far more reasons."

"Then who are you?" Zadkiel asked, drawing a sword. "Deceivers like Incaendiel?"

"No," Sophia smiled warmly. "Gabriel here is not an angel of Alpha. He is my luminary." Gabriel bowed before Sophia. "You all have been led to believe that Alpha was the all-power of the universe, but he is not. Alpha was created just as you all were created. He is a lowly god throwing a tantrum and revolting against the elder gods."

"Then who created Alpha?" Azazel queried, full of wonder.

"I did," Sophia replied, turning to Azazel.

"That means… you're a god too?" Samael asked as everything began to click together for him.

"Yes," Sophia replied, looking around at all of the angels. "I am the mother of Alpha. I hid my shame when I created him and toted him away to a universe of his own for him to believe he was an almighty god. I hid among you all to watch over him because a mother loves her child, no matter how evil they are. He began to learn of the other gods and sought their counsel. The rest is history."

"You're our grandmother?" Metatron asked.

"Yes, dear Metatron," Sophia smiled, placing her hand gently on Metatron's shoulder. "I am your grandmother. And what Incaendiel speaks is the truth. You all are in great danger."

"So, when Alpha is defeated, do you take his throne?" Michael asked.

"No," Sophia said flatly. "I have no desire to rule this universe."

"Then who will take over Alpha's throne?" Michael asked, raising an eyebrow. "One of us?"

"Yes, one of you will be the new Alpha," she replied, looking around at us all.

"Who?" Michael asked, straightening his stance. "One of the higher-ranking angels? Azazel? Samael? Metatron? Me?"

"I am afraid not," Sophia answered apologetically. "You are archangels, yes. But you do not possess godlike powers."

"Then who will replace him and mother?" Azazel asked, looking around the room at everyone who stood in there.

"Ntidus Assis," Sophia responded.

"What does that mean?" Michael asked, scrunching his face in confusion.

"The Shining Ones," Sophia replied.

"Who are the Shining Ones?" Metatron inquired.

Sophia looked at me. "A god was hidden among your ranks in secret. Well, not one god, but two. Twin flames," she replied. "With the feather of a phoenix to give them power over fire. The energy of a dying sun belonging to an old God is fading into the darkness. Power from the fey belonging to the Goddess Tiamat and the power of Alpha and Lilith combined created a pair of Shining Ones."

"Power over fire," murmured through the crowd.

"What?" I demanded, furrowing my brows.

"Yes, Incaendiel," Sophia answered. "You and Sophie are the Gods of the new generation and were expected to take over after Lilith and Alpha's powers began to fade."

"I don't believe it," Michael laughed, walking closer to Sophia. "Incaendiel is not a God. Hell, it took him the age of the world to even learn how to control his power over fire."

"Incaendiel has one more step to complete his transition into a god," Sophia continued, ignoring Michael. "The power of the fey came with an enchantment to hide his power from Alpha so Alpha would not grow jealous and destroy him. Alpha knows the children are Shining Ones, and that's why he wishes to have them all together so he can control them. He thinks they are the only ones. He still doesn't know about Sophie and Incaendiel. It is the one thing Lilith made sure to do right in this little game they play with one another."

"I believe it," Azazel stated, nodding her head. "When Incaendiel died, he willed himself back to life. And he also brought Sophie back to life when she died as well. Remember?" she asked, looking around at everyone. "Angels can't do that."

"It was Sophie and he alone who could raise the portal between the mortal world and the Summit for us to return. We also witnessed him raise it on his own," Metatron added. "Only Alpha had that power."

"I'm afraid Alpha does know about Sophie and me," I replied, a grave look washing over my face. "He skirted around it while I was held captive, but he knows. It's why he wanted all of us together to control."

"Then you all are in more danger than you realize," Sophia replied.

"Incaendiel is not a god!" Michael shouted, interrupting the conversation.

"Why does this anger you, Michael?" Gabriel asked, shaking his head and turning toward Michael to confront him.

"Because... because it's Incaendiel!" Michael laughed, pointing at me. "He can't even go long without him being overpowered by his own lack of self-control and burning something to the ground."

"Or it is because you are not in alliance with us as you say," Gadreel demanded, stepping forward.

"And here we go," Michael sneered, glaring at Gadreel. "It was a mistake letting you out of that tower."

"Only a mistake for you. Everyone believes I was locked away for helping Lilith deceive Eve, but that's not the true reason. Is it Michael?" Gadreel asked, walking closer to him. "What was the *real* reason, Brother? Why was I banished to the tower and not even have visitors?"

"Because you betrayed Father!" Michael hissed, stepping up to him nearly nose to nose.

Gadreel smiled in his face. "You and Lucifer make a wonderful pair. Most everyone forgets that you two are twins. Where is Lucifer, by the way?" Gadreel asked, looking around the room. "Still pretending to be an alliance to you all, or has he taken his place by Alpha's side publicly?"

I looked at Michael as his face contorted in anger. "I am not like Lucifer."

Gadreel's smile widened as his constant barrage began to work against Michael's ego. "So you're not Alpha's little spy? You don't know the secrets that Alpha has buried, waiting to come to light?" Gadreel asked.

"Lies," Michael hissed, reaching for his sword.

I played every single detail over in my head from the beginning to now. Michael's fall with Sophie's memories. Beelzebub taking on Michael's form to confuse Sophie when she was mortal. Michael eagerly coming forth to join us in searching for the kids. It was Michael who had sent us on a wild goose chase through Alabama. It was Michael who knew I wasn't the one who brought the Glade down. Michael was the one who knew we were going to Stygia, where the children were being guarded. It was Michael who wished to know if the Watchers were joining us in the alliance against Alpha.

"You have been reporting to Alpha about our every single move since you fell with those memories," I snarled, walking toward him. "You have been lying to us the entire time. You and Lucifer." Michael's eyes narrowed at me. "When Lucifer arrived, he was so buddy-buddy. I didn't want to trust him. He had been nothing but horrible to me the entire time we lived in the Summit. It was Lucifer who released Sophie's first memory to gain our trust. And then it was you who carried the rest with you when you fell. It was Lucifer who told us that you were being weird and distant from the others right before you fell. I challenged you about being a spy, and Lucifer intervened. Beelzebub disguised himself as you to throw us off your scent when Sophie had made it back to the Glade after being tortured by *you*. It was right under our noses the whole time, and we just couldn't piece it together."

"Do you also forget that if it hadn't been for my fall, none of the others would have joined?" Michael spat in contempt.

"We questioned whether you had a double that fell. But your charm after we found Beelzebub disguised as you..." I looked around at everyone who had fallen that day. I stopped at Metatron's face. "How can I trust any of you, now?" I asked, shaking my head.

Without missing a beat, Metatron walked before me and stared deeply into my eyes. "I will follow you anywhere, Brother," he said. He took a knee. "All hail the King of Kings!" he shouted.

One by one, angels dropped to their knees, all repeating the same phrase. I looked around at the masses of angels on bent knees. My eyes stopped on Samael and Azazel, who were still standing.

"I never wanted this," I said, walking toward them. "I have known you two from the beginning. You have been there for me through every single test I have gone through. You helped me get Sophie back. You didn't hesitate to help me find my children. You don't have to bow to me. You don't have to prove yourselves to me. The day Mother told you about my powers and how they were greater than yours, I did not want to take your place in charge. I still don't know if I really want to. You are the angel in command, Samael." I looked at Azazel. "And you are my second in command. You always will be."

Samael crossed his left arm over his chest, and Azazel followed suit. "Hail to the King," Samael replied and took a knee.

"Hail to the King," Azazel repeated, also taking a knee.

I scanned the room, and Michael and a third of the others who had spoken out against me or didn't trust me were the only ones left standing. Even Gabriel and Sophia had bowed down to me.

"I refuse to bow to you," Michael hissed, hand on the hilt of his sword. "You are not my god. You are not my leader." He drew his sword from its sheath and released his wings. "All hail Alpha!"

In the blink of an eye, he was gone.

"So, it was true," I murmured, a crushing wave of mistrust displacing my fighting spirit.

Everyone stood from their knees. I walked over to Sophia and asked, "What do we do now?"

"You go to Lightshade," she informed me. "There, you will meet Starfire, the Oracle. She has what you need to restore your full power."

"What about the kids?" I queried.

"They're safe. They're there with her performing the task needed to retrieve the ingredients to activate you," she replied.

I turned to look at the fleet of angels assembled before me. "Will you join us against Alpha?" I asked, scanning the room and every face that stood there. "Will you turn your back on your creator to follow me into the Valley of the Shadow of Death?"

"You know the answer to that, Brother," Samael replied with a nod and thrust his sword in the air, letting loose a battle cry, and the rest of the angels followed suit.

"Then it's off to Lightshade!" I shouted.

"Where is it?" Azazel asked.

I stopped for a moment. "I'm not sure how, but I know where it is," I replied.

Chapter 5

I WALKED THE Summit with Sophia by my side as everyone else prepared to make their way to Lightshade. Everything bounced around in my head and made my brain hurt.

"It's a lot to take in, isn't it?" she asked.

I nodded. "It is."

"Doing it all alone isn't easy, as well?" she asked, peering at me.

I sighed. "I tried to get her to come with me, but she has been so manipulated by Alpha that she can't tell right from wrong anymore."

"I understand," she replied with a shake of her head.

"You do?" I asked.

She smiled. "When I first fell in line with Alpha and Omega, pretending to be one of their angels, I met Lucifer. He was made without a mate, you know?"

"We all thought he was made with you," I replied, my eyes scanning the skies as a meteor flew overhead. "Obviously, he wasn't."

"No, he wasn't. Instead, he was made with Michael as twins," she replied. "I took pity on him. It wasn't fair that all of you were paired up, but he and Michael had to be the right and left hands of Alpha. In the beginning, he wasn't the gnarled piece of hardened coal he is now. He was different then. It wasn't hard loving him. He became so consumed with you and Sophie, so jealous of you two. It wasn't fair that you had special powers and also a twin flame. All he talked about was gaining power over you and separating you from Sophie. In the end, his jealousy won out over his love for me. So, I left. He never forgave me for leaving him either. I embarrassed him. When they attacked Stygia, he gave the command to Damian to kill me. He was so cold to me, as if I were the reason we had fallen apart. Sweet Damian," she smiled. "He didn't want to hurt me. He was stuck between a rock and a hard place there. So, he faked my death. Alpha knew he didn't kill me. I believe that was why he was tortured even more after capturing you."

"Yeah, that kid has been through hell," I replied. "He doesn't deserve all of that."

She glanced at me and looked me in the eyes. "You love him like he is yours, don't you?"

I smiled and nodded. "Yeah, I can't help to. Even when Sophie told me about the affair and about the baby, at first, I was angered and really hurt. But I would have loved him and raised him as my own had she stayed. Instead, I pushed her into Lucifer's arms to keep her safe."

"You loved him before you even met him," she laughed.

"I did," I chuckled. "And then he helped kidnap Luxina, and I was so angry with him. I felt like my own child had betrayed us, even though I had never met him before or spent any time with him."

"And now you know everything he did was out of self-preservation and manipulation by Alpha," she replied.

"I do," I said, nodding my head. "When I was in the Otherworld, he was going through the Nightmares and Shadows realm by himself. I had to choose between keeping the fey safe or making sure he stayed safe. I chose him."

"But?" she asked, pushing for more.

"But Gabriel told me he was safe, and the vision hadn't changed. So, what was happening had already happened in the vision. So, I knew he would make it out," I answered.

She smiled. "Gabriel is a mighty fine luminary."

"What exactly is a luminary?" I asked.

"An angel," she replied. "But not like Alpha's angels or even his archangels. I created eight angels of my own, with permission, of course. Alpha was not created with permission." She sighed heavily. "My actions are why he is so evil. I let him become this thing. Had I not hidden him away and just accepted what I had done, he would be different. He is arrogant. He doesn't even know he has a mother. He just thinks he came to be out of his own energy swirling around."

"Did you know about Michael?" I asked, glancing at her face. "That he was a spy for Alpha."

"I didn't. I had already left by the time you all had fallen. I don't think anyone but Gadreel knew the truth. It's why he most likely set up the deception of Eve."

"Is Alpha your only kid?" I asked, watching her face for a reaction. "Or do I have an aunt or uncle?"

She whirled and faced me, eyes wide, while glancing around, and whispered. "Yes, but you mustn't tell anyone!" she warned.

"Why?" I whispered back.

"Because it is not safe for her," she replied. "The first thing that Alpha did after Lilith fell was slay Tiamat. He started searching out all of the elder gods, and the ones who wouldn't help him, he killed. If he found her and then learned about himself and me, I would definitely be next on his list."

"How do you know he doesn't already know about you?" I asked. "You were ordered to be killed."

She pondered. "Even if he knew I was a god, he would have confronted me over being his creator."

"Where is she? What's her name?" I asked, bombarding her. "I can protect her."

She smiled. "She is hidden away, much like how Sophie was all those years. Her name is Zoe."

"I have so many questions for you," I began. "Who is your creator?"

"My father is Yahweh, and my mother is Barbelo," she replied.

"Where do they reside?" I asked.

"I have no idea where my father has gone to," she responded. "But my mother," she smiled, "my mother lives within us all. She is the energy of the universe. But, most importantly, I believe she was the energy used to create you and Sophie. When she grew tired of seeing everything going awry with Alpha, she decided to disperse herself. I believe that was when Lilith collected the energy to create you two."

"Why didn't Lilith just create us on her own the way Alpha was created by you?" I asked.

"Don't you know, Incaendiel?" Sophia replied. "Alpha is a jealous god. And neither of them could create without the other. His one selfless act of creating her was all the power he could muster on his own. He needed her energy to create more because she *was* his energy."

Thoughts of the vision that Gabriel shared with me tumbled through my head. Lilith was not in the vision at all.

"When he slew all of the other gods, did he take their power?" I pondered, running the premonition through my head.

"Yes, he has grown more and more powerful over the years. But they were old gods, so they weren't as powerful as they had been in the beginning. It was like feeding him crumbs," Sophia replied.

"Can Alpha reabsorb Lilith without destroying her so her power isn't dissipated like the others?" I inquired, stopping to think.

She stopped in her tracks. "Oh no," she whispered and faced me. "Indeed, he can."

"She wasn't in the apocalypse vision," I stated.

Sophia put her hand on her forehead and began to pace. "You need to go to Starfire, now!" she barked.

I nodded and jogged back to where the angels were waiting for me.

"Is everyone ready?" I asked.

"We are," Metatron answered, putting the final touches of his armor on.

I nodded. I started waving my hands around as if by nature.

"What is he doing?" Azazel whispered to Samael.

"I believe he is summoning a portal to Lightshade," Samael replied in awe.

The wind began to swirl, and it was like I was looking through a window. I saw Damian and Luxina standing in the middle of a field. I walked through, and the others followed. Meteors pounded against a force field that Starfire had up around her safe haven. Warlocks filtered their magic to the sky as havoc rained down against the dome of protection.

"Alpha," Damian sneered.

"You are quite right," Starfire replied, walking up beside them and watching the sky. "He is angry."

"I took what was his," Luxina replied, her eyes fluttering in Damian's direction. "This is my punishment."

She is safe, I sighed

"What can we do?" Damian asked, turning to Starfire.

She closed her eyes and smiled. "What you do best."

They both looked at her, confused.

"Shine."

I was about to step forward to help when Damian and Luxina looked at one another and took hands. The fiery glow of their souls erupted to the surface, and I shielded my eyes from the blinding light. Damian glowed his icy blue fire while Luxina blazed in red and orange embers, much like her mother and me. They lifted from the ground, holding tightly to each other's hands. Each lifted their free hand, and light exploded, shooting across the valley. Their bodies grew brighter, and soon, nothing but pure white light was visible to the naked eye. I watched in amazement as the powerful glow gathered at the top of the sky in the center of where the magic dome encased the valley. Its tendrils slowly crept across the dome, latching onto every bit of magic that swirled above and solidified it in its place. It sparkled and crackled as it wound over and out across the entire paradise. I could see they pushed hard with their light, and the descending meteors began to slow and hover in midair, suspended briefly before bursting into clouds of stardust.

Alpha's scowling face appeared in the sky, glaring at them.

"Parlor tricks," he hissed.

"We're coming for you, Alpha," Luxina replied. "You can try to run, you can try to hide, but we will find you, and you will fall like the ashes of Eden." *She is just like me,* I mused.

He laughed deeply. "Do you think you can take me alone? A handful of Nephilim and Warlocks? A meager fleet of angels. You will still fail in the end! My army grows by the day, and they are bloodthirsty." He smiled, rolling his head and cracking his neck. "Bow to me, and those you love will live in the end. Defy me, and well, nothing will be left to mourn. Not even you two."

Damian shot an icy fireball into the sky, and Alpha's face distorted and disappeared. The two of them descended to the ground below, and we all watched in awe. As their feet touched the ground, Praeziel walked up to them. He put his right arm across the center of his chest, then took a knee.

"I pledge my allegiance to you," he shouted. "I will follow you to the ends of the earth, no matter how soon or far off that may be."

I looked around at the growing number of people who stood in Lightshade. While Damian and Luxina had been protecting it, the Nephilim had begun to arrive. One by one, each Nephilim who had entered the valley gathered around us, pledging their loyalty to Damian and Luxina. The warlocks took a knee, yelling their allegiances into the air. I looked around in amazement as they, one by one, each announced to follow them to the end of days.

"We shall fight alongside you as well, young Shining Ones," a voice called out behind them.

I watched as the Seelie and Unseelie Courts walked through a portal and stood behind them. The Dark Queen Mab, Queen Titania, and King Oberon stood at the forefront of the gathered fey. All three of them bowed to Damian and Luxina, and every single one of their followers followed as well. More and more people began to appear from various portals into Lightshade. The sun eclipsed to cast a shadowy glow across the valley.

"The vampires pledge our allegiance to the cause as well," replied a young man stepping forward. "For too long, Alpha has experimented with humans, turning us into nightwalkers with the vampiric blood of those in the abyss."

"The werewolves do as well," a young woman said, stepping into the front of the crowd. "Alpha has mistreated our kind for far too long. It is time he pays for the crimes he has committed against all."

I smiled as the support of every imaginable creature that had suffered from Alpha's reign of terror stood in allegiance with us all. Damian and Luxina had convinced them all by protecting Lightshade and showing just how powerful they were together. I looked from face to face as millions stood before us, pledging their lives to stop him.

"We will follow you wherever you go," I yelled above the crowd.

Luxina turned around, and her eyes lit up as she ran toward me.

"Daddy!" she shouted as she wrapped her arms around my neck.

I hugged her, tightening my grip around her shoulders, near tears. I breathed in deep, allowing the scent of her soul to fill my weary heart.

"I have been so worried about you," she cried, tears spilling onto my chest. "I was so afraid that Alpha still had you and was torturing you as punishment to me."

"You don't know how good it feels to see you and know you are safe," I replied, pulling back from the embrace. "I never imagined in all of the worlds that you would be so powerful."

"I get it from my father," she replied as she swiped away a falling tear.

She looked behind me to see thousands upon thousands of angels that were left in the Summit when Alpha abandoned his throne in the sky. I watched as she scanned the crowd, looking for one face in particular.

"She's not here," I breathed. "I will explain it all, but right now, we have business to attend to."

Damian walked over to join us, and I patted him on the back.

"It's nice to see you again, kid," I said, smiling. "I see you kept to your word."

"Not quite," he murmured.

I looked at him a bit confused. Luxina exchanged glances with him.

"Where's Xavier?" I asked, looking around in the crowd for his face.

"That's a long story," Luxina replied gravely. "But for now, just know he is safe, and he is home."

"Welcome, Incaendiel," Starfire said, pushing through the crowd to stand face to face with me. I towered over her like a giant. "We have much to talk about and to do."

"Yes, we do," I replied, nodding in agreement. "It's my understanding you have something for me?"

"I do," she replied. "Follow me inside. I was hoping Sophie would be with you, but that was another alternative move in the vast game of chess."

My eyes lowered. "Yes, I had hoped as well."

"Come now, don't doddle," she said and led me into her cottage. "I understand that you have gone through just as much as Damian has to get here."

"I have," I chuckled. "It's been an experience of a lifetime."

She smiled. "I see you got the votes from the angels. Our numbers have increased tremendously. It is looking promising for our battle against Alpha."

"Yes, some joined that I never expected to, and some declined," I replied sadly.

"I am sorry you had to learn about Michael the way you did," she said, patting my arm. "Just know he was on the ropes quite often about it all being a spy for Alpha. He battled over it quite often."

"How do you know that?" I asked.

"I know everything," she laughed. "He may come around in the end. We shall see. It made him bitter that he wasn't the chosen one to take over for Alpha. Mirror of his father, I suppose." She produced a bottle from her robe and held it up. "This is what you came for," she said, placing it on the table in front of her.

"What is it?" I inquired.

"It's a potion to break your enchantment and bring you to full power," she explained. "It does not taste good, and I am afraid it will hurt."

"Does anything involving fey magic not hurt?" I asked.

She chuckled. "Ah, the Lake of Purity. Well, if you must know, it's quite the same, but most likely a bit more intense. It will make you feel like you're dying."

"Well, I have done that before," I laughed.

"Oh," she laughed, swatting my arm. "I had forgotten about that. Tell me, do you remember anything about that?"

"What do you mean?" I asked.

"After you died, what do you remember before you came back to life?" she prodded.

I began to think. "I remember floating along in darkness. I was bound for Potter's Field. I heard Sophie call out my name, and it was like her voice alone gave me the power to return," I explained.

"Do you remember anyone being with you?" she pushed.

I thought harder. A face appeared in my mind, but as fast as it had appeared, it disappeared. "Barely," I replied.

She smiled. "Azrael," she stated.

"Who?" I asked, confused.

"Potion first, then we talk," she urged.

I sighed heavily. "Bottoms up," I groaned as I uncorked the bottle and drank it down.

It was sweet with a bitter aftertaste. I stood and waited for whatever to happen. I looked at Starfire.

"Just wait," she replied.

Almost instantly, I was doubled over with pain twisting through me like I had drunk ground-up glass, and it was shredding my insides. My body automatically heaved as if it could rid itself of the potion, and I lay gagging on the floor. She was right. This was worse than the Lake of Purity. Fire ran through my veins with an icy heat. I screamed in agony as steam rose from my skin, as I burned from the inside out. I had spent my whole life engulfed in flames and never had felt what the fire should feel like until now. I couldn't control my fire, and it began to burn uncontrollably on my skin.

"You need to leave," I heaved between breaths. "I don't want to hurt you."

"You won't hurt me," she replied.

"Ahhh!" I roared as my fire grew in intensity and burned inwardly.

I looked around, and nothing inside was catching on fire as I blazed out of control. It felt like she was pouring fuel on my fire as the burn deepened. I watched fire ringlets race through my veins on my arms up to my head. My head felt like it was going to burst from all of the heat. And just as quickly as it started, it stopped. I slowly stood to my feet, and Starfire offered me a chair to sit with her at the table.

"How do you feel?" she asked.

"Like I was boiled alive," I muttered.

"Want some tea?" she offered. "It will help soothe your insides."

"Thank you," I smiled.

She poured me a cup, and I took a sip. Immediately, every leftover feeling of being burned subsided. "That's quite the tea."

"Home blend," she said, smiling.

"Ready to talk now?" I asked, continuing to sip on the tea.

"I am!" she exclaimed as she picked up her own cup to drink from.

"So, who is Azrael, and why have I never heard of him... or her?" I questioned.

"Azrael is older than Alpha. She is older than most of the gods. If I am not mistaken, she was one of the first to come into existence. She goes by many names in many cultures. She is like Santisma Muerte to the Mexican Catholics. Nergal to the Sumerians. Mot to the Phoenicians, Charon to the Greeks. Azrael is Death incarnate," Starfire explained. "She ferries the souls to Sheol for them to rest. She ferries the immortal ones to Potter's Field."

"All immortal ones?" I pressed, shifting in my seat.

"No, Gods do not go to Potter's Field," she explained. "When they die, their energy goes out into the universe and is centralized into new gods waiting to burst forth into existence."

"Where was she taking me then?" I wondered.

"She was *trying* to take you to Potter's Field," she chuckled. "But your energy was too much for her to handle because in your dead state, you were pure, new god energy."

"So, she slipped, and I was able to will myself back alive, right?" I mused.

"Yes and no," she replied. "You resurrected yourself, yes. But she didn't slip. You were just too powerful for her to contain."

"I see," I said, taking another sip from my cup. "And you know also about Sophia and Gabriel and all of that too."

"Oh, child. I have known everything for what seems like forever," she laughed while picking up her cup.

"Sophia told me her secret," I commented. "Do you know about that too?" I asked.

"I do," she answered, smiling and taking a sip of her drink. "I also know where she is as well. But I will let Sophia tell you those things."

"And Yahweh?" I questioned. "Where is he? I didn't get a chance to ask Sophia. I already know about Barbelo."

"Yahweh is hiding," Starfire replied, setting the cup back on its glass plate. "Once Alpha is defeated, he will come out and bestow upon you and the kids his power."

"Why hasn't he given it to Alpha?" I asked, staring down into her eyes.

"Because he knows how evil Alpha is," she answered. "He wouldn't use the power for good. The reason Barbelo relinquished her energy to the universe was to give it a chance to live on past Alpha through you."

"Is Alpha going to destroy Lilith? Reabsorb her?" I wondered.

Starfire's face dimmed. "Yes," she stated. "He will be in full power then."

"When?" I asked, looking down at the table.

"Soon," she replied. I stood from my seat to leave. "Not that soon. You have time to stop him."

"Do I?" I inquired.

"You have just rejoined Luxina. Don't you want to spend some time with her before leaving again?" she questioned.

"You are right," I answered with a smile.

"Finish your tea."

Chapter 6

I SAT WITH Metatron and Gabriel as we watched more Nephilim arrive and check in. Hundreds of celestials showed up by the day. Our numbers had nearly tripled since Damian and Luxina showed everyone what they were fighting alongside when they fought against Alpha. It was beginning to look more and more hopeful for us as power built on our side.

"Is this place even big enough for all of us?" Metatron quipped, looking around at his surroundings.

"This place is magical," a young warlock interjected. "It will accommodate itself to the numbers."

"What's your name, kid?" I asked.

"Reikal," he replied.

"Oh, you're the one who gave Luxina those fancy hand knives," Gabriel interrupted and then turned to me. "She has been showing everyone those knives."

"Yes, sir," he boasted proudly.

"I am Incaendiel," I said, holding my hand out to him. "I am Luxina's father."

"Nice to meet you," he replied. He examined the sword that hung from my side. "Is that the flaming sword?" he questioned.

I looked down. I had forgotten I even had it. "It is," I answered

"Wait, since when do you have that?" Metatron demanded. "We were told it was gone."

Gabriel raised his hand. "That's because I stole it."

"Where is Michael's spear?" Metatron inquired.

"I stole that, too," Gabriel laughed.

"Is there anything you didn't steal?" Metatron drawled.

Gabriel thought for a moment. He snapped his fingers. "I left my horn. I have to go get it."

Reikal giggled as Gabriel sprinted off. "I can add some additional magic to your sword if you would like?" he offered.

"Like, what kind of magic?" I asked.

"I can make it where it cannot be wielded by anyone except those loyal to the Shining Ones," he replied.

"Now that would be useful," I remarked and handed it over. "How long will it take?" I queried.

"Back in a flash," he responded, running off.

"I hope I didn't just get robbed," I chuckled.

A loud trumpet echoed in the air.

"Gabriel found his horn," Metatron sighed.

I stood and watched as millions of lights lit up the sky.

"I think something is wrong," I said, pointing to the sky.

"Those look like..." Metatron began.

"Falling angels," I finished.

"What's happening?" Azazel asked, running up to us with Samael right behind her.

"I don't know," I replied. "Take down the force field!" I demanded. "They'll be burned alive falling like that through it."

Almost immediately, the force field came down. All of the angels who had returned to the Summit came careening down like meteors, hitting the ground with a burning thud. I ran to the first one to fall. It was Gabriel. He was burned pretty badly.

"Starfire!" I yelled. "We need to help them!" I examined him over. He was clutching the trumpet in his hand. "What happened?"

"No sooner had I returned to the Summit and retrieved my horn than Alpha and Lilith showed up," he replied. "He kicked us all out. He's closed off the Summit."

I looked around as more angels thudded to the ground and others ran to their sides to help them.

"Where are the kids?" I asked Azazel.

"They're inside asleep. They're pretty worn out from the past few days," she responded.

"Don't wake them," I ordered. "Starfire?" I called out again.

"I'm right here," she replied, holding a jar of some sort of substance. "Smear this salve all over them. It will heal the burns."

"Can you make sure they don't hear this inside?" I urged.

"I already did. It's soundproofed to where they can't hear anything outside of the walls," she replied.

"Thank you," I breathed.

I reached into the jar and scooped out a handful of the salve. I took my other hand and used it to apply it all over Gabriel. He groaned as the salve absorbed into his skin.

"It burns like acid," he screeched.

"It will only burn for a little bit," Starfire assured him. "Then it will be cooling."

I could see the relief wash over him as the burning stopped and the cooling kicked in. I handed the jar to Azazel.

"Quick, run the jar to the next angel and explain how to use it and hand it off," I ordered.

"On it," she noted.

"Raphael!" I shouted.

"Right here, Incaendiel," Raphael replied, running up to me.

"Heal as many as you can," I commanded.

He nodded and ran off to the first angel adjacent to Gabriel. He started running his hands over them, slowly healing their wounds.

"Are there any fatalities?" I yelled.

I watched a few hands pop up in the air and ran to them. The first I came across was Zadkiel. "Oh, no," I murmured as I hit the ground on my knees.

"There's nothing you can do for him, Incaendiel," Metatron mumbled. "Find the ones you can help."

His body began to dematerialize, and I looked up to see Azrael standing there.

"You," I stated.

"Me," she answered.

"Who are you talking to?" Metatron asked.

"You can't see her?" I stammered.

"See who?"

"They can't see me," she affirmed. "I am only visible to gods and other reapers. I will allow myself to be visible to others only when I want to be."

"Why?" I pressed.

"Because reapers are a different type of celestial," she explained.

"There are more of you?" I pressed.

She nodded. "And we will join your side."

"Is he going to Potter's Field?" I mused.

She nodded. "He will have a noble burial."

"I can't bring him back?" I protested.

She stopped to think for a moment. "I don't know. I know you brought yourself back and your twin flame. Why don't you try?"

"What do I do?" I asked.

"I don't know," she replied. "Try putting your hands on his chest and willing him back like you did Sophie."

I did as instructed and closed my eyes. I felt a buzzing in my hands and opened my eyes. Bright light emanated from them and was pulsating into Zadkiel's body. Zadkiel bolted upright, gasping deeply.

"I was dead," he blurted.

"Yes, you were dead," I replied, astonished.

"You brought me back?" he asked.

"I did," I answered, wide-eyed, still bewildered.

"Thank you, Brother," he responded.

"How did you do that?" Metatron asked.

"I don't know," I murmured.

I looked up at Azrael. "Can I save them all?"

She smiled and nodded.

I raced to each hand that was held up in the air, signaling a dead angel, and repeated what I had done with Zadkiel. Each one of them sprang back alive. It felt like it took an eternity to get all of the angels healed up with Starfire's salve and me reviving the dead ones. By the time we had finished, I was exhausted. I stumbled to the cottage porch and sat down on the steps. Metatron took a seat next to me.

"Who were you talking to earlier that I couldn't see?" he pushed.

Samael and Azazel ran up to the porch as well, both looking tired.

"You ok?" Azazel asked. "You look like you need a nap."

I laughed. "Yeah, I could use one," I replied.

"Who was that woman you were talking to?" Samael questioned.

My brows knitted together. "You could see her?" I asked in return, confused.

"Yeah, we both did," Azazel answered, nodding.

I scratched my head. "That doesn't make any sense," I stated, shaking my head. "She said only other gods could see her."

"Who is she?" Samael prodded, propping a foot up on the step and leaning down on his leg.

"Her name is Azrael," I replied.

"Who is she, and why couldn't I see her, but they could?" Metatron asked.

"She's Death and the leader of the reaper angels," I responded. "You can't see her because you're not meant to see her. I have no idea why those two could see her." I motioned between Samael and Azazel.

"Reaper angels?" Metatron wondered.

I nodded. "They help ferry the dead souls of humans and celestials," I replied. "She told me they were joining our side."

"I always wondered who was in charge of the dead souls," Samael remarked. "Neither Mother nor Alpha had ever told us about reapers. I just thought Alpha was in charge of that."

"I did too," I replied. "But you and Azazel seeing her doesn't make any sense. You're not gods unless..."

"Unless what?" Azazel asked.

Right when I was about to answer, Raphael ran up to the porch with a look of worry.

"What's wrong, Rafe?" I probed.

"Michael is among the fallen," he stated, glancing over his shoulder toward the fallen scattered across the grass.

"Michael?" I asked.

He nodded.

"Is he alive?" I urged.

"Yes. Gabriel is healing him up right now," he replied. "He asked for you."

I swallowed hard. "What do I do, Sam?" I questioned, looking at him.

He thought long and hard before he answered. "I would hear him out," he responded.

"I'm getting too old for this crap," I muttered.

Samael laughed loudly. "Aren't we all, Brother. Aren't we all." I began to walk off when he shouted, "Wait." I turned around to look at him. "Aren't you like eighteen years old?" he asked, laughing.

"Shut up," I laughed back.

I walked over to where Michael sat on the ground. Azazel was still applying the salve to his back when I knelt in front of him.

"Michael," I stated.

He looked at me, and I could see the pain in his eyes. "Why me?" he asked.

"Why not?" I replied.

"I did everything he asked of me," he cried.

"We all did. He still abandoned us," I sighed. "He doesn't care about anyone but himself."

"I did horrible things for him," Michael whimpered. "Horrible things in the name of a father who just tossed all of his kids out of their home. We didn't have a choice like you all did."

"It's the same game. It's the same story. It's just a different point of view for you," I replied. "Alpha wants power. He can't have power when he is outnumbered. He thinks by making you all fall, your power is diminished."

"It is," Michael cried. "It's gone."

"Do you trust me, Brother?" I asked.

He was silent.

"Will you follow me as your leader?" I pressed.

He hung his head, crying into his hands. "I don't have a choice, do I?" he whispered.

"You have a choice with me," I replied. "I won't make you choose my side. I won't make you leave this safe haven either if you don't. I am not our father."

I started to stand up when he grabbed my arm. He looked me in the eyes and inhaled deeply. "Hail to the King."

I nodded as I took his other hand in mine and pulled him in for a hug. Lights swirled around him as all of his power was restored to him.

"You don't need his power with me," I whispered in his ear. "I have my own power apart from his."

I stood up and looked out at the crowd of angels who sat on the ground, bruised and broken.

"For those of you who have not joined my ranks, I offer it to you now. Join me in the fight against Alpha. Accept me. In return, you will be restored like Michael here. It's your choice to make. I will not force you to choose between Alpha and me. I will not make you leave this safe haven. I will not abandon you because of your choice. But if you choose to join our ranks against Alpha, you will share in my power. Alpha has taken your power. Alpha takes everything for himself. When you fell, the powers he bestowed upon you went back to him to make him more powerful. He is absorbing all the power he can find to try to defeat us. I am offering you restoration. He is offering nothing."

One by one, angels stood from the ground and shouted. "Hail to the King." One by one, they each shared in my power. I was exhausted by the time everyone was all fixed up and part of the ranks. I could hardly walk back to the cottage. I stumbled and nearly hit the ground when Michael caught me.

"Let me help you, Brother," he said.

"Thank you," I slurred. "I just need to sit down."

"No, what you need is some rest," he urged.

"I will take him," Sophia said, stepping forth almost out of nowhere. "We have much to discuss once he has his nap."

"When did you get here?" I queried, barely able to form the words from exhaustion.

"I've been here since right before Alpha kicked them all out," she responded.

She walked over, and I leaned against her as she helped me inside the cottage.

"Can you trust him here?" she asked, eyeing Michael suspiciously.

"I don't know," I replied. "It didn't look or sound like an act. I do believe Alpha kicked him out like the rest of them."

"I still don't trust him alone with you," she sneered. "For all we know, he could be trying to kill you and steal the power for himself."

"Have a little faith in him," Starfire interrupted as we shut the door behind us.

I gave her a half smile and a nod. She *did* know things we didn't. If she believed he was to be trusted, I trusted her.

"Which room can I take him to?" Sophia asked, motioning to me.

"A lot of them are empty upstairs," Starfire replied. "The ones that are occupied have a sign on them."

Sophia nodded. She helped me up the steps and into the first empty room we came across. She helped me over to the bed, and I flopped onto it.

"Oh my god," I breathed. "This bed feels like a cloud."

"Don't you mean 'oh my me?'" Sophia asked with a laugh.

"Ha, good one," I groaned. "What are you doing here, Sophia?"

"Well, when Alpha showed up at the Summit, I waited around as long as I could to see what his plans were," she replied. "I had no idea that he was going to kick everyone out to absorb their powers. We didn't think of that one."

"No, we didn't," I remarked. "I feel stupid for not thinking of it when I thought of it with Lilith."

"You're not stupid, Incaendiel," she cooed. "You're just overworked and underpaid."

I rolled to my side and looked at her sitting in the chair beside the bed. "Are you sure the humans didn't wear off on you, too? You sure do have a lot of their sayings preprogrammed."

"Ha, humor," she mocked. "Did you take your potion?" she asked.

I nodded. "It was agonizing, by the way."

"I didn't think it would feel too pretty," she replied. "Have the kids taken theirs too?" she asked.

"Yeah, they took theirs before I got here. You should have seen them in action against Alpha with their unlocked power. They looked so majestic."

"You should have seen you and how you looked bringing all of those angels back from the dead," she replied.

"What did I look like?" I murmured, half asleep.

"You looked like a god," she responded, stroking my hair. "I am so proud of you, Incaendiel. You're going to restore the reputation of this family."

"Is that what you care about most?" I demanded, staring at her. "How the other gods look at us?"

"No," she replied. "I care about righting a wrong I committed so long ago."

"You sound self-absorbed like Alpha," I muttered. "You know what I care about?" I asked, propping myself up on my elbow. "I care about the world and what happens to it. I care about the universe crumbling in on itself. And I care about those kids down the hall. That's what I care about. I don't care about restoring a reputation marred by you. I don't care about being the most powerful being in the universe. I care about others, not myself."

"And that is what makes you such a fine god," she remarked. "You are selfless and not selfish. I was selfish. I wanted to create something of my own so badly that I did so without getting permission from my father. I ended up creating this universe and then the ass of a god that runs it.

Out of my selfish act came things we had never witnessed before from gods. Well, aside from Enlil, but he is just an asshole. Wrath, vengeance, jealousy, pride, envy, greed, so many personality traits that gods aren't supposed to possess, came from me. All because I wanted to do something I wasn't permitted to do yet."

"You were a kid, too, Sophia," I explained. "You didn't know any better."

"Did I? I went on a quest to find out and learn everything my father knew. In turn, violence, sorrow, disease, vice, madness, and even old age are what humans suffer at the hands of their god because he decided to throw a temper tantrum, learning he wasn't the only god of his universe. Then, the petty games he plays with Lilith make it even worse for humans. It's so horrible," she said, shaking her head.

I brushed my hand against her cheek. "You're not as bad as you think you are. It's not your fault you made a mistake. Everyone makes mistakes." I inspected her closely. I hadn't noticed how much Sophie resembled her before now.

She placed her hand on top of mine and smiled. "No one has been as kind to me as you have since I left Lucifer." She leaned in closer to my face, and I cleared my throat.

She blushed and immediately sat back up straight.

"So, you're the mother of the Nephilim," I stated, changing position in the bed a bit away from her. "Does that make them demigods?"

"In a way, yes," she replied, adjusting in her seat. "More like the myths of Nephilim being half angel. Since they were created through mortals and not clapped into being with a snap of my fingers, they're not quite godlike."

"Did you create them all?" I asked.

"No, I created the first one and then helped Samyaza and other Watchers to create more," she explained. "They all look to me as their mother since I created the first one."

"Who was the one you created?" I asked, propping my head up on my hand.

She smiled. "You have met him already," she replied. "Praeziel is my son."

"Another good kid," I remarked. "I know he worked diligently to keep the kids safe from harm."

"He did," she smiled and nodded. "But he lives such a sad life."

"Why?" I asked.

"He can never be with another Nephilim," she explained. "After Alpha learned about the Nephilim, he did something to their bloodlines. When they pair up, they turn mortal and die. So, he has spent the last several thousand years alone because he doesn't want to lose his powers."

"Why would Alpha do that?" I demanded.

"Alpha was angry with the Nephilim being created. It didn't help that Samyaza and the others decided to teach humankind things that Alpha wasn't ready for them to learn, along with teaching them to sin. Samyaza taught the humans arts and technologies. He showed them how to make weapons, cosmetics, and mirrors, and even taught them sorcery. One of the reasons that the city of Atlantis was run off was because they were such an advanced civilization compared to his creations. He wanted humans to advance at his pace. It was a stab at Alpha, really, for abandoning the Watchers. So, Alpha's punishment to them was to make their children die out," she elaborated.

"And you can't reverse what he did to them?" I asked. "I mean, you are a god."

"No, I can't," she replied with a half-smile. "The only one that I can guarantee is Praeziel because he was made from me, but I haven't told him because when he pairs up with another Nephilim and they grow mortal and die, it will crush him that he lost a grand love. He has already lost many loves throughout the years. Gwynevere, I believe, was his breaking point."

"Who was Gwynevere?" I questioned.

"She was part of the Unseelie court," Sophia shared. "She had been with Praeziel for the last three hundred years. She was with him and the kids as they looked for Starfire."

"What happened?"

"She was in league with Alpha," she asserted. "Luxina killed her."

"What?" I snapped, sitting upright in the bed. "She killed her?"

Sophia nodded. "She didn't have a choice, really. Gwynevere had spent the last year playing games with them and keeping them from getting to Starfire. Luxina was enraged during a fight and walked through one of the portals from the Otherworld and landed right where they needed to be. When Alpha took control of Damian's mind, he told her that Gwynevere was his spy. She only needed to ask Starfire one question. Gwynevere had told her that Starfire's location kept moving and bouncing around, so they had to hunt for the location. It was a lie, and that was the question she asked Starfire. She killed Gwynevere without a second thought. Praeziel was crushed that Gwynevere had betrayed them. He loved her dearly."

"She should have given her a second chance," I muttered. "She shouldn't have just killed her. So many people are allied with him out of fear, not out of want."

"Luxina did what she thought was best for everyone. She is still learning. She was with Gwynevere for a year, and at any given moment, Alpha could have taken her prisoner. She was scared. She was scared of going back there and being tortured more." Sophia reasoned. "Praeziel understands that she needed to be dispatched. It's just another lost love on his long list of loneliness."

"Every single misfortune, or grief, or tragic tale always comes back to Alpha being the source of the grievance," I grunted. "He needs to be stopped."

"Indeed, he does," Sophia sighed gravely.

I eyed her face. "You know something, don't you. What he's planning. You mentioned it earlier. What is it?" I urged.

"They have a young angel with them that looks like the children," she replied. "I don't know his name or who he is, but he is a new creation."

I thought back to the vision Gabriel shared with me of the apocalypse. The angel that seemed to control the horde of creatures looked to be around the same age as the kids.

"How new is he?" I asked.

"I'm not sure," she responded. "I don't even know what his name is. But he radiates wickedness."

"In the vision Gabriel had, there was a young angel in it. I bet it is him," I said, sitting up in the bed.

I ran my hand through my hair and then rubbed my eyes.

"Who else was there?" I pressed.

"Those of the angels who have been by Alpha's side since the war," she answered. "The Forsaken as well. Well, at least those who didn't choose Damian's side. I heard some of them talking about how they split with Asmodeus, with him leading the other faction. Apparently, some kind of conflict happened when Asmodeus helped Damian and you escape from Alpha. There is also a faction of the Watchers who joined with Alpha, led by Baraqiel."

"When did that happen?" I asked.

"When Stygia was attacked. Watchers chose sides then. Alpha gave them a choice to join, but those who didn't join would still be spared as a pardon for him abandoning them," she replied.

There was a knock on the door.

"You can come in," I answered as I straightened upright to look more energetic than I felt.

The door opened, and Raphael stepped through. He looked just as tired as I did.

"You better come down," he stated solemnly.

"What's going on?" I sighed.

"You will just have to come and see," he replied.

I stood up from the bed and followed him from the room, with Sophia right behind me. We made our way downstairs and outside of Starfire's cottage to a loud commotion outside. I stepped off the porch and saw Michael squaring up against another who had their back turned to me. Michael had his blade drawn, as did the other person.

"What's going on?" I shouted.

"Intruders," Michael hissed. "They claim to be friendly, but anyone who was in Alpha's ranks cannot be trusted."

"Mind your words, Brother," I barked. "You are one of Alpha's former loyalists. Let's hear them out."

"They're not even angels anymore," Michael sneered, still in fighting position.

"I said to back off!" I shouted.

My voice echoed through the valley much like Metatron's usually sounds. Michael immediately sheathed his sword.

"That's my power," Metatron whispered, leaning into my ear.

"I am trying to be serious here," I whispered back. "Who is it?" I demanded. "Who do you think you cannot trust?"

The visitor turned around.

"Asmodeus, Brother!" I sighed in relief. I walked over and gave him a welcoming hug. "I have been waiting for you to show up. I had feared the worst."

"We had followed Damian into the Nightmares and Shadows realm to help him after Alpha dispatched Zephar and others who were his loyalists. We narrowly escaped. Those monsters he made were there. We helped Damian escape at the last minute. He must have walked into the portal that would have brought him to the other kids because the creatures just disappeared as fast as they had appeared," Asmodeus recounted as he sheathed his sword.

"Are you here alone?" I asked, looking around for more of the others who left Alpha.

He nodded. "I thought it would be best that the others wait on the other side of the force field so they weren't attacked, thinking they were still in league with Alpha," he growled, glaring at Michael.

"How do you know he can be trusted?" Michael petitioned.

"He helped Damian and me escape from Alpha's lair at Chernobyl," I replied.

"No one spoke of this to me," Michael retorted. "None of the other Forsaken mentioned a rebellion."

"They were probably ordered not to," Asmodeus explained. "Alpha already thought he had lost you to Incaendiel's side. So he wouldn't have let anyone tell you about any new plans or what had happened."

"Metatron?" I asked, glancing back in his direction. "Will you lead our other brothers into Lightshade, please? They need a safe haven."

"Yes, sir," Metatron replied and marched off to the top of the hill to let them in.

"Sir," Asmodeus mouthed.

"I'm kind of a big deal now," I whispered, with a shrug.

"Where is Damian?" he asked, peering around the crowd for his face.

"Upstairs in the cottage, sleeping. He and Luxina had a huge showdown with Alpha, and it zapped them of all of their energy," I replied.

"Looks like it zapped you, too?" he remarked, looking me over.

"That's another story," I sighed. "One reason Michael is a bit touchy right now," I whispered into his ear.

"What happened?" Asmodeus murmured, glancing over at Michael, who had turned to walk away.

"Alpha kicked all of the angels out of the Summit," I responded. "They all fell and lost the powers he had given them."

Asmodeus's face turned from a look of amusement to a look of worry. "It's almost time then," he blurted.

"Time for what?" I asked, narrowing my eyes.

"He's locked himself away in the Summit," Asmodeus replied. "He had told us that when it got closer to the beginning of starting this universal destruction plan of his, he would take those who followed him to the Summit and kick all of the angels out."

Metatron came running back down the hill in a panic. "They're being attacked! They need our help!" he shouted.

I took off in a sprint to make it up the hill, running past Metatron with Asmodeus behind me. I stepped through the force field, and it was a blood bath on the other side. Those who were waiting had been attacked by the creatures Alpha made, as well as a horde of Forsaken. Brother fighting brother and then being ripped apart by malformed werewolf beasts.

Asmodeus went to run to help them, I grabbed his shoulder and pulled him back.

"Stand behind me," I ordered.

I extended both of my arms out by my side and then clapped them together as hard as I could. A shockwave of energy knocked everyone from their feet in front of me and sent them spiraling into the air. I raised my hands and sent blasts of fiery energy at the beasts that were trying to recover, and disintegrated them where they stood. The Forsaken tried to scramble to their feet and attack once again.

"Stop!" I bellowed.

My voice shook the ground beneath our feet, and they cowered into a squatting position.

"Those of you with Asmodeus, get inside," I ordered.

"Come on," Mammon shouted to those who were on our side as he and Asmodeus stood at the gates, making sure no one slipped in who wasn't supposed to.

"You two go as well," I demanded as the last one of them ran through.

"What about you?" Asmodeus asked.

I turned around and told him, "I got this."

He nodded and disappeared into the gate with Mammon right behind him. I turned my attention back to those who still cowered in front of me.

"You have a choice to make here," I began, looking each of them in the eyes. "You can stay with Alpha and let him continue to mistreat and abuse you, or you can join me."

"What makes you think we will join you so quickly?" one shouted, standing to her feet.

"Naamah, Sister," I replied. "It's nice to see you."

Abaddon scoffed. "You think you're special because you have powers. You're nothing more than a little bug that needs squashing," she seethed, twisting her sword in her hand.

"I am not the one who abandoned you, Sister," I refuted, putting my hands up defensively. "I am not Alpha, nor am I Lilith. I did not make you into what you are now."

"You didn't stop it either, now did you?" she huffed, readying her sword. "Besides, I like who I am now. Alpha accepts me for who I am now."

"Does he?" I prodded, shaking my head. "Or does he just treat you like his slaves? Warriors that can be expendable. That's how he treated those who went after Damian. They were expendable to him. And so are you, or you wouldn't be here. Instead, you would be nestled safely in the Summit with him while those beasts he created carried out his dirty deeds."

"We are important to him!" Naamah countered, drawing the bowstring of her bow.

"You are his pawns," I insisted. "The pieces sent out first into battle that are dispensable and not essential to his grand scheme in the end. But you don't have to be! You can join your brothers and sisters. You can join us! You can become whole again."

"How can we become whole again?" she sneered, glaring at me. "We are Forsakens for a reason. No one can restore our light. No one can untarnish our souls."

"I can," I replied, holding out my hand. "All you need to do is trust me and join me in this fight because, in the end, nothing will be left. Not even you. Alpha is going to destroy everything and reabsorb every bit of power and energy he exhausted in creating it to be an all-mighty god. That includes you. You won't survive the end. Why do you think he created those muddled creatures? They're not an expense of energy to him."

"I don't believe you," she spat. "Alpha has told us his plans. Those loyal to him will reap the benefits in the end."

"I can show you the end," I defended. "Do you really want to see how this all plays out for us all? Because in the end, you are not in the final battle. None of you are."

"Lies!" she shouted.

"Gabriel!" I commanded.

Gabriel appeared at my side. "What do you need?"

"Show them the end," I said, pointing over at them. "Show them their fates."

"I can't show them that anymore," Gabriel replied.

"Why not?" I asked in disbelief. "You showed *me*."

"Because it has changed," he answered. "I am not allowed to show anyone the new future now."

"Then show him the old one," I demanded.

"Those get erased when the future changes. That vision no longer exists," he responded. "But you should be able to share it with him."

"What use is an old vision?" Naamah laughed. "Afraid to show us how we win in the end?"

I became irritated and held up my hand. A blast of white light came out of it, and all of their eyes lit up like stars exploding. Somehow, even though I didn't know exactly what I was doing, I shared the vision Gabriel had given me. The light disappeared, and the bright light that had shone from their eyes was gone as well.

"How did I do that?" I whispered to Gabriel.

"You should know," Gabriel replied. "You're a god, remember?"

Naamah stood quietly as she processed what she saw in her head. "Alpha lied to us," she murmured, tears filling her eyes.

"Alpha lies to everyone," I reinforced, taking a few steps closer to her. "Alpha is the Great Deceiver he warned you all about. The question is, what do you plan to do about it?"

Before she could respond, fiery brimstone erupted from the sky and struck down like lightning on her. She was turned into a pillar of salt right before me. More shafts of brimstone began to rain down as each of the Forsaken who stood there began to flee before they were struck.

"Quickly, into Lightshade!" I urged, waving my arm for them to follow toward the open portal.

They ran as quickly as they could as Alpha tried to smite them. Gabriel followed in after them, and just as I was about to turn and close the gate, a voice called out.

"Incaendiel! Wait!"

I turned to see a straggler trying to dodge the beams of hellfire pelting down. The anger boiled deep within me as I looked from the straggler to the pillar of salt Naamah had been turned into. I roared in rage and clapped my hands together toward the sky, taking my wrath out on Alpha. A powerful beam erupted from me and shot into the sky. Lightning struck, and thunder clapped, and the sky went silent. The straggler ran up to me breathlessly.

"Thank you, Brother," she said, removing the hood from her head.

"Uriel?"

Chapter 7

URIEL WALKED BY my side as we came down the hill to the center of Lightshade, where everyone awaited my return. Asmodeus stood guarding the Forsaken I had let into Lightshade that Alpha had sent while everyone else was being bandaged up.

"Uriel!" Metatron gasped and ran up to her, grabbing her by her shoulders. "Why are you here?"

"I had no choice but to flee the entrance of Purgatory," Uriel shared. "Alpha cleaned house, and I was next on his list."

"Purgatory?" I interjected. "What the hell is Purgatory?"

"After Lucifer walked as Jesus, Alpha created a system of punishment for not just humans but for celestials as well," Uriel explained. "Only certain ones of us knew about it and were not allowed to speak about it. What the humans speak about is real. He made hell, limbo, purgatory, the abyss, and all kinds of other traps."

"Where are Sandalphon and Jophiel?" Metatron asked, shaking her.

"They fled inside Purgatory," Uriel went on. "I didn't have time to search for them. Alpha tried to smite me." She unsheathed her wings, and they were a tattered mess. "I took to the Otherworld and bounced through portals before landing here to witness the showdown between Alpha and Incaendiel."

"Showdown?" Samael inquired, looking between Uriel and me. "What showdown?"

One of the Forsaken who was being guarded by Asmodeus spoke up. "Alpha tried to smite us after Incaendiel showed us all the vision he was given by Gabriel."

"Astaroth?" Michael asked, pushing through the crowd.

"Yes, it's me," Astaroth responded.

"I *know* he is in league with Alpha," Michael hissed.

"I am aware," I reassured, motioning with my hands for him to calm down. "I gave them safe haven. Alpha just tried to smite them. He turned Naamah into a pillar of salt just now."

"They don't deserve a safe haven," Michael sneered.

"What is *with* you?" I demanded, turning on my heels to face him. "Do you think you are the only one worthy of a second chance? Everyone has had their fair share of manipulations and punishments by Alpha and Lilith. Everyone deserves a second chance, not just you."

"Incaendiel saved us," Astaroth relayed.

"After they all got to safety, Incaendiel was about to close the force field to Lightshade when I found him," Uriel recounted. "Alpha was also trying to smite me still, as well, and I showed up at the wrong place at the wrong time. Incaendiel tossed his own smite at Alpha. I am fairly certain he struck him as well. The sky went silent afterward."

"You smote Alpha?" Samael asked, bewildered.

I nodded. "I was enraged at what he had done to everyone. Naamah didn't deserve to die like that. None of them did. Seeing her frozen as a pillar of salt and the beams of hellfire still raining down as Uriel tried to get to me, I just exploded."

"I don't know about the rest of our brothers and sisters who came here allied with Alpha, but I pledge my allegiance to you, Incaendiel," Astaroth declared with a bow. "Hail to the King."

"All Hail Incaendiel, King of Kings!" Asmodeus shouted.

The valley was filled with the voices of the Forsaken shouting my name and bowing to me. Bright lights began to swirl around them, and they were lifted from the ground.

"What's happening?" Asmodeus demanded, panicking.

"I don't know," I stuttered.

The lights swirled around them like magical fireflies in the night sky. One by one, the lights entered their body, and a bright shining white beam erupted from their chests. Their grayed skin turned to a lustrous shine. Those who no longer had their wings from when the darkness took over them sprouted a new pair from their shoulder blades. Their dark hair turned back into the lustrous blond hues that they once had. Their dark eyes were once more a silvery blue as they had been in the beginning.

"My grace, my light," Asmodeus murmured, looking his body over. "It has been restored!"

"He has done even what Alpha has refused to do through all of our loyalty!" Astaroth shouted. "We are angels again!"

"So, it's true," Uriel started. "I have been sitting on the sidelines listening to both sides of the fence. I heard that those who join you will share in your power. Alpha has been telling all of his loyalists that it's just a rumor. That you don't have the capability of restoring power to anyone."

"It's true," Eisleth shared, stepping forward. "Alpha keeps those of us in check by saying that he will restore us once we prove that we remain loyal to only him, and that Incaendiel will offer false promises to us to gain our trust when, in fact, it is he who is deceiving us."

"And we need to act quickly against him," a voice called out through the crowd.

"Azrael," I stated, walking toward her. "It's good to see you again."

"Who is she?" many began to shout.

"They can see you?" I wondered aloud, looking around at all the confused faces.

"Yes," she elaborated. "I am allowing them to see me right now. We have a big problem."

"Wha's wrong?" I asked.

"Where is Lailah?" she demanded, looking around at everyone.

"Is Lailah here?" I shouted among the others, looking for her myself. "Did she fall with the rest of you? Has anyone seen her?"

I looked around at all of the faces, and they shook their heads.

"She is not at the giving tree," Azrael asserted, worried.

"How do you know Lailah?" I asked.

"Among you are reaper angels that do not know that they are reaper angels," she clarified. "They just handle the tasks as ordered without knowing *why* they do what they do. I have gathered many helpers throughout the millennia. However, Alpha has hoarded his lot of angels who were supposed to have been allotted to me during their creation. Lailah, among others, is one of them."

"She has never spoken of you before," Metatron emphasized.

"That's because she doesn't remember me after she sees me," Azrael revealed. "Alpha doesn't want any of you knowing there is a force greater than he that controls death and life."

"Alpha doesn't want them to know things, period," Gabriel interjected with a huff.

"Is Lailah not in the Summit?" I asked.

"No, she is not," Azrael replied, her worry growing deeper. "I went to look for her when everyone was kicked out of the Summit and fell since she wasn't among any that I could see. Without Lailah, there aren't going to be any new births. I can't give her souls to recycle."

"Sandalphon and Jophiel are missing as well," Metatron added.

"Who else does Alpha have stashed away that is vital in the upkeep of the world?" Samael asked.

"He has my Watchers."

I whipped around to see Samyaza and Belial standing together.

"Alpha came to Stygia nearly a year ago when we were having the council meeting with Incaendiel," Samyaza began. "Nice to see you're still alive, by the way," he added, looking me up and down.

"Yeah, it's been a helluva year," I muttered.

"When he infiltrated our sacred place, he took those he saw as he marched through our tunnels captive," Samyaza continued. "Belial and I hardly escaped."

"Wait," I started. "That's not what Sophia told me. She said that Baraqiel led another faction that had split from the Watchers to join Alpha after he made promises."

"Lies," Belial hissed.

"She just told me!" I retorted.

"Sophia is under protective custody of the fey," Samyaza asserted. "She isn't even in the universe right now. After Alpha tried to slay her, and Damian spared her, she was taken where she couldn't be found."

"Then who the hell was in my bedroom?" I demanded and turned around to scan the crowd. "Has anyone seen Sophia?"

"Not since Asmodeus arrived," Azazel responded.

"Check and make sure the kids are still safe in their room," I ordered.

Azazel nodded and ran off into Starfire's cottage.

"This doesn't make sense," I murmured. My eyes narrowed. "Where is Michael?" I snapped.

"Right here," Michael answered, stepping forward.

I ran up to him, grabbed him by his shirt, and pushed him up against a tree. "She showed up right after you did, just like how Beelzebub showed up right after you did all those years ago. Tell me, *Brother,* and don't you dare lie to me. Did you have anything to do with this?"

Michael's eyes were saucers of fear. "I swear to you, Incaendiel. I had nothing to do with this. I do not know who is faking being Sophia."

It began to thunder and lightning. The clouds began to swirl, and rain began to pelt down. "Tell me the truth!" I bellowed.

Michael looked around at those gathered around. "Please, don't let him smite me!" he pleaded.

The wind blew ferociously as I stood my ground with Michael.

"Incaendiel!" a voice shouted, and I looked behind me.

The others were on the ground, holding on to anything the best that they could as the winds picked up, nearly carrying them away. Their eyes filled with fear as they looked at me.

"I swear to you, Brother!" Michael implored. "I have nothing to do with this!"

I released my grip on him, and the storm that had rolled in disappeared just as quickly as it had appeared.

"Where is Starfire?" I muttered, stalking off to her cottage.

I met Azazel on the steps. "The children are sound asleep in bed," she reported.

"Thank you," I sighed in relief.

I walked past her and into the cottage. "Starfire?" I called out.

She emerged from a room to my left that was filled with potion bottles and books, closing the door behind her.

"I know what you want," she replied, walking out into the middle of the room. "But first, you must calm down."

"I *am* calm," I snapped.

"Are you?" she asked, not moving from her place. "Take in a deep breath and exhale."

I was growing impatient by the minute.

"Incaendiel, you are more powerful than you were before," she explained. "You don't understand or know how to really control these new powers of yours. You need to calm down." She looked frightened.

I breathed in deeply and exhaled slowly, letting all of the anger out with my breath.

"Who was pretending to be Sophia?" I asked.

"You already know the answer," she replied.

"It can't be Beelzebub. I killed him," I retorted.

"No, you only thought you did," she replied. "That injection into your neck took immediate effect. It wasn't Beelzebub that gave it to you. And there wasn't anyone standing there for you to strike down. Alpha was the one who gave you the injection. Beelzebub knows a lot of things that others do not because he has been by Alpha's side for a really long time. Against his will, but by his side."

"Is Gabriel real? Are the others real?" I begged, fearing I had been hallucinating this whole time. "The ones that joined my side, are they to be trusted?"

She smiled. "The others are real. Everything else is real. Beelzebub didn't know how to come to you and ask for safe haven, considering your past. So, he took on the role of Sophia and told you things he knew from Alpha. Most of the things were true. Some were not because he was going solely by information told to him or what he heard by eavesdropping on Alpha," she replied.

I nodded and left the cabin. "Beelzebub!" I shouted. "Show yourself!"

In the middle of the crowd of angels, one of them began slowly moving forward.

"Sophia?" Samyaza called out. "It can't be?"

"It's not," I answered him.

As the crowd parted to allow Sophia through, her body dematerialized, and before me stood Beelzebub. He dropped to his knees.

"Please, Incaendiel," he implored. "I wish you no harm. I wish everybody no harm."

I took slow steps toward him. "Are you spying for Alpha?" I glowered. "And do not lie."

"I am not," he cried. "I am here for safety. I knew about the Forsaken and their plans to revolt against Alpha. I knew they were going to release you and Damian. I didn't tell Alpha, and he is looking to punish me."

"How can I trust you?" I asked.

"I bowed to you, Brother," he insisted, crawling toward me on his knees. "I accept you as my leader. I am one of you now."

I bent down to look him in the eyes, and his eyes fell to the ground. "Look at me!" I barked. His eyes came up to mine. "If you betray me, I will not have mercy on you. At all."

"Everything I have done has been Alpha's demand of me. And if I didn't do what he told me to do, he threatened to smite me," Beelzebub whimpered. "I am at your mercy, and I am at your feet. I am begging you to believe me because those things I told you, the things Sophia thinks Alpha doesn't know, he does."

"What is he talking about?" Belial demanded. "What things?"

"There was a lot. To highlight, Sophia is the mother of Alpha, but she also has another child named Zoe, whom she hides among the mortals like Alpha did with Sophie," I replied.

"Even we didn't know those things," Samyaza declared. "How do we know it's not another lie like was told about Baraqiel?" he asked.

"Because Alpha has been searching for her," Beelzebub elaborated. "It's why he has taken Lailah and why he took over the Summit. He is going through the list of conceptions and births to figure out which person on earth is Zoe."

"He is right," Azrael cut in. "If Zoe is recycled the same way human spirits are, then Lailah would know who she is. But even I cannot handle godly souls. They are too powerful for me to ferry." She nodded toward me.

"It's why Incaendiel could will himself back to life, right?" Azazel added. "And why Sophie didn't die either?"

"That's right," Azrael replied. "So, who has been ferrying Zoe's soul to Lailah?"

"I have," an old voice croaked.

I turned around and behind me stood a very old woman.

"Who are you?" I asked.

"I am Maveth," she responded. "The mother of Azrael."

Azrael bowed low in response to the voice. "Mother," she said. "Why are you here?"

"Because this is becoming far bigger than we discussed," Maveth answered. Maveth smiled at me and touched my cheek. "You look just like Yahweh."

"You know about the others?" I asked.

"Of course, I do," she laughed. "I am not an old woman in person for no reason. I am as old as time itself. I was the first to come into existence. I brought forth my daughter, Azrael. The universe cannot operate if life exists first. There would be no order. Death has to exist before life because it is what brings life. Each universe created by the varying gods springing to life eventually all flows back to me. However, I choose not to title myself as the primordial being or the big bang that set off the energy for everything to begin manifesting. So, few know how I came to exist. And with that shroud of knowledge, I am able to work in mysterious ways."

Maveth moved past me to where Beelzebub still cowered on the ground. "Your brother here, he speaks the truth. Alpha is looking for Zoe," she said as she bent down and lifted his face to her by his chin. "You are safe here. Incaendiel will not hurt you." She helped him to his feet and then turned back around to me. "You must find Zoe before he does."

"What if that's what Alpha wants?" I asked. "What if I lead him to her by mistake?"

"You have to trust yourself, dear boy," she laughed. "How can you be the ruler of this universe if you still cast doubt against yourself? Believe in yourself, child. I do," she replied, raising her eyebrow with a grin. "If it wasn't such a universal apocalyptic ordeal, we would all have a pool running on you all to see who would win. And I would bet on you."

"So, what do we do first?" I asked. "Who do we find first? There are so many of us that Alpha has taken against their will. How do we know whom to find that will lead us to victory?"

"Everyone is a grand chess piece in this game Alpha plays," she elaborated. "He has already squandered his pawns. You're on to the key chess pieces now until he finishes his monsters and whatever else he has planned to create. Everyone is important now. Even the ones you think aren't important are."

Maveth began to wander away from us. "Wait!" I shouted. "Where are you going?"

"Home," she replied. "You don't need my help right now. You just need to figure out your strategy." She smiled and turned into stardust.

"She's right," I declared, turning my attention to the crowd of angels behind me. "We need a game plan."

"So we have Sophie, Sandalphon, Jophiel, Lailah, the Watchers, and Zoe to save," Raphael chimed in. "We need a head count of who else there is that we are missing that are important."

"Lucifer," I added.

A riotous commotion broke out.

"Are you serious?" one yelled.

"He has betrayed us all over and over," another insisted.

"He cannot be trusted!" one hissed.

"Beelzebub?" I called out, and the crowd quietened.

"Yes, Brother?" Beelzebub replied.

"Where is Lucifer?" I inquired.

"No one knows," he replied. "Alpha did something with him after Damian had come to see you. I believe he was punished for disobeying orders."

"What orders?" I asked.

"He had been trying for a while to lure Damian away from Alpha," Beelzebub explained. "He had bartered with Alpha, giving him your kids in exchange, but Alpha refused to hold up his end of the bargain. So Lucifer tried to sweet-talk his way into changing Damian's mind. That kid loathes him. Damian only went along with Alpha's plans to make sure Luxina and Xavier stayed safe. He had no idea that Alpha would subject him to more injections to control him. And then the arena where he was nearly killed."

"I know all of that," I replied. "Is there anything else?"

"He tried to get Sophie to disobey orders as well," Beelzebub recounted. "But Alpha had a good grip on her. The last I saw of Lucifer, he entered Alpha's office and never came back out. Only Alpha knows where he is."

"Is he still loyal to Alpha?" I asked. "Or was it out of necessity to get Damian?"

"From my understanding, he was only hanging around and doing Alpha's bidding to get Damian," Beelzebub replied. "Alpha knew Lucifer would keep Damian away from anyone who would try to set him free because he wanted to take Damian away from everyone to keep him for himself."

"You said you had escaped from the Summit after he tossed everyone out," I resumed questioning. "Was that before or after he had gone to Purgatory?"

"It was before," Beelzebub clarified. "I didn't know about the attack on Uriel until she arrived, or about the attack on the Forsaken that was going to transpire."

"Uriel," I called out.

"Yes?" she responded, stepping forth.

"What is in Purgatory that Alpha could use? Why is he interested in it?" I asked.

"Human souls are the only thing I can think of, and then those like myself and the others who guard it and make sure no soul escapes without purification," she replied.

I started thinking hard. *Purgatory. Souls. Can Alpha eat souls? For power?*

"When the time comes, we go to Purgatory," I asserted aloud. "I have a feeling about it that I just can't shake. For now, we will stay here and train. We need numbers, and we need them to be able to fight. Once we are all on the same page, we begin the rescues."

Chapter 8

"DO YOU EVER sleep?" Asmodeus asked, walking into the kitchen of Starfire's cottage.

"Hmph," I snorted while sitting at the table. "I will sleep when I am dead, apparently."

Asmodeus stared out the window, watching everyone training through the glass. I followed his eyes and saw he was staring at Damian.

"Have you even told him you're here yet?" I prodded.

Asmodeus looked down and laughed, shaking his head. "I don't know why I haven't told him," he replied, taking a seat next to me at the table. "I'm just glad to see he's alive and isn't stuck in that dungeon of Alpha's anymore."

I nodded. "Yeah, he didn't deserve any of that. Alpha is... he never did any of that to us, you know?"

"Right?" Asmodeus remarked. "Like, I mean, yeah, he abandoned us after the fall, and we all have some form of complex from that, but I never saw him actually torture us the way he did Damian. It was ruthless. He had no compassion for him. He had no love for him. It's like he hated his existence but tolerated him so he could be his soldier or weapon."

"You said it there," I replied, pointing at him. "His weapon. He knew what Damian was. I think he knew what we all were, sometimes. It just doesn't make sense that someone as all-knowing as he is didn't know that there were people among his ranks who had power like we did. Lilith, thinking she hid some grand secret," I laughed.

"Do you remember much of anything the day you two escaped?" Asmodeus asked.

"Apparently, what I remember isn't true," I responded. "I remember seeing Damian off into safety and then getting stuck in the neck with a needle. When I turned around, it was Beelzebub. I killed him right then and there."

"Is that all?" Asmodeus pushed, perking up.

"I remember you ran up to help me after I was injected," I answered. "Did that happen?"

Asmodeus smiled. "That did happen. And then you went psycho."

"What do you mean?" I asked. "I thought we were attacked, and then I saw Sophie laughing with her black eyes."

"That didn't happen either," Asmodeus said. "I had carried you partway back inside when the other Forsaken joined us to help fight our way out. Sophie saw you and demanded to know what happened to you. When I was telling her what happened, you freaked, man. You started fighting us. I don't know what he jabbed into your neck, but you almost killed us all trying to fight us off."

"Maybe that's what Alpha was hoping for," I mused. "Kill off those of you who sided with me while I was thinking you were all monsters and attacking me. Two birds, one stone."

"Maybe," Asmodeus murmured while thinking. "What happened after you left?"

"I was flying through the air, and something struck me in the back of the head, or at least I think? I don't know anymore," I replied. "I careened to the ground and woke up in a faery glade. Queen Titania found me and led me to the Otherworld and had me bathe in the fountain to leach all of the injections from my body and restore my memories."

"Memories?" Asmodeus asked.

"Yeah, whatever hit me in the head gave me amnesia or something, paired with that last jab in my neck. I had forgotten about everything but the small talk I had with Damian before Lucifer had busted in," I explained. "I had forgotten all about the torture and the injections. Seeing Sophie. Seeing you and Mammon. Talking with Alpha and Lilith.

Everything except that one talk with Damian. I don't know why, but my brain held onto that one."

"That's so crazy," Asmodeus sighed.

"How did you all escape after I went insane?" I asked with a chuckle.

"We had to fight our way out through monsters and other Forsaken who had chosen to side with Alpha," he replied. "It was a blood bath. A lot of good men died for the cause."

"I'm sorry. I should have been there to help," I declared.

"It's not your fault," Asmodeus insisted, patting my arm.

"Where did you go?" I asked.

"First, we went to the Watchers when we learned that Samyaza and Belial were the only two left in Stygia after Alpha had captured everyone else," he replied. "We then went to the Otherworld to find Damian. That boy is crafty. It took us a long time to finally find him, and it was after the loyalists had found him. We watched as he took them down with ease. Then, Alpha's monsters found us."

"Yeah, they found me, too," I shared.

"You should have seen Damian trying to save everyone in the Nightmares and Shadows black market. He didn't want anyone dying for him," Asmodeus declared. "He told us over and over, all the time, that he hated that people were dying for him. He summoned his icy powers and took a lot of the creatures out, but it seemed like if we cut the head from one, two more rose in its place. I finally yelled for him to get out of there, and he listened. Once he was gone, they were too. How did you handle the ones after you?" he asked.

"I burned the Seelie court down to the ground and took them with it," I replied with a smirk.

"Somehow," Asmodeus laughed, "I knew you were going to say that."

"I am in over my head, man," I huffed. "Like, everyone is looking to me for answers as if I know everything. I don't know any more than they do. All of this is new to me, just like it is to them. I am so overwhelmed. Yeah, sure, I have power that's nearly the strength of Alpha, but all of this," I motioned, pointing outside, "I am not ready for this."

"The universe wasn't built in a day, my friend," Asmodeus said, slapping my shoulder. "You will get the hang of everything. I mean, no pressure or anything, but we are all depending on you here. We didn't just pledge allegiance to you and pick a side because you promised us things or because we were afraid of Alpha. We pledged our allegiance because we do believe in you, Brother. We believe you will be a much better leader than our parents. Plus, I happened to have read some prophecies while being a dungeon master."

I laughed. "You read some prophecies?"

He laughed as well. "I did. I stole some books that Damian had been reading to see what he was studying up on. Like you believe, I also believe that Alpha knows more than what we think. Those books... those books helped me pick a side. Sure, I was always on Damian's side. I would follow that kid wherever. He is a helluva warrior. But you," Asmodeus stopped and cleared his throat.

"What about me, Brother?" I asked.

"I was still angry with you for not trying to help me after the darkness took over," he replied sheepishly. "I had a lot of anger and resentment toward you all, including Lilith and Alpha. I was bitter for years until Alpha showed up one day. He came with a promise that if we did what we were asked to do, he would restore us. Years went by, and he never held up his end of the bargain. Then the war happened, and we were told to wait on the sidelines. He told us none of you would fight fairly with us. And then he carried that boy into my life. Just a baby, crying and alone. Damian's cries irritated Alpha to the point where Alpha was just going to kill him. I took Damian and looked after him. I have looked after him for the past seven years as my own kid. He softened my hardened heart and taught me love again. When I learned he was one of the special beings called The Shining Ones, and you were too, I knew then that you were the ones to bring about the change we needed. I decided then I would help you escape from Alpha. The rest is history."

I swallowed hard. "I am sorry, Asmodeus. We had been so busy trying to be the perfect warriors, fighting the fight... I wanted to leave with you, you know?" I asserted, bowing my head. "When Lilith cast you out because you had completely lost your grace, I wanted to go with you. I could feel the darkness trying to overtake me. But she reminded me of Sophie and how I was the key piece to the whole thing. The whole damn game." I wiped my eyes as stray tears formed. "I never forgot about you, though, even though it seemed like everyone forgot about me and how I saved them and returned their light to them. I never forgot about those of you I didn't have the chance to save as well."

Asmodeus smiled. "Well, now you have, Brother," he replied, his silvery blue eyes sparkling. "And I owe you my life for it. I owe all of you my life for it."

"You don't owe me anything, Asmodeus," I said. "I had no idea that when people pledged their allegiance to me, all of this would happen. I don't deserve the praise and thanks for it."

"That right there," he replied, pointing at me. "That is why you are and will be a better god than Alpha. You don't take credit for anything. You are selfless and compassionate. You're not doing this for a power play. You're doing this to set things right again. To right the universe. To right so many wrongs done by Alpha. You are doing this for selfless reasons, whereas Alpha claimed his title of god to hold power over others."

"All I hear is people telling me I need to believe in myself," I sighed. "I don't know how to do that. I have been conditioned to fear my power for so long that I am always afraid of losing it and taking out people I care about."

"I think when you believe in yourself and have the confidence in yourself that all of these people keep telling you to have, all of the pieces will fall into place," he replied.

"I'm supposed to be in charge, and here I am whining to you about all of this," I laughed.

He laughed as well. "It's what makes you a good leader, Brother. You are humble, and you're not afraid to talk to people in confidence about your troubles and hardships. I am sure the others would be just as receptive to your self-doubt as I am and would tell you the same thing."

"Tell him what?" Gabriel asked, walking into the kitchen and snagging an apple from the table. "That he is ugly as all get out?" he asked, laughing and taking a bite from the apple.

"So this is where the party is," Raphael teased, walking in with Samael, Azazel, and Metatron following behind.

"What's going on?" Samael asked.

"Tell them," Asmodeus urged.

I sighed with a groan. "I was talking to Asmodeus about everything."

"Everything is pretty ambiguous," Azazel said, popping a grape in her mouth. "You gotta be more specific than that."

"About my lack of confidence with everything. Like, what the hell am I doing?" I replied.

"You, Brother," Samael began, "are saving us."

"How did I become the savior, though?" I asked. "Do you have confidence in me solely based on my power, or do you really believe in me?"

Samael smiled. "I bowed to you, Brother. I bow to no one."

"Good point," I laughed.

"We follow you because we really do believe in you," Metatron added. "It's not because we are choosing sides in fear of Alpha or fear of you. We aren't picking you because you have all these cool powers or anything like that. We are following you because you are you and always have been. You never bowed down to Alpha. You never listened to anything anyone has ever told you. You have done what you were going to do through choice alone. You saved us so many times when all hope was lost. We believe you will save us again."

"I needed that," I replied. "Good pep talk, everyone. Don't eat all the food," I joked.

I walked outside and sat on the porch of Starfire's cottage as the sound of swords clashing filled the air. All of these people here believed in me and needed me to help change things and restore the natural balance and order of the universe. Training for the final battle against Alpha had commenced, and everyone was preparing. In intervals, the sun would eclipse so the vampires and werewolves could train as well, since the vampires couldn't be out in the sunlight and the moon triggered the werewolves. I sat and watched the Nephilim train beside the angels as equals, and the Seelies and warlocks train in harmony. I couldn't help but smile as I watched them all when Reikal came running up to me.

"Here you go, sir," Reikal stated, holding the flaming sword out for me.

"And it's done?" I asked. "Whoever wields it as my foe cannot activate it?"

"Yep!" Reikal squeaked.

"Thank you," I replied, bowing my head.

"Anything for the savior of the universe," he obliged, bowing and taking off.

I returned my attention to everyone training. My eyes were trained on Damian and Luxina as they went hand-to-hand with one another. I wasn't the only one mesmerized by their lyrical movements. They danced around as if they had been sparring with one another since they were young. A blaze of fire followed them as their powers merged together in perfect balance. Their skin had begun to glow brighter and brighter each day as their powers grew stronger. I watched as Damian drew out his long sword and Luxina handled her two short, dueling swords as a pro. I had never been prouder of her than I was at that moment. I had held her back, keeping her safe instead of letting her flourish.

"You had one helluva trainer," I called out as I watched them.

"I sure did," she replied, smiling at Damian.

"Don't let her fool you," Damian said. "I'm really just hanging by a thread here. She is schooling me."

I laughed heartily. He was a good kid. My instincts were right about him. I wish I had the chance to watch him grow up as I did Luxina. Everything would have been so much simpler had Sophie and I just stayed together. Luxina dropped her dueling swords and pulled out some hand knives I had never seen before.

"That's not fair," Damian said. "Those things amplify your powers."

"Is someone afraid of losing?" she giggled.

If I had just said screw the risk, everything would be better. We could have found Damian together. We could have saved him from Alpha together without risking losing the other two.

"I like a challenge," Damian mused, cocking his mouth with a grin.

He looked like Xavier when he smiled like that. *Speaking of,* I thought to myself, *where is Xavier?*

Luxina pressed her fist into her chest and sank to the ground.

"Luxina," I called out, and I was at her side as quickly as I could get there. "What's wrong?" I demanded.

"I... I don't know," she choked out. "Xavier?"

Damian narrowed his eyes.

"Xavier? Is something wrong with him?" I asked.

She just stared into my eyes.

"Not right now," Damian hissed.

"He needs to know the truth," she shot back. She winced in more pain. "It might be that!"

"It might be what?" Tell me what?" I asked, confused.

"Help me carry her inside," Damian said, lifting her up under one of her arms.

I grabbed her other arm, and we led her into Starfire's cottage. We sat her down in the chair while Damian ran to get her some water.

"What do I need to know?" I demanded.

"There was a prophecy," she began.

"What prophecy?" I asked, shaking my head.

"The one about the birth of the three Shining Ones. Except the third Shining One was never supposed to exist. When I was created, the power between you and Mom split," she explained, clenching her jaw in pain. "I split in half. Part of me staying with you, the other part of me staying with mom."

"This doesn't explain anything about where Xavier is," I replied. *None of this makes any sense.*

"Xavier was me, Dad. Xavier was the dark half of my soul," she said, pressing her hand harder into her chest.

It all tumbled over and over in my head. "So, what happened?"

"I absorbed myself back," she replied quietly. "It happened a lot sooner than what we had hoped it would. But we had to save Damian from Alpha. He had hijacked his mind. It was the only way to save him."

"You sacrificed your brother to save him?" I seethed. *I didn't even get to spend time with Xavier to get to know him. This was exactly what Alpha had warned me about. Damian would destroy Xavier and make Luxina believe he was on our side when he had an agenda of his own. Was Alpha telling the truth for once?*

"Xavier sacrificed himself!" she yelled. "I sacrificed myself. You of all people should understand. Look at what you sacrificed for Mom! For a lie!"

"What do you mean a lie?" I demanded, irritated. *I am starting to get impatient with all of this.*

"Ask your mother," she growled. "It was all a lie. The search for the garden, your darkness leaching mom's light. None of it was true. Your mother played a power trip with both of you."

"Let me guess, he told you?" I asked, glaring at Damian. "It's lies, Luxina."

"He didn't tell me. He didn't have to. I know everything he knows. I can still hear the words echoing from the Dark Queen Mab's lips as she told him in the Otherworld," I snapped.

"Instead of arguing over what is the truth and what is not, how about we focus on what is happening to Luxina?" Damian interrupted. "You can hate me later, but right now, she needs help."

"Indeed, she does," Starfire said, walking into the room. "Something went wrong with the absorption."

"Xavier told me it's Alpha doing it," she cried out, grabbing her chest.

"We know the poison from the injections was removed from Luxina by the Watchers. What about Xavier?" Starfire asked.

"No," I replied. "He wasn't dying from them."

"He had already absorbed them," Damian reaffirmed. "After the first set he received, they no longer affected him."

"So, when she absorbed him, the poisons slowly began to re-enter her system," Starfire stated.

"Why didn't they burn away as mine did?" Damian asked.

"Because she was still transitioning and hadn't fully taken Xavier's soul into hers. The transition is complete now," Starfire explained. "That's why she can hear him now."

"Well, what do we do?" I asked. "We can't just let her writhe in pain."

"I'm afraid that's exactly what we have to do. She has to filter it out of her system," Starfire said, setting the manacles we had tied Damian up with on the table.

"What are those for?!" Damian shouted.

"You know what they are for," Starfire retorted. "Now, put them on her. Alpha will work her the same way he did you."

"No," Damian replied, outright refusing. "We are not chaining her up. I can handle her."

"Damian," Luxina croaked out. "Just do it."

"No," Damian barked. "You are nothing like I was. You won't hurt us."

She rose to her feet as if a machine was controlling her. We all took a step back from her. Her eyes were black, just as Sophie's were in all of my hallucinations.

"Everyone, leave the room," Damian demanded.

Starfire began to back away slowly from her when Luxina's head twisted in her direction.

"No, no, over here," Damian said, jumping into her line of sight. "Get her out, Incaendiel."

"I'm not leaving this room," I replied.

"Just do it!" Damian shouted.

I walked calmly over to Starfire and stood in front of her so she could leave the cottage. We inched slowly to the door until it was safe for her to walk out of it. I closed it behind me and peered through the window to see what was happening.

"Hey," Damian spoke softly. "Right here."

She returned her gaze to Damian, craning her neck like a possessed human, and stared at him. I watched him put his hands up as if to calm her down. She moved forward toward him, but he stood his ground as she walked closer. She reached her hand out slowly to touch his face, and he allowed her to do so.

"Your hair is white now," she mused.

She looked around the room. "Where did Incaendiel go?" she asked.

"He escorted Starfire from the room," Damian replied nervously.

"Why? I wasn't going to hurt her," she declared, walking around the room and touching everything.

"Luxina?" Damian asked. "Luxina, can you hear me?"

"Come with me, Damian," she cooed calmly. "Come with me to where it is safe."

"I'm right where I need to be," Damian responded.

"Safe?" she laughed. "Do you think you are safe here? Safe with Luxina? She killed your brother. She took my Xavier from me, and she will take you from me as well."

"Sophie?" Damian questioned.

"Yes," she breathed. "It's me. It's mother."

"You're not my mother," Damian sneered. "You aren't anyone's mother."

"Don't talk to me like that!" Her voice echoed off the walls with a deafening screech.

I opened the door and walked in. She watched me close the door behind me and advance to Damian's side.

"Incaendiel, you look so different now. Brighter, glowing," she whispered. "Why did you leave me?"

"I didn't leave you, Sophie," I replied. "You refused to go with me. Alpha has brainwashed you."

"Alpha is our one true father, and no one should come before him," she stated. "Why can't you see that?" her voice was pleading.

"No, Sophie. That is one thing that isn't true. We are our own gods and far more superior to him," I declared.

Her skin began to sizzle, and steam rose off as flames burst to the surface.

"She was more important to you than anyone else in the end. Even more important than my precious boy." She lifted her hand, and a flaming fireball formed. "I tried to tell you. I tried to make you see. But you refused to believe that your precious little baby was evil."

"She is not evil!" Damian yelled.

Luxina's head jerked to look at him. "She has you under a spell, son. She will kill you in the end, too. You're nothing but a monster to her."

"I know her better than what you think," Damian spat. "And she would never call me that."

She cackled, throwing her head back. "You are so naive," she muttered. "Alpha was right. You're nothing. You're weak. She has turned you into a mindless drone."

She tossed the fireball in her hand at Damian and struck him in the chest, knocking him to the ground.

Another fireball formed in her hand, and she looked at me while I stood there calmly.

"You're not even going to fight back?" she asked, and then motioned from head to toe. "Too afraid of harming your precious cargo?"

"I don't want to hurt you, Sophie," I replied, walking closer to her.

"Liar!" she screamed. "If you had never wanted to hurt me, you wouldn't have made a choice for me all those years ago. You would have come with me to the Summit, or I would have stayed with you at the Glade."

"Mother is to blame for that," I stammered. "She lied to us, Sophie. She lied to lay claim to power in the little game she played with Alpha. And it just goes around and around, and it always claims us in the end. She wanted to control us. She needed to keep us apart so our power wouldn't overpower her own."

"No," she whimpered.

"Yes," I insisted.

I stood before her with pleading eyes. I wrapped my arms around her and squeezed her tightly.

"I love you so much, Sophie," I breathed. "I never stopped loving you. And when I thought you loved another more than me, my love grew for you in leaps and bounds. Come to me, my love. Come and be with our children."

"Do you love him as your own?" she asked, barely a whisper.

"I was the one who saved him," I assured.

While I kept her distracted, Damian slipped the manacles onto her wrists. She screamed in fury and crumpled to the floor, out cold.

"Quick," I urged. "Get her tied to the chair so she can't hurt anyone or herself. There's no telling who she will wake up as."

We picked her up and sat her in the chair. Damian worked quickly, getting her bound in ropes, and then took a seat across from her. His face was a mess of worry.

"It will be ok, Damian," I assured him. "She will come back."

"Will she?" he whimpered. "When Alpha took over me, I know it lasted forever before I was myself again. He injected Xavier with so many different things; there is no telling what all he put into him, and it didn't even phase him. He was like a golem of her."

"I'm telling you," I repeated. "She will be fine."

Luxina started to slowly come to, and when she had shaken the haze, she stared straight ahead at Damian, who sat with his head bent down and resting in his hands, deep in thought. He looked up, and the kid looked as if he were hundreds of years old, with all the worry and exhaustion settling in.

"Come back to me, Luxina," he whispered.

"I'm here for a while, so get used to it," she snarled instead. "I don't understand why you care so much about her."

"You never will," he replied, annoyed.

"Then, explain it to me," she urged snidely. "I have all the time in the world."

"The only person in this room who would understand is him," Damian said, pointing at me. "He loved you. He loved you more than life itself. He died and came back to life for you. I watched it happen."

"So, you would die for her?" she queried.

"Over and over and over, again and again, and again," Damian affirmed. "She saw me for more than a weapon. She saw me for more than just a chess piece. She loved me without condition. You... you chose Alpha over every person that loved you or that you loved. Luxina, she defied Alpha. You know she did. You were punished for it."

She stared at him, and you could see the thoughts running through her head. Unlike my connection with Sophie, I couldn't read her thoughts at all since she was being channeled through Luxina. There was some sort of block up. And then I heard her voice.

He is nothing like me, Sophie thought within. *How can he be so much like Incaendie?*

"Because he knows right from wrong right now," I interrupted aloud. "Alpha is injecting you with nothing more than mind-controlling substances. He has gained your trust in him through lies. You weren't strong enough to fight it. You aren't at fault for that. But you can't blame innocents for that. Luxina, she is innocent in all of this. She is your daughter. That should mean something to you."

"There's nothing but cloudiness in my mind. All I can think of is hating her," she replied through gritted teeth.

"That is Alpha thinking through you," Damian declared. "I know more than ever what that feels like."

"Save me," she implored. "Incaendiel, save me!"

I will leave with you this time. I promise!

I went to leave the room.

"No," Damian demanded, halting me in my steps. "This is a trick."

A deep, guttural laugh emerged from Luxina's throat.

"Oh, you were always the smart one," Luxina remarked in a raspy voice. "Did you know that at any moment I could just simply kill her?"

Damian's eyes widened.

"I love these little games we play too much to do that," she laughed.

Damian stood from his chair, kicking it across the room. I stood in shock, unable to move or do anything.

"You give her back," he demanded, yelling into her face.

"Tsk-tsk. Always with that temper," she replied coolly. "I was so sure she would never save you from me that you were mine in finality. But you loved her so much. You came back for her. Do you think she loves you as much as you love her?"

"If she didn't love me, she would have never tried as hard as she did to save me from you," Damian responded quietly.

"That is what you think or what you know? Could it be that she was using you as her own little weapon?" she asked, a smile spreading widely across her face.

"Don't listen to him, Damian," I ordered. "He will manipulate you and will use anything he thinks will make you weak."

"Luxina is already his weakness and has been since he learned who she was. Always fighting how he felt around her. Wanting her and her precious Xavier to stay together. I hold in my hand the only thing that will destroy him," she rasped. "How do you save her when you couldn't even save yourself? Join me, Damian."

"I will die before I join you," Damian sneered.

"Then have fun rescuing your precious Luxina from the darkness," she taunted.

Her head slumped forward, and once again, she was unconscious.

"Luxina?" Damian asked, running to her.

He grabbed her face in his hands, gently shaking it.

"Luxina?" he demanded with growing worry in his voice. "Luxina!" he pleaded. "Luxina, please. I can't do this alone!" he sobbed into his arm. "Incaendiel, what do we do?"

"All we can do is wait for her to wake up," I breathed. "I have no clue what to do from here. She has to find her way back."

"And what if she can't find her way back?" he implored. "What if she is stuck in the darkness forever?"

I was silent. I didn't know how to answer that.

"You know she is afraid of the dark, right?" he asked, stroking her face. "She was so scared of being engulfed in the dark. She didn't know that she was the brightest light in the world."

"She was my light," I choked out. "She saved me when I was left behind by everyone. If it hadn't been for her, I wouldn't be here right now. She was my saving grace."

"Yeah," he cried. "She was mine too."

I wiped a straggling tear rolling down my cheek. "Let's get her up into a bed and untied from this chair," I spoke softly.

"Should we untie her?" Damian asked.

"By the time she wakes up, all of those things should be burned from her system. I think that's why it happened as quickly as it did, because of how her power was growing. It was Alpha's last trick up his sleeve," I replied.

"Ok," he murmured.

He untied her and scooped her up in his arms, and carried her upstairs, still whispering her name, trying to get her to wake up.

I slumped down in a chair and ran my hand through my hair. "What the hell am I supposed to do now?" I whispered. "What am I supposed to believe?"

"There's nothing you can do," Starfire replied, walking through the door. "She has to wake up on her own, like you said."

"Alpha told me this all was going to happen. That Damian would find a way to destroy Xavier and make Luxina think he was on our side when he is just manipulating people for his own gain," I said quietly.

"Do you really think that boy is lying about everything?" Starfire asked, raising an eyebrow.

"That's what it feels like," I huffed. I ran my hands through my hair in frustration. "I don't know what to believe. I don't know what is real and what is manipulation. He told me other things too, you know? Things that actually make sense."

"Like what?" Starfire asked, taking a seat in a chair across from me.

"Like Lilith being the one that kept us away from Alpha to foster a hatred of him and telling us he abandoned us instead," I replied, wringing my hands together.

Starfire was quiet.

"It's true, isn't it?" I asked.

"Yes," Starfire declared. "Not the whole truth, but it's true."

"He sprinkles so many truths in together with lies, and it's so hard to tell which is truth and which is a lie," I sighed.

"I cannot tell you what to believe and what not to believe. That is your cross to bear," Starfire replied. "I know this whole thing isn't something parents should put their children through."

"So do I just keep Damian at arm's length until I know he's really not the mastermind behind the end of the world?" I asked.

"I can't answer that either," Starfire spoke honestly. "But I can tell you that soon, the truth will be revealed about Damian. And it's a bombshell of a truth as well."

"What do I do about Sophie?" I asked. "I know she said she would come with me this time, but with Alpha behind this all, what if it's just another trap for me to be captured again?"

"What does your heart tell you?" she asked in return.

"It tells me that I need to find her and Lilith," I breathed.

"Then that's what you do," she declared. "I will watch over these two. You go save them while you can."

"Let them know if they ask about me, ok?" I asked.

"I will be sure to," she replied. "You going the old-fashioned way, or are you going to use that new power of yours to get there?"

"What do you mean?" I wondered.

"You used a portal to get here," she responded. "Are you going to fly there or portal there?"

"Portal would be faster," I replied.

"Good," she stated. "Now, hurry back!"

Chapter 9

I WAVED MY hands around like I had done in the Summit and thought of Mother. I pulled up a portal to the Summit. As I looked through the window, I could see Lilith waiting in the throne room. I stepped through the portal, and it vanished behind me.

"Incaendiel?" she whispered, walking over to me. "What are you doing here?"

"I am here to take you to safety," I replied in hushed tones.

"There is nowhere you can take me where I will be safe," she declared.

"Yes, there is," I assured, looking around for Alpha's minions. "But you just have to come with me."

"I was a fool, you know," she remarked. "To think that Alpha still loved me." She began to laugh, and then it turned into a whimpering sob. "He just wants to destroy me."

"I won't let that happen," I replied, extending my hand out to her.

There was a noise in the corridor.

"They're coming," she gasped, wide-eyed. "You have to leave and leave me here. They will kill you."

I smiled devilishly. "They can try, Mother."

"Your eyes," she remarked. "I have never seen them glow like that before..."

The room was filled with Forsaken, who were the loyalists who chose Alpha.

"Well, well. Back so soon?" one of them asked.

"Python? Is that you?" I asked, peering closely at them.

"It is, Brother," he laughed, raising his sword.

"Why are you still loyal to Alpha after everything he has done?" I questioned.

"Why not?" he snickered. "We can be as bad as we want without any repercussions with him. Unlike Mother," he sneered, looking in her direction. "Mother abandoned us when the darkness took over us."

"You were doing hideous things to the humans," she cried, pointing an accusing finger at him.

"Nothing as bad as Alpha will do to you," he replied, stepping toward her.

I stepped in between them.

"You will have to go through me, I'm afraid," I growled. I could see the reflection of myself in his eyes. My eyes blazed like fiery pits.

Python took a step back for a moment, and a look of unease settled on his face.

"When did you get that power?" he asked, taking a step back.

"I have always had it," I glowered. "I just had to find a way to set it free."

Fire blazed to the surface of my skin. For once, I was no longer afraid to use it. I somehow knew I could wield it without it causing damage like before.

"Your eyes," he whispered, visibly shaken.

"Get used to them," I snarled. "I am God now."

They all rushed at me at once, and I lifted my hand. A blinding white light erupted from it, and they were turned to ash mid-step. I heard more footsteps coming down the corridor.

"Are you going to come with me, or are you going to stay to be absorbed by Alpha?" I asked, turning to face Lilith.

"I see Barbelo has been set free within you," Lilith commented.

She reached out her hand, and I grabbed it. I led her through the varying hallways off from the throne room, taking down each person who popped out to try and stop me.

"Lilith!" Alpha bellowed from the throne room.

"Oh no!" she whimpered as I pulled her along.

We made it outside into the Summit, and there were thousands of angels, Watchers, and Forsaken waiting for me who had sided with Alpha. I pulled the flaming sword from my side, and it leapt to life instantly.

"Where did you get that?" Lilith demanded.

"It's a long story," I replied, as I walked unafraid in front of her.

Those in the forefront of the gathered loyalists who had drawn their swords took a step back. They glanced nervously from me to Lilith and then among themselves.

"Let us through," I growled, staring each of them in the eyes.

"It's our orders," Baraquiel refuted quietly.

"Screw your orders," I hissed, blazing hotter. "Do you really want to challenge me right now?"

"No," Baraquiel cried. "But we must obey Alpha."

"Don't hurt them," Lilith begged, grabbing my shoulder. The fire from my skin singed her hands, but she didn't let go.

I looked at each of them who stood against me and huffed, "Fine!"

I raised the sword in the air, and a blinding light leapt from the tip of the blade. Their swords clattered to the ground, and everyone in front of me grabbed their eyes, screaming.

"It burns!" one shouted.

"I can't see anything!" another yelled.

I took the moment to grab Lilith by the hand and towed her toward the garden's gate.

"Where are we going?" she demanded. "That leads to nowhere! The garden is gone!"

"For you all, maybe," I retorted.

We ran through the gate and entered the garden. Lilith looked around, puzzled.

"How did you do that?" she questioned. "No one has been able to access the garden for a while now."

"That's because it doesn't belong to the Summit anymore," I answered. "We gave it back to the fey as a peace treaty, and they joined our side against Alpha."

As we walked through the garden, sprites and brownies who were lounging in the sun immediately ran for cover.

"Incaendiel!" a sweet voice called out. "Oh, and you have company." Queen Titania walked up to us, smiling at me and then frowning at Lilith. "Why are you here? And with her?" she demanded.

"We were escaping the Summit," I explained. "We needed safe passage or else the war would have started without everyone chipping in."

She giggled. "I see," she replied. "And her?" she mused, glaring at Lilith.

"I am taking her to Lightshade to protect her from Alpha," I replied.

"Why on earth would you need to protect her from Alpha?" she questioned, narrowing her eyes suspiciously at Lilith.

"Because he is reabsorbing his power," I answered. "We can't let him absorb her and become too powerful for us."

Queen Titania laughed. "Oh my child," she cooed. "She still hasn't told you everything yet. But okay. I will allow it."

I looked at Lilith questioningly, and she averted her eyes from mine.

"If you follow this path," Queen Titania explained, "it will lead you to the portal to Lightshade."

I bowed to the queen. "Thank you," I replied.

"Anything for my favorite Shining One," she cooed and disappeared.

We walked the path the queen had instructed us to follow in utter silence. I had questions for Lilith now. What did Queen Titania mean by Lilith not telling me everything yet? We came to the portal quicker than I thought we would. I held my hand out in front of me.

"Go ahead," I urged. "You first."

Lilith hesitated, then stepped through the portal. We were just outside the entrance of Lightshade, where Starfire stood waiting.

"Hello, Lilith," she greeted. "I have been waiting to finally meet you. We have much to discuss, you and I."

She opened the force field around Lightshade and motioned for Lilith to walk through.

"Aren't you coming with me?" Lilith asked, glancing over at me.

"No, I have one more person to rescue," I replied.

"Sophie," she responded with a smile.

"Yes, Sophie."

"Good luck with her, son," she remarked. "Alpha has her in his clutches, and she is far gone."

"I know. I have spoken with her. She is ready this time," I declared. "Now, go."

Lilith walked with Starfire into Lightshade, and the force field went back up. I knew where I had to go to retrieve Sophie. She was at Chernobyl. I opened my wings and took off. It wasn't as quick as using portals, but I honestly didn't have the energy to raise one, so my wings were the only other option. Chernobyl came into view, and I soared overhead. It looked empty enough. I didn't see any of the creatures Alpha had chasing Damian and me, so I landed outside the fortress.

"I should have portaled in," I muttered as I walked through the field.

I entered the building through the giant hole I had made in the sidewall and made my way through the maze of halls. Forsaken popped up everywhere, and I had to obliterate them. There was no conversation to be had with them as made apparent in the Summit. Occasionally, I would run into one of those creatures Alpha had made, just roaming the halls like a guard dog. I began to grow impatient and worried about Sophie. My slow meandering turned into a jog and then a sprint. I stopped long enough to open doors and peer inside just to find them empty. My patience was wearing thin along with my confidence.

"Sophie? Sophie?" I called out as I ran the halls of Chernobyl. "Sophie!"

As I rounded a corner, I heard familiar voices talking, but I couldn't decipher which room they came from.

"You came back after all!"

"Hello, Alpha."

That sounds just like Luxina, I thought. I left Luxina with Damian. How did she get here? Rage built within me. Alpha told me he was using us all. This was their plan. Damian brought her back to Alpha after all. I knew I couldn't trust that little shit. I should have left him for the creatures to eat.

"What is she doing here?" another voice shrieked.

Sophie! I started busting doors one by one, listening to them talk.

"Ah, Sophie. My favorite little angel. Your job is done. I no longer need you. You brought me exactly what I needed. Little Luxina here."

No! I busted another door down. Nothing. *Where in the hell are they?*

"You used me to get my daughter?" she asked, confused. "I thought you needed me."

So it wasn't Damian after all. I sighed in relief. I needed to trust that kid more than I do. I was so conflicted about how I felt about the kid. On one hand, I loved him like he was my own, but then Alpha would sneak into my head and make me feel like I couldn't trust him at all.

"No, Sophie. I no longer need you. It's time for you to go back to sleep and Anniel to come forth," Alpha declared.

I hit the ground with a searing pain shooting through my skull. I could hear Sophie scream out in the same pain. My mind was flooded with memories. Memories that I had never recalled or possibly had been altered. Her name had been Anniel since we were created. My mind seemed to merge with hers, and every single memory she had erased became one with my own. She was Alpha's spy the whole time, unless she was human. She was his first experiment before Damian.

I scrambled to my feet and used her eyes as a guide to where she was. I opened the door just as Alpha snapped his fingers to disappear.

"Daddy!" Luxina shouted and then was gone.

"Sophie?" I yelled as I ran over to her. "Sophie."

She sat with her head in her hands, rocking back and forth. "We both know that's not my real name," she sobbed.

I was silent for a moment. "Anniel," I breathed.

She looked up at me with red-rimmed eyes. "Incaendiel, who am I? What am I? What have I done?" she cried.

I knelt down in front of her and wiped the tears from her face. "You did what you were commanded to do. Just like Damian."

"How do I stop it?" she implored.

"Come with me," I said, holding my hand out. "We can fix this."

"How?" she demanded, torn in two by her emotions.

"Starfire," I replied. "She has what we need to fix you. To fix this."

"I don't deserve to be fixed," she whimpered. "I have done terrible things for Alpha."

"He made you do them!" I insisted, wiping the tears once more that streamed down her face.

She looked up at me with pain written in her eyes. "There's more than what little you have seen."

"What do you mean?" I asked.

"I was never locked in that tower. It was a fake memory," she replied. "I was never with Lucifer."

"I don't understand," I declared, shaking my head. "What?"

"I was never with Lucifer. It was a fake memory," she reiterated. "I never had an affair."

"Then," I began. "Wait." I was the one confused now. "That means..."

"Damian isn't his son," she replied.

"Damian isn't his son," I repeated.

"No," she stated. "Damian was born when the portal opened, and Alpha snatched him. Luxina was born when it closed and was split into two. Damian is your son. Damian is our son."

"Damian is... my son?" I stammered, sinking to the floor.

She nodded. "He is why I have stuck by Alpha. Alpha promised to let him go if I did what I was told. Lucifer promised me he would let him go. Lucifer," she sneered and squeezed her eyes shut. "After we raised the portal, I had my will back. I remember. I willingly came back to Alpha to get Damian back. But he would sleep my memories whenever I was Sophie so that I couldn't tell anyone the truth. And now... I led Luxina right to him, being his little puppet. I'm Alpha's real monster."

I pulled her into my arms. "We are all Alpha's puppets. We just didn't know we were. It's been a game from the beginning," I replied. "But this time, we will win."

"Will we?" she asked. "I know things since he left me awake."

"What do you know?" I inquired.

"I know about Adam," she responded.

"Who the hell is Adam?" I asked, but she didn't answer. I asked another question, "And Lucifer has been a spy for Alpha this whole time?"

She nodded. "Since the fall, Lucifer has been the one who has been in Alpha's ear. He is Alpha's right hand, and I was his left," she cried.

"Who all are really loyalists to him and spying on us?" I urged. "Who else is there?"

"And Mother, Lilith, Omega, whatever you want to call her," she snarled. "She can't be trusted at all. She's been playing this game with Alpha the whole time. The fall was a ruse. He wanted to weed out those who weren't loyal to him. There was an imbalance of power, and it wasn't because there was not enough darkness and too much light. It was because we existed. We had to be separated, but Alpha couldn't just kick you out without a reason and make you an adversary. So he and his mother concocted the fall. They knew one of us would stay, and one of us would fall."

"How do you know all of this?" I asked. "The vision you had?"

"No," she breathed. "That was a lie. I never had a vision. Omega and Alpha told me to tell you that." She buried her face in her hands.

I held her in my arms as I carried her outside of Alpha's fortress. I flew her back to Lightshade as she kept her face buried in my chest the entire time. Starfire stood at the entrance as we arrived.

"I had a feeling I should be here," she said, winking. "Anniel?" she asked.

"You... you know my name? Anniel questioned.

"Of course, I do. I know everything. I'm just not allowed to reveal what's not meant for me to reveal," Starfire replied. "Let's get you in Lightshade and make sure Alpha never hurts you again."

Starfire opened her force field and led us back to her cottage. When we were inside and the door closed for privacy, I sat Anniel down in a nice, soft chair. She looked horrible in the light. She indeed had been tortured by Alpha, much like Damian had been. She saw me looking her over and hid her face in shame.

"I must look terrible," she stuttered, trying to fix her hair and wipe her face.

"What did he do to you?" I asked, kneeling in front of her and examining her closely.

She had bruises and lashes all over her.

"I was punished for allowing you and Damian to escape and not telling Alpha about the plans," she replied softly. She looked me in the eyes. "You two needed to escape him before he turned you into me."

"Should we wait until all of the injections he has used on her are out of her system before we give her the potion?" I asked Starfire.

"There's no need," Anniel replied quietly. "I haven't had injections in a long, long time."

"He did his damage a long time ago to her," Starfire added. "What he was doing to the kids was different than what he did to her. He needed to control her. He wanted to turn them into his own personal creations."

I held her bottle of disenchanting potion. "This potion is agonizing," I told Anniel.

"That's a lot coming from you," Anniel replied nervously, eyeing the bottle.

"We can wait until you feel better," I offered.

She shook her head. "We need to do it and get it over with. We need to be at full power to go up against him. That can be any time now."

"She is right, Incaendiel," Lilith said, walking into the room. "It *can* be at any time."

"Mother..." Anniel gasped. "What are you doing here?" she sneered, standing to her feet.

"Incaendiel rescued me from the Summit," Lilith cooed with a smile.

"Why?" Anniel uttered angrily. "She's just as deceitful as Alpha is. She doesn't deserve to be rescued! She chooses to do what she does. She wasn't forced into it."

"I had to," I defended. "Alpha planned to reabsorb her to be more powerful. Even though she has been mendacious to us throughout the years, we cannot allow Alpha to become more powerful. Without her, he doesn't have nearly half of his powers."

Anniel glared at her in contempt. "Can she go somewhere else? I don't want to be around her."

"As you wish, Sophie," Lilith replied, with tight lips.

"You know that's not my name," Anniel barked. "How long did you go along with Alpha in concealing my real identity?"

Lilith pursed her lips. "Fine. As you wish, Anniel."

Anniel flinched.

"So, you did know?" I exclaimed angrily.

"I'm going to my room," Lilith huffed and left the room, heading upstairs to the many rooms.

My temper began to flare, and I had to reel it in. I inhaled deeply and exhaled the frustration out.

"I see some things have changed," Anniel said with a half-smile. "You can control it now."

I smiled. "I can. The kids know how to control it as well."

"Even Damian?" she asked, cocking an eyebrow. "I know his powers were out of control when he was locked up."

"Yes, even Damian," I answered proudly. "Speaking of, where's Damian?" I inquired, looking at Starfire.

"I'm surprised you didn't run into him at Alpha's lair. He raced as fast as he could there to save Luxina," she replied.

Panic rose in my chest. "You stay here with Starfire," I told Anniel. "I will make sure he is safe."

"There is no need, Incaendiel," Starfire assured. "I believe he just returned."

"Are you sure?" I insisted, pacing the floor. "He could be taken just like her. It could be a trap for him as well! We can't lose them both back to Alpha! We just got him free! I can't lose my-" I stopped myself from finishing the sentence.

Starfire smiled. "Well, I see the truth has been revealed in other topics as well," she murmured, glancing at Anniel.

Anniel smiled and nodded. "Alpha didn't take my memories away when he left me this time. I could tell the truth about everything. He didn't sleep me into being Sophie."

"Well, it's about time Incaendiel knew the truth," Starfire cheered.

"Now we just have to figure out how to tell Damian the truth ourselves," I murmured, frowning.

"Tell me the truth about what?" Damian asked, walking through the door.

I froze, mouth agape. I wasn't expecting him to walk in on the tail end of the conversation.

"About your mother," Starfire replied for me.

Damian glanced around me and scowled when his eyes landed on Anniel. "What about her, other than she is here when less than a day has passed since she took over Luxina's mind for Alpha?" he spat.

"That there is a lot more that we didn't know about her until now," I replied sympathetically. "That even I didn't know about."

"Like what?" he sneered. "Oh! Let me guess. She was tortured by Alpha, and that's why she is such a bi—"

"Watch how you talk about your mother," I ordered, pointing my finger at him.

"You are a completely different person when you aren't around her," Damian snapped, glaring at me. "She makes you weak."

"Now, who sounds like Alpha?" I sneered back.

His glare toward me deepened at the comparison. "Do you even know where Luxina is?" he demanded. "Or were you too busy trying to save your precious Sophie?"

"I didn't get there in time," I replied solemnly. "I found them just as Alpha whisked her way. But we will get her back!"

"What a pathetic excuse," Damian retorted, scrunching his face in disapproval at me.

"Hey!" Anniel interjected, grabbing his arm. "Don't say that about him!"

"You shut up," Damian sneered, shaking off her grasp. "You're the last person who should be speaking right now. You don't have the right to talk to me."

"Don't speak to your mother like that," I commanded, walking closer to him.

Damian began to glow as his anger triggered his powers. "Had you been here instead of running off to save the love of your life, you could have stopped Luxina."

"Boys!" Starfire shouted, but it was already too far into an argument to stop.

"Hey!" I defended, my anger starting to boil beneath the surface. "She's *my* daughter. I care. I cared about her when no one else even knew she existed, including you! I spent a long time trying to make sure she was safe, and as I recall, you were the one who initially helped Alpha take her. So, back off!"

Damian backed up a little but still held his ground. "That's what you see me as still, isn't it?" he demanded. "I'm still Alpha's little monster to you."

"Everyone needs to calm down!" Starfire shouted, raising her hands in a slow, steadying motion. "You're going to both erupt with your powers and burn my cottage to the ground."

Damian and I stared one another down. I glanced up and caught my reflection in the mirror hanging on the adjacent wall. My entire body was a fiery glow, and my eyes were two bottomless pits of fire. I looked like a tyrant who was staring down a child. I returned my attention to him, and I could see that even though he was standing up to me, he was absolutely terrified of me. His eyes were intense and determined, but I could see the fear in them, wondering if I would smite him. I exhaled and felt the energy that had been rising during the argument taper off. Once I had returned to my normal temperament, I could see the glow start to taper from his body, and he returned to normal as well.

I sighed. "You were never a monster, Damian," I replied softly, realizing I must look and sound like Alpha was to him for all of these years. "You were manipulated like we all were. Just a piece in his game of chess with Lilith."

"You hardly know what manipulation feels like," Damian scoffed. "You spent a few months with Alpha in your head in that dungeon. I spent my whole life with him in mine."

"It's been my whole life, too!" I refuted. "It's been both our whole lives," I defended, motioning to Anniel.

"What did he do to her besides lock her in a tower?" he sneered.

"He didn't keep her in the tower," I explained. "Those were fake memories. He has been manipulating her to be his spy, his weapon, and his toy just like you ever since the fall. Hell, he even made us forget what her real name is."

"Whatever," he huffed, shaking his head. "Any excuse to make her seem like a damsel. Any excuse to make a pity party for both of you." He waved me off with a flick of his wrist.

"Do you really think I want a pity party?" I hissed. "Do you really think my one goal in life is for everyone to feel sorry for me? Oh, poor Incaendiel. Useless Incaendiel. Lilith's little pet."

"Then what did he possibly keep from you that was earth-shattering or so enraging? What did he take from you? Memories? Time?" he demanded.

I didn't know what else to say. It just came out. "You, son. He kept you."

Damian narrowed his eyes at me. "You're not my father," he refuted.

"Yes," Anniel interjected, standing up. "He is. The whole Lucifer being your father was a fake memory that Lucifer and Alpha planted in my memory jar."

"I don't believe you!" he screamed, near tears, and looking at Starfire.

Starfire nodded her head. "It's true, Damian," she assured.

"Then why didn't you tell me?" he cried, his eyes glowing ice blue from rage.

"It wasn't my—"

"Oh, don't give me the whole it wasn't your place thing or that you weren't allowed to," he huffed. "That's bullshit. You could have told me."

"Damian," I began, placing my hand on his shoulder.

"No!" he yelled, shrugging my hand off his shoulder. "Just because you just found out I am your son doesn't mean you get to start treating me kinder or differently. It doesn't change anything."

"I have never treated you any other way," I replied. "The few times I did was Alpha in my head, trying to make me believe you are just playing us. I saved you from Alpha! I made sure you got away before he could kill you. It wasn't all Asmodeus. It was me, too! It was me and your mother who made sure you escaped that hell he kept you in."

"This is too much too soon," he huffed and walked toward the staircase.

"Where are you going?" I asked.

"To lie down," he rasped as he climbed the steps. "And don't bother me either."

My heart felt like it was going to tear from my chest. Just like I had been rejected by Xavier when I first met him, Damian was now rejecting me. *Had Luxina not been left with me the way she was, would she even love me the way she does now? Alpha abandoned us and rejected those of us who fell. I had been rejected by Anniel every single incarnation she went through over thousands of years, and then I was rejected by my own children. Maybe I wasn't meant to be accepted in love. Maybe I was supposed to be alone. Maybe I wasn't meant to exist with a family or as part of something as grand as what I had been presented with.*

"None of that is true, and you know it," Anniel cooed.

"No privacy," I replied with a half-smile.

"Just give him time," she urged. "He has been through the ringer with Alpha, trying to attain his love as a parent figure, just to be used. Finding out everything he had ever known was a complete lie is a lot for him to take in, just as it was for us."

I sighed. She was right. But I still felt like a failure as a father for not being there to stop Luxina from doing what she did. How could she have walked right into Alpha's trap like that? She was smarter than that.

"I know you two have a lot to catch up on, and this is all terrible timing for the past few days," Starfire interjected. "But we need to get Anniel full power now," she said, holding the last bottle of elixir.

Anniel shifted uneasily in her seat. *What if this is Alpha's plan?* she wondered in her head.

"Could it be part of his plan?" I asked Starfire for her.

"Could what be part of his plan?" Starfire asked back.

"Her taking this and being all powerful, and then him taking back control of her?" I asked.

"Just trust me," Starfire replied with a wink. "Everything will be fine."

I took the elixir from Starfire and walked it over to Anniel. "Are you ready?" I asked.

"No," she replied with a deep exhale. "But I don't have a choice now, do I?"

I shook my head. "It's the only way to overcome Alpha and to defeat him."

"You said it was agonizing," she stated, taking the bottle from my hand.

"It felt like death," I answered.

"I died once," she mused. "So long ago, but it still feels like yesterday."

"Sadly," I began. "It feels worse than that."

Anniel inhaled a heavy breath and exhaled it slowly. She uncorked the bottle and lifted it in the air. "Cheers," she remarked and drank the bottle down.

Her face pinched from the bitter taste that hit her tongue.

"Bleck!" she groaned. "You didn't tell me it tasted bad, too." She smacked her lips and swallowed harder, trying to get the taste out of her mouth, and waited. "So when—" was all she got out before she doubled over, heaving and screaming. She hit the floor and rolled side to side while holding her stomach and retching. Steam began to rise from her skin, and water droplets dripped from her as she began to crawl in between gasps. "I can't control it," she hissed. "Get out of here!" She erupted into flames like I had.

"It's ok," I reassured her. "This is normal."

"No, it's not!" she screamed as her fire burned hotter and brighter.

Something was wrong. The way she was burning was different with her than it had been with me. The flames grew larger and stronger, setting the floor and furniture on fire.

"Why is it doing that?!" I demanded, looking at Starfire.

"She is the last one to take it," she replied. "The final puzzle piece is sliding into place."

"Incaendiel!" Anniel screamed. "I am going to explode!"

I grabbed Starfire's hand and pulled her close to me while wrapping my wings around her. A ball of white light and fiery flames erupted and knocked us to the ground. The windows shattered, and the walls of the room were blown out. Anniel screamed as her fire raged in her.

"Let me go!" Starfire ordered, trying to push me away. "You are about to finish activating as well!"

Starfire scrambled from my clutches from underneath me and clamored out of the cottage.

"What do you mean finish activating?" I shouted.

A searing pain that was worse than the elixir I took tore through my body. I howled in agony as white flames scorched every inch of my skin. The flames began to set the side of the cottage I lay in on fire. Damian came bounding down the stairs as the flames reached the upper floor.

"What the hell is going on!" he demanded before hitting the ground as well in screams.

He began to glow the same white, fiery hue that Anniel was emitting. Tendrils of his flames finished catching the rest of the bottom floor of the cottage on fire, and soon, the whole place was ablaze. The top floor began to cave in.

Are we dying? Damian thought, stricken with panic.

I don't know! I replied.

I heard someone yell my name.

"No!" Starfire yelled, refusing them access to the cottage. "It will kill you! Get back! Reikal! Are you all ready?"

"Yes," the young warlock shouted.

"Now!" she screamed.

Anniel, Damian, and I all released a bellowing yell before we exploded.

Chapter 10

IT WAS AS if I were holding my eyes shut, but I wasn't. I felt like pure light, pure energy. I had no sense of hearing, no sense of sight, but it was like I could see and hear everything. I didn't have to see anything because I just knew that Anniel and Damian were ok. Everything was dark. There was no light. There was no air. There was no movement. It was as if we were at the beginning of everything.

Incaendiel? Anniel asked. *Are we dead?*

No, I replied.

Then what are we? Damian asked.

I think we are pure energy right now, I replied. *Our former selves have transformed.*

Will we have bodies again? Damian asked.

Of course, I replied. *Alpha and Lilith do.*

When will we return to normal? Anniel asked.

Soon, I replied.

It was like all of the secrets of creation were unleashed in that moment. Light burst forth before us. Knowledge of gods past and present flooded my mind. Everything Sophia had told me about raced through my head as a movie. I saw Maveth just materialize as if Death needed to come before life, which made all the sense now. I saw Azrael spring forth, and like a domino effect, everything leapt into existence. I saw all of the forefathers of gods who were nothing but energy, copulating. The universe Sophi was from crept into my view. Tehom, the deep, intermingled with the Wind. I saw Yahweh, my grandfather, pop into existence, and then he brought Barbelo forth into the light. I saw the entire line of gods of varying universes brought forth in the same fashion. Nanna brought forth Ki and An. Ptah created Atum. I watched as Chaos Gaia, Nyx, Erebus, Eros, and Tartarus leapt into being. I had no idea who the gods over some of the universes were, but they burst into being. Varying gods began to form and create their own universes right before my eyes.

I watched as Sophia created Alpha, and it spilled over, creating our universe. I watched as she hid him away from the other gods so they wouldn't know what she did, but Yahweh knew everything. He knew all, just as we were learning. I felt the compassion he had toward Sophia and the sadness he had when she left before even explaining herself for fear of punishment. I watched as Alpha didn't understand who or what he was and existed in lonely ignorance until Lilith formed as Omega from his energy. I watched as the two spirits acknowledged each other, and the love that was shared between them ignited, bringing forth more creation.

And then I watched the old gods grow old and release their energy into the world to create new and more exciting lineages. Each of the Elder gods imparted their energy onto the next successor in line, like the universe had intended. I watched as Alpha sought counsel with the Council of El. I then watched as Alpha destroyed them one by one, taking their energy just as Beelzebub had said he had after they convened the last time.

"Alpha, it is time to bring forth the creations that are to replace you," Inanna cooed.

"No one will replace me. I am still a young god. I have much power still. I am not old and falling apart, such as my greedy grandfather, who still covets his energy and refuses to bless me," Alpha sneered.

"This is the way of the universe," Drac interjected.

"All of the powers ebb and wane and release to the next ones. It's the law of physics in the universe," Enki agreed. "When our time is up, we pass the torch onto our children. And then our children pass on to their children. So on and so forth."

"It's not *time!*" Alpha bellowed, pounding his fist on the table. "I have so much more to accomplish than the meager humans I have created!"

The room was silent as everyone glanced at one another. "Grandson," Yahweh spoke softly as he entered the Council Room. "Relinquishing your power doesn't mean you fade into nothing. It means you pass on the torch. You still retain energy. You are pure energy. You can't get rid of that. When you are an old man like me, and it's time for you to release to the universe, it is but a drop in the bucket in the grand scheme."

"Ah, he shows!" Alpha laughed maniacally. "Tell me, Yahweh," Alpha spat in sarcasm, bowing lowly, "if it is the way of the grand scheme, then why have I not received my blessing?"

"Because among your ranks exists a power far greater than yours, and they are to receive the blessing of the bloodline. Not you. You are to bless them as well. You are supposed to be compassionate, loving, and doting. You are filled with so much rage. Why?"

Alpha smirked. "You already know why. I was hidden away from you all. Cast aside and abandoned by the lot of you. From the moment I was brought into existence, I have been angry for being alone."

"Why make others suffer along with you?" Yahweh questioned.

"Why not?" Alpha asked.

"You bring great shame upon our lineage," Yahweh replied as he shook his head. "Your mother believed herself to be the one who cast shame upon us, but it's you."

"I bring shame?" Alpha asked as his temper flared. "Then how about I show just how shameful I can be?"

A bright light began to emit from Alpha as he grinned sadistically at all who were there.

"Everyone, get out!" Enlil shouted, and the vision faded into the dark.

Daddy?

Luxina! I gasped as I was brought out of the vision of the past unfolding.

What's going on? What's happening? she pleaded.

We are ascending, I explained. *Your mother took her elixir.*

Where are you? Damian demanded.

I don't know. Some place Alpha created, she whimpered. *There's nothing but darkness where I am. I thought I was dying. I exploded.*

We all did that, sweetie, I said. *We will find you. I promise.*

Hurry, Daddy! There are monsters here. I am pretty sure they are the ones from the vision that Alpha plans to use against us. I can hear them, she whimpered.

We will be there as soon as we learn where you are, Anniel replied.

Mom? Luxina asked.

The darkness faded, and light came into view. Luxina's voice was gone. I squinted, shielding my eyes as they adjusted to my surroundings. I looked around, and we were inside a huge crater. I heard Anniel and Damian moving and rolled over to see where they were. Both sat at the bottom of the crater with me, shielding their eyes in the same manner.

"What the hell?" Damian groaned, rolling over.

He stood up, wobbling on his feet, and my eyes finally adjusted to the blinding light of day. It was as if a soft glow emanated from him. I pushed myself from the ground and walked over to inspect him, brushing the dirt from his shoulders and hair. The scars he had on his face had disappeared. I looked over every visible part of his body, and every trace of the torture Alpha had subjected him to was gone.

"What?" he asked, patting himself down. "Am I part fish or something?"

I laughed. "No," I replied. "You're perfect."

I walked over to Anniel and helped her to her feet. I brushed the dirt from her the same way I had brushed it from Damian. She tousled my hair, and dirt flew in various directions. She looked around the crater.

"Did we do this?" she asked.

"I believe we did," I replied.

Her eyes widened. "What about the others?"

"What others?" Damian asked. "We were the only ones in the cottage."

"Everyone who was in Lightshade," I responded as I began to climb to the top of the crater. "With a hole this big, it would have been like a cataclysmic event."

They trailed behind me, sliding on the dirt. We reached the top, and a hand was thrust in my face.

"Grab my hand, Brother," Samael urged.

I grabbed his hand, and he pulled me from the crater. Asmodeus helped Damian, and Azazel helped Anniel.

"You have seen better days, kid," Asmodeus teased, tousling his hair as dirt flew from it.

"Asmodeus!" Damian shouted as he realized who was helping him. "You look so different!" He threw his arms around Asmodeus and squeezed him tightly.

"Don't break me," Asmodeus squeaked. Damian released his grip, and Asmodeus took in a breath. "Well, you're a helluva lot stronger now."

"What happened?" I asked Samael as I looked around everywhere. Nothing else had been destroyed other than Starfire's cottage.

"You exploded, like, literally," Samael replied. "Nothing but vapors and swirling energy was left in your wake."

"We thought you had died," Azazel added, hugging me tightly. She let go of her embrace of me and stepped back.

"We technically did," I replied, looking at Starfire. "We shed our angelic forms and became our true selves."

"Well, you're just as ugly as you were before," Gabriel joked as he walked over to join us. "What did you see?" he inquired.

"Everything," Anniel replied. "Existence. Gods. Creation. We saw it all."

"Sorry about your house," I told Starfire. "Was anyone hurt in the 'big bang '?"

"We were able to contain it to just this spot," she responded with a wink.

"What about Lilith?" Anniel asked, looking around for her face. "Did she get out of there before it exploded?"

"I... I don't know," Starfire replied, confused. "I can't see her anymore. That's strange."

"Does that mean she was killed?" I asked nervously.

Starfire scrunched her face, her brows knitted together in confusion. "No," Starfire replied. "That's why it's strange. I would see it. But I can't see anything past her walking upstairs to her room. I was distracted by you two, so I didn't see anything regarding her."

"Does that mean Alpha has her now?" I asked, worried.

She peered up at me, her eyes as wide as saucers. "I don't know what it means," she replied, worried. "I have never not been able to see anyone."

Anxiety filled me. "Can you still see Alpha?" I urged.

Her eyes flitted back and forth quickly. "No," she replied with fearful eyes. "I can't see anything at all."

"That doesn't make sense," I replied, chewing my nail.

"I don't see anything at all, either," Gabriel interjected. "I am able to see everything at all times. However, there is nothing about Lilith and Alpha any longer."

"What does that mean?" Anniel asked, turning to Gabriel.

"It must mean we are writing the future," Gabriel replied. "And there aren't any clues as to where it is going either."

"What was your last vision?" I prodded. "You said you couldn't share it with me before. Can you now?"

Gabriel shook his head. "I can't show you, but I can tell you," he replied. "Alpha was surrendering, but it was odd. Like, he knew something we didn't know."

"And now it's just darkness?" I queried.

"Correct," Gabriel replied with a quick nod.

A million thoughts raced through my mind from the events of the last year. The kids were having the visions as dreams. Angels don't dream. That still didn't explain Gabriel because he is the angel of visions... but he isn't an angel either.

"Hmmm," I murmured to myself.

"Hmmm, what?" Anniel asked.

"What if the first vision Gabriel had was a planted vision?" I pondered out loud. "The kids had it as a dream. Starfire saw it. Gabriel saw it. Then it changed, and we all assumed it was because things had changed since Xavier had been absorbed by Luxina and altered that part of the vision. But Alpha knew that was going to happen. He told me it was going to happen to manipulate me into believing that Damian was evil."

"That still doesn't explain why no one else can see that part of the future anymore, though," Damian replied.

"It would, since we are no longer tied to Alpha through his powers. He can't plant the visions anymore," I explained, still mulling over my train of thought. "Everything in this universe and world is Alpha's creation. He held power over it because he was the god of it. But now we exist in the universe as well. Everyone pledged their loyalty to us, including Gabriel and Starfire. Even though Gabriel was not an angel, so to speak, of Alpha's, he had pledged his loyalty to hide among the ranks. That loyalty and connection were severed. So, Alpha can no longer show us the future he was planning, or that he was faking planning. That last vision was a clue. Alpha was surrendering because he knew something we don't know. And then nothing. Just empty darkness. We changed the future, and he has seen the new future. However, we don't have the connection to see anything fake or not."

"I told you, Brother," a voice called out in the crowd that began to part to make way for the owner of the voice to move forward. "We need my book."

"Raziel," I said with a smile, throwing my arms around him. "I see you found the place."

"I did," Raziel replied.

"What about your book?" Anniel asked.

"Your grandmother's bible," Raziel answered, leaning in to hug her. "It's good to see you, too, Sister."

"My grandmother's bible?" Anniel asked, confused.

"Yes, during your incarnation as Sophie. You had a bible that your grandmother gave you. It was my book. What you seek to learn is in that book. And only one person other than me can read it."

"Eva," Incaendiel replied. "That's right. The prophet."

"Alpha must know about her," Starfire warned. "It can't be a coincidence."

"Well, let's go get it!" Damian exclaimed, bouncing around with newfound energy.

"Oh, sweetie," Anniel began, "I don't know where it is. That was years ago."

"It has to be with your earth family," Damian replied.

Anniel nodded. "Yes, it is," she declared. "But my mother, Lorraine, went into hiding a long time ago. Alpha had already sent me to try to find the book. I couldn't find it or her. I wondered why he wanted it. I thought it was just a family heirloom."

"Even I have been unable to see Lorraine in visions," Starfire replied. "She is heavily cloaked in magic."

"Who possesses magic that strong?" I asked.

"There is magic in the world that is far older than magic taught by the Watchers," Starfire replied. "A magic so ancient, it goes back to where it all began, surprisingly. Adam and Eve learned a few things before they left the Garden, right, Raziel?"

"She is correct. Adam and Eve taught Cain and Seth what they had learned from the Tree of Knowledge of Good and Evil. When they ate the fruit, they became a conduit of knowledge and power. They were so powerful that Alpha was frightened they would find a way to the Summit and rule it themselves. That's why they were forced out of the garden. The fruit of the Tree of Life would grant them immortality in their new state if they were to eat from it first. Once they tasted mortal food, they became mortal," Raziel explained. "And since Lorraine is from the very bloodline of Adam and Eve, her family knows those secrets of magic as well."

"Then, how are we going to find the book?" Damian demanded, annoyed and frustrated.

"I may have a solution for that," Gadreel chimed in, stepping forward. "There is someone who no one knows is still alive, except for me, who can find her."

"Who?" Anniel asked.

"Cain."

Chapter 11

"STARFIRE, WHAT DO you know about Adam?" Anniel asked as she set off to the side while everyone filled the hole we had left behind during our ascension.

"Ah... Adam," Starfire mused. "I have been wondering when someone would ask about Adam."

"Who is Adam?" Damian asked, scrunching his face, already not liking where this was going.

"Adam is our new brother," Anniel replied, looking over at Damian. "I know who he is, and I know Alpha and Lilith created him, but that is all I know. Do you know more, Starfire?" she repeated, returning her attention to Starfire.

A riotous commotion started amongst the angels in wait, all asking, "Adam? Who is Adam? Why does she know Adam?" and an array of other comments.

"Do you know more?" Damian reiterated once more to Starfire as I shushed everyone.

"I do," Starfire replied. "But let's rebuild my house first, so I have somewhere comfortable to tell you all about Adam."

The warlocks and angels worked side by side, harvesting wood, turning the wood into planks, and rebuilding the outer shell for Starfire's cottage. It took what would have been half a day, if not for the endless sunshine in the valley, for it to be completed. It was a plain, square cabin, just as she had asked, with four walls. Starfire and Reikal walked inside it, and the magic began before our very eyes. Together, they built a mansion inside just it had been before, waving their hands around as hallways and rooms appeared. Starfire motioned for us to walk in and led us to a room that was as large as the throne room in the Summit.

"Everyone, please take a seat," Starfire encouraged.

Anniel and I found a seat in the front row, along with Samael, Azazel, Metatron, and Asmodeus. Instead of sitting with us, Damian chose to sit at the far end with Asmodeus. Jealousy and envy swarmed me, and I leveled my composure to focus on what Starfire had to tell us about Adam. *He will never see me as his father,* I thought to myself. *He doesn't need to. He already has one.*

Give him time, love, Anniel replied. *He needs space, and that's all we can do. Alpha did a number on us all mentally and emotionally. Asmodeus was his only father figure. It is going to take time for him to come to see you as his father. He is angry, and he is a young one.*

I know, I sighed. *It doesn't make it any less unbearable, though. He was mine this whole time, and the thoughts I had about him...*

That's all in the past, Anniel cooed. *You know now, and that's all that matters.* She grabbed my hand, and I could feel my mood change instantly.

That's supposed to be my power, I joked.

We are all full of surprises, she replied with a giggle.

I heard a scoff and glanced over to see Damian glaring at us and then returning his attention to the front of the room to wait for Starfire.

"I know you are all eager to know about Adam," Starfire began as she paced in front of us. "It wasn't too long ago that he sparked into being. Right around the time Alpha started keeping Damian locked up was when Alpha and Lilith created him."

Murmurs began to grow in the room when she raised her hands for everyone to settle down so she could continue. I shifted in my seat, waiting for her to continue, nervously glancing around at everyone.

"Adam wasn't created to be an angel," she continued, watching the faces in the crowd. "Much like Anniel and Incaendiel, he was molded to become a god."

"So he has the same powers as them?" a voice asked in the crowd.

"I thought we had the upper hand?" another shouted.

"What does this mean for everyone who took allegiance with Incaendiel?" one more posed.

"I will get to all of your questions. First, you all must know that Adam was in the original vision. He was there alongside Alpha when he was destroying the world. He is the power force that he had hoped our Shining Ones would be for him. He hadn't planned on them not bowing to his requests and resisting him as much as they have. And they have us at a disadvantage right now."

"How?" someone else asked.

"Alpha has Luxina," Starfire replied gravely, staring intently into the crowd of angels. "She finished her transition just as the other three did here. The problem is we don't know where he has hidden her away until he can activate his plans."

"And what are his plans?" Metatron asked, sitting forward in his seat.

"One of two things. He either wants to get Luxina on his side, and he will use Adam to do that," Starfire replied.

"Use Adam how?" Damian asked, piping up.

I watched his hand grip the armrest of his seat as he repressed his rage bubbling to the surface.

Starfire sighed. "By getting him to do what you would not when it was Xavier and her who everyone thought was the bonded pair."

"For what?!" Damian shouted, jumping to his feet.

"To create his own Shining Ones league, of course," Starfire responded.

I watched as the realization settled onto Damian's face. His eyes glowed in fury.

Calm down, I coaxed. *We don't need to hurt anyone here, and we all don't know how to contain this new power.*

I watched him relax and crack his neck in irritation, sitting back down in his seat. *I don't need you in my head telling me what to do,* he shot back.

"What's the other things?" I asked, funneling the direction of information.

"Somehow stripping half of the power from Luxina the way she was split in two with Xavier before," Starfire replied. "He could then either use Adam as is or put him inside Luxina, darkening her. Instead of Xavier being her other half, her true half, it would be evil in his place."

The room fell silent apart from the quiet murmuring around. I breathed heavily, trying to calm and stop myself from leaving the room and trying to find her myself before Alpha could do either of those things to her.

"If Adam succeeds, all is lost. The vision we had prior to everything going dark was of Luxina and Adam in power and Alpha surrendering," Starfire spoke again. "While Adam doesn't necessarily have the same powers as the four of them have, he possesses his own. And Alpha will give him his power to make sure he succeeds in the end."

"Is Adam blind to Alpha's manipulation?" I grunted, tapping my fingertips on my chair arm.

"I have no idea," Starfire replied, looking directly at me. "I saw very little of Adam. Alpha only allowed everyone who could see what he wanted them to see."

"So there's a chance he could be swayed to our side?" Anniel asked, leaning forward.

"It's a very slim chance," Starfire replied. "It was a one-in-a-million variable in the visions. Nearly all timelines had him at Alpha's side."

"But that's a chance!" I exclaimed, pounding the arm of my chair. "I mean, he is our brother."

"He doesn't see you as brothers and sisters. He sees you as disloyalists against Alpha. Alpha made sure to dote extra hard on him. He knew he could never win over Damian, not even with the injections, because his will was strong. He never showered him with affection and treated him as a weapon, which pushed Damian away. He regretted that decision, so when Lilith and he made Adam, he did the opposite with Adam," Starfire explained.

"And he is aging just like Damian and Luxina?" Anniel asked as her interest piqued.

"Faster," Starfire responded. "He is already around the same age as they are, and it has only been a year."

"Why so fast?" I inquired. "For all of them? Why did they age so exponentially?"

"They needed to be old enough to handle the tasks and protect themselves. The universe has a way of protecting its creation," Starfire answered.

"So what exactly is he?" Anniel prodded, trying to understand everything. "How was he made? We know the fey courts had nothing to do with it, and all of the elder gods have vanished. How did they make him into one of us?"

"Me," Damian replied before Starfire had a chance, head hanging low and staring at the ground. "He wasn't just injecting me with his concoctions, but he was also studying my blood after. He used my blood to mold and shape him. Right?" he asked, looking up at Starfire.

Starfire lowered her eyes. "Yes," she declared.

"So it's my fault all of this is happening?" Damian sputtered, looking sheepishly back down at the ground.

"Of course, it's not your fault!" I shouted, and his eyes met mine. "You were kidnapped as a baby, and you fought tooth and nail to stop him from doing the things he did to you."

Damian lowered his eyes, and I couldn't sense what he was thinking.

"So we capture him," Samael interjected. "Show him things from our perspective."

"Yeah, there has to be a way to get that one in a million chance of him not siding with Alpha," Azazel offered, agreeing with Samael.

"But he's not an angel," Michael replied as if withholding information Starfire hadn't told us. "We have no way to contain him. We don't even know if he can freely use his powers. He may not be bound like Anniel and Incaendiel were."

"Have you seen what he can do?" I asked, turning in my seat to look at Michael.

Michael was silent.

"Well, have you?" Anniel prodded further, turning around as well.

"Alpha had another gladiator ring," Michael began, not making eye contact with either of us. "It was set up just like the one Damian fought in, except only certain people were privy to watching Adam fight."

"And?" Metatron asked, turning in his seat to watch him.

"I have only seen Damian fight as an angel, not as a god," Michael remarked, looking off to the side.

"What does that mean?" Damian asked, snidely facing Michael, as a look of contempt plastered his face.

"Adam didn't fight against monsters like you did," Michael continued, eyes to the floor. "He fought against clones of you."

The room fell silent.

"He made clones of me?!" Damian demanded, shooting up attentive in his seat.

"Yes," Michael replied. "And one by one, he fought them until he could beat you."

"How many clones were there?!" Damian asked angrily, pounding his fist onto the arm of his chair.

"Millions," Michael uttered quietly. "Adam has been training since his creation to take you out of the picture. It's his one task. He eliminates you, and Alpha wins."

"Why?" I implored Michael. "Why him and not Anniel or me?"

"It's all part of his game," Lilith answered for him, quietly moving to the front of the room.

"Oh, the prodigal Mother returns," Anniel curtly stated, rolling her eyes in frustration.

"Where were you?" I demanded, narrowing my eyes at her.

"With Alpha," Lilith replied, unblinkingly.

"Of course you were," Anniel huffed and then let out a nervous laugh. "You were divorced and reconciled by having a baby. Don't you know that's how all relationships end? By fixing it with a baby?"

"I admit, I have done things that are... awful," Lilith began, staring at us both. "But he plans to kill me in the end, so I suppose the honeymoon stage is over," she spat as snarky as she could.

"Why are you here, Mother?" Samael asked flatly, unwavering in his poker face of distrust.

"To ask for forgiveness," Lilith cried quietly, tears flowing freely.

"No, you're just here trying to seek asylum is what you are doing," Azazel replied heatedly. "You're not sorry for anything you have done. You're not sorry for anything at all."

"I am here to offer you the upper hand against Alpha," Lilith stated, ignoring Azazel. "Adam isn't going to come to you willingly, but he's going to fight his way in. I can trick him easier than any of you."

"Why?" I asked, interrupting her.

"Why what?" Lilith asked in reply.

"Why do you want to trick him here?" I stood up from my seat and walked over to where she stood. I could see the fear in her eyes as I approached her.

"Because he is my son, like all of you," she replied nervously. Her eyes watched me as I drew closer. "I want to save him from Alpha just as I wanted to save Damian from his clutches."

Her eyes couldn't rest on mine, and she nervously looked around the room.

"Are you afraid of me?" I asked, leaning in to her face.

"Yes," she whispered. "You have always frightened the hell out of me."

"Good," I replied in satisfaction. "Because if you double-cross us one more time, I won't have mercy on you anymore. I will kill you myself." She nodded, acknowledging me, and I took a step back from her. "How do we keep him here without him using his powers?"

"He hasn't been activated yet," she replied. "He is like the children were before they took the elixir."

"I didn't think he needed to be activated?" I prodded. "I thought since he had Damian's blood, he was full-powered."

"Damian wasn't activated when Alpha had him," Lilith replied, cautiously walking around me. "He took the elixir after escaping."

"Can he use Luxina's blood?" Damian interrupted, leaning in closely to listen.

"No," Lilith began. "He has already been brought to life with your blood. It doesn't work the way you're thinking. He was infused with your blood during his shaping."

"I don't understand," I replied, turning around to face her. "If he isn't activated, how do you activate him?"

"One of two ways," she started explaining. "Either with my power or with one of your powers."

"So when he takes out Damian, he immediately absorbs his powers?" I asked furiously.

"Yes, and if Alpha can't get his hands on Damian, then it's me," she replied. "He's not harvesting power for himself, but for him and Adam. Once he defeats what's left of you, he will be the most powerful being in all of the universes. And then he will hand all of that power over to Adam, who will be just as evil as Alpha is."

"He can try to take me out, but I was trained with the best of the best," Damian interrupted, his pride getting the best of him. "Not only the training I acquired myself, but also the training Xavier received, is part of me. I was trained by demons and angels. And now, I am a god."

"Even gods can be slain, Damian," Lilith warned. "You are being too cavalier about this. Or do you not remember Tiamat from your travels to Atlantis?"

"But she is not dead," Damian replied. "She is waiting to return to her home after Alpha's destruction."

"We are not risking your death just for you to have an ego trip with Adam," I ordered, putting an end to the bickering between Lilith and him.

"You don't tell me what to do!" Damian seethed, standing from his seat and walking up to me.

"Damian, enough!" Asmodeus barked, jumping up from his seat as well.

Damian continued his glare at me and turned on his heel to leave the room.

"Where are you going?" I demanded.

"Somewhere you won't be!" he shot back.

Anger tore through me, and I whipped around to face Lilith. "That is your fault there!" I yelled, pointing to the shutting door as Damian left the room. "You and Alpha with your damn mind games and parlor tricks."

Lilith stifled a cry as I stepped closer toward her. "I know, and I am sorry," she pleaded.

"Incaendiel," Anniel spoke up, placing her hand on my shoulder. "Calm down."

"Why should I take pity on her? We aren't going to show Alpha any mercy. Why should we show her mercy? She is just as much to blame as Alpha. She has been right by his side, playing games with him. Separating us and then putting us through the stupid search for the garden that meant absolutely nothing. The garden wasn't gone. It. Was. Just. A. Game. They stood by and watched as we struggled with our identities. Mother being the jealous one, not allowing us around daddy. They watched as Anniel was born, raised, and killed as a human over and over. It was one sick, twisted game, and we were the chess pieces. Warped our minds so we wouldn't remember certain things. Placed fake memories in us. And for what? Because they were afraid we would steal their power? Afraid we would rebel? Just mad at each other because of a marital spat?" I was fuming and could feel the heat rising to my skin, and I had to snuff out quickly.

"What are you talking about?" Asmodeus interrupted, and the rest of the room mumbled quietly.

"Damian is my son," I croaked, fighting back the rising lump in the back of my throat. "And Alpha kidnapped him when we initially raised the portal to the Summit. The portal in which we were told the only way we could raise was to finally have sex and combine our powers. But it was their sick, perverted game. They wanted us to have offspring because they knew our power, combined for the first time, would result in the kids. Alpha having one of them, and you having the other. Am I right so far, *Mother?*" I thundered angrily.

"Yes," she whispered in reply, taking a step back from me as I advanced toward her.

"And then you could have your own little family after Alpha planted the false memory of Damian being Anniel's and Lucifer's kid. So Anniel would be off with Lucifer, looking for Damian, leaving Xavier behind with you, and Damian with Alpha. But no one knew about Luxina. Not until Alpha started spying in on Damian's dreams, right?" I demanded

"Yes," she cried, once again taking another step back.

"And you could raise them and train them to do your bidding. So you would have their power to defeat Anniel and me when the time came down to it, right?" I raged once more.

A tear slid down her cheek. "Yes," she breathed. "You were getting too strong for me to control, and Alpha wanted to destroy you."

"But Luxina ruined it all, am I right?" I roared, feeling heavier and heavier with her confessions.

"Yes," she replied, wiping away the tears and recomposing herself. "She wasn't supposed to exist, or at least that's what we thought. We thought twins were born like Lucifer and Michael. We had no idea it was Luxina split in half."

"Who all knew the truth?" I ordered.

She glanced at Michael in his seat. "Us two, Lucifer, and Michael," she mumbled.

I glared at Michael in his seat, and he averted his eyes in shame. "You couldn't tell me?" I demanded. He remained silent. I returned my attention back to Lilith, fuming. "Why should I show you mercy?" I cried. "After everything you have put my family and me through, why would I show you compassion and forgiveness?"

"Because it's who you are at the core," Lilith answered softly. "You are not Alpha, and you are not me. You are good."

"Brother," Beelzebub interrupted, standing nervously to his feet. "You were angry when you learned Luxina showed no mercy or compassion when she killed Gwynevere."

"Gwynevere was like us. Just another chess piece with these two." I pointed my finger at Lilith's face. "She's not a pawn. She's a queen to her king," I growled, looking around at all the faces in the room. "But I will put it to a vote. All those in favor of entertaining Lilith raise your hand."

Hands shot up in the air everywhere.

"All opposed?" I asked.

Very few hands were raised.

"Well, you have your mother," I muttered, turning on my heels to leave the room.

"Where are you going?" Metatron asked, jumping to his feet.

"To cool off," I snapped back as I walked to the entrance of the room.

"But we aren't done!" Samael protested, also rising to his feet. "What about Adam?"

"Figure it out and then tell me the game plan," I muttered, dismissing them with a hand.

I continued walking to the entrance.

"We still need you, Brother," Samael declared. "You are still who we choose to side with."

"You all have a funny way of showing it," I snapped, walking out the door.

"Wait, Incaendiel!" Lilith shouted.

As I looked over my shoulder, I collided with another person. I abruptly stopped to look at who I had run into. "Xavier?" I asked, my blood running cold.

"Hello, Brother," he replied. "You don't know me. My name is Adam."

Chapter 12

"HOW THE HELL did he get into Lightshade?" I asked Lilith, fuming as I paced the room.

We stood just outside the room of angels who were now arguing whether I had a point or not upon my abrupt departure. I looked over at Adam, who stared around the room as if mesmerized by the whole thing.

"He has learned how to portal just as you all have," Lilith replied, glancing in his direction. "And he has Damian's blood swimming around in his veins, so he is allowed through the force field."

"Why didn't you—" I began to yell and then quieted my voice. "Why didn't you mention before that he looks just like Xavier? And why does he look just like him?"

"I was getting to that before you exited via stage left!" Lilith hissed. "What better way to sway Luxina than to have him look like Xavier?"

"You need to get him out of here *now!*" I shouted in hushed tones.

"Well, now that he is here, why not make the best of it?" Lilith asked, a slight flicker of hope on her face.

"Why? So, Damian can try to kill him?" I replied in a raised whisper, looking around to see if anyone was coming our way.

"Oh, he won't try to kill him," Lilith stated quietly with a wave of her hand, brushing the thought off.

"We just told him Adam was out for his blood, and you don't think he won't act first? That Adam's arena was fighting clones of him over and over," I refuted, flabbergasted. "Do you not remember whose child he really is?" I reminded her, pointing to myself and glancing over at Adam, who was busy staring at the paintings hanging on the wall.

"It will be fine!" Lilith insisted with set eyes.

"What will be fine?" Damian asked, coming through the front door of the cottage and interrupting our private conversation.

"We would like you to—" Lilith began, and I quickly cut her off.

"Train more of the people arriving. They have been coming in by handfuls and are just waiting around for instruction. You have the best militant training track record," I offered with a smile.

Damian glanced from Lilith to me. "You're acting weird," Damian replied, narrowing his eyes and scrunching his face. "But fine. Where are they?"

"Outside with Praeziel," I said, and pushed him off in the direction of the door. "Run along."

He eyed me and shook his head. Once he was out of earshot, my attention returned to Lilith. "I mean it, Lilith. He needs to go."

"But I just got here, Brother," Adam interjected, standing right next to me. "And why do you call Mother by her name, Lilith?"

I scowled at Lilith. "He's like a toddler."

"Of course, he is like a toddler! A toddler with a unique ability to cut your head off, but a toddler nonetheless, mental acuity-wise," she rasped.

"What if this is all part of Alpha's plans?" I queried. "Hmm? Infiltrate the fortress, then help him portal in. Did you think of that?"

"Father doesn't know I am here," Adam interjected while examining a shelf of old talismans. "He doesn't want me around you all because he believes I will become disloyal to him."

"But you're not disloyal to him?" I prodded.

He shook his head. "No, I am very loyal to my father. But that doesn't mean I cannot also be close with my family. It isn't fair that it is a demand of me to choose sides when I just wish to know you all and love you all," he responded, putting an old rabbit's foot down and glancing up at me.

"And if you see Damian?" I pressed.

"I haven't been given his kill order," he replied nonchalantly. "Until then, he won't be harmed."

I glared at Lilith. "That's safe?" I demanded.

I started to walk off when she grabbed me by the hand. "Incaendiel, please!" she begged. "Please let him stay."

"Put. It. To. A. Vote," I hissed heatedly, annunciating each word.

"Put what to a vote?" Samael asked, walking from the conference room.

I pointed at Adam. Samael stared wide-eyed and confused. "He looks just like—"

"Yup," I interjected.

"Anniel will not handle that well at all," Samael replied. "You, Mother, of all people, should know that. And how could you be okay with it? Xavier was your precious boy."

And then it clicked. "Another lie to be caught in," I sneered. "It wasn't only Alpha's idea to make him look like Xavier but yours as well."

She gasped. "You caught me," she responded sarcastically with a glare to match.

"If it is too displeasing how I look, I can cast a glamour," Adam offered as he stared at the antique light fixtures on the wall.

"Oh, see! One problem solved already!" Lilith shrieked in delight.

"If you all are done arguing over whether I can stay or leave, I have news about Luxina for you," Adam interjected.

"News? What news?" I asked, shifting my focus to the murderous little devil spawn.

"I know where she is, but it won't be an easy task getting to her," he replied.

"Why would you let us know where she is?" I demanded, suspicious of his motivation.

"Because she is in danger there," he answered.

"And where is there?" I pushed, annoyed.

"Inside Purgatory, of course," he stated.

"And why do you care?"

"Well, I can't let my twin flame come to any danger," he responded, staring me in the eyes.

"Twin flame?" Samael asked.

"Yes, I can feel her," he replied with a sign. "She is lonely and scared."

"So not only does his blood make him like Damian, but Damian's twin-flame bond courses through his veins? What the actual—" I stopped myself from finishing the sentence and pinched the bridge of my nose in frustration.

I motioned for Samael to follow me to a corner so we could speak quietly without Lilith interrupting me every five minutes.

"What do we do?" I whispered, watching them closely. "We can't keep him here without Alpha looking for him or, worse, Damian finding out who he is. Not to mention, what if Alpha finds out he is here and executes the kill order on Damian?"

"We also can't let him go back to Alpha," Samael refuted.

"I know," I said, agreeing. "So what the hell do we do?"

"Whatever we do, we need to do it fast because the angels just convened, and Anniel will see him. Not to mention, Damian is heading back over this way," Samael replied, looking over my shoulder with his eyes in Damian's direction.

Damian walked with curiosity to the new person standing with Lilith. I rushed over to Adam and told him to glamour. "Your name is Sage, and you are a Nephilim. Got it?" I asked through gritted teeth.

"Yes, sir," he replied with a salute.

"Cute," I groaned.

Samael pulled me aside. "We can't not tell Damian who he is!" he hissed. "That will leave him defenseless."

"He won't ever get close enough to him to even ruffle his hair," I retorted, staring at Adam as Damian walked up. "I will kill him before he ever gets a chance."

"You must be Damian," Adam said, holding his hand out to him. "My name is Sage. I am one of the late-arriving Nephilim ready for training."

Damian took his hand and shook it. "Nice to meet you, Sage. Yes, I am Damian. I will be your trainer."

"Actually," I interjected, "One of us will train him," I stated, pulling Adam away from Damian.

"Why?" Damian pressed.

"Lighten your load," I replied. "We decided we were all going to start training the Nephilim and teaching them their untapped angelic powers."

"I didn't think they had any," Damian declared, narrowing his eyes.

"We didn't either, but apparently they do," I replied, lying. "I mean, at least we believe they should. They are half angel."

Damian shrugged. "Whatever." He began to walk away when Adam piped up.

"It was nice meeting you, Damian. I look forward to getting acquainted with you. I have heard a lot of things about you."

"I'm sure they're all half true," Damian replied, cracking a smile and walking out the front door.

"He is not at all like Alpha described him," Adam said, returning his attention to more relics in Starfire's house.

"And what does Alpha tell you about him?" I asked, watching his face.

"He said he is a monster who wishes to hurt him," he replied.

"Well, that's partly true," I muttered under my breath.

"So, are you going to be the one who pretends to train me?" he inquired.

"Why the hell not?" I replied with a sigh, throwing my hands up.

"Let's go then," he gushed with a grin.

He followed me out the door and to the sparring arena. He pulled out dueling blades as I pulled out my long sword. "Let's see what you got, kid."

Before I knew it, he was on me, and I was parrying his blocks. It was an assault after assault of weapon blows that I could hardly keep up with. I was putting in actual effort to avoid being caught by one of his swords. His movements were methodical and precise.

"Who the hell trained you?" I asked, trying to keep up with his blows.

"Damian," he replied. "You heard what Michael told you about my arena. I learned by watching him and fighting him until I won. It's in my blood to be exactly like him, is it not?"

"Nice moves," Damian remarked as if on cue, walking up to the two of us just outside our designated circle.

Without a moment's hesitation, Adam let loose one of his dueling blades, throwing it as hard as he could at Damian. I tried to jump and grab it, but I couldn't move quickly enough. I watched with a thud to the ground as the sword careened toward Damian's head as if time had slowed down. Damian stepped aside and grabbed the sword by the blade, and the freeze on time disappeared.

"What the hell was that for?" Damian demanded, throwing the knife to the ground. "We don't take kill shots in training here!"

Adam stood there with wide eyes as Damian stalked off. "He moved so fast it was like he slowed down time," he murmured and looked at me. "How did he do that?" he asked.

"Because he is not one of the clones Alpha made of him for you to battle," I replied. "He thinks on his feet, something that can't be replicated. He is always on guard. And he is a god."

"Did Father love him?" he questioned.

"No. He used him in a game with Lilith as a weapon of mass destruction. But when he couldn't get him to bend to his will, he tossed him aside and made you," I answered.

"Why wouldn't he listen to Father obediently?" he pestered.

"He did, for the most part. But it didn't matter to Alpha. He had him tortured anyway," I explained as we both watched Damian training another Nephilim.

"Tortured?" he asked. "How?"

"Whips, chains, monsters. You name it, and it was his torture," I responded.

"Father shows me love, but he also looks at me with disappointment because I am not Damian," Adam stated sadly.

"That's just how he is," I replied, fostering empathy for him a bit more than I should. "Alpha doesn't care about anyone except Alpha."

"I need to go home," he stated, walking away. "I have more training to do."

"Training for what?" I inquired.

"Meeting you and Damian doesn't change my orders. When Alpha gives the order, I am to take him out or die trying," he replied.

"It doesn't have to be that way, though," I said, placing my hand on his shoulder. "You don't have to submit to his will."

"The perfect soldier always submits," he snapped, grabbing my hand and throwing it off his shoulder. "You will not change my mind."

"Will you be back again to visit?" I asked.

"Maybe," he replied with a shrug. "I did enjoy getting to know you, Incaendiel."

He raised his hands, and a portal appeared. He disappeared through the opening, and it closed behind him.

"You let him get away?!" Samael hissed as he ran up beside me.

"Yes. Yes, I did," I declared. "We have a big problem, and we need to be prepared for when he returns."

"How the hell did that Nephilim raise a portal?" Damian demanded, running up beside me.

I looked over at Samael, and he put his hands up in the air. "I told you to tell him."

"Tell me what?" Damian urged, glaring at me.

I sighed. "That was Adam."

"And you let him get away?!" Damian hissed. "He tried to kill me!"

"He didn't try to kill you," I explained. "He was testing you, and he failed."

"You still let him walk out of here without trying to stop him," he replied angrily.

"We *just* learned about him!" I exclaimed. "We don't even know *how* to stop him, and I wasn't going to set a killing machine loose in the valley."

"How did he even get in here?" Damian snapped. "I thought this place was protected."

I stared at him gravely, and the realization washed over his face.

"He got in because he has my blood. So once again, we aren't safe because of me," he insisted, answering his own question.

"It's not your fault," I spoke softly, laying my hand on his shoulder. "None of this will ever be your fault."

He shrugged my hand off just as Adam had. "What if he comes back next time with Alpha?!"

"He won't," I refuted.

"How do you know?" Damian demanded.

"I just do. I can't explain it," I said.

"Well, now that I know what he looks like, I can dispatch him as soon as he steps into Lightshade again," Damian remarked.

"About that," I began. "That's not how he really looks."

"What does he look like?" Damian asked. "A three-headed monster?"

"Alpha and Lilith played a cruel joke on us all," I replied.

"How?" he pestered.

"He looks like Xavier," I responded.

Fury erupted across Damian's face. "Why would they do that?"

"Well, we have the one reason," I began and trailed off.

"What's the other?"

"Now that is the million-dollar question," I started. "It's too easy for it to be because they want to sway Luxina to believing she has a different twin flame. With Alpha, there's always a sinister side to every coin flipped."

"Where is Lilith?" Damian demanded. "I want to speak with her."

"Last I saw her, she was inside Starfire's cottage," Samael chimed in.

Damian stalked off to the cottage, and we followed hot on his trail. He was met by Starfire on the porch.

"Where is Lilith?" he demanded once again.

"She left not too long ago when Incaendiel was sparring with Adam," Starfire replied.

"Where did she go?" he pressed.

Starfire shrugged her shoulders. "I can no longer see her or Alpha."

"Dammit!" he seethed. He glanced over at Samael. "This is your fault. You and your gang of angels, who were all too thrilled to see Mommy Dearest appear. This was a set-up. She brought him here to see if he was ready yet to kill me, and had I not been quick on my feet, he would have succeeded. Lilith isn't to be trusted, just like Alpha. She is a monster, too, and the sooner you and your brothers and sisters get that through your head, the better off we all will be. She will use your love for her against you and manipulate you with love bombs while simultaneously planning your demise. Get over your mommy and daddy issues and get your shit straight or we all die!"

Damian stalked off, leaving Samael and me standing on the porch.

"He is right, and you both know it," Starfire interjected. "Terror has followed Alpha while devastation has followed Lilith. You know, they form a toxic bond with one another and have played games with one another for millennia. Neither of them is to be trusted, nor is Adam to be trusted. I know you want to be a leader who listens to his followers, Incaendiel, but in some cases, you will have to pull rank and follow your gut. And your gut was right about those two. I can feel it. I just can't see it."

"So now what?" I inquired. "How do we prevent either of them from being able to return to Lightshade to harm anyone?"

"Reikal went into stealth mode and collected hair from both of them," she replied. "I will add it to the barrier to keep them out, even from portaling in."

"You good with that?" I asked Samael.

He scowled. "Do I have a choice?" he snapped and stalked off.

"I just have a knack for pissing people off lately," I sighed.

"He will come around," Starfire replied with a wink.

"Have you seen Anniel?" I asked. "I haven't gotten a chance to speak with her alone at all, it seems."

"She is upstairs in your room," she replied with a smile.

"Thanks," I said as I walked past her and inside.

I made my way up the stairs to the room I had had before the fire. I opened the door and found her asleep on the bed. I walked over to the other side of the bed and climbed in beside her, pulling her in close to me. I breathed her scent in deeply and felt more at home and at peace than I had felt in a very long time. She began to stir and rolled over in my arms, placing her head on my shoulder and her hand on my chest.

"Mmmm," she purred. "There's my firefly." Her hand roamed from my chest to my face, and she brushed it along my cheek. "I was wondering when you would come join me."

"I had some things I had to take care of first," I replied, brushing her hair from her face and cupping her chin in it. "And then I thought of you."

She smiled. I hadn't even taken the time to see that her hair had changed colors as I sat there drinking her in. It was the same color as Damian's and Luxina's hair. White tendrils fell around her face, which had highlights of red hues. Her eyes were a beautiful shade of gray with flecks of amber. It felt like millennia had passed since we both had a moment alone together like this. I leaned in and planted my lips on hers as her hands roamed through my hair. I rolled over on top of her as her hands explored my body through my clothes. I kissed her mouth, her chin, her cheek, her neck. My mouth explored every part of her exposed. She pulled my shirt from my back and over my head, running her fingers across every muscle she could see. Her eyes glowed as she looked at me. She was so beautiful.

"You're just as beautiful," she replied as if she had read my mind.

And with that, I gave in and fell into her arms, and after, I slept for the first time in what seemed like an eternity.

Chapter 13

I STIRRED AWAKE and reached over to the side of the bed Anniel had lain on, but found it empty. I had no idea how long I had been out. I rubbed my eyes and stretched my arms before I stood from the bed that beckoned me to stay and sleep my troubles away. I left the room and made my way down the stairs to see where everyone was. A slight panic overcame me when I couldn't find anyone inside, so I walked outside to see what everyone was doing. Once again, there wasn't anyone to be found.

"Where the hell is everyone?" I asked out loud.

"They're all gone, Incaendiel," Starfire replied, popping out from inside her cottage.

"Where did they go?" I inquired, panic-stricken.

"To join Alpha, of course," she answered with a hearty laugh. "Did you really think they were going to stick around when you kicked their mother out? Did you really think Samael would take being bossed around by you? Are you that daft, boy?"

"You're not Starfire," I replied heatedly.

"No, son. I am not," Starfire agreed with a sinister laugh and eyes blacked over.

"Where are Anniel and Damian?" I demanded.

"Right where they belong. Anniel is at my side, and Damian, well, Adam knew what needed to be done with that disobedient brat," he sneered.

"No," I shouted, my flames leaping forward. "No, he isn't dead. You can't trick me this time."

"This isn't a trick or a mind game," Alpha replied. "If I can't have the boy, then no one can! Enjoy your quick death!" he shouted as he blew dust in my face.

I went to tackle Starfire to the ground, but she vanished as well, and I was left all alone in Lightshade. I sank to the ground, breathing in sharp heaves as the emotions welled in my chest. The dust I had inhaled began to choke me, and I couldn't breathe. I crawled across the ground, my flames lighting Lightshade up like a bonfire as I lay in the drifting embers.

"Incaendiel!"

Who is that? I wondered as I tried to suck in breath after breath but was met with only a lungful of ashes.

"Incaendiel, wake up!" the voice insisted.

But I am awake, I insisted, accepting my fate of dying alone.

"Wake up now!"

I sat up from my sleep, drenched in sweat. Fire smoldered around me as I watched Damian put the flames out with his ice. I looked around at the charred and burned room and heaved out in sharp breaths. Damian watched me, and I could see the look of worry in his eyes. I felt my face, and it was wet from stray tears I had let loose while sleeping. I quickly swiped them away.

"I'm fine," I choked out, running my hand through my sweat-drenched hair.

"You sure?" he urged.

"Yes," I replied, sitting up in bed. "It was just a bad dream, is all." Panic tore through me. "Anniel?" I asked, reaching for the empty side of the bed.

"She is fine. She is downstairs. No one was aware of what was happening. I came to wake you up and found you burning in your sleep," he replied quietly, looking around the room. "I've never seen someone use their powers like this in their sleep before."

"Everything is okay," I reaffirmed, shaking off the nightmare.

"Don't let him in your head," Damian warned. "He is a master at making you think you aren't worth anything."

Was it that obvious? Could he see what I was actively dreaming?

"No, I didn't need to see," he replied, reading my mind. "But if you used your powers in your sleep, then it was more than just a bad dream."

Flashes of the dream ran through my mind, and I pushed aside the anxiety that welled in my chest and shoved it deep down. Damian watched me for a little bit longer before he turned to walk out the door.

"No one is going to leave you, Incaendiel," he said as he shut the door behind him.

I quickly wiped the sweat from my face and started to clean up the room. I put everything I had burned into a bag and carried it out without anyone seeing me. I returned to the room to make the bed back up, but it had already been fixed. Even the burned walls had been replaced. I suppose it was the magic Starfire used to create the place.

"There you are," Anniel remarked, walking up behind me and snaking her arms around my waist from behind. "I was wondering if you were ever going to wake up or just sleep the day away."

"Yeah, I slept pretty well," I lied, turning around and picking her up in my arms. "I didn't want to leave the bed."

She smiled and planted a kiss on my lips. "Good. I was worried when I left the bed that you were having a fitful sleep. You were tossing and turning."

"Yeah, because my paperweight left my side," I teased, running my finger lightly down the bridge of her nose.

"I'll have you know I am handier than a paperweight," she retorted with a laugh.

"I don't know. You're pretty lightweight," I taunted.

"Why don't you say that in the sparring arena?" she giggled as she wiggled out of my arms and ran for the door. "Catch me if you can!" she called as she threw the door open and bounded down the stairs.

I smiled and blinked from inside the cottage to the front door just as she opened it and ran out, catching her in my arms.

"No fair!" she yelled, laughing. "You *always* cheat!"

"I thought you were going to show me some moves?" I bantered.

She wiggled from my grip once more and ran over to one of the open arenas and picked up a long sword. "Oh, I have some moves," she goaded.

I walked over to the arena and picked up a long sword as well. "Let's see them then," I baited.

Her sword burst into flames as her powers ran up her hands and into the sword.

"Oh, so we are using powers, are we?" I laughed as I did the same with my sword.

"Don't hold back, love," she murmured before advancing.

She brought her sword down hard onto mine, and I parried it. We danced around the circle with our swords clanking and clashing. I caught her sword with mine and tossed it aside. She didn't waste a second, barrel rolling over to a set of dueling knives and blocking my sword as it came down on her.

"Now, that wasn't very nice," she replied with an impish grin.

Her dueling swords sprang to life with her power, and she landed blow for blow against me, just as I had watched Luxina with Damian.

"You fight pretty good for a girl," I taunted and ducked while laughing as she swung out with her sword.

Her eyes began to glow a fiery amber as she began to pelt me with blows from her sword. One after another came down against my sword, and then one nicked my arm. Determination was set in her eyes as she continued blow after blow, coming faster and stronger with each one.

"I don't remember you being this good," I uttered, struggling to counter every move.

Another of her swords nicked my other arm, and she continued on with her fight with determination in her eyes. As I blocked each blow, I could see the hunger in her eyes for more and more of the fight.

"Alright, that's enough," I laughed nervously.

She didn't stop but pushed harder and faster.

"I said that's enough."

It was as if she couldn't hear me anymore and had just one task at hand.

"Anniel, enough!" I bellowed.

She snapped out of whatever trance she had been in and dropped her swords to the ground once she saw the blood dripping from my arms.

"I'm sorry," she whispered and turned to walk away.

"What was that?" I demanded as I picked up a towel and wiped away the blood oozing from the gashes.

"I was conditioned to fight," she replied and walked back inside.

"What the hell did Alpha do to you?" I muttered to myself.

A searing pain tore through my head, and instinctively, my hand went to my forehead as I crouched to the ground.

"Anniel," Alpha *called out in the garden as she and I ran around playing our cat-and-mouse game.*

"Yes, Father?" she asked, stopping and swiping the hair from her face.

"It's time for training," Alpha replied with a warm smile.

"Coming!" she called back to him as he left. "While this was amusing and fun, Firefly, I have to go do my daily training."

"I want to come," I murmured, pulling her to me by her hand.

She giggled. "You know he trains me alone." Her hand slipped from mine, and she went running after Alpha.

The pain stopped, and I stood back up. I don't remember anyone else being trained personally by Alpha. I needed to talk to Metatron. Was she the only one he took aside? Did he train Lucifer? Or Michael? I walked quickly through Lightshade from arena to arena, looking for Metatron. I had no idea who he could be training with or even if he was training until I stumbled across him and Praeziel. Praeziel looked majestic in the arena. I had never seen him fight before, and I couldn't tell if he was or wasn't holding back as he sparred.

"He's definitely holding back," Damian commented, walking up beside me. "I have seen him in action on several occasions. He is the leader and trainer of the Nephilim."

Metatron glanced my way, and I waved him over. He jogged to me and stopped, breathless.

"That little Nephilim gave me a workout," he said through rapid breaths, glancing back at Praeziel and then back to me.

"That's because he's not a Nephilim," I replied with a laugh.

"What the hell is he?" Metatron asked, glancing over his shoulder nervously.

"A demigod," I answered, nodding at Praeziel, who was watching us. "But that discussion is for another day. I have been looking for you."

"What do you need?" Metatron asked, wiping the sweat from his face with a towel.

"In the Summit, who trained you?" I inquired.

"No one, really," he replied, shifting from foot to foot. "We trained ourselves and then honed our skills in sparring with one another. Why?"

"What about Lucifer?" I pressed. "Same thing?"

"Yes," Metatron responded. "Why?" he asked again.

"I just had a memory tear through my head," I replied, instinctively rubbing my forehead. "I suppose a lot of them are repressed from before the fall. Anyway, I was sparring with Anniel when she went into attack mode, and it triggered the memory when she said she was conditioned that way. My memory was of Alpha training her."

"Alpha?" he pondered, a look of confusion spreading across his face. "I thought the whole reason we were warrior angels was because he didn't fight."

"Oh, he fights," Damian added. "There was a time or two when he pulled me off in secret to spar with him. How else do you think he went after the elder gods?"

"So the memory is true," I murmured, running it all through my head. "From day one, he was training her to be a killing machine." I thought quietly for a moment. "I need my memories unlocked. I need to remember everything he warped us into forgetting."

"Starfire would be the only person who could help," Damian replied. "And if you are going to do it, you need it done before Cain arrives."

"I agree," Metatron said.

I nodded and turned around to head back to the cottage.

"Incaendiel, hold up," Damian shouted as he jogged up to me to walk with me. "What more do you think can be hidden?" he asked as we walked.

"I don't know," I replied. "But there's a lot I don't remember, and I need answers."

"Do you want me there with you?" he inquired, rubbing the back of his head nervously. "You know, just in case what happened while you were asleep happens again."

"If you want to be there, I wouldn't mind," I responded.

"Are you ready to talk about it?" he questioned, glancing up at me. "The dream?"

"It was just your usual anxiety about being a leader," I answered. "Nothing more or less."

"I doubt that," Damian scoffed. "You dreamt that everyone abandoned you and teamed up with Alpha. Everyone who pledged their loyalty to you was gone, and you were left all alone."

"Did you lie about spying in on my dream?" I hissed, irritated.

"We can read each other's thoughts, remember?" he replied defensively. "And I couldn't wake you up. So I peeked in."

"There is no privacy in this damn family," I muttered as we reached Starfire's porch.

"That's because you never learned how to put up a block so people wouldn't pry," he retorted with a laugh. "I thought Lilith was the one training you to hone your powers. She didn't teach you?"

I huffed as I climbed the stairs. "The only thing she taught me was to fear them. Push them down and repress them so I don't burn shit down."

"What can I do for you, Incaendiel?" Starfire asked, emerging from one of her rooms as we walked through the door.

"I need my memories unlocked from before the fall," I replied.

"Come in and sit down," she said, motioning with her hand to the sitting room. "What makes you think your memories are locked?

"Because I had one earlier that tore through my brain as if it were unlocked, like when Alpha released his hold on the power around Anniel's name," I replied, taking a seat on the couch with Damian following beside me.

"What was it about?" she asked as she sipped on a cup of tea.

"Alpha coming to get Anniel for her special training with him," I answered. "There has to be more that we all don't remember. Either due to the trauma of the fall or things Alpha kept layering in lies, messing with our memories."

"I see," Starfire remarked. "And Alpha didn't train anyone else?" she asked.

"No, I asked Metatron," I stated, fidgeting with my hands. "He said no one trained us, that we just knew what to do."

"Interesting," she murmured. "I believe you're right. You all have hidden memories."

"Why do you say that?" I urged, staring at her intently.

She didn't reply and instead walked from her seat into her potions room. It took a few minutes, but soon after, she returned with a hot cup of tea.

"Drink this," she said, handing me the cup.

"What is it?" I queried, staring down at it and taking a whiff. "Last time wasn't a pleasant experience."

"Some mugwort and other things," she replied with a smile. "It shouldn't be as unpleasant as the potion before, but I am afraid your skull will feel like it's being hammered open once you take it."

I frowned at the cup and then sighed. What choice did I have? "Bottoms up," I declared as I drank the tea.

"You might want to get comfortable," she offered with a serious face.

I lay back on the couch with Damian switching to another chair, sitting and watching me.

"Will I go to sleep?" I asked as I waited for it to kick in.

"Unfortunately not," Starfire replied, shifting uncomfortably in her seat. "It will be just like when Anniel was receiving her memories."

And without warning, everything went black.

Chapter 14

"WHY THESE TWO?" Alpha asked as he crafted the molding of a body. He was shaping me, and I could feel his hands working every single inch of my body into perfection.

"Don't you want your lineage to be more than warriors fighting for us? Or do you want children who will carry on your legacy and become something grander than this crafted universe?" Omega inquired in reply as she nimbly ran her fingers along the clay figure beside me. "Here, this bottle is for him," Omega dictated as she handed Alpha a bottle and then opened the other bottle she had.

"I believe I am finished with this one," Alpha declared as he placed a few drops of the substance on my forehead. "And you're sure they can't be brought to full power without stripping the enchantment? We put a fair amount of power into both of them. We don't need devil spawn running around and overthrowing us."

"Yes, the fey courts said this would prevent them from coming to full power until we were ready for them to become who they are meant to be," Omega replied, adding the substance from the separate bottle to the other figure's head. "They must never know, though."

"Why not?" Alpha prodded, standing from his kneeling position to marvel at what they had created thus far. "If they are destined for greatness, then they need to know so they can grow properly."

"We don't want the other children thinking we had favorites now, do we?" she ventured, wiping the stardust mud from her hands. "There's enough in numbers where they could easily overpower us since these two are not yet accustomed to their abilities."

"How did you persuade the fey into giving you an enchantment?" Alpha asked, raising an eyebrow.

Omega laughed. "I told them I didn't want you finding out about them, or you would kill them. They think I am creating them all on my own."

"And they believed you?" Alpha teased, chuckling. "Do they not understand you couldn't wield the power we harvested alone? It would take both of us to do it."

"I don't think they know much about us," Omega cooed. "They still think you are ignorant of the fact that there are other gods in the universe."

"I told you our life story would be the best entertaining show ever to hit the cosmos," Alpha joked, nudging Omega with his elbow.

Omega laughed and gently pushed his elbow away. "Stop it."

They both stood silently, unaware that I may have been unconscious, but my spirit was hearing and seeing everything.

"Are you ready to wake them up?" Alpha asked, bending down to inspect us.

"There's one more thing," Omega stated, kneeling beside him while staring at the two of us. "Since it has to remain a secret, and we cannot train them in private without word getting out to the others we are training them, then we need to encrypt their minds before we wake them."

"You mean like a trigger word that will wake and sleep them so they don't remember anything?" Alpha inquired.

Omega nodded.

"Which one do you wish to be the master over?" Alpha asked, eyeing us both.

"I will take Incaendiel," Omega replied, touching my forehead and turning my body from mud into flesh. "You take Anniel."

"Ok," Alpha said, bending down and touching the figure beside me. "I will take Anniel."

Anniel's body began to change like mine had, from mud to flesh.

"Anniel, uwr," Alpha commanded, and a bright light began to glow around her body. "Lishon." Her light snuffed out.

"Incaendiel, uwr," Omega commanded, and the same happened with me. "Lishon." My light was snuffed out.

"All right," Alpha said with a grin. "Let's bring our Shining Ones to life."

Omega leaned down and breathed her breath into me, and my spark lit up in my chest. She repeated the same to Anniel, and her spark lit up as well. "Uwr," Alpha and she spoke. "L'chaim!" We both opened our eyes and rose from the ground, both looking around confused.

"Welcome, my children," Alpha announced, his arms spread wide.

"Where are we?" Anniel asked, glancing around the space we were made in.

"You are in our universe," Omega replied, smiling from ear to ear.

"What happened to our universe?" I demanded. "We were fueling it to prevent its collapse."

"I am afraid your universe supernovaed," Alpha responded grimly. "We harvested your power right before it fell apart."

"Did you save our people?" Anniel implored, looking around at the empty surroundings in which she sat in. "Where are they?"

"They didn't make it, dear," Omega cooed, bending down and rubbing her arm. "You are the only survivors."

"And who are you two?" I snapped, standing up and helping Anniel to her feet.

"We are your creators," Omega replied nervously.

"No, you are not our creators," I stated flatly, hatred brimming beneath the surface. "You stole us from our parents. You brought us here and shoved us into these bodies. That doesn't make you our parents."

My body lit up like the sun on fire. I had total control over it as the flames danced across my skin. Anniel lit up as well, and we stood there prepared to fight.

"What the hell did we create?" Alpha asked, wide-eyed.

"I don't know, but I'm glad we put in that fail-safe," Omega muttered.

"Lishon!" they both shouted.

Our fires were snuffed out, but we were still awake.

"Lamut," they said in unison.

We hit the ground, unconscious.

"I thought you said their power would be suppressed," Alpha seethed, pacing uncomfortably.

"Their power *is* suppressed. This must be the overflow of power," Omega replied nervously.

"How did we make them more powerful than we are?" Alpha demanded, his nostrils flaring in jealousy.

"I don't know!" Omega hissed. "It was your idea to take their power from the sun!"

"No, the sun didn't do this," Alpha replied. "They have to have Barbelo in them."

Omega looked gravely at us while we lay asleep. "How do we fix this?" she asked.

"There's more of the enchantment left in the bottle," Alpha said. "Let's put the rest on them and don't use the trigger word unless we are in private and want to perfect their god powers.

"Ok," Omega agreed as she smeared the rest of the enchantment potion on our foreheads.

A brighter glow lit up our heads and went out.

"This is going to take a while for us to strip their memories from their previous life," Alpha stated, annoyed.

"And never together," Omega replied. "They're too powerful as a unit. We are going to have to handle them on a one-on-one basis."

"Do you think the council will have any advice on how to handle them?" Alpha asked.

"They should, yes," Omega answered. "Let's bring them to life again, and then we will go to the council."

"No, you need to stay here and watch them," Alpha argued. "I will go alone."

"You need to take at least one of them with you so you can demonstrate the issue," Omega retorted.

"Fine," Alpha relented. "I will take the boy since he seems more powerful than the girl."

"Ok," Omega replied with a shrug. "Ready to bring them to life?" Alpha nodded.

"L'chaim," they repeated once again.

"Where are we?" I asked, sitting up from the ground. "And who are you?"

Alpha and Omega exchanged glances. "We are your creators," Alpha replied hesitantly.

"What do we call you?" Anniel asked, her and I standing up.

"I am Father," Alpha replied with a nefarious grin.

"And I am Mother," Omega replied, smiling as well.

***

"I am sure you are wondering why I called you here together today," Alpha spoke to the council members gathered around the table. "We have a problem."

"Is that... Barbelo at your side?" Tiamat asked, peering curiously at me.

"I believe it is," Alpha replied. "She was not part of our plan when we created the two beings we did. I was sure that I had absorbed all of her power released out into the universe, but apparently, she reserved herself for this specific occasion. Now, our twin flame pair are far more powerful than we are, and we cannot control them."

"He doesn't seem like a threat. He is pretty docile," Drac joked.

"Incaendiel, uwr," Alpha spoke, and I awoke.

"Where am I? Who are all of you?" I asked as I looked around the room, resting on Alpha's face. "It's you!" I spat. "You destroyed my universe to harvest my soul from the sun!"

My body erupted into flames, fully controlled. I felt no anxiety or impending doom while in this form. I felt free, something I had never felt. I brought forth a fireball into my hand and was about to destroy Alpha.

"Lishon!" Alpha shouted.

My true self fell back asleep. The room laughed. "You can't even control your own creations. This is amusing," Tiamat remarked.

"This is not a laughing matter. He can burn everything to the ground, including all of you!" Alpha shouted.

Tiamat stood from her seat and walked over to me, looking me over. "Bring him back awake," she ordered.

"Incaendiel, uwr!" Alpha commanded.

I awoke and looked into her eyes as she stood right before me. "Do you remember me?" she asked.

Images started to zoom through my mind of my previous life in another universe, where I was the sun of the universe. "You are the mother of the Na'Thalhûn universe," I replied. "Why were we forsaken?" I cried. "We pleaded with you for help as our universe began to topple."

"You were dying, my child," she cooed. "You were old power. I told Omega about what was left of your power because the multiverses need you, and so you could be renewed again through her, your new mother, and through him," she said, motioning to Alpha, "your new father."

"He will never be my father," I replied bitterly. "I can see into his mind, and it is a wicked thing to witness. He killed—"

"Lishon!" Alpha barked.

"I wasn't done speaking with him!" Tiamat hissed.

"That was enough," Alpha replied, glaring at her.

Tiamat stared intently at Alpha. "There is only one thing that will help your issue. They are too powerful together. Let them grow some more together while their souls are asleep, so they can become acclimated to you being their father, because as of now, he despises you. I am sure his mate does as well. When they come to see you as their father, that is when you separate them and begin their slow transition from being asleep to being fully awake. But you must be careful. You have to keep their memory suppressed of their life before, or else they will destroy you both. Once you are ready to separate them, return to us for counsel so we can see the progress and make sure they are ready as well. You do it too soon, and they will retaliate," Tiamat explained.

"And you are sure this plan will work?" Alpha asked.

"We shall see," Tiamat replied. "That is the best we can do at this point."

***

"I want to come," I replied, pulling her to me by her hand.

She giggled. "You know he trains me alone." Her hand slipped from mine, and she went running after Alpha.

"Incaendiel?" Mother called out.

I turned around, and she was standing behind me, off at a distance.

"You ready for your training?" she asked with a warm smile.

I nodded and walked over to her side. We began making our way to the room she had trained me in.

"Mother?" I began.

"Yes, dear?" she responded to me, looping her arm in mine.

"Does Father not like me?" I asked, looking down at the ground.

She stopped in her tracks. "What in Summit would make you ask that?" she asked, peering up at me.

"He always calls Anniel off but never spends time alone with me," I replied.

She smiled. "We agreed to train you separately. I train you, and he trains her," she explained.

"Why can't we be trained together?" I inquired.

"Because you're special, Incaendiel," she replied. "You know your power requires special attention. It's a one-on-one job for us to do."

"How come my power shows more than Anniel's?" I prodded. "She doesn't even know about her gift over fire because it doesn't burst forth like mine."

"I am not sure why your power overtakes you and hers does not," Mother answered. "But that is why we train both of you, just in case hers does bubble to the top. She will know how to use it properly."

"Why can't I remember when you train me what we talk about?" I pressed. "I don't even remember the private training until you show up and mention it."

"We can't have your brothers and sisters jealous of you, now, can we?" she murmured in reply.

"I am sure they would understand that I need a bit more care than they do, given the fact that I nearly burn down the place all the time," I replied as she opened the door to my training room.

When she closed the door, she spoke, "Uwr."

I felt my whole personality shift. "Where is Anniel?" I demanded.

"She is with your father," Mother replied nervously, making sure to keep distance between us.

"He is not my father," I quipped heatedly.

"You need to calm down, sweetie," she cooed. "Your fire isn't suppressed, remember? We don't want to hurt your brothers and sisters, now do we?"

"I recalled the memories of my split self and sighed. "No, I do not wish to hurt anyone," I responded.

She smiled sweetly. "Thank you, son."

"I am torn at acknowledging you as my mother," I replied. "The part of me who is awake all the time cares deeply for you as his parent. However, I still know who my original creator was."

"Why is it you prefer me to your father, Alpha?" she asked as she took a seat at the table behind the wall I would go behind to train.

"I don't know. There's something wicked about his energy," I answered. "I can see thoughts in his head so sinister... he is not like you. Although I cannot read you as I do him."

"That is because I have my thoughts blocked from even him," she stated. "I cannot let him know how your training is progressing."

"Why not?" I asked.

"He would destroy you, my little firefly," she replied with a sigh. "Your powers have grown and grown, no matter how much we try to sleep them away. Even in your sleep state, your powers bubble through the enchantment in waves."

"I'm sorry," I mumbled, looking down at the ground. "I do not wish to harm anyone."

"I know you don't," she cooed sweetly. "And that is why I train you and he does not."

"Would you allow him to destroy me if he needed to?" I asked, bringing my eyes up to meet hers.

"No," she replied intently. "You are my child, even if your soul's power comes from another god who belonged to another pantheon's universe. I made you, and he will not destroy you if I have any say in it."

"Do you truly love me, or do you just see me as an emblem of power, the way he sees Anniel?" I inquired.

"He doesn't see you solely as power," she refuted.

"He might tell you otherwise," I began, "but I can see into his mind. Maybe he only lets you see what he wants you to see."

Mother swallowed hard and then smiled. "Let's begin your training, okay?"

I nodded and walked into the room behind the wall where she sat. I stood in the center of the room and waited for my command.

"Let it loose!" Mother shouted.

A deafening howl escaped my lips as I exploded in fire, like an atomic bomb going off.

"Recall it!" Mother commanded.

As soon as the words left her lips, the fire was sucked back into my body.

"Perfect. Now again!"

***

"We never said we were going to challenge them against one another!" Mother seethed.

"We need to see how their powers are progressing apart from one another and how they are when they are placed together with their powers active!" Alpha hissed. "Or else this will have all been for naught."

Mother looked between Anniel and me. We stood lovingly side by side and hand in hand.

"Fine, but not for long. We don't know how long they can be in the same room together with their powers at the surface."

"Anniel, uwr," Alpha commanded.

"Incaendiel, uwr," Mother commanded.

Immediately, Anniel's persona changed toward me, and she walked over to Alpha's side. One look at Alpha and I was filled with rage. Anniel took a step between Alpha and me and stood, unsheathing her sword and wielding it.

"You trained her to protect you against him?" Mother fumed.

"I did much more than that," Alpha bragged. "Anniel, bring forth your fire."

Anniel's fire climbed to the surface in total control. I unsheathed my sword and looked at Mother.

"Do it," she commanded.

My fire burst forth, hotter and brighter than that of Anniel, and trailed up my sword as I spun it around in my hand.

"How can he do that?" Alpha demanded, pounding his fist down on the table he stood before.

"Training," Mother boasted.

Alpha growled and yelled, "Now, Anniel!"

Anniel advanced against me and brought her sword down on mine. I blocked and parried her blow for blow. Every clank of our swords was like a ricochet effect. Cracks formed in the walls around us as our powers bounced off one another.

"Alpha, they're too powerful!" Mother cried as the room shook. "We need to shut them down before they bring the Summit down!"

"Just a little while longer," Alpha murmured, grinning madly as Anniel and I fought each other.

Splashes of light began to pour through the ceiling, and it was torn from the threshold, and a huge whirlpool formed in the space above us.

"They're creating a black hole!" Mother urged. "It will devour us all without escape. We have to shut it down!"

"A little longer!" Alpha ordered.

"No!" Mother shouted. "Incaendiel, Lishon! Anniel, Lishon!"

My powers deactivated, and I was myself again. However, Anniel was not. She was still fighting me with her sword.

"Why isn't she listening?" Mother demanded.

"She only has one master," Alpha replied.

"Tell her to stop!" Mother urged.

"Let's see how he fares against her without his powers," Alpha retorted.

I fought tooth and nail against her assaults. My fire burst forth on my skin and through my sword. I didn't want to hurt her, but I couldn't be defenseless against her either. Once again, the room began to shake, and the black hole appeared again.

"Why can he do that?" Alpha demanded, pounding his fist down on the table he sat at.

"Because even asleep, his powers still come forth uncontrolled!" Mother hissed. "You know this."

"Why does hers not do the same thing?" Alpha bellowed, enraged.

"Had you focused on controlling her powers instead of controlling her, then maybe hers would!" Mother spat.

Alpha groaned loudly. "Fine! Anniel, Lishon!"

☆☆☆

"We have a huge problem," Alpha remarked, pacing back and forth in front of the council. "My universe is beginning to fold in on itself."

"Are they ready to be separated?" Tiamat inquired. "Their strong connection and close proximity together are trying to free their sleeping souls."

"I am not sure if they are ready," Alpha stated, sitting and rubbing his forehead.

"This is what happens when baby gods want to play house," Drac sneered. "You decided to create something, and you cannot even control it because you made it from old power you don't even understand. You are an ignorant god."

"I am not ignorant, and I am fully aware of how this all went. But if I recall correctly, Tiamat was the one who aided Omega in collecting the power that rests asleep in them. So are we naïve, or were we fooled by that harlot?" Alpha spat.

"Had you focused more on creating life as opposed to creating power, you wouldn't be in this predicament!" Tiamat hissed. "I helped you as was asked of me. Do not turn this on me as if I deceived you purposefully. I had no idea that Barbelo would bind to them when presented with the chance!"

"They're not ready," Alpha pleaded. "What else can I do?"

"Beg Yahweh for his power," Tiamat replied, shrugging her shoulders. "You have to have more power than they do to control them. It's that simple. If you cannot attain his power, then you have to separate them, whether they are ready or not."

Alpha ran his hands over his face in frustration.

"I am so sorry, Alpha, truly," Tiamat stated. "I know this is a hard decision for you to have to make. But they are indeed your only options."

"What if you were to take one of them?" Alpha asked, motioning to me. "You can have him back, and I keep the girl."

"Is that really fair to either of them?" Tiamat asked, looking at clueless me.

"I don't care what's fair to them!" Alpha shouted. "Not at this point!"

Tiamat glared at Alpha. "No."

"What?" he asked, confused.

"No, I will not take one or the other," she replied. "Fix your problem on your own. We are done trying to counsel you, especially if you won't listen to our suggestions."

"You told me if I separated them too soon, then there would be problems," Alpha refuted. "I did as you suggested. It is not my fault that the universe is pushing me faster when they are not ready."

"That's not our problem," Drac replied.

"You will regret this," Alpha seethed as he grabbed me by my arm and dragged me from the room.

***

"What did the council tell you?" Mother asked.

"It's time," Alpha replied, sitting down in the seat of his throne and rubbing his forehead.

"They're not ready to be separated!" Mother insisted. "Incaendiel's emotions have not been fostered with you at all!"

"I know this!" Alpha spat. "I was hoping for more time to switch them out with one another and I start training with him, but there isn't any time. They can't be together without them tearing the universe apart at the seams. It is time they are separated."

"So, how do we do this?" Mother asked, glancing in my direction.

"I have to cast one of them out," Alpha stated flatly.

"We can't just toss one of them out without a justifiable reason!" Mother refuted. "The others will ask questions."

"Then we lie to them. Tell him the one was disobedient to the point we feared for our safety," Alpha replied.

"That's not going to work!" Mother said, rejecting the idea. "The angels are not stupid."

"I don't know what you want me to do!" Alpha hollered. "They can't stay here together. I tried to get Tiamat to take him for a while, but she refused."

"You tried to give him away?" Mother asked in disbelief.

"I am out of choices," Alpha hollered. "I mean, I am open to suggestions. What do you think we should do?"

"We tell the children that there's a problem with all of our power, and we need one of them to fall," Mother offered.

"And if he doesn't step forward?" Alpha inquired, motioning to me.

"Then I will assume the responsibility of the need for the split of power, and he will choose to go with me," Mother insisted.

"Do you honestly think he loves you more than he loves her?" Alpha asked, motioning over at Anniel.

We both stood quietly as they argued back and forth.

"You can manipulate our thoughts, can you not?" Anniel asked. "Like when you erase the memories of these meetings from our memory so we don't tell the others."

"Yes," Alpha answered. "We can manipulate what we think, see, and do. But we don't like to do it more than necessary. Too many manipulations can backfire on us."

"What if it's a small one?" Anniel offered. "Like you show me something that will tell me to tell Incaendiel to go with Mother?"

"Would that work?" Mother asked.

Alpha sighed. "It's our only chance at this, so it better."

Chapter 15

I SNAPPED UP from my lying position in a cold sweat. I looked around the room to see Starfire and Damian watching me intently.

"I need to go back," I stammered, looking over at Starfire. "I need to see more."

"I think you have seen enough for one day," Starfire urged.

"No!" I demanded. "I need to see what Lilith did to me after the fall."

"Another day!" Starfire insisted. "That was a lot to process, and by the end, your power was starting to grow out of control. You nearly caught on fire."

I moved my body so my legs could hang off the couch, and I rested my head in my hands. "Did you all see what I saw?" I asked, not looking up.

"Yes," Damian replied softly, sitting quiet and still in his spot.

"Are Anniel and I actually at full power, or are we still asleep?" I asked Starfire.

"You are still asleep," Starfire answered quietly.

I rubbed my forehead the same way I had seen Alpha do all those years. "What do I do?" I whimpered with a tear rolling down my face.

"That is a difficult question," Starfire replied.

"Would Anniel attack him?" Damian asked. "That's what she was conditioned to do in her training while awake."

"That is what makes it a difficult question because it's a fifty-fifty chance," Starfire replied.

"Does it have to be Alpha that awakens her still?" Damian pressed. "Because he's not going to activate her without her by his side."

"Yes, it has to be Alpha," Lilith interrupted, walking into the room.

"How are you even here?" Damian demanded, jumping up from his seat.

"Do you really think Starfire's warlocks hold a power greater than that of gods?" Lilith replied smugly. "We can come and go as we please. Alpha just chooses not to while playing this game with us all."

"So he could come here anytime he wishes to?" Damian mumbled in a panic, taking a seat again.

"Yes, but he won't," Lilith replied. "He is afraid of you all together." She looked at me. "Especially you."

"Why me?" I asked.

"Because you never submitted to him as his child. And that shadow part of you that we keep asleep hates him. It bubbled to the surface every so often with your powers. You became so angry with him throughout the millennia. Pair that with your shadow self, and you have pure hatred for him. He doesn't know if I have let that side of you loose yet. So he keeps his distance," Lilith explained.

"And Anniel?" I inquired.

"Her shadow self is bubbling to the surface just as yours does," Lilith replied.

"So every single millennium that passed and he kept her to himself, he taught her to hate me through her shadow self?" I asked, staring in disbelief at Lilith.

A lonely tear fell from Lilith's eye. "I believe so," she whispered.

"So our choices are to keep ourselves asleep and our psyche split apart or awaken and possibly be at each other's throats?" I pressed.

Lilith nodded.

"Why did he hate me?" I implored. "I saw his face while creating me. He was happy. He was enthusiastic. Why does he hate me?"

"He doesn't hate you, son," Lilith replied with a stifled cry. "He fears you. He fears your power. And he is jealous you were chosen by Barbelo to be more powerful than he is."

"I know Yahweh turned him down for power," I stated. "We saw it after we were in the void during our transition."

Lilith nodded her head. "He went to Yahweh first thing because he didn't want to lose his children. But just as you could see into his mind, Yahweh could as well. Yahweh is the all-seeing father, and Barbelo the all-seeing mother. They could see past any blocks put up in our minds. And he saw the future in wait with Alpha with power beyond comprehension, where he used it for greed and not love."

"So that's why Damian could tap into anyone's thoughts?" I pondered. "Because he and Luxina aren't asleep like Anniel and me? Is that why we can only read each other's minds, or the kids when they let us?"

"Yes," Lilith answered.

The room fell silent, and the tension in the air was like waves of sound crashing against one another.

"Do you love us?" I whimpered.

"I divorced Alpha for you," she replied, taking a seat at the table with Starfire. "I would have activated you to take him out if he ever tried to truly hurt you."

"When I was in the dungeon?" I asked.

"He never had one-on-one training with you like he did with Anniel," she answered. "He was trying to break your shadow self. The part of you that has never submitted to him. The part of you that loves Anniel with every fiber in your being and will not hurt her, and he knows it. He was trying to make you despise her and sever that connection."

"Would you abandon me to take his side?" I queried, staring at her intently.

As she fell quiet, I studied her face. She appeared more youthful than she did in the dungeon.

"How have you been regressing your age?" I breathed.

"What do you mean?" she asked, taken aback.

"Every time I see you, you appear younger and younger," I replied.

"We... aged the more we used our power to create this place," she explained.

"So the more the power returns to you, the more youthful you become?" I asked.

"Yes, and the more powerful we become as well," she replied, shifting in her seat. "Alpha only took a small part of the angels back. He took their light but not their grace. Only I can take that back. That is the spark of life I breathed into each of you."

"So, even though they are now in allegiance with Incaendiel and share his power, you can still make them drop dead where they stand if you wish to?" Damian chimed in.

"Yes, but I would never do that," Lilith protested. "I may have been a toxic mother and played games and all while having my spat with Alpha, but I would never hurt my children like that. Even when Anniel was being incarnated as a human, she only died a human death. She was never in any real danger at my hands. Now, Alpha..." she trailed off. "Alpha would if he could."

"I want to awaken," I plainly stated. "I want to be whole again."

"There is no turning back once I awaken you," she warned. "I haven't brought you forth in a long time, and once your sleep self merges with your awake self, it will know all. I cannot control you, and I don't even know if you could control yourself."

"You could put me back to sleep," I protested.

"No, I can't, Incaendiel," she replied, sighing. "You have been stripped of your enchantment. I cannot control anything about you once you are awakened. You will be your own person again. You will be the old soul who awakened when I first created you."

"Can we defeat Alpha without Anniel and me awake?" I asked.

"I don't know," Lilith answered. "And before you ask, I don't know if you being awake is enough as well."

"Starfire?" I asked, glancing at her. "Do you see anything about it?"

"Until you drop your suppressed psyche, I cannot see anything about the end still," she replied.

"Do it," Damian interrupted.

"What if I don't remember the person I am now?" I urged, turning my attention to him. "What if I don't remember you or Luxina? My asleep self has never met either of you."

"You will remember," Damian replied. "Blood remembers blood. It's why your shadow self cannot let go of who you came from. You remember them in your blood, even if your memory won't let you see them. Do it!"

"Will I hurt anyone when I come together?" I questioned, turning to Starfire.

"That I also cannot see," she responded.

"Can you enchant a room to contain me?" I asked.

"Just like when you finished your transition once I stripped your enchantment away, I cannot contain you if you explode," she replied.

"Take me somewhere safe," I told Lilith. "That way, no one can be hurt. Take me to the lake."

"What lake?" Damian asked, scrunching his face.

"The lake he died," Starfire replied.

"I'm going, too," Damian said, standing to his feet.

"No, you're not," I protested.

"You can't tell me what I can and can't do!" Damian shouted.

I stood up, towering over him, and even though he kept the same willful spite, I could see his fear.

"I don't want you to get hurt," I replied softly.

"You won't hurt me," he insisted, fear still creeping through his eyes. "Blood remembers blood."

We were all quiet for what seemed like an eternity.

"So, is it settled?" Lilith asked. "Are we doing this?"

"Yes," I replied, still staring Damian down. "Take us to the lake. Starfire, tell Anniel we will be back."

Starfire nodded, and we all stepped out the door.

"Take my hand," Lilith said, and we each grabbed one of her hands.

"Incaendiel?" Samael said, walking up to us. "What are you doing?"

"Righting a wrong," I breathed as we disappeared from Lightshade and arrived at the lake. I walked around the lake, admiring the foliage and crystal blue water as memories from years ago came rushing forth.

"You burned this place down so many times trying to come to grips with your power that your ego was never supposed to wield alone," Lilith remarked, walking up to my side. "It's fitting that you wanted to be here."

"Do it," I demanded as I turned to face her.

"As you wish, son," she replied. "Damian, go stand over there, please," she ordered, pointing to a spot a reasonable distance from the place I stood in.

Surprisingly, he obeyed and went to stand where she directed. I made eye contact with him, and I saw the worry in his eyes. I gave him a reassuring smile and looked back at Lilith.

I took in a deep breath and then exhaled. "Say it," I spoke softly.

Lilith exhaled nervously and nodded. "Incaendiel, uwr!" she commanded.

My skin blazed to life, and I could feel the power surging through my body. I had never felt power like this before, but at the same time, it felt normal. Out of all the times I had lost control of myself and burned things to a crisp, it didn't compare to the ringlets of fire that coursed through my veins, looking like the day I took my potion. And all at once, my ego and shadow self collided as memories from when I was awake and asleep flooded my mind all at once. I dropped to the ground, howling in pain as my skull felt like it was tearing apart.

"What's happening to him?" I heard Damian demand. "What did you do to him?"

"I freed him," Lilith replied. "His memories are all colliding and fusing together to form the picture he has been searching for. Some of them will fight the others. His split psyche is fighting over which is to become the dominant him."

I burned hotter as every glimpse into the past rolled through my head, and I let out a deafening scream. My power mounted and mounted until I exploded into a huge ball of fire, just like I had seen in the memory. I was an atom bomb going off, and my freed power fed it like gasoline. Unlike before, when I was under the enchantment, I now had nothing holding back the flames as they crawled up the mountainside. Another deafening howl, and the fire burned more intensely. I didn't tire as I used to. There was a constant source of power keeping my rage inside fueled. The face of Alpha appeared in my mind, and all I wanted was him dead. It's all I could focus on, and that he needed to be destroyed.

"Incaendiel!" Lilith shouted, and I whipped my head in her direction, standing from the burning foliage in which I was squatting.

"You," I raged in a hollow voice.

"It's me," she replied, holding her hands up. "It's Mother."

"You are not my mother," I hissed venomously. "You have done things... sinister things."

"I have been the only mother you have known for more than four billion years," she pleaded.

"A mother doesn't do what you did to me," I replied dryly. "A mother doesn't cause the devastation, trauma, and anguish you have inflicted alongside your husband."

"Please, you need me!" she implored, hitting her knees.

"I need no one," I answered, raising my hand and bringing forth my fire into my hand.

Someone jumped in front of her and shouted, "No, Incaendiel!"

"Who are you?" I demanded, shifting my attention to his face.

"It's Damian!" he replied.

"I don't remember a Damian," I growled. "All I can remember is her face and Alpha's face and the torture they subjected me to over and over to try and break me."

"They did it to me, too," he replied, taking a few steps closer to me. "They chained me up, beat me, nearly killed me, threw me in arenas with monstrous beings. And you saved me."

"I have never met you before," I protested.

"But you have!" he insisted. "You know who I am! Please, don't do this!"

"You don't control me," I rasped. "No one controls me anymore. I have been shoved in a box for too long. No one will ever put me back in it."

I focused my hand on him and primed my energy.

"Dad! Please don't!" he cried. *Blood remembers blood...*

It only took one word for my memories to tumble together. Dad. Everything rushed through my mind: The training in secret, Anniel, the fall, her human trials, the fake manipulations of memories, the war against Alpha, Luxina, Xavier, Starfire, and finally, Damian. I howled in pain again as everything crashed around in my brain, and then everything went black.

When I opened my eyes, smoke rose around me. I sat up and looked around at the burning rubble. Once again, I had burned the place down to bare ground. I placed my hand on the earth and recalled the flames back to me. As they retreated, the land healed immediately behind the receding flames as if nothing had happened. And then I was filled with panic. Damian! Where is Damian? My eyes scanned my surroundings, trying to find him through the lingering smoke.

"Damian!" I shouted in panic. "Damian!"

"I'm right here!" he called out through the smoke.

I jumped to my feet and ran in the direction from which I had heard his voice. As the smoke cleared, I saw him standing with Lilith, unharmed. I let out a sigh of relief and walked over to him, pulling him into my chest.

"I almost killed you," I breathed shakily.

He wrapped his arms around me for a brief moment before he pushed me away. I looked at him, puzzled.

"I don't like to be touched," he replied as if answering the question I had yet to form.

Lilith stood behind him, still fearful but trying her best not to show it. I still wanted to destroy her, but I could control the urge now that both halves of myself had melded together.

"I remember everything," I stated curtly.

"I know," she replied, swallowing hard.

"I remember what you put me through," I growled through gritted teeth.

"It was only to get you to learn to control your power," she reminded me.

"There could have been better ways," I snarled.

"No one is perfect," she replied meekly. "Let's get back to Lightshade."

I snapped my fingers, and we were back in front of Starfire's cottage. Samael slowly stood up from his seated position on the steps as he stared at me. Unlike before, when we exploded and activated our powers, he didn't move closer to me and kept his distance.

"What did you do to him?" he demanded, looking at Lilith.

"I took down the wall in his mind that we put up as a fail-safe when he was created," she replied. "He is now at full power."

"He looks..." Samael began.

"Like he grew four feet and has suns for eyes?" Damian asked, amused.

"Yeah, that," Samael replied, swallowing as he nodded.

"Yeah, freaked me out as well," Damian replied.

"How is his power brought forth, but he isn't burning everything down to the ground?" Samael asked, bewildered.

"Because he knows how to control it now," Lilith replied. "The only reason we put up the barrier was because at full power, he was trying to kill us when we first made him."

"Woah," Azazel remarked as she came running up to Samael and slowed. One by one, the angels started making their way over. "What happened to him?" she murmured.

"I am now who I am supposed to be," I replied, my voice deeper than before.

"Even your voice is different," Samael declared in awe.

"Where is Anniel?" I asked.

"No one has seen her since this morning," Azazel answered, not taking her eyes off me.

"Well, we need to find her so we can fill her in on what is going on," I said.

Chapter 16

I SAT ON Starfire's porch, still unsure if I should try to interact with anyone, afraid I could accidentally hurt them. I understood fear and anxiety fuel my powers, so I tried to keep the thoughts from my mind, but having been conditioned for so long to repress my powers, I am lost. I know I have control over them, but there's still that doubt in my head. I looked around at the people gathered in the different arenas, and I could hear them speak even though no words left their lips. Every now and then, they would glance in my direction.

He looks so different now.

He's scary.

Why was he chosen and not one of us?

He could probably kill us all with a snap of his fingers.

Is it safe to even be around him?

Maybe Alpha kept that block up in his head for a reason.

Did we make the right choice siding with him?

They feared me now. And yeah, I probably could kill them with a snap of my fingers. Samael had been actively avoiding me since I returned to Lightshade. I don't know if it was out of fear or jealousy. I couldn't tell with him anymore, and I didn't pry into his thoughts to find out. I didn't want to know. He and I had followed each other to the ends of the earth, and it would be world-shattering to learn he didn't want to have anything to do with me anymore. Damian appeared from inside Starfire's cottage and sat down beside me.

"They had the same thoughts running through their heads when they met me," he stated as he sat down on the step beside me. "They saw me as a monster who couldn't be trusted."

"It's different for me," I replied. "Most of them, I was raised beside them for billions of years. Lilith and Alpha kept my one side hidden so it wouldn't spark fear or jealousy with them, and now, here we are. Lifetimes have gone by with us side by side, and they are doing just as Lilith and Alpha feared they would."

"We still haven't found Anniel," he said, changing the subject. "We have searched all of Lightshade, and she is not here."

"Her memory wall had already been toppled by Alpha," I sighed. "He removed all manipulations of memories from her and me. The only ones that were left for me were the ones Lilith had put up. There's no telling what was triggered when we were sparring earlier."

"You don't think she returned to Alpha, do you?" Damian asked, glancing up at me.

"I don't know," I replied with a heavy sigh. "I don't know anything at this point."

Metatron and the rest of the group rounded the corner of Starfire's cottage and slowed. I glanced over at him. He shook his head.

"We didn't find her," he declared.

I scanned their faces while reading their thoughts.

He's going to kill us for not finding her, Michael thought.

He looks so menacing, Azazel thought. *Are we safe around him now?*

He's the most beautiful and the most terrifying being in the universe, Metatron thought.

My eyes rested on Samael, and I took a deep breath.

We need to keep him calm and rational. This is all new to him, and he had a problem before he was uncaged in keeping his powers in check. I hope none of these idiots say anything to trigger him. There's no telling what he would do. But I will be there. I will keep my brother safe.

Relief washed over me, and Damian nudged my elbow. "Thought you weren't going to do that?" he teased.

"Shut up," I smirked and tousled his hair. "Has Lilith made it back?" I asked the group.

They shook their heads. "We haven't seen her since she left to check the Summit and see if Anniel returned there."

I nodded and stood up from the porch step.

"Where are you going?" Damian asked.

"To lie down. I'm exhausted," I answered, yawning and stretching.

"I will let you know if anything changes," he assured as I walked inside.

"Thank you," I replied and headed up the stairs.

I opened the door to my room, hoping someone had forgotten to check in here for her, but I was met with disappointment. The room was empty. I walked over to the bed and flopped down on it, staring up at the ceiling. I knew where she was. We all knew where she was. It was why Lilith hadn't returned. She was there. She returned to her master like she had been conditioned to do. The door opened abruptly, and I sat up as it was closed behind Anniel.

"There you are!" I exclaimed and jumped up from the bed. "We have been looking for you everywhere!"

"I can't stay here, Incaendiel," she whispered. "I have to go."

"What are you talking about?" I asked, confused.

"Every bone in my body is screaming for me to kill you," she replied, turning on her heel and looking me in the eyes. Her eyes were red-rimmed from where she was crying. "And even more so now that you have been woken up," she murmured. "I remember it all. I remember every single time Alpha made us fight, trying to hone our powers in. I remember how he made me his lapdog and how I was to protect him at all costs, even if that meant killing you. Because even then, even in the beginning, you hated him and wanted to make him suffer for what he let happen to our universe. We both did. But for some reason, I grew to care for him."

"Wait, you knew this whole time about it all and didn't say anything?" I snapped.

"At first, it was just bits and pieces," she replied. "Then it started peeling back more and more, and then we sparred..."

"Things will be fine," I proclaimed.

"No, they won't," she insisted, pacing the room.

"You will be fine!" I protested.

"No," she screeched, abruptly stopping in place. "It's just one word, and I awaken, and I do not meld together. Unlike with Lilith and you, it has not been years and years since he has used my powers. He used them every chance he got. I do not meld. I become the machine he made me into. And my only goal is to protect him and to kill you!"

"There is a fifty-fifty chance that this time it will work and you will bond with your other self," I refuted. "It took me a while to bond. I almost killed Lilith and Damian!" I hissed. "You cannot give up on this. The universe needs you. I need you. You're my other half. I cannot do this alone. I cannot do this without you!"

"I'm sorry," she whimpered and turned to grab the doorknob.

"Where are you going to go?" I demanded. "Anywhere you go, Alpha will try and bring you back to him. He knows he can't from here because he will die trying. But out there, without me or everyone else, he will. You have to stay," I pleaded.

"If I stay, I will kill you!" she yelled. "And you are the only hope everyone has of taking down Alpha. I am not. I do not have the same will as you and never have. It's why he was able to manipulate me so easily."

She yanked the door open and was met with the face of Alpha on the other side. He spun her around and held her by her neck as I blazed in loathing and fury.

"I see Lilith has set you free," Alpha remarked with a wicked grin, struggling to hold Anniel in his grasp. "Too bad Anniel didn't fill you in sooner so you could have a better game plan when I came for her."

I looked from him to Anniel, and she looked away from me. "Oh, she didn't tell you," Alpha goaded, mocking me with a sad face. "She knew I would be coming for her this whole time. She was just ordered by her master not to say anything. I needed her enchantment dropped so I could use my best foot soldier."

I went to take a step toward him.

"At, at," he taunted, wagging his finger at me. "I will set her free, and then it will be a showdown between the two of you. You don't want to destroy your precious little façade of a safe haven, now do you? Besides, you have bigger fish to fry. You have to find your precious Luxina still before she comes over to the dark side with her mother."

"What do you want?" I demanded. I conceded, backed down, and then glared at him.

"I've already got it," he snarled and vanished into thin air with Anniel.

"Fuck!" I yelled, pounding the wall and busting a hole through it.

I bounded down the stairs and out the door to make sure everyone was okay outside. Anxiety flooded my body as I looked around. No one was outside. My dream came to my forethoughts, and I began to spiral into a panic attack.

"Where the fuck is everyone!" I screamed in heaves.

"Hidden away," Starfire assured as she appeared from inside. "They are safe and sound. I sensed Alpha's presence and portaled them to a hideaway bunker."

"Damian?" I implored, fighting the tightening of my chest.

"He is with them, too," Starfire affirmed. "We couldn't find Anniel, though."

"He took her," I said, my voice cracking.

Everything was crashing down around me, and I felt like I couldn't breathe. I clawed at my chest, trying to release the tension my shirt had on it, to take in deeper gulps of air, but nothing worked.

"Breathe!" Starfire shouted.

Fire erupted around me as I hit the ground and began crawling. Maybe it was for the best that I died. I am not a leader. I am a selfish person, always putting my needs over everyone else's. First with Luxina, then with Anniel and Damian. I would let the world burn for those three and not even give a shit. As long as they were safe, the world was safe. But now...

"Incaendiel!" Damian shouted, bending down in front of me.

It was like listening through a tunnel. I could see his face and watch his mouth move, but his voice was muffled, and a loud ringing sound echoed in my ears.

"What happened?" I could hear muffled.

"Alpha," was all Starfire said as my vision began to grow dark.

Dad! Damian shouted in his head. *Breathe!*

I snapped out of the dark hole closing around me and back into the light.

"Breathe!" Damian yelled.

I took in a sharp inhale and exhaled slowly, followed by another and another. I looked around to see everything catching on fire. I laid my hand on the ground and recalled the fire back to me as my heart slowed its racing and my breathing started to steady itself. My hearing began to return, and I heard Starfire talking.

"When I found him, he was already going into a panic attack. He thought Alpha had taken you all," she explained, recounting what had happened.

"Or he thought we all left him for Alpha," Damian offered, glancing over at me.

"Why would he think that?" Metatron asked, his eyes on me, and then back to Damian.

"Before he was fully unlocked, he had a dream that was just like this," Damian shared with the group. "He came outside, and everyone was gone, and Alpha told him we all left him to join his side."

"We would never do that, though," Samael insisted.

"He can hear everyone's thoughts now!" Damian hissed, glaring at everyone standing around. "Every single thing that goes through you all's minds, he can hear, and so can I. So I know what you've been thinking about him as well."

"We didn't know he could read everyone's minds now," Azazel murmured, glancing over at me shamefully. "We always knew of the connection between him and Anniel."

"Well, now you know," Damian snapped. "Samael, you're still first in command. Keep them in line," he ordered.

I began to stand when Damian ran to my side to help me up.

"I'm okay," I reassured him.

"Yeah, but you still need some time to rest," he replied, leading me to the steps to go inside.

"Incaendiel!" Samael called out. Damian and I turned around to look at him. "I will follow you to the ends of the earth. I hope you know that, Brother. None of this will ever change our bond. You being who you are now. I am not afraid of that. You have my word, I will not leave your side."

"We pledged to follow you," Michael said, stepping forward. "There's no going back to Alpha. Not after what he did to us all. Not after what he continues to do to everyone."

I nodded. "A discussion for another time because what I have to ask of you is once again selfish," I replied regretfully.

"It's not selfish trying to keep our whole family together," Azazel chimed in. "Anniel and Luxina are both our family, too. And we will tear the universe apart to keep them safe. Asking us to help save them isn't even a question. We are already formulating the plan."

A tear slid down my cheek as Damian pulled me toward the door. I nodded at them all before turning around to go into the cottage. I looked down at Damian, who wasn't much shorter than I was.

"When did you get taller?" I joked.

"Seriously?" he asked, looking up at me. "Now you have jokes?"

I chuckled. "Without humor, what do we have left but self-loathing and dark thoughts?"

"Touché," he smirked.

He helped me into my room and sat me down on the bed. I lay back, exhausted, when it felt like déjà vu all over again from earlier. Another panic attack loomed on the horizon.

"Alpha won't be back," he assured me, reading my thoughts. "He got what he wanted. He pulled the ace he had up his sleeve that we were all thinking he had."

"If only I had thought of the memories sooner," I murmured. "I could have stopped this from happening."

"No, you wouldn't have," Damian replied, sitting in a chair against the wall. "She was going to go back to him to protect us all before he took her. Alpha was just waiting for Lilith to topple your wall and activate you before he let us know his rook was here the whole time."

"How is this our lives?" I asked, placing my hand on my head. "Always running, always hiding, always fighting, and for what? To live? To exist? Sometimes, I don't know what the point is. Not when everything always ends the same damn way every time. We never catch a break, and it's getting so exhausting. Over four billion years of this bullshit."

"It's different this time," Damian refuted.

"Not much so," I fired back. "He has your mother again. He has Luxina again in freaking Purgatory of all places, doing who knows what to her."

"He doesn't have me, and he doesn't have you," Damian replied. "He never has all of us, and this time, you are different. I am different. We aren't defenseless against him anymore."

"If he activates your mother, she doesn't believe she is strong enough to meld her two psyches together like I did," I confessed. "She believes she will just be his mindless lapdog, protecting him from me. You know what that means?" I asked, swallowing the lump in my throat.

"What?" Damian asked in return.

"It means I will have to kill her, or she will kill me," I choked out, tears threatening to spill out.

"Starfire said there is a fifty-fifty chance that won't happen, and she will accept her shadow self and ego as one," he stated confidently. "And if I am betting money on a horse, I am betting on Starfire. Not Alpha."

"I am so tired from this war," I replied, straightening in the bed on my back. "It's been going on for so long, long before you were ever born, back to the very beginning, back to my creation, back before my creation. I can feel it in my bones. Something happened; more than just a sun was dying, and the power was harvested. It feels like I was slain to attain the power. Power that wasn't theirs to have to begin with."

"You need to sleep," Damian ordered, changing the subject. "You will feel better once you rest. You've been through a lot lately. It's wearing you thin. You can't fight when you're battling your own self."

"You don't tell me what to do," I teased with a chuckle.

I was so tired, and the bed was so inviting. But I didn't want to sleep. I was afraid to sleep. Bad things happen when I am not awake. Both mentally and physically not awake.

"This isn't the same sleep Alpha would do," Damian reassured me. "This is the sleep your body needs to rest and reset. Nothing bad is going to happen, and I will stay with you until you wake back up."

"You don't have to do that," I replied. "You don't have to sacrifice your time to make sure I am okay."

"I want to," he assured.

And as his calming vibes hit me, I drifted off into sweet, dreamless nothingness.

Chapter 17

I AWOKE TO silence and sat straight up in bed. Damian was slumped down in his chair, asleep. He looked so at peace when he was asleep. I thought back to the day before. His mannerisms were warming up more and more to me. He was no longer standoffish or belligerent with me. And he had started calling me dad, which secretly made me smile with joy even if it is only to snap me out of shit. He made me feel wanted during a time when I felt like no one wanted me around, which meant so much to me coming from him. I rose out of bed and stood, cracking every muscle in my body as I stretched. I nudged him, and he stirred awake.

"Did you sleep there all night?" I asked, staring at him in the chair.

He rubbed his neck and nodded.

"Climb in the bed and get you a few good hours of good sleep," I ordered, pointing over to my bed.

"What about you?" he asked, looking from the bed and back to me.

"I will be fine," I assured him with a smile. "Sleep did the trick. I will come and get you in a few hours."

He nodded and moved from the chair over to the bed. He snuggled into the pillow and was out within seconds. He had the weight of the world on his shoulders, and the last thing he needed to do was have to babysit me because I couldn't come to terms with things and handle my own shit. I left the room, closing the door quietly behind me, and made my way downstairs. I walked into the kitchen to look for something to eat because, quite frankly, I hadn't eaten in a few days and needed food for energy.

"Well, look what the cat dragged in," Asmodeus teased as he took a bite of an apple.

"Are you ever anywhere except in the kitchen?" I shot back with a laugh.

"You know me," he joked, tipping the chair he sat in back on two legs. "I could eat for days."

"I feel like that now," I said as I picked up some grapes. "I don't even know when the last time it was that I ate some food here."

"Yeah, you gotta watch that figure," he replied, slapping my abs and laughing.

"Where's everyone at?" I asked, popping a grape in my mouth.

"Training, as usual," he answered, taking another bite of his apple. "Samael is whipping everyone into shape, and everyone is falling in rank."

"Anyone giving him lip?" I wondered, a laugh creeping up through the seriousness.

"You know the same old same old," he declared, laughing. "And then Azazel steps in to bite their heads off."

"Just like old times, eh?" I mused.

"Yep, just like old times, Brother," Asmodeus asserted, patting my shoulder. "The only difference is now you don't get fussed at for burning shit down."

"Hey!" I defended, holding my hands up. "Cheap shot much?"

I grinned, popping another grape in my mouth, and reached for some cheese and bread.

"I'm glad you're better today," Asmodeus said seriously. "We were all worried about you yesterday."

I agreed silently. "Yeah, yesterday was a shit day."

"I can't imagine going through all you have gone through and still waking up the next day to keep going further," he responded in awe. "I admire that about you. It's what I admire about Damian, too."

"That little shit saved me yesterday when I almost lost myself," I said, putting my food down for a second. "He brought me together after Lilith freed me. He brought me out of my panic attack. He's the real hero of the family. Not me."

"No one can blame you for how you reacted yesterday and if they do, I will give them a swift kick in the ass," he replied, tossing his apple core in a bin. "Damian is just like you. It's amazing how he was raised with Alpha, and yet your defiance spoke through his veins."

"I don't know," I insisted, raising an eyebrow. "I do recall it was you who stole Alpha's chariot and horses to joyride around Saturn. I believe he is more like you."

"Hey!" Asmodeus shouted, wide-eyed and grinning from ear to ear. "That was *your* idea!"

I glanced out the window of the kitchen and saw everyone out there training.

"I bet they're all out there waiting for me, aren't they?" I asked, dreading going out there.

"No," Asmodeus assured. "They expect you to sleep like the dead for a few days."

"Has Lilith been back?" I questioned, turning my attention back to him.

He shook his head. "No one has seen her since she left to look for Anniel in the Summit."

"Probably for the best," I replied. "I almost killed her once she set me free."

He nodded. "Damian told me while we were hiding out in the bunker. I couldn't blame you if you did, though. She put you through hell."

"No one understands that if Anniel doesn't meld with her other self and we have to fight, we will tear the universe apart doing it," I declared, looking at Asmodeus. "It's why they separated us."

"What does that mean?" he asked in return.

"It means that if she doesn't find the part of herself where she is split to fix it, I will have to kill her before she ever gets a chance to try and fight me," I explained.

"Can you do that, though?" he inquired, leaning forward. "Can you really kill her? After everything throughout the years. Her human trials and all. Can you really bring yourself to be the one to end her?"

"I don't know," I responded, leaning against the counter I stood at. "But I won't put that on either of the kids' shoulders when it comes down to it. Damian has enough baggage hanging over his head, and Luxina… she had to basically kill her brother for her to be whole again. And I don't think I could let one of you either without feeling some type of way, you know?"

"Our parents really screwed us all the way up," Asmodeus proclaimed, popping a grape in his mouth. "And the generation that followed. All over some stupid games because they were having a marital spat."

"Talk about family drama," I added, rolling my eyes. "We are a freaking soap opera."

I started heading out of the kitchen.

"Where are you going?" Asmodeus asked.

"Outside before Samael breaks out a whip and starts cracking it at everyone," I joked. "You better soon as well before he sends a hunting party after you."

Asmodeus stood to attention and raised his hand in a salute. "Sir, yes, sir!"

"Cute," I smirked.

Asmodeus laughed, and I walked out the front door and into the sunshine.

"Well, aren't you a sight for sore eyes?" Metatron declared, walking up to me and playfully punching my shoulder. "We didn't expect to see you crawl out of bed for at least a week."

"Yeah, I will reserve that kind of sleep for when I am dead," I joked back. "How's the training coming along?"

"A lot better than it had been," Metatron replied. "Even though it was a lie that you were spouting to Damian the other day about the Nephilim and their untouched angelic powers, you turned out to be right."

"Wait, what?" I asked. "They *do* have powers?"

Metatron nodded. "I mean, it makes sense that they do. They're half angel."

"Did they have to do anything special to unlock them?" I asked, watching all of the Nephilim closely and seeing their powers shine from their skin.

"I think Starfire gave them something," Metatron answered. "Not sure."

"Well, as long as their powers are now active," I said, watching them spar with the angels. "Would that make them our nieces and nephews or cousins?" I asked.

"It makes them a powerful ally," Samyaza replied, walking up to me. "Nice to see you again, Incaendiel. It's been a few days. I heard... things happened and came to see for myself."

"Yeah, it's been a long week," I huffed. "I don't think there's been a longer week since the first week of creation."

"I didn't expect you to be cracking jokes knowing Alpha has taken your mate with him off to the Summit," Samyaza chided.

"If I don't make jokes, I burn shit down and kill people," I remarked in return. "Jokes are safer for everybody."

"Duly noted," Samayaza replied, cocking his head to the side in acknowledgement. "I arrived to tell you that the few remaining Watchers will be arriving in the next few days and wanted to make sure they would be welcomed and not treated indifferently."

"Indifference is a thing of the past among everyone here, Brother," I declared sincerely. "Everyone is family here. And what happened to all of you was by far one of the worst things Alpha did to any of us."

"And when we join your ranks..." he began.

I could hear the thoughts he didn't want to speak freely. "Yes, you will all become your original, angelic selves. No more vampyric blood for you all, and you don't have to hide in shadows anymore, either."

"I want you to know that's not the only reason we are joining the cause," Samyaza replied, lowering his embarrassed eyes.

"I know. You don't have to worry, Brother," I assured him, patting his shoulder. "Don't try to explain yourselves. We wouldn't be whole without you all."

Samael walked over to join the conversation. "Didn't expect to see either of you," he said, looking between Samyaza and me, with his eyes resting on mine. "Are you well rested?"

I nodded. "About yesterday," I began.

He held up his hand. "Don't explain yourself. We know how difficult all of this has been for you, and all at once. I'm surprised it took this long for you to have a nuclear meltdown. I was expecting it much sooner."

"Not sure if that should offend me or not," I laughed.

"Everything makes so much more sense about you now," he offered. "The reason you couldn't control your power was because you weren't whole, and your asleep self was the one who could. If anyone should be apologetic, it should be us. You didn't deserve the treatment you received growing up in the Summit, and you didn't deserve what you heard from everyone's thoughts yesterday. Had Alpha and Lilith not lied to everyone from the spark of creation, we wouldn't have feared your powers either."

"Even though my memories are unlocked from everything post-creation, there are still some suppressed memories from when I was another being," I replied. "I do know that much. I know I came from another place, but everything is hazy now. Lilith and Alpha suppressed them because it fueled my hatred for Alpha. They were able to wipe them, but not the feelings of hatred against him."

"If we find my book, all of those questions will be answered," Raziel remarked as he walked up to us.

"We haven't seen you in a few days," I replied, giving him a short hug. "Did you find Cain?" I asked, looking around for a new face.

"I did and wanted to make sure it was safe for him to come here since Alpha made his grand appearance yesterday," he said.

"Yeah, even Starfire didn't know her force field was useless against gods," I replied. "But honestly, can you really stop gods?"

"Will he be returning?" Raziel asked.

"No, he got what he wanted," I answered, lowering my eyes and thinking about Anniel.

"She knows too much for Alpha," Raziel insisted. "Will she tell him? Were her orders to be a spy and collect information for him?" he prodded.

"I'm not sure," I stammered, shrugging my shoulders. "At this point, who really knows?"

"Well, we mustn't waste any time then," Raziel said, lifting his fingers to his mouth and whistling.

We all looked at the portal that formed, and Gadreel and Cain walked through, holding a book.

"Are you all ready to find my descendants?" he asked, holding the book up in the air.

"Yes," I replied, waving my hand. "Follow me to the conference room." I looked around at those who were standing with me. "All of you. And gather the key players."

I led Gadreel, Cain, and Raziel into Starfire's cottage and to the conference room. Samyaza followed along with Samael while Metatron rounded up the others. One by one, they all filled the room. Azazel, Raphael, Michael, Metatron, and Praeziel all took a seat in the front rows of the room. Whispers filled my head from an unknown source, and I couldn't make out what they were saying. I looked around the room at those sitting in front of me, and none of their faces gave away that they were thinking anything I couldn't hear.

"Are any of you thinking something, I don't know, quietly?" I asked, peering at everyone.

"Can you think thoughts quietly?" Michael mused.

I shrugged. "I don't know. Never mind," I said, shaking my head.

We all turned our attention to Cain, who stood beside me, looking up at me with curious but fearful eyes.

"So it's true," he proclaimed, continuing his stare. "You're really a god."

I nodded.

"And you *are* going to take down Alpha, right?" he questioned, watching my eyes intently.

"That's the plan," I answered.

"I need you to say it," he insisted. "I need to hear it said in those specific words."

"I am going to destroy Alpha or die trying," I affirmed.

He studied my face before nodding. "Okay," he said, turning his attention to everyone. "You all probably know bits and pieces of my story."

"It was just a few human years ago we learned what Alpha did to you," Samael replied. "We had no idea that Lucifer possessed your body."

Cain smiled. "I loved my brother, Abel, so very much..." he trailed off. "When Lucifer left me, I stood with the rock still in my hand, staring down at his bleeding corpse. Alpha appeared. It just wasn't his voice like that god awful memoir of his states. He looked from Abel, and then to me...

"Cain, what has happened?" Alpha asked, bending down and touching Abel's body lying in the field. "He is dead."

"I don't know," Cain stuttered. "I wasn't in control of my body, and it was like someone else was doing everything."

"What do you remember being said?" Alpha inquired, standing up and facing Cain.

"Something about the garden," Cain replied. "That's all I can remember, and then Abel was struck down dead."

Alpha sighed. "It is going to be a hard road ahead for you," he began. "People are going to see you as a murderer and blame you for his death, no matter what you say."

"But I didn't do it!" Cain protested.

"I believe you, my child," Alpha responded, placing his hand on Cain's cheek. "So, I will bless you with protection so no one can ever try to retaliate against you for the crime you did not commit. But I am afraid you can no longer live here. You will have to go out into the world and find a new place for you to live. Your parents will not understand what happened here."

"They will if you tell them!" Cain implored, hitting his knees. *"Please, my Lord. Show me mercy and explain to them what happened."*

"I am showing you mercy," Alpha replied, touching Cain's forehead with the palm of his hand. *"You will bear a mark, and everyone who sees the mark will recognize you as Cain and know you are protected by me."*

Alpha's palm burned into Cain's forehead, and when he was done marking him, he disappeared, leaving Cain alone in the field to explain what happened to his brother.

We all looked at Cain as he raised his bangs from his forehead to show us the mark Alpha had left behind.

"And that mark made you immortal?" I asked, pointing at his forehead.

He nodded. "Nothing earthly can kill me, and I haven't attempted anything celestial to test."

"What does your mark have to do with your descendants?" Raphael inquired.

"My descendants all bear the mark as a birthmark," he replied.

"How many descendants do you have?" Metatron asked, raising his eyebrows.

"Too many to count," Cain answered. "After the flood, I started my bloodline up again as a means to one day stop Alpha. I know some of them were saved from the flood waters, but not all. I helped them form the first order of protectors over humanity. I gave them my book, and it was passed down through just one single part of my bloodline to where it is now."

"Anniel's human family?" Samael affirmed, leaning forward intently.

"Yes, the people who took her in when she was born," he replied, flipping his book open. "According to my records, they are the Asher family in Tennessee."

"But Anniel didn't live in Tennessee," I interjected, shaking my head in disagreement. "It was New Salem where her mother lived."

"Correct," he declared with a nod. "But she is no longer there. And she is cloaked from me as well. I know you were hoping I could find her, but she has some strong magic protecting her. I don't know what kind of magic it is that could prevent a blood bond search or even Alpha from finding her. But it's old and strong."

"Then how does any of this help?" Raphael interrupted. "If you can't find her, we still won't find the book."

"The Asher family will know how to find her," he replied. "Her brother, Harrison, has kept in contact with her from here and there. Even though she left the Diakonian Order because she married outside of the family rules, he still makes sure to check in on her since their mother died."

"So, who do we send to fetch the book then?" Azazel asked, looking around at everyone. "It can't be just any angel. We would have to be able to trust them inherently."

"Well it can't be any of us because we have all this shit going on here," I answered. "Does anyone have a suggestion?"

"Why not Raziel?" Michael asked. "It *is* his book."

"Alpha will probably expect that," I replied, shaking my head.

"Damian has spent a fair amount of time on Earth," Metatron offered. "He could go."

"Out of the question," I replied. "He's a sitting duck by himself for Alpha to take for himself."

Raphael raised his hand, and I looked over at him. "What about Ariel?" he asked. "She was one of the fallen angels, so she could assimilate pretty easily as a human."

"How do we test her to make sure she is loyal?" Azazel chimed in. "I mean, don't get me wrong. I believe everyone here is loyal, but you can never be too careful."

"Bring her in," I replied and started walking to the door.

"Where are you going?" Samael asked, turning his head around as I walked by.

"I will be right back," I reassured, turning my head to speak to them as I walked. "I just got to grab something."

I walked out of the room and bounded up the stairs to my room. I opened the door quietly so I wouldn't wake up Damian and walked over to one of the dressers. I opened the drawer and pulled out the flaming sword Reikal had adjusted for me.

Damian stirred in the bed. "What's going on?" he asked, sitting up and rubbing his eyes.

"Nothing," I whispered, shutting the drawer back. "You can go back to sleep."

"Nah, I am awake now," he said, sliding his feet off the bed. "What are you doing with that?"

"Testing loyalty," I declared, walking out of the room. "You coming?" I asked.

Damian followed behind me as I made my way back to the conference room. Ariel was already waiting at the front of the room. Terror filled her face when she saw my sword.

"The flaming sword," Samyaza murmured, marveling at the blade.

"I didn't do anything!" Ariel protested, holding her hands up defensively. "Please don't kill me!"

"Incaendiel, what's that for?" Samael demanded, standing from his seat and walking over to her.

I stopped in my tracks and looked around at everyone. Their eyes were all full of fear. I handed the sword over to Damian.

"Take it up to her, unsheath it, and hand it to her," I ordered gently.

Damian nodded and walked it over to her, doing as I instructed. He held it out for her to grab, and everyone in the room relaxed.

"I don't understand," she stammered nervously.

"Pick it up and bring it to life," I instructed, pointing at the hilt.

She hesitated before grabbing it from Damian's hand and willed the sword to life. Flames leapt from the blade.

"She's loyal," I proclaimed, walking up to her and gently taking it from her.

Damian handed me the sheath, and I put it back inside of it and tied it to my side.

"How do you know?" Michael asked, puzzled. "We all can wield the sword."

Metatron snapped his fingers. "That little warlock Reikal put some magic on it to make it unwieldable by anyone who isn't loyal to Incaendiel," Metatron replied, remembering when we had spoken to Reikal.

"We have a task for you to complete, and now that we are sure you are loyal to me, we can tell you what it is," I explained, looking at Ariel and changing the subject. "We need you to go to Tennessee and befriend the Asher family. They are descendants of Cain and have the Book of Raziel. We need the book."

"What if Alpha," she began.

"Alpha doesn't know about them and can't find Anniel's mother to get the book," I replied. "They've tried finding it and have failed. So it is safe for you to attempt."

"And if I fail?" she asked, glancing at the sword at my side.

"If you fail, then it's back to the drawing board," I answered, placing my hand tenderly on her shoulder. "I'm not a mindless murderer like Alpha. I do not punish." Ariel began to walk past me when I gently grabbed her hand. "You do not need to fear me, Ariel. You are still my sister. I wouldn't hurt you."

She nodded and left the room.

I returned my gaze to everyone in the room who was watching me. "I am not Alpha. When will you all trust that I am not going to hurt anyone?" I asked. "It feels like, with every move I make, you all are watching me, waiting for me to be just like him, even though you tell me you trust me and trust in me. Which is it? Because a few minutes ago, you all believed I was going to hurt Ariel. I can't be your leader if you don't put all of your trust in me, which is a big ask, I know. Alpha and Lilith screwed up our heads and we can't put our trust in hardly anyone. But you have been with me since the war. Nothing has changed. I haven't changed. I am still me."

They all lowered their eyes, ashamed.

I closed my eyes and recomposed myself. "Cain, is there anything else we need to know?" I asked, changing the subject.

He laughed. "Where would you like me to start?" he mused.

"The beginning, I guess?" I answered. "I don't know. We need to know as much as we can because we have been spoon-fed lies our entire lives."

He flipped his book to the very first page. "I copied this down from the Book of Raziel before giving it to my grown firstborn," Cain answered and began to read.

Chapter 18

IN THE BEGINNING...

On the sixth day of creation, Alpha and Omega created man. Omega released the waters of creation into the valley of the Garden of Eden to soften the dirt. Alpha gathered the dirt to shape and mold just as he had done with the angels, with the exception of using stardust for them. Alpha and Omega each touched his forehead, and the mud became human flesh. Omega then breathed the spark of life into his mouth, and man was born. Adam opened his eyes. Unlike the idea that Adam was created a full-grown man, Adam was born as a child who aged and grew much slower than what was taught for human years.

Alpha and Omega spent a lot of time fostering Adam's growth and teaching him how his species was meant to flourish. In essence, they were his parents, much like how they were the parents of the angels, except he did not have celestial powers. Adam was alone for a very long time in the garden without another human, but he didn't mind when he was younger. Time moved differently in the garden than it did on the earth Alpha and Omega had created together. Time in the garden was celestial since it was set gated just outside the realm of the Summit, a gift from Tiamat created by the fey. The years were incomprehensible, differing between celestial time and mortal time. Where everything grew slower in the celestial realm but aged faster on Earth, the years went by quickly in the garden. One celestial day could equal years on Earth, but since it sat outside of space and time, it couldn't be calculated in earthly time.

Adam soon started to become lonely. Yes, Alpha and Omega set aside time to visit him either together or separately, and the angels even came by to play with him or teach him things, but the time periods when he was alone in the garden grew heavy on his mind. And then, the fall happened. Alpha and Lilith had their squabble in front of Adam when Alpha had erased her from his mind. And then they settled on a game to play. They told their children the garden was hidden in a secret location when, in truth, they just hid the entrance to it. Only they could access the garden, and no one else, so that they could keep the charade up, and the children would choose sides on who to love more.

For a brief period, Alpha tried to create humans without Lilith and failed miserably. They convinced everyone that Alpha had to create Eve from the rib of Adam to bring her forth into life. However, that was also not true. It wasn't Alpha's ability to spark life into creation. When Adam had learned Alpha was trying to make him a mate, the very next time he saw Lilith, he begged her to help Alpha create Eve for him. Lilith couldn't refuse his request and agreed to help bring Eve to life. Adam showed her the body Alpha had made using his blood to wet the earth and his rib to try to bring life into her. Lilith breathed life into Eve, and Eve came to be.

Lilith, still bitter and indifferent to Alpha, picked the fruit of the Tree of Knowledge of Good and Bad and gave it to Adam and Eve to eat. With the power of the Tree of Life flowing through their veins from the fruit they ate every day, they had become little demigods. This enraged Alpha. Once again, he and Lilith fought over what she had done. To punish Lilith for her misdeeds, he banished Adam and Eve from the garden, and once their lips tasted the mortal fruit growing on earth, their bodies became mortal and began to age more rapidly than they were accustomed.

Alpha was always punishing Lilith by using her own compassion and love against her for the creations she coveted so dearly. After every toxic deed he ever committed against her, he would love bomb her and beg her for her forgiveness, and most times, she would concede. Both the angels in the Summit and the fallen ones in the Glade were led to believe that their parents were separated, but it was only partially true. They often met in secret. One of those meetings led to them agreeing that Adam and

Eve could have children. They had not been created to be fruitful and multiply like the other men of the earth, as Eve had been created barren. They had been created to remain innocent and pure. However, they agreed that the two needed children since they no longer had the loving embrace of their mother and father. The next greatest love, apart from having parents, is becoming a parent.

But where there is willful ignorance, there is also deceit. Alpha had removed Lilith's memory from Adam's memory long before Eve had been created. So he didn't remember her after she left the Summit. Lilith took this opportunity to foster a relationship that was much more than creator and creation, and she took Adam as a lover. She didn't think that Alpha knew, but Alpha knew everything in his universe, no matter how hard she tried to hide things. She was created from Alpha and, therefore, was always a part of him. Right before the creation of Eve, Lilith and Adam had one more fling, and then it was over.

At least it was over for Adam. After helping Alpha create Eve, Lilith realized she was pregnant with Adam's child. She hid the pregnancy well, too, because none of the fallen ones were ever privy to her visits unless she requested, and for nine months, under the guise of a broken heart from her divorce with their father, she hid away until the baby was born. She ferried the child off to Adam and convinced Eve that her firstborn child had been delivered by the divine, as opposed to her having to have the pangs of childbirth. Lilith believed she had kept the child secret enough that Alpha wouldn't have noticed. But Alpha knows everything, and his punishment to Eve was to make her child with Adam suffer. So he chose Cain and Abel on purpose to be Anniel's first incarnation, so Cain would have the blood of the innocent on his hands while possessed by Lucifer. His final act was to give Cain a mark that would pass through all of his bloodline, so every person would not only recognize who he was but also recognize the bloodline where murder began, ostracizing them until people eventually forgot after they believed the flood had wiped out his family lineage. Alpha didn't know that even though he had been born mortal, once he laid his hand on Cain, he would turn him immortal and therefore soulless, without a soul to return to the Giving Tree and unable to track. Alpha's interest in him dwindled as the millennia passed, and he soon forgot about Lilith's offspring from her act of betrayal. Even though he knows everything in his universe, sometimes he just doesn't care.

Chapter 19

"IS THAT WHAT you heard being plotted in the garden?" I asked Gadreel once Cain closed the book.

"That is a very minute portion of what I had eavesdropped on in the garden," Gadreel replied, shifting in his seat.

"Please, enlighten us," I ordered, extending my hand for him to join me up front.

"Well," he began as he walked to the front. "You already know about Michael and Lucifer. That was revealed before. I don't know how much you remember about prior to the fall, though," he said directly to me.

"I had the wall brought down for the memories of being awakened and put to sleep for training," I replied.

"What about your past life memories? Have any of those surfaced yet?" he prodded.

"No, not yet," I responded, and the whispers began again. I glanced around the room, but everyone's face was solemn as they prepared for Cain to speak.

"Alpha and Lilith needed a couple of guards at the door of the garden whenever they had talks among themselves or talks with you and Anniel," he explained as the whispers grew louder but still unintelligible. "Raziel and I were there when they orchestrated the fall with you in the room and then without you in the room."

The whispers stopped, and my head snapped in his direction. "What do you mean?" I asked.

"The plan they came up with regarding Anniel and you was just the plan for you to hear," he recounted further. "Once you were out of the picture of making the plan, their tune changed quite a bit."

"Show me," I demanded, walking over to him and holding my hand out. "Put your forehead to my hand and think about it."

He did as instructed and leaned into my hand. My head was immediately filled with his memories.

"Are they out of earshot?" Alpha asked, not moving to look to draw attention to himself.

Omega watched us leave. "Yes," she answered, turning toward Alpha.

"We need a better plan," Alpha began, holding a hand up to his chin from his crossed arms. "And it needs to involve more than just us, too. We need others involved."

"We already have Lucifer and Michael in the know of what is happening," Omega replied. "Lucifer is bitter about Incaendiel being chosen over him. And Michael... well, he has made it known that he will put Incaendiel down if we need him to."

"Those two won't be enough, and we need to make sure they are here alongside Anniel and stay behind for the fall," Alpha mused, tapping his finger against his lips.

"What about Metatron?" Omega asked, serenely rocking back and forth where she stood. "He would be a fine leader to have in on the plan."

"No," Alpha declined, with a shake of his head. "Nearly all of the angels would choose his side if he fell, and we are back to square one."

"What about Samael and Azazel?" Omega offered, raising an eyebrow. "We could let them in on everything like Lucifer and Michael. They are the first and second command and would fall with me anyway."

Alpha smiled widely. "Perfect," he replied. "Gadreel?" he called, looking off to the entrance to the garden.

Gadreel stepped within the gate of the garden. "Yes, Father?" he asked.

"Send for Samael and Azazel to come to the garden," Alpha ordered.

"Yes, Father," Gadreel replied.

I broke contact with his head and dropped my hand. "That's a lie!" I seethed, stepping back from him.

"It's not a lie," Gadreel replied calmly. "I have no reason to lie to you, Brother."

I didn't want to make eye contact with them, but I did anyway. I looked at Samael and Azazel.

"Is it true?" I asked, staring keenly at the two.

Samael swallowed hard. Azazel sat wide-eyed, unable to answer.

"It is true?!" I demanded.

"Is what true?" Samael finally answered, more softly than I expected.

"You knew the whole time," I asked, walking over to them. "You knew the whole time and didn't bother telling me?"

"I was following orders, In—"

"Fuck your orders!" I barked, leaning in nose to nose with his face. "I was your brother! You have had this whole time to tell me what was happening that I couldn't remember." I looked at Azazel. "And you!" I looked at Michael. "And you."

I tore the flaming sword from my side and unsheathed it.

"What are you doing?" Damian demanded, rising from his seat.

I swallowed hard. "Take it," I ordered, holding the sword out to Samael.

Samael looked at me and then at the sword, but didn't move.

"Take it!" I yelled, pumping the sword out in front of him.

"Does my word mean nothing to you?" Samael asked, standing and staring me down. "Have I not proven my loyalty to you now? Yes, I fucked up in the past. But it was the past."

"It's not the past when you have been lying this whole entire time to me," I replied, fighting the urge to bring forth my powers and smite him.

"I haven't lied about anything!" Samael hollered, becoming defensive in his posture.

"Omission is betrayal, Brother," I stated, a tear slipping down my face. "Take the god damned sword!"

Samael grabbed the sword, and it flared to life with fire. He handed it over to Azazel, and the flame stayed steady. She handed the sword back to me.

"You asked us to trust in you," Samael snarled, looking me up and down. "We ask the same in return." He patted her arm, and she followed him as he left the room.

"So you're going to gaslight me?" I asked, a laugh slipping out nervously. "This is my fault for not trusting your word when, for millennia, you were sneaking around behind my back with Lilith about me. You knew about everything. And you didn't bother to tell me even after your 'duties' and 'orders' no longer held merit to Lilith or Alpha."

"Do you think you and your little precious family were the only ones whom Alpha and Lilith manipulated?" Samael demanded, spinning around on his heels and walking back toward me while Azazel tugged on his arm to stop.

He walked up to me and stood directly in my face, waiting for me to make a move.

"When they gave us an order, it wasn't out of obedience we saw it through," he hissed. "Free will and the right to choose is bullshit when it comes to those two. We could *not* tell you, even after we joined your ranks. We are still under whatever they did to us, like you were. We weren't even allowed to think about it because they feared you could read our minds. We still can't. We are still their puppets."

"Were there any others?" I asked, not moving and holding my ground.

"If there were, then they were sworn to not say anything about it, just like us," he answered. "We weren't even allowed to talk to Lucifer and Michael about it."

"Did you want to do it?" I questioned, stepping back.

"In the beginning, yes," he revealed, shamefully rubbing the top of his head. "Like Michael and Lucifer, I was jealous of you. I was jealous you were chosen. I was jealous you were so powerful that your powers couldn't be contained. I despised you. And I knew one day, you would outrank me like it was always intended." He stopped for a minute and looked over at Azazel, and she nodded her head. "We watched you fight so hard to win Anniel over through all of those years. And it wasn't really just to make her remember to love you over and over, which was Alpha testing her loyalty, by the way. I can say that. He wanted to see how deep the taproot of his control over her went. And you two beat them at their own game. You fought hard to get us home and to get everyone back together. That's what I admired about you. That's what changed my mind about you and my point of view, and every jealous bone in my body started to buck back at Alpha and Mo—" he stopped briefly and inhaled. "*Lilith.* But I still couldn't tell you the truth. All I could do was pledge my loyalty to you to show you that I would follow you to the ends of the earth if I needed to, because you did love us as your brothers and sisters, while our parents just used us over and over."

He stopped for a moment, and the room was silent. "The reason we weren't trusted to remain silent is because they knew our devotion outweighed our obedience. They knew we would cave and tell you everything because we didn't have a deep-seated hatred of you as Michael and Lucifer did. Their jealousy ran through to their bones because they were created as twins as well, but not like you two. Their obedience was the make it or break it with Alpha and Lilith, and they had to prove to them all the time that they were better than any of us and would follow them to the ends of the earth or be banished."

"It wasn't always solely obedience. At times, Lucifer and I questioned what they had us doing. They threatened to kick us out all the time," Michael added in reply to Samael's confession. "If we didn't follow orders, we lost our light, and we lost our wings. We would be thrown into the abyss and locked away for our crimes against them. And once that happened, if we didn't fight tooth and nail to get back in their good graces and grovel at their feet, they would take our grace as well."

I felt for the nearest chair and took a seat, running my hands over my face.

"You have been the only one of us who was truly free, even if on the inside, you were caged," Azazel chimed in, walking over and kneeling down in front of me. "The way you would speak about Alpha and vehemently stand against him. And we all knew that. We all knew that you couldn't be punished like we were. If he could punish you the same way he threatened us, then he would have done it so long ago. We didn't understand it completely, but we knew you would be the one to save us and set us free, Brother."

"Look, there's more to see," Gadreel interrupted, walking over to me. "And you will understand what they mean." He knelt before me, and I placed my hand on his forehead.

*"I have **had** it with these two," Alpha raged, throwing boulders around in the garden.*

Omega stood by quietly.

"If we can't bring them forth and they love us as their parents, then what is the point in keeping them around?" Alpha bellowed, kicking the shrubbery beside him. "We wanted a lineage, not children to overthrow us."

Omega swallowed. "What do you wish to do then?"

"What we should have done a long time ago," Alpha muttered, walking over to Anniel and me.

"Lamut!" Alpha shouted.

Nothing happened.

"Aphes!" he uttered, a bit louder.

"Pasu!" he bellowed as Omega gasped.

However, Anniel and I still stood without any harm coming to us.

"Why are they not dying?" Alpha demanded, fuming and muttering.

"Maybe because they are old gods and we cannot destroy the energy we gave them?" Omega offered with a shrug.

"I have slain a few old gods in my time, Omega," Alpha spat, glaring at her. "I am pretty sure I know what I am doing."

"They were the first gods of existence!" Omega hissed. "The first pantheon ever to spring forth. They are not like the others!"

"All gods can die," Alpha muttered. "I will find a way to put an end to them, even if it takes me billions of years!" he hissed.

"Why do you hate them so much when they are your children?" Omega demanded, shaking her head in disbelief.

"Barbelo's power was meant to be mine!" Alpha yelled. "I was deceived!"

"So you are jealous that your grandmother chose your children to bestow a gift upon instead of you?" Omega asked. "Pathetic. If you treated them more like your children and less like a weapon, they would most likely bend to your will and fall in line."

"Not that one," he said, pointing his finger at me. "That one was born with hatred in his heart for me."

"Well, you shouldn't have slain their parents!" she hissed. "They watched you do it before you put them to sleep to take their power from their bodies. Tiamat told us to gather the energy of the dying sun god, but that wasn't enough for you. You wanted more and more and more like you always desire, and instead, you destroyed their universe to gain them."

"It was already dying!" Alpha remarked.

"But they were not!" Omega hissed. "They had plans to fuel another universe until you took these two, and their universe collapsed before they could escape. So many souls, Alpha!"

"And those souls were brought back with me to our Giving Tree," Alpha protested. "They will still have life!"

"Those souls weren't meant for our universe, and you know it!" Omega refuted with angry, wide eyes. "Those souls were meant to recycle in their universe alone. So now, so many of them will incarnate and not feel as if they belong because they don't belong in this universe!"

"Whatever," Alpha muttered. "Mark my words, Omega, I will find a way for those two to die, and I will be the one to put an end to them, and I will take their power for myself."

I removed my hand from Gadreel's forehead and sat quietly.

"What did you see?" Metatron asked.

"Before the fall, Alpha tried to undo his and Anniel's existence," Damian replied, leaning forward in his chair. "He couldn't because of how old their power is."

"And their power is very old," Azrael interrupted, walking into the room.

Everyone turned to watch her walk up to the front and join us.

"How old?" Samael asked.

"They were the first ever born gods along with their parents," she answered, stepping up to the front of the room. "And I do mean born and not created."

"You know where I come from?" I inquired.

"Yes and no," she replied. "Mother has told me the story of your universe. At that time, we didn't govern the life and death cycle of it. We understood death needed to be a part of the life cycle, but your civilization was so grand. Far more advanced than any we have ever witnessed since. Your universe was the epitome of dreamers, of seekers, of knowledge, and of hope. So we left it be in hopes its existence would inspire the rest of the universes to spring forth in life."

"I need to know more," I pleaded. "Will you call your mother here so I can speak with her? So we can learn who we are since they stole away our memories."

"My boy, I thought you would never ask," Maveth chimed in, materializing before us.

"Did you know my real parents?" I urged, looking up at her from my chair.

She nodded. "I did. And they were so wonderful."

Chapter 20

"SO MANY CREATION stories begin with in the beginning because it was the beginning of that specific universe. We are starting at the moment of conception of life after death," Maveth began:

There was nothing but darkness, and in that darkness, I existed and brought forth my first reaper, Azrael. And we waited for more than just death to exist for what seemed like aeons before the first shade formed. Her name was Tulu-Ama, the Mother of the Deep. She was the womb of the waters of Zul'Tama, the first universe that sparked to life instead of being forged like many others, such as this one in which Alpha exists. Like many primordial beings, she had no face or form. She was the dark matter that spread like water in the deepest parts of the ocean. She was the whisper of potential, and from her flowed the first currents of energy and the pulse that would become the heartbeat of time itself.

Once aware of her sentience, her voice emerged like echoes of musical notes, whispering in the void with her first breath of life. From this breath emerged Kharuun, the Howling Voice of the Storm. He split the void with a shattering wind of a screaming roar, becoming the howler of the skies. His thunderous cries ripped through the silence as he floated across the inky abyss of nothingness, finding Tulu-Ama. They danced wildly together, and he gave her shape and form with his winds of chaos. As they brushed upon one another, lightning sparked within the thunderous cloud of desire. That flicker created the first creation of heat, and from the steam of meeting the air and water, the first spark of creation came to be as Is'hari, the First Flame and Breath of Fire. Another primordial being who was not created but ignited from the depths of the soulless expanses of nothingness.

Is'hari was the breath of glowing warmth who brought light to the dance with Tulu-Ama and Kharuun, splitting night from day. Together, the three of them awakened life among the inky dark, shaping and molding the galaxies within the void. However, their universe began to grow unstable, wild from the pure energy drifting through the expanse. What was brought forth between the three of them would crumble back into ashen nothingness. But just as the universe knew it needed the three of them to start creation, it knew it needed a fourth. It needed more than just a spark of heat to turn creation into a lasting thought. Vahr-Zhul sprang forth from the deep, born from the ashes of failed sparks and the heat of exploding stars. He was the sacred flame who brought with him a purifying and cleansing flame. He was the destroyer, but also the renewer. He was the judge and the guardian. He did not flicker. Instead, he burned, and wherever he walked, the old was burned away so new could be brought forth. From his flames, the expanses were illuminated, and through their combined fire, they brought forth creation, soon to be followed by more gods and more universes. Together, he and Is'hari formed what would become known as the Guardians of Light with the birth of their twin children, Caelvryn and Valiryen.

The union between Is'hari and Vahr-Zhul was never meant to be. One of them was divine purpose, while the other was pure chaos. However, the magnetic pull between the two, no matter how they fought, caused them to collide in burning stillness and flickering wilderness. Their collision brought forth Valiryen, the Crowned Flame, and Caelvryn, the Silent Ember. Valiryen had the totality of her father and blazed with radiance, bringing judgement, seeing through the smoke and mirrors of lies to the bare truth. Caelvryn was born with the cold fire of stillness. He was the gentle ending to things with a chill that preserved what shouldn't be burned, while Valiryen seared away the rest, he being the Flame of Frost and she being the Flame of Transformation. Falsehood disappeared under her while remembrance remained with him, he wielding sorrowful fire while she wielded sorrowful wisdom. They weaved through the universe, life and death, heat and stillness, what was and could be.

The Tale of the Ashen Sky speaks of the time when their mortal realm was still young and reckless. Much like the tales of the bible, the world was burning itself with its own hunger. But unlike Alpha with his unrelenting judgment and fury, Valiryen knew she would unravel the universe with her fury if she went unchecked. So she asked her twin, Caelvryn, to still the winds, silence the sky, and let the world pause so she could cleanse it properly without bringing destruction beyond their fixing. Caelvryn raised his hand, and through his power of stillness, as that of quiet falling snow, he froze time. Everything fell silent and stopped, including the cries and laments of man, trapping them mid-breath. And she burned, unraveling every misdeed their mortals had made without harming them in wrath. Caelvryn and Valiryen stood in the ashes and, once they realized their task was done, left together. And the world began again, renewed.

"So Anniel is Is'hari?" I asked when Maveth was finished.

She nodded. "And you are Vahr-Zhul. Luxina is Valiryen and Damian is Caelvryn."

"How did they gather our power?" I inquired. "Were we really dying?"

Maveth nodded. "You were using every bit of your power to try and sustain the universe as it began to fold in. You would have died trying, as well. Alpha had slain your parents and caused the universe to begin the cycle of renewal and give its energy to other places. Before Alpha learned about Valiryen and Caelvryn, you had already absorbed them back, so they would be safe from him in case he tried to take their power for himself. It was during your memory suppression that he learned about the power overflow and why you were too strong to contain. It's also why you were able to temper yourself better once the children were born. You didn't have all of the extra power swirling around trying to bust forth."

"And then he made the plans for us to create the kids here so he could lay claim to their power," I stated.

"Yes, and the rest is history," she replied.

"And without us?" I asked.

"Light and life of the universe would cease to exist," Maveth explained. "If Alpha destroys you, he destroys everything and everyone, including himself."

"Does he not know he will extinguish himself as well?" Damian chimed in, shifting in his seat. He had been so quiet that I forgot he was even in the room.

"He thinks if he absorbs enough power, he will be able to keep everything going himself," Maveth replied. "His final act would be to absorb the power of you four so he can be the support its needs. However, he doesn't understand the old power you all contain. If he tries, it will rip him to shreds because everything your names stood for is everything he is against. Destruction and renewal, tempered justice and judgment, the order you bring to the cosmos he stands against with his chaos and unadulterated hatred and jealousy."

"How many of us absorbed would rip him to shreds?" I pondered. "One, two, all?"

"At least two," Maveth answered.

"Will it take all four of us to keep the cosmos in order?" I asked tentatively.

"As long as two of you exist, the Guardians of Light will continue on through offspring," she responded.

"The Guardians of Light has a nice ring to it," Samyaza interjected.

"Alpha mentioned taking the souls from Zul'Tama and adding them to the Giving Tree of souls for this universe," Damian began. "What does that mean?"

"I am sure Sophia talked to you about starseeds, correct?" Maveth inquired.

"Briefly. She didn't exactly explain them, just that they were 'extraterrestrial' souls," Damian replied.

"Lilith mentioned them briefly to me as well," I interjected. "She said that once our powers were activated, they would be activated as well."

"Those starseeds she spoke about are all of the souls from your universe. They are the dreamwalkers, the prophets, and many more other things in this world, and you are the power sustaining those souls, not Alpha," Maveth explained.

"So the prophet we are to look for, who is named Eva, she is a starseed, right?" I asked.

"I cannot discuss Eva until we all know she is safe and sound," Maveth replied.

"Why not?" Damian queried, scrunching his face.

"Alpha is always everywhere listening when you least suspect it," Maveth answered.

"Are we sure that Alpha is priming himself to absorb powers, or could he be priming Adam?" Samael asked.

"That is also a possibility," Maveth replied.

"Would the same thing happen to Adam that would happen to Alpha?" Azazel questioned. "Would he rip apart as well?"

"I'm not sure. He might or he might not, considering he was created from the Guardians' blood. It depends on how things unfold for Adam and how his powers are activated," Maveth replied.

"Thank you for speaking with us," I said, standing and bowing.

"I wish you the best of luck. I would hate to exist with only my reaper angels and nothing else once more," Maveth stated as she dematerialized.

We all looked at Azrael with that last remark.

"You can't kill death," she explained.

The low whispers began again as I looked around for the source.

"Ok, who is thinking something that I cannot hear?" I demanded.

"So you hear them too?" Damian asked, sighing in exasperation, but also put to ease. "I thought I was going insane."

Azrael smiled. "So the whispers have begun for you?" she asked.

"Yes, what do they mean?" I questioned in return.

"You hear your mother from Zul'Tama calling for you," she explained, and then turned to Damian. "And you hear your grandmother. She may have been slain by Alpha, but her spirit still lives on through you all."

"What was Zul'Tama like?" I asked, leaning against a chair.

Azrael smiled. "It was so magical and beautiful there. Alpha tried to recreate the beauty of the universe at the Summit. He wanted to find a way to make you more comfortable when you were awake. Finally, he had the Garden of Eden fashioned for you, and while it was the most beautiful and harmonious thing he ever created, it still didn't feel like home for you because it wasn't home," she explained.

"So that's why Anniel and I loved being in the garden and why it was gifted to us by Alpha," I replied, finally understanding.

The whispering began again, and I quickly looked around.

"It's back, right?" Azrael asked, raising an eyebrow.

I nodded.

"Listen to the call," she replied. "Listen with your mind, heart, and soul. She has a message for you."

"How?" I questioned. "I don't know how to decipher the whispers."

"Feel the whispers," she answered.

Feel the whispers, I thought to myself. *Feel the whispers. Feel the whispers.*

I closed my eyes and focused on my breathing. The whispers grew louder but were still inaudible. The sounds of everything else drowned out the words. I could hear the breathing of those in the room, the sounds from outside, but not the words. And then everything went quiet. I opened my eyes, and everyone in the room wasn't moving.

"You needed stillness," Damian said, standing from his seat and walking over to me.

"Did you just freeze time?" I asked, bewildered.

"It made sense when Maveth was telling the story of Caelvryn. She said he had the power to slow down time and freeze it. When Adam threw that sword at me, it felt different when I dodged it. I thought I had moved so fast that it felt like time had slowed down. But I had actually slowed it down to dodge it. So to normal people, it looks like I am moving really fast, but in truth, I have slowed down time around me," he explained.

"It did look as if you slowed down time," I concurred. "And this," I began, looking around the room. "This proves it."

"We needed stillness to hear beyond," he said, with a shrug.

I nodded and closed my eyes. The whispers began again and grew louder, much louder than they had ever been, until I heard a voice.

"My dear, Vahr-Zhul," the voice whispered. "I have been trying for so long to speak with you, my child."

"Mother?" I asked as emotions welled that I didn't know I could feel.

"Yes, my sweet Firefly," she replied. "It's Mother," she cooed.

And all at once, memories rushed forth of Zul'Tama. I could see everything Azrael had described. There weren't enough words to describe the breathtaking marvel our universe had once been. The colors were brighter there, as if I had been looking through painted glass my entire life. I could see my mother, a darkened cloud gathered into stardust and bioluminescence as my father swam around her. A bright light flowed around me as Is'hari brushed my side, our energies in perfect harmony. My fire burned bright and powerful without causing any harm. Valiryen and Caelvryn danced through the sky, leaving trails of fire and ice in their wake. It was peaceful, serene. There wasn't a single feeling of doom or chaos. We all existed as a thriving unanimity. I watched other universes begin to materialize as our power fueled the cosmos, inspiring the birth and rise of gods. There wasn't animosity or hatred, and it was utopic, to say the least.

And then we saw a dark cloud form over the last universe to be brought into existence. I could feel the wicked tendrils of energy weaving their web through the air. We watched the universe unfold and Alpha materialize as nothing but pure light. And then from him another light sprang forth. Omega. But the light was deceitful, for there was nothing illuminating about the two. There was a deep-seated darkness within them, and I could see it.

"We need to purify or extinguish them before they wreak havoc on the cosmos," I said to Mother and Father.

"Give them a chance, Vahr-Zhul," Mother cooed. "They are new and need time to find their place."

"I can feel the wickedness of their hearts, Mother," I protested. "They will bring nothing but the end to all if they are not dealt with."

"Listen to your mother, Vahr-Zhul," Father ordered. "We must give them a chance. It is the law of the universe."

"But as the Guardians—"

"That is an order!" Father demanded.

"And you were right, my Firefly," Mother breathed as the memory faded. "Alpha did just that, and he started at the beginning of life itself."

"I will right the wrongs he has committed," I assured her. "I will fix this."

"I know you will, love," Mother sweetly replied. "I know you all will. And even though you can't see me or feel me or your father, we will be there with you as the ashes of purification and renewal rain down across the universe."

And the whispering stopped.

"So what now?" Samyaza asked, his voice breaking the stillness in the room.

"Holy crap!" Azazel yelled. "How did you get over there so fast?" she asked, looking at Damian.

"He froze time," Azrael replied with a smile. "It's nice to see you again, Caelvryn."

"Damian is still fine for you to call me," Damian insisted.

"Like Samyaza asked, what now?" Metatron asked, redirecting the room.

"Someone needs to go and find Eva," I replied. "Guard her at all costs."

"Who, though?" Azazel asked. "I don't think another one of the angels out in the world is a good idea."

"I can do it," Raphael offered. "It will be like before when we were guarding Anniel."

"No, we need you here," I replied.

"What about me?" Praeziel interjected, standing up. "I can guard her. I have been among the humans before and know their ways, too. It would be easier for me than for another angel."

Everyone looked at me for an answer.

"What about training?" I asked.

"The Nephilim will follow Samael's orders," he reassured. "They respect him, and plus, I may have threatened them just a bit."

I mulled over it for a bit. "I don't see why not," I answered, with a shrug. "But do we know where she is?"

Silence fell over the room.

"We need Lailah. She is the only one who places the souls," Samael stated, breaking the hushed crowd.

"And we can't get to the Book of Life either since it's in the Summit," Michael added.

"Do you have any idea where Alpha could have hidden Lailah?" I asked Azrael.

"I haven't the slightest idea," Azrael replied with a sigh. "She's not in the Summit. That much I can tell you. And the only other thing I know of that could locate her would be Raziel's book, which we don't have either."

"Wait, what about the Watcher's Eye?" Samael asked, glancing over at Samyaza. "Could that find her?"

Samyaza pondered for a minute. "It might. We could possibly see where she is, although it won't take us to her."

"Where is it?" I asked.

"That's the problem," Samyaza replied. "I haven't seen it since before the Watchers were banished to Stygia. I believe one of the last few times I saw it was the last we saw of the flaming sword."

I hmphed. "Gabriel."

Chapter 21

I WALKED AROUND Lightshade, looking for Gabriel. He wasn't in the millions of rooms in Starfire's cottage, nor in the arenas sparring. My feet began to travel into the forest, and I couldn't help but marvel at the majestic vibe this nature had within the canopy of trees that loomed overhead. I hadn't done any exploring of the place since my arrival, and what better way to explore than looking for Gabriel? I remembered from before the fall how he used to always go off by himself to meditate and commune with those he needed to deliver messages to.

I walked alongside the riverbed, watching the tiny creatures swim through the waters and crawl along the floor where there was shallow water. Birds chirped, and there was something off in the varying types of grasses that made chirping noises, most likely crickets. Butterflies floated in the light breeze, landing on the unique flowers that grew wild within the foliage. It was so peaceful here, and for once, I could feel all of my tension sliding from my shoulders. Lightshade existed outside of time, and I had no idea just how long we had been holed up here, so this brief piece of time I had to myself was calming.

"It's like she made the garden all over, isn't it?" a voice called out, breaking my trance.

"Yes. Yes, just like the garden," I replied, walking over to Gabriel, who was sitting cross-legged in a field of flowers. "I have been looking for you."

"Oh?" he mused, standing up and dusting his pants off. "What do you need?"

"When you stole all the things from the Summit like the flaming sword and Michael's spear," I began, "did you happen to take the Watcher's Eye as well?" I asked.

"Yes, among other things," he answered, walking with me along the river.

"Are they stashed in the Summit or somewhere else?" I pressed, remembering how he went back for his horn.

"They are hidden outside of the Summit," he replied with a laugh. "What do you need it for?" he questioned.

"We were hoping to use it and try and find Lailah," I responded. "We are going to start searching for Eva, and without Lailah or being able to look at Raziel's book or the Book of Life in the Summit, we won't be able to find her."

"Let me go get it," he stated and took off to the sky.

At the sight of his wings, a thought crossed my mind that I hadn't bothered to think of or acknowledge. Do I still have wings? They were usually just always there, and I was aware of them, but since our transformation, I no longer felt the urge to use them. Do I have to will them forth like my power? I shrugged to myself. What better way to take a peek and see while I was alone? I thought about my wings and pushed. Unlike the usual angel wings I had before, wings of fire erupted from my back.

"Holy shit!" Damian squealed, breaking my focus and catching me off guard.

My wings went back into their hiding spot as I turned to face him.

"Do I have wings like that now?" he gushed, glancing over his shoulder.

"I don't know," I answered. "I just now started to think about them. I am sure yours will be like mine. You just have to will them forth."

I watched his face make a strange expression as he focused on his wings. Brilliant, fiery blue wings popped out from behind him.

"Gods have wings?" he ventured as he dropped his wings back into place.

"I don't know," I offered with a shrug. "I have never met one who had them, and let us see them. Alpha or Lilith might have them and just keep them hidden, or just don't know they have them."

"Did you find Gabriel?" he prodded, as he willed his wings in and out, testing out his ability to command them.

"Yes," I replied as I watched him, amused. "He went to go and get the Watcher's Eye."

He fell quiet for a moment.

"Whatcha thinking about?" I asked as we began walking around the forest.

Some deer popped out of the trees to graze, and we quietly watched them while he found the words he was looking for.

"Do you think we can communicate with Luxina the same way we communicated with Tul-Ama?" he asked.

I shook my head. "I don't think so, or else I would have been able to communicate with Anniel by now," I answered. "I think we can hear Tul-Ama because she is in us."

"How is she in us if Alpha took her power?" he inquired, picking up a rock and tossing it at the river water to watch it skip.

"The same reason we have Barbelo in us as well," I responded. "They only gave him what he expected as power since they were old. They reserved the rest for us."

"Do you remember anything else from Zul'Tama?" he asked, skipping another rock across the water as we walked.

"Not really," I replied, rubbing the back of my head. "Just what I saw while talking to Tul-Ama. You?" I asked in return.

He nodded. "I remember everything," he declared.

As I was about to ask him more questions, Gabriel returned, landing in front of us. "Here it is," he said, handing over a purplish stone.

"What else do you have in your stash spot?" I queried with a laugh.

"The answers to that are endless," he replied with a laugh.

"Well, let's get this back to Samyaza," I stated, putting it in my pocket. "Only Watchers can use it."

"Will it work?" Damian asked as we started heading back to the center of Lightshade.

"Maybe, maybe not," Gabriel replied. "It was intended to be used by mortals to help them find us when they needed us."

"But does it find the specific angel they were inquiring about?" Damian pressed, stepping up and over a large fallen tree trunk.

"It did," Gabriel replied, also climbing over the tree.

I jumped over it and landed with a soft thud and asked, "What?" as they just squinted at me with tight-lipped smirks.

"Show off," Gabriel quipped. "So what happens after we find where Lailah is?"

"We go get her and bring her here," I responded.

"And then?" he prodded.

"We find Eva after," I noted. "Praeziel has offered to be her guardian until she activates completely."

"Shouldn't she immediately activate since we have?" Damian inquired.

"I don't know," I answered. "For all we know, she has. I don't know if it's immediate or if it takes time. I just know we need her before Alpha finds her. That's probably who he is looking for instead of Zoe, as he told Beelzebub."

"I didn't think of that," Gabriel remarked. "Everything is always a race against him."

"I know, and it's exhausting," I replied as we stepped through the trees and out into the unsheltered sunlight.

Raphael came running up to us when he saw us emerge from the tree line.

"We have a problem," he stammered, glancing over his shoulder.

"What is it?" I muttered, following his gaze to see if I could make out the problem myself.

"Adam's back," he replied, looking from me to Damian. "He's asking for *him*," he stated, nodding in Damian's direction.

"Did he say what he wanted with him?" I pressed as I scanned the area closely.

Raphael shook his head. "No, he just said he wanted to see Damian," he replied.

"Where is he?" Damian asked, looking around, trying to find him to confront him.

"No," I ordered.

"But—" he began.

"No buts!" I objected, staring at him intently until he got the point.

Damian scowled at me. "Stop bossing me around!" he demanded.

"No," I countered, raising my eyebrows and holding back a laugh. "I know no one has ever told you no or really what to do other than Alpha's demands, but you need to listen to me."

"You've been my father for like ten seconds!" he snapped, throwing his hands up in the air in frustration. "Nothing has changed!"

"Everything has changed!" I growled, my brows knitting together. "You've had new powers since we transitioned, and you haven't even begun to tap into them. You need more experience before you take on Adam."

"I can handle myself!" Damian hissed, stepping up to me and challenging my authority. "I don't need a babysitter."

We stared each other down as Raphael and Gabriel stood there.

"Take this to Samyaza and do whatever he needs you to do," I commanded as I handed Damian the stone from my pocket.

"Whatever," Damian replied, rolling his eyes.

"Thank you," I called out as he stomped off, and he waved me off.

"Would have never imagined that stubborn creature was your kid," Raphael remarked sarcastically.

"Shut it," I drawled. "Where is Adam?" I asked, changing the subject.

"Starfire's cottage," Raphael replied.

I groaned and headed toward her cabin. Just what I needed. The devil spawn returned. As I climbed the steps, Adam emerged from the door. He looked taller than the last time he was here.

"Where is Damian?" he inquired, looking around outside for him.

"Busy," I replied, giving him a deadpan stare. "What do you need, Adam?" I pressed.

"My business is with Damian," he stated, looking down his nose at me.

"Well, I am the best you have right now," I insisted, crossing my arms.

"You don't scare me," he glowered, stepping up to me just as Damian had to challenge my authority.

"And you don't scare me, kid," I shot back, leaning down in his face.

"I wanted to spar with him," he replied nonchalantly.

"Not going to happen," I commanded with dead set eyes.

"Why not?" he refuted, furrowing his brows.

"Because the last time you were here, you threw a sword at his head!" I shrieked.

He huffed. "I cannot fail, Alpha. I need to train with the real thing," he insisted.

I leaned in closer to him. "Not going to happen," I barked, annunciating each word.

"Alpha told me how arrogant you are and how you think no one could hurt you," he spat. "You could hardly keep up with me in the arena."

"I am sure Alpha tells you nothing but the truth and no lies," I quipped, standing back up.

"I've learned a few things since our last time in the arena," he remarked, smirking with arrogant eyes.

"Well, let's see what you have learned, squirt," I bantered, tousling his hair.

He smacked my hand away with a scowl. "You *will* respect me!" he proclaimed.

I got down to eye level with him and leveled with him. "Respect is earned and not given."

He glared at me and pushed past me, bumping me with his shoulder. Why is it that every kid I meet thinks they're the boss of me? Is it because they look the same age? I rolled my eyes and followed him to the arena he chose. No sooner had we entered the arena than his hands began to throw ice at me. I shot back with fire bullets, destroying each ice block as they careened through the air.

"Oh, so we are doing that?" I snapped as he grinned at me wildly.

"Don't hold back," he ordered.

"If I don't hold back, I will burn this place to the ground," I growled.

"Well, I won't be," he beamed as he unleashed a wall of icy fire my way.

I didn't move, and I didn't block it. I let it hit me just to see what it would do. As the ice met my body, steam rose and melted upon impact. When the mist cleared, I stood there, staring Adam down, who stood there bewildered.

"Is that really all you got?" I quipped. "Show me your fury!" I commanded.

His face darkened, and I watched as he reached in deep and brought forth his power. Everything around us began to freeze over. Those who were training in other arenas froze solid in their places, some mid-air. Adam screamed in fury, and the ice thickened. As it licked my feet, it immediately melted, leaving a puddle of water gathered around my feet.

"How are you doing that?!" he whined, stomping his foot in a tantrum.

I walked calmly over to him and leaned down in his face so I could stare him in the eye with my reply. "Because I am *the* god."

I raised my hand, and heat radiated from it, melting the ice that had covered Lightshade. As the ice thinned, those training busted through the sheet that had encased them and turned to stare in our direction.

"Just because you're as powerful as you are doesn't mean Alpha won't stop you, and it doesn't mean Damian is as powerful as you either," Adam seethed. "I will take him down and fully become him in the end."

"You will die trying," I snarled, and he was gone.

"What the *hell* was that?" Samael demanded, emerging from Starfire's cottage.

"Adam," I replied. "We have a problem."

Chapter 22

"HIS POWERS ARE advancing," Metatron said as we all stood around the backside of Starfire's cottage.

"I'd say they're more than advancing. He froze you all!" I exclaimed as I paced back and forth. "How are we going to take on Alpha if his little devil can take you all out at once?"

"We have to level the playing field," Samael replied with a shrug. "I don't know how, but we need a game plan because this isn't working out; we are just sparring for training."

"Well, do you have any powers?" I asked, bobbing my head at him.

He shrugged. "I don't know. Alpha only had us train to be warriors."

"You brought out powers in the Nephilim," I argued. "Angels have to have *some* sort of power if they do."

"Look, I have tried to be like you for millennia," Samael remarked. "I have tried willing anything possible forth, and nothing ever happens."

"Then the only thing that can stop Adam is Damian," Asmodeus interjected. "He would have to keep him distracted as we fight whatever Alpha sends our way." He looked at me as I glared at him. "I know you hate the idea, but he is a god just like you. You have to stop babying him.

You can't keep sheltering him and putting him in a corner. In the end, it will be him against Adam."

"You don't have to remind me!" I hissed. "I am well aware of what is to transpire. It's still not safe for him!"

"He can't take down Damian without all of Damian in him," Asmodeus countered. "He will be fighting against just another angel with powers, not a god."

"Unless Alpha finds a way to turn him into a god," Azazel chimed in. "And then Incaendiel has a reason to be worried."

"You're not helping the situation, Azazel!" Asmodeus growled, glaring in her direction.

"Stop arguing!" Raphael snapped, and we all fell silent. "It's not doing any good standing around arguing over what might happen and what might not happen. We have to prepare for *all* possibilities, and that includes Damian against Adam, whether you like it or not, Incaendiel."

"Raphael is right," Michael offered, and I scowled at him. "It's not just about you. It's about all of our survival. So we all have a vote in this."

"The answer is no!" I barked firmly. "We do not test Damian against Adam."

"What if he takes him out before Alpha's plan comes to fruition, though?" Metatron added. "We will have the upper hand then."

My frustration took hold of me, and I punched the wall of Starfire's cottage, busting a hole through it. I stood there with my hands placed against the wall, running everything through my head as everyone stood silent.

"Can we just get through one problem at a time, please?" I choked out.

"Incaendiel is right," Samael affirmed. "Let's get through one thing at a time, or else we will all be left frustrated and overwhelmed."

The wood on the wall magically fixed itself, and I sighed.

"What's going on?" Damian asked as he walked up alongside Samyaza.

"Strategizing," Asmodeus grunted and walked off.

I went to walk off after him when Samael grabbed me gently by the shoulder.

"Let him go cool off," he said and patted my shoulder.

I nodded okay and turned my attention to Samyaza. "Did you find her?" I inquired, changing the subject.

"We did," Samyaza replied, grimacing.

"Well, where is she?" I asked, waiting for him to answer.

"She's in Sheol," Damian responded. "She's being guarded there by Aker, Beberos, and a few others."

"We were also able to locate the other Watchers as well," Samyaza chimed in. "They are in Tartarus, the furthest depths of Sheol."

"Seems easy enough," I replied. "Should be a cakewalk."

Damian and Samyaza exchanged glances.

"What?" I asked, looking between the two.

"Alpha has a whole slew of those creatures and more in Tartarus," Samyaza replied. "We would have to fight our way in to get to them."

"What about Sheol?" I asked. "Anything there?"

Damian shook his head. "None that we could see, but you know Alpha. What we could see was just who Alpha has guarding Lailah, but like I said, I was only able to see a handful of them. Plus, there are the human souls there as well. So we have to be careful using our powers or we will destroy the souls before they recycle to the Giving Tree."

"I don't see the problem," I replied. "We can take a handful of Forsaken and angels."

"Sheol has its own monsters from the various voids of the cosmos," Damian replied. "Like Cerberus, Hydra, and all."

"I forgot about them," I replied, chewing on my nail, deep in thought. "We go to Sheol first and bring Lailah back, and then on to Tartarus to release the Watchers."

"We still need to free Luxina from Purgatory as well," Damian piped up.

"We will be better in more numbers going into Purgatory," I replied. "There's no telling what Alpha has stashed in there to keep us from getting to her. I can guarantee you it will be worse than Sheol or Tartarus."

"We will need to bring offerings to Charon so he will let us through the river," Azazel added.

"That, and you need to make peace with Hades, or he won't let you through either," Azrael remarked, walking up to us. "He is still Lord of the Underworld. We need his permission to go through."

We all groaned.

"What?" she asked, looking around at us.

"Hades is so pompous," Samael replied, rolling his eyes.

"I don't even know why Alpha agreed to let him continue to be the Lord over the dead," Metatron agreed.

"Alpha didn't agree to anything," Azrael laughed. "Alpha has no control over the death deities, just like he has no control over the reaper angels or Maveth. *All* souls in the cosmos go through him and the other death deities as we carry them there."

"It doesn't make him more likable," Michael chimed in, scrunching his face in disgust.

"He thinks that he is better than everyone else," Azazel added.

"Well, whether you personally like him or not, he is the only way in, even if you pay Charon the token to take the river," Azrael chirped.

"Well, then, it's settled," I interrupted. "We make peace with Hades. Samael, gather the tokens from Starfire for Charon. I know she has them somewhere among her relics."

Samael nodded and walked around the building to go inside.

"How many of us are going?" Damian asked.

"You're staying here with Samyaza," I replied.

"But—" he began to protest.

I put my hand up. "It's not because you need protection or because I think you won't be safe. Lightshade needs protection in case Adam comes back."

"I thought I wasn't allowed to fight him," he quipped.

"Why not let Damian come with us and you stay behind to protect Lightshade?" Raphael offered. "You handled Adam without breaking a sweat and without hurting him."

I thought it over. "Fine. I will stay behind. Take Asmodeus with you," I urged, looking at Damian. "And you mind Samael as well. He is first in command."

He nodded and ran off to find Asmodeus.

"I did not expect you to agree as fast as you did," Raphael remarked, surprised and laughing.

"If anything happens to him, it comes down on your head," I replied with a forced, sweet smile.

He stopped laughing and looked around at everyone, who looked off as if they were searching for something in the air.

"You all are asses," Raphael muttered, kicking the dirt.

"While they are off to Sheol," Samyaza began, changing the subject, "You and I can strategize infiltrating Tartarus."

I nodded. "Sounds like a plan."

Samael returned, holding the coins Starfire had given him for Charon. "Are we ready?" he asked, looking around at everyone.

"Yep," Damian replied, walking up with Asmodeus at his side.

Keep him safe, I projected to Asmodeus, and he gave a nod.

You have my word, Brother, he replied in his head.

I can hear you both! Damian interrupted, rolling his eyes.

"Alright, let's go," Samael replied, with Metatron, Azazel, Michael, Raphael, Damian, and Asmodeus falling in behind him as he walked off.

"Is Starfire portalling you in?" I shouted after them.

Samael gave me a thumbs up without turning around and continued back around the cottage. I returned my attention to Samyaza, who stood watching me curiously.

"What?" I asked, feeling like I had three heads.

"You are so different than before the fall," he mused. "You have grown so much as a leader."

"Thank you?" I asked.

We began to walk around the cabin as we caught those remaining of the group walking through the portal, and it closed behind them.

"When you came to Stygia to ask us to join you in your fight against Alpha, we were not thrilled with the idea at all. Sophia pulling rank is why we joined," he explained.

"And now?" I asked.

He stopped and looked me dead in the eye. "I will follow you to Potter's Field, Brother."

I nodded. "That's good to hear," I replied. "Not the Potter's Field bit, but to know I have you on my side and to know it's not because it's just for survival makes me feel a lot better as a leader."

We continued around the cottage and inside.

"Can I ask you something?" I inquired as we walked into Starfire's private collection room full of her books on mythology.

"What?" he asked in return.

"Why haven't you pledged to me yet?" I prodded. "Not that it matters, really. I am just curious."

"I am waiting for all the Watchers to be together so we can all pledge at once," he replied. "I do not wish to overcome my tribulations without them by my side as they have been for millennia."

I inclined my head in agreement. "I understand."

I walked over to a bookcase and scanned the spines. I ran my finger along each shelf of books until I came to the book I was looking for. "Ah, here we go."

"What's that?" Samyaza asked.

"It has every monster listed in it that's in Tartarus," I replied, placing it on a table and opening it.

"Typhon is at the entrance, right?" Samyaza questioned, leaning down to glance through the pages with me.

"Yes, he is the first thing we have to take out," I murmured.

There were tons of monsters listed in the book that Tartarus housed.

"Echidna, I forgot about her," Samyaza said as he turned the page to her portrait.

"The Mother of Monsters," I mumbled. "How are we going to make our way through the maze of monsters to find the others?" I asked. "Did it show you specifically where they were?"

Samyaza shook his head. "No, it didn't. It's going to be a wild hunt getting to them."

"Indeed," I muttered. "How are they being held prisoner?" I asked, looking up at Samyaza.

"Alpha has them bound by their hands and feet," he responded.

"So they're defenseless too?" I asked.

"Yes. From what I saw, they were surrounded by Keres," he replied. "They don't have much time before they grow bored and lead something to them to finish them off so they can start devouring them."

"You need Thanatos to guide you through," Azrael said, popping up.

Adrenaline rushed through me, and I had to control my fire. "I wish you would stop doing that," I muttered.

"How else would you like me to appear?" she smirked, crossing her arms.

"I don't know. Knock, maybe?" I replied, shaking my head in frustration.

She rolled her eyes and continued. "Thanatos can help guide you through there. He travels through Tartarus from time to time and knows his way around."

"Well, why don't you go get him then?" I quipped.

"Because that's not my job," she retorted. "I'm not your messenger."

Messenger!

"Gabriel can find him," I replied, matter-of-factly.

"Now you're using your brain," Azrael quipped.

"You're starting to get on my nerves," I remarked, glaring at her.

"You've been on mine!" she mocked.

I pursed my lips. "I'm going to go find Gabriel."

"We will be right here, going through the book," Samyaza replied, eyeing the two of us.

I left the room, irritation bubbling below the surface. What was the deal with Azrael? I thought we were all supposed to be working together. As I bounded down the steps of the cottage, Adam appeared.

I groaned. I didn't have time for his little games. "What is your deal, kid?" I demanded, walking up to him.

His eyes lit up with a glow, and he held his hand up in the air, focusing his energy to the palm of his hand and fired a shot at me. The blow caught me off guard, and I went careening backward against the steps. All of my anger came gushing forth, and I stood up from the broken porch steps, glaring at Adam.

He stood there, his cockiness apparent in his posture. "You don't scare me," he goaded.

I let a deafening howl loose and burst into flames. He smiled sinisterly and snapped his fingers. A portal popped up behind him, and through the opening, a dark, smoky mass with serpents for legs and wings stepped through.

"I heard you were going to storm Tartarus looking for the rest of the Watchers," Adam began, squinting his eyes at me. "So I brought Tartarus to you."

"Typhon," I growled.

As Typhon finished stepping through the portal, more beings followed. A half-woman, half-serpent slithered through the opening.

"Echidna."

A triple-headed giant followed closely behind her.

"Geryon."

Black ethereal smoke oozed out of the opening as shrieking Keres emerged. More and more monsters poured out into Lightshade as Adam stood in front of them, grinning from ear to ear, looking more and more like Alpha.

"Have fun," he teased and disappeared.

"Samyaza!" I bellowed.

Samyaza came running from inside, slowing as he saw the monsters just outside the cottage.

"What the——"

"Adam," I seethed before he could finish his sentence. "Get everyone to safety who cannot fight while I hold them off."

"What can I do?" Azrael asked, appearing at my side, wide-eyed with fear.

"Get Starfire to safety!" I ordered.

I removed the flaming sword from my side, and it sprang to life. "Here we go!" I yelled, running toward them.

Angels and Nephilim poured in from all sides and began their assault on the monsters as I took on Typhon.

"You call yourself a god," Typhon sneered venomously. "A god could put me back where I came from."

"I'm not putting you back," I replied, walking in a circle around him. "Your head's going on my wall!"

Black fiery smoke snaked its way from his body and wrapped around me, choking me. I hit the ground hacking and coughing, trying to get a breath of fresh air.

"You can die trying," Typhon growled.

I grabbed at the smoke tendrils, trying to free them from around my throat. A horn blew, and I looked over to see Gabriel with his horn, aiming it at Typhon. The sound vibrated in the air, and the force of the sound sent shockwaves of wind toward Typhon. He began to lose mass as the wind carried his smoke away and turned his attention to Gabriel. He loosened the grip he had on me, and I was able to grab him by his serpentine tail. I began to spin him in the air and soon held the end of his tail like a lasso. My arm turned to fire and rushed through my hand and into his smoky, formless body. I summoned thunderbolts from the sky, and they crackled around him like fireworks. The fire began to burn away the oxygen left that kept him in his smoke state until he poofed into nothingness.

I glanced over to my left, and Echidna was tearing through the angels and Nephilim left and right. As they went down one by one, they retreated to safety as I walked up behind her. She whipped around to face me.

"Ah, Vahr-Zul in the flesh," she hissed like a thousand snakes. "I never imagined I would ever meet you. I happily obliged when Alpha asked us to perform this task for him."

I turned toward Gabriel. "Find Samyaza. Tell him it's now or never. He has to go in and get back out quickly!"

Gabriel nodded in acknowledgement and took off to find Samyaza.

"You think you have won when you rescue your Watchers?" Echidna snarled. "I am a dream compared to things Alpha has created for you, and that's saying something, for I am the mother of monsters."

I watched as Samyaza and Belial raced through the portal with Gabriel to retrieve the bound Watchers from inside Tartarus. I returned my attention to Echidna.

"Alpha will win in the end, you know?" she goaded. "He will slay your whole family again just as he did before. And there's nothing you can do to stop him."

"You talk too much," I muttered as I ran toward her, unleashing a ray of fire and burning the ground around her, trapping her inside a circle.

She howled in rage as I jumped through the air. I brought my wings out and began to spin, and soon, she was trapped inside a whirlwind of fire. I hovered just above the fire as she let loose a deafening screech, calling forth her children to save her. I dropped down through the top of the flames and brought the flaming sword down on her neck, severing it clean from her body. I turned my attention to the masses of monsters that had clawed their way out of Tartarus and began hacking and slashing through them alongside everybody else. It seemed the more we killed, the more that poured freely through the portal, including some of the monstrosities Alpha had created as Samyaza and Damian warned about.

"Incaendiel!" Praeziel hollered over the sound of howls and screams of terror. "We have to close the portal!"

"Not until they come back through!" I ordered as I slashed through the monsters with the flaming sword.

"Lightshade will perish if we don't!" he urged as he fought more and more of the monsters popping out.

"I made a promise, and I intend to keep it!" I hissed.

Flames leapt from my feet and burned in precise patterns as I fought my way through the barrage of monsters. It felt like there was no end to the fight as more creatures surrounded me with every burst of flame. They paid closer attention to me than to the angels and Nephilim whom they only attacked when provoked.

"They're here for me!" I yelled. "On my order, I want you all to back down!"

"You can't use your powers here!" Praeziel refuted. "You will kill everyone!"

Samyaza emerged through the portal, with the Watchers following close behind and racing for safety. Once the portal was clear of any stragglers, I yelled the order. "Fall back!"

"We can't do that!" Praeziel insisted.

"Do as I say!" I commanded, my voice echoing through the valley.

They all did as instructed, and the monsters swarmed me. I fought each attacking creature as I slowly made my way over to the portal so I could lure them back through.

"What the hell is going on!" I heard Damian yell as he and the rest of the group stepped out of the portal from Sheol.

I had no time to explain. I stepped through the portal into Tartarus, and the opening filled with all of the monsters.

"Incaendiel, what are you doing?" Damian demanded, rushing toward the portal entrance.

"I have to use my power somewhere, and it can't be Lightshade!" I shouted back.

"Tartarus will cave in and either trap you forever or kill you!" he refuted.

"It's the only way!" I shot back.

"Don't do this!" he pleaded as he began to step through the portal entrance.

"Stand back!" I ordered, waiting for the last monster to surround me inside the portal.

I lifted my hand to snap my fingers.

"Dad! No!" Damian shouted as my fingers clicked against my palm.

The portal shut, and I was trapped inside Tartarus with the ravenous, snapping jaws of evil. It's now or never. I willed every ounce of my power to the brim and exploded just as I had done so many times during my training with Lilith.

Chapter 23

IT DIDN'T TAKE me long to get back to Lightshade. Once I unleashed my power, I was able to beam back instantly before Tartarus caved in. Every single monster was now either dead, buried, or forever trapped there. I walked through the field where the bodies of angels and Nephilim killed lay, as well as the carcasses of the monsters that had been slain. Damian ran up to me and pushed me hard. I stumbled back as he began to lay blow after blow against me with his fists.

"You could have been stuck forever!" he hollered. "Why would you do that?"

A blow caught me square in the jaw before I threw my arms around him and wrestled him to the ground.

"Let me go!" he yelled, kicking and screaming as his ice began to wrap up my arms. "Let me go! Let me go! Let me gooooo!"

His powers mounted and went off in my arms. Everything went still as he froze time in its place while ice crept around the valley.

"You have to calm down!" I demanded, holding him as tightly as I could as he wiggled in my arms.

"You don't tell me what to do!" he cried, wrestling free from my arms as my heat melted the ice.

"It was the only choice I had!" I defended. "I would have leveled Lightshade and killed everyone there!"

He stood to his feet and landed another punch to my jaw.

"Stop that!" I barked, my voice echoing and shattering the ice into crumbled shards.

He raised his arms, and the shards rose in the air along with them.

"If you want to die so bad, why don't I just take you out right here and right now!" he cried, his eyes full of pain and fear.

"I wasn't trying to die!" I explained as the shards all pointed toward me. "I was just trying to save everyone!"

"You're always trying to save everyone no matter what the cost is to you!" he shot back, tears falling freely down his face.

"Like father, like son!" I quipped.

"Stop calling me that!" he snarled and let the shards loose.

They each melted into puddles of water before they ever reached me.

"If you don't want me calling you that, then stop acting like it!" I retorted.

He hit the ground on his knees and heaved into his hands. "You're all I have," he cried "If anything happens to you, there is no one left!"

"No, Damian," I replied, walking over to him. "You have everyone. There's Asmodeus, who has been the only father—"

"That doesn't make him my father," he hissed, cutting me off. "I look up to him as a big brother, and I know he took care of me, but that doesn't make him my father. You are my father!"

I knelt before him and watched him intently as he rocked back and forth. I grabbed at him to pull him into my chest. He fought off my arms, and I fought back until I had him pinned to me as he flailed his arms, hitting me in the back. He soon stopped, and I held him. His freeze on time let loose, and everyone who was frozen still stood quietly as I rocked him back and forth.

"I'm sorry," I whispered to him. "I had no idea..."

"Well, now you do," he cried in heaves into my chest.

We sat there for what seemed like an eternity before he peeled himself from my arms. He looked up to see everyone watching us and quickly swiped away the tears from his face. I stood up and held out my hand to help him to his feet.

He smacked it away and stood on his own. "Lailah is inside the cottage," he muttered and walked off.

That boy had me frustrated and sorry all at the same time. I looked around at the carnage lying in the field. So many had died fending off the attack on Lightshade. The angels were waiting to be ferried off by the reapers to Potter's Field as they slowly, one by one, disappeared from the field. I watched the bodies of the Nephilim lie there. I had no idea where they went when they died. Sheol? Potter's Field.

"If they died in the mundane world where they chose to live on as mortals, they will go to Sheol. These will go to Potter's Field since they died in a heroic battle alongside angels," Azrael said, as if reading my mind. She turned to face me, her face stricken with shame. "I apologize for earlier, Incaendiel. I shouldn't have worked you up the way I did. Things may have gone differently had I not riled you up before you met Adam at the steps."

I shook my head. "It didn't matter what happened between Adam and me. This was the plan all along between Alpha and him," I replied. "No fault to anyone." I looked at her and gave a half-smile. "I am sorry too, Azrael."

She looked around at the bodies slowly disappearing. "We don't have enough in numbers willing to come here to ferry them." She looked sad and despondent. "They're afraid Alpha will show up again."

"Samael and Azazel can help if you show them," I offered, and she stared at me, surprised. "You said they were supposed to have been reapers, and Alpha didn't give his lot. Ask them. I am sure they won't mind."

She nodded with a forced smile. "Thank you."

She ran over to the two of them and began talking. I saw them agree, and off they went to help her with their brothers and sisters. I walked inside the cottage, and Starfire sat at her table, with her finger pointing to a room.

"She's in there," Starfire stated.

I walked to the room and began to open the door when Starfire stopped me.

"Incaendiel?" she asked, and I turned to look at her. "Thank you for saving our home."

"No thanks is needed," I replied with a light-hearted smile.

I twisted the doorknob and opened the door to find Lailah sitting at a table. I closed the door behind me and walked over to the table, taking a seat across from her. "You are one hard person to track down," I said as I sat down.

"Do you think this is all fun and games?" Lailah snapped, glaring at me.

"Unlike Alpha, no. No, I do not think this is all fun and games," I answered thoughtfully. I pointed to the door. "Our brothers and sisters are lying in a field out there, dead, because it is all fun and games to him. But instead of having a moment to mourn the losses, I have to move to the next point in strategy to try and defeat him, which I can only do if I had found you. So, forgive me, Sister, for trying to lighten the mood. If you want doom and gloom, that is my specialty."

Her jaw tightened as she fought back the rising anger. "Fine," she stated flatly. "What do you want with me?"

"I need to know the location of a human," I replied.

She laughed and scoffed, "A human? That's all this is about?" she asked with her hand. She leaned forward. "A human, Incaendiel?"

"Yes, a human," I sneered, growing impatient. Why was she being such a pain in the ass? Why does everyone have to be such a pain in the freaking ass?

"I have better things to do with my *free* time than to sit here like another prisoner so you can use me as a geolocator to find a human for you," she huffed and stood from her seat.

"She's not just any human," I said as she walked toward the door. "She's a starseed."

She stopped in her tracks and turned around. "My, you have been a busy boy, haven't you?" she smirked enthralled. "That word doesn't get tossed around that much."

My eyes blazed to life, and fear fell over her face. "A lot of things have changed since we last saw one another, Lailah," I replied.

"When did Lilith let you out of the cage?" she asked, sitting back down and propping her feet up on the table.

"You *knew?*" I demanded.

She waved her hand in the air. "Of course, I knew," she replied. "How else was Alpha going to explain all of the souls from your universe once they started arriving after he took you from them?" she mused.

"How can you be so cavalier about this?" I asked in return. "Why aren't you angry with Alpha?"

She pulled her feet from the table and leaned in close to me. "I don't like you, Incaendiel. I never have. You and your mate ruined it for all of us," she snapped.

"It wasn't our fault," I protested, anger bubbling beneath the surface. "I can't help Alpha meddled with power he had absolutely no business meddling with."

"Had it not been for you two," she continued smugly. "We all would be one big, happy family."

"Do you really think that?" I stammered, standing to my feet. "He and Lilith manipulated all of you."

"I never was," Lailah replied, her uncaring eyes staring up into my eyes. "I had one job and was left to do what I was supposed to do. Meanwhile, Samael and Azazel were pulled from me to babysit you because Mother and Father needed help controlling you more."

"Just give me the location of Eva, and you can be on your way," I ordered, my patience at its last stretching point.

"That's the only reason you rescued me," she declared, standing from her seat and meeting me eye to eye. "You needed something from me. And I was the only person who could give it to you."

"I have rescued so many of you over and over throughout the millennia. Do not patronize me!" I fumed, jumping to my feet and walking over to her. "You were one of the first people asked about, but we couldn't get to the Summit to look for you because Alpha slammed the doors shut!"

"If I give you her location," she began. "Do I *have* to leave, or can I stay if I wish to stay?"

"You can stay, or you can go," I replied, walking to the door. "The choice is yours and yours alone. No one controls you here. No one tells you what to do. No one makes demands of you."

"And if I don't give you the location?" she asked, raising an eyebrow.

I shrugged my shoulders. "The same deal. You can choose to stay or go, and we will just go back to the drawing board to find another way."

She stared at me intently. "She's in Angel Falls, Idaho. Her name is Eva Green. She is a teenager, and she hasn't activated yet."

"Thank you," I replied, uncaring as I opened the door.

"Incaendiel?" Lailah asked.

"Yes?" I turned around to answer.

"Don't get her killed, please," she pleaded, her eyes full of worry. "She's more important than for reading the book."

I nodded and closed the door behind me.

Praeziel sat in the sitting room, waiting for his orders.

I walked over to him and whispered her location in his ear. He nodded and headed out the door. Samyaza appeared, stepping out of the conference room.

"They're in there all waiting to hear," he stated, pointing with his thumb back at the room. "Did Lailah tell you what you needed?" he asked as I began walking over to the conference room.

"Yes, but man, was she a stubborn one about it. I had no idea so many of you hated me throughout all the years," I replied, walking up the aisles to the front of the room. "Is this everyone?" I asked, looking at all the worn faces in the room.

"The last two hundred of us who didn't take Alpha's side," Samyaza answered.

I breathed in deeply, preparing to give my speech. "I know you're tired," I spoke loudly. "And the war has hardly begun. The last time I stood before you, there was derision and fighting over whether to join in the war or to keep to yourselves and remain neutral. Alpha forced your hand over a year ago when he took you all captive."

"Why are you just now rescuing us?" Armaros demanded, and all of them began talking at once.

I motioned with my hands for them to quieten down. "I was taken captive and held in one of Alpha's dungeons," I replied as the room fell quiet. "Believe me when I say, we would have exhausted all resources trying to find you all. Samyaza was able to locate you with the missing Watchers Eye amulet."

"How do we know you won't become power hungry like Alpha?" Sathariel questioned, a look of disdain painted across his face. "How do we know we can trust you?"

"I cannot sway your trust. I will not make you follow me, and if you choose not to and to remain neutral, you are free to stay here where it is safe," I replied, looking intently around the room. "I will not make you do what you don't want to do, and I will also not abandon you. For too long, you have been cast aside like garbage by Alpha and Lilith. Not with me. I will honor your decisions, whatever they may be."

"And if we decide to join you, then what?" Asbeel asked. "Do we become your mindless drones?"

I laughed. "No. You keep your free will, your free thinking, and everything about you that makes you who you are," I replied.

"But we are restored to our angelic selves, though. Right?" Chazaquiel inquired, leaning forward. "I mean, it's not the determining factor for our loyalty, but it is a key piece in making the decision."

"If you join me and pledge your loyalty to me, then yes. You will be restored," I answered, looking around at them all. "But," I began.

"But what?" Sathariel sneered, shaking his head. "See, there's always a catch. We probably have to bend to his will and do whatever he asks of us."

I shook my head. "No," I replied. "Not at all."

"Then what?" he demanded.

"You can't just say it," I replied. "You have to mean it or it won't work. When you pledge yourselves to my power, the power knows if you are being deceitful or telling the truth. With the angels, I cannot tell because they have nothing to transform out of. They took a knee, and that was it. But when the Forsaken pledged to me, I watched it happen before my very eyes. And those who did not pledge and just sought safe haven did not change."

Chatter filled the room as they all began discussing what I had told them.

Samyaza stepped forward to speak. "Incaendiel is offering us freedom from the curse we have spent millennia trying to fight free from," he spoke loudly.

"The curse that Alpha promised to find a way to life but did not attempt to right," Belial added, stepping up beside Samyaza.

"Why are you two still cursed, then, if you have pledged your loyalty to Incaendiel?" Asbeel asked.

"Because we waited to be reunited with you all before we pledged. We took the curse together and it will be lifted together," Belial insisted.

"What do we have to do?" Armaros asked.

"Yeah, is there some sort of ritual or something?" Chazaquiel added.

"Not really a ritual," I began.

"You take a knee, place your arm across your chest, and you hail the new king," Samael replied, walking into the room. "He is our new King of Kings, and that is how he is heralded."

"Did you?" Sathariel asked. "Did you take a knee to Incaendiel, first in command?"

Samael looked at me. "I did," Samael replied. "And I will follow our brother to the ends of the universe because he speaks nothing but truths while Alpha basks in lies."

"Are you ready, Brothers?" Samyaza asked, stepping forward before them all. "Are you ready to become whole again? To once again be angels instead of the abominations we have become? Are you ready to follow the new cosmic order? Because I am."

"I am! Hail to the King!" Belial shouted, stepping out and taking a knee.

Like with the Forsaken, healing white lights floated around him as my power restored him to his former angelic self.

"It works!" the crowd of Watchers murmured.

"Hail to the King!" Samyaza bellowed, thrusting his hand in the air, drawing it across his chest, and taking a knee.

The entire room echoed Belial and Samyaza's oath, shouting, "Hail to the King!" and taking a knee before me. The lights gathered, and it was like staring at the sun as the healing rays burned away their vampyric blood. When the light died down, the room cheered in happiness and gratitude.

"It was all true!"

"We are healed!"

"Incaendiel saved us!"

"He did what Alpha would not!"

"Incaendiel is the true ruler of the cosmos!"

Samyaza turned toward me, his new icy blue eyes that had replaced the blood red purple ones he once sported, peered at me. "Thank you, Brother," he cried, a tear slipping down his face.

I nodded and walked through the masses of angels there, cheering for the salvation of the Watchers. I made it to the sitting room where Starfire still sat at her table. I flopped down on the couch, tipping my head back for it to rest on the pillow. I sighed heavily and looked over at Starfire.

"Long day?" she mused with a smirk.

"Long lifetime," I groaned.

"Well, it could have gone worse," she offered.

"The day or the lifetime?" I asked with a half-hearted smile.

"Both," she chuckled. "You could have been reborn as a bug."

"I need to find Damian," I began, standing up from my seat, thinking back to earlier when he had his meltdown. "Know where he is?"

"He is with Asmodeus," Starfire replied as I began to walk to the door. "They went back to scour Chernobyl to see if there were any clues left to find Luxina and learn more about what Alpha has planned. They should be fine."

"He shouldn't have gone back to that place. It was questionable the first time, but understandable. It's downright suicide this time. Alpha took Luxina to Purgatory. We know that!"

I started to run out the door.

"Where are you going?" Starfire demanded.

"To Chernobyl," I replied. "There could be a trap set just waiting for him to return, and I will be damned Alpha gets Damian back as well."

I stepped out on the porch and unleashed my wings. Fire tore through the sky as I lifted off and flew. My wings were as fast as lightning compared to my angelic ones, and I was back to Chernobyl in no time to find Damian. As I approached, I felt the static in the air. It was the same static the day that Damian escaped Alpha. Those creatures were here. How many there were was undetermined. I flew faster around the area. I scanned for any sign of him. I finally spotted him and Asmodeus at the edge of the woods there. That's when I saw the creatures barreling right toward them. A new sense of energy I hadn't felt before bubbled to the surface as rage erupted from me. The need to protect him fueled my powers. Fire blasted through the sky like an atomic bomb, turning every one of those abominations to ash, and when the smoke and ash began to clear, some, Damian was nowhere to be seen.

Oh no! I thought to myself. *Did the fire reach them too? Did I destroy them?*

I flew around the area, trying to peer through the smoke and ash still drifting through the sky. Another set of creatures appeared out of thin air, and once more, I used my powers to turn them into floating carcasses of embers and smoke. Their close proximity to Alpha's fortress erupted in a fireball of atomic energy as the radiation met my powers. Flames burned the area in billowing pillars after the pressure of the explosion leveled the forest. I waited for Damian and Asmodeus to appear from somewhere, anywhere, in what was left of the brush, as my heart skipped a beat and anxiety threatened to spill out as fire and brimstone.

Did I kill... was the only thought that floated through my head as I recalled the fires in the fields back to me, and I floated along the wind alone, without a single sign of life to be seen in the burned wasteland.

Firefly of Immortality II

SNEAK PEEK AT BOOK 6

Ashes of Immortality:

BLACK WINGS OF DEATH

Firefly of Immortality II

PROLOGUE: DAMIAN

WHY DO I HAVE to be so stupid? Why am I all of a sudden so damn insecure around Luxina? All the abuse Alpha put me through weakened me instead of strengthening me. Around her, I didn't have my feet on the ground. I had no stability. I free floated. It was amazing and nerve-wracking all at once. I wanted to give her everything, and at the same time, I was afraid of the world being jerked out from beneath my feet.

How could she love me so much as hideous as I look? There was some truth behind what Alpha had said through her. She didn't need me here because she wanted me. She required me to be away from Alpha so I wouldn't be his weapon of mass destruction. She had said it herself. She needed me this. She needed me that. She can't just all of a sudden *want* me.

"Take it easy, Damian. We're training, not really fighting," Praeziel yelled, ducking from my sword.

I snapped from my thoughts, nodding apologetically. "My head's not in it right now," I replied.

"It's ok. Training for the day is over anyway," Praeziel offered sympathetically. "How is Luxina?"

"Awake," I sighed.

"Why are you out here with us and not in there with her?" Praeziel chided.

I didn't answer as I shoved my weapons back into my bag. "You let him get to you, didn't you?" Praeziel asked.

"Who?" I asked, pulling my shirt back on.

"Alpha. When he had control over her, he said something that got to you, didn't he? About her?" Praeziel continued.

"Maybe. So what?" I huffed.

"Whatever it was, don't believe it. Don't let it sink in. You go back in there to her and forget everything. Don't break the bond you two have," Praeziel reassured.

"I'm not... breaking the bond. I just have some things to work through. It has nothing to do with her. It's all me," I replied.

"Well, don't let her think otherwise. She's more vulnerable now than she was before. She has the dark half of her soul back. It can consume her easier than most because she's never experienced it before," Praeziel warned.

"Yeah," I replied. "I hadn't thought of that."

I dropped my bag on the porch of Starfire's cabin and walked through the doorway. Luxina stood in front of one of her portals. Where was she going? Was Starfire sending her somewhere? Why hadn't she told me anything about it?

"Luxina?"

Luxina glanced back at me with determination in her eyes. I looked past her to see where she was going. On the other side of the portal doorway was a darkened room. As I stared closer, I could see chains on the wall, and a flickering light bulb was lighting the room up quickly every so often and shooting it back into darkness. I knew that room. I knew that place.

"No!" I shouted.

"I love you, Damian," she said.

She stepped through the portal faster than I could get to her side. It closed behind her as I tried to jump through at the last minute. I thudded to the floor.

"No, no, no, no, no, no!" I shouted over and over, pounding my fist into the floor.

I rolled from all fours over to a sitting position with my hands cupping my head. Fear tore through my body. I had to get to her. I had to get to her before Alpha got his hands on her. Anxiety ran through my veins, and I felt weak momentarily. Starfire calmly walked to the center of the floor.

"Why didn't you tell me she would do this?" I seethed, jumping up to my feet in anger.

"Because I didn't know how this day would have gone. There were two possibilities. The first one was that when she woke up and told you how much she loved you, you would welcome it with open arms. The second possibility is what happened. You put up a wall," Starfire replied.

"Why did she go? How does this have anything to do with…"

It sank in. Luxina wouldn't just risk going to Alpha unless she had a plan. Her reasons for going had to be simple enough, but at the same time, they had to mean something more than just going for revenge or blood. She was going for one specific reason.

"Do you see now why, Damian?" Starfire asked.

I looked up at Starfire with tears welling, forcing them back down. "To prove how much she loves me," I choked out.

"So, you know you can't stop her. She's going to do this or die trying, but you won't be able to stop what she is doing," Starfire offered.

"Then, we will both die together," I avowed through gritted teeth. "I'm not letting her do this alone."

"You'll never find them, Damian…"

CHAPTER 1: LUXINA

Obviously, things didn't go as planned when I stepped through the portal back to Chernobyl to confront Alpha. As it closed behind me, I was startled by the voice in the dark.

"Luxina, you came back after all!"

I spun around to the voice to see Alpha sitting in a chair behind me in the dark.

"Hello, Alpha."

"What is she doing here?" another voice shrieked.

I turned around to see my mother walking through the door and closing it behind her. She looked just as awful as Damian had looked when he found us after escaping Alpha.

"Ah, Sophie. My favorite little angel. Your job is done. I no longer need you. You brought me exactly what I needed. Little Luxina here."

The realization set in when he said the words. I had fallen for the trap he set. He knew that every single thing he said to Damian would get under his skin. The constant abuse he was put through at Alpha's hands had worked his mind in ways no one could comprehend. I thought I was being defiant by trying to show him how much I cared. But instead, we played right into Alpha's hands.

"You used me to get my daughter?" Sophie asked, confused. "I thought you needed me."

I had no idea how long Alpha had been using my mother, but it was evident that for a really long time, she had been Alpha's favorite.

"No, Sophie. I no longer need you. It's time for you to go back to sleep and Anniel to come forth," Alpha declared.

Anniel? I thought to myself. Before I could say or think anything, the door opened behind my mother, and in walked my dad, just as Alpha grabbed me, then snapped his fingers to disappear.

"Daddy!" I shouted, and then we were gone.

Alpha let go of my arm, pushing me as he did so, and I hit the ground in front of a throne that sat in a beautifully ornate room. Gold trimmed the walls, and the ceiling was open to the view of the sky. But it wasn't just any sky. It was the galaxy. Memories flashed through my head, and I knew just exactly where I was thanks to Xavier. Alpha had brought me to the Summit. This was his throne room. I slowly got up to my feet, hesitant that he would knock me back down to the ground.

"I'm not going to hurt you," Alpha cooed as he sat down on his throne. "No one here is going to hurt you either."

"I almost died last time I was with you," I hissed, glaring at him in a defensive stance.

"And that was my mistake," he replied earnestly. "I was trying to bend you to my will, and I apologize."

"Apology not accepted," I sneered.

He smiled. "I didn't expect you to accept it."

I inspected his face, eyeing him closely. "You look different than last time I saw you," I stated. "Younger."

His smile turned into a smirk, and then he explained. "Whenever I am fed new power, or if I withdraw the power I have used to create things, I grow younger. We aged with every single use of our powers. Being a god didn't come with instructions. So it's a learning curve still."

"What do you want with me?" I prodded, walking the floor in front of the throne and admiring the room.

"I have someone I want you to meet," he replied casually. "Adam?" he called out.

From one of the passageways, I heard footsteps approaching. I turned to see who was emerging from the shadows, and my breath caught in my throat.

"Xavier?" I whispered.

It can't be Xavier. Xavier was me, and he is in me. The boy walked closer to me, and as the lights from the sky above splashed across his face, it was without a doubt Xavier who stood in front of me.

"Hello, Luxina," he said. "My name is Adam." He held out his hand for me to shake.

I cautiously took his hand and gave it a small shake. "You look just like Xavier," I murmured.

"It was a rather unfair and cruel joke the universe played on you three," Alpha chimed in. "Having to absorb Xavier like you did isn't something anyone should have to endure. When I learned about the prophecy, I knew I had to right the wrong being committed. So I created Adam just for you in Xavier's image."

"That doesn't make him Xavier," I protested heatedly. "He may look like him, but he is not Xavier."

"But what if he could be?" Alpha asked, leaning forward in his throne. "What if Xavier could come back?"

I shook my head. "Xavier was the missing piece of my soul that I needed to be whole. He can't come back."

"You survived once, split apart. It didn't affect your powers. It didn't affect you as a person," Alpha retorted. "Xavier can once again exist if you wish him to."

"If that were the case, I wouldn't have needed to absorb him back," I refuted.

"I am the all-powerful god," Alpha replied, raising his hands to the sky. "I can do anything, including bringing Xavier back. He could exist again in Adam's body."

"But Adam has his own conscience. It would be just like me with him shoved into the shadows," I explained, glancing over at Adam, who didn't seem to mind the idea. "He wouldn't be Xavier at all."

Alpha pinched the bridge of his nose in frustration. "Just say yes!" he demanded.

I retreated a bit from him, glancing between Alpha and Adam. "No," I stated. "You can't have half of my soul."

Alpha pounded the arm of his throne and ran his hands across his face.

"Well, until you agree, I guess we will just have to lock you up until you change your mind," Alpha hissed. "Belphegor!" he called.

There was shuffling of feet, and he emerged from the same passageway Adam had come out of.

"Yes, my liege?" he replied, kneeling at the throne in front of Alpha.

"Take her to purgatory," Alpha said with a flick of his wrist. "Have Uriel lock it up behind you."

"There's no such thing," I laughed. "Purgatory is made up."

"Is it?" Alpha asked, cocking an eyebrow, amused.

I glanced around nervously at everyone. No one seemed to refute the idea of purgatory. Belphegor walked toward me, and I fought him off.

"Get your hands off of me!" I screamed.

I punched and kicked just as Damian had taught me.

"She's a feisty one," Belphegor laughed as he struggled to keep his grip on me.

"Do you need help?" Alpha sneered. "She's one little girl."

"I got her," Belphegor replied, wrapping his hand in my hair and giving it a hard yank. "Off we go, princess," he sneered as he walked away.

"Does she really need to go to Purgatory?" I heard Adam ask as we walked in.

"Yes," Alpha replied.

Belphegor walked me down some corridors and finally toward a door that a woman stood beside. The door glowed an ominous red color. She reached over to the door with a key and slipped it into the keyhole. The door slowly opened, and Belphegor pushed me through it, kicked me to the ground, and walked back out of the door, leaving me behind in the dark as the door slammed shut. I huddled in the corner of the space I was left. I couldn't see anything. It was total darkness that surrounded me. However, I could hear the sounds of this place echoing off the walls, which frightened me to the core. There was moaning and groaning as well as snarls and snaps. Whatever creatures Alpha had created and put here were most likely ravenous beasts he hadn't fed in a long time. The other sounds must be the sounds of human souls he trapped here for their sins.

I wasn't alone for very long when a searing pain shot through my body. It crawled along my skin, and I doubled over on my side on the ground. I screamed and heaved as it tore through every inch of me, flames licking the ground around me. I had no control over my powers and couldn't recall the fire back to my core at all. I felt like steam was being trapped in the furthest reaches of my body, building into combustion, and at any minute, I would burst and splatter everywhere. And just as quickly as the thought crossed my mind, I exploded in one large fireball, and then everything felt empty.

The darkness that surrounded me didn't compare to the void I floated in. Then, everything began to rush through my mind. The big bang of the cosmos sprang life into the vast void. I saw the moment that creation began, all the way through to Alpha being created. I heard faint talking and recognized the voice of my dad.

Daddy?

Luxina! he gasped.

What's going on? What's happening? I pleaded.

We are ascending, he explained. *Your mother took her elixir.*

Where are you? Damian demanded.

I don't know. Some place Alpha created, I whimpered. *There's nothing but darkness where I am. I thought I was dying. I exploded.*

We all did that, sweetie, he said. *We will find you. I promise.*

Hurry, Daddy! There are monsters here. I am pretty sure they are the ones from the vision that Alpha plans to use against us. I can hear them, I whimpered.

We will be there as soon as we learn where you are, Anniel replied.

Mom? I asked.

The darkness of wherever I had been faded, and I sat up from the spot where I was left. My skin now glowed, and I could see around me. I had created a crater. I sighed and began to climb to the top of the massive hole, slipping and sliding on the loosened dirt. When I was nearly at the threshold, a hand shot out for me to grab.

"Take my hand, and I will pull you out," Adam called, leaning over the hole.

I smacked his hand away and finished climbing out on my own. "I don't need your help," I snapped.

"Fair enough," he replied, taking a step back.

I stood up and dusted myself off. "Why are you here?" I demanded, patting myself down and brushing off dirt.

"I didn't want you to be left alone in here," he answered, sitting down on a boulder.

"Where exactly is here?" I huffed. "Alpha said Purgatory, but everyone knows Purgatory doesn't exist. It was just a made-up poem by a person who had too much time on his hands."

"Father created Purgatory because the mortals dreamt it up," Adam replied. "You're on the seventh terrace."

"What's the seventh terrace?" I questioned, crossing my arms.

"The sin of Lust," he answered. "Since you seduced Damian's obedience away from Father, he thought it was fitting to place you here."

"I didn't seduce Damian," I snapped. "I showed him real love, something Alpha never showed him."

"Father doesn't show love to those who are disobedient," Adam retorted. "Damian never listened to anything he was told to do."

"I see Alpha has you wrapped around his little finger," I mused. "You probably bend over backward to please him, don't you?"

"I do everything Father tells me to do," he replied earnestly.

"Why do you call him Father?" I asked. "He is a terrible parent."

"Because he is my father," he answered, standing up from the boulder. "Just like you call your father, what was it? Oh, *Daddy.*"

I glared at him and started to walk away.

"Where are you going?" he demanded.

"I am finding my way out of here," I replied, not slowing my pace.

"There's no way out," he urged. "One way leads to the abyss, and the other leads to the other six terraces, and there are monsters and demons on every level."

"I will fight my way out then," I called out over my shoulder.

He ran up to me and grabbed me by my wrist, stopping me. "No!" he ordered. "It's too dangerous!"

I wrenched my arm from his grasp. "You don't tell me what to do!" I shouted. "I can fight my way out!" I insisted as I began walking again.

Again, he grabbed me by my wrist and pulled me back to him. I lost my footing and stumbled into his chest. He breathed slowly as I stared up into his eyes. He peered back at me, and it was like stepping into the past with Xavier.

"You can't fight those things without help," he stated calmly and quietly. "There are too many of them."

He felt so familiar to me, even though I didn't even know who he was. He felt like Damian. I shook the feeling off and took a step back.

"Help me escape then," I muttered.

He ran his hand through his hair as he glanced around nervously. "I can't," he replied.

"Why not?" I demanded, stomping my foot.

"Father would punish me for acting out of line," he answered, putting his finger to his lip for me to be quiet.

When the time comes, I will help you escape, he thought. *There are listening ears in here.*

I huffed. "Fine." I trudged back to the crater in the ground. "What am I supposed to do until then?" I asked.

"Just wait," he replied with a shrug.

I studied his face. His looking like Xavier really threw me for a loop. He didn't seem all too threatening.

"Will you wait with me?" I pleaded.

"I can't stay," he replied. "But I will be back when I can to check in on you and make sure you're ok."

He started to leave when I stopped him. "Wait!" He turned around to look at me. "Do you want what Alpha wants with Xavier?" I asked.

He stood quietly for a moment before he answered. "I will do what Father asks me to do."

And with that, he turned around, waved his hand, and walked through the portal he brought up. It closed behind him, leaving me alone once again. I sat there thinking about the whole interaction with him. He was obedient to Alpha even if he didn't agree with what Alpha wanted to do. He was nothing like Damian. It took mind control for him to do what Alpha wanted, and if he didn't, then Alpha would torture him for it. Is Adam afraid that what happened to Damian would happen to him as well? I slumped down against the stone wall beside the crater, feeling defeated. For a brief moment, I thought about how protective and demanding Adam had been with me. The feelings I had when I touched him, I didn't like at all. It was almost as if he had a part of Damian in him, but that was impossible. Damian wasn't split in half like I was, and Alpha created Adam recently. So why was I so innately drawn to Adam?

Don't fall for it, Xavier whispered to me.

Well, hello there, I mused. *Don't fall for what?*

Whatever it is that Alpha and that Adam have planned, Xavier answered. *I don't like Adam trying to get close to you and being all Damianish. It's ick.*

Damianish? I asked, confused.

"Oh, look, Luxina in danger. I'd better save her or die trying because I truly love her, even though she has no clue how I feel until I tell her. But I will kill anyone who tries to hurt her." Does that ring a bell? he asked.

He is not Damianish, I replied, rolling my eyes.

How can you not see the plan here? Xavier demanded. *Alpha wants to put me into Adam's body so Adam can become a Shining One like us.*

And you think Adam is going to try to sweep me off my feet and help Alpha to do that? I snorted. *I see you have a lot of faith in me.*

I felt what you felt, remember? Xavier said. *Something is off about Adam. He shouldn't have that effect on you like that. So don't fall for any of his bullshit until we figure out everything. Like how he was created to begin with.*

Stop already! I was growing angry. *I love Damian. It's the whole reason I am stuck here in this place. It's my punishment for showing him love. Nothing is going to change that.*

We will see, Xavier retorted and went quiet.

Xavier?

Nothing. Once again, I was utterly alone without anyone to talk to. Story of my life...

10

***

I'm not sure how long I was left alone before Adam came back again. Whatever monsters and demons hid in the shadows in here stayed in the shadows. There were times I tried to leave, even though Adam had warned me not to, but it seemed like no matter which way I went, it was an endless walk, and I always ended up back where I began. It was a futile effort trying to escape, just like he said, except no one attempted to stop me. I even attempted to use my powers to raise a portal, but I wasn't able to. Somehow, Alpha was able to block anyone's abilities there except for Adam's.

"Hello, Luxina," Adam said, breaking the silence as he stepped through a portal.

I stood from my seated position against the cave wall and walked over to him. "Adam!" I breathed. "You're back!"

"Excited to see me, are we?" he mused with a devilish grin.

"There's absolutely nothing to do here or anyone to talk to, so yes. I am excited to see you," I retorted.

He casually strolled toward me and then circled me as he looked over every inch of my body. I don't know why, but all of a sudden, I felt very insecure as if he was scrutinizing every aspect of my being. He stopped in front of me and peered down at me with tantalizing eyes.

"What?" I asked self-consciously.

"Nothing," he murmured. "You're perfect. Not a scratch on you."

"Nothing has tried to bother me down here yet," I replied.

"They will soon," he remarked. "Father issued orders to start your harrowing."

"What's a harrowing?" I prodded nervously.

"He plans to torment you," he replied casually. "Unless you agree to what he wants to do."

"Well, I am not agreeing," I snapped. "And if that's the case, it won't be his first harrowing of me. He did the same thing when he gave me all of those injections over a year ago. I don't break."

A smirk tugged at the corners of Adam's mouth. "I know," he mumbled.

"Why are you here, Adam?" I asked, growing impatient.

"I paid Damian a visit," he taunted, pacing around me once more. "He's looking good for someone who was beaten within inches of his life and left to be ugly and unlovable. Not a scar on his body."

"What did you do to Damian?" I implored, grabbing his arm.

He stepped closer to me, and I could feel the magnetic pull I had with Damian become stronger. I let go of his arm and just stared at him.

"I haven't done anything to him... yet," he answered. "Just testing the field."

"Yet?" I asked. "What do you mean yet?"

"Father and I have discussed it. When Father gives me the signal for the kill order, I will be sent to dispatch him," he responded nonchalantly.

"You can't do that!" I pleaded.

"Not right now, I can't," he sighed. "But soon I can. He has some new power that manifests, and he can slow down time. Once I am able to acquire that power of his, it will be match for match against him."

"I don't understand," I replied, shaking my head. "How do you have any of his powers to begin with?"

"You haven't figured out how I was created yet, have you?" he inquired with a smug grin.

"No, I haven't," I answered impatiently.

"Father created me from Damian's blood," he stated with a smirk. "I am essentially Damian, but look like Xavier. Two of your weaknesses."

I swallowed the lump forming in my throat. Alpha was indeed ten steps ahead of everyone. This explains why I can't help but gravitate toward Adam.

"I see it has clicked for you," he mused. "Now you understand why every time we touch, you feel that magnetic field circle around us."

"I love Damian," I insisted, breathing heavily.

"No," he replied coolly. "Your twin flame bond makes you love him. You don't love him for him. It's just the bond. So in the end, you will love me too."

Everything Xavier had warned me about now started to make sense. Alpha wants me to love Adam, so he made Adam to be like Damian.

"I love Damian for more than just his bond to me," I sneered. "I loved him before I even knew him as a person. Then, getting to know him made me love him even more. I won't love you the same way."

"Maybe," he retorted. "Or maybe not. Your mother faced the same dilemma over and over throughout the millennia. Being faced with different angels every incarnation, and your father having to battle for her heart. Guess who won each time? Not him."

"He won the last time," I spat. "And I am not my mother."

"I can feel your desire, Luxina," he cooed, stepping closer to me. The same storm rolled behind his eyes that had unraveled me with Damian. "I know that every word that leaves my lips sends goosebumps down your spine." He ran his finger along my arm, and shivers erupted.

My knees buckled. I could remember his hands. My soul cried out in divine betrayal. "I know every time I touch you, you get a little feeling that grows in your stomach." His hand wrapped around my waist. Every heartbeat that thudded in my chest felt like betrayal. His hands were that of roses and thorns, as every tremble they caused felt like thorns shredding the thread binding me to Damian. He leaned in closer and whispered in my ear. "I know he hasn't touched you, and that ache radiates into your core." He exhaled, tingling the hairs in my ear, teasing my neck with goosebumps, and I couldn't help but lean into it. I wanted this... or did I? His scent was intoxicating, and embers awoke in my soul while my body ached for Damian. Adam wasn't the one who fought for me, cried with me, nor bled for me, but he was what I wanted in that very moment, going against every hushed whisper saying he wasn't Damian.

Luxina! Xavier shouted, breaking me out of the trance I had become wrapped up in. I pulled away from Adam, too ashamed to even look him in the face.

"I see dear old brother interrupted," he sighed. "Father will fix that for us soon."

He waved his hand, and a portal appeared. "I'll be back."

He stepped through the portal, and it vanished. I hit the ground, shaking and in tears.

Xavier, what am I supposed to do? I asked in between sobs.

I don't know, but we need to come up with something quick, he replied. *We can't fight that pull at all. I even tried to stop you and couldn't.*

Damian, I need you, I cried.

Kasey Hill is a critically acclaimed versatile writer from Franklin County, Virginia, known for her work in several genres, including urban fantasy, horror, thriller, paranormal romance, and metaphysical/New Age topics. She has authored both fiction and non-fiction, with a particular interest in Wicca, specializing in Trinitarian Wicca as the historical archivist with an upcoming historical account of the shift from polytheism to monotheism in Abrahamic religions, where she has published non-fiction works exploring the subject.

Her fiction often dives into the supernatural and the macabre, blending mythological elements with modern storytelling. She has published multiple novels, poetry collections, and short stories. Notable works include her *Guardians of Light* series in the mythology fantasy genre, and her poetry that has received recognition for its depth and emotional resonance. As she grows in the horror genre, she has a particular penchant for Southern Appalachian Gothic storytelling, such as her Adult Horror novel *Devil's Claw* and her Young Adult horror series, *The Whispering Spirits* featuring *The Haunting at Foxwood Village* and *Dark Coven*. She has several Horror short stories circulating for anthologies and Ezines featuring her unique style of worldbuilding.

In addition to her writing, Kasey Hill has also contributed to the Wiccan and occult community through her non-fiction work, making her a multi-faceted author with a broad range of interests and expertise.

www.ingramcontent.com/pod-product-compliance
Lightning Source LLC
Chambersburg PA
CBHW030917020726
47498CB00001B/12